THE
STRANGER'S
CHILD

THE STRANGER'S CHILD

Alan Hollinghurst

ALFRED A. KNOPF   NEW YORK · TORONTO   2011

Library of Congress Cataloging-in-Publication Data
Hollinghurst, Alan.
The stranger's child : a novel / Alan Hollinghurst. — 1st ed.
p. cm.
ISBN 978-0-307-27276-8
1. Triangles (Interpersonal relations)—Fiction.   2. Families—England—
London—Fiction.   3. Family secrets—Fiction.   4. Families—
History—Fiction.   I. Title.
PR6058.04467S77 2011
823'.914—dc22   2011010256

Library and Archives Canada Cataloguing in Publication
Hollinghurst, Alan
The stranger's child / Alan Hollinghurst.
Issued also in electronic format.
ISBN 978-0-307-39842-0
I. Title.
PR6058.0484S77 2011   823'.914   C2011901892-6

Jacket illustration: painting by Eugene Speicher,
from the collection of J. D. McClatchy
Jacket design by Chip Kidd

Manufactured in the United States of America
First North American Edition

IM

MICK IMLAH

1956–2009

AUTHOR'S NOTE

I am very grateful to the Belgian literary organization Het Beschrijf for a month's residency in the Passa Porta writers' apartment in Brussels, where part of this novel was written.

ONE

"Two Acres"

I

SHE'D BEEN LYING in the hammock reading poetry for over an hour. It wasn't easy: she was thinking all the while about George coming back with Cecil, and she kept sliding down, in small half-willing surrenders, till she was in a heap, with the book held tiringly above her face. Now the light was going, and the words began to hide among themselves on the page. She wanted to get a look at Cecil, to drink him in for a minute before he saw her, and was introduced, and asked her what she was reading. But he must have missed his train, or at least his connection: she saw him pacing the long platform at Harrow and Wealdstone, and rather regretting he'd come. Five minutes later, as the sunset sky turned pink above the rockery, it began to seem possible that something worse had happened. With sudden grave excitement she pictured the arrival of a telegram, and the news being passed round; imagined weeping pretty wildly; then saw herself describing the occasion to someone, many years later, though still without quite deciding what the news had been.

In the sitting-room the lamps were being lit, and through the open window she could hear her mother talking to Mrs. Kalbeck, who had come to tea, and who tended to stay, having no one to get back for. The glow across the path made the garden suddenly lonelier. Daphne slipped out of the hammock, put on her shoes, and forgot about her books. She started towards the house, but something in the time of day held her, with its hint of a mystery she had so far overlooked: it drew her down the lawn, past the rockery, where the pond that reflected the trees in silhouette had grown as deep as the white sky. It was the long still moment when the hedges and borders turned dusky and vague, but anything she looked at closely, a rose, a begonia, a glossy laurel leaf, seemed to give itself back to the day with a secret throb of colour.

She heard a faint familiar sound, the knock of the broken gate against the post at the bottom of the garden; and then an unfamiliar voice, with an edge to it, and then George's laugh. He must have brought Cecil the other way, through the Priory and the woods. Daphne ran up the narrow half-hidden steps in the rockery and from the top she could just make them out in the spinney below. She couldn't really hear what they were saying, but she was disconcerted by Cecil's voice; it seemed so quickly and decisively to take control of their garden and their house and the whole of the coming weekend. It was an excitable voice that seemed to say it didn't care who heard it, but in its tone there was also something mocking and superior. She looked back at the house, the dark mass of the roof and the chimney-stacks against the sky, the lamp-lit windows under low eaves, and thought about Monday, and the life they would pick up again very readily after Cecil had gone.

Under the trees the dusk was deeper, and their little wood seemed interestingly larger. The boys were dawdling, for all Cecil's note of impatience. Their pale clothes, the rim of George's boater, caught the failing light as they moved slowly between the birch-trunks, but their faces were hard to make out. George had stopped and was poking at something with his foot, Cecil, taller, standing close beside him, as if to share his view of it. She went cautiously towards them, and it took her a moment to realize that they were quite unaware of her; she stood still, smiling awkwardly, let out an anxious gasp, and then, mystified and excited, began to explore her position. She knew that Cecil was a guest and too grown-up to play a trick on, though George was surely in her power. But having the power, she couldn't think what to do with it. Now Cecil had his hand on George's shoulder, as if consoling him, though he was laughing too, more quietly than before; the curves of their two hats nudged and overlapped. She thought there was something nice in Cecil's laugh, after all, a little whinny of good fun, even if, as so often, she was not included in the joke. Then Cecil raised his head and saw her and said, "Oh, hello!" as if they'd already met several times and enjoyed it.

George was confused for a second, peered at her as he quickly buttoned his jacket, and said, "Cecil missed his train," rather sharply.

"Well, clearly," said Daphne, who chose a certain dryness of tone against the constant queasy likelihood of being teased.

"And then of course I had to see Middlesex," said Cecil, coming forward and shaking her hand. "We seem to have tramped over much of the county."

"He brought you the country way," said Daphne. "There's the country way, and the suburban way, which doesn't create such a fine impression. You just go straight up Stanmore Hill."

George wheezed with embarrassment, and also a kind of relief. "There, Cess, you've met my sister."

Cecil's hand, hot and hard, was still gripping hers, in a frank, convivial way. It was a large hand, and somehow unfeeling; a hand more used to gripping oars and ropes than the slender fingers of sixteen-year-old girls. She took in his smell, of sweat and grass, the sourness of his breath. When she started to pull her fingers out, he squeezed again, for a second or two, before releasing her. She didn't like the sensation, but in the minute that followed she found that her hand held the memory of his hand, and half-wanted to reach out through the shadows and touch it again.

"I was reading poetry," she said, "but I'm afraid it grew too dark to see."

"Ah!" said Cecil, with his quick high laugh, that was almost a snigger; but she sensed he was looking at her kindly. In the late dusk they had to peer closely to be sure of each other's expressions; it made them seem particularly interested in each other. "Which poet?"

She had Tennyson's poems, and also the *Granta*, with three of Cecil's own poems in it, "Corley," "Dawn at Corley" and "Corley: Dusk." She said, "Oh, Alfred, Lord Tennyson."

Cecil nodded slowly and seemed amused by searching for the kind and lively thing to say. "Do you find he still holds up?" he said.

"Oh yes," said Daphne firmly, and then wondered if she'd understood the question. She glanced between the lines of trees, but with a sense of other shadowy perspectives, the kind of Cambridge talk that George often treated them to, where things were insisted on that couldn't possibly be meant. It was a refinement of teasing, where you were never told why your answer was wrong. "We all love Tennyson here," she said, "at 'Two Acres.' "

Now Cecil's eyes seemed very playful, under the broad peak of his cap. "Then I can see we shall get on," he said. "Let's all read out our favourite poems—if you like to read aloud."

"Oh yes!" said Daphne, excited already, though she'd never heard Hubert read out anything except a letter in *The Times* that he agreed with. "Which *is* your favourite?" she said, with a moment's worry that she wouldn't have heard of it.

Cecil smiled at them both, savouring his power of choice, and said, "Well, you'll find out when I read it to you."

"I hope it's not 'The Lady of Shalott,' " said Daphne.

"Oh, I like 'The Lady of Shalott.' "

"I mean, that's my favourite," said Daphne.

George said, "Well, come up and meet Mother," spreading his arms to shepherd them.

"And Mrs. Kalbeck's here too," said Daphne, "by the way."

"Then we'll try and get rid of her," said George.

"Well, you can try . . . ," said Daphne.

"I'm already feeling sorry for Mrs. Kalbeck," said Cecil, "whoever she may be."

"She's a big black beetle," said George, "who took Mother to Germany last year, and hasn't let go of her since."

"She's a German widow," said Daphne, with a note of sad realism and a pitying shake of the head. She found Cecil had spread his arms too and, hardly thinking, she did the same; for a moment they seemed united in a lightly rebellious pact.

2

WHILE THE MAID was removing the tea-things, Freda Sawle stood up and wandered between the small tables and numerous little armchairs to the open window. A few high streaks of cloud glowed pink above the rockery, and the garden itself was stilled in the first grey of the twilight. It was a time of day that played uncomfortably on her feelings. "I suppose my child is straining her eyes out there somewhere," she said, turning back to the warmer light of the room.

"If she has her poetry books," said Clara Kalbeck.

"She's been studying some of Cecil Valance's poems. She says they are very fine, but not so good as Swinburne or Lord Tennyson."

"Swinburne . . . ," said Mrs. Kalbeck, with a wary chuckle.

"All the poems of Cecil's that I've seen have been about his own house. Though George says he has others, of more general interest."

"I feel I know a good deal about Cecil Valance's house," said Clara, with the slight asperity that gave even her nicest remarks an air of sarcasm.

Freda paced the short distance to the musical end of the room, the embrasure with the piano and the dark cabinet of the gramophone. George himself had turned rather critical of "Two Acres" since his visit to

Corley Court. He said it had a way of "resolving itself into nooks." This nook had its own little window, and was spanned by a broad oak beam. "They're very late," said Freda, "though George says Cecil is hopeless about time."

Clara looked tolerantly at the clock on the mantelpiece. "I think perhaps they are rambling around."

"Oh, who knows what George is doing with him!" said Freda, and frowned at her own sharp tone.

"He may have lost his connection at Harrow and Wealdstone," said Clara.

"Quite so," said Freda; and for a moment the two names, with the pinched vowels, the throaty *r*, the blurred *W* that was almost an *F*, struck her as a tiny emblem of her friend's claim on England, and Stanmore, and her. She stopped to make adjustments to the framed photographs that stood in an expectant half-circle on a small round table. Dear Frank, in a studio setting, with his hand on another small round table. Hubert in a rowing-boat and George on a pony. She pushed the two of them apart, to give Daphne more prominence. Often she was glad of Clara's company, and her unselfconscious willingness to sit, for long hours at a time. She was no less good a friend for being a pitiful one. Freda had three children, the telephone, and an upstairs bathroom; Clara had none of these amenities, and it was hard to begrudge her when she laboured up the hill from damp little "Lorelei" in search of talk. Tonight, though, with dinner raising tensions in the kitchen, her staying-put showed a certain insensitivity.

"One can see George is so happy to be having his friend," said Clara.

"I know," said Freda, sitting down again with a sudden return of patience. "And of course I'm happy too. Before, he never seemed to have anybody."

"Perhaps losing a father made him shy," said Clara. "He wanted only to be with you."

"Mm, you may be right," said Freda, piqued by Clara's wisdom, and touched at the same time by the thought of George's devotion. "But he's certainly changing now. I can see it in his walk. And he whistles a great deal, which usually shows that a man's looking forward to something . . . Of course he loves Cambridge. He loves the life of ideas." She saw the paths across and around the courts of the colleges as ideas, with the young men following them, through archways, and up staircases. Beyond were the gardens and river-banks, the hazy dazzle of social freedom, where George and his friends stretched out on the grass, or slipped by in punts. She said cautiously, "You know he has been elected to the Conversazione Society."

"Indeed . . . ," said Clara, with a vague shake of the head.

"We're not allowed to know about it. But it's philosophy, I think. Cecil Valance got him into it. They discuss ideas. I think George said they discuss 'Does this hearth-rug exist?' That kind of thing."

"The big questions," said Clara.

Freda laughed guiltily and said, "I understand it's a great honour to be a member."

"And Cecil is older than George," said Clara.

"I believe two or three years older, and already quite an expert on some aspect of the Indian Mutiny. Apparently he hopes to be a Fellow of the college."

"He is offering to help George."

"Well, I think they're great friends!"

Clara let a moment pass. "Whatever the reason," she said, "George is blooming."

Freda smiled firmly, as she took up her friend's idea. "I know," she said. "He's coming into bloom, at last!" The image was both beautiful and vaguely unsettling. Then Daphne was sticking her head through the window and shouting,

"They're here!"—sounding furious with them for not knowing.

"Ah, good," said her mother, standing up again.

"Not a moment too soon," said Clara Kalbeck, with a dry laugh, as if her own patience had been tried by the wait.

Daphne glanced quickly over her shoulder, before saying, "He's extremely charming, you know, but he has a rather carrying voice."

"And so have you, my dear," said Freda. "Now do go and bring him in."

"I shall depart," said Clara, quietly and gravely.

"Oh, nonsense," said Freda, surrendering as she had suspected she would, and getting up and going into the hall. As it happened Hubert had just got home from work, and was standing at the front door in his bowler hat, almost throwing two brown suitcases into the house. He said,

"I brought these up with me in the van."

"Oh, they must be Cecil's," said Freda. "Yes, 'C. T. V.,' look. Do be careful . . ." Her elder son was a well-built boy, with a surprisingly ruddy moustache, but she saw in a moment, in the light of her latest conversation, that he hadn't yet bloomed, and would surely be completely bald before he had had the chance. She said, "And a most intriguing packet has come for you. Good evening, Hubert."

"Good evening, Mother," said Hubert, leaning over the cases to kiss her on the cheek. It was the little dry comedy of their relations, which somehow turned on the fact that Hubert wasn't lightly amused, perhaps didn't even know there was anything comic about them. "Is this it?" he said, picking up a small parcel wrapped in shiny red paper. "It looks more like a lady's thing."

"Well, so I had hoped," said his mother, "it's from Mappin's—," as behind her, where the garden door had stood open all day, the others were arriving: waiting a minute outside, in the soft light that spread across the path, George and Cecil arm in arm, gleaming against the dusk, and Daphne just behind, wide-eyed, with a part in the drama, the person who had found them. Freda had a momentary sense of Cecil leading George, rather than George presenting his friend; and Cecil himself, crossing the threshold in his pale linen clothes, with only his hat in his hand, seemed strangely unencumbered. He might have been coming in from his own garden.

3

UP IN THE SPARE BEDROOM, Jonah settled the first suitcase on the bed, and ran his hands over the smooth hard leather; in the centre of the lid the initials C. T. V. were stamped in faded gold. He shifted and sighed in his private quandary, alert to the sound of the guest in the house. They were making each other laugh, down below, and the noise came upstairs without the sense. He heard Cecil Valance's laugh, like a dog shut in a room, and pictured him again in the hall, in his cream-coloured jacket with grass stains on the elbows. He had lively dark eyes and high colour, as though he'd been running. Mr. George had called him Cess—Jonah said it in a noiseless whisper as he traced the *C* with the tip of his finger. Then he stood up straight, sprang the catches, and released the heady and authentic gentleman's smell: toilet water, starch, and the slowly fading reek of leather.

As a rule, Jonah only came upstairs to carry cases or shift a bed; and last winter, his first at "Two Acres," he had brought the coals up for the fires. He was fifteen, short for his age, but strong; he chopped wood, ran errands, went up and down to the station in Horner's van. He was the boy, in all the useful senses of the word, but he had never "valeted" before. George and Hubert seemed able to dress and undress by themselves, and Mustow, Mrs. Sawle's maid, took down all the laundry. This morning, however, George had called him in after breakfast and told him to look after his friend Valance, who he said was used to any number of servants. At Corley Court he had a marvellous man called Wilkes, who had looked after George as well when he stayed there, and given him some good advice without appearing to do so. Jonah asked what sort of advice it had been, but George laughed and said, "Just find out if he needs anything. Unpack his bags as soon as he comes, and, you know, arrange the contents convincingly." This was the word, enormous but elusive, that Jonah had had on his mind all day, sometimes displaced by some other task, then gripping him again with a subtle horror.

Now he unbuckled straps and lifted tissue-paper with hesitant fingers. Though he needed help, he was glad he was alone. The case had been packed by some expert servant, by Wilkes himself perhaps, and seemed to Jonah to call for some similar skill in the unpacking. There was an evening suit with two waistcoats, one black and one fancy, and then under the tissue-paper three dress-shirts and a round leather box for the collars. Jonah saw himself in the wardrobe mirror as he carried the clothes across the room, and saw his shadow, from the lamp on the bed-side table, go rearing across the slope of the ceiling. George said Wilkes had done a particular thing, which was to take away all his loose change when he arrived and wash it for him. Jonah wondered how he was going to get the change off Cecil without asking for it or appearing to steal it. It occurred to him that George might possibly have been joking, but with George these days, as even Mrs. Sawle had said, it was hard to tell.

In the second case there were clothes for cricket and swimming, and a number of soft, coloured shirts which Jonah thought were unusual. He spaced them out equally on the available shelves, like a display in a draper's. Then there was the body linen, fine as a lady's, the drawers ivory-coloured, vaguely shiny, catching on the roughness of his thumb before he stroked them flat again. He listened for a moment for the tone of the talk downstairs, then took the chance he had been given to unfold a pair and hold them up against his round young face so that the light glowed through them. The pulse of excitement beating under his anxiety made the blood rush into his head.

The lid of the case was heavy; it had two wide pockets in it, closed with press-studs, and holding books and papers. Jonah took these out with a little more confidence, knowing from George that his guest was a writing man. He himself could write neatly, and could read almost anything, given the time. The handwriting, in the first book Jonah opened, was very bad, and ran uphill at an angle, with the *g*s and *y*s tangling the lines together. This appeared to be a diary. Another book, rubbed at the corners like the cash-book in the kitchen, had what must be poems in it. "Oh do not smile on me if at the last," Jonah made out, the words quite large, but then after a few lines, where the crossing-out began, getting smaller and scratchier, sloping away across the page until they were crowded and climbing over each other in the bottom right-hand corner. There were dog-eared bits of paper tucked in, and an envelope addressed to "Cecil Valance Esqre, King's College" in the careful writing which he knew at once to be George's. He heard rapid steps on the stairs and Cecil calling out, "Hallo, which is my room?"

"In here, sir," said Jonah, pushing the letter back and quickly squaring up the books on the table.

"Aha, are you my man?" said Cecil, suddenly possessing the room.

"Yes, I am, sir," said Jonah, with a momentary sense of betrayal.

"I shan't need you much," Cecil said, "in fact you can leave me alone in the morning," taking off his jacket at once and passing it to Jonah, who hung it up in the wardrobe without touching on the stained elbows. He planned to come back later, when they were having dinner, and deal with the dirty clothes unseen. He was going to be very much involved with all Cecil's things until Monday morning. "Now, what shall I call you?" said Cecil, almost as if choosing from a list in his head.

"I'm Jonah, sir."

"Jonah, eh . . . ?" The name sometimes led to remarks, and Jonah started rearranging the books on the table, unsure if they showed in some way that he'd looked inside them. After a moment Cecil said, "Now those are my poetry notebooks. You must make sure you never touch them."

"Very well, sir," said Jonah. "Did you want them unpacked, then?"

"Yes, yes, that's all right," said Cecil fair-mindedly. He tugged his tie off, and started unbuttoning his shirt. "Been with the family long?"

"Since last Christmas, sir."

Cecil smiled vaguely, as if he'd forgotten the question by the time it was answered, and said, "Funny little room, isn't it." Since Jonah didn't answer, he added, "Rather charming, though, rather charming," with his yap of a laugh. Jonah had the strange feeling of being intimate with someone who was simultaneously unaware of him. In a way it was what you looked for, as a servant. But he had never been kept in talk in any of the other, smaller, bedrooms. He peered respectfully at the floor, feeling he mustn't be caught looking at Cecil's naked shoulders and chest. Now Cecil took out the change from his pocket and slapped it on the wash-stand; Jonah glanced at it and bit his cheek. "And will you run me a bath," said Cecil, undoing his belt and wriggling his hips to make his trousers fall down.

"Yes, sir," said Jonah, "at once, sir," and slipped past him with a pang of relief.

4

HUBERT FORWENT HIS BATH that evening, and had what he felt was an unsatisfactory wash in his room. He wanted their guest to admire the house, and took some pleasure in hearing the tremendous splashes coming from next door; but he frowned as well, as he tied his tie in the mirror, at the virtual certainty that the sacrifice of his own half-hour in the tub would go unrecognized.

Having some time to spare, he went downstairs to the gloomy little room by the front door, which had been his father's office, and where Hubert too liked to write his letters. In truth he had very little private correspondence, and was dimly aware of not having the knack of it. When there was a letter to write, he did it with businesslike promptness. Now he sat down at the oak desk, fished his new gift from his dinner-jacket pocket, and laid it on the blotter with faint unease. He took a sheet of headed paper from a drawer, dipped his pen in the pewter ink-well and wrote, in a rolling, backward-leaning hand:

My dear old Harry—
I can never thank you enough for the silver cigarette case. It's an absolute ripper, Harry old boy. I have told no one about it yet but

will hand it round after dinner & just watch their faces! You are too generous, I'm sure no one ever had such a friend Harry. Well, it is nearly dinner-time, & we have a young friend of George's staying, a poet! You will meet him tomorrow, when you come over, he looks the part I must say though I have read not a word from his pen! Tons of thanks, Harry old boy, & best love from yours ever,
    Hubert.

Hubert turned the paper over on the blotter and thumped it tenderly with his fist. By writing large he had got the final few words on to the third side of the small folded sheet, which was a sign one hadn't merely written dutifully; the letter ran on pleasantly, and reading it over again he felt satisfied with the touches of humour. He tucked it into an envelope, wrote "Harry Hewitt Esq., Mattocks, Harrow Weald" and "By Hand" in the corner, and placed it on the tray in the hall for Jonah to take over in the morning. He stood looking at it for a moment, struck by the solemn rightness of living just here, and of Harry living where he did, and of letters passing between them with such noble efficiency.

5

GEORGE WAS THE LAST to come down, and even so he stopped on the stairs for a minute. They were almost ready. He saw the housemaid cross the hall with a salt-cellar, caught the odour of cooked fish, heard Cecil's high overriding laugh, and felt the chill of his own act of daring, bringing this man into his mother's house. Then he thought of what Cecil had said to him in the park, in the half-hour they had made for themselves by pretending he'd missed his train, and felt his scalp, his shoulders, his whole spine prickle under the sweeping, secret promise. He tiptoed down and slipped into the drawing-room with a nearly dizzy-making sense of the dangers ahead. "Ah, George," murmured his mother, with a hint of reproach; he shrugged and smirked slightly as if his only offence had been to keep them waiting. Hubert, with his back to the empty grate, had ensnared them all in talk about local transport. "So you were stranded at Harrow and Wealdstone, eh?" He beamed over his raised champagne glass, as proud of the rigours of life in Stanmore as he was of the blessings.

"Didn't matter a bit," said Cecil, catching George's eye and smiling curiously.

"As a wit once said, it sounds like some medieval torture. Harrow and wealdstone—can't you just see it!"

"Oh, spare me the wealdstone!" said Daphne.

"We're devoted to Harrow and Wealdstone, whatever a wit may have said," said his mother.

George stood for a moment with his hand pressed flat against Cecil's lower back and gazed into his friend's glass. He wiggled his fingers to play the secret notes of apology and promise. "Well, the Valance motto," Cecil said, "is 'Seize the Day.' We were brought up not to waste time. You'd be amazed what one can find to do, even at a suburban railway station." He gave them all his happiest smile, and when Daphne said, "What sort of things do you mean?" he carried on smiling as if he hadn't heard her.

"I gather you came up through the Priory," said Hubert, genially determined to follow every step of his journey.

"Yes, indeed we did," said Cecil, very smoothly.

"You know Queen Adelaide used to live there," said Hubert, with a quick frown to show he didn't want to make a big thing of it.

"So I gather," said Cecil, his glass empty already.

"Later I believe it was a very excellent hotel," said Mrs. Kalbeck.

"And now a school," said Hubert, with a bleak little snuffle.

"A sad fate!" said Daphne.

Jesus Christ! thought George, though all he came out with as he crossed the room was a sort of distracted chuckle. He poured himself the last of the bottle of Pommery, and glanced into the window, where the lamplit room was reflected, idealized and doubled in size, spread invitingly across the dark garden. His hand was trembling, and he kept his back to them as he picked up the fullish glass, steadying it with the other hand. It was impossible to imagine such a weakness in Cecil, and a consciousness of this added subtly to George's shame. He turned and looked at them, and they seemed all to be looking at him, as if they had gathered at his request, and were waiting for his explanation. All he had intended was a quiet family supper, to introduce his friend. Of course he hadn't reckoned on old Kalbeck, who seemed to think "Two Acres" itself was a hotel—it was really the limit how she'd fished, in her cunning oblivious way, for an invitation to stay on, his mother magnanimously lending her a wrap and dabbing her in her own familiar Coty scent. Now he watched with horror as she questioned Cecil about the Dolomites, her head on one side; her great brown teeth made her smiles both gauche and menacing. But a minute or two later Cecil was yarning with her in German, and almost making a virtue of her presence. Cecil, of course, lived in Berkshire: there was little danger of Frau Kalbeck turning up just before meals at Corley Court. He spoke German nicely, keeping an amused pedantic eye on the slowly approaching end of his sentences. When the maid announced dinner, Mrs. Kalbeck made it seem like an unexpected intrusion on their happy meeting of minds.

"Will you sit here, Mrs. Kalbeck," Hubert was saying, standing by his chair at the head of the table and smiling thinly as he watched them find their places. George smiled too, a little disconcerted from his glass of champagne. He felt a twinge of shame and regret at having no father, and forever having to make do. Perhaps it was just the memory of Corley, with its enormous oriental dining-room, that made the present party seem cramped and airless. Cecil stooped as he entered the room, in a possibly unconscious gesture to the cosiness of scale at "Two Acres." A father like Cecil's set a reassuring tone for a dinner, being very rich and an authority on shorthorn cattle. He had immense grey side-whiskers, brushed outwards, and themselves like a pair of brushes. Hubert was twenty-two, and wore a soft red moustache; he went to an office every day by train. This of course was what their own father had done, and George tried to picture him in Hubert's chair, ten years older than when he'd seen him last; but the image was blurred and unavailing, like any much-handled memory, the pale blue eyes soon lost among the flowers and candles crowding the table.

Even so, his mother was very pretty, and really a great beauty compared to Lady Valance, "The General," as Cecil and his brother called her, or sometimes "The Iron Duke," on account of her very faint resemblance to the first Duke of Wellington. Tonight Freda was wearing her amethyst drops, and her red-gold hair seemed to glimmer, like the candle-lit wine in her glass. The General naturally was a strict teetotaller—and now George wondered if Cecil himself had been shocked to see his hostess drinking before dinner? Well, he'd have to get used to it. They were doing things in their best festive style for him, the napkins belaboured into lilies, the small silver items, bowls and boxes of uncertain use, polished up and set down between the glasses and candlesticks. George reached forward and moved slightly to the left a vase of white roses and trailing ivy that obstructed his view of Cecil opposite. Cecil held his eye for a long moment—he felt the jolt of simultaneous danger and reassurance pass through him. Then he watched his friend blink slowly and turn to answer Daphne on his right.

"Do you have jelly-mould domes?" she wanted to know.

"At Corley?" said Cecil. "As a matter of fact, we do." He said the word "Corley" as other men said "England" or "The King," with reverent briskness and simple confidence in his cause.

"What are they," Daphne said, "exactly?"

"Well, they're perfectly extraordinary," said Cecil, unfolding his lily, "though not I suppose strictly domes."

"They're sort of little compartments in the ceiling, aren't they," said George, feeling rather silly to have bragged to the family about them.

Hubert murmured abstractedly and stared at the parlour-maid, who had been brought in to help the housemaid serve dinner, and was taking round bread-rolls, setting each one on its plate with a tiny gasp of relief.

"I imagine they're painted in fairly gaudy colours?" Daphne said.

"Really, child," said her mother.

Cecil looked drolly across the table. "They're red and gold, I think—aren't they, Georgie?"

Daphne sighed and watched the golden soup swim from the ladle into Cecil's bowl. "I wish we had jelly-mould domes," she said. "Or compartments."

"They might look somewhat amiss here, old girl," said George, pulling a face at the oak beams low overhead, "in the Arts and Crafts ambience of 2A."

"I do wish you wouldn't," said his mother. "You make us sound like a flat above a shop."

Cecil smiled uncertainly, and said to Daphne, "Well, you must come to Corley and see them for yourself."

"There, Daphne!" said her mother, in reproach and triumph.

"Do you have brothers and sisters?" asked Mrs. Kalbeck, perhaps already envisaging the visit.

"There are only two of us, I'm afraid," said Cecil.

"Cecil has a younger brother," said George.

"Is he called Dudley?" said Daphne.

"He is," Cecil admitted.

"I believe he's very handsome," said Daphne, with new confidence.

George was appalled to find himself blushing. "Well . . . ," said Cecil, taking a first moody sip of soup, but, thank heavens, not looking at him. In fact anyone would have said that Dudley was extremely good-looking, but George was ashamed to hear his own words repeated back to Cecil. "A younger brother can be something of a bane," Cecil said.

Hubert nodded and laughed and sat back as if he'd made a joke himself.

"Dud's awfully satirical, wouldn't you say, Georgie?" Cecil went on, giving him a sly look over the white roses.

"He works on your mother's patience," said George with a sigh, as though he'd known the family for years, and aware too that this repeated "Georgie," never used by his own family, was showing him to them in a novel light.

"Is your brother at Cambridge also?" asked George's mother.

"No, he's at Oxford, thank heavens."

"Oh, really, which college?"

"Now, which one is it?" said Cecil. "I think it's called something like . . . *Balliol?*"

"That certainly is one of the Oxford colleges," said Hubert.

"Well, that's it, then," said Cecil. George sniggered and gazed with nervous admiration at his pondering face, above the high starched collar and lustrous black tie, the sparkle of his dress-studs in the candlelight, and felt a quick knock against his foot under the table. He gasped and cleared his throat but Cecil was turning with a bland smile to Mrs. Kalbeck, and then as Hubert started to say something idiotic George felt the sole of Cecil's shoe push against his ankle again quite hard, so that the secret mischief had something rougher in it, as often with Cecil, and after a few testing and self-conscious seconds George regretfully edged his foot out of the way. "I'm sure you're absolutely right," said Cecil, with another solemn shake of the head. The fact that he was already mocking his brother made George queasily excited, as if some large shift of loyalties was about to be demanded of him, and he soon got up to deal with the wine for the fish, which the maids were hopelessly dim about.

Mrs. Kalbeck tackled a small trout with her customary relish. "Do you hunt?" she asked Cecil, in a square, almost jaunty way, rather as though she were always on a horse herself.

"I get out with the VWH now and then," said Cecil, "though I'm afraid my father doesn't approve."

"Oh, really?"

"He breeds livestock, you see, and has a tender feeling for creatures."

"Well, how very sweet," said Daphne, shaking her head with dawning approval.

Cecil held her eye with that affable superiority that George could only struggle to emulate. "As he doesn't ride to hounds, he's gained the reputation locally of being a great scholar." She smiled as if mesmerized by this, clearly having no idea what he meant.

George said, "Well, Cess, he is something of a scholar."

"Indeed he is," said Cecil. "He's seen his *Cattle Feeds and Cattle Care* go into a fourth edition, the most successful literary production of the Valance family by far."

"*So* far, you mean," said George.

"And does your mother share his views on hunting?" asked Mrs. Sawle teasingly, perhaps not sure whom to side with.

"Oh, Lord, no—no, she's all for killing. She likes me to get out with a gun when I can, though we keep it from my papa as much as possible. I'm quite a fair shot," said Cecil, and with another sly glance round in the candlelight, to see that he had them all: "The General sent me out with a gun when I was quite small, to kill a whole lot of rooks that were making a racket—I brought down four of them . . ."

"Really . . . ?" said Daphne, while George waited for the next line—

"But I wrote a poem about them the following day."

"Ah! well . . ."—again, they didn't quite know what to think; while George quickly explained that the General was what they called Cecil's mother, feeling keenly embarrassed both by the fact and by the pretence that he hadn't told them this before.

"I should have explained," said Cecil. "My mother's a natural leader of men. But she's a sweet old thing once you get to know her. Wouldn't you say, George?"

George thought Lady Valance the most terrifying person he'd ever met, dogmatic, pious, inexcusably direct, and immune to all jokes, even when explained to her; her sons had learned to treasure her earnestness as a great joke in itself. "Well, your mother devotes most of her time and energy to good works, doesn't she," George said, with wary piety of his own.

With the serving of the main course and a new wine, George suddenly felt it was going well, what had loomed as an unprecedented challenge was emerging a modest success. Clearly they all admired Cecil, and George's confidence in his friend's complete mastery of what to say and do outran his terror of his doing or saying something outrageous, even if simply intended to amuse. At Cambridge Cecil was frequently outrageous, and as for his letters—the things he wrote in letters appeared dimly to George now as a troupe of masked figures, Pompeian obscenities, hiding just out of view behind the curtains, and in the shadows of the inglenook. But for the moment all was well. Rather like the deep in Tennyson's poem, Cecil had many voices . . . George's toe sought out his friend's now and again, and was received with a playful wriggle rather than a jab. He worried about his mother drinking too much, but the claret was a good one, much commended by Hubert, and a convivial mood, of a perceptibly new kind for "Two Acres," suffused the whole party. Only his sister's stares and grins at Cecil, and her pert way of putting her head on one side, could really annoy him. Then to his horror he heard Mrs. Kalbeck say, "And I understand you and George are members of an ancient society!"

"Oh . . . oh . . . ," said George, though at once it was a test above all for Cecil. He found his failure to look at him a reproach in itself.

After a moment, with an almost apologetic flinch, Cecil said, "Well, no harm in your knowing, I dare say."

"And since candour is our watch-word!" George put in, glancing with lurking fury at his mother, who had been sworn to secrecy. Cecil must have seen, however, that a light-hearted embrace of the occasion was wiser than a haughty evasion.

"Oh yes, absolute candour," he said.

"I see . . . ," said Hubert, who clearly knew nothing about it. "And what are you candid about?"

Now Cecil did look at George. "Well that," he said, "I'm afraid we're not allowed to tell you."

"Strict secrecy," said George.

"That's right," said Cecil. "In fact that's our other watch-word. You really shouldn't have been told that we're members. It's a most serious breach"—with the steel of a real displeasure glimpsed through his playful one.

"Members of what?" said Daphne, joining the game.

"Exactly!" said George, with almost too much relief. "There is no society. I trust you haven't mentioned it to anyone else, Mother."

She smiled hesitantly. "I think only Mrs. Kalbeck."

"Oh, Mrs. Kalbeck doesn't count," said George.

"Really, George . . . !"—his mother almost tumbled her wineglass with the sweep of her sleeve. By luck, there was only a dribble left in it. George grinned at Clara Kalbeck. It was a teasing taste of candour itself, which at Cambridge overrode the principles of kindness and respect, but perhaps wasn't readily understood here, in the suburbs.

"No, you know what I mean," he said smoothly to his mother, and gave her a quick look, half smile, half frown.

"The Society is a secret," said Cecil, patiently, "so that no one can make a fuss about wanting to get into it. But of course I told the General the minute I was elected. And she will have told my father, since she's a great believer in candour herself. My grandfather was a member too, back in the forties. Many distinguished people were."

"We have nothing to do with politics, however," said George, "or worldly fame. We're thoroughly democratic."

"That's right," said Cecil, with a note of regret. "Many great writers have been members, of course." He looked down, blinking modestly, and at the same time, sitting forward, gave George a vicious kick under the table. "I'm so sorry!" he said, since George had yelped, and before anyone could quite understand what had happened the talk jumped on to other things, leaving George with a sense of guilty resentment, and beyond it a mysterious vision of screens, as of one train moving behind another, the large collective secret of the Society and the other unspeakable one still surely hidden from view.

By the time the pudding was brought in George was longing for dinner to be over, and wondering how soon he could politely arrange to get Cecil to himself again. He and Cecil ate everything with rapacious speed, while the others were surely dawdling wilfully and whimsically with their food. In the later phases of a meal, he well knew, his mother might go into trances of decoy and delay, a shivering delight in the mere fact of being at table, playful pleadings for a further drop of wine. After that, half an hour over port would be truly intolerable. Hubert's friendly banalities were as wearing as Daphne's prying prattle—"This will interest you," he would say, before launching into a bungled account of something everyone knew already. Perhaps tonight, being so few, they could all get up together; or would Cecil think that very bad form? Was he hideously bored? Or was he, just possibly, completely happy and at ease, and puzzled and even embarrassed by George's evident desire to get through the meal and away from his family as soon as possible? When his mother pushed back her chair and said, "Shall we . . . ?" with a guarded smile at Mrs. Kalbeck, George glanced at Cecil, and found him smiling back—a stranger might have thought amiably, but George knew it as a look of complete determination to get his way. As soon as the three females had passed through into the hall, Cecil nodded nicely to Hubert and said, "I have a horrible habit, anathema to polite society, which can only decently be pursued out of doors, under cover of darkness."

Hubert smiled anxiously at this unexpected confession, whilst producing from his pocket a silver cigarette case which he laid rather bashfully on the table. Cecil in turn drew out the leather sheath that held, like two cartridges in a gun, a brace of cigars. They seemed almost shockingly designed for an exclusive session *à deux*. "But my dear fellow," said Hubert, with a note of perplexity, and a shy sweep of the hand to show that he was free to do as he pleased.

"No, really, I couldn't possibly fug up in so"—Cecil was caught for a second—"so *intimate* a setting. Your mother would think very ill of me. It would be all over the house. Even at Corley, you know, we're fearfully strict about it," and he fixed Hubert with a wicked little smile, to suggest this was an exciting moment for him as well, a chance to break with convention whilst still somehow doing the right thing. George wasn't sure Hubert did see it quite like that, and not waiting for any further accommodations on his part, he said, "We'll have a proper jaw tomorrow night, Huey, when Harry comes."

"Well, of course we will," said Hubert. He seemed only lightly offended, puzzled but perhaps relieved, acquiescent already to the pact between the Cambridge men. "You'll see we don't stand on ceremony here, Valance! You go and make as much stink as you like outside, and I'll . . . I'll just shuffle through and have a gasper with the ladies." And he flourished his cigarette case at them with an air of cheerful self-sufficiency.

6

AFTER LEAVING the dining-room Daphne went upstairs and came back down in her mother's crimson shawl with black tassels, and with a feeling of doing things that were only just allowed. She saw the housemaid glance at her in what she sensed was a critical way. Coffee and liqueurs had been brought in, and Daphne asked absent-mindedly for a small glass of ginger brandy, which her mother passed to her with a raised eyebrow and the mocking suppression of a smile. Hubert, standing on the hearth-rug, was fiddling with a cigarette case, tapping a cigarette on the lid, and flexing his face as if about to complain, or make a joke, or anyhow say something, which never came. Cecil, apparently not wanting to pollute the house, had seized the moment to open the french windows and take his cigar outside; and George had followed. Mrs. Kalbeck sat down in her armchair with a preoccupied smile, and hummed one of her familiar leitmotifs as she looked over the various bottles. Everyone seemed to be quite drunk. To Daphne the lesson of these grown-up dinners was the way they went at the drinks, and what happened when they'd done so. She didn't mind the general increase in friendliness and noise, and people saying what they thought, even if some of the things George thought were quite strange. What troubled her was when her mother got flushed and talked too much, a development that the others, who were drunk themselves, seemed not to mind. The Welsh came out in her voice in a slightly embarrassing way. If they had music she tended to cry. Now she said, "Shall we have some music? I was going to play Cecil my Emmy Destinn."

"Well, the window's open," said Daphne, "he'll hear it outside." She felt drawn to the garden herself, and had put on the shawl with a vague romantic view to going out.

"Help me with the machine, child."

Freda swept across the room, brushing against the small round table with the photographs on it. She was wide-hipped and tightly corseted, and the gathered back of her dress twitched like a memory of a bustle. Daphne watched her for several abstracted seconds in which her mother's form, known more deeply and unthinkingly than anything in her life, appeared like that of someone quite unknown to her, a determined little woman in front of her in a shop or at the theatre. "Well . . . I have a few letters to write!" said Hubert. Mrs. Kalbeck smiled at him blandly to show she'd still be there when he got back.

The gramophone, in its upright mahogany disguise, was a recent gift of their neighbour Harry Hewitt; apart from the handle sticking out on the right it looked just like a nice old Sheraton cabinet, and part of the fun of playing it to people was to raise the lid and open the drawers and reveal it for what it was. There was no visible horn, and the drawers were really doors, concealing the mysterious louvred compartment from which the music emerged.

Now her mother was stooping and pulling records out from the cupboard at the bottom, trying to find Senta's Ballad. There were only a dozen records but of course they all looked the same and she didn't have her spectacles.

"Are we having the *Holländer*?" said Mrs. Kalbeck.

"If Mother can find it," said Daphne.

"Ah, good." The old woman sat back with a glass of cherry brandy and a patient smile. She had heard all their records several times, the John McCormack and the Nellie Melba, so the excitement was mixed with a sense of routine, which she seemed to find almost as pleasing.

"Is this it . . . ?" said Freda, squinting at the difficult small type on the label.

"Oh, let me do it," said Daphne, dropping down beside her and nudging her until she went away.

It was Daphne's own favourite, because something she couldn't describe took place inside her when she heard it, something quite different from the song from *Traviata* or "Linden Lea." Each time, she looked forward to running again through the keen, almost painful novelty of these particular emotions. She set the disc on the mat, took another big sip from her glass, coughed shamefully, and then cranked up the handle as tight as it would go.

"Careful, child . . . !" said her mother, one hand reaching for the mantelpiece, eyes fixed as if about to sing herself.

"She's a strong girl," said Mrs. Kalbeck.

Daphne lowered the needle and at once walked towards the window, to see if she could spot the boys outside.

The orchestra, they had all agreed, left much to be desired. The strings shrilled like a tin whistle, and the brass thumped like something being thrown downstairs. Daphne knew how to make allowances for this. She had heard a real orchestra at the Queen's Hall; she had been taken to *The Rhinegold* at Covent Garden, where they'd had six harps as well as anvils and a giant gong. With a record you learned to ignore the shortcomings if you knew what this piping and thumping stood for.

When Senta started singing it was spellbinding—Daphne said this word to herself with a further shiver of pleasure. She sat on the window-seat with the shawl pulled round her and a mysterious smile on her face at the first intimacies of the ginger brandy. She'd had a real drink before, a half glass of champagne when Huey came of age, and once long ago she and George had done a small but rash experiment with Cook's brandy. Like the music, a drink was marvellous as well as alarming. She was gripped by the girl's eerie calls, *Jo-ho-he, Jo-ho-he,* which had a clear warning of tragedy to them; but at the same time she had a delicious sense of having nothing whatever to worry about. She looked casually at the others, her mother braced as if for the impact of salt waves, Mrs. Kalbeck tilting her head in more mature appraisal. Daphne saw the beauty of being spontaneous, and had to hold back a number of things she suddenly felt like saying. She frowned at the Persian rug. There were two sections, which recurred: there was the wild storm music, where you saw the men hanging in the rigging, and then, when the storm was stilled, the most beautiful tune she'd ever heard came in, dropping and soaring, rapturous and free and yet intensely sad, and in either case somehow inevitable. She didn't know what Senta was saying, beyond the recurrent sounding of the word *Mann,* but she sensed the presence of passionate love, and felt the air of legend, which had a natural hold on her. Emmy Destinn herself she saw as a wild waif with long dark hair, somehow marked out by her own peculiar name. Almost at once she sang a high note, the brass fell downstairs and Daphne ran over to lift the needle off the disc.

"It is sadly shortened," said Mrs. Kalbeck. "In truth there are two more strophes."

"Yes, dear, you said before," said Freda rather sharply; and then, softening as always, "There is only so much they can squeeze on to the record. To me it's a marvel that they do that."

"Then shall we have it again?" said Daphne, looking back at them.

"Oh, why not!" said her mother, in a tone of harmless female conspiracy, given more swagger by what Daphne saw as a small crowd of empty glasses. Mrs. Kalbeck nodded in helpless agreement. Records were indeed marvels, but they were only tiny helpings from the ocean of music.

During the second helping Daphne moved very slowly across the room, picked up her glass and drained it, and put it down again with a complicated feeling of sadness and satisfaction that was thoroughly endorsed by Wagner's restless ballad. She slipped out into the garden just as the music hurtled to its end. "Oh darling, should you?" wailed her mother. It was simply that the lure of the other conspiracy, the one she had entered into with the boys in the wood, was so much more urgent than keeping company with the two old women. "There may be a dewfall!" said Freda, in a tone that suggested an avalanche.

"I know," Daphne called back, seizing her excuse, "I've left Lord Tennyson out in the dew!" Things seemed to come to her.

She went quickly past the windows of the house, and then stood still on the edge of the lawn. The grass was dry when she stooped and touched it—it was still too warm for dew. Warm and yet not warm. Seeing the house from outside she remembered her earlier twinge of loneliness, when the sun was setting and the lights came on indoors. She did have to find her books, which would be lying just where she'd left them, by the hammock. She wanted to prepare for the Tennyson reading that Cecil had proposed, she was already imagining it . . . "I'm to be Queen o' the May, mother, I'm to be Queen o' the May . . . ," or, " 'The curse is come upon me!' cried the Lady of Shalott" . . . completely different, of course—she couldn't decide. But where were the boys? The night seemed to have swallowed them up completely, leaving only the whispering of the breeze in the tree-tops. All she could see was vague silhouettes of black on grey, but the smells of the trees and the grass flooded the air. She felt that Nature was restoring itself in a secret flow of scent while people, most people, stayed heedlessly indoors. There were privet smells and earth smells and rose smells that she took in without naming them in her heady swoop across the lawn. Her heart was beating with the undeniable daring of being out here, and being slightly adrift, coming suddenly on the stone bench and stopping to peer around. Up above, the stars were gathering all the time, sliding out between high faint trails of cloud as though they had grown used to her. She heard a sort of moan, just ahead of her, quickly stifled, and a run of recognizable giggles; and of course that further smell, distinct from dry grass and vegetation, the gentlemanly whiff of Cecil's cigar.

She went a few steps towards the clump of trees where the hammock was slung. She didn't know if she'd been seen. It was oddly like the minute of uncertainty before, in the wood, when Cecil had just arrived, and she couldn't tell if she was spying. Now, though, it was far too dark for spying. She heard Cecil say something funny about a moustache, "quite an adorable moustache"; George murmured something and Cecil said, "I suppose he wears it to make himself look older, but of course it has just the opposite effect, he looks like a boy playing hide and seek." "Hmm . . . I'm not sure anyone's seeking especially," said George. "Well . . . ," said Cecil, and there was a little stifled rumpus of giggles and grunts that went on for ten seconds, till George said, rather loudly, gasping for breath, "No, no, besides, Hubert's a womanizer through and through."

A womanizer . . . ! The word lay, sinuous and poisonous, in the shadowy borders of Daphne's vocabulary. For a moment she pictured it, and behind it a vaguer image still, of a man dancing with a woman in a low-cut dress. The drunkenness of her own evening was lurchingly intensified in this imaginary room, where it was really the woman she saw, and certainly not Hubert, who was quite the most awkward figure when it came to dancing. A strange silence fell, in which she heard her own pulse in her ear. Part of her, she realized, needed to learn more. Then, "What is it, Daphne?" said George.

"Oh, are you here?" she said, and she pushed on, under the low branches that screened the hammock on that side. "I've left my books out here, in the dew."

"Well, I haven't seen them," said George, and she heard the hammock rope shift and creak against the tree.

"No, you wouldn't have seen them, of course, because it's the night." She laughed mockingly and slid her foot forward over the invisible ground. "But I know where they are. I can picture them."

"All right," said George.

She edged forward again, and could just make out the slump of the hammock as it tilted and steadied. Again, she stooped to pat the grass, and half fell forward, startled and amused by her own tipsiness. "Isn't Cecil with you?" she said artfully.

"Ha . . . !" said Cecil softly, just above her, and pulled on his cigar—she looked up and saw the scarlet burn of its tip and beyond it, for three seconds, the shadowed gleam of his face. Then the tip twitched away and faded and the darkness teemed in to where his features had been, while the sharp dry odour floated wide.

"Are you both in the hammock!" She stood up straight, with a sense that she'd been tricked, or anyway overlooked, in this new game they were making up. She reached out a hand for the webbing, where it fanned towards their feet. It would be very easy, and entertaining, to rock them, or even tip them out; though she felt at the same time a simple urge to climb in with them. She had shared the hammock with her mother, when she was smaller, and being read to; now she was mindful of the hot cigar. "Well, I must say," she said. The cigar tip, barely showing, dithered in the air like some dimly luminous bug and then glowed into life again, but now it was George's face that she saw in its faint devilish light. "Oh, I thought it was Cecil's cigar," she said simply.

George chortled in three quick huffs of smoke. And Cecil cleared his throat—somehow supportively and appreciatively. "So it was," said George, in his most paradoxical tone. "I'm smoking Cecil's cigar too."

"Oh really . . . ," said Daphne, not knowing what tone to give the words. "Well, I shouldn't let Mother find out."

"Oh, most young men smoke," said George.

"Oh, do they?" she said, deciding sarcasm was her best option. She watched, pained and tantalized, as the next glow showed up a hint of Cecil's cheeks and watchful eyes through a fading puff of smoke. Quite without warning *The Flying Dutchman* began again, startlingly loud through the open windows.

"God! What's that, the third time . . . !" said George.

"Lord," said Cecil. "They are keen."

"It's Kalbeck, of course," George said, as though to exonerate the Sawles themselves from such obsessive behaviour. "God knows what the Cosgroves must think."

"Mother loved Wagner long before she met Mrs. Kalbeck," said Daphne.

"We all love Wagner, darling. But he's quite repetitious enough on his own account without playing the same record ten times."

"It's Senta's Ballad," Daphne said, not immune to it herself this third time, in fact suddenly more moved by it out in the open, as if it were in the air itself, a part of nature, and wanting them all to listen and share in it. The orchestra sounded better from here, like a real band heard at a distance, and Emmy Destinn seemed even more wild and intense. For a moment she pictured the lit house behind them as a ship in the night. "Cecil," she said fondly, using his name for the first time, "I expect you understand the words."

"*Ja, ja,* clear as mud," said Cecil, with a friendly though disconcerting snort.

"She's a mad girl in love with a man she's never seen," said George, "and the man is under a curse and can only be redeemed by a woman's love. And she rather fancies being that woman. There you are."

"One feels no good will come of it," said Cecil.

"Oh, but listen . . . ," said Daphne.

"Would you like a go?" said Cecil.

Daphne, taking in what she'd just been told about Senta, leant on the rope. "In the hammock . . . ?"

"On the cigar."

"Really . . . ," murmured George, a little shocked.

"Oh, I don't think so!"

Cecil took an exemplary pull on it. "I know girls aren't meant to have them."

Now the lovely tune was pulsing through the garden, full of yearning and defiance and the heightened effect of beauty encountered in an unexpected setting. She really didn't want the cigar, but she was worried by the thought of missing a chance at it. It was something none of her friends had done, she was pretty sure of that.

"No, it is a fine song," said Cecil, and she heard how his words were a little slurred and careless. Now the cigar was being passed to George again.

"Oh, all right," she said.

"Yes?"

"I mean, yes, please."

She leant on George and felt the whole hammock shudder, and held his arm firmly to take the item, taboo and already slightly disgusting, from between his thumb and forefinger. By now she could half-see the two boys squashed together, rather absurd, drunk of course, but also solid and established, like a long-ago memory of her parents sitting up in bed. She had the smell of the thing near her face, almost coughed before she tasted it, and then pinched her lips quickly round it, with a feeling of shame and duty and regret.

"Oh!" she said, thrusting it away from her and coughing harshly at the tiny inrush of smoke. The bitter smoke was horrible, but so was the unexpected feel of the thing, dry to the fingers but wet and decomposing on the lips and tongue. George took it from her with a vaguely remorseful laugh. When she'd coughed again she turned and did a more unladylike thing and spat on the grass. She wanted the whole thing out of her system. She was glad of the dark, and wiped her mouth with the back of her hand. Beyond her, in the friendly familiar house, Emmy Destinn was still singing, in noble ignorance of Daphne's behaviour.

"Want another puff?" said Cecil, as though satisfied with her reaction to the first.

"I think not!" said Daphne.

"You'll like the second one much more."

"That seems unlikely."

"And the third one will be better still."

"And before you know where you are," said George, "you'll be strolling through Stanmore with a pongy old cheroot clamped between your teeth."

"Don't I detect Miss Sawle's cigar?" said Cecil facetiously.

"That would never happen," said Daphne.

But she was really very happy after all, standing there, peering some-what speculatively into the smoky darkness. "Is ginger brandy consid-ered a strong drink?" she was saying. It must be the drink that gave this lovely spontaneity to things, so that she spoke or moved without decid-ing to do so.

"Oh dear, Daph," said George. And before she knew what she'd done, she was heaving herself, gasping and laughing, onto the near end of the hammock, where the boys' feet were.

"Mind out!" said George. "That's my foot . . ."

"You'll break the blasted thing," said Cecil.

"For God's sake . . . !" said George, tilting sideways in the effort to leap out, and in a second she was jolted on to the ground. Cecil was tum-bling; his foot caught her, rather hard, between the ribs.

"Ow!" she said, and then "ow . . . ," but she despised the shock and fright; she was laughing again as the boys reached awkwardly for each other, and then she let herself be pulled up. She knew she had heard her shawl tearing as she fell, and that this was one part of the escapade she would not get away with; but again she didn't terribly care.

"Perhaps we should go in," said Cecil, "before something truly scan-dalous happens."

They shepherded each other out on to the lawn, with little pats and murmurs. George spent a moment tucking his shirt in and getting his trousers straight. "At Corley, of course, you have a smoking-room," he said. "This sort of thing could never happen."

"Indeed," said Cecil solemnly. Emmy Destinn had finished, and in her place Daphne saw the figure of her mother coming to the lighted window and peering vainly out.

"We're all here!" Daphne shouted. And in the darkness, under the millions of stars, with the boys on either side of her, she felt she could speak for them all; there was a hilarious safety that seemed a renewal of the pact they had made without speaking when Cecil arrived.

"Well, hurry in," her mother said, in a hectic, ingenious tone. "I want Cecil to read to us."

"There you are," murmured Cecil, straightening his bow-tie. Daphne glanced up at him. George went responsibly ahead on the path, and as they followed behind him Cecil slipped his large hot hand around her, and left it there, just where he'd kicked her, until they reached the open french windows.

7

AFTER BREAKFAST next morning she found Cecil in a deckchair on the lawn, writing in a small brown book. She sat down too, on a nearby wall, keen to observe a poet at work, and just close enough to put him off; in a minute he turned and smiled and shut his book with the pencil in it. "What have you got there?" he said.

She was holding a small book of her own, an autograph album bound in mauve silk. "I don't know if you can be prevailed upon," she said.

"May I see?"

"If you like you can just put your name. Though obviously . . ."

Cecil's long arm and blue-veined hand seemed to pull her to him. She presented the book with a blush and mixed feelings of pride and inadequacy. She said, "I've only been keeping it a year."

"So whom have you got?"

"I've got Arthur Nikisch. I suppose he's the best."

"Right-oh!" said Cecil, with the delighted firmness that conceals a measure of uncertainty. She leant over the back of the deckchair to guide him to the page. He was like an uncle this morning, confidential without the least hint of intimacy. Last night's rough-house, apparently, had never happened. She noticed again that smell he had, as if he'd always just got back from one of his rambles, or scrambles, which she pictured as fairly boisterous affairs. Oh, it was so typical of boys, they got on their dignity, they kept closing the door on some interesting scene they had let you witness a moment before. Though perhaps it was meant as a reproach to her, for last night's foolery.

"I got him when we went to *The Rhinegold*."

"Ah yes . . . He's quite a big shot, isn't he?"

"Herr Nikisch? Well, he's the conductor!"

"No, I've heard of him," said Cecil. "You may as well know that I have a tin ear, by the way."

"Oh . . . ," said Daphne, and looked for a moment at Cecil's left ear, which was brown and sunburnt on top. She said, "I should have thought a poet had a good ear," with a frown at the unexpected cleverness of her own words.

"I can hear poems," said Cecil. "But all the Valances are tone-deaf,

I'm afraid. The General's almost queer about it. She went to *The Gondoliers* once, but she said never again. She thought it was never going to end."

"Well, she certainly wouldn't like Wagner, in that case," said Daphne, rescuing a kindly superiority from her initial sense of disappointment. And still not quite sure she had got to the bottom of it, "Though you said you liked the gramophone last night."

"Oh, I don't hate it, it's just rather lost on me. I was enjoying the company." His ear coloured slightly at this, and she saw that perhaps she'd been given a compliment, and blushed a little herself. He said, "Did you care for the opera when you went?"

"They had a new swimming apparatus for the Rhinemaidens, but I didn't find it very convincing."

"It must be hard work swimming and singing at the same time," said Cecil, turning the page. "Now who's this Byzantine fellow?"

"That's Mr. Barstow."

"Should I know him?"

"He's the curate in Stanmore," said Daphne, unsure if they were both admiring the elaborate penwork.

"I see . . . And now: Olive Watkins, you could read that at twenty paces."

"I didn't really want to have her, as it's supposed to be only adults, but she got me for hers." Underneath her signature Olive had written, with great force, "A friend in need is a friend indeed," the indentations of the pen being readable on the following pages. "She has the best collection, certainly that I know," said Daphne. "She has Winston Churchill."

"My word . . . ," said Cecil respectfully.

"I know."

Cecil turned a page or two. "But you've got Jebland, look. That's special in another way."

"He's my other best," Daphne admitted. "He only sent it me the week before his propeller broke. I've learned that you can't wait with airmen. They're not like other autographs. That's how Olive lost Stefanelli."

"And does Olive have Jebland?"

"No, she does not," said Daphne, trying to subdue the note of triumph to one of respect for the dead aviator.

"I see it's rather morbid," said Cecil. "You make me feel a little anxious."

"Oh, everyone else in it is still alive!"

Cecil closed the book. "Well, leave it with me, and I promise I'll think something up before I go."

"Do feel free to write some occasional verse." She came round the chair and stood looking at him full-face. He was fingering his own book again as he squinted up at her, smiling tensely against the light. She felt the momentary advantage she had over him, and gazed with a novel kind of licence at his parted lips and his strong brown neck where it emerged from his soft blue shirt. He was surely writing a poem now, the pencil was waiting in the cruck of the notebook. She felt she couldn't ask about it. But nor could she let him alone. She said, "Have you seen over the garden?"

"D'you know, I have. I rambled right round it with Georgie, first thing."

"Oh . . ."

"Oh, long before you were up. I went and tipped him out of bed."

"I see . . ."

"I'm a pagan, you see, and I worship the dawn. I'm trying to instil the cult in your brother."

"I wonder how you'll get on." Cecil closed his eyes languidly as he smiled, so that she had a further sense of screened-off mysteries. "Perhaps tomorrow you could tip me out of bed too."

"Do you think your mother would approve?"

"Oh, she won't mind."

"Well, we'll see."

"I could show you all kinds of things." She felt the grass with her hand before sitting down beside Cecil's chair. "I can't believe George showed you the whole of 'Two Acres.' "

"Well, possibly not . . . ," said Cecil, with a quick snigger.

Daphne peered encouragingly at the view—the neat parched lawn, the little tor of the rockery, the line of dark firs that hid the Cosgroves' potting-shed and motor-garage. To her the "Two" in her house's name had always been reassuring, a quietly emphatic boast to schoolfriends who lived in a town or a terrace, the proof of a generous over-provision. But in Cecil's presence she felt the first shimmer of uncertainty. Sitting side by side, she hoped to make him share her view, but wondered if she hadn't started sharing his instead. She said, "You know, the rockery was my father's contribution."

"He must have put a good deal of work into it," said Cecil.

"Yes, he worked terribly hard at it. Those large red stones came all the way from Devon—which of course *he* did!"

"They will be a strange geological conundrum to later ages," said Cecil.

"Yes, I suppose they will."

"They will be like the monoliths of Stonehenge."

"Mm," said Daphne, sensing teasing where she'd hoped for something better. She pressed on, "My father wasn't artistic like my mother, but she gave him a free hand with the rockery. In a way it's his monument."

Cecil stared at it with a chastened expression. "I suppose you don't really remember your father," he said. "You must have been too young."

"Oh, I remember him quite well." She nodded up at him. "He used to come home from work, and have his Old Smuggler while I was in the bath."

"You mean he drank whisky in the bathroom?"

"Yes, while he was telling me a story. We had a nanny of course, who used to bath me. Frankly, I think we had rather more money then, than we have now."

Cecil gave her the fleeting wince of merely abstract sympathy that she'd noticed already when it came to money or servants. "I can't imagine my father doing that," he said.

"Well, your father doesn't go to work, does he."

"That's true," said Cecil, and giggled attractively.

"Of course Huey works very hard. My mother says one of us needs to get married."

"Well, I've no doubt you will," said Cecil, his dark eyes holding hers and his eyebrow rising slightly for emphasis and a hint of amusement, so that her heart thumped and she hurried on,

"One day, we'll see. I dare say we all will." She wanted to say she had overheard them last night, and to tell him they were wrong, he and George: Hubert wasn't a womanizer at all, he was really intensely respectable. But she was frightened by this unknown subject, and worried that she might have misunderstood.

"I don't think George has a particular girlfriend?" said Cecil, after a minute.

"We all thought you would know," she said, and then regretted the suggestion that they'd been talking about him. Something in Cecil of course demanded to be talked about. She tore up a few blades of grass, and glanced at him, feeling still the great novelty and interest of his presence. He shifted in the deckchair, crossed his right ankle on his left knee, a glimpse of brown calf. He was wearing white canvas shoes, scuffed at the heel. It would be amusing if they could explain George to each other behind his back. She said, "We all thought there might be someone when he started getting letters; but of course they were from you!"

Cecil looked both pleased and embarrassed by this, and glanced over his shoulder at the house. "But what about your mother, do you think?" he said, in a sudden sensitive tone. "She's still quite young, and really most attractive. She might marry again herself. She must have many admirers . . . ?"

"Oh, I don't think so!" Daphne frowned and blushed at the question. It was one thing to talk about poor George's prospects, quite another to ask about those of a middle-aged lady whom he hardly knew. It was most inappropriate; and besides, the last thing she wanted was a stepfather. She pictured Harry Hewitt standing on her father's rockery—worse, ordering its demolition. Though actually, almost certainly, they would all have to move to Mattocks, with its peculiar pictures and statues. She sat looking at Cecil's white shoes, and thinking rather hard. He didn't press her for an answer. She saw it was a new kind of talk, which she wasn't quite ready for, like certain books, which were in English obviously, but too grown-up for her to understand. He said,

"I didn't mean to pry. You know how Georgie and I and all our lot are devils for speaking candidly."

"That's all right," she said.

"Tell me it's none of my business."

"Well, there's a man who's coming to dinner tonight that I think likes my mother a lot," she said, and a sense of betrayal discoloured the following seconds.

"Is this Harry?"

"Yes, it is," she said, feeling her shame still more.

"The man who gave you the gramophone."

"Oh, yes, well he's given us all kinds of things. He's given Hubert a gun, and . . . lots of things. The Complete Works of Sheridan."

"I imagine Huey might appreciate some of these gifts rather more than others," said Cecil, again familiar and casual.

"Well . . . He gave me a dressing set, with a scent bottle, which I'm not old enough for, and silver-backed brushes."

"He sounds like Father Christmas," said Cecil; and with a hint of boredom, looking round, "What a jolly fellow."

"Hmm. He's very generous, I suppose, but he's not a bit jolly. You'll see." She glanced up at him, still strangely indignant both with him and with Harry, but he was gazing at the top of the spinney, where they'd met last night, as if at something much more intriguing. "He goes to Germany a great deal, he does import-export, you know. He brings us back things."

"And you think all these presents are his way of . . . paying court to your mamma," said Cecil.

"I fear so."

Cecil's splendid profile, the autocratic nose and slightly bulbous eye, seemed poised for judgement; but when he turned and smiled she felt the sudden return of his attention and kindness. "But, my dear child, you've no need to fear unless you think she returns his feelings."

"Oh, I don't know . . . !" She was flustered, by having come so far, and by this unexpected word *child,* which was what her mother herself called her, quite naturally, though often with a hint of criticism. She had got it last night, once or twice, when she was trying to make Cecil feel at home and asking him questions. He must have heard her say it. Now she felt some not quite nice rhetorical advantage had been taken of her—he'd humbled her at the very moment he was meant to be cheering her up.

Cecil smiled. "I tell you what. I'll have a good look at him, as a total outsider, and let you know what I think."

"All right . . . ," said Daphne, not at all sure about this compromise.

"Ah!" said Cecil, sitting forward in his chair. George was coming across the lawn, his jacket hooked over his shoulder, and whistling cheerily. Then he stood looking down at them, with a question hidden somewhere in his smile.

"What is that thing you're always whistling?" said Daphne.

"I don't know," said George. "It's a song my gyp sings, 'When I sees you, my heart goes boomps-a-daisy.' "

"Really . . . ! I'd have thought if you had to whistle, you'd have chosen something nice," and seeing a chance to bring them all back to the subject of last night—"such as *The Flying Dutchman,* for instance."

George pressed his hand to his heart and started on the lovely part of Senta's Ballad, staring at her with his eyebrows raised and slowly shaking his head, as if to throw his own self-consciousness over to her. He had a sweet high swooping whistle, but he put in so much vibrato he made the song sound rather silly, and soon he couldn't keep his lips together and the whistle became a breathy laugh.

"Hah . . . ," muttered Cecil, seeming slightly uncomfortable, standing up and slipping his notebook into his jacket pocket. Then, with a cold smile, "No . . . I can't whistle, I'm afraid."

"Well, with your tin ear!" said Daphne.

"I'm just going to take this precious book inside," he said, holding up Daphne's little album. And they watched him cross the lawn and go in by the garden door.

"So what were you talking about to Cess?" said George, looking down at her again with his funny smile.

She picked over the grass in front of her, in a teasing delay. Her first thought, surprisingly strong, was that her own relations with Cecil, going on quite independently of George's, if not entirely satisfactorily, must be kept as secret as possible. She felt there was something there, which mustn't be exposed to reason or mockery. "We were talking about you, of course," she said.

"Oh," said George, "that must have been interesting."

Daphne gave a soft snort at this. "If you must know, Cecil was asking if you had any particular girlfriends."

"Oh," said George, more airily this time, "and what did you say?"— he had started blushing, and turned away in a vain attempt to conceal the fact. Now he was gazing off down the garden, as if he'd just noticed something interesting. It was quite unexpected, and it even took Daphne, with her sisterly intuition, a few moments to understand, and then shout out,

"Oh, George, you have!"

"What . . . ? Oh nonsense . . . ," George said. "Be quiet!"

"You have, you have!" said Daphne, feeling at once how the joy of discovery was shadowed by the sense of being left behind.

8

ONCE THE GENTLEMEN had gone out, Jonah set off upstairs, and was almost at the top when he found he'd forgotten Mr. Cecil's shoes, and turned back to get them. But just then he heard voices in the hall below. They must have gone into the study for a minute, to the right of the front door: now they were by the hall-stand, getting their hats. Jonah stood where he was, not hiding, but in the shadows, on the turn of the stair.

"Is this one yours?" Cecil said.

"Oh, you ass," said George. "Come on, let's get out. I'll bring this, I think, just in case."

"Good idea . . . How do I look?"

"You look quite decent, for once. Jonah must be doing all right for you."

"Oh, Jonah's a dream," said Cecil. "Did I tell you, I'm taking him back to Corley with me."

"Oh no, you don't!" There was a little tussle that Jonah couldn't see, giggling and gasping, voices under their breath—". . . ow! . . . for God's sake, Cecil . . ."—and then the noise of the front door opening. Jonah went up three steps and peeped out of the little window. Cecil vaulted the garden gate, and George seemed to think about it, just for a moment, and then opened it and went out. Cecil was already some way down the lane.

Jonah waited a minute longer where he was, looking up the last three stairs and across the landing towards the spare-room door. *Jonah's a dream*—what a way they talked . . . though it must mean things were going all right, he was doing it all convincingly. He didn't think Mrs. Sawle would let Cecil take him away, and he certainly didn't want to leave home. He'd been into Harrow, of course, many times, and Edgware, and once to the Alexandra Palace to hear the organ . . . He went on up. The landing was dark, with its oak panelling and thick Turkey carpet, but the bedrooms were flung open so as to air and were full of light. He could hear Veronica, the housemaid, in Mr. Hubert's room, her grunts as she shook and thumped the pillows; she talked to herself, in a pleasant, businesslike mutter, ". . . there you are . . . up we go . . . thank you *very* much . . ." Jonah felt he had understood something, they had decided he was ready. He looked forward to straightening the room and taking his time with Cecil's things, examining the buttons and pockets in more detail. He would never have said it to anyone downstairs, but he thought if he learned valeting it could be a job for him, in a year or two's time. One day, perhaps, he would let Mr. Cecil, or someone very like him, take him away after all.

Then he pushed open the door, and saw at once he knew nothing, they'd told him nothing about what went on between bedtime and breakfast. It was like stepping into another house. Or else, he felt, as he took two or three short steps into the room, or else this Mr. Cecil Valance was a lunatic; and at this thought he gave a sort of staring giggle. Well, he would have to wait for Veronica. The bed was all over the floor as if a fight had taken place in it. He looked at the shaving-water cold and scummy in the basin, the shaving-brush lying in a wet ring on top of the bookcase. He frowned at the clothes strewn over the floor and across the little armchair with a new and painful feeling that he'd known them in an earlier and happier time, when things were still going convincingly. And the roses were as good as dead—yes, Cecil must have knocked them over and then jammed the stems just anyhow into the vase with no water. Their heads had dropped after a few hours of neglect, and a patch on the patterned rug was dark and damp to the back of the hand. On the dressing-table the scribbled sheets of paper were more what Jonah had expected. "When you were there, and I away," Jonah read, "But scenting in the Alpine air the roses of an English May." Then he snatched up the shaving-brush and stared at the oily pool it had made.

Jonah went over to the waste-paper basket, as if routinely tidying a barely occupied room, and took out the handful of bits of paper. He saw one of them was written by George, and felt embarrassed on his behalf that his guest should have made such a mess. It was hard to read . . . "Veins," it seemed to say, if that was how you spelt it: "Viens." The poetry notebook, which Jonah had been told never to touch, still lay within reach, on the bedside table. Later, he thought, he almost certainly would have a look at it.

"I see he's made himself at home," said Veronica from the door, and her competent tone cheered Jonah up. "Yes, Cook said he'll make a mess but he'll give you ten shillings—could be a guinea if you're lucky."

"I expect so," said Jonah, as though used to such treatment, stuffing the bits of paper awkwardly into his trouser pocket. Then he couldn't help smiling. "Cook said that?"

Veronica plucked the pillows off the bed. "Well, he's an aristocrat," she said, with the air of someone who'd seen a few. "If they make a mess they can pay for it." She pulled the rucked bottom sheet tight and looked at it with a raised eyebrow and a strange twist of the mouth. "Well, Jonah, look what I see."

"Oh yes . . . ," said Jonah.

"Your gentleman's had a mission."

"Oh," said Jonah, with the same look of suppressed confusion.

Veronica glanced at him shrewdly but not unkindly. "You don't know what that is, do you? A nocturnal mission, they call it. It's something the young gentlemen are very much prone to." She tugged off the sheet with surprising strength, the mattress shuddering as it came free. "There you are, smell it, you can always tell."

"No, I won't!" said Jonah, feeling this wasn't right, and colouring up at the sudden connection it made with a worry of his own.

"Well, you'll know all about it soon enough, my dear," said Veronica, who had just taken on in Jonah's mind the character of someone alarmingly older and rather wicked. "Ah! Don't you worry. You should see Mr. Hubert's. Have to change his sheets two or three times a week. Mrs. S. knows—I mean, she didn't say anything exactly, she just said, 'Any marks or stains, Veronica, kindly change the boys' sheets.' It's a fact of nature, my dear, I'm afraid."

Jonah busied himself picking up and folding clothes, unsure if the items that had been worn should be put back in the wardrobe or politely hidden somewhere else until Cecil left and they could be packed again; he couldn't ask Veronica anything while her upsetting little speech was still burning his ears. Here was the cast-off dress-shirt from last night, a grey smear across its stiff white front, cigar ash perhaps, and the beautiful singlet and drawers, fine as ladies' wear, now thoughtlessly stained in ways he wouldn't be able to look into until later, when he was by himself. He took the wash-basin out of the room and across the landing and emptied it carefully into the lavatory. A thousand tiny bristles in a scum of soap still clung to the curved surface, and he stared at them, as he did at everything of Cecil's, with an awful mixture of worry and pride.

Later he went out to the privy, and in the grey light through the frosted-glass square in the door he took out the rubbish from his pocket and sat turning it over, turning it round and reading the crossed-out words on it. He had a clear sense of giving way to "idle curiosity," which was something Cook was very censorious about. The ripe collective stink beneath him, thinly smothered with coke ash from the kitchen, made his actions feel more furtive and wicked. He wasn't quite sure even why he was doing it. The gentlemen's talk was different from normal talk, and George was different too, now his friend was here . . . "A hammock in the shade," Jonah made out. "A larch tree at your head and at your feet a pussy willow." He was slow to make the connection with anything he knew, and it was only when he'd read a bit more that the uneasy recognition dawned on him. Mr. Cecil was writing about their own hammock, which Jonah himself had helped Mr. Hubert to sling up at the start of the summer. He wondered what he was going to say about it. "A birch tree at your feet, And overhead a weeping willow"—he couldn't make up his mind! Then written up the edge of the page, "As wood-lice chew willows, So do mites bite pillows!"—this was crossed out, with a wavy line. The muddled worry that he was saying something shocking, that there might be mites in the bedding here, in Mrs. Sawle's best goose pillows, took a moment to rise and fade. He remembered it was poetry, but wasn't sure if that made it more or less likely to be true. Another piece of paper had been torn in half, and he held the two edges together, wondering if Wilkes ever did anything like this, when he emptied his master's waste-paper basket.

> *Within that ~~thronging~~ singing woodland round*
> *Two blessed acres of English ground,*
> *And ~~leading~~ roaming by its outmost edge*
> *Beneath a darkling ~~cypress myrtle~~ privet hedge*
> *With hazel-clusters hung above*
> *We'll walk the ~~secret long dark~~ wild dark path of love*
> *Whose secrets none shall ever hear*
> *Twixt ~~set of sun~~ late last rook and Chaunticleer.*
> *Love as vital as the spring*
> *And secret as—XXX (some<u>thing</u>!)*
> *Hearty, lusty, true and bold,*
> *Yet shy to have its honour told—*

here there was a very dense crossing out, as if not only Cecil's words but his very ideas had had to be obliterated. Jonah heard the well-known scrape of the scullery door and footsteps on the brick path—and in a moment the bulk of a large person outside (Cook, was it, or Miss Mustow?) cut off his light, and now his hand shook as the latch was rattled and he fumbled the papers back into his pocket. "Just a minute!" he called out, wondering for a second if he should throw the bits of paper down into the privy, but then thinking better of it.

9

FREDA LIFTED HER GLASS and surveyed the table with the open-minded smile of someone who has not been paying attention. But yes, indeed, it was Germany again, and now Harry said how "each day brings us one day nearer to the German war"—a catch-phrase of his that was beginning to irritate her. "I'm in and out of Hamburg a good deal on business," he explained, "and I know what I've seen." Freda didn't care at all for the idea of a German war, and felt impatient with Harry for predicting it so insistently; but Cecil seemed ready to fight at once—he said he would jump at the chance. It was touching, and slightly comical, to see George's indecision. Anyone less inclined to fight it would be hard to imagine, but he was clearly reluctant to disappoint Cecil. "I suppose I would, would I?—if it came to it," he said.

"Oh, no question, old chap," said Cecil, and managed, with a slow turn of the head, to give them all a look at his profile. He'd told them already how much he liked killing, and clearly Germans would represent an exciting advance on mere foxes, pheasants and ducks. Freda was glad Clara wasn't here tonight: her brother, who seemed to be her only relative, was in the Kaiser's army, though in a clerical job of some kind, thank heavens. She said,

"I'm not quite certain I want my boys getting hacked to pieces"—in a droll tone, but the image startled them all, the boys themselves gleaming in the candlelight, Huey wiping his moustache with a white napkin. Huey said sternly but kindly,

"Let us hope it doesn't come to that, Mother."

"I think our boys are ready for a scrap," said Elspeth.

"Yes, but you don't have any boys to get in a scrap, my dear," said Freda. Elspeth was Harry's spinster sister, and one had to wonder, if Harry were to marry, where Elspeth would go. She'd kept house for him for so many years that it was hard to imagine her in a house of her own. But she would have to go somewhere . . . But then, *Harry marry*, wasn't there something absurd in the very phrase?

The pudding was a macédoine of fruits, the apples from the orchard. Cecil, on Freda's right, ate quickly and without apparent pleasure, even with a vague air of annoyance. Disheartening for a hostess, but was it perhaps a sign of good breeding not to dwell on food? Something put in front of you by servants, something that stopped you talking, however briefly, about matters that were more important. George tonight was beside Cecil, and somehow teamed with him; now and then he put a hand on his sleeve and murmured to him under the louder talk all around, but Cecil's preference was to speak to the whole table. Cecil too had been to Germany, and produced rather crushingly a good deal of information on the military and industrial side—much of it seemingly untranslatable. Freda, whose German was limited to heroic expressions of love, loyalty and revenge, and how to ask for a brandy and water, soon felt sad and somewhat squashed. Her Germany was hot, formal though not well organized, a maze of arrangements all shot through and redeemed for ever by the love of the Volsungs, the Forest Murmurs, and Wotan's Farewell, the keenest ten minutes in the ten years of her widowhood. A shudder ran up her spine and her lower lip drew back at the thought of it.

An awkward seating, with Daphne facing the two boys, and flanked by Harry and Elspeth. Daphne looked crushed herself, but revived in a moment whenever Cecil turned his attention to her. Normally Harry brought a glow, almost at times a sparkle, to Hubert—he was the one among her friends who paid him the most attention; but this evening Huey seemed somewhat preoccupied—was he even a little jealous of Cecil's evident fascination for Harry? Harry, who seemed to see all the new books, had a number of questions for him about Cambridge figures. "I wonder if you know young Rupert Brooke?" he asked.

"Oh, Rupert Brooke," said Freda, "what an Adonis!"

Cecil gave a snuffly smile as if at some rather basic misapprehension. "Oh, yes, I know Brooke," he said. "We used to see a lot of him in College, but now of course rather less."

"My mother thinks Rupert's work rather advanced," said George.

"Really, my dear?" said Elspeth, with twinkling concern.

Freda thought it best not to protest—as a mother one had to play the fool from time to time. "I didn't awfully care to read about his being seasick," she said, "to be perfectly honest."

"Oh, gobbets up I throw!" said Daphne.

"Thank you, child, I said I didn't care for it." In fact it was one of their own silly catch-phrases, those puerile tags that reduced the family to weeping laughter but were strictly not for the outside world. Freda gave her daughter a sharp pinch of a frown, in part to stop herself smirking. She felt Cecil would be forming a very poor impression of all of them.

"I'm no expert on poetry," said Hubert, with sweet redundancy, and seemed ready to head them off in another direction.

"I'm less up to date with *English* poetry," said Elspeth.

Harry said, "I always enjoy Strachey's pieces in the *Spectator*—you must know him, I suppose?"

Again, perhaps, was the boys' Club in the air, that fearfully important "Conversazione Society" she wasn't allowed to mention? "We do see Lytton from time to time," Cecil said, with an air of discretion.

"Now he's awfully clever," said Elspeth.

"Who's that, dear?" said Freda.

"Lytton Strachey—you must have seen his *Landmarks in French Literature.*"

"Oh . . . I . . . ?"

"Harry thought less highly of it than I did."

"I prefer a heavier ratio of fact to hot air," said Harry.

"We all believe Lytton will do something brilliant one day," said Cecil suavely.

"I don't care for him," said George.

"Now, why's that, dear?" said Freda mockingly, though she didn't think she'd ever heard of this man Strachey before a minute ago.

"Oh, I don't know," muttered George, and blushed, and then looked rather cross.

"No one could deny," said Cecil, "that poor Strachey has the most unfortunate speaking voice."

"Oh . . . ?" Freda knew she mustn't catch Daphne's eye.

"What you musical types I believe call a *falsetto*. It makes any sort of public speaking impossible for him."

"Even his private speaking's pretty impossible," said George.

"Well, happily, we don't have to hear the fellow," said Harry; "or, in your mother's case, read him either." He looked at Freda beside him with a smirk of almost parental collusion, and then at Hubert, who laughed uncertainly. It would be something one had to put up with, his cool good humour curdling into sarcasm. He was a kind and generous man, oddly generous perhaps for one so cool, but you couldn't be sure he would make the right effect.

"Well, on the matter of at least semi-public speaking . . . ," said Cecil archly, and gave a strange look at Daphne.

"Oh yes!" said Daphne, with a child's alertness at the sudden touch of attention. "What about our readings, Cecil?"

"Oh, my dear, what's this?" said Freda, fearing Daphne was about to bore their guests.

"It was Cecil's idea," said Daphne.

"He may have said it just to be kind," said Freda.

"Not a bit of it," said Cecil.

"Mother, Cecil has offered to read to us!" said Daphne, almost as if Freda were deaf, as well as mad to ignore such an offer.

Freda said, "Well, that is very kind, Cecil, whatever you may say. If you're sure . . . ?" She herself, of course, had suggested something similar the night before, to get them in from the garden.

"Perhaps you'll read us some of your own work?" Harry said, with a solemn look, to show Cecil that its fame had gone before him.

Cecil smiled and looked down again. "Well, Daphne and I hatched this plan, do you see, that everyone would read out their own favourite poem of Tennyson's."

"Goodness, I don't know," said Freda, thinking she couldn't without her glasses. And Hubert said warmly,

"Oh no, old chap, we'd much rather listen to you."

"Well, if you'd really like that . . . ," said Cecil, with a clever little show of discomfort.

Freda looked at Daphne, whose own desire to perform for them all seemed sunk in her fascination with Cecil. To a hostess such a reading was potentially awkward, but of course it might turn out to be a triumph and a thing they'd remember for years. Harry had asked for it, and she didn't want to disappoint him. She had a dread of Harry being bored. She said, "Well, then—after dinner . . . !" And then, "You know we met him, of course . . . ?"

"Now this will interest you, Cecil," said Hubert.

"Met whom, my dear?" said Elspeth.

"Oh, Lord Tennyson. Yes, indeed," she said warmly, laying a hand for a minute on Cecil's sleeve. Cecil smiled courteously at the hand, until after a quick squeeze she took it away. "We were on our honeymoon, so it seemed auspicious." She looked round the table with the satisfaction of having their attention, but made anxious by George's expression, his eyebrows raised in mocking indulgence. She felt he was trying to deflect the story which she'd now found a chance to tell. She knew she had a way of telling it, and knew from experience that she was liable to leave something out. "It was our honeymoon," she repeated, to steady herself; she let her eyes rest speculatively on Harry, as that intriguing word glowed in the candlelight. She didn't think he'd heard the story before, but she wasn't completely sure. "We went to the Isle of Wight—Frank said he wanted to take me over the water!"

"Very typical of him," said Hubert, with a fond shake of the head.

"You know you go over on the ferry, from . . . Lynmouth, isn't it?"

"Lymington, I believe . . . ," said Harry.

"Why do I always get that wrong?"

"You can go across from Portsmouth too, of course," said George; "but it's a little further."

"Do let Mother tell the story," said Daphne, sounding frustrated equally with the story and the interruptions.

Freda let Harry fill her glass, and took a rich long sip of wine. "It must have been the early evening. Have you been on that ferry? It seems to wander over to the Isle of Wight, as if it had all the time in the world! Or perhaps we were just impatient . . . I remember the Queen was at Osborne, and Frank said he'd seen the Equerry, with the red boxes— everything had to go back and forth on the ferry, of course, it must have been a business for them."

"I don't suppose they minded," said Hubert. "She was the Queen, after all, and that was their job."

"No . . . probably they didn't. Anyway—we were sitting inside, as I was feeling rather cold, but Frank was always very curious about ships!"

"One could say that my father was fascinated by all kinds of transport," said Hubert.

"And Frank said," said Freda, "would I mind, though it *was* our honeymoon, if he went outside and had a look round."

"And he ran into Tennyson," said Cecil, who had leant forward over his plate in a twisted posture of attention.

"Well, I didn't know it was him!" said Freda, rather flustered by Cecil's narrative economy. "You know, Frank always liked to have a talk with the captain and that kind of thing. Well, after a while I looked out and saw him leaning on the rail beside a most extraordinary figure."

"I'm sure," said Cecil. "He must often have been on the ferry, going to Farringford."

"Well, I'm sure . . . But I felt quite alarmed!" said Freda. And she started, with a faint sense of panic, on the bit of the story she knew best, knew word for word from her earlier tellings: "It was a tall old man, even then he was taller than Frank, though I believe he was eighty. I can see him now, he had a cloak on over his clothes and"—here she always made large swooping gestures above her head—"an extraordinary, very wide hat, and from behind—"

"A wide-awake hat," said George.

"Yes . . . and from behind you saw his"—she always dropped her voice—"*filthy*-looking hair. I can see him now. My first thought was he was bothering Frank, you see, I mean that he was a beggar or something! Imagine!"

"The Poet Laureate of England!" said Hubert.

"Well, you know they talked for some time. Apparently the captain had told him we were newly-weds." She had another drink of wine, looking at Harry over the glass. Her heart was beating absurdly.

"And what did they talk about, darling?" prompted George, with a rather tight smile.

"Oh, I forget . . ."

"Oh dear!" said Cecil, slumping back as if he'd paid good money for nothing, but also, surprisingly, as if he knew her well enough now to tease her. She laughed at herself and again put her hand for a moment on his sleeve.

"Lord Tennyson said—I shouldn't really say." She felt a knot of incoherence in her chest.

"We won't tell," said Elspeth, kindly, but as if to a slightly trying child.

Daphne said loudly, in a gruff and approximately regional voice, "He said, 'We need more *bloody*, young man.'"

"Really, child . . . ," said Freda, laughing and flushing.

" 'Less *awfully*, young man, more *bloody*!' " boomed Daphne.

"I can tell you, he was very down-to-earth!" said Freda.

Cecil laughed now, in his brief, loud way, and mild amusement and relief spread round the table, the laugh in part at the girl's absurd bit of play-acting.

"So that was all they got out of that great poet," Daphne explained in her normal voice. "No occasional verse, just"—and here she tucked in her chin again—" 'More *bloody*, young man!' "

"Enough, child . . . !" said Freda.

"I suppose one sees what he meant," said Harry.

"He was fed up with fine words by that stage," said Hubert, clearly quite proud of this family anecdote, and seeing the interest in it.

"Poor Frank was a little disconcerted," said Freda, feeling uncertainly for the ebbing hilarity, and realizing she'd missed out what Tennyson had said about honeymoons. That too was a little disconcerting, and she thought it best to let it go.

"No, he could be very blunt," said Cecil, splintering a brazil nut in the silver jaws of the nutcracker.

"Bloody blunt, you might say," said George, smirking round.

"If you can't be blunt at eighty . . . ," said Daphne.

"He could be very blunt indeed," said Cecil again, through a mouthful of nut, and a sudden uncouth appearance of being quite drunk. "I remember my grandfather saying so—he knew him pretty well, of course."

"Oh, really?" said Freda—it was almost a wail.

"Oh, Lord, yes," said Cecil, his loud emphasis followed by a total loss of interest; his face went blank and heavy and he turned away.

When the ladies withdrew for coffee the dining-room door was firmly closed, but the louder sounds carried across the hall—Cecil's yap, and now and again the awkward note of Huey's laughter. One never knew what went on, as they pushed the decanter round; whatever it was, it stayed in the room. All they ever brought in with them afterwards was a sporting sense of solidarity and the comfortable stink of cigars. The women's team, by contrast, was plainly unfocused and without a strategy.

"Oh, my dear, goodness . . . ," said Freda, vaguely motioning Elspeth to a chair.

"I'll stand for a while," said Elspeth, taking up her coffee cup, declining a liqueur with a tiny shudder, and walking to the end of the room on a brisk inspection of ornaments and pictures. At Mattocks, of course, there was quite an advanced collection of pictures, strange symbolic works of various Continental schools. One glanced around with a degree of apprehension.

"And you, child?" said Freda. "A little ginger brandy, perhaps?"

"No, thank you, Mother."

"No, indeed!" said Elspeth.

"Oh, well," said Daphne, "perhaps just a small one, Mother, thank you so very much."

Elspeth was combative, but not easily rattled. She came back across the room and perched on the edge of the window-seat. Straight-backed, smartly but staidly dressed in shades of grey, she had something of Harry's sharp-eyed handsomeness and, it had to be admitted, coolness. "I think your young poet so striking," she said.

"Yes, isn't he striking," said Freda, sipping off the top from a perilously full glass of Cointreau. She sat down carefully. "He's made quite an impression here."

"He has charm," said Elspeth, "but not too much of it."

"I find him most charming," said Daphne.

Freda glanced at her daughter, who looked flushed and slightly reckless as though she'd already had her drink. She said, with a vague desire to annoy, "Daphne finds him charming, but she thinks he speaks too loud."

"Oh, Mother!" said Daphne. "That was before I knew him."

"He only arrived here last night, my lamb," said Freda. "None of us knows him at all well, as yet."

"Well, I feel I know him," said Daphne.

"One can see that George is very attached to him," said Elspeth, "in the Cambridge way."

"Of course George is devoted to him," said Freda. "Cecil has done so much for him. Helped him up and, you know, what have you . . ."

Elspeth took a quick sip of coffee. "A touch of hero-worship on George's part, I would say, wouldn't you!"

This seemed to put George in a rather foolish light. "Oh, George is no fool!" said Freda. She saw something pleasurable dawn in Daphne's face, the way, over and over, a child slyly seizes on a new phrase, a new conception.

Daphne said, "Oh, I think he does hero-worship him," with a frank little shake of the head. A great collective laugh was heard from across the hall, which rather showed up the ladies' thin attempts at enjoying themselves. "I wonder what they're talking about," Daphne said.

"Best we never know, I think, don't you," said Freda.

"What would it be, though, that isn't thought fit for our ears?" said Daphne.

"I think that's a lot of nonsense," said Elspeth.

"What is, dear?"

"You know," said Elspeth.

"Do you mean they talk about women?" said Daphne.

"They must know some very amusing women, in that case," said Freda, as another burst of laughter was heard. She had a disquieting sense of Harry, who was always so solemn with her, taking quite another character when the ladies were absent. She said, "Frank always said the secret was they didn't want to bore us, but didn't mind boring themselves. He always hurried them through. He wanted to get back to the women." The thought was intensely poignant.

Daphne said, with a pretence of indifference, "Do you have many dinner parties of your own, Miss Hewitt?"

"At Mattocks? Oh, not a great many, no," said Elspeth. "Poor Harry is so extremely busy, and of course he's often away."

"So you dine in solitary splendour, poor thing!" said Freda. "In that palace . . ."

"I can't say I mind," said Elspeth drily.

"Among all your marvellous pictures," said Daphne, slightly over-doing it, Freda felt. She said,

"Harry must be doing awfully well . . ." But at this Elspeth's pride seemed to knit up tight and in getting up to return her coffee cup she effectively swept the matter of her brother's prospects aside. Freda said, artificially, she felt, "And your dress, dear, I've been wanting to ask—is it from our splendid Madame Claire?"

Elspeth wrinkled her nose in pretended apology—"Lucille," she said. "Ah, well!"

"Oh, yes," said Elspeth, "I can't deny Harry keeps me in fine style."

"No, indeed!" said Freda, with a quickly spreading feeling she'd been put in her place. Of course Elspeth might have been hinting that he would do the same for his wife, but Freda was fairly clear she was saying she hadn't a chance.

There was the sound of a door opening, and Daphne said, "Ah, here come the gentlemen."

"Ah, yes," said Freda, looking up at the group as they reappeared, with their funny discreet smiles. It was as if they had reached a decision, but were not at liberty to reveal what it was. Harry deferred to Cecil in the doorway, and then waited a few moments to defer to Hubert as well: he came in with an arm lightly round his shoulders, as if to thank and reassure him. Huey had drunk more than usual, and had a hot, uncertain look, the host to three men cleverer than himself. "Now then . . . ," he was saying, surely as glad as his father would have been to have got through that part of the evening. "Now then, how are we going to do this?"

There was a brief discussion of where Cecil was going to be, and how the chairs should be rearranged. George said wasn't it frightfully hot in the room, and opened the french windows. "Shall we all sit outside?" said Daphne.

"Don't be absurd," said Freda. There were hazards enough in the reading as it was. She watched Harry, hoping that in the shunting back of the chairs he would sit by her. He took up a small armchair in a masterful hug, with a pleasant effect of tension in his well-trousered legs as he lifted it out of the way. A rough semi-circle was formed in front of the window. Cecil set a lamp on a small table, actually outside, on the brick path, and a chair beside it. It was a miniature theatre. The lamp lit up the shrubs, the leaning hollyhocks and little lightless Chinese lanterns immediately behind him, but made everything else beyond and above seem the more thickly dark.

"Since someone so kindly asked," said Cecil, with a confident glance at Harry, "I'll read a poem or two of mine *before* scaling the heights of, er, Mount Tennyson." He sat down, with a copy of the *Granta* held out under the lamp at arm's length. "I hope it won't seem immodest to read a poem about Corley. The place seems to call poems forth—somehow!" Varied murmurs of indulgence and respect were heard. Cecil raised his chin, and his eyebrows, and then, as if addressing a gathering, or rather congregation, of a hundred or so people, began: "The lights of home! the lights of home! / Clear through a mile of glimmering park, / The glooming woods, the scented loam, / Scarce seen beneath the horse's feet / As through the Corley woods I beat / My happy pathway through the dark." The effect was so far from modest, Cecil chanting the words like a priest, and with so little suggestion of their meaning, that Freda found herself completely at a loss as to what he was talking about. Her eyes went straight to Daphne, who was grinning and blinking with the sudden need to master her feelings. Hubert looked pretty astonished for several seconds, then quickly assumed a cunning frown, as if measuring it against other readings he'd heard. Harry and Elspeth, more truly accustomed to literary soirées, maintained calmly appreciative near-smiles. George had turned so as to look straight into the garden, and his face was hidden; was it just the lamplight that made his ears burn red?

Freda took a furtive fortifying swig from her glass, and smiled approvingly in Cecil's direction. The same thing always happened when she was read to, even when the reading was a more thoughtful and quiet one: at first she could barely take it in, as if nonplussed by her own concentration; then she settled and focused; then after ten minutes or so it seemed to be going on and on, Cecil's voice had its own patterns, everyone's did, that carried on more or less the same up the hills and down the dales of the poems, so that the words themselves all came to seem the same. "The footings of the fawn among the fern"—she saw what he meant, but it made her want to giggle. "Love comes not always in by the front door," said Cecil, in his most homiletic tone. She let her head fall back and peeped abstractedly at Harry's profile, stern but fine, and his strong left leg jutting out, jumping unconsciously with his pulse. Had he perhaps been injured, heart-wounded, in some earlier romance? She thought that must be it. One couldn't imagine adoring him, exactly; but he was rich, and generous with it, she came back to that, his touching sweetness to Hubert: few "got" poor Huey, as Harry did. But there was something difficult about him, no doubt—his singleness was perhaps a warning as much as an invitation. She looked away with a wistful smile. Nothing had been said about the scale of this event; as each probable limit was reached and passed without any remark of surprise or prediction Freda grew restless, and then, the opposite of restless, when she closed her eyes to try and savour the sense and not have actually to look at Cecil, and the warm electric rush of noises, the confident stride of whole new situations with all their pre-existing logic, talking with Miriam Cosgrove on a beach in Cornwall, they had to pack, there was so little time before the train pulled out, and they mistook the way to the hotel, they were hopelessly lost, and then, was it just a silence that had woken her, with its own queer tension, and she sat up and reached again for her empty glass. "Perfectly marvellous," she muttered, now slightly giddy as well as bleary. She forced herself awake. "A memorable evening!"

"I'll read you my favourite section," said Cecil, and took a preoccupied sip from his tumbler—was it water he was drinking, or whisky? "Unwatch'd, the garden bough shall sway—"

"Oh, yes, I love this one," said Freda, over-compensating; her daughter glanced furiously at her.

"The tender blossom flutter down—"

"Ah . . ."

"Unloved, that beech will gather brown, / This maple burn itself away." Large gestures of his raised right arm took in the garden beyond him.

Feeling suddenly delightfully awake, Freda smiled round, gave an almost conspiratorial look to Harry, who nodded, very slightly, but pleasantly. Elspeth glanced down, having noticed. It was a beautiful poem, beautiful and sad. "Unloved, the sun-flower, shining fair, / Ray round with flames her disk of seed . . ." Again she could imagine it more

sensitively read—or did she mean less sensitively?—anyway, without a
certain atmosphere of Westminster Abbey. Poor Huey was fast asleep; it
might have been a great pitiless sermon. She wondered if she could poke
him discreetly or otherwise get at him, and felt another giggle hiding in
her consternation. Oh, let him sleep. Her other two children, in supporting postures, flanked the stage, George subtly reflecting Cecil's
importance, while Daphne's silly face was tense with the desire to
respond. Freda could tell she wasn't taking a word of it in.

> *Unloved, by many a sandy bar,*
> *The brook shall babble down the plain,*
> *At noon or when the lesser wain*
> *Is twisting round the polar star;*

and once more Cecil's long and powerful fingers, commanding their
attention, twisted in front of him, throwing his face into dramatic
shadow—

> *Uncared for, gird the windy grove,*
> *And flood the haunts of hern and crake;*
> *Or into silver arrows break*
> *The sailing moon in creek and cove—*

here he glanced upwards with a surprising note of comic disadvantage,
but carried on determinedly—

> *Till from the garden and the wild*
> *A fresh association blow,*
> *And year by year the landscape grow*
> *Familiar to the stranger's child—*

the first hesitant drops, like soft footsteps or tactful throat-clearings, had
quickly gained confidence, a rush of pattering had begun, and Cecil too,
no stranger to the elements, was rushing through, raising his voice just
when he needed to bring the poem to rest: he went on emphatically,

> *As year by year the labourer tills*
> *His wonted glebe, or lops the glades;*
> *And year by year our memory fades*
> *From all the circle of the hills—*

but now all of them were getting up to move the lamp and close the windows and his last words rose against the settling roar of the rain in a determined shout.

IO

HUBERT WOKE EARLY, with a sharp ache above his left eye, where a number of oppressive thoughts seemed to have gathered and knotted. His pyjamas were twisted and damp with sweat. Social life, though it had its importance, often left him confused and even physically out of sorts. The rain on the roof had got him off to sleep, and then woken him again to his own heat. He had a muddled apprehension of people moving about; his mother had restless nights, and now, as he dozed and woke again, his worries about her wove their way through his uneasy recall of moments at dinner and afterwards. Then the sun rose with merciless brilliance. Like Cecil Valance, Hubert hated to waste time, but unlike Cecil he was sometimes at a loss to know quite what to do with it. He decided he must go to early Communion, and leave the rest of the party to go to Matins without him. Twenty minutes later he closed the front gate and set off down the hill with an air of sulky rectitude. It had turned into a fresh, still morning; the great vale of northern Middlesex lay before him, with the answering heights of Muswell Hill rising mistily beyond, but he searched in vain for his usual sober pleasure in belonging here.

He paid scant attention to the service, conducted by Mr. Barstow, the laborious curate; but it gave him a measure of satisfaction to sit in his pew, and to kneel on the hard carpet of the sanctuary steps. Afterwards he walked home through the Priory, and was still quite warm from the climb when he joined the others at breakfast. Cecil was talking, in his trying, amusing way, and though Hubert greeted them all properly, and asked them if they'd slept well, he sensed that Cecil had taken charge.

"I slept almost troublingly well," said Cecil, showing by his frown at his boiled egg that he expected a laugh; then went on where he'd been interrupted, "No, I shall leave that to you, if you don't mind."

"You know Cecil's a pagan, Mother," said George.

"Cecil worships the dawn," said Daphne.

"I see . . . ," said their mother, with the strained brightness of her early mornings.

Cecil said, "I confess I was relieved when Georgie told me Stanmore church was a roofless ruin."

"He may not have mentioned," said Hubert, "but there's a first-rate new church bang next door to it. I can recommend it."

"I think I rather prefer the ruined one," said Daphne experimentally.

"Really, child," said her mother, pouring tea into her cup with a wandering hand. "Well, we will have to go without you."

"Oh . . . !"

"Cecil, I mean, not you."

"You know we had rather hoped to show you off to the village," said George.

"Daphne will repeat the sermon for you over lunch," said his mother.

"And what will Cecil do while we're at church?" asked Daphne.

Cecil gave a hesitant smile, and then rather mumbled, "Oh, I expect I'll have a look at a poem."

"There," said Daphne; and George too looked vindicated.

Hubert, feeling a little queasy, poured out a cup of coffee and stood up. "I hope you won't mind," he said, "if I excuse myself," and he left the room with the clear feeling that no one did. He crossed the hall and went into his father's office, and closed the door.

> My dear Harry [he wrote]
> I will certainly take the cigarette-case in to Kinsley's & have your name put on it—I think not in my writing, which as one wit remarked looks like a man's attempt at knitting!

He looked gloomily out of the little leaded casement, that was half-obscured by leaves; and went on,

> You were a bit upset with me last night Harry, and I'm not sure you were being altogether fair. I'm afraid I always rather shun demonstrations of affection between men.

Here he paused again, and then, with a firmness belied by his flinching expression, inserted "and dislike" after "shun"; he turned his full stop into a comma, and went on:

as being unmanly, and "aesthetic." I know the rest of the Sawle clan are more that way, but it has never been in my nature. You know no one ever had a better friend than you, Harry old boy. I should not have told you about our situation, it is not "desperate" by any means, and I hope we manage pretty well. We are not yet "mortgaged to the last sod" as you put it! But the small comforts of life make all the difference, whatever anyone says. I am not the demonstrative sort Harry, as you must know by now, but we are all very grateful.

Hubert sat back and smoothed his moustache down over his mouth in vexation. He felt his letter wasn't going well. He looked briefly at the photograph of his father that hung above the bookcase, and wondered if he had ever had to deal with a similar problem. It was very hard, when you did get a friend, who was so ready to help, and then this happened. And then not knowing exactly what it was that was happening. He felt he must say something before Harry took him out for a run to St. Albans in the car. Still not sure if he would actually send the letter, he closed it anyway, with a touch of coolness, "Yours ever Hubert." Remembering an idea he had had, which he hoped might not offend Harry, and might even be thought to have a certain elegance, he added: "PS, I wondered last night whether a simple H might not do just as well, on the cigarette-case, as standing for us both—"

Then he thought he'd better start the whole letter again.

II

THEY LEFT THE GARDEN through the front gate and went up the lane towards the Common, Cecil instinctively leading the way. "So what did you really do while we were flopping and droning?" said George. He'd found the hour at church, away from Cecil, unexpectedly painful.

"Oh, much the same," said Cecil. "I flopped on the lawn; and I droned to the parlour-maid."

"Little Veronica?"

"Poor child, yes. We assessed the chances of a war with Germany."

"I'm sure she was a fund of pertinent views."

"She seemed to think it was on the cards."

"Oh, dear!"

"I fear little Veronica is rather smitten with me."

"Darling Cecil, not everyone at 'Two Acres' is in love with you, you know," said George, and smiled with private satisfaction and a hint of mistrust. He did wonder if Cecil hadn't been almost too much of a success.

"She's an attractive young girl," said Cecil, in his most reasonable tone.

"Is she?"

"Well, to me." Cecil gave him a bland smile. "But then I don't share your fastidious horror at the mere idea of a cunt."

"No, indeed," said George drily, though a blush quickly followed. His face was hot and stiff. He saw how easily Cecil could spoil the walk, the day, the weekend altogether, if he wanted to, with his airy aggressions. "She is only sixteen," he said.

"Exactly," said Cecil, but relented, and put his arm through George's, and pulled him to him tightly as they strode along. "Weren't you possessed by the wickedest thoughts when you were sixteen?"

"I never had a wicked thought at all till I met you," said George. "Or at least until I saw you, staring at me so brazenly, and longingly, across the lawn." This was a favourite scene or theme for both of them, their little myth of origins, its artificiality a part of its erotic charm. "Little did I know that one day you would be my Father." Here they were by Miss Nichols's cottage. George straightened himself, knowing they would be seen, but not sure what impression he wanted to create. He felt a half-hearted desire to startle Miss Nichols, but in the event merely raised his hat and shook it in a feebly cavalier way.

"You looked so perfectly . . . suitable," said Cecil, with a sudden drop of the arm and quick sharp squeeze of George's bottom.

"Is that what you call it?" said George, wriggling free and looking quickly round.

"I wouldn't say your brother Hubert was particularly suitable."

"No," said George firmly.

"Though one can't help being just a little in love with his moustache."

"Don't go on about it," said George. "You're only saying it because I said Dudley had splendid legs. I'm not sure anyone's ever admired poor Hubert. Besides, he's a womanizer through and through." And they both laughed like mad again, and somehow amorously, at the silliness of their slang. George felt a wave of happiness rise through him. Then Cecil said,

"I'm afraid you're wrong about that, though."

"About what?"

Cecil glanced round. "I would say your brother Hubert has one very ardent admirer—in the person of Mr. Harry Hewitt."

"What, Harry? Don't be idiotic. Harry's after my mother."

"I know that's the idea. Your sister's worried sick about it. But I promise you she needn't be."

"I don't know what's put this into your head."

"Well, there's his taste in art—you know, he told me the sort of thing he collects. But mainly, I must admit, there's his tendency to manhandle your brother on every possible occasion."

"Does he?" said George, with a frown of repudiation but also of dull recognition. "He's certainly very generous to him."

"My dear, the man must be the most arrant sodomite in Harrow."

"A large claim!" said George, sparring a little for time.

"I just happened to catch an extraordinary moment, after dinner, when I'll swear the old monster tried to kiss him in the inglenook. They didn't know I could see them. Poor Hubert was most frightfully put out."

George gasped and laughed. "You call him old," he said, "though I believe he's not yet forty." The Cecil-type shock of this, the lightly brutal worldliness, brought its own little train of resistance, concession and in this case amusing relief. Cecil was always right. And of course there was something perversely delightful in the situation. It was only later that he saw the hazard to his mother. "Well, I'll be jiggered," he said.

"Yes, indeed," said Cecil, and gave him an odd hard look, as though he thought him a fool. Now they were passing the gryphon-capped gate-piers of Stanmore Hall, a mansion almost as imposing as Corley Court; Cecil glanced in across the lawns, but if he had any feelings of curiosity he repressed them. He was smooth and unseeing after his little triumph about Harry. The Sawles barely knew the Hadleighs; their friends in the top end of the village were Mrs. Wye, who took in sewing, and the Cattos, who bred show-birds in a straggle of huts and runs behind their cottage—people dear to George since childhood, but useless and even embarrassing for present purposes. He saw the deeply familiar paths and pavements, trees, walls and white-railed fences with renewed alertness, half-loving and half-critical, and longed for Cecil, with his poet's eye, to give them his blessing.

"Well, this is the first pond," he said, pulling him up by the muddy slipway where a small wild girl in a cloth hat was submerging a toy boat.

Cecil looked across the circle of brown water and green duckweed with a pursed, absent smile. "I don't think even I could take my clothes off here," he said, "right next to these people's cottages, and so on."

"Oh, we're not swimming here," said George. "I've got somewhere much more pretty, and indeed private, in mind for that."

"Have you, Georgie?" said Cecil, with a mixture of fondness and sauciness, and suspicion, since he liked to make the plans himself.

"I have. There are three ponds here; I dare say the village lads will be swimming in the big one, beyond those trees, if you'd like to have a look at them . . . ?"

Cecil peered pityingly at the little girl, who was perhaps too young to think sailing better than sinking; while the wooden block of the boat kept bobbing up and the sodden triangle of sail struggled to right itself. "As it happens," he said, distantly, "I only want to look at you," and then turned to smile at George, so that the remark seemed to have curved in the air, to have set out towards some more obvious and perhaps deserving target, and then swooped wonderfully home.

They went on across the open field towards the woods, no longer arm in arm, Cecil again a little ahead, in his habitual fashion, so that the lovely certainty of a minute before seemed vaguely called in question. The tiny separation felt to George like a foretaste of what would happen next morning. He planned to go down to the station in the van with Cecil, but was flustered and miserable already when he tried to picture it, there would be no time, no chance . . . Really everything rode on this last afternoon. "Wait for me!" he said.

Cecil slowed and turned and smiled so widely and yet so privately that George felt almost faint with reassurance. "I hardly can wait," Cecil said, and kept smiling; then they went on, side by side, with a funny tongue-tied singleness of purpose. George was aware of his own breathing, his own pulse, as the ragged line of oaks rose up in front of them. His feelings absorbed him so completely that he seemed to float towards them, weak with excitement, across a purely symbolic landscape. Away to their right a middle-aged couple whom he didn't recognize were also approaching the woods, with a pair of snuffling and bickering spaniels. He took them in exactly, but with no sense of their reality. The woman wore a bright blue blouse, and a low brown hat with a feather in it; the man, in country flannels, had a button-topped cap like Cecil's, and raised his stick in amiable greeting. George nodded and quickened his pace, in a rush of guilt and exultation. He would easily be able to avoid these people. Other walkers were so predictable. There was a riding trail that ran for a mile or more along the wood's edge; and other tracks led on from glade to glade across the whole breadth of the Common. Thinner pathways, under lower branches, had been made by the deer. George ducked in through one of these, a tight green tunnel through the oak and beech saplings, and Cecil was obliged to follow, with an odd sort of cough of surrender. "I can tell you know the way," he said.

The truth was that George had played in these woods for years, with his brother and sister, but just as often, since he was big enough, alone. There were half-a-dozen tall trees he had worked out, through long hours of held breath and anxious daring, how to climb without help; there were hiding places and burial places. To show them to Cecil was to admit to something very far from Cambridge, and the Society. He stood up in the small clearing at the tunnel's end, and reached back to help Cecil and get in his way as he came up behind him.

Cecil stifled his usual yelp of a laugh and patted George's side and held his forearm in a tight grip, to keep him at a distance but not to let him go. He seemed to be listening, his head raised and eyes warily sliding, his posture self-conscious. They heard the dogs barking and bothering each other, close by. For a second or two the blue of the woman's blouse could be seen among the leaves, and the man called out "Mary! Mary!," which George thought was the woman's name but then she called it too. There was something unaccountably funny about a dog called Mary, perhaps it was after the Queen, and he giggled to himself as he stood, with his arm burning from Cecil's grip; though that was nothing to the tantalized ache in the back of his thighs and the thick of his chest at Cecil's muscular closeness, his shushing lips, the blatant evidence of his arousal. George was breathing half-forgetfully, in sighs, while his heart raced. They heard the dogs yelping again, a bit further off, and the notes, though not the words, of the couple talking, the strange flat tone of marriage. Cecil took a few cautious steps across the leafy floor, still gripping George at arm's length, peering round. They were very close to the wood's edge—below the green translucent fringe of beech leaves you could see the open field. Still, Cecil was being a little absurd—if Mary's owners thought of them at all it would be their silence that puzzled them, their abrupt disappearance that seemed queer.

"Let's go a bit further," said Cecil. George sighed and followed behind him, rubbing his wrist with an air of grievance. He saw that this little mime of prudence, air of woodcraft, had just been Cecil's way of getting on top and taking control of a scene which George for once had planned. Well, they were dreams as much as plans, memories mixed up with wild ideas for things they'd not yet done, perhaps could never do. Cecil, under other circumstances, was bold to the point of recklessness. George let him go ahead, pushing springy branches aside, barely bothering to hold them back for his friend, as if he could look after himself. It was all so new, the pleasure flecked with its opposite, with little hurts and contradictions that came to seem as much a part of love as the clear gaze of acceptance. He watched Cecil's back, the loose grey linen jacket, dark curls twisting out under the brim of his cap, with a momentary sense of following a stranger. He couldn't think what to say, his yearning coloured with apprehension, since Cecil was demanding and at times almost violent. Now they'd emerged by the huge fallen oak that George could have led him to by a much quicker path. It had come down in the storms several winters ago and he had watched it sink over time on the shattered branches beneath it, like a great gnarled monster protractedly lying down, bedding down in its own rot and wreckage. Cecil stopped and shrugged with pleasure, slipped off his jacket and hung it on the upraised claw above him. Then he turned and reached out his hands impatiently.

"THAT WAS VERY GOOD," muttered Cecil, already standing up— then walking off for a few paces as he roughly straightened his clothes. He stood looking over the low dense screen of brambles, smiled mildly at a squirrel, cricked his neck both sides, ran a hand through his hair. He had a way of distancing himself at once, and seemed almost to counter the bleak little minute of irrational sadness by pretending that nothing had happened. His words might have followed a merely adequate meal, his thoughts already on something more important. He squared his shoulders, smiled and snuffled. The squirrel twitched its brown tail, scrabbled up its branch, watched him again. Perhaps it had watched his whole performance. It seemed to be applauding, with its tiny hands. George, still lying in the leaves, watched them both. He was amazed each time by Cecil's detachment, unsure if it was a virtue or a lack. Perhaps Cecil thought it rather poor form of George to be so shaken by the experience. The tender comedy of George's recovery, the invalidish wince and protesting groan at his ravishment, were ignored. Once in college he had been back at his desk within a minute, with a paper to finish, and seemed almost vexed when he turned a while later to find George still lying there, as he was now, spent but tender, and longing for the patient touch and simple smile of shared knowledge.

"Funny little creature," said Cecil whimsically.

"Oh . . . thank you," said George.

"Not you," said Cecil, raising his chin and mimicking the rodent's spasms of nibbling.

George gave a rueful laugh, and sat forward with his hands round his knees. He wanted Cecil to know how he felt, but he feared that what he felt was wrong; and even so, to tell him would be to praise him, since he had produced this wild effect in him. "Help me up, sir," he said.

Cecil came back and took his raised hands and pulled him up. And he wasn't so distant—they kissed, for a second or two, long enough for reassurance but not to get anything started again.

THE STREAMS RAN DOWN at two or three places in the woods, threading and pooling and dropping again, among the huge roots of the oaks. They were hardly noisy, you came on them by surprise, just when you heard their busy trickling. They brought down leaves that caught and gathered on twigs and roots to make little grey-gold dams, with clear pools behind them. At a low point, by the wood's edge, two streams ran into one behind the dike of a fallen tree, silted and half-submerged, and made a bigger pond; in high summer it could be too shallow for bathing, but the recent rains had filled it up again.

"The lowest pond is deeper than it looks," said George.

"Aha . . . ," said Cecil.

"If you want to have a dip . . . ?" He felt he shouldn't show how much he wanted him naked again, and then he would get it. The weekend so far had been hobbled and hampered by dropped trousers and half-unbuttoned shirts.

"You go first, and report on conditions," Cecil said.

George gave him a sideways smile, ready but a little disappointed. "All right," he said; and he started to unlace his shoes.

"Do it slowly," said Cecil. "And keep looking at me." He went over to the great oak above the pond, scanning its twisted and bulbous trunk for footholds, then in five seconds scrambled up to the low landing where it divided, and eased himself out on his bottom a short way along a broad, almost horizontal branch. He sat there, suddenly owning the wood as much as George had believed himself to do. "I can see you," he said.

"And I can see you," said George, unbuttoning the top of his shirt and then pulling it over his head.

"I said slowly," said Cecil.

George was slower, accordingly, when it came to his trousers. He found a certain shyness clouding his desire to please. Cecil maintained a provoking half-smile, arousal masked in amusement. "You're like some shy sylvan creature," he said, "unused to the prying eyes of men. Perhaps you're a hamadryad."

"Hamadryads are female," said George, "which I think you can see I'm not."

"I still can't really see. You look a bit like a hamadryad to me. I expect you live in this oak tree I'm sitting in."

George folded his trousers loosely and laid them on an old stump; but he turned away to slip off his white drawers, and saw with a twinge of regret that they were stained with mud from the tussle ten minutes earlier. "Oh, you are shy," said Cecil, almost crossly. George glanced over his shoulder, and forgot his anxiety about the mud in the larger strangeness of his nakedness, in the dappled woods, where any other walker could see him, and with Cecil, in his shirt and trousers and shoes, watching him steadily. He stepped down carefully across the dead leaves and oak mast towards the loose ellipse of water. The day was warm, but in and out of the patchy sunlight he shivered at the air on his back. He saw he was excited by the part he was playing, the new little scene of obedience, in which none the less his own worth and beauty were enhanced. It was something to know you were what Cecil wanted more than anything. He crouched down, still with his back to him, and peered into the water, which was brownish, loamy, stirred gently and continuously by the little rill that fell into it. Sunlight sparkled on the far side, twenty feet away. He slid a leg through the cold surface, and at once, when he felt the gripping chill of the water, flung himself in too. He circled and steadied and gasped out, "It's delicious!"

After that it was his turn to watch Cecil, a readier and more practised undresser. Cecil's way was just to be out of his things with a tug and a wiggle and a kick. He pranced down the leafy slope like a satyr, sunburnt and sinewy, calves and forearms darkly hairy. Then he leapt into the little pond almost on top of George, drowned him for a second or two, their legs tangling violently as George gripped at him, frightened and excited. He wanted to calm Cecil and keep him. They circled each other, spitting out water, laughing, the surface settling and bubbling. Underneath, their feet kicked branches, stirred up leaves and slime. Cecil reached for him, had an arm round his shoulder, then closed with him inexorably underwater.

THEY LAY OUT to dry for a few last minutes at the edge of the wood, where the sun shone in under the high fringe of leaves. The field beyond had already been ploughed, and the tussocky grass of the headland was faded and trampled. The small stream that trickled down from the pool where they'd swum ran away behind them through a long ditch thick with brambles, its noise hardly louder than the miscellaneous birdsong. George had put his drawers back on, but Cecil spread out still naked, raised on his elbows, frowning lightly at his own body. George loved the confident display, and was vaguely, half-pleasurably, alarmed by it; he thought of the spaniel called Mary, and looked across the curve of the wood's edge half-expecting to see the blue blouse and hear the dry chatter of the couple on the breeze. He looked back almost shyly at Cecil— he felt he would never stop taking him in. He loved the beautiful rightness of his bearing, that everyone saw, and he loved all the things that fell short of beauty, or redefined it, things generally hidden, the freckled shoulders swollen with muscle, knees knotty with sinew, black body-hair streaked flat, dark blemishes of the summer's mosquito-bites fading on his arms and neck. Behind him rose the dim pillars and dappled shadow of the woodlands, "the Common," which to George was the magical landscape of his own solitude. This was the man who had entered it, unaware of its secrets: he had quickly surveyed it and possessed it; now here he was, stretched out full length in front of it. Here he was, rolling over with an absent-minded stare and settling on top of him, twitching experimentally as he squashed him, big trickles of cold water running suddenly off his hair into George's wincing and gasping face.

It was the hat that he saw first, over Cecil's shoulder, while his friend moved rhythmically on top of him: red and white, distant, but clearly on the move, above the bracken, where the woodland curved out round the far edge of the field. "No, no . . . !"—he tried to draw up his knees, pushed at Cecil with his fists, tried to twist and topple him.

"No . . . ?" said Cecil, sneering and panting in his face.

"No, don't, Cess—no! Stop!"—jerking his head up to see more clearly.

"Yes . . . ?" said Cecil, more rakishly now.

"It's my sister—coming down the path."

"Oh, Christ . . . ," said Cecil, slumping, then rolling off him pretty smartly. "Has she seen us?"

"I don't know . . . I don't think so." George sat up and rolled over at the same time, reaching for his trousers. Cecil's own clothes were further off, and required a quick soldier-like scramble, white buttocks wriggling through the grass.

"No harm in a sun-bath, is there?" he said. "Where is she?" For the moment the red hat had disappeared. He pulled on his silk drawers, and then sat back, insouciant, but flushed and still notably excited.

"Best get your trousers on," said George.

"Just been having a bathe . . . ," said Cecil.

"Even so . . . ," said George sharply, the sense of a very tricky moment still thick about him.

"A bit of a rough-house . . . ?" Cecil smirked at him. "And anyway, what was it?—only a bit of Oxford Style, Georgie, hardly the real thing."

"Trousers!" said George.

Cecil tutted, but said, "Well, perhaps you're right. We can't have your sister exposed to my *membrum virile*."

"I feel a gentleman would have put that the other way round," said George.

"What can you mean?" said Cecil. "I'm a gentleman to the tip of my . . . toes"—and he pulled on his trousers crouchingly, peering across the undergrowth. "I can't see the darned girl," he said.

"It was definitely her. She has a hat I would know half a mile off."

"What, a sort of sou'wester?"

"It's a red straw hat, with a white silk flower on the side."

"It sounds frightful."

"Well, she likes it. And the main thing is it shows up."

"If she does, you mean . . ."

George was trying and re-trying various phrases in his head—buttoning his shirt he ran through facial expressions suggestive of bafflement and surprise at his sister's questions. "Well, perhaps she didn't see us . . . ," he said, after a minute.

Cecil looked at him narrowly. "You didn't invent this sighting of your sister, did you, Georgie, just to put me off a bit of Oxford with you? Because you know that sort of trick never, ever works."

"No, my darling Cess, I did not," with momentary anger. "For heaven's sake, I'm losing you tomorrow, I want as much of you as . . . as I can manage."

"Well . . . good," said Cecil, faintly abashed, standing up and stretching, then reaching down again to help him up.

When they were back in their shoes and jackets, Cecil said, "Allow me," and as he kissed him quickly on the lips he snatched off their two hats and switched them round, cocking George's boater on his own damp curly head, and whisking his green tweed cap on to George's bigger, rounder bonce—it perched there in a way he clearly found amusing. They scrambled up, past the pond, the little trickling stream, its noise quickly lost. George started talking quite loudly about College matters, virtually nonsense, but as they regained the path they had caught the stride of two friends out walking, with the woods to themselves. When they spotted Daphne, it was clear that in her solitary way she was doing the same, pretending to be merely out for some air, but hoping above all to find them and tag along. She knew enough not to search for them openly. Where the path she had been following crossed their own she turned down demurely towards them, red hat among the bushes, like a girl in a fairytale. George felt furious with her, but felt also the need for exceptional tact. Something in her demeanour told him that she hadn't seen them in the grass. Cecil called out, "Daphne!" and waved pleasantly. Daphne looked up in surely genuine surprise, waved back, and hurried towards them. "What do you think?" muttered Cecil.

"I think we're fine," said George. "Anyway, she knows nothing about these things." His anxiety was not that she'd have known what they were doing, but that in her general astonishing innocence she wouldn't have had the first idea. He saw her talking to their mother about it, and their mother taking a colder and cannier guess.

"Miss Sawle . . . !" said Cecil, raising his borrowed boater as she approached.

"Daphne!" said George and touched the peak of Cecil's cap, with a facetious smile.

Daphne stopped three yards off and looked at them. "This is nice," she said. "There's something funny about you."

"Oh . . ."—the two boys gaped comically at each other, patted themselves, George tense with worry that something else funny might show. Surely Cecil's whole person glowed with unmentionable lust; but Daphne simply gaped back at him, and then looked away in the warm uncertainty of being teased. "Well, I don't know," she said. It was very strange, and in its way reassuring, that she couldn't work out the obvious thing.

"What an exceptionally pretty hat, if I may say so," said Cecil, as they started back together up the path.

Daphne looked up at him with an idiotic smile. "Oh, thank you, Cecil!" she said. "Thank you." And as they walked on: "Yes, I've received any number of compliments on this hat."

To George it was entirely irksome having Daphne with them for the walk home—twenty minutes that he and Cecil might have spent alone. He wondered what further chances they would have before the van came in the morning. After supper, perhaps, they might slip outside for a cigar. And of course they could start very early indeed and walk to the station, and Jonah could go in the van with Cecil's bags. He thought intently about how to propose these arrangements, only sharing in the chatter with a tone of wan good cheer. Wherever they paused to let one another go ahead through a gap in the undergrowth George patted Cecil, and sometimes Cecil abstractedly patted him back. Soon they left the woods by a different path, and then they were out in the lane . . . a high load of straw creaking past on a wagon, a motor-car caught behind it, banging and fuming. It seemed to him Cecil was taking quite unnecessary interest in Daphne, bending to her, shielding her as they scooted past the smelly car; but he had a picture too of his own silly jealousy, scuffing along behind this comical couple, the tall dark athlete with his ears curled outwards by an oversized boater and the little girl in a bright red hat trotting eagerly beside him.

And there, already, was the steep red roof of "Two Acres," the low wall, the front gate, the row of dark-leaved cherry-trees outside the dining-room window. The front door stood open, in the summer way, into the shadowy hall. Beyond it, the garden door too stood open, the afternoon light glinting softly on polished oak, a china bowl—one could pass right through the house, like a breeze. Over the door was the nailed-up horseshoe, and beneath it the old palm cross. George felt the unseen jostling of different magics, varying systems of good luck. It was something extraordinary they were doing, he and Cecil, a mad vertiginous adventure. On the hall-stand hung Hubert's irreproachable bowler, and their father's old billycock hat that was always left there, as if he might return or, having returned, feel the need to go out again. Cecil looked round, with George's boater in his hand, and tossed it with a slight spin through the air so that it landed on a free peg. "Ha!" he said, with a little smirk of satisfaction at George and at himself. George found his hand was trembling as he hung up Cecil's cap beside it.

12

"CECIL, you've performed a miracle," said Daphne.

"My dear girl . . . ," said Cecil complacently.

"You've turned water into wine."

"Well," murmured Hubert, with a quick glance at his mother, "a special occasion."

"We not infrequently have wine on Sunday," said George.

"A very sad occasion," said their mother, shaking her head as she raised her glass. "We can't have Cecil drinking water on his last night with us. Whatever would he think."

"I should think you jolly insensitive," said Cecil, knocking back his glass of hock.

"Indeed!" said Daphne, who was still forced to keep their normal Sunday commons. Sunday was Cook's night off, and they had sat down to a bare supper of jellied chicken and salad. They had given up the festive style, there was a sense of looking ahead—after the champagne and Tennyson of their earlier dinners, the table tonight seemed tactfully to prepare them for the prose of Monday morning.

"Yes, we'll be sorry to see you go, old chap," said George.

"Such a pity . . . ," said his mother, with an uncertain little smile at Daphne.

Daphne in turn peered at George, who did look oddly wretched— she knew the way his face went stiff with feeling, just as she knew his irritable frown when he found he was being stared at. "You'll be back in Cambridge in a fortnight," she said.

"Oh, I think we'll get by," said Cecil absently.

Daphne said, "I mean, George is all right, but we won't see Cecil for ages, perhaps never again!"

Cecil seemed pleased by this histrionic claim, and his dark eyes held hers as he laughed, and said, "You must come to Cambridge too. Mustn't she, Georgie?"

"Oh, rather . . . ," said George dully.

"Hmm . . . ," said Daphne.

"No, of course you must," said George in a sincere tone; though she knew that George didn't want her in Cambridge, "tagging along," breaking in on his important discussions with Cecil, and all the other things she was prone to do.

"You might all come up for the French play," said Cecil.

"I suppose so," said Daphne, though she felt she heard in this general invitation a note that she hadn't suspected before, the note of a general boredom.

"What are you doing?" said her mother.

"The *Dom Juan* of Molière," said Cecil, as if it was something they all knew well. Daphne knew enough to know what it was about—a lady's man—a womanizer, in fact! "I'm taking Sganarelle—rather a fine part, though of course a great deal to learn."

"It's in French, you know," said George, which if it was meant to put his sister off was fairly effective.

"I see," said Daphne. "I'm not sure I'd be able to follow a whole play in French." She hardly thought it worth it just to watch Cecil prancing around, with a cloak and sword, probably. But at once she had a pang at the thought of missing it.

"How marvellous," said her mother graciously, excusing herself as well.

A little later Cecil said to George, as if the others weren't there, "I'll have to get ahead with my paper on Havelock this week," so that Daphne had a clear sense that he had already left them, might even have preferred to go today, after lunch.

When supper was over, George was sent round to the Cosgroves' on some mission he clearly thought beneath him, Hubert claimed he had letters to write, and their mother, trailing into the drawing-room, paused, raised a finger, and went out again. Cecil and Daphne were left for a minute on the hearth-rug. Daphne saw this as the threshold to the grown-up end of the evening, with social requirements she wasn't quite sure of.

"I don't suppose you want to hear the gramophone," she said. She had a sense of opportunity, made more incoherent by her new fear of boring Cecil.

"Not specially," he said, casually but kindly, with a smile she hadn't seen before, a candid gape that slightly startled her, and was probably a

Cambridge thing: it was hard to work out, but at Cambridge it seemed it was almost a sign of respect to be disrespectful, to say just what you felt at any time. Well, candour was their watchword! Cecil was fingering in his waistcoat pocket, then brought out his little clipper. He said, "I wonder if Miss Sawle would care to keep me company while I enjoy my cigar?"

"Oh, yes!" said Daphne. "Oh, I'll get a coat," and she ran to the cloakroom under the stairs. It was such an exciting idea that there were bound to be strenuous arguments against it. But that was part of Cecil's atmosphere and appeal. She came back, not with her own dull coat, but with one of George's old tweed jackets round her shoulders. She liked the air of improvisation; a man's jacket seemed to show she was up for a lark, and to carry some chivalrous hint of her need for protection. "It's a little bit smelly," she said; though she hardly imagined that would worry Cecil.

"Well, I'm going to make a smell too."

"Well, quite."

"I may be being too sensitive," said Cecil, glancing towards the door. "The General's so down on smoke, at home we all sneak off to the smoking-room. She's made it into quite a guilty pleasure."

"No, no," said Daphne.

Cecil drew out a cigar case from a surprising pocket. "I've got two, if you're tempted to try again," he said, and uncapped the stiff leather sheath to show her the tops of them. They made her think of soldiers, or the cartridges in Hubert's rifle. She saw it might be wittier not to answer, and he seemed amused by her condescending smile. She knew she should call to her mother, but sighed just to think of the objections, and followed Cecil out into the garden, leaving the french window ajar.

It was quite a bit colder than last night, though she was not going to mention it. She said, "Cecil, I think I shall always associate *In Memoriam* with you!"

"Well . . ."—Cecil was fussing with a lighted match and making impatient appreciative noises as he drew on the cigar. Then the newly conjured smoke was all around them.

"Shall we sit here?"

"Let's walk on," said Cecil, moving her along past the windows of the sitting-room. "We'll see what the stars are up to, shall we?"

"All right," said Daphne, and as he crooked his arm she reached up to slip her hand through it. As well as everything else, there was something

entirely proper about Cecil; he perhaps wasn't even aware of her happy
sense of play-acting, her toss of the head in the dark as she took his arm.
Then George's jacket, merely slung round her shoulders, slipped off.

"Here, let me help you." In the gloom on the edge of the lawn Cecil
held the coat and patted her shoulders when she'd got it on.

"I must look like a tramp," she said, her hands covered by the sleeves,
silky linings cold for a moment on bare arms, the weight and smell of the
thing hugged round her.

"Do it up," said Cecil, his cigar between his teeth. And again his large
hands seemed to take care of her, to be larger and more capable than
ever. Then he offered his arm once more.

They went on a few leisurely paces, Daphne happily self-conscious,
Cecil a touch reserved, though she wasn't sure of his face, and perhaps he
was merely working out the stars. She wondered if he was thinking of the
hammock again—and was embarrassed to think of it herself after what
had happened. She knew he'd had three or four glasses of wine; decisions
would come easily to him, though to a sober person they might seem
whimsical and delayed. She looked up, above the silhouette of the tree-
tops. "I fear it's too cloudy tonight, Cecil," she said.

Cecil huffed out another cloud of rich, sour smoke, and cackled
vaguely. "Were you in the woods for long this afternoon?" he said.

"This afternoon, oh, not really."

"You didn't get much of a walk."

"Well, when I met you I came home, of course."

She felt him press her arm more tightly against his side, and the beautiful grown-up presence of Cecil, his height and his muscular warmth
under evening dress, and even his voice, which she'd once thought so
cutting and grand, slightly turned her head. "It must have been someone
else we saw earlier on. I said to Georgie, 'Isn't that Daph?' but by the
time he looked whoever it was had gone."

"Well, it could have been. Did you call?"

"You know, I wasn't sure."

"Lots of people do walk there."

"Of course," said Cecil. "Anyway, you didn't see us."

Daphne felt again she was missing something, but was carried along
by the excitement of making conversation, and squeezed his arm reassuringly. "I would have said hello if I had."

"I thought you would."

"To be honest, it's George. He doesn't want me tagging along."

Cecil made a low disparaging murmur, and they turned round. "You can see a bit better now," he said. "There's the famous rockery!"

"I know . . ." She felt he was still rather mocking the rockery, and it emboldened her. "Cecil," she said, "when may I come to Corley?"

"Mm . . . ? To Corley?"—it was as though he'd never heard of such a place, and certainly had no memory of his earlier invitation. Then he laughed. "My dear girl, whenever you like."

"Oh . . . thank you."

"Whenever you like . . . ," he said again, expanding into his decision in a tone which seemed oddly to undermine it. "I suppose it won't be till the Christmas vac now, will it, probably."

This seemed as good as never to Daphne. "No, I suppose."

"Get Georgie to bring you over."

They moved on, towards the dark outline of the rockery, which at night might truly have been taken for a greater and more distant outcrop. Daphne said, huskily casual, "I imagine I could come by myself."

"Would your mother allow that?"

"I am quite grown up, you know," said Daphne.

Cecil said nothing. He pressed forward with his usual confidence; she thought she should say, "There's a step there"—she half-yelled it as he stumbled and lurched down hard on his right leg, caught himself but pulled her with him, and then lurched again to save her and grip her.

"Oh Christ, are you all right?"

"I'm fine . . . !"—wincing where he'd trodden heavily on the edge of her foot.

"Whenever we go out, we seem to end up taking a tumble, don't we!"

"I know!"

"And now I've lost my dratted cigar."

They were face to face, her heart still lively from the shock, and he put his arms round her waist and pulled her against him, so that she had to turn her cheek to his cold lapel. He moved a hand up and down on her back, over the warm tweed of George's jacket. "Blasted steps . . . ," he said.

"I'm all right," said Daphne. She rather dreaded looking at her shoe, when they got in, but Cecil was at a disadvantage, and she knew at once that he could never be blamed for anything. She said quietly, "I can't think how those steps got there"; then went one better, "Those bloody steps!"

Cecil gave a sigh of a laugh across her hair. "Oh child, child . . . ," he said, with a softness and a sadness she had never heard before, even from her mother. "What are we going to do?"

Daphne eased herself a fraction freer. She wanted to play her part, felt the privilege of Cecil's attention—it was awfully nice being held so tightly by him—but there was something in his tone that worried her. "Well, I suppose you're going to have to pack."

"Hah . . . ," said Cecil, again with a strange despairing note, like his poetry voice.

"I think . . . shall we go back in?"

"Yes, yes," he said. "Can you keep a secret, Daph?"

"As a rule," said Daphne.

"Let's keep this a secret."

"All right." She wasn't sure if she understood. Falling over a step wasn't much of a secret, but Cecil was clearly embarrassed by it.

His hands relaxed slightly, and travelled down almost to her bottom as he smiled and murmured, "You know, it's been splendid getting to know you."

"Oh . . . well . . . ," she said, somehow paralysed by his hands. "That's what we're all saying about you. There's never been anything like it!"

He bent his head and kissed her on the forehead, like sending her to bed, but then the tip of his nose moved down her cheek and he kissed her beside her mouth, in his cigar breath, and then, completely without expression, on her lips. "There," he said.

"Cecil, don't be silly," she said, "you've been drinking," and he tilted his face sideways and pushed his open mouth over hers, and worked his tongue against her teeth in a quite idiotic and unpleasant way. She pushed herself half-free of him; she was alarmed but kept her composure, even laughed rather sarcastically.

"You don't mind if I kiss you?" said Cecil dreamily.

"I don't call that kissing, Cecil!" she said.

"Mm . . . ?" said Cecil. "What would you call kissing, then, Daphne?" his tone dopy and mocking, slightly annoyed, tugging her back into his grasp like a dancer with a mere flourish of his suddenly inescapable strength. "More something like this?"—and he started again, just darting his lips all over her face, like a tormenting game, allowing her to dodge and turn her head a little but holding her so tightly about the waist that she was quite hurt by the hard shape of the cigar case in his trouser pocket thrusting against her stomach. She found she was giggling, in quick shallow breaths, and before she could help it

they'd turned into hot little sobs, and then a hushed wail of childlike surrender and failure.

"Hello . . . ?" It was George, back from the Cosgroves', coming to
look for them, surely? Childish timid relief mixed almost at once with
pride. But no, it was Huey, in a funny voice, apologetic but actually
rather cross. "I say . . ."

Cecil loosened his grip, sighed acceptingly, though the little snigger
he gave her seemed to say he hadn't given up. He looked round, over the
top of the bushes, to see who it was, perhaps he too thought it was
George, and again she felt the special subject of her own secret with
Cecil. They both had to be careful: she'd been frightened by him, but she
still had a sense that he would know what to do. "We're over here," she
said, her voice clotted with crying.

"Are you all right?"

"I fell down the blasted step," said Cecil in a drawl. "I seem to have
trodden on your sister."

Hubert stood there, in silhouette, conveying an indignant but undecided impression. "Can you walk?" he said, very distinctly, as though
speaking over the telephone.

"Of course I can walk, we're just coming in."

"It's really a bit dark for rambling round," Hubert said.

"That was the point," said Cecil. "We were studying the stars."

Hubert peered upwards doubtfully. "It's a bit cloudy for that," he
said, and turned back to the house.

DAPHNE LAY FIRST on one side, then on the other side, tired out by
her thoughts and kept alert by them too. Her right foot throbbed
impressively in evidence, and was already bruising.

Sometimes she drifted sideways into near-unconsciousness, but woke
at once with a sprint of the heart at the thought of Cecil's closeness, his
strength and his breath. His body was exceptionally hard, his breath
warm, moist and bitter.

Cecil was drunk, of course, she'd seen two bottles of wine emptied at
dinner, the hock it was, with the black German lettering. Daphne knew
what drink did to people, and after Friday night, and her own tipsy
episode with the ginger brandy, she knew something more about the
strange freedoms of drinkers. They were intriguing, but unnecessary, and
the truth was they were generally somewhat revolting. Afterwards one

didn't talk about them, out of the vague sense of shame that attached to them. One sobered up. Cecil would surely have a headache in the morning, but he would get over it. Her mother was often absurd at bedtime, but perfectly sensible again by breakfast. It would probably be a mistake to make too much of it.

And yet the whole thing showed Cecil in a very poor light, or half-light . . . so much of their dealings had happened in the dark, and if she saw him at all it was by the glow of a cigar end or the faint glimmer of the suburban night. When he'd come he'd put them all on their mettle by his sheer distinction, his cutting voice, his cleverness and money. And now, as she rolled on to her other side in excited despair of ever sleeping, she wondered just what George would say if he were told the extraordinary unwholesome thing his friend had tried to do. And she went through it all in her mind again, in the order it had happened, to savour the shock of it properly.

Well, she wasn't naïve, she knew perfectly well that the upper classes could behave appallingly. Perhaps George should be told what his precious friend was really like. Though perhaps she would keep it to herself, with the choice then of bringing out the facts on some later occasion. It soon seemed more adult not to make a fuss. She started thinking about Lord Pettifer in *The Silver Charger,* and, her mind chasing and confirming and losing the story in the vivid fragments of memory, she wandered off through lighted rooms into the welcoming jabber of dreams but then almost grunted herself awake, and lurched at once into a seventh or eighth rehearsal of her own story, in the garden with Cecil Valance.

With each retelling, the story, with its kernel of scandal, made her heart race a fraction less, and its imagined impact on George, or her mother, or Olive Watkins, their fury and bewilderment, grew stronger in compensation. Daphne felt the warm flood of the story surge through her and grip her whole person; but each time the wave seemed a little weaker than the time before, and her reasonable relief at this gradual change was coloured with a tinge of indignation.

Or could that be what kissing was really about? It seemed more like some childish dare, to stick your tongue into someone else's mouth, and took a good deal of forbearance on their part, even if they liked you a lot. Alas there was no one she could ask. If she brought it up with her mother she would instantly grow suspicious. Could Hubert conceivably have kissed a woman like that? Maybe George, if he did have a girl, had had a go at it. She imagined asking him, and the secret fact of it having happened with his best friend made the idea slyly amusing.

What she was almost conscious of not thinking of was the way he had rubbed himself rhythmically against her. All her feelings were fixed on the easier, and after all rather comic, liberties of licking her mouth and feeling her bottom.

Later she found she had slept, and the dream she had just come out of kept its magic as she lay with open eyes in the deep grey dark. Then she thought she had been a silly child before. "Child, child," he had called her, and that's what she was. She thought about what Cecil had actually said, how it had been so wonderful getting to know her, and she flopped on to her back and wondered quite coolly if he had fallen in love with her. She gazed at the shadowy zone of the ceiling, the first powdery gleam of light above the curtains, as a sort of image of her own innocence. What evidence was there? Cecil had a very particular way of looking at her, even when others were present, of holding her eye at moments in their talk, so that another unspoken conversation seemed also to be going on. She had never known such a thing before, the boldness and the absolute privateness as well. It was still rather awful that Cecil had gone behind George's back like that, but she felt a certain thrilled complacency at the choice he had secretly made. And of course he had to do it like this, his love had to be concealed, and it had to come out. There was something very touching as well as alarming in Cecil's passion. Now she leapt forgivingly over the muddle in the garden, and thought of the life they would share together. Would he want to do that kind of thing again? Not when they were married, presumably. And another perspective of lighted spaces opened before her: she saw herself sitting down to dinner beneath the jelly-mould domes, or anyway compartments, of Corley Court.

She slept unusually late, slept on with only a momentary murmur and swallow through the rustling and bumping on the landing, the fact of voices downstairs; and when she at last came up into fuddled life her little clock said a quarter to nine. After that, and a further helpless three minutes of gaping sleep, she found she had attuned to something, to the loss of something she was amazed to find she had already grown used to, the noise of Cecil in the house. Of course he had gone! There was a thinness in the air that told her, in the tone of the morning, the texture of the servants' movements and fragments of talk. And all her plans for him were thwarted, the witty thing she was going to say to him, as he climbed into Horner's van . . . It would be weeks, perhaps months, before she saw him again. Moaning with a lover's pangs, as well as with a certain sulky relief at this tragic postponement, she thrust herself out of bed, and on to her instantly tender right foot.

In the thick of her solitary breakfast, with the maid looking in once a minute to see if she'd finished, there was George coming past the window, back home from the station and seeing Cecil off. He had a bleak, faraway look which annoyed her the moment she saw it and felt its meaning. It was a time of reckoning for him—his guest, his first one ever, had left, and now the family could take him back and tell him, more or less, what they thought. He would be moody and delicate, unsure who to side with. And then she remembered her book. Oh, what had Cecil done with it? Had he written in it? Where had he put it? She was suddenly sick with anger at Jonah for packing it with Cecil's other books. Even now it would be trapped unbeknownst between other books in his suitcase, in a crowd of other cases on Harrow and Weald-stone station.

"Oh, Veronica," she said.

"Sorry, miss!" said Veronica.

"No, not that," said Daphne. "Did you see, did Mr. Valance leave anything for me, my autograph book, I mean?"

"Oh, no, miss." And knotting her duster in a pretence of interest, "Is that the one with the vicar in?"

"What . . . ?" said Daphne. "Well, it has a number of important men in it." She didn't quite trust Veronica, who was more or less her own age, and treated her more or less like a fool.

"I'll ask, miss, shall I?" Veronica said. But then George looked round the door, gave a rueful smile, and said,

"Cecil says goodbye." He hovered there, feeling the atmosphere, seeming uncertain whether to share the subject of Cecil any further with his sister.

"I'm afraid I slept somewhat badly," said Daphne, aware of her own adult tone. "And then I must have overslept . . ."

"He was up fearfully early," said George. "You know Cecil!"

"Perhaps Mr. George has got it, miss," said Veronica.

"Oh, really, it doesn't matter," said Daphne, and coloured at the disclosure of her private worry.

"Got what?" said George, with an anxious look of his own.

So Daphne had to say to him, "I wondered if Cecil had found a chance to write in my little album, that's all."

"I expect he wrote something or other. Cess is rarely at a loss for words."

"I expect he's left it somewhere," Daphne said, and spread some butter on her toast, though really her smothered anxiety had squeezed up her appetite to nothing. She looked at her brother with a cold smile. "So what are you doing today, George?" she said, conscious of denying him a talk on the obvious subject.

"Eh? Oh, I'll find something," he said, with a hint of pathos. He was leaning against the doorpost, neither in nor out, the maid sidling past him back into the hall. Daphne saw him decide to speak, and as he started airily, "No, it was a shame Cecil couldn't stay longer . . . ," she said, "I've invited Olive for tea tomorrow, I haven't seen her since they got back from Dawlish." She knew Olive Watkins was small beer after Cecil, and Dawlish after the Dolomites, and she felt ashamed and almost sad as well as defiant in mentioning her. But she couldn't indulge George in his present mood. It rubbed up too closely against her own.

"Oh, have you . . . ," said George, startled and bored. Daphne saw she'd produced a particular kind of family atmosphere, and that itself was depressing after the wider horizons of Cecil's visit. Also, she really wanted her book back, to show Olive whatever it was that Cecil had written. This had been her main purpose in asking her to tea.

Then Veronica, with her own bored persistence, looked back in and said, "I asked Jonah, miss. He's having a look."

"Thank you," said Daphne, feeling oppressed now by the public nature of the search.

"Jonah's looking in his room now. I mean he's looking in Mr. Valance's room!"

And George, without saying anything more, drifted away, and then Daphne heard him going, rather stealthily she thought, upstairs as well, two at a time. She told herself, without fully believing it, that probably, after all, Cecil would have put nothing but his name and the date.

A minute later George came back down, with Jonah at his heels, and Daphne's mauve album open in his hands. "My word, sis . . . ," he said abstractedly, turning the page and continuing to read; "he's certainly done you proud!"

"What is it?" said Daphne, pushing back her chair but determined to keep her dignity, almost to seem indifferent. Not just his name, then: she could see it was much, much more—now that the book was here, open, in the room, she felt quite frightened at the thought of what might come out of it.

"The gentleman left it in the room," said Jonah, looking from one to the other of them.

"Yes, thank you," said Daphne. George was blinking slowly and softly biting his lower lip in concentration. He might have been pondering how to break some rather awkward news to her, as he came and sat down across from her, placing the book on the table, then turning the pages back to start again. "Well, when you've finished," Daphne said tartly, but also with reluctant respect. What Cecil had written was poetry, which took longer to read, and his handwriting wasn't of the clearest.

"Goodness," said George, and looked up at her with a firm little smile. "I think you should feel thoroughly flattered."

"Oh, really?" said Daphne. "Should I?" It seemed George was determined to master the poem and its secrets before he let her see a word of it.

"No, this is quite something," he said, shaking his head as he ran back over it. "You're going to have to let me copy this out for myself."

Daphne drained her teacup completely, folded her napkin, glanced across at the two servants, who were smiling stupidly at the successful retrieval of the book, and also formed a somewhat inhibiting audience to this agitating crisis in her life, and then said, as lightly as she could, "Don't be such a tease, George, let me see." Of course it was a tease, the latest of thousands, but it was more than that, and she knew resentfully that George couldn't help it.

"Sorry, old girl," he said, and sat back at last, and slid the album towards her.

"Thank you!" said Daphne.

"If you could see your face," said George.

She pushed her plate aside—"Will you take all this, please," to the maid; who did so, with gaping slowness, peering at the columns of Cecil's black script as though they confirmed a rather dubious opinion she'd formed of him. "Thank you," said Daphne again sharply; and frowned and coloured, unable to take in a word of the poem. She had to find out at once what George meant, that she should be flattered. Was this it, the sudden helpless breaking of the news? Perhaps not, or George would have said something more. The harder she looked at it, the less she knew. Well, it was called, simply, "Two Acres," and it ran on over five pages, both sides of the paper—she flicked back and forth.

"Formally, it's rather simple," said George, "for Cecil."

"Well, quite," said Daphne.

"Just regular tetrameter couplets."

"That will be all," said Daphne, and waited while Veronica and Jonah went off. Really they were most irritating. She flicked further back for a moment, to the Revd. Barstow, with his scholarly flourish, "B. A. Dunelm"; and then forward to Cecil, who had broken all the rules of an autograph book with his enormous entry, and made everyone else look so feeble and dutiful. It was unmannerly, and she wasn't sure if she resented it or admired it. His writing grew smaller and faster as it sloped down the page. On the first page the bottom line turned up sideways at the end to fit in—"Chaunticleer," she read, which was a definite poetry word, though she wasn't precisely sure of its meaning.

"I suppose he'll be publishing it somewhere," said George, "the *Westminster Review* or somewhere."

"Do you think?" said Daphne, as levelly as she could, but with a quick strong feeling that the poem was hers after all. Cecil hadn't just written it here, in her book, by chance. She was still trying to see if it said things about her personally, or if it was simply about the house—and the garden:

> *The Jenny nettle by the wall,*
> *That some the Devil's Play-thing call—*

that was a conversation she'd had with him—now quite simply turned into poetry. Her father had called stinging nettles Devil's Play-things, it was what they called them in Devon. She felt thrilled, and a little bewildered, at being in on the very making of a poem, and at something else magical, like seeing oneself in a photograph. What else would be revealed?

> *The book left out beneath the trees,*
> *Read over backwards by the breeze.*
> *The spinney where the lisping larches*
> *Kiss overhead in silver arches*
> *And in their shadows lovers too*
> *Might kiss and tell their secrets through.*

Again the minutely staggered and then breathtaking merging of word, image and fact. She was really going to have to read this somewhere apart, in private. "I think it would be most appropriate to read this *in* the garden," she said, getting up and feeling very slightly sick; but just then her mother appeared in the doorway, with her heavy morning face, and her bright morning manner. In fact her manner was flustered; there was something behind her smile. Word must already have got through. Beyond her Veronica loitered, the informer.

"Well, child . . . !" her mother said, and gave Daphne a strange, eager look. "What excitements."

"Everyone can see it when I've finished reading it," said Daphne. "People seem to be forgetting that it's my book."

"Well, of course, dear," said her mother, going round the table and opening a window as if to show she had other useful things to do; and then, "You've obviously made quite an impression . . . on him"—not using Cecil's name, out of some awful delicacy. She gave Daphne a teasing glance that had something new to it—a sense of girding herself for some welcome parental obligation.

"Mother, he was only here for three nights," said George, almost crossly. "All Cecil has done, with his customary generosity, is to write a poem about our house as a thank-you for the visit."

"I know, dear," said their mother, with a little flinch at her two prickly children. "He's been most generous to Jonah too."

George got up, and went to the window, and looked out in the manner of someone who wants to say something firm but difficult. "The poem's really nothing to do with Daphne."

"Isn't it?" said Daphne, shaking her head. Wasn't it? It was there, she had seen it at once, the lovers' kiss in the shadows, telling their secrets; but of course she couldn't say that to either of them. "I suppose I should be sorry he didn't write a poem for you."

George's pitying look was focused on the cherry-trees outside. "As a matter of fact, he has written a poem for me."

"Oh, George, you never said," said their mother. "You mean just now?"

"No, no—last term sometime—it really doesn't matter."

"Well!" said their mother, trying to maintain a tone of bewildered amusement. "Rather a fuss about a poem."

"There's no fuss, darling," said George, now in a brightly patient tone.

"It's too lovely to have a poem written for you at all, in my view."

"I quite agree!" said Daphne, and the feeling that everything was being spoiled welled up inside her.

"I'm beginning to feel very sorry that I mentioned it. If Cecil's visit has to end in this kind of childish bickering."

"Oh, read it if you want to!" said Daphne, pursing her lips against tears, and flapping through the book to give it to her open at the right page. Her mother looked at her sharply, and after a moment, and quite gently, took it from her.

"Thank you . . . now if the girl could run for my glasses." And when Veronica came back, their mother sat down at the dining-table and addressed herself, with a quizzical but sporting look, to the poem that had just been written about her house.

TWO

Revel

Man must say farewell
To parents now,
And to William Tell,
And Mrs. Cow.

—Edith Sitwell,
"Jodelling Song"

I

FROM WHERE SHE SAT, in the window of the morning-room, the two figures seemed to hurry towards each other. Above the long hedge at the end of the formal garden, a man's head, jerking with the lurch of a limp, moved impatiently along. "Rubbish!" he shouted. "Rubbish!" Whilst away to the right, between the hazily green horse-chestnuts of the park, a shiny beige car was approaching, its windscreen flashing in the sun.

"D," she wrote, and hesitated, with her nib on the paper. Not "Darling," so "Dear" certainly, and then another pause, which threatened to turn into a blot, before she added "est": "Dearest Revel." One went up and down the scale with people—certainly among their set there were startling advances in closeness, which sometimes were followed by coolings just as abrupt. Revel, though, was a family friend, the superlative quite proper. "It is too awful about David," she went on, "and you have all my sympathy"—but she thought, what one really needed was a scale below "Dear," since often one had no time whatever for the person one was warmly embracing on the page: "Untrustworthy Jessica," "Detestable Mr. Carlton-Brown."

She heard the car stop outside, the swift jangle of the bell, footsteps and then voices. "Is Lady Valance in?" "I believe she's in the morning-room, madam. Shall I—" "Oh, I won't disturb her." "I can tell her"—Wilkes giving her a clear chance to do the right thing. "No, don't bother. I'll go straight through to the office." "Very good, madam." It was a small contest of wills, in which the subtle but hamstrung Wilkes was trounced by the forthright Mrs. Riley. A minute later he came in to cast an eye at the fire, and said, "Mrs. Riley has come, my lady. She went through to the office, as she calls it."

"Thank you, I heard her," said Daphne, looking up and lightly covering the page with her sleeve. She shared a moment's oddly intimate gaze with Wilkes. "I expect she had her plans with her?"

"She appeared to, madam."

"These plans!" said Daphne. "We're not going to know ourselves soon."

"No, madam," said Wilkes, passing his white-gloved hand into the black mitten that was kept in the log-basket. "But they are still only plans."

"Hmm. You mean they may not come off?"

Wilkes smiled rather strictly as he lodged a small branch on the top of the pyre, and controlled the ensuing tumble of ash and sparks. "Perhaps not fully, madam, no; and in any case, not . . . irreversibly." He went on confidentially, "I understand Lady Valance is with us on the dining-room."

"Well, she's rarely an advocate for change," said Daphne a little drily, but with respect for the butler's old allegiances. With two Lady Valances in the house, there were niceties of expression which even Wilkes was sometimes tripped up by. "Though last night she claimed to find the new drawing-room 'very restful.'" She turned back to what she had written, and Wilkes, after a few more testing pokes at the fire, went out of the room.

"Perhaps best not to come this weekend—we have a *houseful* with much family &c (my mother)—on top of which Sebby Stokes is coming down to look at Cecil's poems. It will be somewhat of a 'Cecil weekend,' and you would barely get a word in! Though perhaps"—but here the bracket clock whirred and then hectically struck eleven, its weights spooling downwards at the sudden expense of energy. She had to sit for a moment, when the echo had vanished, to repossess her thoughts. Other clocks (and now she could hear the grandfather in the hall chime in belatedly) showed a more respectful attitude to telling the hour. They struck, all through the house, like attentive servants. Not so that old brass bully the morning-room clock, which banged it out as fast as it could. "Life is short!" it shouted. "Get on with it, before I strike again!" Well, it was their motto, wasn't it: Carpe Diem! She thought better of her "perhaps," and signed off blandly, "Love from us both, Duffel."

She took her letter into the hall, and stood for a moment by the massive oak table in the middle of the room. It seemed to her suddenly the emblem and essence of Corley. The children tore round it, the dog got under it, the housemaids polished it and polished it, like votaries of a cult. Functionless, unwieldy, an obstacle to anyone who crossed the room, the table had a firm place in Daphne's happiness, from which she feared it was about to be prised by force. She saw again how imposing the hall was, with its gloomy panelling and Gothic windows, in which the Valance coat of arms was repeated insistently. Would those perhaps be allowed to stay? The fireplace was designed like a castle, with battlements instead of a mantelpiece and turrets on either side, each of which had a tiny window, with shutters that opened and closed. This had come in for particular sarcasm from Eva Riley—it was indeed hard to defend, except by saying foolishly that one loved it. Daphne went to the drawing-room door, put her fingers on the handle, and then flung it open as though hoping to surprise someone other than herself.

The off-white dazzle of it, on a bright April morning, was undeniably effective. It was like a room in some extremely expensive sanatorium. Comfortable modern chairs in grey loose covers had replaced the old clutter of cane and chintz and heavy-fringed velvet. The dark dadoed walls and the coffered ceiling, with its twelve inset panels depicting the months, had been smoothly boxed in, and on the new walls a few of the original pictures were hung beside very different work. There was old Sir Eustace, and his young wife Geraldine, two full-length portraits designed to glance tenderly at each other, but now divided by a large almost "abstract" painting of a factory perhaps or a prison. Daphne turned and looked at Sir Edwin, more respectfully hung on the facing wall, beside the rather chilling portrait of her mother-in-law. This had been done a few years before the War, and showed her in a dark red dress, her hair drawn back, a shining absence of doubt in her large pale eyes. She was holding a closed fan, like a lacquered black baton. Here nothing came between the couple, but still a vague air of satire seemed to threaten them, in their carved and gilded frames. In the old drawing-room, where the curtains, even when roped back, had been so bulky that they kept out much of the light, Daphne had loved to sit and almost, in a way, to hide; but no such refuge was offered by the new one, and she decided to go upstairs and see if the children were ready.

"Mummy!" said Wilfrid, as soon as she went into the nursery. "Is Mrs. Cow coming?"

"Wilfrid's afraid of Mrs. Cow," said Corinna.

"I am not," said Wilfrid.

"Why would anyone be afraid of a dear old lady?" said Nanny.

"Yes, thank you, Nanny," said Daphne. "Now, my darlings, are you going to give Granny Sawle a special surprise?"

"Will it be the same surprise as last time?" said Corinna.

Daphne thought for a second and said, "This time it will be a double surprise." For Wilfrid these rituals, invented by his sister, were still sickeningly exciting, but Corinna herself was beginning to think them beneath her. "We must all be sweet to Mrs. Cow," Daphne said. "She is not very well."

"Is she infectious?" said Corinna, who had only just got over the measles.

"Not that sort of unwell," said Daphne. "She has awful arthritis. I'm afraid she's in a great deal of pain."

"Poor lady," said Wilfrid, visibly attempting a maturer view of her.

"I know . . . ," said Daphne, "poor lady." She perched self-consciously on the upholstered top of the high fender. "No fire today, then, Nanny?" she said.

"Well, my lady, we thought it was almost nice enough to do without."

"Are you warm enough, Corinna?"

"Yes, just about, Mother," said Corinna, and glanced uneasily at Mrs. Copeland.

"I *am* rather cold," said Wilfrid, who tended to adopt a grievance once it had been pointed out to him.

"Then let's run downstairs and get warmed up," said Daphne, in happy contravention of Nanny's number one rule, and getting up briskly.

"No two-at-a-time, mind, Wilfrid!" said Nanny.

"You can be sure he will be all right with me," said Daphne.

When they were out in the top passage, Wilfrid said, "Is Mrs. Cow stopping for the night?"

"Wilfrid, *of course,*" said Corinna, as if at the end of her patience, "she's coming on the train with Granny Sawle."

"Uncle George will take them home on Sunday, after lunch," said Daphne; and finding herself holding his hand, she said, "I thought it would be nice if you showed her up to her room."

"Then I will show Granny up to her room," said Corinna, making it harder for Wilfrid to get out of.

"But what about Wilkes?" said Wilfrid ingeniously.

"Oh, I don't know. Wilkes can put his feet up, and have a nice cup of tea, what do you think?" said Daphne, and laughed delightedly until Wilfrid joined in on a more tentative note.

On the top stairs, they trotted down hand-in-hand, and in step, which did require a measure of discipline. Then from the window on the first-floor landing she saw the car arriving from the station. "They're here . . . oh, darlings, run!" she said, shaking off the children's hands.

"Oh, Mummy . . . ," said Wilfrid, transfixed with anxious excitement.

"Come on!" said Corinna; and they pelted down the three bright turns of polished oak, Wilfrid losing his footing on the last corner and bumping down very fast over several steps on his hip, his bottom. Daphne tensed herself, with a touch of annoyance, but now he was limping across the hall and round the table (looking just like his father), and by the time he started self-righteously to wail he was already distracted by the need to do the next thing.

Wilkes appeared, with the new Scottish boy, and Daphne let them go ahead and tackle the car for a minute while she watched from the porch. Awful to admit, but her pleasure at seeing her mother again was a touch defensive: she was thinking of the things her husband would say about her after she'd gone. Wilkes deferred to Freda very properly and smilingly, with his usual intuitive sense of what a guest might need. To Daphne herself she seemed an attractive figure, pretty, flushed, in a new blue dress well above the ankle and a fashionable little hat, with her own anxieties about the visit peeping out very touchingly. The handsome boy was helping Clara Kalbeck, a tactfully physical business: she came over the gravel slowly and determinedly, swathed in black, on two sticks, following Freda like her own old age.

2

WILFRID GLANCED ACROSS at his sister, and then put his eye back to the chink between the shutters. His leg was burning, and his heart was thumping, but he still hoped to do it right. He saw Robbie come in to the house with the suitcases—he leant forward to watch him and nudged the door open with his cheek. "Not till I say," said Corinna. Robbie looked up and gave them a wink.

"I know," muttered Wilfrid, and peered at her in the shadows with a mixture of awe and annoyance. The others seemed stuck in the porch, in endless adult talk. He could tell they were talking nonsense. He wanted to shout out at once, and he was also quite scared, as Corinna had said.

The weekend loomed above him, with its shadowy guests and challenges. More people were coming tomorrow—Uncle George and Aunt
Madeleine, he knew, and a man from London called Uncle Sebby. They
would all be talking and talking, but at some point they would have to
stop and Corinna would play the piano and Wilfrid would do his dance.
He felt hollow with worry and excitement. When a fire was lit in the
hall, this little cave-like passage was warm and stuffy, but today it smelt
of cold stone. He was glad he had someone with him. At last Granny
Sawle stepped in through the front door, and just for a second she
glanced at the fireplace, with a dead look, so that Wilfrid knew she was
expecting the surprise—though somehow this didn't spoil it, in a way it
made it better, and as soon as she'd dutifully turned her back he flung
open his shutters and shouted, "Hello, Granny—"

"Not yet!" wailed Corinna. "You've got it wrong, Wilfrid," but
Granny had spun round already, a hand pressed to her heart.

"Oh!" she said, "oh!"—and so Corinna pushed open her shutters too
and shouted the correct announcement, which was, "Welcome to Corley
Court, Granny Sawle and Mrs. Kalbeck!" with Wilfrid in hilarious uni-
son, riding roughshod over his own mistake, and even though Mrs.
Kalbeck hadn't yet made it into the house.

"It's too amazing!" said Granny. "The very walls have voices." Wilfrid
giggled in delight. "Ah, Dudley, dear"—now his father had come in, and
the dog barking. She raised her voice—"This ancient fireplace has miraculous properties!"

"Rubbish, Rubbish!" his father shouted, as the dog ran yelping and
shivering towards the front door. "Here, Rubbish, come here! Pipe
down!"; though Rubbish as usual did no such thing, and wanted to give
everyone a Corley welcome of his own.

"Quite magical!" Granny held on.

"Well, it won't be magical for much longer," said his father, in his
meaning voice, kissing her on the cheek. "Come on out of there, will
you!" though it wasn't clear now if he was shouting at the children or
the dog.

"Wilfrid messed it up," said Corinna in a further announcement, as
Mrs. Kalbeck leant in through the front door, on one stick after the
other, clearly alarmed as Rubbish leapt up and waltzed with her for a
moment with his front paws on her tummy—she took two panting steps
backwards, and the dog dropped down and sniffed excitedly round her
legs, her round black shoes. After that it took a while for her to see where
the young girl's voice was coming from.

"Frau Kalbeck, marvellous to see you again," said Dudley, limping quickly but very heavily across to her, so that he seemed to be playing with her, aping her or just joining in, you couldn't tell. "Please ignore my children."

"Oh, but darling," said their mother, "the children have asked to show the guests up to their rooms."

Dudley swung round with what they called the "mad glint." The mood thickened, in a familiar way. But he seemed to let them off by saying simply, "Oh, the little dears."

Mrs. Kalbeck was awfully slow on the stairs. Wilfrid watched the rubber tip of each stick as it felt for its purchase on the shiny oak. "It *is* very dangerous," he assured her. "I've fallen down here myself." Being responsible for her, he found her interesting as well as frightening. He bobbed up and down the stairs beside her, encouraging and assessing her much slower progress. Corinna and Granny Sawle had gone on ahead, and he was worried, as always, about being late, and about what his father would say. "This house is Victorian," he explained.

Mrs. Kalbeck chuckled amongst her sighs, and looked him in the face, levelly but sweetly. "And so am I, my dear," she said, in her precise German voice, her large grey eyes casting a kind of spell on him.

"Do you like it then?" he said.

"This marvellous old house?" she said gaily, but peering past him up the polished stairs with anxious blankness.

"My father can't warm to it," said Wilfrid. "He's going to change it all."

"Well," she said disappointingly, "if that's what he wants to do."

Mrs. Kalbeck had been put in the Yellow Room, at the far end of the house, and Wilfrid went a step or two ahead of her along the broad strip of carpet on the landing. They passed the open door of Granny Sawle's room, where Corinna had already been given a present, a bright red scarf which she was looking at in the mirror. It was a cheerful irresistible room, and Wilfrid started to go into it, but then did resist, and walked on. The next door on the other side was his parents' bedroom. "I'm afraid you're not allowed in that room," he said, "unless my parents ask you to go in, of course." He was embarrassed that he didn't exactly know Mrs. Cow's name; though at the same time he enjoyed thinking of her by her rude name. He didn't want to get too close to her black dress, and her smell, white flowers mixed up with something sour and unhappy. "Mrs. Ka . . . ," he said tentatively.

"Yes, Wilfrid."

"My name's not Vilfrid, you know, Mrs. Ka . . . !"

The old lady stopped and pursed her lips obediently. "*Wil*–frid," she said, and coloured a little, which confused Wilfrid too for a moment. He looked away. "You were saying, *Wil*–frid, my dear . . . ?" But of course he couldn't say. He danced on, down the long sunlit landing, leaving her to catch up.

The door of the Yellow Room was open, and the maid Sarah, not one of his favourites, was standing over Mrs. Kalbeck's old blue suitcase, going through its contents with a slightly comic expression. When Mrs. Kalbeck saw her, she lurched forward, almost fell as a rug slid away under her stick. "Oh, I can do that," she said. "Let me do that!"

"It's no trouble, madam," said Sarah, smiling coolly.

Mrs. Kalbeck sat down heavily on the dressing-table stool, panting with indecision, though there was nothing she could do. "Those old things . . . ," she said, and looked quickly from the maid to Wilfrid, hoping he at least hadn't seen them, and then back again, as they were carried ceremoniously towards an open wardrobe.

"Well, goodbye," said Wilfrid, and withdrew from the room as if not expecting to meet her again.

On the landing, by himself, he couldn't shake off the feeling that he should have said something. He trailed his fingers along the spines of the books in the bookcase as he passed, producing a low steady ripple. He covered his unease with a kind of insouciance, though no one was watching. He'd done what he'd been told, he'd been extremely kind to Mrs. Cow, but his worry was more wounding and obscure: that he'd been told to do it by someone who knew it was wrong, and yet pretended it wasn't. Three toes on his father's left foot had been blown off by a German shell, and the man he had learned to call Uncle Cecil was a cold white statue in the chapel downstairs, because of a German sniper with a gun. Wilfrid ran down the corridor, in momentary freedom from any kind of adult, his fear of being late overruled by a blind desire to hide—ran past his grandmother's room and round the corner, till he got to the linen-room, and went in, and closed the door.

3

"HAVE A DRINK, Duffel," said Dudley genially, rather as if she were another guest.

"We're having Manhattans," said Mrs. Riley.

"Oh . . . ," said Daphne, not quite looking at either of them, but crossing the room with a good-tempered expression. She still felt distinctly odd, like the subject of an experiment, whenever she came into the "new" drawing-room; and having Mrs. Riley herself in the room only made her feel odder. "Should we wait for Mother and Clara?"

"Oh, I don't know . . . ," said Dudley. "Eva looked thirsty."

Mrs. Riley gave her quick smoky laugh. "How do you know Mrs. . . . um—?" she said.

"Mrs. Kalbeck? She was our neighbour in Middlesex," said Daphne, making a moody survey of the bottles on the tray; and though she loved Manhattans, and had loved Manhattan itself, when they'd gone there for Dudley's book, she set about mixing herself a gin and Dubonnet.

Mrs. Riley said, "She seems rather . . . um . . . ," making a game of her own malice.

"Yes, she's a dear," said Daphne.

"She's certainly an enormous asset at a house party," said Dudley.

Daphne gave a pinched smile and said, "Poor Clara had a very hard war," which was what her mother often said in her friend's defence, and now sounded almost as satirical as Dudley's previous remark. She'd never been fond of Clara, but she pitied her, and since they both had brothers who'd been killed in the War, felt a certain kinship with her.

"Just wait till she starts singing the Ride of the Valkyries," Dudley said.

"Oh, does she do that," said Mrs. Riley.

"Well, she loves Wagner," said Daphne. "You know she took my mother to Bayreuth before the War."

"Poor thing . . . ," said Mrs. Riley.

"She's never quite recovered," said Dudley in a tactful tone, "has she, Duffel, your mother, really?"

Mrs. Riley chuckled again, and now Daphne looked at her: yes, that was how she chuckled, head back an inch, upper lip spread downwards, a huff of cigarette-smoke: a more or less tolerant gesture as much as a laugh.

"I don't rightly know," said Daphne, frowning, but seeing the point of keeping her husband in a good humour. A certain amount of baiting of the Sawles would have to be allowed this weekend. She came over with her drink, and dropped into one of the low grey armchairs with a trace of a smirk at its continuing novelty. She thought she'd never seen anything so short, for evening wear, as Eva Riley's dress, only just on the knee when she sat, or indeed anything so long as her slithering red necklace, doubtless also of her own design. Well, her odd flat body was made for fashion, or at least for these fashions; and her sharp little face, not pretty, really, but made up as if it were, in red, white and black like a Chinese doll. Designers, it seemed, were never off duty. Curled across the corner of a sofa, her red necklace slinking over the grey cushions, Mrs. Riley was a sort of advertisement for her room; or perhaps the room was an advertisement for her. "I know this weekend has been consecrated to Cecil," Daphne said, "but actually I'm glad that Clara was persuaded to come. She has no one, really, except my mother. It will mean so much to her. Poor dear, you know she hasn't even got electricity."

Dudley snorted delightedly at this. "She'll revel in the electrical fixtures here," he said.

Daphne smiled, as if trying not to, while the quick unmeaning use of the word *revel* lodged and sank in her, a momentary regret; she went on, "It's really rather a hovel she lives in, I mean clean of course, but so tiny and dark. It's just down the hill from where my mother used to live." Still, she knew she had been right to tell Revel not to come.

"And where you grew up, Duffel," said Dudley, as if his wife were getting airs. "The famous 'Two Acres.' "

"Oh, yes," said Mrs. Riley. "What was it . . . ? 'Two blessèd acres of English ground!' "

"Indeed!" said Dudley.

"I suppose that was Cecil's most famous poem, wasn't it?" said Mrs. Riley.

"I'm not sure," said Daphne, with another little frown. There was perhaps something reassuring after all about Eva Riley's long bare legs. A clever woman aiming to seduce a rich man right under his wife's nose would surely wear something more discreet, and dissembling. Daphne looked away, and out through the window at the garden, already losing colour in the early spring evening. At the top of the central section of each window the Valance coat of arms appeared, with the motto beneath it on a folded strip in Gothic letters. The gaudy little shields looked cheerfully at odds with the cold modernity of the room.

Dudley sipped piously at his cocktail, and said, "I can't help feeling slightly mortified that my brother Cecil, heir to a baronetcy and three thousand acres, not to mention one of the ugliest houses in the south of England, should be best remembered for his ode to a suburban garden."

"Well," said Daphne stoutly, and not for the first time, "it was quite a lovely garden. I hope you're not going to say things like that to Sebby Stokes." She watched Mrs. Riley's heavy-lidded smile indulge them both. "Or indeed to my poor mother. She's very proud of that poem. Besides Cecil wrote far more poems about Corley, masses of them, as you well know."

"Castle of exotic dreams," said Dudley, in an absurd Thespian tone, "mirrored in enamelled streams . . ."—but sounding in fact quite like Cecil's "poetry voice."

"I'm sure even Cecil never wrote anything so awful as that," said Daphne. And Dudley, excited by mockery of anything that others held dear, grinned widely at Eva Riley, showing her, like a flash of nakedness, his glistening dog-teeth. Mrs. Riley said, very smoothly, jabbing her cigarette out in the ashtray,

"I'm surprised your mother didn't marry again."

"The General, dear god!" said Dudley.

"No . . . Lady Valance's mother," said Eva Riley.

"It never seemed to come up, somehow . . . I'm not sure she'd have wanted it," said Daphne, suppressing, in a kind of ruffled dignity, her own uncomfortable thoughts on the subject.

"She's a pretty little thing. And she must have been widowed rather young."

"Yes—yes, she was," said Daphne, absently but firmly; and looked to Dudley to change the subject. He lit a cigarette, and steadied a heavy silver ashtray on the arm of his chair. It was one of over a hundred items that he had had stamped on the bottom: *Stolen from Corley Court.* Up in his dressing-room he kept a pewter mug of no great value with *Stolen from Hepton Castle* invitingly engraved on its underside, and he had followed the practice back at Corley, overseeing the work himself with fierce determination.

"When's the Stoker getting here?" he said, after a bit.

"Oh, not till quite late, not till after dinner," said Daphne.

"I expect he's got some extremely important business to attend to," said Dudley.

"There's some important meeting, something about the miners, you know," said Daphne.

"You don't know Sebastian Stokes," Dudley told Mrs. Riley. "He combines great literary sensitivity with a keen political mind."

"Well, of course I've heard of him," said Mrs. Riley, rather cautiously. In Dudley's talk candour marched so closely with satire that the uninitiated could often only stare and laugh uncertainly at his pronouncements. Now Mrs. Riley leant forward to take a new cigarette from the malachite box on the low table.

"You don't need to lose any sleep about the miners with Stokes in charge," said Dudley.

"I'm sleeping like a top as it is," she said pertly, fiddling with a match.

Daphne took a warming sip of her gin and thought what she could say about the poor miners, if there had been any point to it at all. She said, "I think it's rather marvellous of him to do all this about Cecil when the Prime Minister needs him in London."

"But he idolized Cecil," said Dudley. "He wrote his obituary in *The Times,* you know."

"Oh, really . . . ?" said Mrs. Riley, as if she'd read it and wondered.

"He did it to please the General, but it came from the heart. A soldier . . . a scholar . . . a poet . . . etc., etc., etc. . . . *etc.* . . . *and* a gentleman!" Dudley knocked back his drink in a sudden alarming flourish. "It was a wonderful send-off; though of course largely unrecognizable to anyone who'd really known my brother Cecil."

"So he didn't really know him," said Mrs. Riley, still treading warily, but clearly enjoying the treacherous turn of the talk.

"Oh, they met a few times. One of Cecil's bugger friends had him down to Cambridge, and they went in a punt and Cecil read him a sonnet, you know, and the Stoker was completely bowled over and got it put in some magazine. And Cecil wrote him some high-flown letters that he put in *The Times* later on, when Cecil was dead . . ." Dudley seemed to run down, and sat gazing, with eyebrows lightly raised, as if at the unthinkable tedium of it all.

"I see . . . ," said Mrs. Riley, with a coy smirk, and then looked across at Daphne. "I don't suppose you ever knew Cecil, Lady Valance?" she said.

"Me, oh good lord yes!" said Daphne. "In fact I knew him long before I met Dud—," but at that moment the door was opened by Wilkes and her mother came in, hesitantly it seemed, since she was waiting for her friend, on her two slow sticks, to cross the hall, and Clara herself was in distracted conversation with Dudley's mother, who came in briskly just behind her.

"My husband, you could fairly say, disliked music," said Louisa Valance. "It wasn't that he hated it, you understand. He was in many ways an unduly sensitive man. Music made him sad."

"Music is sad, yes," said Clara, looking vaguely harassed. "But also, I think—"

"Come in, come and sit," said Daphne, with a rescuing smile at Clara's shabby sparkle, the old black evening dress tight under the arms, the old black evening bag, that had been to the opera long before the War, swinging around the stick in her left hand as she thrust forward into the room. The Scottish boy, handsome as a singer himself in his breeches and evening coat, brought forward a higher chair for her, and propped her sticks by it once she'd sat down. Eva and Dudley seemed lightly mesmerized by the sticks, and gazed at them as if at rude survivals from a culture they thought they had swept away. The boy hovered discreetly, smiled and acted with proper impersonal charm. He was the first appointment Wilkes had made under Daphne's rule at Corley, and in some incoherent and almost romantic way she thought of him as her own.

"Sebastian hasn't arrived?" said Louisa.

"Not yet," said Daphne. "Not till after dinner."

"We have so much to talk about," said Louisa, with buoyant impatience.

"Ah, Mamma . . . ," said Dudley, coming towards her as if to kiss her, but stopping a few feet off with a wide grin.

"Good evening, my dear. You knew I was coming in."

"Well, I hoped so, Mamma, of course. Now what would you like to drink?"

"I think a lemonade. It's quite spring-like today!"

"Isn't it," said Dudley. "Let's celebrate."

Louisa gave him the dry smile that seemed partly to absorb and partly to deflect his sarcasms, and looked away. Her eyes lingered on Mrs. Riley's legs, then switched for reassurance to Daphne's, and her face, not naturally tactful, seemed frozen for five seconds in the forming and suppressing of a "remark." She was standing, perhaps by design, beneath her own portrait, which in a way made remarks superfluous. This was the house she had ruled for forty years. She was gaunter now about the brow than when she'd been painted, sharper about the chin. Her hair had gone from russet to ash, the red dress changed irreversibly to black. Every time she "came in" from the set of rooms she now occupied, and where she often chose to dine alone, she moved with a perceptible shiver of shaken dignity, made all the clearer by the sunny bits of play-acting that accompanied it. "I do think you've been so clever, my dear," she said to Mrs. Riley. "You've changed this room out of all recognition." At the corner of her eye she had the abstract painting, which so far she had affected not to have seen at all.

"Oh, thank you, Lady Valance," said Eva, with a slightly nervous laugh.

"It's most unexpected," said Clara, with her involuntary German air of meaning rather more.

Louisa gazed around. "I find it really most restful," she said, as if restfulness were a quality she specially cared for.

"You haven't seen anything yet," said Dudley, lurching towards his mother with her favourite drink. "We're going to brighten the whole place up."

"I'd be sorry to see the library changed," said Louisa.

"If you say so, Mamma, the library will be spared, it will retain its primeval gloom."

"Well . . ." She took a sip of lemonade, and smiled tightly, as if relishing her own good humour. "And what of the hall?"

"Now the hall . . . I believe Mrs. Riley has quite set her sights on the fireplace."

"Oh, not the fireplace!" said Freda, rather wildly. "But the children adore the fireplace."

"One would *have* to be a child, surely, to adore the fireplace," said Eva Riley.

"Well, I must be a child in that case," said Freda.

"Which makes me the child of a child," said Daphne, "a babe in arms!"

Dudley looked round the roomful of women with a glint of annoyance, but at once recovered. "You know, a lot of the best people nowadays are getting rid of these Victorian absurdities. You should run over and see what the Witherses have done at Badly-Madly, Mamma. They've pulled down the bell-tower, and put an Olympic swimming-pool in its place."

"Goodness!" said Louisa—which alternated with "Horror!" in her small repertoire of interjections, and was more or less interchangeable with it.

"At Madderleigh, of course," said Eva Riley, "they got to work long ago. They boxed in the dining-room there in the Eighties, I believe."

"There you are! Even the man who built it couldn't stand it," said Dudley.

"The man who built this house was your grandfather," said Louisa. "He loved it."

"I know . . . wasn't it odd of him?"

"But then you never showed any feeling for the things your grandfather held dear, or your father either." She grinned round at the others, as though they were all with her.

"Oh, not true," said Dudley, "I love cows, and claret."

"Now won't you sit down, Louisa?" said Freda warmly, smoothing the expanse of plumped cushion beside her. Daphne knew she hated the candour of talk at Corley since Sir Edwin had died, the constant sparring she herself had quickly become inured to.

"I prefer a hard chair, my dear," said Louisa. "I find armchairs somewhat effeminate." She sighed. "I wonder what Cecil would have made of all these changes."

"Mm, I wonder," said Dudley, turning away; and then facetiously, as if only half-hoping to be heard, "Perhaps you could ask him, the next time you're in touch?"

Daphne slid a horrified glance at Louisa; it wasn't clear if she'd heard. Dudley's head was nodding in noiseless laughter, and his mother went on with tense determination, "Cecil had a keen sense of tradition, he was never less than dignified—," but at that moment the door flew open, and there was Nanny, with a hand on each child's shoulder. She held them to her, perhaps a moment too long, in a little tableau of her own efficiency. "Well, here they are!" she said. When Granny Sawle visited, they were brought down at six, between nursery supper and bed. Wilfrid broke away and ran to greet her, with a low sweeping bow, which was his new game, while Corinna walked in front of the fireplace with her hands behind her back, as though about to make one of her announcements. They each found a moment to peep nervously at their father—but Dudley's high spirits didn't much falter.

"Say hello to Mrs. Riley," he said.

"Hello, Mrs. Riley," said the children, promptly but with no great warmth.

"My dears . . . ," said Mrs. Riley over her cocktail-glass.

Wilfrid ran round politely to bow to Granny V as well, who said warily, "Look at you!" as with a quick panting sound and the thwack of his tail against chairs and table-legs Rubbish bustled across the room from the open garden door and excitedly circled his master.

"Oh, do we really want the dog in?" said Daphne, with a flutter of panic as her mother raised her drink away from its thrusting nose and made a face at the gamy heat of its breath. She got up to grab it, but Dudley was growling indulgently and provokingly, "Oh, Wubbishy Wubbishy Wubbish!" and had already produced from somewhere one of the bone-hard black biscuits that Rubbish was said to like, which after a bit of teasing he threw into the air—it went down in one. Clara was still nervous of the dog, and smiled keenly at it to suggest she was not. She hid her shyness in a bit of pantomime, stretching out a hand in childish reconciliation, but she had no biscuit, and Rubbish walked past as if he hadn't seen her.

Corinna had moved in a discreetly purposeful way towards the piano, and now perched on the edge of the stool, studying her father for the best moment to speak. "You're not going to play for us, or anything, are you, old girl?" said Dudley.

"Oh, does she play?" said Eva, with a sly spurt of smoke.

"Play? She's a perfect fiend at the piano," said Dudley. "Aren't you, my darling?" At which Corinna smiled uncertainly.

"I'll play for you tomorrow," she said.

"Good idea. Play for Uncle George," said Dudley, tired already of his own sarcasm, as well as the subject itself.

"And Wilfie can do his dance," said Corinna, reminding her father of the terms of the deal.

"Well, exactly . . . ," said Dudley after a minute.

Louisa, still rather fixed on Eva, said, "I imagine you might care for music, Mrs. Riley?"

Mrs. Riley smiled at her to prepare her for her answer: "Oh, awfully—certain music, at least."

"What, Gounod and what have you?"

"Not Gounod particularly, no . . ."

"I should think one would draw the line at Gounod."

"Now Wilfie," said Dudley, with a loud cough, as if reproving him; but then went on, "have you heard about the Colonel and the Rat?"

"No, Daddy," said Wilfrid softly, hardly daring to believe that a poem was starting, but perhaps apprehensive too about its subject.

"Well . . . ," said Dudley. "The Colonel was there, with bristling hair, and a terrible air, of pain and despair."

Wilfrid laughed at this, or at least at the awful face his father had pulled to go with it; anything awful could be funny too. "Oh ducky," said Daphne, "is Daddy doing doggerel for you."

"It's not doggerel, Duffel," said Dudley, tightly suppressing a snort at so much alliteration, "it's called Skeltonics, it dates from the time of King Henry VIII. If you remember, Skelton was the poet laureate."

"Oh, in that case," said Daphne.

"Well, if you don't want me to tell you a poem."

"Oh, yes, Daddy!" said Wilfrid.

"Your uncle Cecil was a famous poet, but what people tend not to know is that I have quite a talent that way myself."

Daphne glanced at Louisa, who had an unprovokable look, as though she found her son and her grandson equally beyond comprehension.

"I know, Daddy," said Wilfrid, and stood yearningly by his father's knee, almost as if he might be going to lay his hand on it.

4

AFTER BREAKFAST the next day Daphne appeared in the nursery, just as Mrs. Copeland was getting the children ready for a walk: "No, Wilfrid, not those white trousers, you'll be all over mud."

"Mud will be all over me, you mean, Nanny," he said.

"Mother, we're walking to Pritchett's farm," said Corinna, with a stoical wince as Mrs. Copeland pulled a band over her hair.

"Don't worry, Nanny," said Daphne, "I'll take them myself. We've got photographers."

"Indeed, my lady!" said Nanny, with a keen smile and a hint of pique, scanning her charges with a sharper eye. "Shall we be in the papers again, then?"

"Well, *we* shall," Daphne wanted to say, "not you," but she made do with, "It's the *Sketch,* I think."

Mrs. Copeland tugged a little harder at Corinna's hair. "My sister in London sent Sir Dudley's picture from the *Daily Mail.*"

"I fear publicity is all a part of being a successful writer," said Daphne, "these days! No, leave those trousers on, my duck—we'll just be sitting about in the garden."

Wilfrid frowned at her bravely for a moment, but then turned and went to the window as if suddenly remembering something outside. "Wilfrid was promised to see the new foal," said Corinna, in a pitying, almost mocking voice, "and the little chicks in the incubator," but she was touched already by the strange contagion of grief, and when a wail went up from the window she started to crumple too, which was worse for her because of the loss of status. She didn't make much noise, but she attended to her doll's overnight bag with a swollen face, jamming in the parasol and the tiny red cardigan.

"Oh, are you bringing Mavis, darling?" said Daphne. Corinna nodded vigorously but didn't risk speaking.

"Oh dear, oh dear!" said Nanny smugly.

"Oh, Wilfie, don't cry," said Daphne, picturing the new foal nuzzling its mother and then running off with a nervy sense of untested liberty; but she hardened herself: "You don't want to look all blotchy in the paper."

"*I don't want to be in the paper,*" said Wilfrid tragically, his back still turned. Again, Daphne saw the sense of this, but she said,

"My duck, what a thing to say. You'll be famous. You'll be there with Bonzo the Dog, think of that. All over England people will be asking themselves"—here she ran over and snatched him up with a grunt and a slight stagger at his six-year-old weight—" 'Who is that lucky, *lucky* little boy?' "

But Wilfrid seemed to find that idea even more upsetting than the missed muddy walk.

Out among the maze-like hedges and commas of lawn in the flower-garden, Daphne saw him brighten and perhaps forget. After half a minute his dragging sorrow had a skip in it, there was a glance of reconciliation, a further ten seconds of remembered sorrow, rather formal and conscious, and then the surely unselfconscious surrender to the game of the paths. Gravel, or flagged, or narrow strips of grass, the paths curled between hedges, flanked the long borders, or opened into circles that had nearly identical statues in them, and presented a further compass of decisions, on which the children rarely tried to agree. Now Corinna marched ahead, down the main grass walk that was flanked with clematis grown along chains, dipping and rising between tall posts—in a week or two it would be a blaze of white, like the route of a wedding. She clutched, not

Mavis, but Mavis's red leather reticule. Wilfie avoided the processional way—he cantered around to left and right, talking in an odd private voice, sometimes sounding furious with himself or with some imaginary friend or follower. "Come along, my darling, let's see what those fish are up to," said Daphne.

A pool of dumb goldfish struck her as a wan consolation for the hot breath and smells and squelch of a farmyard, and Wilfie himself, when they all arrived at the central pond, took a bit of encouraging to focus on it. "Can they all be under that leaf?" said Daphne. The pool was ringed by a flagged path, and then four stone seats between high rose arches, thick with red and dark green leaves and only the tips of one or two buds as yet showing pink or white. Daphne sat down, with a passive conventional sense that it would make a good place for a photograph.

"Mother, is Sebby coming here?" said Corinna, setting her case on the bench between them.

"I don't know, darling," said Daphne, glancing round. "He's talking to your father."

"What on earth is Uncle Sebby doing?" said Wilfrid.

"He's not Uncle Sebby," said Corinna, with a giggle.

"No, ducky, he's not . . ." Poor Wilfie was haunted and puzzled by phantom uncles. Uncle Cecil at least was in the house, in a highly idealized marmoreal form, and was often invoked, but Uncle Hubert was mentioned so rarely that he barely existed for him—she wasn't sure that he had ever even seen his picture. All he had to go on, for uncles, was an occasional appearance by Uncle George, with his long words. When most uncles no longer existed, it was natural to co-opt one or two who did.

"Well, you see," said Daphne, "it's been decided that there's going to be a book of all Uncle Cecil's poems, and Sebby's come down to talk to your father about it, and Granny V, and well, talk to everybody really."

"Why?" said Wilfrid.

"Well . . . there's to be a memoir, you know . . . the story of Uncle Cecil's life, and Granny V wants Sebby to write it. So he needs to talk to all the people who knew him."

Wilfrid said nothing, and started on a game, and a minute later, staring into the pond, said, "A memoir . . . !" under his breath, as if they all knew it was a mad idea.

"Poor Uncle Cecil," said Corinna, in one of her calculated turns of piety. "What a great man he was!"

"Oh . . . well . . . ," said Daphne.

"And so handsome."

"No, he was," Daphne allowed.

"Was he more handsome than Daddy, would you say?"

"He had enormous hands," said Daphne, looking round at the first bark of the dog, which must mean Dudley, and everyone coming.

"Oh, Mother!"

"He was a great climber, you know. Always clambering up the Dolomites or somewhere."

"What's the Dolomites?" said Wilfrid, stirring the fishpond tentatively with a short stick.

"It's mountains," said Corinna, as Rubbish busied in through the rose arch behind them, went rather fast round half the circle, and came back, nose low and lively over the flagstones, scruffy grey tail flickering. Wilfrid pointed his wet stick bravely at him and Corinna commanded, "Rubbish!" but Rubbish only gave them a perfunctory sniff; it was almost hurtful to the children how little they counted for in the dog's stark system of command and reward, though a relief too, of course. "Bad dog!" said Wilfrid. Sometimes Rubbish explored by himself, sometimes he joined you flatteringly for the outset of a walk and then doubled off on business of his own, but mainly he was Dudley's running herald, hounded himself by his own shouted name. Daphne waited for the shouts, ignoring the dog, and rather disliking it; but no shouts came and in a minute Rubbish, oddly polite, stepping forward and stopping, gave a long cajoling whine, and when she looked round there was Revel under the arch.

He made a little picture of himself, in its frame. "My dear," said Daphne, "you made it!" as though she'd encouraged him rather than put him off. She felt she put a hint of warning in her welcome, in the look she gave him, which searched his charming sharp little face for signs of distress. He almost ignored her, bit his lip in mock-penitence, while his dark eyes went from one child to the other. He made everything depend on them—he was the opposite of the dog. "Rubbish told me I'd find you here," he said, coming forward to kiss Corinna on the silky top of her hair, pulling Wilfie quickly against his thigh, while the dog barked brusquely and then, its duty done, trotted back towards the house without looking round.

"Uncle Revel," said Wilfrid, taking the surprise more easily than his mother, "will you draw a brontosaurus?"

"I'll draw anything you like, darling," said Revel. "Though brontosauruses are rather hard." He came towards Daphne, who stood up, without quite wanting to, and felt his cheek and chin harsh against hers for a second. He said quietly, "I hope you don't mind, I rang up Dud and he said just to come."

"No, of course," she said. "Did you see someone? Did you see the photographer?" She felt somehow that Revel's visit, if it had to happen, should be kept out of the papers—and of course, if the photographers saw him they'd want him: he seemed to her to come emphasized, transfigured, set apart by success in a light of his own that was subtly distinct from the general gleam of the April day. Everyone was talking about him, not as much perhaps as they were about Sebby and the Trade Unions, but a good deal more than about Dudley, or Mrs. Riley, or of course herself! And now he'd had a frightful row with David, so the gleam about him was that of suffering as well as fame. Surely the last thing he needed was to see himself splashed all over the *Sketch*.

"There was a chap in a greasy trilby I don't think I've seen before," Revel said.

"Hmm, that'll be him," said Daphne.

"And I think I spotted your brother and his wife."

"Oh, really?" said Daphne, rather heavily.

"Fair, balding, wire-framed glasses . . . ?"

"That sounds like Madeleine . . ."

"But nice-looking," said Revel, with the little giggle she loved. "Madeleine more severe. Heavy tread, awful hat. If I may say so."

"Oh, say what you like," said Daphne. "Everyone does here."

"Is Uncle George here?" said Wilfrid.

"He is," said Revel. "I think they were going up to the High Ground."

"How perfectly obstreperous of him," said Corinna.

"Don't be an idiot," said Daphne.

"How entirely preposterous," said Corinna.

"Well, perhaps we should join them," Daphne said. And taking charge, she went out under the further rose arch, with the children eventually following, and Revel ambling between them and Daphne, speaking in the pointed way one did with other people's children, to amuse them and amuse the listening parent in a different way. "Certainly I don't think any brontosauruses have been spotted in Berkshire for several years now," he said. "But I'm told there are other wild beasts, some of them fiendishly disguised in smart white trousers . . ." Daphne felt the magnetic disturbance of his presence just behind her, at the corner of her eye as she led them up the steps and passed through the white gate under the arch. You were wonderfully safe of course with a man like Revel; but then the safety itself had something elastic about it. There were George and Madeleine—so odd that they'd set straight off on a walk. Perhaps just so as to be doing something, since Madeleine was unable to relax; or possibly to put off seeing Dudley for as long as they decently could.

The High Ground was an immense lawn beyond the formal gardens, from which, though the climb to it seemed slight, you got "a remarkable view of nothing," as Dudley put it: the house itself, of course, and the slowly dropping expanse of farmland towards the villages of Bampton and Brize Norton. It was an easy uncalculating view, with no undue excitement, small woods of beech and poplar greening up across the pasture-land. Somewhere a few miles off flowed the Thames, already wideish and winding, though from here you would never have guessed it. Today the High Ground was being mown, the first time of the year, the donkey in its queer rubber overshoes pulling the clattering mower, steered from behind by one of the men, who took off his cap to them as he approached. Really you didn't mow at weekends, but Dudley had ordered it, doubtless so as to annoy his guests. George and Madeleine were strolling on the far side, avoiding the mowing, heads down in talk, perhaps enjoying themselves in their own way.

The children hastened, at a ragged march, towards their uncle and aunt—and seemed unsure themselves how much of their delight was real, how much good manners; Corinna by now took delight in good manners for their own sake. George stood his ground, in his dark suit and large brown shoes, and then squatted down with a wary cackle to inspect them for a moment on their own level. Madeleine, wrapped in a long mackintosh, held back, with a thin fixed smile, in which various doubts and questions were tightly hidden.

"Aunt Madeleine, I've learned a new piece to play for you," said Corinna straight away.

"Oh," said Madeleine, "what is it?"

"It's called 'The Happy Wallaby.' "

"Well, my dear," said Madeleine, as if seeing something faintly compromising in this, "we'll have to see."

"She's been practising, haven't you, Corinna," said Daphne, and saw her glance at Wilfrid.

"And Wilfie's going to do his dance," Corinna said.

"Oh, that will be capital," said George. "When will you do it? I don't want to miss that," making up for his wife's lack of warmth.

"After nursery tea," said Daphne. "They're allowed down." The thing about seeing George with Madeleine was that it made you fonder of George; he stood up, and they kissed with a noisy firmness that amused them both. "How's Brum?" said Daphne.

"Brum's all right," said George.

"It's a great deal of work," said Madeleine; "you don't see us at our best, I fear!"

"I don't think you've met Revel Ralph, Madeleine . . . Revel, my brother George Sawle."

George looked keenly at Revel as he shook his hand. "Madeleine and I have been reading a lot about your show . . . congratulations! Your designs sound marvellous."

"Oh, yes," said Madeleine uncertainly.

"I wonder if we'll get down," said George, now smiling rather anxiously at Revel. "I'd love to see it."

"Well, let me know, won't you," said Revel.

"You've been, Daph, of course?" said George.

"I'd have to stay with someone, wouldn't I," said Daphne.

"You ought to have a little place in Town," said Revel.

"Well, we did have that very nice flat in Marylebone, but of course Louisa sold it," said Daphne, and changed the subject before it got going—"Watch out . . ." The donkey was plodding rapidly towards them, and they set off to the mown side of the lawn, damp grass cuttings clinging to their shoes. "God knows why they're mowing today," she said, though she took a kind of pleasure in it too, different from her husband's—it was something to do with labour, and running a place with twenty servants.

"How *is* Dudley?" said George.

"I think all right," said Daphne, with a quick glance at the children.

"Book coming on?"

"Oh, I find it best not to ask."

George gave her a strange look. "You've not seen any of it?"

"No, no." She took a bright, hard tone: "You know he's very excited about boxing things in."

"Oh, yes, I want to see this," said George, with his taste for controversy as much as for design. "How far is he taking it?"

"Oh, quite far."

"But you don't mind," with a sideways smile at her.

"Well, there are some things. You'll see."

"What do you think, Ralph?" said George. "For or against the egregious grotesqueries of the Victorians?" And now Daphne saw they were back in common-room mode, after a brief spontaneous holiday. The children smirked.

Revel thought and said, "Can I be somewhere in between?" with an appealing wriggle in his voice.

"I'd want to know why. Or rather where."

"I suppose what I feel," said Revel, after a minute, "well, the grotesqueries are what I like best, really, and the more egregious the better."

"What? Not St. Pancras?" said George. "Not Keble College?"

"Oh, when I first saw St. Pancras," said Revel, "I thought it was the most beautiful building on earth."

"And you didn't change your mind when you'd seen the Parthenon."

Revel blushed slightly—Daphne thought perhaps he had yet to see the Parthenon. "Well, I feel there's room in the world for more than one kind of beauty," he said, "put it that way," firmly but graciously.

George took this in, seemed even to blush a little himself. He stopped and looked away towards the house: turrets and gables, the glaring plate glass in Gothic windows, the unrestful patterns of red, white and black brick. Creeper spread like doubt around the openings at the western end. Daphne felt she wouldn't have chosen it, felt it had in a way chosen her, and now she would be sick at heart to lose it. She turned to Madeleine. "I remember when George first came to stay here, Madeleine," she said: "we thought we'd never hear the end of the splendours of Corley Court. Oh, the jelly-mould domes in the dining-room!" But such comical alliances with her sister-in-law rarely stuck—Madeleine smiled for a second, but her allegiance to George's intellect was the firmer. "No grotesqueries then!" insisted Daphne.

George clearly thought it wise to laugh at himself for a moment: "Cecil liked them, and one didn't argue with Cecil." It seemed not to bother him that he was mocking his sister's home.

"I see," said Revel, with that mixture of dryness and forgiveness that was so unlike Dudley's humour. "So you know the house quite well."

"Oh, quite . . . ," said George absently, the question of why he so rarely came to Corley perhaps embarrassing him. "You're too young to have known Cecil," he said.

"I'm afraid so," said Revel solemnly, and with the faintest smile, since his youth was generally thought to be in his favour, it was what all the articles in the magazines dwelt on—his being so brilliant so young.

"But you've been over Corley before," said George, now a touch proprietary.

"Oh, heaps of times," said Revel; and a strange sort of tension, of rivalry and regret, seemed for a moment to flicker in the two men's different smiles.

"Anyway, you'll meet Mrs. Riley," said Daphne, "she's staying for the weekend."

"Oh, is she . . . ," said Revel, as if seeing a disadvantage after all in his visit.

"She hung around for ages, you know, measuring things up or whatever she does and dropping ash on the carpet; and then Dud for some reason asked her to stay. And would you believe it, she had all her evening clothes in the boot of her car."

"Why did she?" said Wilfrid.

"She'll have been on the way to someone else's house, old chap," said George.

"Well, she designs clothes," said Corinna. "She's got tons of skirts and dresses in the car. She's going to make one for me, green velvet, with a low waist and no particular bust."

"No particular bust!" said Daphne. And then, "Is she indeed!"

"Is she all right?" said Revel. "I dare say she is—we come at things from different ends."

Daphne was a little unsure about the turn she'd given the talk. "I'm sure she's a genius," she said. "I'm just not awfully good with very fashionable people." And she thought, *and where is she now?*—in a scurry of anxiety which she quickly brought to heel.

"I don't expect she comes cheap," said Revel.

"No. In fact she's quite violently expensive," said Daphne, in a way that suggested a more than reasonable cause of annoyance.

They strolled back, their group still tentative and self-conscious, towards the white gate under the stone arch, and the broad path back to the house. Freda and Clara had come out for some air, and were moving at their own peculiar pace among the spring beds and low hedges of the formal garden. Daphne saw the man that Revel had mentioned, in a brown trilby, lope across and engage them in talk—they seemed confused, earnestly helpful, and then somewhat defensive. Clara raised one stick, and pointed it, as if sending him off. He had a camera-case slung round his neck, but didn't seem interested in using the camera on them. "Go on, my darlings, rescue Granny Sawle," said Daphne. But just then the man, backing away and glancing round, saw Dudley himself emerge through the garden door, with the look of tricky geniality that he put on for the press, and with Sebby just behind him, jammed in the doorway by the excitable dog, and clearly more reluctant to be seen.

"Here we are," said Dudley, as they all came up, shaking hands with George, shaking hands, rather pointedly, with Madeleine, though grinning at her fiercely as he did so. "And Revel, my dear, you've made it." He turned with a lurch to embrace the whole group in his grin. "What a lovely reunion!" Daphne glanced at her mother, who she felt was the one most vulnerable to Dudley's performance, but she was too caught up in her own reunion with George to notice it.

"Hello, George!" said Freda, with a brave little quiver, the tone of someone not quite sure of being remembered. And perhaps this tiny glimpse touched George as well—he enveloped his mother in a firm hug, sweetly, and guiltily, protracted.

"Maddy, dear," he said, and Madeleine too held Freda's shoulder and angled in for a kiss under the tilting brims of their hats.

"Now, I'm sorry to say, ladies and gentlemen," said Dudley, "that our little weekend idyll has been infiltrated by one of the tireless and pitiless agents of Fleet Street. What's your name?"

"Oh, I'm Goldblatt, Sir Dudley," said the photographer, swallowing Dudley's harsh tone, "Jerry Goldblatt," lifting his trilby an inch as he looked over the group.

"Jerry Goldblatt," said Dudley, and paused unpleasantly, "is just going to take a few snapshots for the *Sketch*."

"I prefer to say portraits," said Goldblatt, "portrait groups."

"So if you wouldn't mind awfully doing what he says for ten minutes, then we can get the damn fellow out of here."

"Much obliged," said Goldblatt. "Well, ladies and gentlemen—"

But they saw very quickly that it was Dudley who'd be telling them what to do. A trying hour or more of sittings ensued, different groupings around various stone seats, or posed, with a hint of awkward clowning, under the raised arms and bare breasts of bronze and marble statues. The Scottish boy made himself useful, and quickly set up the croquet lawn, where they started a pretend game which immediately got serious, and was abandoned with bad grace for work at another location. Really there were three of them the photographer wanted, Dudley, Sebby and Revel, with Daphne and the children as decorative extras. Dudley of course knew this, but in a complicated rigmarole brought in all the others, and nearly pretended not to want to be involved himself at all.

Dudley said: "But look here, Goldblatt, you must have a snapshot of our friend Frau Kalbeck. You know, she's one of the original Valkyries of Stanmore Hill."

"Oh, yes, Sir Dudley?" said the photographer warily.

"No, no, please . . . !" said Clara, tickled but mortified at the same time. She seemed ready to tuck her sticks out of sight. Daphne said,

"But not if you don't want to, dear," and indeed thought it quite impossible that they'd use such a photograph, which would make it, in the longer view, even sadder for her.

"Perhaps not, I think," said Clara, and hid her tiny disappointment in a histrionic call—"But where is dear Mrs. Riley?" It was unexpected, but she seemed to have taken a shine to Eva.

"Dudley dear, where's Mrs. Riley?" said Daphne coolly.

"Oh lord . . . ," said Dudley, the mad glint showing for a second through his puzzled tone. "Robbie, run and look for Mrs. Riley"—and as Robbie went swiftly away, "She may be just too busy . . ."

"Is that Mrs. Eva Riley, sir?" said Jerry Goldblatt, with a cunning glance at the house. "The interior decorator?"

"Yes, yes," said Dudley, "Mrs. Riley, the famous interior decorator of the Carousel Restaurant," as if writing the copy for the *Sketch* as well.

"That is a stroke of luck, Sir Dudley," said Goldblatt.

Daphne saw that Dudley had got almost everything he wanted; he'd rescued a stylish, amusing and important party from the jaws of the other one that bored him to madness, and posed it, for as long as the camera's flashes lasted, for the world to see. Sebby Stokes in fact declined to join in, suspecting that he shouldn't be seen playing croquet while the nation stood on the brink of a general strike; he shrewdly told Goldblatt he would be "working on Cabinet papers in the library." George, quite new to the world of publicity, acted up determinedly, followed Revel's instructions for new poses, and whisked the children along in a hectic and rather touching show of affection. He seemed to like Revel— perhaps the little friction in their views on St. Pancras Station had excited him. Madeleine, with the unhappy solidarity of the shy, had perched beside Clara, and in effect opted out of the photographs. As for Revel himself, Daphne saw that she needn't have worried, in fact there was almost some further friction in his eagerness to direct arrangements himself. "Well . . . yes . . . ," said Dudley, frowning, "no, no, my dear, you're the designer!"—shaking his head none the less in slight bafflement, while Jerry Goldblatt pleaded, "If I could just have Lady Valance and the kiddies?" Then Eva Riley arrived, her long legs white in sheeny stockings, almost laughably fashionable, a pearl-coloured cloche hat pulled down tight on her black bob. "Do you really need me?" she wailed, and Jerry Goldblatt called back that he certainly did.

Revel and Daphne had their picture taken together, back by the fishpond. They stood on either side of a rose arch, each with one arm raised like a dancer to gesture at the view beyond it. Daphne laughed to show she was not an actress, not certainly a dancer, and looked across at Revel, who kept a straighter face. She felt her laughter had a touch of panic to it. She had an apprehensive image of next week's *Sketch* on the morning-room table, and their silly faces vying for attention with the antics of Bonzo the Dog.

5

AT THE END of lunch George slipped out from the dining-room and set off for a distant lavatory, treasuring the prospect of four or five minutes alone. He felt stifled already by the subject of Cecil, and by the thought of a further twenty-four hours devoted to his brilliance, bravery and charm. What things they all found themselves saying. Perhaps in certain monasteries, or in finishing schools, the conversation at meals was as strictly prescribed. The General threw up a topic, and the rest of them batted it gingerly to and fro, with Sebastian Stokes as umpire; even Dudley's sneering had been edgily reined in. George had met Stokes once before, in Cambridge, when they'd all gone out in a punt, Cecil clearly exciting his guest by his lordly thrust and toss of the pole and intermittent recital of sonnets. Stokes seemed not to remember that George had been of the party, and George didn't remind him, when the talk turned to their Cambridge days. He felt undeniably uneasy, and drank several glasses of champagne, in the hope they would relax him, but they had only made him hot and giddy, while the dining-room itself, with its gaudy décor, its mirrors and gilding, had appeared to him more ghastly than ever, like some funereal fairground. Of course one indulged the dead, wrote off their debts; one forgave them as one lamented them; and Cecil had been mightily clever and fearless, no doubt, and had broken many hearts in his short life. But surely no one but Louisa could want a new memorial to him, ten years after his passing? Here they all were, submissively clutching their contributions. A dispiriting odour, of false piety and dutiful suppression, seemed to rise from the table and hang like cabbage-smells in the jelly-mould domes of the ceiling.

As he crossed the hall, the door under the stairs was shoved open by Wilkes, with the surprising look, for just a second, of a man who has a life of his own.

"Ah, sir . . . !" said Wilkes, turning to catch the door, the age-old benignity back at once like a faint blush.

"Thanks so much, Wilkes," said George. And since he had him there, "I hope you're well."

"*Very* well, thank you, sir, very well indeed," as if made even fitter by George's solicitude.

"I'm so glad."

"I trust you're well, too, sir; and Mrs. Sawle . . ."

"Oh, yes, both frightfully busy and burdened with work, you know, but, thank you, pretty well."

George and Wilkes were both holding the door, while Wilkes gazed at him with his usual flattering lack of impatience, of any suggestion that a moment before he had been rushing elsewhere. "It's good to see you back at Corley, sir." Though it struck George that Wilkes's mastery of implicit moral commentary was conveyed in the same smooth phrase.

He frowned and said, "We don't get down as often as we should like."

"It's possibly not very convenient for you," allowed Wilkes, letting his hand drop.

"Well, not terribly," George said.

"I know Lady Valance is especially pleased you've come, sir."

"Oh . . ."

"I mean the old Lady, sir, particularly . . . though your sister, too, I'm sure!"

"Oh, well it's the least I could do for her," said George, with adequate conviction, he felt.

"Since you and Captain Valance were such great friends."

"Well, yes," said George quickly, and rather sternly, over his own incipient blush. "Though goodness, it all feels a world ago, Wilkes." He

looked around the hall, with a kind of weary marvelment that it was still
there, the armorial windows, the brightly polished "hall chairs" no one
would dream of sitting on, the vast brown canvas of a Highland glen,
with long-horned cattle standing in the water. He remembered looking
at this painting on his first visit, and Cecil's father telling him it was "a
very fine picture," and what sort of cows they were. Cecil was behind
him, not quite touching, a latent heat; he had said something, "That's
MacArthur's herd, isn't it, Pa?"—his interest as smooth and confident as
his deceit; the old boy had agreed, and they'd gone into lunch, Cecil's
hand just for a moment in the small of his guest's back. "Of course I
remember it all," said George, and even working it up a bit in his embarrassment: "I always remember that Scottish picture." The picture itself
could hardly have been duller, but it was eloquent of something—the
drinking cattle seemed almost to embody Sir Edwin's artless unawareness
of what his son got up to.

"Ah, yes, sir," said Wilkes, to show it meant something, surely rather
different, to him too. "Sir Edwin cared greatly for 'The Loch of Galber.'
He often said he preferred it to the Raphael."

"Yes . . . ," said George, not sure if Wilkes's eyebrows, raised in amiable remembrance, acknowledged the general opinion about the
Raphael. "I was thinking, Wilkes, Mr. Stokes should have a word with
you about Cecil while he's here."

"Oh, it hasn't been suggested, sir."

"Really? You probably knew him better than anybody."

"It's true, sir, in some ways I did," said Wilkes modestly, and with
something else in his hesitancy, a hazy vision of all the people who
nursed the illusion of "knowing" Cecil best of all.

"Lady Valance made it clear at luncheon that she wants a full picture
of his childhood years," said George, with a hint of pomp. "She has a
poem he wrote when he was only three, I believe . . ."

Wilkes's pink, attentive face absorbed the idea of this new kind of
service, which would evidently be a very delicate one. "Of course I have
numerous memories," he said, rather doubtfully.

"Cecil always spoke of you with the greatest . . . admiration, you
know," said George, and then put in the word he'd just dodged, "and
affection, Wilkes."

Wilkes murmured half-gratefully, and George looked down for a
moment before saying, "My own feeling is that we should tell Mr. Stokes
all we can; it's for him to judge what details to include."

"I'm sure there's nothing I wouldn't be happy to tell Mr. Stokes, sir," said Wilkes, with a geniality close to reproach.

"No, no," said George, "no, I'm sure . . ."—and again he felt a little flustered by this courteous saunter round an unmentionable truth. "But I mustn't keep you!" And with a snuffle and a little bow, which seemed unintentionally to mimic the butler himself, and made George colour suddenly again, he turned through the door, which he closed softly behind him, and started down the long passage.

It was a strange sensation, this passage. He went along it with the natural rights of a guest, a slightly tipsy adult free to do as he pleased, but breathless at once with the reawoken feelings of his first visit, thirteen years before. Nothing had changed: the dim natural light, the school-like smell of polish, the long row of portraits of almost rectangular bulls and cows. He was dismayed to find himself blushing so soon and so much. He wondered anxiously if Wilkes, a valet in those days, who had been so helpful and tactful with him, and always somehow to hand, hadn't also been present, unremembered, in other scenes. Had he come and gone, silently, unnoticed? Was it indeed part of a very good valet's duties to spy, to read letters, to go through waste-paper baskets, the more fully to know his master's thoughts and anticipate his needs? Would that increase or diminish his respect for his master? Was it not said, by one of the French aphorists, that great men rarely seemed great to their valets? And it was here, where you turned the corner, that Cecil had grabbed him and kissed him, in his very first minutes at Corley, while showing him where to wash his hands. Kissed him in his imperious way, with a twist of aggression. George's heart jumped and raced, for a moment, remembering. The kiss, together with the tension of arrival at a country house and his own keen desire to impress and deceive Cecil's parents, had made George suddenly mad with worry. He had struggled with Cecil, who was proud of his strength. The cloakroom was thick with coats, as if a meeting or a concert were going on next door, and Cecil pushed him against them, lifting a tall stiff mackintosh off its peg—it toppled slowly over them and put a comical kind of stop to things, for the time being.

Beyond the coats was the sombre marble and mahogany washroom, and then the third room, with its towering cistern and high-up prison-like window. George locked the door with a remembered sense of refuge; and then with a gasp of confusion that the man he was hiding from was long dead.

On his way back along the passage he saw the charm of avoiding the

party for a little longer, and decided to visit the chapel and look at Cecil's
effigy. On the occasion of Daphne and Dudley's wedding, the tomb had
been unfinished, a brick box that one had to go to left or right of. To tell
the truth, he'd avoided looking at it. There had seemed to be some awful
lurking joke that they were getting married over Cecil's dead body. Now
there was no one in the hall, no sound of voices, and he skirted the mon-
strous oak table and went out into the glassed-in arcade, half cloister,
half conservatory, which ran along the side of the house to the chapel
door. Here too everything seemed the same, everything old and old-
fashioned, muddled and habitual, waiting no doubt for Mrs. Riley's
ruthless hand. Hard to bear in mind it was only fifty years old, younger
than his own mother. It looked sunk in habit and history. Gothic plinths
held up stone tubs of flowers; three brass chandeliers, crudely wired for
electricity, hung to just above head-height; the floor was of diapered tiles,
crimson and biscuit. George felt how the dark oak door of the chapel
loomed, seemed to summon and dishearten the visitor with the same
black stare. He gripped the cold ring of the handle, the latch shot up
inside with a clack, and again he saw Cecil, bustling him through on that
first afternoon, with a glance back over his shoulder, in case they were
being followed—"This gloomy hole is the family chapel"—and holding
him tightly round his upper arm. George had peeped about, in an
excited muddle, trying to smother his awe in the required show of disdain for religion, while sensing none the less that Cecil would expect
some sign of admiration at there being a chapel at all. Surely they were
both rather thrilled by it. The chapel was tall for its modest size, the timber roof shadowy, the thwarted light through the stained-glass window
giving the place, by afternoon, the atmosphere of the time just after sunset. Pale things glowed weakly, but others, tiles and tapestries, were dull
until the eyes adjusted.

Now what he saw, among the grey shadows, was Cecil's white figure,
stretched out flat, and seeming to float above the floor. The sun had long
since gone off the garish glass of the east window, and what daylight
there was, oblique and qualified, seemed all to be gathered in Cecil. His
feet pointed away, towards the altar. It was as if the chapel had been built
for him.

George pushed the door to, without quite closing it, and stood by the
first pew's end, with a stern expression and a very slight feeling of fear.
He was alone with his old pal again, almost as though he'd come into a
hospital ward rather than a chapel, and was afraid of disturbing him,

half-hoped to find him asleep and to slip away, having kept his word. That was a kind of visit he'd paid many times, in the War, and after, dreading to see what had happened to a fellow, afraid of the horror in his own face. Here there was a sickly smell of Easter lilies rather than disinfectant. "Hello, Cecil, old boy," he said, pleasantly and not very loudly, with a dim echo, and then he laughed to himself in the silence that followed. They wouldn't have to have an awkward conversation. He listened to the silence, chapel silence, with its faint penumbra of excluded sounds—birdsong, periodic rattle of the distant mower, soft thumps that were less the wind on the roof than the pulse in his ear.

Cecil was laid out in dress uniform, with rich attention to detail. The sculptor had fastened his attention on the cuff-badges, the captain's square stars, the thin square flower of the Military Cross. The buttons shone dully in their strange new light, brass transmuted into marble. Who was it . . . ? George stooped to read the name, which was dashingly signed along the edge of the cushion: "Professor Farinelli"—dashing and a touch pedantic too. The effigy lay on a plain white chest, with less readable lettering, Gothic and plaited, running right round it in a long band: CECIL TEUCER VALANCE MC ✠ CAPTAIN 6TH BATT ROYAL BERKSHIRE REGT ✠ BORN APRIL 13 1891 ✠ FELL AT MARICOURT JULY 1 1916 ✠ CRAS INGENS ITERABIMUS AEQUOR. It was a thoroughly dignified piece of work, in fact magnificently proper. It struck George, as the chapel itself had on that first day, as a quietly crushing assertion of wealth and status, of knowing what to do. It seemed to place Cecil in some floating cortège of knights and nobles reaching back through the centuries to the Crusades. George saw them for a moment like gleaming boats in a thousand chapels and churches the length of the land. He gripped Cecil's marble boot-caps, and waggled them sulkily; his hand waggled, the boot-caps eternally not. Then he edged round to look at the dead man's face.

His first polite thought was that he must have forgotten what Cecil looked like, in the ten years and more since he'd been in a room with him alive. But no, of course, the long curved nose . . . the wide cheekbones . . . the decisive mouth: they were surely what he remembered. Naturally the rather bulbous eyes were closed, the hair short and soldierly, as it must have been latterly, pushed back flat about a central parting. The nose had grown somehow mathematical. The whole head had an air of the ideal that bordered on the standardized; it simplified, no doubt, in some acceptable accord between the longings of the parents and the limits of the artist's skill. The Professor had never set eyes on Cecil—he must have worked from photographs, chosen by Louisa, which only told their own truth. Cecil had been much photographed, and doubtless much described; he was someone who commanded description, which was a rareish thing, most people going on for years on end with not a word written down as to what they looked like. And yet all these depictions were in a sense failures, just as this resplendent effigy was . . . So George reasoned for half a minute, looking over the polished features, the small seamed cushions of the closed eyes that once had seen right into him, thinking already what phrases he would use when he spoke to Louisa about it; whilst he tried to hold off some other unexpected sadness—not that he had lost Cecil, but that some longing of his own, awakened by the day and the place, some occult opportunity of meeting him again, had been so promptly denied.

None the less, he thought he would sit for a minute or two, in the flanking pew—he couldn't quite have said why; but when he was there he dropped his forehead to his raised hand, leant forward slightly and prayed, in a vague, largely wordless way, a prayer of images and reproaches. He looked up, on a level now with Cecil's sleeping form, the obdurate nose pointing roofwards, the soldierly commonplace of the body, posed perhaps by some artist's model, not completely unlike Cecil, not a runt or a giant, but not Cecil in any particular way. And pictures of the particular Cecil rose towards him, naked and dripping on the banks of the Cam, or trotting through the Backs in his rugger bags and clattering studs, white and unassailable before a match, filthy and bloody after it. They were beautiful images, but vague as well with touching and retouching. He had others, more magical and private, images less seen than felt, memories kept by his hands, the heat of Cecil, the hair-raising beauty of his skin, of his warm waist under his shirt, and the trail of rough curls leading down from his waist. George's praying fingers spread in a tentative caress of recollection. And then of course the celebrated . . . the celebrated *membrum virile,* unguessed for ever beneath the marble tunic, but once so insistently alive and alert . . . How Cecil went on about it, pompously and responsibly—it might have been the Magna Carta from the way he talked of it. Absurd but undeniable, even now, so that the colour came to George's face and he thought of Madeleine, as a kind of remedy, though it didn't seem to work like that, in fact didn't seem to work at all.

George dropped his head again, rather wondering about this probing of old feelings. It was awful that Cecil was dead, he'd been wonderful in many ways, and who knew what he might not have gone on to do for English poetry. Yet the plain truth was that months went past without his thinking of him. Had Cecil lived, he would have married, inherited, sired children incessantly. It would have been strange, in some middle-aged drawing-room, to have stood on the hearthrug with Sir Cecil, in blank disavowal of their mad sodomitical past. Was it even a past?—it was a few months, it was a moment. And then might there have been another moment, in the study one night, which Cecil now occupied as surely as his father had done, some instinctual surrender to the old passion, George bald and professorial, Cecil haggard and scarred? Could passion survive such changes? The scene was undeniably fantastic. Did he take off his glasses? Perhaps Cecil by then had glasses too, a monocle that dropped between them just as their lips approached. Only young men kissed, and even then not frequently. He saw the charming trouble-some face of Revel Ralph, and pictured himself in the same tense proximity with him, with a sudden canter of the heart of a kind he had almost forgotten.

There was the sharp moan of the door on its hinges, and Sebby Stokes stepped in, with his quiet official air, gleam of high white collar and silvery head. He pushed the door almost closed, as George had done, and came forward—clearly he thought he was alone, for these first few moments, and for George, half-hidden by the tomb, his unguarded expression had an odd, almost comic interest. Stokes surely felt the slight but unusual thrill of his imminent encounter with Cecil. George saw more clearly something feminine and nervous in his walk and glance; but there was something else too in the set of his mouth, his frown of appraisal—something hard and impatient, not glimpsed at all in the infinite diplomacy of his social manner. George stood up abruptly and enjoyed his jump of alarm, and humorous recovery, in which a trace of irritation lingered for a minute. "Ah! Mr. Sawle . . . You startled me."

"Well, you startled me," said George equably.

"Oh! Hmm, my apologies . . ." Stokes walked around the tomb with a firmer expression, frank but respectful, so that now you couldn't tell what he thought. "Quite a fine piece of work, don't you think? May I call you George?—it seems to be the style here now, and one hates to appear stuffy!"

"Of course," said George, "I wish you would," and then wondered if he was meant to call Stokes Sebby, which seemed an unwarranted jump into familiarity with a man so much older and so oddly, almost surprisingly, distinguished.

"It's not a bad likeness, by any means," Stokes said. "Often I'm afraid they don't quite get them if they haven't known them. I've seen some very hand-me-down efforts."

"Yes . . . ," said George, out of courtesy, but feeling, now the subject was being aired, more critical and proprietary. "Of course I didn't see him later on," he admitted. "But I don't quite feel I've found him here." He drew his fingers thoughtfully down Cecil's arm, and glanced for an abstracted moment at the marble hands, which lay idly on his tunicked stomach, almost touching, the hands of a sleeper. They were small and neat, somewhat stylized and square, in what was clearly the Professor's way. They were the hands of a gentleman, or even of a large child, untested by labour or use. But they were not the hands of Cecil Valance, mountaineer, oarsman and seducer. If the Captain's neat head was a well-meant approximation, his hands were an imposture. George said, "And of course the hands are quite wrong."

"Yes?" said Stokes, with a momentary anxiety, and then, a little reluctantly, "No, I think you're right," a sense of their unequal intimacies in the air.

"But when did you last see him yourself, I wonder?"

"Oh . . . well . . ." Stokes looked at him: "It must have been . . . ten days before he was killed?"

"Oh, well, there you are . . ."

"He was on leave unexpectedly, you know, and I invited him to dine at my club." Stokes said this in a natural, practical tone, but it was clear the invitation had meant a great deal to him.

"How was he?"

"Oh, he was splendid. Cecil was always splendid." Stokes smiled for a moment at the marble figure, which certainly seemed to encourage this view. George felt, as he had with Wilkes, that the older man's words lightly censured some suspected impropriety in his own. "Of course I first met him in a *punt*," said Stokes, while George's pulse quickened at the chance for disclosure, a diverting little episode.

"You came to Cambridge . . . ," he said, neutrally, with a quiet sense of the chance flowing away. There had been four or five of them in the punt, Ragley and Willard certainly, both now dead, and someone else George couldn't see. His own focus, like Sebby's evidently, had been on the figure with the pole at the rear.

"Lady Blanchard's son, Peter, had asked me down to meet Cecil, and meet some of the new poets."

"Of course . . . ," said George, "yes, Peter Blanchard . . ."

"Peter Blanchard was full of Cecil."

"Yes, wasn't he just . . . ," said George, looking away, distantly bewildered to think how jealous of Blanchard he'd been. The absolute torments of those days, the flicker of gowns in stairwells, the faces glimpsed as curtains were closed, seemed now like distant superstitions. What could any such emotions mean years later, and when their objects were dead? Stokes gave him a quick uncertain glance, but pushed on humorously,

"I can't remember them all now. There was a young man who never said a word, and who had the job of keeping the champagne cold."

"Did he have the bottles on strings in the water . . . ?" said George, now feeling terribly foolish, in retrospect as well as in the present moment. The bottles used to knock against the hull with each forward thrust of the boat; when you loosened the wire the corks went off like shots into the overhanging willows.

"Exactly so," said Stokes, "exactly so. It was a splendid day. I'll never forget Cecil reading—or not reading, reciting—his poems. He seemed to have them by heart, didn't he, so that they came out like talk; but in quite a different voice, the poet's voice. It was distinctly impressive. He recited 'Oh do not smile on me'—though one could hardly help it, of course!"

"No, I'm sure," said George, blushing abruptly and turning away. He peered at the altar, beyond its polished brass rail, as though he had found something interesting. Was he doomed to glow like a beacon throughout the whole weekend?

"But you were never one of the poets?"

"What . . . ? Oh, never written a line," said George, over his shoulder.

"Ah . . ."—Stokes murmured behind him. "But you have the satisfaction of having inspired, or occasioned, or anyway in some wise brought about perhaps his most famous poem."

George turned—they were rather penned in in this space between the tomb and the altar. The question was laboriously genial but he ran over it again carefully. "Oh, if you mean 'Two Acres,' " he said. "Well that of course was written for my sister."

Stokes smiled vaguely at him and then at the floor. It was as if a mist of delicacy had obscured the subject. "Of course I must ask Lady

Valance—Daphne—about that when we talk this afternoon. Do you not see yourself in the lines, what is it? 'I wonder if there's any man more / Learned than the man of Stanmore'?"

George laughed warily. "Guilty as charged," he said—though he knew "learned" had not been Cecil's original choice of epithet. "You know he wrote it first in Daphne's autograph book."

"I have it," said Stokes, with the brevity that lay just beyond his delicacy; and then, "She must have felt she'd got rather more than she bargained for," with a surprising laugh.

"Yes, doesn't it go on," said George. He himself felt sick of the poem, though still wearily pleased by his connection with it; bored and embarrassed by its popularity, therefore amused by its having a secret, and sadly reassured by the fact that it could never be told. There were parts of it unpublished, unpublishable, that Cecil had read to him—now lost for ever, probably. The English idyll had its secret paragraphs, priapic figures in the trees and bushes . . . "Well, Daphne can tell you the story," he said, with his usual disavowal of it.

Stokes said, in a most tactful tone, "But you and Cecil were clearly . . . very dear friends," the tact being a continued sympathy for his loss, of course, but suggesting to George some further, not quite welcome, sympathy, of a subtler kind.

"Oh, for a while we were terrific pals."

"Do you recall how you met?"

"Do you know, I'm not sure."

"I suppose in College . . ."

"Cecil was very much a figure in College. It was flattering if he took an interest. I think I'd won . . . oh, one of our essay prizes. Cecil took a keen interest in the younger historians . . ."

"Quite so, I imagine," said Stokes, with perhaps a passing twinkle at George's tone.

"I'm not really able to talk about it," said George, and saw Stokes's ghost of a smile stiffen with repressed curiosity. "But still . . . you must know about the Society, I imagine."

"Ah, I see, the Society . . ."

"Cecil was my Father." It was striking, and useful, how one set of secrets nested inside another.

"I see . . . ," said Stokes again, with the usual faint drollery of an Oxford man about Cambridge customs. Still, the exchange of esoteric fact was very much his line, and his face softened once more into a ready reflector of hints and allusions. "So he . . ."

"He picked me—he put me up," said George curtly, as if he shouldn't be giving even this much away.

Stokes smiled almost slyly over this. "And do you still go back?"

"So you do know about us, perhaps everyone knows."

"Oh, I don't think by any means."

George shrugged. "I haven't been back for years. I'm immensely busy with the department in Birmingham. I can't tell you how it nails me down." He heard his own forced note, and thought he saw Stokes hear it too, absorb it and conceal it. He went on, with a quick laugh, "I've rather left Cambridge behind, to be frank."

"Well, perhaps one day they will call you back."

Stokes seemed to speak from the world of discreet power, of committees and advisers, and George smiled and murmured at his courtesy. "Perhaps. Who knows."

"And what about letters, by the way?"

"Oh, I had many letters from him," said George, with a sigh, and choosing Stokes's word, "really *splendid* letters . . . But I'm afraid they were lost when we moved from 'Two Acres.' At least they've never turned up."

"That is a shame," said Stokes, so sincerely as to suggest a vague suspicion. "My own letters from Cecil, only a handful, you know, but they were marvellous things . . . *joyous* things. Even up to the end he had such spirit. I will certainly give some beautiful instances."

"I hope you will."

"And of course if yours were to be found . . ."

"Ah," said George, with a laugh to cover his momentary vertigo. *Was ever such a letter written by a man to a man? How the world would howl and condemn if it read over my shoulder, yet everything in it is as natural and true as the spring itself.* He slid past Stokes to look at the tomb again and thought he could ask practically, "I suppose you're his literary executor?"

"Yes," said Stokes; and perhaps hearing something more in the question, "He didn't appoint me, to be completely frank, but I made a promise I'd look after all that for him." George saw he couldn't ask if the promise had been made to Cecil in person or was purely a duty Stokes had imposed on himself.

"Well, he's very lucky, in that at least."

"There has to be someone . . ."

"Mm, but someone with judgement. Posthumous publication doesn't always enhance a writer's reputation." He took a frank, almost academic note. "I don't know how you would rate Cecil Valance, as a poet?"

"Oh . . ." Stokes looked at him, and then looked at Cecil, who now seemed to cause him a slight inhibition, his marble nose alert for any disloyalty. "Oh, I think no one would question," he said, "do you? that a number, really a goodly few, of Cecil's poems, especially perhaps the lyrics . . . one or two of the trench poems, certainly . . . 'Two Acres,' indeed, lighter but of course so charming . . . will be read for as long as there are readers with an ear for English music, and an eye for English things . . ."

This large claim seemed rather to evaporate in its later clauses. George glanced at Cecil's knightly figure and said kindly, "I just wonder if people aren't growing sick of the War."

"Oh, I don't think we've heard the last of the War," said Stokes.

"Well, no," said George. "And of course much of Cecil's work was done before the War."

"Quite so, quite so . . . but the War made his name, you'd have to agree; when Churchill quoted those lines from 'Two Acres' in *The Times,* Cecil had become a war poet . . ." Stokes sat down, at the end of the first pew, as though to mitigate the strict air of debate, as well as to show he had time for it.

"And yet," said George, as he often had before, with a teacher's persistence, " 'Two Acres' itself was written a full year before war broke out."

"Yes . . . ," said Stokes, with something of a committee face. "Yes. But isn't there often, in our poets and our artists, a prophetic strain?" He smiled in concession: "Or if not that precisely, a fore-knowledge, a sense, perhaps, of the great inevitable that most of us are deaf and blind to?"

"It may be so," said George, wary of this sweeping talk, which in his view bedevilled too much of what passed as literary criticism. "But to that I'd say two things. You'd agree, I'm sure, that we were all talking about war long before it happened. You didn't need prophetic gifts to know what was going on, though Cecil certainly, who went to Hamburg and Berlin, and had been sailing up on the Frisian coast, was very much in the picture. My second point is that as I'm sure you know Cecil appended that further little section to 'Two Acres' when it came out in *New Numbers.*"

" 'The greyhound in its courses, / The hawk above the hill,' you mean."

" 'Move not more surely to their end / Than England to the kill,' " said George, pleased to cap the quotation, though far from pleased by the words themselves. "Which of course has nothing to do with 'Two Acres' the house, though it turns the poem 'Two Acres' into a war poem of—in my view—a somewhat depressing kind."

"It certainly changes the poem," said Stokes more leniently.

"For us it was a bit like finding a gun-emplacement at the bottom of the garden . . . But perhaps you think rather better of it. I'm a historian, not a critic."

"I'm not sure I allow a clear distinction."

"I mean I'm not a reader of new poetry. I don't keep up, as you do."

"Well, I try," said Stokes. "I admit there are poets writing at this moment whom I don't fully understand—some of the Americans, perhaps . . ."

"But you keep up," George assured him.

Stokes seemed to ponder. "I think more in terms of those individuals I can help," he said, something at once noble and needy in his tone.

"And now . . ."

"And now . . . well, now I must get all Valance's things up together," said Stokes, standing up, with the air of someone late for work.

"How much is there, would you say?"

Stokes paused as if considering a further confidence. "Oh, it will be quite a book."

"A lot of new things . . . ?"

A tiny flinch. "Well, a good many old ones."

"Mm, you mean the infant effusions."

Sebby Stokes looked around, with his almost comical air of simultaneous candour and caution. "The infant effusions, as you so justly put it."

"Not omittable?"

"All addressed to Mamma!"

"Of course . . ."

"Most unfortunate."

"Touching, in a way, perhaps?"

"Oh, touching, certainly. Certainly that."

George giggled ruefully. "And then Marlborough, I suppose?"

"There the view grows a good deal brighter. Some of the schoolboy work we know from *Night Wake,* of course, but I shall comb the *Marlburian* with much keenness."

"But again . . . later unknown things?"

Stokes looked at him keenly, even pleadingly, for a second. "If you know of any . . ."

"As I say, we'd rather lost touch."

"No . . . The fact is I am a little troubled by something." Stokes glanced at the tomb. "When I last saw Cecil that night in London, he showed me a handful of new poems, some of them unfinished. We went back to my flat after dinner, and he read to me, it must have been for half an hour or so. Very striking: both in itself and, somehow, in the way he read: very quiet and . . . thoughtful. It was a new voice—you might say a personal voice, as much as a poetical one, if you see what I mean. I was most taken, and stirred." Stokes was brusque for a moment with reawoken feeling.

George pictured this scene with a forgiving sense of the Cecil that Stokes had never known, the nudist, the satyr, the fornicator; and with a twist of envy too—the bachelor flat, Cecil in uniform, the bewildering brevity of a soldier's leave, the luxury of talk about poems over a coal fire. "And what subjects was he dealing with?"

"Oh, they were war poems, poems about his men, trench life. They were very . . . *candid*," said Stokes frankly but airily, briefly searching George's face.

"Mm, I'd like to see them." (No, the coal fire was nonsense, some memory of his own—it must have been June, windows open on to the London night.)

Stokes nodded impatiently. "So indeed should I."

"Ah. He didn't leave them with you."

"He said he'd send them," said Stokes, with a touch of petulance; and then, with an accepting snuffle, "but of course he went back to France without finding occasion to do so."

"He had other things on his mind," said George.

"I'm sure he did . . . ," said Stokes, clearly not in need of a lesson.

"And these poems weren't among his effects?" George had a sense of Stokes's pretty formidable efficiency rattled by this lapse.

Stokes shook his head, and looked up quickly, almost furtively, at the groan of the door behind them. "Anyway . . . here is your wife!"

George turned and saw Madeleine step cautiously into the gloom. He raised a hand reassuringly and called, "Hello, Mad"—the echoes reawoken.

"Ah, there you are," said Madeleine. She came forward, adjusting her eyes to the shadows and perhaps to something else in the atmosphere. "Are you praying, or plotting?"

"Neither," said George.

"Both," said Stokes.

"We've been communing with Cecil," said George.

"Well, it's Cecil I've come to see," said Madeleine, in her own tone, with its possible tremor of humour; George had seen people peer at her, trying to make it out. The two men stood silent and observant as she approached the effigy and looked it over, with her scholarly firmness of interest and her cool immunity to all aesthetic sensations. "Is it a good likeness?" she said.

"As it happens," said Stokes, "we weren't quite able in the end to decide; were we, George? Is it Cecil, or is it, as it were, someone else?" He had a slight air of taking sides and teasing Madeleine, which George entirely understood and keenly resented. He said,

"I'm afraid I don't think it's him."

Madeleine stood by the head of the tomb, with the straight-backed look of a senior nurse. Impossible to guess how much she knew; or even to know how much she guessed. "Was he not bigger?" she said.

"Oh . . . possibly . . . ," said George, coming over to face her across the body, with a clear, disingenuous desire to be open, casual, critical if need be. "But it's not that."

"Not more muscular?" said Madeleine, giving a glimpse perhaps of what she'd been encouraged to believe about the dead hero.

George stood, with his eyebrows raised, gently shaking his head . . . "What can I say?—just more alive, simply."

"Ha, yes," said Madeleine, and gave him a quick puzzled look. "Have you been having a useful discussion?"

"Your husband has been moderately forthcoming," said Stokes. "Though I feel I haven't finished with him yet."

"Sebastian has a great deal to do," said George, and laughed.

Stokes bowed his head with courteous humour. "Indeed, and I must get on—I've promised to interrogate your dear mother . . ." And he went out, with that slight hardening of the face again at the prospect of further work and new calculations.

George looked up at his wife, and then down again at Cecil, who seemed somehow to have turned into a piece of evidence, ambiguous but irreducible, lying between them. He had an almost physical sense of changing the subject as he turned away and said, "You know, old Valance has been quite bearable, so far."

Madeleine smiled tightly. "So far. But then we have only been here for three hours."

"I imagine it's pretty galling for him to have this fuss kicked up about Cecil, all over again."

"I don't see why," said Madeleine, naturally contrary.

"One sees the anniversaries stretching ahead for ever."

"Dudley Valance is a very strange man. I think it very sad, if he's jealous after all this time."

"A bad war, of course."

"Though you might think not so bad as Cecil's. Louisa was just telling me about the death. How they went out to France themselves to see him."

"Yes, he hung on, didn't he, for several days . . . ?" George had an idea that "Fell at Maricourt" was a sonorous formula, rather than the strict and messy truth.

"They got permission to bring his body back. I say 'they,' but I had the impression it was Louisa's doing."

"She's not called the General for nothing."

"One can sympathize with them wanting to see their son," said Madeleine fairly.

"Well, of course, darling."

"Though immediately one thinks of the thousands of parents who simply couldn't do that."

"Very true. My own dear mother, for instance."

"Well, there you are," said Madeleine, but as if arguing rather than agreeing—it was their way, their own odd intimacy, though charged now with something more anxious. "They brought him back here, and he was laid out in his own room, facing the rising sun."

"Oh, god. What, in the coffin?" George pursed his lips against a horrified giggle.

"I wasn't quite clear," said Madeleine.

"No . . . Where was he hit exactly?"

"Well, I could hardly ask, could I. I suppose he might have been very disfigured."

George saw how he'd been able to avoid such questions before; and had a certain sense, too, of Madeleine choosing her moment to raise them.

"I don't think you've ever told me," she said, "about when you heard the news."

"Oh, didn't I, Mad . . . ?" George blinked, and frowned at the floor. His thoughts ran along the diagonals, the larger red lozenge of the tiles. Well, she'd asked him, and he must answer. "I do remember one or two things about it very well. I was up at Marston, of course, I remember it was very hot, and everyone was tired and tense about what was happening in France. Then after dinner I was called to the telephone. As soon as I heard it was Daphne, I felt quite sick with dread that something had happened to Hubert, and when it turned out to be Cecil, awful to say but I remember the news had to fight with a sort of upsurge of relief." He glanced at his wife. "I remember blurting out, 'But Huey's all right!' and old Daph saying, rather crossly, you know, 'What . . . ? Oh, Huey's fine,' and then, her exact words, 'It's beautiful Cecil who's dead'—and then she sort of wailed into the telephone, an extraordinary sound I've never heard her make before or since." George himself, looking at Madeleine, gave a weird gasp of a laugh. She looked back, showing in her blankly pondering face that she had other questions. "Beautiful Cecil is dead," said George quietly again, in a tone of amused reminiscence. Well, he would never forget the words, or the sudden wild licence of grief so startling in someone as close as a sister. Even then he had resisted them, their sudden appeal to something shared but never said till now. In truth, more than most deaths that summer, Cecil's death had seemed both quite impossible and numbly unsurprising. Within a week or so he had seen it as inevitable.

6

"Darling: *Piccadilly* . . . ," said Mrs. Riley: "two *c*s?"

"Well, yes!" said Daphne.

"Oh, I think two," said her mother, after a moment.

"I'm not entirely stupid," said Mrs. Riley, "but there are one or two words . . ." She drew a bold line beneath the address, and smiled mischievously at what she'd written. None of them knew what the letter was, but the address in Piccadilly seemed designed to make them wonder. They were in the morning-room, with its chintz and china, and a small fire disappearing in the sunlight. Freda gazed at the pale flames and said, as Daphne knew she would,

"The sun will put that fire out."

Mrs. Riley lit a cigarette with a hint of impatience. "My dear, do you believe that?" she said.

"You may laugh," said Freda, and then, "At least, that's what I believe," and smiled at her rather timidly. She had clearly registered her daughter's dislike for the woman, but herself perhaps found her no more than disconcerting.

Daphne said pleasantly, "Well, we'll hardly miss it, Mummy, will we, it's such a warm day." She smiled across at her mother, who was sitting with another letter in her lap, an old one, whose envelope, half-ripped in the long-ago moment of opening it, she was pressing and smoothing with her thumb.

"This is all I have," she said. "I hardly knew Cecil."

"It really doesn't matter," said Daphne. "Anyway, you did."

"I didn't know he was going to be a great poet."

"Mm, well, I'm not sure anyone thinks that . . ." The far door led to the library, and there Sebby Stokes was having his little chats. She thought Wilkes was in there now, being pressed for recollections, early signals of genius. The talk of course wasn't audible, but none the less somehow present to those in the morning-room, sitting like waiting patients half-expecting to hear cries from the surgery. Freda looked at her daughter, with a fretful effort at concentration.

"I do remember one or two things about him . . . Was it twice he came to the house? I've only the one letter, you see."

"Twice perhaps, yes."

"He was very energetic," said Freda.

"Well, he could be, couldn't he . . ."

Though nothing was ever said, Daphne felt that her mother hadn't specially cared for Cecil. She saw him again, larger than life in their house, stooping briefly to their low-beamed ways. They had given him special rights, as a poet and a member of the upper classes; he'd been allowed to break things, to stay up all night, worship the dawn . . . They'd done their best to treat his absurdities as virtues, enlightening novelties. He'd been welcomed, as a friend of George's, which was a novelty in itself. Had Freda picked up on the goings-on in the garden, after nightfall? There was much that she'd missed in those years, with the bottles in the wardrobe, and who knew where else. She had been excited by the poem, and really quite encouraging when Cecil started writing to Daphne—she saw a future in it, no doubt; she had allowed them to meet, when Cecil was on leave. Even so, something was amiss. It seemed possible Cecil had done or said some particular small thing, some slight that Freda could never mention and never forget—and in fact rather treasured for the reliable throb of indignation it caused . . . Now he was just an excuse for her—Daphne knew she'd come for the weekend so as to see the children. But Freda's frown softened: "I'll never forget him reading to us that night in the garden—reading Swinburne, was it, and in such a voice . . ."

"Oh yes . . . Was it Swinburne? I know he read *In Memoriam.*"

"Ha, indeed, how apt," said Freda, and then looked blankly again at the thin flames. "Didn't he read us his own things?"

"He kept us up all night listening to him," said Daphne.

"We were out on the lawn, weren't we, under the stars . . ." Daphne didn't think this was right, but nor was it worth correcting. Freda's gaze wandered round the room and out, beyond Mrs. Riley, to the present-day lawns and the trees of the Park beyond. "I sometimes think how different things would have been if George had never met Cecil," she said.

"Well, yes . . . !" said Daphne, with a short laugh. "Of course they would, Mother."

"No, darling, you know," Freda said, "but I do think some of his ideas were rather silly . . . I don't know . . . one can't say that, I suppose."

"His ideas . . . ?" Daphne felt she half-knew what her mother meant. "I think you can say what you like."

Freda seemed to weigh up this privilege. "He certainly turned your head," she said, in a rather bleak tone.

"I was very young," said Daphne quietly, wishing more than ever that Mrs. Riley wasn't occupying her desk, toying with her fountain pen, and observing the conversation, in her disappointed and reducing way: now she said almost slyly,

"You must have been a mere girl, my dear."

"Yes, I was."

"She was very susceptible," Freda explained, "weren't you, Daphne?"

"Thank you, Mother!"

"And then he wrote his most famous poem for you, you must have been swept off your feet," said Mrs. Riley, enjoying the picture.

"No, he did," said Freda.

Daphne said, "Well . . . he wrote it for all of us, really, didn't he." She felt vaguely amazed now by the whole business of the poem, by the awkward memory of what it had once meant to her. She would never have been allowed to keep it to herself. That morning she knew it was the most precious thing she had ever been given, and even then she had felt it being taken away from her. Everyone had wanted a part of it. Well, now they had it, they were welcome to it; if she tried to claim it back it was only as mortifying evidence of her first infatuation. Sometimes she acted her role: when people found out the story, and gloated over her, she agreed what a very lucky young lady she had been; but where possible she went on to say that she no longer cared. Within a week she had learned from George that other people were reading it. It appeared in *New Numbers,* a good deal rewritten. Then, when Cecil died, it was quoted by Churchill himself, in *The Times.* She had just lent the famous autograph book to Sebby Stokes; it was a bit greasy and frayed, the other entries before it and after it looking sweetly strait-laced and proper in comparison. But the poem itself . . . "It's entered the language, hasn't it," she said.

"It's a bit of a jingle," said Freda, which Daphne had heard her say before.

"You must be awfully proud," Mrs. Riley insisted.

"Well, you know," said Freda.

Mrs. Riley shook her head. "I can't help wondering what Cecil would think of us all talking about him like this."

"Oh, I'm sure he'd be pleased to find he was still the centre of attention," said Daphne.

"Cecil was awfully fond of Cecil!" said Freda. "If you know what I mean."

Mrs. Riley looked round for a second before saying, rather archly, "Does your mother-in-law still get messages from him, I wonder?"

"Not any more," said Daphne. "Anyway, it was all nonsense, all that, and all very sad."

"What's that, dear?"

"Oh, nothing, Mother . . . Louisa's book tests, you remember."

"Oh, that, yes . . . ," said Freda with a little stricken look. "So sad."

"I'm sure it must be nonsense," said Mrs. Riley, "but I've always thought it would be fun to try."

"I don't think fun comes into it very much," said Freda, frankly bemused.

"We could try and get through to old Cecil . . . ," said Mrs. Riley jauntily. But here the door opened and with an effect both tactful and inescapable Sebby Stokes came in.

"Dear Mrs. Sawle . . . ," he said, smiling and cushioning his formality.

"Oh, well!" Freda said, with a humorous tremor, reaching for her handbag.

Daphne watched her mother cross the room, saw her distinctly, her comic note of bravery, knowing she was watched, flustered but making a go of it, an amenable guest in her daughter's house. There was a little stoop of humility as she passed through the door, into the larger but darker library beyond, a hint of frailty, an affectation of bearing more than her fifty-nine years, a slight bewildered totter among the grandeur that her daughter now had to pretend to take for granted. Daphne saw what was sturdy and capable and truthful in the mother she'd always known, the bigger woman, morally big, that no one else but George perhaps could see; and at the same time she saw exactly how shaken and vulnerable she was. She was a grieving mother herself, though in the hierarchy of mourning here her grief was largely overlooked. Sebby glanced back with an abstracted nod as he pulled the door to. The dry click of the lock seemed oddly momentous.

Mrs. Riley got up from the desk and came over towards her. She had a sort of sloping and swooping walk, with a nerviness that was plastered over in her drawling talk. She crossed the hearthrug and flicked her ash into the fire. "This whole thing's getting rather like one of Agatha Christie's," she said, "with our Sebastian as clever Monsieur Poirot."

"I know . . . ," said Daphne, getting up too, and moving towards the window.

"I wonder who did it. I don't think I did . . ."

"I suppose you'd remember?" said Daphne, resisting the game. Outside, on the far side of the lawn, Revel was sitting on a stone bench drawing the house.

"D'you think he'll have us all in together at the end for the solution?"

"Somehow I doubt it," said Daphne. There was something so charming in his posture, his look, the look he had of being himself a figure in a picture, that she couldn't help smiling, and then sighing. He'd done it, *seized the day*—he was outside in the late April sunshine, while Daphne was in here like a child held back for some futile punishment. She looked down at her desk, where the letter lay on the blotter, but with Mrs. Riley's lacquered cigarette-case hiding the address.

"I see your friend Revel's making a drawing," said Mrs. Riley.

"I know, I feel very lucky," said Daphne, turning away from the window.

"Mm, he's clearly got something," said Mrs. Riley. She smiled abstractedly. "Quite a feminine touch—more feminine, probably, than me!"

"Oh . . . well . . ."

"He's still terribly young, of course."

"That's true . . ."

"How old is he?"

"I believe he's twenty-four," said Daphne, slightly confused, and went on quickly, "I'm so pleased he's drawing the house. He's always had a great deal of feeling for Corley Court."

"You mean, you want him to capture it before I pull it down!" said Mrs. Riley, acknowledging her sense of rivalry with a laugh and a hint of a blush—a peculiar effect under so much pale powder. "Well, you needn't worry."

"Oh, I'm not worried," said Daphne, with a tight little smile, but feeling rattled. Mrs. Riley gazed out rather drolly at Revel, so that Daphne hoped he wouldn't look this way and see her.

"How did you get to know him?"

This was easy. "He drew the jacket for *The Long Gallery.*"

"Oh, your husband's book, you mean?" said Mrs. Riley unguardedly.

"You remember, the pretty drawing of the old Gothic window . . ."

Mrs. Riley threw her cigarette away, and became very simple. "To tell the truth, I feel rather foolish," she said.

"Oh . . ."

"I mean, not having known Cecil."

"It's hardly foolish not to have known Cecil," said Daphne, with dry indulgence. So much of her own foolishness, she thought, stemmed from the fact that she had.

"Well . . . ," said Mrs. Riley, and she made a little grimace of reluctance, and went on, "Are you absolutely sure you wouldn't rather I pushed off?"

"Oh . . . *Eva* . . . ," said Daphne, with a gasp, "no, no," frowning and colouring uncomfortably in turn. "How could you?"

"Are you sure? I feel like some ghastly 'gate-crasher,' as they say." Daphne had an image of Mrs. Riley's smart little car smashing into the wrought-iron gates of Corley Court. "I'm not at all poetical. I'm not literary, like you are."

"Well . . ."

"No, you are. You're always reading, I've seen you. Well, you're married to a writer, for heaven's sake! I only ever read thrillers. I was frankly surprised"—and she crossed the room again for her cigarette case—"you know, when your husband asked me to stay."

"Well . . . ," said Daphne awkwardly, "I dare say he wanted some light relief from all this talk about his brother."

"Oh, perhaps, I wonder . . . ," said Eva, not immediately adjusting herself to this role.

"I mean we can't talk about Cecil every minute of the day—we'd go mad! Do you think I might have one of your cigarettes?"

"Oh, my dear, I didn't know," said Eva, coming back, offering the case languidly, but with a sharp glance.

"Thank you." Daphne was urging her blush to subside, with its clear disclosure of her mutinous feelings, and the proof it gave Mrs. Riley of her own clever tactics. She struck a match, away from her, awkwardly, and held it out to Eva, hiding her nerves by moving it around absentmindedly, so that Eva stooped and laughed. When they were both puffing, Eva looked at her frankly, with a hint of amusement as she angled her smoke sideways. She said,

"Well, I'm glad you think it's all right." And then, "Tell me truly, don't you ever find it just a teeny bit depressing having Cecil lying around next door—don't you sometimes just want to forget about all that, really? I have to say I'm thoroughly sick of the War, and I think a lot of people feel the same."

"Oh, I like having him there," said Daphne, not quite truthfully, but seeing with a little run of the pulse another channel for her larger resentment of Eva to push into. "You see, I lost a brother too, though no one ever remembers that."

"Darling, I'd no idea."

"No, well, how could you have," said Daphne grudgingly.

"You mean in the War . . ."

"Yes, a bit later than Cecil. There weren't any articles about it in *The Times*."

"Won't you tell me about him?"

"Well, he was a dear," said Daphne. She pictured her mother, beyond the heavy oak doors of the library, and keeping the whole matter to herself.

Eva sat down, as if to pay more solemn attention, and threw back the loose cushion to make a space beside her, but Daphne preferred to remain on her feet. "What was he called?"

"Oh . . . Hubert. Hubert Sawle. He was my elder brother." She felt the odd prickly decorum of telling Eva but very little of the solemn heartache which she hoped none the less to convey. When she went to the window, it seemed that Revel had gone; her spirits sank for a moment, but then she saw him again, talking to George—their heads and shoulders could be seen as they moved slowly away among the hedges. Now George stopped him and they laughed together. A twinge of jealous irritation went through her. "No, Hubert was very much our mainstay, as my father had died young."

"He wasn't married, then?"

"No, he wasn't . . . He did get very close to a girl, from Hampshire . . ."

"Oh . . . ?"

Daphne turned back into the room. "Anyway, nothing happened."

"A lot of brave girls were left high and dry by the War," said Eva, in a strange defiant tone. Then, with a little gasp, "I hope I didn't upset your mother by what I said earlier about, you know, getting in touch with Cecil—I mean actually I do think it's ridiculous, but of course I didn't know about your brother."

"I think she did go to a séance once, but it didn't work for her."

"No, well . . ."

Daphne found she didn't want to talk about Louisa's spiritualist obsession, which she and Dudley both deplored, to anyone outside the family; a feeling of loyalty was sharpened by her indignation at Eva's mockery, which at the same time she perfectly understood. Then the bracket clock struck three-thirty, banishing all thought. "What a brute that thing is!" said Eva, with a tight shake of the head, as though to say even Daphne surely wouldn't regret getting rid of it. Then she was saying, "No, your husband read me that bit in his new book, you know, about the famous book tests—awfully funny, isn't it, actually, the way he does it—that's what put it in my mind."

"Oh, *really* . . . ," said Daphne, dawdlingly, though she knew her whole face was stiffening by the second, ungovernable, with hurt and indignation. "Will you excuse me for a moment," and she turned and went out quickly into the hall, where the grandfather clock was now mellowly stating the time, and the clock in the drawing-room beyond, with no sense of the mortifying scrumple of her feelings as she hurried to the front door and out into the porch. She stood looking across the gravel, at the various trees, and up the long slope of the entrance drive, to the inner set of gates, with the whole blue Berkshire afternoon lying hidden beyond them. She puffed at the last half-inch of the cigarette with a certain revulsion, and then trod it under her heel on the doorstep. She wasn't going to mention it to Dudley, and she certainly wasn't going to tell Eva Riley herself that no one had ever seen a word of "his new book," much less had awfully amusing bits of it read to them. Some occasion in his "office," no doubt, over the plans. The awful undermining evidence that all her own scruples of loyalty to Louisa, to the family, weren't actually shared by the head of the family himself. She felt foolish, in her simple high-mindedness, and furious much more than hurt. She touched her hair and her neck as though in front of a mirror and then she did what one always did at Corley, and went back in.

Eva looked glad to see her. She went on, "You know, I feel very fortunate to have met your husband"—modest but also subtly possessive.

"It's silly of me," said Daphne, "I don't quite know how you did." She knew what Dudley had said, of course.

"Well, I fitted up Bobby Bannister's place in Surrey, didn't I, and he must have told . . . your husband about me. I rather think he gave him the whole idea for improving Corley."

This was exactly Dudley's version too, though the cool nerve of "improving" made Daphne laugh. She said, "It's become a bit of a thing with Dud—I think he's doing it mainly to upset his mother."

"Oh, I do hope it's rather more than that," said Eva. "I must say I love working here"—and she gave Daphne a look of rather unnerving sweetness.

"Well . . ." Daphne went back towards the window to see where Revel and George had got to, but there was now no sign of them. Then there was the click of the library door, and Daphne turned, expecting her mother to be shown back in, amid reassuring murmurs and thanks—but it was Sebby alone, head cocked, with an apologetic half-smile. It seemed Freda had been shown out the other way, into the hall: this was oddly confounding for a second or two, as though she had vanished in some more permanent sense. "She seemed anxious about her friend," Sebby said.

"Ah yes, I fear she's not at all well." Daphne gave a bland nod to Eva and went in, and when he closed the door behind her, the click confirmed her earlier sense of the process: you watched for a bit, and then you were part of it. A slight awkwardness, at being a guest in her own house, coloured the first moments for both of them, but they smiled through it. "I feel rather like a doctor," said Sebby.

"Mrs. Riley thought a detective," said Daphne.

Sebby was hesitant but sure. "Really I hope no more than a well-meaning friend," he said, and waited for Daphne to sit down. On the big table he had laid out the publications in which Cecil's verses had appeared—a small pile of periodicals, the anthologies, *Georgian Poetry,* the *Cambridge Poets,* and the one book he'd published in his lifetime, *Night Wake and Other Poems,* in its soft grey paper covers easily dog-eared and torn. Another pile seemed to contain things in manuscript—there was her autograph book, given up this morning. Daphne was impressed, and again unsettled by the evidence of a clear procedure. She saw that she hadn't prepared. This was because she hadn't been able to, her mind wouldn't fix on any of the things she knew she might say; she had had an unaccountable confidence that inspiration would come to her as soon as Sebby's questions began. Now she regretted the past ten minutes spent sparring with Eva, when she could have been putting her thoughts in order.

"Forgive me for one moment," Sebby said, turning to the table and starting to search through the pile of handwritten things. Daphne glimpsed her own letters from Cecil, which she had also dutifully sur-rendered—again she didn't want to think about them. She looked at his stooped back and then at the long dim room beyond him. Though she was, as Eva had said, a reader, she had never exactly taken to the library—like Dudley's study, which she never entered, it was a part of the house outside her sway. Sometimes she came in to look for a book, a novel from the great leather sets of Trollope or Dickens, or an old bound volume of *Punch* for Wilfie to work out the cartoons, but she couldn't quite shake off the feeling of being a visitor, as if in a public library, with rules and fines. As the scene of her mother-in-law's now "famous" book tests, too, it had an unhappy air. Of these Sebby probably knew nothing, but to her the room was tainted by earlier attempts to contact Cecil—all nonsense, of course, as she and Eva agreed, but like much nonsense not entirely easy to dismiss.

Sebby sat down, on the same side of the table as she was, and again with an evident awareness of the niceties, she half his age, but a titled lady, he far more clever, a distinguished guest who'd been asked to per-form a peculiar service for his hosts. "I hope this isn't distressing for you," he said.

"Oh, not at all," said Daphne graciously, her smile expressing a mild amazement at the thought that perhaps it should be. She saw Sebby's own undecided glance. He said,

"Dear Cecil aroused keen feelings in many of those who crossed his path."

"Indeed he did . . ."

"And you would seem, from the letters you've so generously shared with me, to have had a similar effect on him."

"I know, isn't it awful," said Daphne.

"Hah . . ." Sebby again unsure of her. He turned to pick up a clutch of the letters. She hadn't been able to read them again herself, out of a strong compound embarrassment at everything they said about both of them. "There are beautiful passages—I sat up late with them last night, in my room." He smiled mildly as he turned over the small folded pages, re-creating his own pleasure. Daphne saw him propped up in the very grand bed in the Garnet Room and handling these papers with a mixture of eagerness and regret. He was used to dealing with confidential matters, though not as a rule perhaps the amorous declarations of excitable young men. He hesitated, looked up at her, and started reading, with an affectionate expression: " 'The moon tonight, dear child, I suppose shines as bright on Stanmore as it does on Mme Collet's vegetable garden and on the very long nose of the adjutant, who is snoring enough to wake the Hun on the far side of the room. Are you too snoring—do you snore, child?—or do you lie awake and think of your poor dirty Cecil far away? He is much in need of his Daphne's kind words and . . .' "—Sebby petered out discreetly at the slither into intimacy. "Delightful, isn't it?"

"Oh . . . yes . . . I don't remember," said Daphne, half-turning her head to see. "The ones from France are a bit better, aren't they?"

"I found them most touching," said Sebby. "I have letters of my own from him, two or three . . . but these strike quite another tone."

"He had something to write about," said Daphne.

"He had a great deal to write about," said Sebby, with a quick smile of courteous reproof. He looked through a few more letters, while Daphne wondered if she could possibly explain her feelings, even had she wanted to; she felt she would have to understand them first, and this unnatural little chat was hardly going to help her to do that. What she felt then; and what she felt now; and what she felt now about what she felt then: it wasn't remotely easy to say. Sebby was every inch the bachelor—his intuitions about a young girl's first love and about Cecil himself as a lover were unlikely to be worth much. Cecil's way of being in love with her was alternately to berate her and to berate himself: there wasn't much fun in it, for all his famed high spirits. Yet he always seemed happy when away from her (which was most of the time) and she had sensed more and more how much he enjoyed the absences he was always deploring.

The War when it came was an absolute godsend. Sebby said, "Tell me if I am being too inquisitive, but I feel it will help me to a clearer vision of what might have been. Here's the letter, what is it, June 1916, 'Tell me, Daphne, will you be my widow?' "

"Oh, yes . . ." She coloured slightly.

"Do you remember how you replied to that?"

"Oh, I said of course."

"And you considered yourselves . . . engaged?"

Daphne smiled and looked down at the deep red carpet almost puzzled for a moment that she had ended up here anyway. What was the status of a long-lost expectation? She couldn't now recapture any picture she might then have had of a future life with Cecil. "As far as I remember we both agreed to keep it a secret. I wasn't altogether Louisa's idea of the next Lady Valance."

Sebby smiled back rather furtively at this little irony. "Your letters to Cecil haven't survived."

"I do hope not!"

"I have the impression Cecil never kept letters, which is really rather trying of him."

"He saw you coming, Sebby!" said Daphne, and laughed to cover the surprise of her own tone. He wasn't used to teasing, but she wasn't sure he minded it.

"Indeed!" Sebby rose, and looked for a book on the table. "Well, I don't want to keep you too long."

"Oh . . . ! Well, you haven't." Perhaps she had rattled him after all, he thought she was simply being flippant.

"What I hope you might do," said Sebby, "is to write down for me a few paragraphs, simply evoking dear Cecil, and furnishing perhaps an anecdote or two. A little memorandum."

"A memorandum, yes."

"And then if I may quote from the letters . . ."—she had a first glimpse of his impatience—the impersonal logic of even the most flattering diplomatist. Of course one had to remember that he was burdened with far more pressing things.

"I suppose that would be all right."

"I expect to call you simply Miss S., unless you object"—which Daphne found after a mere moment's fury she didn't. "And now I might ask you just to run through 'Two Acres' with me, for any little insights you might give me—local details and so on. I didn't like to press your mother."

"Oh, by all means," said Daphne, with a muddled feeling of relief and disappointment that Sebby had failed to press her too—but that was it, of course, she saw it now, and it was good not to have wasted time on it: he was going to say nothing in this memoir of his, Louisa was in effect his editor, and this weekend of "research," for all its sadness and piquancy and interesting embarrassments, was a mere charade. He picked up the autograph album, the mauve silk now rucked and stained by hundreds of grubby thumbs, and leafed delicately through. There was something else in it for him, no doubt—a busy man wouldn't make this effort without some true personal reason. Sebby too had been awfully fond of Cecil. She gazed up at the carved end of the nearest bookcase, and the stained-glass window beyond it, in a mood of sudden abstraction. The April brilliance that threatened the fire in the morning-room here threw sloping drops and shards of colour across the wall and across the white marble fireplace. They painted the blind marble busts of Homer and Milton pink, turquoise and buttercup. The colours seemed to warm and caress them as they slid and stretched. She pictured Cecil as he had been on his last leave; she had a feeling that when she met him that hot summer night he had just come from dinner with Sebby. Well, he was never going to know about that. For now, she had to come up with something more appropriate; something that she felt wearily had already been written, and that she had merely to find and repeat.

7

FREDA CROSSED THE HALL and started up the great staircase, stopping for a moment on each frighteningly polished tread, reaching up for the banister, which was too wide and Elizabethan in style to hold on to properly, more like the coping of a wall than a handrail. It must be nice for Daphne to have a coat of arms, she supposed—there it was, at each turn, in the paws of a rampant beast with a lantern on its head. She too had dreamt of that for her daughter, in the beginning, before she knew what she knew. Corley Court was a forbidding place—even in the sanctuary of her room the dark panelling and the Gothic fireplace induced a feeling of entrapment, a fear that something impossible was about to be asked of her. She closed the door, crossed the threadbare expanse of crimson carpet, and sat down at the dressing-table, close to tears with her confused relieved unhappy sense of not having said to Sebastian Stokes any of the things she could have said, and had known, in her heart, that she wouldn't.

The one letter she'd shown him, her widow's mite, she'd called it, was mere twaddle, a "Collins." She saw his courteous but very quick eye running over it, his turning the page as if there still might be something of interest on the other side, but of course there was not. He'd sat there, like the family doctor, he'd said, though to her he was a figure of daunting importance, toughness and suppleness, someone who spoke every day with Sir Herbert Samuel and Mr. Baldwin. He was charming but his charm was the charm of diplomacy, charm designed not only to please but to save time and get things done; it was hardly the unconscious charm of a trusted friend. She had felt very foolish, and the pressure of what she was not going to say drove even the simplest conversation out of her mind. She did say that Cecil had made a terrible mess in his room, and it had sounded petty of her, to say such a thing of a poet and a hero who had won the Military Cross. She alluded, in addition, to his "liveliness" and the various things he had broken—widow's mites, again, pathetic grievances. What she couldn't begin to say was the mess Cecil Valance had made of her children.

She waited a minute and then got up her handbag and opened it—inside was a bulging manila envelope torn and folded around a bundle of other letters . . . She couldn't really bear to look at them again. She ought simply to have destroyed them, when she'd found them, during the War. But something had kept her back—there was a great bonfire going, all the autumn leaves, she went out and opened it with a fork, a red and grey winking and smouldering core to it, she could have dropped the commonplace-looking packet in without a soul knowing or caring. That was what she told George she had done; but in fact she couldn't do it. Was it reverence, or mere superstition? They were letters written by a gentleman—that surely in itself meant little or nothing; and by a poet, which gave them a better right to immortality, but which needn't have swayed her. Disgusted by her own unresolved confusion, she tugged out the bundle on to the dressing-table and stared at it. Cecil Valance's impatient handwriting had a strange effect on her, even now; for a year and more it had come dashing and tumbling into her house, letters to George, then letters to Daphne, and the bloody, bloody poem, which she wished had never been written. The letters to Daphne were splendid enough to turn a young girl's head, though Freda hadn't liked their tone, and she could see that Daphne had been frightened by them as much as she was thrilled. Of course she was out of her depth with a man six years older, but then he was out of his depth too: they were horrible posturing letters in which he seemed to be blaming the poor child for something or other that was really his own failing. And yet Freda had not discouraged him—it seemed to her now she'd been out of her depth as well. And perhaps, who knew, it would all have turned out all right.

It was the letters to George, hidden at once, destroyed for all the rest of the family knew, mentioned only breezily—"Cess sends his love!": they had turned out to be the unimagined and yet vaguely dreaded thing. There they had lain, in his room, all the time that George was away in the army—"intelligence," planning, other matters she couldn't be told about. Those endless summer evenings at "Two Acres," just her and Daphne—she would drift through the boys' rooms, take down their old school-books, fold and brush their unused clothes, tidy the drawers of the little bureau beside George's bed, all the childish clutter, the batched-up postcards, the letters . . . Without even touching them now, her mind saw certain phrases, saw them twisting dense and snakelike in the heart of the bundle. Well, she wouldn't read them ever again, there was no need to put herself through that. Letters from King's College, Cambridge, from Hamburg, Lübeck, old Germany before the War, Milan; letters of course from this very house. She edged them back into the brown envelope, which tore open a little more and was now next to useless. Then she tidied her hair, made her face look no less worried with a few more dabs of powder, and set off once again down the long landing to Clara's room.

Clara had had her fire made up, and sat beside it, dressed as if ready to be taken somewhere, but without her shoes on: her brown-stockinged legs, which gave her such pain, were propped on a bulging pile of cushions.

"Have you had your chat?" she said.

"Yes. It was nothing much."

"Mm, you were very quick," said Clara, in that half-admiring, half-critical tone that Freda had grown so used to.

She said, "One doesn't want to waste his time," in her own murmur of suppressed impatience. "Have they been looking after you?" She bustled round the room as though doing so herself, then went restlessly to the window. "Would you like to go outside? I've made enquiries and they've still got Sir Edwin's old bath-chair, if you want it. They can get it out for you."

"Oh, no, Freda, thank you very much."

"I'm sure that handsome Scotch boy would be happy to give you a push."

"No, no, my dear, really!"

If she wouldn't be pushed, in any sense, there was little to be done. Freda knew they both wanted to go home, though Clara obviously couldn't say so, and from Freda it would have been a pitiful admission. She missed her daughter, and loved her grandchildren, but visits to Corley were generally unhappy affairs. Even the cocktail hour lost something of its normal promise when cocktails themselves had such alarming effects on their host.

"Shall we hear Corinna play the piano," Clara said, "before we go?"

"This evening, I think—Dudley's promised them."

"Oh, in that case," said Clara.

This bedroom, at the end of the house, looked out over an expanse of lawn towards the high red wall of the kitchen garden, beyond which the ridges of greenhouses gleamed in the sun. Not normally a walker, Freda dimly planned a little solitary "trudge" or "totter," to calm her feelings— though she knew she might well be snared by some chivalrous fellow-guest. She was frightened of Mrs. Riley, and undecided on the charm of young Mr. Revel Ralph. "I might go out for a bit, dear," she said over her shoulder. Clara made a sort of preoccupied grunt, as if too busy getting herself comfortable to take in what her friend was saying. "Apparently there's a magnolia that has to be seen to be believed." Now, from the direction of the formal garden, two brown-clad figures came slowly walking, George with his hands behind his back, and Madeleine with hers in the pockets of her mackintosh. Their hands seemed somehow locked away from any mutual use they might have been put to, and although the two of them were busily in conversation, George throwing back his head to lend weight to his pronouncements, they looked much more like colleagues than like a couple.

Standing at the window, Freda saw herself already crossing the grass, and saw for a reckless and inspired moment that having the letters with her she should give them back to George; perhaps that would prove to be the real achievement of this arduous visit. It would be a kind of exorcism, a demon cast out of her at last. Her heart was skipping from the double impact of the thought and the opportunity—almost too pressing, with too little space for reflection and stepping back. And then it was as if she saw the letters hurled furiously in the air, falling and blowing across the lawn between them, trapped underfoot by a suddenly game Louisa, fetched out from beneath the bushes by an agile Sebby Stokes. She remembered what she had always felt, that they couldn't be let out— though the feeling now was subtly altered by the momentary vision of release. They were George's letters, and he should have them, but to give them to him after all this time would be to show him that something was live that he had surely thought dead ten years ago.

"Well, I'll get out for a bit, dear," she said again. Now George and Madeleine had gone. Probably she could tell all this to Clara, who out of her difficult existence had garnered a good deal of wisdom; but in a way it was her wisdom that she feared—it might make her look, by contrast, a fool. No one else could possibly be told, since no one keeps other people's secrets, and Daphne in particular must never know of it. Now young Mr. Ralph had come strolling into view, in conversation with the Scotch boy himself, who seemed to be leading him towards the walled garden. He had his sketchbook with him, and Freda was struck by the relaxed and friendly way they went along together; of course they were both very young, and Revel Ralph no doubt was anything but stuffy. They disappeared through the door in the wall. The sense that everyone else was doing something filled her with agitation.

Back in her room she put on a hat, and made sure that the letters were safely stowed. It was absurd, but they had become her guilty secret, as they had once been George's. She went down one of the back staircases, which she probably wasn't supposed to, but she felt she would rather run into a housemaid than a fellow-guest. It led to something called the Gentlemen's Lobby, with the smoking-room beyond, and a small door out on to the back drive. She skirted the end of the house, and then the end of the formal garden, which she'd had enough of. She had an idea of getting into the woods for half an hour, before tea. In a minute or two she was under the shade of the trees, big chestnuts already coming into flower, and the limes putting out small brilliant green shoots. She pushed back her hat and looked upward, giddy at the diamonds of sky among the leaves. Then she walked on, still unusually fast, and after a short while, stepping over twigs and beech mast, rather out of breath.

She started to think she shouldn't go too far, and ducked her way out under the edge of the wood into the grassland of the Park. A long white fence divided the Park from the High Ground, and she drifted along by it for a moment or two in one of those intense unobserved dilemmas as to whether she should try to climb over it; that she was unobserved had first, very casually, to be checked. There were two slender iron rails, the upper at hip height, and a flat-topped post every six feet or so, to hold on to. She rehearsed the lifting of her skirt, with another look round, then quickly steadied her walking shoe on the lower rail, while gripping the upper one, but in the same second she knew that of course she couldn't get over it, and she went on to the distant gate, in a flustered pretence of being in no particular hurry.

The High Ground had just been mown, and as soon as Freda had shut the gate behind her, she found the cuttings, still green and damp, were clinging to her shoes. And there they were again, George and Mad, crossing the far end of the enormous lawn, which must have been a good two acres in itself. She felt she had been ambushed by the very thing that she was hoping to avoid; but also perhaps that it was futile to try to avoid it. They kept to themselves, always talking, always walking; Freda sensed no one cared for them much, and George had always been somewhat shy and stiff—until (there it was again) Cecil had come on the scene. She had tried not to watch him at lunch, knowing what she knew: this weekend must be distinctly uncomfortable for him; she was surprised in a way that he'd come. Though if he had, in whatever fashion, loved Cecil . . . Now she saw the gleam on his glasses, his bald brow quite distinctive; they spotted her and said something to each other—then George waved. She hurried on for a moment, but no—she saw them so rarely . . . she stopped and picked up a black feather, its tip sheared off by the mower, then she turned and strolled slowly towards them, with a frown and smile, and awkward side-glances, and the air of nurturing an amusing remark.

The fact was that this whole business with the letters was kept alive by her own sense of guilt—dormant, forgettable, easily slept with for much of the time, but at moments like this crinkling everything she said to him into bright insincerity. She should never have read them; but once she'd found them, taken one from its envelope with a shifty but tender curiosity, and then read its astounding first page, she found she couldn't stop. She wondered now at her own grim curiosity, her need to know the worst when surely she would rather have known nothing. She glanced at George, beaming mildly, fifty yards away, and saw him on the morning she'd confronted him, George in uniform, grieving for his brother, fighting a war. Her own grief must have triggered it, licensed it. And he hadn't known what to do, any more than she had: he was angry with her as he had never been, they were private letters, she had no right, and at the same time he was haggard with shame and horror at his mother's knowing what had gone on. "It was all over," he said—which was obvious, since Cecil was dead—"it had all been over long ago." And then before the war was out he had proposed to this dreary bluestocking, so that she felt, at her most candid and unhappy moments, that she had condemned him herself to a life of high-minded misery. "Hello! Hello!" said George.

Freda raised her chin and grinned at them.

"Enjoying your walk, Mother?" said Madeleine.

"It's been rather lovely"—she looked up at them with the raffish twinkle of a parent dwarfed by her children.

"I didn't know you liked walking," said Madeleine, suspiciously.

Freda said, "There's a lot you don't know, my dear," and then looked at her own words with a touch of surprise.

"You've had your little chat with Sebby," said George.

"Yes, yes"—she dismissed it.

"All right?"

"Well, I really had nothing to say."

George gave a little purse-lipped smile, and gazed around at the woods. "No, I suppose not." And then, "Are you going back to the house?"

"I'm very much ready for a cup of tea."

"We'll come with you."

As they walked they looked at the house, and it seemed to Freda they were each thinking of something they might say about it. Their self-consciousness focused on it, with an air of latent amusement and concern, but for at least a minute none of them spoke. Freda glanced up at George and wondered if the incident that was gnawing at her self-possession was equally present to him. In the nine years since, it had never once been mentioned; bland evasiveness had slowly assumed the appearance of natural forgetfulness.

"Oh, have you looked at the tomb?" said Madeleine, as they went through the white gate and into the garden.

"Well, I've seen it before," said Freda. She disliked the tomb very much—for strong but again not quite explicable reasons.

"Quite splendid, isn't it."

"Yes, it is!"

"I was thinking about poor old Huey," said George, in this at least chasing her own thoughts.

"Oh, I know . . ."

"We must go, darling," said George, taking his mother's arm with what felt to her like extravagant forgiveness.

"To France . . . ?"

"We'll go this summer, during the long vac."

"Well, I'd love that," said Freda, gripping George to her, then glancing almost shyly at Madeleine. It seemed to her a mystery, another of the great evasions whose nothingness filled her life, that they hadn't been already.

She left them in the hall, and went up to her room, freshly, nearly tearfully, preoccupied with Hubert. Really, his death should have put all these other worries in proportion. The heavy ache of loss was quickened by a touch of indignation. She felt that at some point she must finally and formally talk to Louisa about Hubert, and ask her to acknowledge that the worst possible thing had happened to her as well. That Huey wasn't clever or beautiful, had never met Lytton Strachey or written a sonnet or climbed anything higher than an apple-tree—all this she was somehow forced to acknowledge at each tentative mention of his name to Cecil's mother. She took off her hat, sat down, and attended rather violently to her hair.

She knew it was pointless, heartless, to begrudge Louisa the consolation of having been with Cecil at the end, the aristocratic reach across the Channel that had brought him back, when tens of thousands of others were fated to stay there till doomsday. Daphne said it was the reason the old lady resisted moving out of the big house: she wanted to stay where she could visit her son every day. Freda was picturing Huey, back at "Two Acres," on his last leave—and now the tears welled up and she dropped the comb and fiddled in her sleeve for her handkerchief. In the letters that were sent to her after his death, they had spoken of the wood where he had fallen, trying to take a machine-gun post that was concealed in it: Ivry Wood. Over and over in those weeks she had looked out across her own modest landscape, her own little birch-wood, with a rending sense that Huey would never set foot there again. Almost impossible to grasp, on that first day, that he'd been buried already in France—under shell-fire, they said, with a reading from Revelations. Already he'd been put away for ever, out of the air. And whenever she thought of it, and pictured Ivry Wood, it was her own little spinney she saw, for want of anything better, strangely translated to northern France, and Huey running into it, into the desultory spray of the guns.

Later he had been reburied, and she had photographs of the grave, and of the interment itself. A padre in a white surplice, under an umbrella, men firing a salute. Well, now at last George would take her, and Daphne too perhaps, over to France, they would all go, and she would look at it. She had only been abroad once, before the War, when she and Clara made their pilgrimage to Bayreuth, two widows on the smutty ferry, the stifling trains with German soldiers singing in the next carriage. The thought of this new visit, of the resolute approach to the place, squeezed at her throat.

8

WHEN DAPHNE was getting dressed that evening Dudley strolled in to her room and said, almost in a yawn, that he hoped Mark Gibbons wouldn't take against Revel. "Oh," said Daphne, faintly puzzled but more concerned about dinner, and the horrors of the seating-plan, where she felt her skills as a hostess most exposed. "It seems to me Revel gets on with everyone." She slithered her pearl-coloured petticoat over her head, and smoothed it down with her palms, pleased to hear his name at such a moment. She would have him sit near, though not next to her. Naturally her mother must sit on Dudley's right, but if Clara was tucked away safely in the middle was it better to have Eva or Madeleine on his left? Daphne thought she might well inflict Madeleine on him. "Anyway," she said, "there's no urgent reason they should meet, is there?" And then it came out that Dudley had asked Mark to dinner, and Flora, and also the Strange-Pagets—on the grounds that "we haven't seen them for ages."

"Christ, you might have told me!" said Daphne, feeling her colour flare up. "And the bloody S-Ps, of all people . . ." She caught herself in the mirror, helpless in her underwear, her stockinged feet, her panic slightly comic to Dudley in the glinting freedom of the background. First and foremost she thought of the langoustines, already stretched by Revel's arrival.

"Oh, Duffel . . . ," said Dudley, frowning a little at the jet studs in his shirt-front. "Mark's a marvellous painter."

"Mark may be a bloody genius," said Daphne, hurrying with her dress, "but he still has to eat."

Dudley turned to her with that unstable mixture of indulgence and polite bewilderment and mocking distaste that she had come to know and dread and furiously resent. "Well Flora's a vegetarian, Duffel, remember," he said: "just throw her some nuts and an orange and she'll be as happy as a pig in shit." And he gave her his widest smile, his moist sharp dog-teeth making their old deplorable appeal, but horrible now as his trench language. Daphne thought she had better go down herself and see the cook. It would be one of those ghastly announcements that was all too clearly a plea.

Mark Gibbons, who had painted the large abstract "prison" in the drawing-room, lived on a farm near Wantage with his half-Danish girl-friend Flora. Daphne liked him a good deal without ceasing to be frightened of him. He and Dudley had met in the army, a strangely intimate locking of opposites, it seemed to Daphne, Mark being a socialist and the son of a shopkeeper. He showed no interest in actually marrying Flora, and very little in dressing for dinner, which was the more immediate worry, with Louisa coming in, and Colonel Fountain, who'd been Cecil's superior officer, driving over from Aldershot. Rattling down the back-stairs two at a time, Daphne saw her seating-plan collapse in a jumble of incompatibilities, her husband and mother-in-law like repelling magnets. The Strange-Pagets at least were easier, a dull rather older couple with a lot of money and a country house of their own on the other side of Pusey. Dudley had known Stinker Strange-Paget since boyhood, and was defiantly loyal to him, treating his dim parochial gossip like the wisdom of some gnomic sage.

SEBBY STOKES CAME DOWN FIRST, and Daphne, who'd popped in to the drawing-room for a gin and lemon, was caught for several minutes in distracted conversation with him, a certain warm relief none the less creeping in from the drink. Their earlier chat in the library was a coloured shadow, an attempted intimacy that would never be repeated. She perched on a window-seat, glancing out on to the gravel, where any moment cars would appear. She had done what she could, she must relax. Sebby seemed still to be talking about Cecil, whom she'd forgotten for a moment was the pretext for this whole party. Wasn't this what would happen to all of them, remembrance forgotten in the chaos of other preoccupations? "I've been reading all the letters your mother-in-law received from Cecil's men."

"Aren't they splendid!" said Daphne.

"By George, they loved him," said Sebby, in what she felt was an odd tone. She looked at him, standing stiffly with his glass and his cigarette, such a sleek and perfect embodiment of how to behave, and again she saw what she had glimpsed that afternoon, that *he* had loved him, and would do anything for his good name. She said, mildly but mischievously,

"We had splendid letters about my brother too. Though I suppose they're always likely to be splendid, aren't they. No one ever wrote and said, 'Captain Valance was a beast.' "

"No, indeed . . . ," said Sebby, with a twitch of a smile.

"What are you going to call the book, just *Poems,* I suppose?"

"Or *Collected Poems,* I think. Louisa favours *The Poetical Works of,* which your husband feels is too Mrs. Hemans."

"For once I think he's right," said Daphne. And then there was a warning drone like a plane in the distance and in a moment a brown baker's van, which was Mark and Flo's form of conveyance, came roaring and throbbing down the drive.

"He finds it so useful for his paintings!" Daphne found herself explaining, shouting gaily, and feeling she really wasn't ready for this evening at all. When Mark clambered out from the cab in a full and proper dinner-suit, she felt so relieved that she kissed both George and Madeleine, who had just come in, and were not expecting it. Behind them in the hall was her mother, and then Revel looking at the fireplace while Eva Riley stuck her head out of one of the turret windows. "Absurd!" she was saying. "Too sickening!" Well, it was quite a party, it had been set in motion, and Daphne was gamely pretending to drive it—it was understandable surely if she felt slightly sick herself as it gathered speed. Her mother said quietly that Clara was very tired, and had asked for supper in her room—Daphne felt it was bound to happen, yet a further change to the seating-plan, but she merely told Wilkes, and asked him to sort it out. Then she went and got another gin.

It turned out that Mark knew Eva Riley already, which was a good thing and also vaguely irritating. He called her "old girl" or "Eva Brick" in his cheerful, slightly menacing way. This pre-existing friendship was put on display, and even exaggerated, in front of the other guests. They had a number of acquaintances in common, none of them known personally to anyone else, and Mark kept up conversation about these fascinating absent people with a certain determination, as if aping some polite convention: "What's old Romilly up to?" he asked, and then, "How did you find Stella?"

"Oh, she was on killing form," said Eva, with her secretive smile, perhaps even a little embarrassed. Mark's painting, hanging so prominently in the room, seemed to encourage him, and somehow represent him, as a challenge, a wild figure several moves ahead of them all.

As on the previous day Dudley had a look of risky high spirits, having wrestled his own party out of the one his wife and his mother had so carefully planned. Even Colonel Fountain's arrival was an occasion for mischief. "Colonel, you know the General," said Dudley when he was shown in, which rather threw the old boy for the first minute or two. Daphne had pictured Colonel Fountain as an ebullient figure who liked a drink, but in fact he was a quiet, ascetic-looking man, who'd been deafened in one ear in France, and had trouble with casual conversation. He attached himself courteously to Louisa, and stuck to her, like some old uncle at a children's party, a rout of names he couldn't be sure he'd caught.

Last of all, the Strange-Pagets were delivered by their chauffeur and shown in to the noisy drawing-room, Dudley hailed them histrionically, the party was complete, and just at that moment the door opened again, and there was Nanny with the children, down for their half-hour. This was less than ideal. Daphne saw Nanny looking at Dudley, and Dudley's stare back, the expressionless mask behind which outrage is forming and focusing. There seemed something faintly mutinous mixed in with Nanny's normal servility. It was an evening the children might better have been kept upstairs—but by the same token an evening when they specially wanted to come down. Nanny raised her hands and released them into the crowd, and Daphne swooped over to them with a rare rather shameful desire to tidy them away. In these ultra-modern drawing-rooms there was nowhere to hide. They ran in among the legs of the others, looking for affection, or at least attention. Granny Sawle of course was reliable, and Revel talked to children so pleasantly and levelly they might have thought themselves adults. Stinker and Tilda, who had no children, always viewed them with curiosity and a hint of fear—or so Daphne felt. Again she remembered she must simply leave them to it.

She talked for a while determinedly to Flo, whom she liked very much, about the forthcoming fair at Fernham, and an exhibition that Mark was having in London, but with a slight sense she was turning her back on other responsibilities. She glanced round: it was all right, Corinna was being charming to the Colonel, Wilfie was discussing the miners' strike with George and Sebby Stokes. She introduced Flo to her mother, and they quickly got on to the *Ring;* Flo had been last year to

Bayreuth, and Daphne watched her mother warm to the unexpected pleasure of the subject. "I wish you could meet my dear friend Mrs. Kalbeck," she said, "she's just upstairs! We went to Bayreuth together before the War." In a moment they were naming singers, Freda doubting them as soon as she said them. "We had the great thrill of meeting Madame Schumann-Heink," she said, "who sang one of the Norns, I think it was."At which point they all heard a quiet but momentous arpeggio from the piano across the room. And following, but with the accidental quality still of a rehearsal, the maddening little tune that Daphne had been pretending for days to greatly admire. "Oh, no . . . !" said Dudley, crisply but gaily, like a good sport, over the general noise of the talk. There was an amused, half-distracted turning of heads. Wilfie had gone to stand beside the piano, with his back to the room, tellingly like a child being punished. Madeleine and George, whose special treat this was, stood close by, with the look almost of parents who have sent their own child up on to the stage; but the others had no idea of the plans and promises coming inexorably into play. Louisa had put on a comical sour face, shaking her head, and telling Colonel Fountain in his good ear about how sensitive Sir Edwin was to music. The talk regained confidence, with a certain sense of relief. For forty years, after all, the piano had been untouched, disguised beneath a long-fringed velour shawl, a sturdy platform for all manner of useful or decorative objects, and if anyone after dinner had uncovered the keys and facetiously picked out a phrase the noise that came forth, from under the heaped-up folios and potted plants and the arena of framed photographs, was so jangled by time and neglect as to discourage any further idea of music. Now, however, Corinna was playing the start of the piece, the misleadingly peaceful prologue . . . "Not tonight, old girl," called Dudley from across the room, still humorously, but emphatically, and expecting to be understood—he gave Mark a matey grin. Wilfrid had cleared a little space in front of the piano, asking people in the preoccupied way of some official or commissionaire to stand back. There was a moment of silence, in which it seemed their father's order had been understood, but which Corinna, with a touch of self-righteousness, took as proper expectancy for their performance, and pitched vigorously into "The Happy Wallaby." After three bars, Wilfrid, with a look of selfless submission to order and fate, took the first few steps of his dance, which of course involved crouching and then jumping as far forward as he could. The guests shifted back, shielding their drinks, with little cries of friendly alarm, some clearly thinking this shouldn't be allowed to happen. Stinker carried on talking loudly as if he hadn't noticed—"One awfully clever thing he said was . . ."—but Dudley had put down his drink and stomped across the room, his face already square and staring with ungovernable emotion. He stood by the piano and said, in fact quietly, "I said not tonight."

"But, Daddy, you did say tonight," said Corinna pertly, playing on.

"And tonight I said not! Change of orders!"—and a bark of a laugh at the Colonel to suggest he was more in control than he was. Daphne strode forward—it was what she knew they said about Corley, how it had changed in Dudley's time, the rum mix of folk, the painters and writers, it was bedlam. She felt defiant and apologetic all at once. Wilfrid had stopped jumping, his trust in his sister's plan abandoned, but Corinna played on.

"Perhaps not now, darling," Freda said, stretching out a lace-cuffed hand to her granddaughter's shoulder, just as Dudley, bending over them both, his horrible grimace the sudden focus of the crisis, pounded his fists repeatedly on the keys at the high plinky end of the keyboard and maddened by the silly effect elbowed Corinna off the stool and pounded repeatedly at the more resonant and furious octaves at the bottom. Then he slammed the lid shut.

"Come along," said Daphne quietly, and led the two children out of the room, clinging to her hands. Nanny, the one time you wanted her, was nowhere to be seen. Then she found her mother was following her too, which was welcome in a way, except that an awful strain of unexpressed pity and reproach for her, being married to Dudley Valance, a mad brute, would be in the air. Corinna's lip was trembling, but Wilfrid was already sobbing steadily as he marched along.

When Daphne came back into the drawing-room three minutes later a collective effort at repair had been made. She murmured that the children were fine—she felt an undertow of support hedged with a certain timorous reluctance to go against Dudley. "Little devils, eh?" said the Colonel, and patted her on the arm. Mark and Flo and the S-Ps had seen the like before, and were having an ideally boring conversation about shooting to show that things were under control. Dudley himself, with the touchy geniality of a man who is never in the wrong, was talking to Sebby Stokes, whose natural diplomacy just about carried him through. It was understood that no Valance would ever apologize for anything. Louisa said nothing, though Daphne as usual read her unspoken thoughts very clearly; then she heard her say with necessary clarity to the Colonel, "We never saw our boys after six o'clock." Daphne knew the person who would be most upset was her own mother, who didn't come back in before dinner. The best thing to do was to have a stiff drink. And she found within a minute or two that a wary hilarity of recovery had gripped the whole party.

By the time they went into dinner Daphne's mood was one of non-sensical amusement veering into breathless semi-alarm at not knowing what was going on. She thought she had better bring out Colonel Fountain before the mad atmosphere of the evening engulfed them all. After the fish was served she asked him clearly about Cecil, and heard her words cantering on into a sudden general silence—her voice sounded not quite her own. The Colonel was sitting halfway along the table, on Louisa's right, and glanced around keenly, almost challengingly, as he spoke, as if at a briefing of a different kind. Those looking at him found themselves watching Louisa as well, who took on a solemn and anxious expression, her eyes fixed on the silver salt-cellar in front of her. It was not the story of Cecil's death, thank heavens, but of the famous occasion when he'd won his MC, bringing back three of his wounded men under fire. The Colonel outlined the situation in large terms, enlisting the salt-cellar as a German machine-gun post. The more detailed account he gave of the episode itself was done with honour and a sense of conviction somehow heightened by his reticent manner; but Daphne—and possi-bly others round the table—had a disappointing sense that he no longer distinguished it clearly from a dozen such episodes. He had written a splendid letter to Louisa at the time, and of course recommended Cecil for his medal, and his form of words now was very close to those ten-year-old accounts. Perhaps Dudley and Mark, who had been in similar "shows," envisaged it more freshly. Daphne's eye roamed round the room as Colonel Fountain spoke. It was the room she had associated most with Cecil, from the day they'd first met, and now it looked at its exotic best, with candles reflected in the angled mirrors and in the dim gold leaf of the jelly-mould domes overhead. At the far end, in the glow of an electric lamp, hung the Raphael portrait of a bonneted young man. "I don't know quite how he did it," the Colonel said. "The mist had pretty well cleared—he was horribly exposed." She knew Revel loved the room as much as she did, and she took her time to let her eyes come to rest on him, when he seemed immediately to know, and glanced up at her.

The rest of dinner passed in the blur of three successive wines, but

Dudley, though drunker, was making a better effort not to be rattled. Daphne had decided she must ration the number of times she looked pointedly at Revel, and she soon felt he had come to a similar agreement with himself—it was amusing, and then threatened to become awkward. Sebby naturally was questioned a certain amount about the miners and his answers gave them all the feeling they were at the heart of the crisis without anything much being revealed at all. Mark was more provoked by this than the others, and had clearly taken against Sebby altogether. He talked a good deal of unnecessary rot, or sense that sounded like rot, about his experience growing up behind a butcher's shop in Reading, until Dudley, who was the only person who could, said, "You really must learn, Mark dear, not to look down on those who have grown up without your own disadvantages," and a big licensed laugh ran round the table. To Daphne it was hauntingly like the early days of their marriage, the trance of pleasure and purely happy expectation that Dudley could cast her into. He gleamed in the candlelight and the certainty of his own handsomeness. Then she found her reawakened longing focused on Revel's thin artistic fingers lying loosely spread on the tablecloth, as though waiting for someone to pick them up. And then already it was time for the ladies to withdraw—the easy but decisive initiative in which she still felt, on a night like this, a callow usurper of her mother-in-law.

When the men came through, Colonel Fountain's driver was fetched out from the servants' dining-room—they were setting off straight away to Aldershot. Daphne saw him off from the front doorstep, feeling terribly squiffy and incoherent. She shook the Colonel's hand between both her own, but could think of nothing to say. Though the old boy had been a bit of a disappointment she felt incoherently that they had also let him down.

Back in the drawing-room she found there was talk of a game. Those who were keen half-smothered their interest, and those who weren't pretended blandly that they didn't mind. Louisa, who hated to waste time, was hemming a handkerchief for the British Legion sale. "Wotsit?" she said, squinting down her nose as she tied off the thread.

"Well, I wonder," said George, with a look that Daphne had known since childhood, the concealed excitement, the cool smile that warned them that, should he condescend to play, he would certainly win.

"Before the War," Louisa explained to Sebby Stokes, "we played Wotsit for hours at a time. Dudley and Cecil went at it like rabbits. Of course Cecil knew far more."

"Cecil was so terribly clever, Mamma," said Dudley. "I'm not sure rabbits are *specially* known for their General Knowledge, are they . . . ?"

"Or what about the adverb game," said Eva, "that's always a riot."

"Ah yes, adverbs," said Louisa, as if recalling an unsatisfactory encounter with them in the past.

"Which ones are they?" said Tilda.

"You know, darling, like *quickly* or . . . or *winsomely*," said Eva.

"You have to do something in the manner of the word," said Madeleine, unenthusiastically.

"It can be rather fun," said Revel, giving Daphne a sweet but uncertain smile: "it's about how you do things."

"Oh, I *see* . . . ," said Tilda.

Daphne felt she didn't mind playing, but she knew that Louisa wouldn't like anything boisterous or dependent on a sense of humour for its success. They had played the adverb game once with the children, Louisa baffling them all by picking *seldom*. And in fact she said now, "I don't want to be a wet blanket, but I hope you'll forgive me if I bid you all goodnight." The men leapt to their feet, there was a warm overlapping chorus of goodnights, light-hearted protests; amid which Sebby said quietly that he had papers to read, and Freda too, with a sadly cringing smile at Dudley, announced that she had had a lovely day. Daphne went out with them as far as the foot of the stairs, with a certain apologetic air of her own; though she was grateful of course to see them clamber off to bed.

They all had another drink, the idea of a game still hanging in the air. Madeleine started prattling, in a painful attempt to ward off the threat. Tilda asked if anyone knew the rules for Strip Jack Naked. Then Dudley rang for Wilkes and told him to get the pianola out; they were going to have some dancing. "Oh, what fun," said Eva, with a hard smile through her cigarette-smoke.

"I'm going to play it for my guests," said Dudley. "It's only right."

"And the carpet . . . ," murmured Daphne, with a shrug, as though she didn't really care, which was the only way to get Dudley to do so.

"Yes, remember my carpet!" said Eva.

"In the hall, Wilkes," said Dudley.

"As you wish, Sir Dudley," said Wilkes, managing to convey, beneath his rosy pleasure at the prospect of the guests enjoying themselves, a flicker of apprehension.

The pianola was kept in the cow-passage. In a minute Dudley came out into the hall to watch Robbie and another of the men wheel it roaringly across the wide oak floor. He went down the passage himself, and came back with an awkward armful of the rolls: he had a wild look, mockery mixed up with genuine excitement. It was the moment when Daphne knew she had lost what frail control of the evening she might ever have had—she gave it up in a familiar mixture of misery and relief.

Some of the rolls were just well-known numbers, foxtrots and the like; one or two were the special ones made by Paderewski, of short pieces by Chopin, which were supposed to sound like him playing it himself. Dudley only ever played these to send them up with his absurd imitation of a wild-haired virtuoso. Now he threaded a roll in, drunkenly concentrating, smiling to himself at the treat he was preparing for them, smiling at the machine itself, which he had a childish reverence for. Then he sat down, flung his head back, and started pedalling—out came the foxtrot they'd had a hundred times, and which Daphne knew she would have on the brain if something bigger and better couldn't be made to replace it. The keys going up and down under invisible hands had something almost menacing about them.

Mark, who was as tight as Dudley, immediately seized hold of Daphne, and they shimmied off at a lively stagger across the hall; she felt Mark's warm but undiscriminating interest in her as a member of the opposite sex, they were both breathless with laughter and then Mark bumped quite hard into the table and almost fell over, still holding on to her. She freed herself, and looked around at the others, Madeleine virtually in hiding, doubled up behind the pianola, as if looking for something she'd dropped, and George pretending to praise Dudley's playing with a keen facetious grin, entirely ignored by Dudley himself. Of course she wanted to dance with Revel, but he, quite reasonably, she supposed, had presented his hand to Flo, and moved off with her very confidently, steering as if by magic past the various hazards of hall chairs, plant-stands and the grandfather clock. Daphne only half-followed them, then she saw Revel smiling at her over Flo's shoulder in a perfectly open way from which, none the less, she felt allowed to draw something quite private. The roll came to an end, and Dudley jumped up to choose a replacement, which turned out to be the other foxtrot he always played. He had no ear for music, but was obsessively attached to these two numbers, or at least to playing them, with a staring pretence that anyone who really did care for music would love them too. So Daphne took hold of Stinker, with a certain mischievous determination, and he bumped along beside her and somewhat on top of her, gasping, "Oh, my dear girl, you're too fast for me . . ." In a moment Dudley started singing raucously as he pedalled, "Oh, the lights of home! . . . the lights of home! and a place I can call my own!"

"What's that?" shouted Stinker over his shoulder, trying boldly to wriggle out of dancing.

"What? You can't be so Philistine. It's a lovely song by my brother Cecil"—and he pounded on, jamming the words in to the rhythm nonsensically, and soon with tears of laughter running down his cheeks. Above him the large unapprehending cows in "The Loch of Galber" gazed on. The roll came to an end.

"Goodness, I'm hot after all that," said Stinker, and murmuring extravagantly about what tremendous fun it all was he steered his way back into the drawing-room. Cautious clinking and crashing could be heard and the hoarse gasp of the gazogene; then the pianola started up again. "Come on, Stinker!" shouted Dudley, "it's the 'Hickory-Dickory Rag'—your favourite!"

"Come on, Stinker!" cried Tilda, with exceptional high spirits, so that people laughed at her a little, but then immediately joined her, "Come on, we're starting!"—Flo was darting around already, and Eva, taking the man's part, seized her shoulders and trotted her briskly down the room, head jerking up and down like a hen in a new kind of move she seemed to have designed herself. The women's beads could just be heard, rattling against each other. "Oh!" said Tilda, "oh, my golly!" She followed them with a wide-eyed smile that Daphne had never seen before, something touching and comical in her pleasure, gazing at each of the others to see if they shared it; she peered almost cunningly at George, whose own smile was broad but slightly strained, and suddenly she had hooked his arm round her somehow, and they were moving off together, Tilda doing some intent little back-kicks and George, with shouts of "Whoops!" and "Oh, my word!" randomly trying something similar. "Oh, do come on, Stinker!" shouted Dudley again, rocking from side to side like a cyclist on a steep hill as he worked at the treadles, something mad and relentless in his grin. "Stinker!" shouted Mark, "Stinker-winker!" But Stinker resisted all these calls, and a minute later Daphne saw him wander past the window with a tumbler in his hand, and disappear into the relative safety of the garden. There was a large moon tonight, and he seemed to be peering around for it.

When the dancing stopped, Flo said, "Let's all go outside and get some air." Daphne glanced at Revel, who said, "Oh, good idea," with a sweeping smile which lingered for a moment on her before dropping thoughtfully aside. There was a rush to the front door, even shoving and protesting, then Mark, already out on the drive, singing lustily, to the tune of "Auld Lang Syne," "We're here because we're here because we're here because we're here," which seemed to Daphne rather rude, though preferable no doubt to many of the other army songs that he and Dudley sang when they were drunk, such as "Christmas Day in the Workhouse," which he started to sing next.

"Tell Mark to stop singing," said Daphne to Flo, who seemed to get the point. On a still night every word would be audible in Louisa's bedroom.

"You coming out, Dud?" said George, still panting a bit, and letting his high spirits run on over his brother-in-law.

"Eh . . . ? Oh—no, no," said Dudley, swivelling round on the stool, and then back again to reach for his drink. "No, no—you all go out. I'm going to stop in and read."

"Oh . . . ," said Tilda, still breathless and delighted. Dudley stood up with a fixed but already absent smile, shuffled sideways and dropped back on to the edge of the stool, which shot away across the bare floor— he lunged for the edge of the keyboard as he fell, George jumped from the flying cut-glass tumbler, and Daphne started forward but merely snatched his elbow as he thumped heavily backwards, with a furious shout of "Watch out!" as if someone else was behaving dangerously. "Oh!" said Tilda again. He lay there for several seconds, then sat up like the Dying Gaul, leaning on one hand, staring at the floor as though only just containing his patience, then raised his other hand, whether for help or to ward help off it was hard to tell. Daphne found herself gasping with alarm and pity and almost giggling with childish hilarity.

"No, I'm perfectly all right," said Dudley, and sprang up quite smartly, in the soldier-like way he still had, though unsteady for a moment as he gained his feet. A wince of pain was covered by a sarcastic laugh at the whole situation. His shirt-front and lapel were wet with whisky.

"Are you sure, old man?" said George. Dudley didn't answer or even look at him, but crossed the hall with uncertain dignity, flung open the door and disappeared into the cow-passage, the door swinging loudly shut behind him.

"You go on out," said Daphne to the others. With a familiar resolve she went after Dudley, but with a newer sense looming beyond it that it wasn't just repetition, it was getting much worse.

She found him in the washroom, and his dripping face as he raised it from the basin was alarmingly red. The veins in his temples stood out as if he'd been throttled. But when he had dried himself and sleeked back his hair the colour receded and he looked almost normal. Daphne thought of various futile reproaches and suggestions. She watched him dab at his lapel with the damp towel and then throw it on the floor, as he always did. Then she found he was smiling at her in the mirror, just a moment of doubt as he hooked her glance, the old trick he did without thinking. "Oh my god, Duff"—he turned and lurched into her, his teeth moist and gleaming, his arms went heavily round her shoulders, not her waist, he was kissing her and kissing her, squashing and probing as though to get at something; she didn't know what if anything she gave: all she got from it herself was a compounded sequence of discomforts, the sour flare of drink and cigars into her face. He hadn't done this for ages, it was like a violent little visit from the days when they still made love. He stood back, shaking her lightly, encouragingly, like a good old friend, then he was limping off, head down, head up, with the oblivious sense of a new mission, the unspoken agreements of the demented and the drunk. "Come on, Duffel," he called over his shoulder as he opened the door into the hall. She stood where she was, and watched the door swing closed again behind him.

"Oh, my dear, isn't Dudley joining us?" said Eva, when she got out on to the flagged path.

"No, he can't," said Daphne, with some satisfaction, pulling her wrap round her. "You know, he doesn't go out at night."

"What, not at all?" said Eva. "How very funny of him . . ." She sounded archly suspicious, and then Daphne wondered if Eva had in fact been out at night with Dudley, though she could hardly think when.

"You know, he doesn't talk about it, but it's one of his things."

"Oh, is it one of his things."

"Dud not coming out?" said Mark, suddenly behind them, and now with a hand round her waist—round both their waists.

"He doesn't, darling, as you know," said Daphne; and then she explained, for Eva's benefit, and trying to ignore Mark's quite purposeful grasp for a moment: "It's a thing from the War, as a matter of fact. I probably shouldn't say . . ."—and on the hard path, finding her way in the long spills of light from the drawing-room windows, which only deepened the shadows, she made a little mime of her hesitation. "You know, it was a great friend of his who was killed in the War. Shot dead by a sniper right beside him. They'd seen him in the moonlight, you see, and that's why he can never bear moonlight."

"Oh Lord," said Eva.

Daphne stopped. "He heard the shot and he saw the black flower open on the boy's brow, and he was dead, right beside him." She'd rather muffed the story, which Dudley told, on very rare occasions, with a shaking hand and choked throat, and which wasn't really hers to tell. She felt the horror as well as the rather striking poetry of it all so keenly that she hardly knew if she was Dudley's protector or betrayer—she seemed inextricably to be both. "And then of course Cecil, you know . . ."

"Oh, was he killed in the moonlight too?" said Eva.

"Well, no, but a sniper, it all connects up," said Daphne. In truth, other people's traumas were hard to bear steadily in mind.

In a minute Mark left them—she saw him running at a crouch behind the low hedges to ambush Tilda and Flo, who were walking together between the moonlit chains of clematis. She didn't much want to be alone with Eva; she looked around for Revel, whom she could hear laughing with George nearby . . . still, it presented an opportunity. "I was never sure," she murmured, "well you've never said, you know, but about *Mr.* Riley."

"Oh, my dear . . . ," said Eva, with a quiet smoky laugh, amused as well as embarrassed.

"I don't mean to pry."

"About old Trev . . . ? There's not a very great deal to say."

"I mean, is he not still alive?"

"Oh yes, good lord . . . though he's, you know, a fair age."

"I see," said Daphne. Of course no one knew how old Eva was herself. "I thought perhaps he'd been killed in the War."

"Not a bit," said Eva. She sounded cagey but somehow excited. Barebosomed nymphs raised their arms above them as they turned, by some silent consensus, into the path towards the fishpond. There was no colour, but the garden seemed more and more on the brink of it in the moonlight, as if dim reds and purples might shyly reveal themselves amongst the grey. Daphne turned and looked back at the house, which appeared at its most romantic. The moon burned and slid from window to window as they walked.

"So: *Trevor* . . . ," she said, after a minute. "And you're not divorced or

anything." It was slyly amusing to stick at the question, and after quite a
lot of drinks you didn't care so much about good manners.

"Not actually," said Eva, "no." Daphne supposed she must have married him for money. She saw Trevor Riley as a man who owned a small
factory of some kind. Maybe the War, far from killing him, had made
him a fortune. She found Eva slipping her arm through hers, and with
her other hand giving the long-fringed scarf she was wearing a further
twist round her neck—she felt the silky fringe brush her cheek as it
whisked round. Eva shivered slightly, and pulled Daphne against her. "I
do think marriage is often a fearful nuisance, don't you?" she said.

"Well . . . ! I really don't know."

"Mm?" said Eva.

"Well, it's something that sometimes has to be endured, I dare say."

"Indeed," said Eva, with a throb of grim humour.

"I don't know if Trevor was unfaithful," said Daphne, and shivered
herself at the closeness of the subject. They paced on, in apparent amity,
whilst Eva perhaps worked out what to say. Her evening bag, like a tiny
satchel slung down to the hip, nudged against her with each step, and
evidence about her underclothes, which had puzzled Daphne a good
deal, could obscurely be deduced in the warm pressure of Eva's side
against her upper arm. She must wear no more than a camisole, no need
really for any kind of brassière . . . She seemed unexpectedly vulnerable,
slight and slippery in her thin stuffs.

"Can I tempt you?" said Eva, her hand dropping for a second against
Daphne's hip. The nacreous curve of her cigarette case gleamed like
treasure in the moonlight.

"Oh . . . ! hmm . . . well, all right . . ."

Up flashed the oily flame of her lighter. "I like to see you smoking,"
said Eva, as the tobacco crackled and glowed.

"I'm starting to like it myself," said Daphne.

"There you are," said Eva; and as they strolled on, their pace imposed
by the darkness more than anything else, she slid her arm companion-
ably round Daphne's waist.

"Let's try not to fall into the fishpond," Daphne said, moving slightly
apart.

"I wish you'd let me make you something lovely," said Eva.

"What, to wear, you mean?"

"Of course."

"Oh, you're very kind, but I wouldn't hear of it," said Daphne. Having her redesign her house was one thing, but her person quite another. She imagined her absurdity, coming down to dinner, kitted out in one of Eva's little tunics.

"I don't know where you get your things mainly now, dear?"

Daphne laughed rather curtly through her cigarette-smoke. "Elliston and Cavell's, for the most part."

And Eva laughed too. "I'm sorry," she said, and snuggled against her again cajolingly. "I don't think you know how enchanting you could look." Now they had stopped, and Eva was assessing her, through the fairy medium of the moonlight, one hand on Daphne's hip, the other, with its glowing cigarette, running up her forearm to her shoulder, where the smoke slipped sideways into her eyes. She pinched the soft stuff of her dress at the waist, where Daphne had felt her eyes rest calculatingly before. In a hesitant but almost careless tone Eva said, "I wish you'd let me make you happy."

Daphne said, "We simply must get back," a tight stifling feeling, quite apart from the smoke, in her throat. "I'm really rather cold, I'm most frightfully sorry." She jerked herself away, dropping her cigarette on the path and stamping on it. The lights from the house threw the hedges and other intervening obstacles into muddled silhouette, but it was hard to retreat with complete dignity; nor was the moonlight as friendly as she'd thought. She cut across the grass, found her heels sinking in loam, stumbled back and around an oddly placed border. It was like a further extension of being tight, a funny nocturnal pretence of knowing where she was going. She felt Eva might be pursuing her, but when she looked over her shoulder she was nowhere to be seen—well, she must be there somewhere, lingering, plotting, blowing thin streams of smoke into the night. Daphne reached the firm flags of the path by the house, and in the second she noticed the dark form curled sideways on the bench beside her, her hand was grasped at—"Don't go in . . ."

"Oh, my god!—who's that? Oh, Tilda . . ."

"Sorry, darling, sorry . . ."

"You frightened the life out of me . . ." Tilda wasn't letting her hand go.

"Isn't it a lovely night?" she said brightly. "How are you?" And then, "I'm just rather worried about Arthur."

For a moment Daphne couldn't think who she was talking about. "Oh, Stinker, yes . . . why, Tilda?" She found herself sitting very temporarily on the bench, on its edge. As if with a child, she put away the unmentionable matter of Mrs. Riley. She found Tilda was staring at her, her white little face had forgotten the gaiety of the earlier evening. Had the drink turned on her? In her anxiety she seemed to invest Daphne with unusual powers.

"Have you seen him?" she said.

Daphne said, "Who . . . ? Oh, Stinker . . . isn't he wandering around, I'm sure he's all right . . . darling," which wasn't what she usually called her, any more than Stinker was Arthur. She'd always thought of Tilda as a youngish aunt, perhaps, silly, harmless, hers for life.

"He's so strange these days, don't you think?"

"Is he . . . ?" In so far as Daphne could be bothered to think about it, she wished he was a good deal stranger.

"Am I mad? You don't think, do you, he might be seeing another woman?"

"Stinker? Oh, surely not, Tilda!" It was easy and allowable to smile. "No, I really don't think so."

"Oh!—oh good"—Tilda seemed half-relieved. "I felt you'd know." She flinched, and peered at her again. "Why not?" she said.

Daphne controlled her laugh and said, "But it's obvious Stinker adores you, Tilda." And then perhaps thoughtlessly, "And anyway, who could it be?"

Tilda half-laughed but hesitated. "I suppose I thought perhaps because we haven't, you know . . ." And just then Daphne saw Revel step out through the french window and frown along the path to where he evidently heard their voices. She knew Tilda meant because they didn't have children.

"Come along," said Daphne, getting up, but now in turn grasping Tilda's hand, to conceal her own brusqueness. Any more on this subject would be unbearable.

"Well, I'm just going to sit here and wait for him," Tilda said, not see- ing what was happening, still adrift in drink and her own worry.

"All right, darling," said Daphne, feeling fortune free her and claim her at the same moment. She almost ran along the path.

"Oh, Duffel, darling," said Revel, touching her arm as they came back in together, and taking a smiling five seconds to continue his sen- tence, "do let's pop up and look at the children sleeping."

"Oh," said Daphne, "of *course*," as if it were hopeless of her not to have offered this entertainment already. She gazed at him and her giggle was slightly rueful. She didn't think she herself could have slept, even two floors up, through the "Hickory-Dickory Rag." And then the earlier horror, at the real piano, came back to her—it was wonderful, a blessing, that she'd forgotten it for a while.

"Dudley's gone to bed," said Revel, plainly and pleasantly.

"I see." After the garden the drawing-room was a dazzle; and in their absence, it had been perfectly tidied—everything was always tidied. "Now, have you got a drink?" she said.

"I've got a port in every one," said Revel, a bit cryptically.

"I think I've had enough," said Daphne, looking down on the tray of bottles, some friendly, some perhaps over-familiar, one or two to be avoided. She sloshed herself out another glass of claret. "Oh, Tilda's outside!" she explained to Stinker, who had just come in, stumbling on the sill of the french window. "You've just missed her." He leant on a table and gazed at her, but found nothing immediate to say.

She led the way down the cow-passage and up the east back-stairs, Revel touching her at each half-landing very lightly between the shoulders. His face when she glanced at it was considerate, with inward glints of anticipated pleasure. She was excited almost to the point of talking nonsense. "All rather back-stairs, as Mrs. Riley would say," she said.

"I don't think this is quite what she had in mind, do you," said Revel coolly, so that a leap had been taken, several unsayable matters all at once in the air. Daphne's heart was beating and she felt herself gripped at the same time by a strange gliding languor, as if to counter and conceal the speed of her pulse. She said,

"I've got to tell you about the oddest scene just now, with old Mrs. Riley. I'm absolutely certain she was making love to me."

Revel gave a careless laugh. "So she does have good taste, after all."

Daphne thought this rather glib, though charming of course. "*Well* . . ."

"You see I thought she'd set her sights on Flo, who has a bit of a look of all that, doesn't she."

"You see I thought . . ."—but it was too much to explain, and now a housemaid was coming along the top landing with a baby, no, a hot-water bottle wrapped in a shawl. "You're so sweet to the children," Daphne said loudly, "they'll be thrilled to see you," giving the servant an absent-minded nod as she came past and thinking all would be explained by this, her virtue as a mother touchingly asserted after the frightful racket from downstairs. "If they're not asleep, of course, I mean!" She kissed her raised forefinger and pushed open the door with preposterous caution. Then she had the drama of the light behind her for a minute, before they both came in and Revel closed the door with a muffled snap. Now a sallow night-light glowed from the table and heaped large shadows on the beds and up the walls. "No, Wilfie darling, you go back to sleep," she said. She peered down at him uncertainly in the stuffy gloom—he had stirred and groaned but was not perhaps awake . . . then across at Corinna, by the window, who looked less than lovely, flat on her back, head arched back on the pillow and snoring reedily. "If only she could see herself," murmured Daphne, in wistful mockery of her ceremonious child.

"If only we could see ourselves . . . ," said Revel. "I mean, I expect if you saw me . . ."

"Mm," said Daphne, leaning back, almost feeling with her shoulders to where he was, feeling his left hand slip lightly round her waist, confident but courteous and staying only a moment. "Mm . . . well, there you have them!"—stepping aside in a way that felt dance-like, a promise to return. She muttered into her wineglass as she swigged. "Not a terribly pretty picture, I'm afraid." She felt a run of trivial apology opening up in front of her, the children perhaps not pleasing to Revel. He must be aware of the smell of the chamber-pot, she seemed to see Wilfie's yellow tinkle. "Of course their father never looks at them—when they're asleep, I mean—well, as little as possible at other times—when they're awake!— they can't contrive to be picturesque at all times of the day and night—" She shook her head and sipped again, turned back to Revel. Revel was picking up Roger, Wilfie's brown bear, and frowning at the creature in the pleasant quizzical way of a family doctor: then he looked at her with the same snuffly smile, as if it didn't matter what she said. Her own mention of Dudley hung oddly in the half-light of the top-floor room.

She went round to the far side of Wilfrid's little bed, set her glass down on the bedside table, peered down at him, then perched heavily on the side of the bed. His wide face, like a soft little caricature of his father, all mouth and eyes. She thought of Dudley kissing her just now, in the cow-passage, all her knowledge of him that had to be kept from a child, their child, facing blankly upwards, one cheek in shadow, the other in the gleam of the night-light. She didn't want to think of her husband at all, but his kiss was still there, in her lips, bothering away at her. She gently straightened and smoothed and straightened again the turned-over top of Wilfrid's sheet. Dudley had a way of trapping you, he stalked your conscience, his maddest moments were also oddly tactical. And then of course he was pitiable, wounded, haunted—all that. Wilfrid's head twitched, his eyelids opened and closed and he turned his whole body in a sudden convulsion to the right, then in a second or two he thumped back again, murmured furiously and lay the other way. He had bad dreams that were sometimes spooled out for her, formless descriptions, comically earnest, too boring to do more than pretend to listen to. He claimed to dream about Sergeant Bronson, which Daphne deplored and felt very slightly jealous of. She leant over him and straddled him with her arm, as if to keep him to herself, to say he was spoken for. "Uncle Revel," said Wilfrid sociably.

"Hello, old chap!" whispered Revel, smiling down at him, setting Roger down safely by the pillow. "We didn't mean to wake you up."

Wilfrid gave him a look of unquestioning approval and then his eyes closed and he swallowed and pursed his lips. As they both watched him, the happy look slowly faded from his face, until it was again a soft witless mask.

"You see how he adores you," said Daphne, almost with a note of complaint, a breathless laugh. She gave him a long stare over the child's head. Revel's smiling coolness made her wonder for a moment more soberly if she was being played with. He went to the table and pulled out the diminutive child's chair and sat down with his knees raised. He pretended drolly that life was always lived on this scale. She watched him, vaguely amused. The night-light made a study of his face as he worked quickly at a drawing. It seemed the very last moment of a smile lingered there in his teasing concentration. He used the children's crayons as though they were all an artist could desire, and he was the master of them. Then with a louder snort Corinna had woken herself up and sat up and coughed uninhibitedly.

"Mother, what is it?" she said.

"Go back to sleep, my duck," said Daphne, with a little shushing moue, affectionate but slightly impatient with her. The child's hair was tousled and damp.

"No, Mother, what's the matter?" she said. It was hard to tell if she was angry or merely confused, waking up to these unexpected figures in her room.

"Shush, darling, nothing," said Daphne. "Uncle Revel and I came up to say goodnight."

"He's not Uncle Revel actually," said Corinna; though Daphne felt this was not the only matter on which she might put her in the wrong.

The child had a fearfully censorious vein; what she really meant was that her mother was drunk.

Revel looked over his shoulder, half-turned on the little chair. "We were wondering if we might still see that dance, if we asked very nicely," he said, which actually wasn't a very good idea.

"Oh, it's too late for that," said Corinna, "far too late," as if they were the children pleading with her for some special concession. And getting out of bed she thumped across the room and went out to the lavatory. Daphne slightly dreaded her coming back and making more of a scene, allowing herself to say what she thought. If they all said what they thought . . . And now Wilfrid had woken again at the noise, with a furtive look, like an adult pretending not to have slept. She watched Revel finishing his drawing. There was the clank and torrent of the cistern, suddenly louder as the door was opened. But now Corinna seemed more balanced, more awake perhaps. She got back into bed with the little twitch of propriety that was part of her daylight character.

"Shall I just read you something, darling, and then you both go back to sleep," Daphne said.

"Yes, please," said Corinna, lying down and turning on her side, ready for both the reading and the sleeping.

Daphne looked by Wilfrid's bed, then got up to see what books Corinna had. It was rather a bore, but they would be asleep again in a moment. "Are you reading *The Silver Charger*—how I adored that book . . . though I think I was a good deal older . . ."

"There you are, little one," said Revel, getting up from the desk and holding his picture in front of Wilfrid to catch the light. The child pondered it, with a conditional sort of smile, against the pull of sleep. "I'll put it over here, shall I?"

"Mm," said Wilfrid. Daphne couldn't quite make it out; she saw the great bill of a bird.

"It's chapter eight," said Corinna. Did she think that she ought to have a drawing too? Perhaps, tomorrow, Revel could be asked to make her one, if he wouldn't mind—he might even draw her likeness . . .

" 'So Lord Pettifer climbed into his carriage,' " Daphne read, rather cautiously in the dim light, " 'which was all of gold . . . with two handsome footmen in scarlet livery with gold braid, and the coachman in his great cockled hat—cocked hat—and the green'—I'm so sorry!—'the *great* coat of arms of the Pettifers of Morden emblazoned upon the doors. The snow had begun to fall, very gently and silently, and its soft white flakes sat—*settled*—for a moment on the manes of the four black horses and on the gold . . . panaches of the footmen's hats'—oh lawks, I remember them—or how do we say it?—*panaches,* French . . ." She looked up over the edge of the book at Revel, who was a dark column against the low light, perhaps a little impatient with her performance. He was a man of the theatre, after all; it was just that reading aloud brought out how much you'd had to drink. " ' "I shall return before dusk on Sunday!" said Lord Pettifer. "Pray tell Miranda, my ward, to prepare . . . herself." ' " She wasn't sure how much feeling to put into the speeches; and in fact at that moment there was a snort from Corinna's bed, and Daphne saw that her mouth had opened, and she was already asleep. She peered hopefully at Wilfrid, who was gazing at her clearly, though he couldn't have had the least idea what was going on. "Well, I'll just read a little bit more, shall I?" she said. And lowering her voice she read on, skipping a fair bit, through the wonderful description of Lord Pettifer's journey to Dover through the falling snow, which she hadn't read since she was a girl. How quaint it looked—part of her didn't want to read it like this, distracted by Revel, stumbling over the words; but partly she kept it up out of simple disquiet about stopping. " 'In the distance they saw the lights of a lonely house—that she could never return,' " read Daphne, turning over two pages at once, and taking a moment to realize. She glanced at Wilfrid, then carried on, quite at a loss as to what was happening herself. He smiled distantly, as if to say now it made sense, and to thank her politely, and turned away from the light and pulled up his knees under the covers, which she felt she could take as a sign to stop.

When they were outside in the passage again, things were both more urgent and more awkward. She felt it might go wrong if it wasn't acted on quickly, it would wither on the stem in a horrible embarrassment of delay and indecision. But then Revel put his arms round her lightly. "No," she whispered, "Nanny . . . !"

"Oh . . ."

"Let's go down."

"Really?" said Revel. "If you like." For the first time she had a sense that she could wound him, she could add to his other hurts; though he pressed his little flinching frown into a look of concern for her.

"No, you'll see," she said, and kissed him quickly on the cheek. She led him round, through the L-shaped top passage and out on to the top of the main stairs, with their sudden drama, the gryphons or whatever they were with their shields and raised glass globes of light descending beneath them. She thought, *the glare of publicity.*

"They're wyverns," she said, "I think," as they went down.

"Ah," said Revel, as if he had indeed asked.

In the enormous mirror on the first-floor landing there they went, figures in a story, out of the light into the shadow. She thought she was calmer now but then she started gossiping under her breath, "My dear, I simply have to tell you what Tilda Strange-Paget said"—she peered round—"about Stinker!"

"Oh, yes," said Revel, half-listening, like someone driving.

"I'm not at all sure I should. But apparently he's got another woman, tucked away."

Revel chuckled. "Mm, I wonder where he, um, tucks her." He slowed and turned outside the door of his room. "Are you sure?"

"Well, how can one be sure . . ."

"No, I mean . . ." He looked from her to the door. What she wanted was so simple and she felt suddenly lost. She had an odd, quite super-human sensation of hearing her mother's breathing in her room, and then an image of Clara in hers, miles away, and Dudley of course, but she couldn't think of that.

"No, not here," she said; and taking him on she went round the cor-ner. A single lamp burnt on a table for the guests, and when she opened the linen-room door it flung a great shadow up like a wing across the ceiling. "Will you come in here?" She was solemn but she giggled too.

It was dark, which was the beauty of it, and then the skylight was seen to glimmer—the moon, of course, throwing other shadows down into the well of the room. Again there was no colour, just the white gleam of the high-piled sheets on the shelves among realms of grey. "You can climb out at the top on to the roof," said Daphne.

"Not now, I think," murmured Revel, and putting his hands on either side of her face he kissed her. She rocked in front of him for a moment before she put her arms round him, gripped the loose bulk of the dinner-jacket over his wiry unknown body. She let him kiss her, as though it were still reversible, a mere gambit, and then with a violent grunt of assent she started to kiss him back.

They kissed and kissed, Revel respectfully holding her and stroking her, a faint comedy of self-consciousness creeping into their murmurs and half-smiles between kisses, the little mimicking rhythms of the kisses themselves. Still, it was completely lovely, a forgotten pleasure, to be pleasing someone who sought simply to please you. She had never been kissed by two men in one evening before—well, she'd only been kissed by two or three men ever. The contrast, in so intimate a thing, was bewilderingly beautiful. The of course unmentioned fact, that it was men that Revel liked to kiss, made it the more flattering, though perhaps more unreal. Revel had something more than a man's normal experience in all this, it shone in his mischievous eyes. Daphne couldn't be sure, now it had finally started, that it was serious after all. But if it wasn't serious, perhaps that would be its charm, its point. She stood away for a moment—in the monochrome gleam from the skylight she touched Revel's face, his clever nose, his brow, his lips. He took her hand as she did so and kissed it. Then he kissed her again on her cheek. It was almost odd he didn't push her further. She wondered now if he had ever kissed a woman before. She supposed when men kissed each other it was a pretty rough business; she didn't quite like to think about it. She knew she must encourage Revel, without making him feel at all inadequate or in need of encouragement. He was younger than her, but he was a man. In some strange romantic way, to please him, she wished she could be a man herself. "We can do whatever you like, you know," she said, and then wondered, as he laughed, what she was letting herself in for.

9

THEN FOR TWENTY MINUTES the world belonged to the birds. Thickly in the woods, and out on the High Ground, all through the gardens, on benches and bushes, and high up here among the roofs and chimneys, finches and thrushes, starlings and blackbirds were singing their songs to the daybreak all at once. Wilfrid opened his eyes, and in the greyish light he saw his sister, sitting up in bed, peering at her book. With a cautious turn of the head and a little steady concentration he worked out that it was half past six. There was something strange on the bedside table, which held his attention for a minute, with its shadowy glimmer, but he didn't want to think about it. It made no sense, like a window where no window could ever be. He let his eyes close. The birdsong was so loud that after it had woken you it drove you back to sleep. Then, when you woke again, it was really day, and the birds by now were

further off and much less important. You forgot all about them. He saw
the door was half-open: Corinna had already gone to wash and he
needed to ask her one or two things about the night, about the noises
and music and coming and going that were tangled up with it like
dreams. He turned over and there on the mantelpiece, propped up by
the Toby jug, was Uncle Revel's flamingo, standing on one leg, and giving him a crafty smile. A bit of the dream had stayed in the solid world,
as a proof or a promise, and he slipped out of bed and took it down.
Uncle Revel had been here, with his mother, laughing and joking, and he
had done a drawing, very quickly, like a magic trick. Wilfrid took the
drawing back to bed with him—of course the strange thing on the table,
misleading him before with its magic gleam, was his mother's wineglass,
with the last bit of dark red wine still in it, and bits of black rust in the
wine. He peered into the glass, and confusingly the sour smell was the
smell of his mother's latest kisses. He heard Nanny in her bedroom next
door, the worrying creak of her floorboards, rattle of curtain-rings. She
was talking to someone, it sounded like the maid Sarah. They came on
to the landing. "Another of their wild nights," Nanny was saying. "God
knows what they'll be like this morning." Sarah groaned and laughed.
"Duffel up here at god knows what time, with her young artist friend, to
have a look at the little ones sleeping, she said. Of course, how can they
sleep through that, it upsets them. They'll be little horrors after a night
like that."

"Aah . . . !" said Sarah, who sounded nicer today. Wilfrid hated what
Nanny said about his mother.

"Well, my day off, dear, I don't have to deal with them!"

"Robbie says they were playing at sardines," said Sarah.

"Sardines! Silly buggers, more likely . . . ," said Nanny, and the two
women cackled and seemed to go away down the corridor. "I suppose
you heard the music . . . ," Nanny was saying, as the door at the top of
the stairs thumped shut. Well, they'd all heard the music, Wilfrid
thought. His mother had been dancing with Uncle Revel in the hall, and
he had the scene still bright in his head. Now he wanted to sleep; but in
his heart and mind there was a muddled stirring of protest, at the abuse
and disrespect to his mother but also at the restless and broken night she
had given him. He was exhausted by dreams.

Almost at once, various things happened, perfectly normal but none
the less oddly upsetting in their way of keeping on happening. Very early
a message came up that Mr. Stokes was leaving and her ladyship wanted

the children down. Corinna was already practising the piano, and the maid brought Wilfrid down by himself. He felt lonely and reluctant, and frowned a good deal so as not to give way. In the hall the pianola still stood, with its keyboard closed, at an angle to the wall. He loved the pianola, and once or twice his father had worked the pedals for him and let him run his hands up and down over the dancing keys, while Corinna looked on in disdain. But today it seemed only a jangling reminder of the night before, a toy that others had played on without him. He wished intensely they would take it away. He went out to examine the Daimler. Even Robbie's wink, as he brought out the luggage for Uncle Sebby, was displeasing and lacking in respect. Why did he always have to wink at him? "And how are you, Master Wilfrid?" said Robbie.

"Well, I'm very overwrought," said Wilfrid.

Robbie pondered this for a minute, with a tiny smile. "Overwrought, you say? Now, why would that be?" He handed the bags to Sebby's chauffeur, and Wilfrid came round to see them stowed in the boot. The great interest of the boot, with its unusual door and trench-like black interior, struggled feebly with his mood of discontent.

"Well, I had a bad night, if you must know," said Wilfrid.

"Ah," said Robbie, and nodded sympathetically, but still with an unsettling hint of amusement. "Kept you awake with their dancing, did they?" At which Wilfrid could only look up at him and nod back.

Granny V came down to see Sebby off, and they talked interminably for two or three minutes while Wilfrid wandered round the Daimler, looking at the lamps and at his own reflection looming and folding in the dark grey bodywork. Then Sebby came over and shook his hand, and unexpectedly gave him a large coin before getting into the car, which took off up the drive in a sudden cloud of blue oil-smoke. Wilfrid smiled at the departing car, and at his grandmother, who was watching him keenly for the proper reactions, though in fact he felt bothered and slightly indignant. "Goodness!" said Granny V, in a gloating but critical voice, "a crown!" He put it in his trouser pocket but he felt it was Wilkes who should have been given it.

Then almost at once the trap was brought round, to take Corinna and both her grandmothers to church in Littlemore. Lady Valance herself would drive the mile and a half each way, and Corinna was bleating a promise extracted earlier, that she would be allowed to take the reins for some of the time. The pony could be heard through the open front door twitching its harness, the stable-boy talking to it. There was a flutter in the hall, gloves and hats being found. Granny V always wore the same sort of thing, which was black and took no time, but Corinna had a new dress and a new bonnet, which Granny Sawle was helping her to tie on firmly.

"It seems such a shame not to use the chapel here," said Granny S, as Uncle George and Aunt Madeleine appeared.

"Nowadays," said Granny V, with strange emphasis, "the use of the chapel is restricted to the major festivals"; and she went out into the drive.

" 'Nowadays,' " said George, "seems to have become Louisa's favoured term of opprobrium." He looked comically at his mother. "You don't have to go at all, darling," he said. "We never do, you know."

She fussed with the bow under Corinna's chin. "Louisa does seem to count on my going."

"Mm, but you needn't be bullied," said George.

"Oh, please come, Granny," said Corinna.

"Oh, I'm coming, child, never fear," said her grandmother, holding her at arm's length and looking at her rather sternly.

Wilfrid traipsed out again with his aunt and uncle to see the party leave. As Granny V settled herself on the bench the pony dropped a quick but heavy heap of dung on to the gravel. Wilfrid giggled, and Corinna held her nose up unhappily. The trap jolted and moved off at a brisk pace, as if nothing had happened, leaving the boy to bring a shovel. At the top of the drive Granny Sawle turned and waved. Wilfrid stood beside his aunt and uncle and waved back, half-heartedly, with the sun in his eyes. "Well, here we are, Wilfrid," said Aunt Madeleine, which he felt just about summed it up. She stood stiff above him, blocking his view of some much happier morning, in which he was sitting at a table with Uncle Revel, drawing pictures of birds and mammals. When they went back into the house his mother appeared from the morning-room with a strange fixed smile.

"I hope you slept for a minute or two?" she said.

"Oh, far more," said Uncle George, "ten minutes at least."

"I had a full half-hour," said Aunt Madeleine, apparently not joking.

"What a night," said George. "I feel bright green this morning. I don't know how you take the pace, Daph."

"It requires some getting used to," she said. "One has to be broken in."

Wilfrid stared at his uncle for signs of this exotic colouring. Actually, his mother and George both looked very pale.

"And how are you, Mummy?" he said.

"Good morning, little one," his mother said.

"Do you do this every weekend?" said Madeleine.

"No, sometimes we're very quiet and good, aren't we, my angel," said his mother, as he ran to her and she stooped and pulled him in. He felt a quick shudder go through her, and held her tighter. Then after a moment she stood, and he had more or less to let go. She reached for him vaguely again, but somehow she wasn't there. He looked up into her face, and its utterly familiar roundness and fairness, the batting of the eyelashes, the tiny lines by her mouth when she smiled, beauties he had always known and never for a moment needed to describe, seemed to him for a few strange seconds the features of someone else. "Well, I must get on," she said.

"No, Mummy . . . ," said Wilfrid.

"Hardly the best moment," she explained to Madeleine, "but Revel has offered to draw my picture, which feels too good an offer to refuse, even with a hangover."

"I know what you mean," said George, and smiled at her very steadily. "No, that should be quite something."

"Oh, Mummy, can I come too, can I come and watch?" cried Wilfrid.

And again his mother gave him a strange bland look in which something hurtfully humorous seemed also to lurk. "No, Wilfie, not a good idea. An artist has to concentrate, you know. You can see it when it's done." It was all too much for him, and the tears rose up in a stifling wail. He longed for his mother, but he pushed her off, shouting and gulping, fending them all off, with the tears dripping down on to his jersey.

So after that he was left, for an undefined period, with Uncle George and Aunt Madeleine. They went into the library, where George leant by the empty fireplace and talked to him encouragingly. Wilfrid stood listlessly spinning the large coloured globe, with its well-known splodges of British pink, first one way, then the other. His hands smacked lightly on the bright varnished paper, and the world echoed faintly inside. As often after a great explosion of tears he felt abstracted and weak, and it took him a while to see the point of things again.

"I don't suppose you've seen your father this morning," said George.

Wilfrid thought about how to answer this. He said, "We don't see Daddy in the mornings."

"Oh, really?"

"Well, not as a rule. You see, he's writing his book."

"Oh, yes, of course," said George. "Well, that's the most important thing, isn't it."

Wilfrid didn't agree to this exactly. He said, "He's writing a book about the War."

"Not like his other book, then," said Madeleine, who with her head back and her glasses on the end of her nose was gaping at the shelves above her.

"Not at all," said Wilfrid. "It's about Sergeant Bronson."

"Oh yes . . . ," said George vaguely. "So he tells you about it? How exciting . . ."

The constraints of strict truth felt more threateningly present in this room full of old learning. He wandered off to the centre table with a smile, keeping his answer. "Uncle George," he said, "do you like Uncle Revel's pictures?"

"Oh, very much, old boy. Not that I've seen very many of them. He's still very young, you know," said George, looking less green now than pink. "You know he's not really an uncle, don't you?"

"I know," said Wilfrid. "He's an honourable uncle."

"Well, ha, ha! . . . Well, yes, that's right."

"You mean an *honorary* uncle," said Madeleine.

"Oh," said Wilfrid, "yes . . ."

"I expect you mean both, don't you, Wilfie," said George, and smiled at him understandingly. Wilfrid knew his father couldn't stomach Aunt Madeleine, and he felt this gave him licence to hate her too. She hadn't brought him a present, but as a matter of fact that wasn't it at all. She never said anything nice, and when she tried to it turned out to be horrible. Now she tucked in her chin and gave him her pretend smile, staring at him over her glasses. He leant on the table, and opened and shut the hinged silver ink-well, several times, making its nice loud clopping noise. Aunt Madeleine winced.

"I suppose this is where Granny does her book tests, isn't it," she said, wrinkling her nose, her smile turning hard.

"I'm sure the child doesn't know about that," said Uncle George quietly.

"Actually, I'm learning reading with Nanny," said Wilfrid, abandoning the table and going off towards the corner of the room, where there was a cupboard with some interesting old things in.

"Jolly good," said George. "So what are you reading now? Why don't we read something together?" Wilfrid felt his uncle's grateful relief at the idea of a book—he was already sitting down in one of the slippery leather chairs.

"Corinna's reading *The Silver Charger*," he said.

"Isn't that a bit hard for you?" said Madeleine.

"Daphne loved that book," said George. "It's a children's book."

"I'm not reading it," said Wilfrid. "I don't really want to read now, Uncle George. Have you seen this card machine?" He opened the cupboard, and got the card machine out very carefully, but still banging it against the door. He carried it over and handed it to his uncle, who had assumed a slightly absent smile.

"Ah, yes . . . jolly good . . ." Uncle George wasn't very clever at understanding it, he had it round the wrong way. "Quite a historic object," he said, ready to hand it back.

"What is it?" said Madeleine, coming over. "Oh, yes, I see . . . Historic indeed. Quite useless now, I fear!"

"I like it," said Wilfrid, and something struck him again, by his uncle's knee, with his aunt bending over him, with her smell like an old book. "Uncle George," he said, "why don't you have any children?"

"Well, darling," said Uncle George, "we just haven't got round to it yet." He peered at the machine with new interest; but then went on, "You know, Auntie and I are both very busy at our university. And to be absolutely honest with you, we don't have a very great deal of money."

"Lots of poor people have babies," Wilfrid said, rather bluntly, since he knew his uncle was talking nonsense.

"Yes, but we want to bring up our little boys and girls in comfort, with some of the lovely things in life that you and your sister have, for instance."

Madeleine said, "Remember, George, you need to finish those remarks for the Vice-Chancellor."

"I know, my love," said George, "but it's so much pleasanter conversing with our nephew."

Nevertheless, a minute later George was saying, "I suppose you're right, Mad." A real anxiety started up in Wilfrid that he would be left alone with Aunt Madeleine. "You'll be all right with Auntie, won't you?"

"Oh, please, Uncle George"—Wilfrid felt the anxiety close in on him, but offset at once by a dreary feeling he couldn't explain, that he was going to have to go through with whatever it was, and it didn't really matter.

"We'll do something lovely later," said George, tentatively ruffling his nephew's hair, and then smoothing it back down again. He turned in the doorway. "We can have your famous dance."

When he'd gone, Madeleine rather seized on this.

"Well, I can't do it by myself," said Wilfrid, hands on hips.

"Oh, I suppose you'd want music."

"I mean, can you play?" Wilfrid asked, shaking his head.

"I'm not awfully good!" said Madeleine, pleasantly enough. They went out into the hall. "I suppose there's always the pianola . . ." But happily, the men had already wheeled it back down the cow-passage. Wilfrid didn't want to play the pianola with her. Not meaning to initiate a game, he got under the hall table.

"What are you doing, dear?" said Aunt Madeleine.

"I'm in my house," said Wilfrid. In fact it was a game he sometimes played with his mother, and he felt unfaithful to her but also a kind of security as he squatted down with the huge oak timbers almost touching his head. "You can come and visit me," he said.

"Oh . . . ! Well, I'm not sure," said Madeleine, bending over and peering in.

"Just sit on the table," said Wilfrid. "You have to knock."

"Of course," said Madeleine, with another of those glimpses of being a good sport that complicated the picture. She sat down obediently, and Wilfrid looked out past her swinging green shoes and the translucent hem of her skirt and petticoat. She knocked on the table and said loudly, "Is Mr. Wilfrid Valance at home?"

"Oh . . . I'm not quite sure, madam, I'll go and look," said Wilfrid; and he made a sort of rhythmical mumbling noise, which conveyed very well what someone going to look might sound like.

Almost at once Aunt Madeleine said, "Aren't you going to ask who it is?"

"Oh God, madam, who is it?" said Wilfrid.

"You mustn't say 'God,' " said his aunt, though she didn't sound as if she minded very much.

"Sorry, Aunt Madeleine, who is it, please?"

The proper answer to this, when he played with his mother, was, "It's Miss Edith Sitwell," and then they tried not to laugh. His father often laughed about Miss Sitwell, who he said sounded like a man and looked like a mouse. Wilfrid himself laughed about her whenever he could, though in fact he was rather afraid of her.

But Madeleine said, "Oh, can you tell Mr. Wilfrid Valance that it's Madeleine Sawle."

"Yes, madam," said Wilfrid, in a sort of respectful imitation of Wilkes. He "went away" again, and took his time about it. He had a picture of his aunt's face, smiling impatiently as she sat and waited on the hard table. A wild idea came to him that he would simply say he wasn't at home. But then a shadow seemed to fall on it, it seemed lazy and cruel. But the game, which his aunt had failed to understand, really depended on the person pretending to be someone else. Otherwise you came to the end of it, and a feeling of boredom and dissatisfaction descended almost at once. Then his deep underlying longing for his mother rose in a wave, and the pain of thinking of her, and Uncle Revel drawing her, stiffened his face. It was a burningly important event from which he had been needlessly shut out. Madeleine suddenly said, "Wilfrid, will you be all right there for half a moment, I just have to go and do something."

"Oh, yes, all right," said Wilfrid; and he saw her slide and then jump the six inches down on to the floor, and her clumpy green shoes going off rather fast towards the stairs.

Wilfrid stayed under the table for ten minutes, in the odour of polish, feeling relief at first, and then the bleak little prickle of abandonment, and then a spreading and anxiously practical sense of the things he might now be able to do. The floorboards were faintly sticky with polish under the crepe rubber soles of his sandals. These unprepared freedoms in his closely minded life were exciting, but shadowed by worry that the system designed to protect him could so easily break down.

He crawled out, over the thick oak stretcher of the table, stood up, and went slowly and indirectly towards the foot of the stairs. Without his aunt to license his escapade, he was in the random and irrational jurisdiction of his father. "Daddy, I wasn't," he said, as he climbed the stairs, "I wasn't playing on the landing"—and as each little wounded lie of a denial dropped behind unneeded, the growing sense of freedom was haunted by a blacker sense of guilt. The freedom seemed to stretch uncomfortably, like a held breath. He strolled along the wide landing, still talking inaudibly to himself, head dropping from side to side, in a guilty mime of being alone. Round the corner hung the Blue Lady, with her frightening eyes, and a picture of Scotland, also known as "The Goat's Bottom." A maid came out of a room and crossed to the backstairs but magically without seeing him, and he got to the laundry-room door. The black china handle was large in his child's hand, and slightly loose in the door, so that it joggled betrayingly as he turned it and the door creaked quickly open, outwards across the landing, and swung wide if you didn't hold it, to bang against the chair beside it.

WHEN HE OPENED the door again he was pretending that not long had passed. The clock in the hall was sounding, far away, down below, quarter past, half past, quarter to, though the hour itself hung undisclosed in the grey light of the landing window. He looked both ways with a sense of dread that had been magically banished in the laundry-room itself, and a tense tactical excitement at the prospect of the long corridor and the stairs. His dread was partly still guilt and partly a different kind of awkward feeling, that maybe no one had missed him. It seemed best to take the other back-stairs, at the far end of the main landing, and get round to the nursery that way, and then simply insist he had been there all along. He closed the laundry-room door, with cautious control of the handle, and went along by the wall and looked round the corner.

Mrs. Cow was lying face down, her right hand loosely gripping her stick, which had pushed the long Persian runner up in a wave against the legs of a small table, knocking off the little bronze huntsman, who also lay on his face on the floor, with his pike sticking out. Her other stick was some feet away, as if she'd tossed it in a sudden spasm or attempt to ward something off, and her left arm was trapped under her at an angle that would have been painful for a conscious person. Wilfrid stared, looked away, approached very cautiously, heel to toe in his sandals, not wanting to be heard, least of all by the old lady herself. Then he said "Oh, Mrs. Cow . . . ?"—almost absently, as if starting on some question that would come to him if he kept talking: the point was to get the adult person's attention and keep it. Part of him knew of course that she wouldn't answer, would never answer a question again, in her wilful German voice. But something advised him to pretend politely, for a little while more, that she was still up to a chat. He came round her head, which was turned sideways, her left cheek to the carpet; and saw her right eye, hooded, half-open. Therefore not looking at him, but seeming to be part of her speechless search for something out of range, something that might have helped her. Trembling, slightly but uncontrollably, he squatted down and turned his own head sideways to try to meet her gaze, which in a normal person would have brought about a flicker of engagement. He saw how her mouth, also half-open, had let out a small slick of saliva, its shine fading as it darkened the red of the carpet.

The old lady's left arm was pinned under her, but the hand was poking out: there it lay on the carpet, small and thick, humped and dimpled. Wilfrid stared at it, from his squatting position, then stood up and walked around her again. He was frightened that the hand might move, and also, oddly, almost sickeningly, tempted by it. Looking both ways, holding his breath, he bent down, reached his fingers towards it; then picked it up. In a second he dropped it, and clutched his own warm hands together, then thrust them into his armpits, in a way that he had. He stared at Mrs. Kalbeck's dropped hand, and then in the second he turned away it stirred and retracted slightly, and lay back as it had been before.

On the stairs he was crying so much he hardly saw where he was going—not a mad boo-hoo but wailing sheets of tears, shaken into funny groans by the bump of each step as he hurried down. Helplessly he marched to the door of his father's study. It was the most unapproachable room in the house, a room of unrememberable size and everything in it, clock and fender and crackling waste-paper basket, dark with prohibitions. His father's anger, unleashed last night, at the piano, had withdrawn into it, like a dragon to its lair. Wilfrid stood for a moment outside the door, and wiped his nose thoroughly on his sleeve. Though he was helpless, he was oddly lucid. He knew that to knock would introduce more suspense into the thing than anyone could bear, and risk bringing further wrath upon his head in advance; so, very tactfully, he turned the handle.

The room was unexpectedly dark, the heavy curtains almost closed, and he moved forward not really listening to the clock but with a sense that the spaces between its deep ticks were stretching, as if it was thinking of stopping. The stripe of light across the red carpet made the shadow even deeper, for the first few seconds. Wilfrid knew his father had headaches in the morning, and avoided the light, and this sent another wave of despairing apology over him. At the same time the one line of light showed up ridges and knots in the carpet, which itself had the half-strangeness of something in a dream—in a house where he knew all the carpets as territories, castles, jumping squares, there was this other room with a carpet he had never jumped on. For a long time they seemed not to see him, and as he stepped forward it was as if he still had a chance to step back—the first they would know of his presence would be the click of the door behind him. Nanny was turned away from him, lying with her legs up on the settee, and watching his father, on the other side of the band of light, by the fireplace. His father was still in his dressing-gown, and with his sword in his hand looked like a knight. The fender here was a castle, with brass battlements, and on the black hearthstone beyond it there was a wild heap of smashed plates— other curved splinters of china were scattered across the carpet too. Again Wilfrid took in the pattern: they were the thick French plates with a cockerel on them, the wedding present they all said was hideous and ghastly. Nanny heard him, and glanced round, she half sat up and hugged a cushion to her. "Captain," she said.

"What is it?" said his father, turning to look at him, frowning, not angrily, exactly, but as if trying to make something out. He laid the sword down on the mantelpiece.

And Wilfrid knew he couldn't say. He stepped further into the light. He hoped his own blotchy cheeks and sniffy nose were proof that something serious had happened, but there was no question of saying what. He said, "Oh, Daddy, I've just seen . . . Mrs. Cow."

"Oh, yes," said his father, at once visibly disappointed.

"I think she's fallen over."

His father tutted and went to stand beside his desk, switched on the lamp, peered at some papers as if already getting on with something important. His hair, normally black and shiny, stood up at one side like a wing. Nanny seemed entirely uninterested; she had stood up, straightened her skirt, shifted the cushions on the settee to find her handbag. Without looking at him, Dudley said, "And have you told her to get up?"

"No, Daddy," said Wilfrid, feeling another wail rising in his chest at his father's perversity. He said, "She can't get up, you see, as a matter of fact."

"Broken both her legs, has she?"

Wilfrid shook his head, but couldn't say more, for fear of crying, which his father couldn't stand.

"I wonder if I should look, Sir Dudley?" said Nanny, with odd reluctance, patting her hair. It was her day off, anyway: she probably didn't want to be involved. Slowly, with the playful menace he brought to telling a story, Dudley turned his head, and stared at Wilfrid.

"I wonder if what you're trying to tell me, Wilfrid," he said, "is that Frau Kalbeck is dead?"

"Yes, Daddy, she is!" said Wilfrid, and in the relief of it he was very

nearly grinning at just the same moment the saved-up tears poured out
of him again.

"Of course she should never have come here," said his father, still
maddeningly unexcited, but no longer blaming Wilfrid himself, it
seemed. He looked sharply at Nanny. "Upsetting my son like this." And
then he gave a surprising laugh. "Well, it's taught her a lesson, what? She
won't be coming here again."

Nanny stood behind Wilfrid, and laid her hands hesitantly on his
shoulders. "Now, don't cry, there's a good boy," she said. He struggled to
obey her, as he wanted to, for a moment, but when he thought of the
dead woman's face again, and her hand moving by itself, it was all
beyond him and over him like a wave.

"Run along to Wilkes's room and telephone Dr. Wyatt, would you,
Nanny?" said his father.

"At once, Sir Dudley," said Nanny. Wilfrid of course would go with
her, but she turned uncertainly at the door, and his father nodded and
said,

"You stay here, old boy."

So Wilfrid went to his father, and was pulled experimentally for a
second or two against the heavy strange-scented skirts of the brocade
dressing-gown. It was the touch of privilege, a feel of the luxurious con-
cessions allowed when something awful had happened, and in the interesting surprise of it he at once stopped crying. Then they went together,
snapping odd sharp fragments of china underfoot, to the window, and
each drew back a curtain. Nothing was said about the dinner service; and
his father already had the mischievous preoccupied look that sometimes
announced a treat, an idea that had just surprised him and demanded to
be shared. It was like the mad glint, but usually nicer. Staring into the
garden, fixing his eye so hard on something that Wilfrid thought for a
moment it must be the source of his amusement, he started to talk, too
quietly and rapidly at first for him to follow—"The body was found—it
lay on the ground—without a sound"—

"Oh, Skeleton, Daddy," he said, and his father grinned tolerantly.

"—old fat Mrs. Cow—with her face like a sow—you won't hear from
her now"—he turned and walked excitedly round the room, Wilfrid had
a distracted sense of how he really never noticed his father's limp—"with
her Wagner and Liszt—and her hair in a twist—and always pissed—like
a terrible Hun—with a twelve-bore gun—what?—"

"Yes, Daddy . . ."

"—smelly old Valkyrie—rosewater talc-ery—came down to Corley—and said she was poorly—took it quite sorely . . ." A little flick of
spit from his father's mouth danced in the light as he turned. Wilfrid
couldn't follow or understand a lot of the words themselves, but the joy
of improvisation caught at him as well as the sense of horror that his
father's poems always challenged you not to feel. He had got to the door
and flung it open—"And that, young man," he said, "is more than I've
written of my book for the past six months."

"Really, Daddy?" said Wilfrid, unable to decide from his father's tone
if this was a cause for celebration or despair.

THREE

"Steady, boys, steady!"

I

AT FIVE O'CLOCK, when they were all getting their things, Miss Cobb, the Manager's secretary, made a rare appearance in the staff-room. "Oh, Mr. Bryant," she said, "with Miss Carter away, I wonder if you would walk with Mr. Keeping."

"Oh," said Paul, glancing round at the others, "I don't know . . ." In his mind he was already halfway home, in the high summer evening.

"I'll do it," said Heather Jones.

"Mr. Keeping did ask for Mr. Bryant," said Miss Cobb. "He likes to get to know the new staff."

"Well, of course I will, in that case," said Paul, blushing, with no idea, really, what he was being asked.

"I'll tell Mr. Keeping. In five minutes, in the Public Space? Thank you so much . . ."—and Miss Cobb withdrew, with her sad flinch of a smile.

In a week he had got to know all their names, which were still coloured and almost physical for him, made distinct by their newness and the need to tell them apart. Heather Jones and Hannah Gearing; Jack Reeves, the chief cashier; Geoff Viner, the second cashier, a bit of a looker; Susie Carter, a good-natured chatterbox, who was off today, attending a funeral in Newbury. Her empty chair and shrouded type-writer had quietened the office behind him. He slid his thermos into his briefcase and said quietly to Heather, "What does Susie do with Mr. Keeping exactly?"

Heather seemed to think for a moment. "Oh, she just walks home with him."

Hannah, with her more maternal note, said, "Mr. Keeping likes someone to keep him company. Normally Susie goes because she lives up past the church. It's a nice little walk, really—it'll only take you five minutes."

"Just don't say, 'How are you, Keeping?'" said June Underwood.

"I won't," said Paul, to whom the whole business sounded odd and euphemistic. From what he had seen of him, Mr. Keeping was a cool and formal sort of man, with a sarcastic streak, but he'd noticed the staff took a strangely protective attitude to him. If they'd ever thought it odd for a middle-aged man to need walking home, they treated it now as the normal thing. He said, "Isn't the Manager meant to live over the bank?" He'd seen upstairs, where the sitting-room of the bank house was lined with filing-cabinets and the bedrooms were stacked with old desks and junk.

"Well, this one doesn't," said Jack Reeves, who'd just got his pipe going, the coarse dry smoke like a sign of his authority.

Geoff Viner, taming his hair with a comb and the flat of his hand, said, "I assume you don't know Mrs. Keeping."

"Oh, you know her, Geoffrey, do you!" said June, and a bit of a laugh went round the room.

Jack Reeves said, "I assure you Mrs. Keeping has no intention of living over the shop."

"I'd hardly call the Midland Bank a shop," said Heather.

"Her words, not mine," said Jack.

"Well, she's got the boys to think of too," said Hannah. "They need a proper garden to run around in."

"What children have they got?" said Paul.

"Well, I say boys . . . John's at college, isn't he."

"John, the elder boy, is at Durham University"—Jack Reeves frowned over his pipe, out of his greater intimacy with the Manager. "Julian is in the Sixth Form at Oundle School, and doing very well, I believe." He sucked and nodded and gazed over their heads. "They talk of Oxford"— and he went out, leaving them half a roomful of smoke.

In the Gents Paul washed the money smell, copper and nickel and grubby paper, from his hands. The geyser rumbled. Grey-black suds speckled the basin. He was bothered about the imminent walk, but it was an opportunity, as his mother would say, and it looked a little easier if the Keepings had sons, one of them about Paul's own age. John and Julian: he saw them, seductive images spun from nothing; already they were showing him around their large garden. He smiled narrowly at himself in the mirror, turning a little to left and right: he had a long nose, the "Bryant nose," his mother said, disclaiming it; his hair was cut horribly short for the new job, and the strip light, which spared nothing, brought out its odd coppery sheen and the stipple of spots across his forehead. Then he started grinning, to see what that looked like, but immediately Geoff came in behind him and went to the urinal; it was a double one, on a raised step, and Paul looked furtively at Geoff's back in the mirror.

"No, the thing about the boss, young Paul," Geoff said, with a quick glance over his shoulder, "is he had a very bad war."

"Oh, did he, right . . . ," said Paul, busying himself with the taps and then with the damp curtain of roller towel.

"Prisoner of war," said Geoff. "He never talks about it, so for god's sake don't mention it."

"Well, I wouldn't, would I," said Paul, "obviously."

Geoff finished, jiggled, zipped up his wonderfully tight fly, and came over to the basins, where he looked at himself in the mirror with no sign of the dissatisfaction Paul had felt. He jutted his jaw, and turned his head both ways with a stroking hand. His roundish, full-lipped face was sharpened up by a pair of handsome sideburns, shaved forward at the bottom into dark points. "Sorry to say," he said, "he's a bit of a nervous wreck. Pathetic, really. He ought to have a much bigger branch than this. Brilliant brain, they say, but can't take the strain. Feels he can't go any-where alone. There's a word for it . . ."

"Yes. Agoraphobia?"

"That's it. Hence the girls walking him home." He ran the hot tap and the geyser flared up again. "At least he says that's the reason . . ." Paul found he was looking at him in the mirror, one eyebrow raised, and he sniggered and coloured and looked down. He wasn't nearly ready to joke about the other staff. He knew he had picked up on certain atmospheres between them, thought he glimpsed little histories; but any sort of sexual joke seemed to threaten him with exposure too. He knew he couldn't bring them off. Geoff came up close to him to use the towel; he had a sharp five o'clock smell, smoke, bri-nylon and faded aftershave. "Well, mustn't keep My Fair Lady waiting," he said. He was walking out with a girl from the National Provincial, the rival bank across the square, a fact which the girls at the Midland seemed to think a bit off.

When Paul got back into the Public Space Mr. Keeping was just com-ing out of the Manager's office. He held a light raincoat folded over his arm, and carried a dark brown trilby. Paul scanned him nervously for signs of his weakness, his war-time trauma. The dominant impression, of course, was his baldness, the great square blank of brow the home and symbol of that brilliant brain. Below it his features seemed rather small and provisional. He had dry, oddly rimless lips, and his smiles drew the corners of his mouth down with a confusing suggestion of distaste. When they were outside he stayed on the step to hear the successive muffled shocks of the door being locked and bolted from within. Then he settled his hat, with a forward tilt, low on his brows. At once he had a charming and even mischievous look. His guarded grey eyes, in the shadow of the brim, now seemed almost playful. And with a little bow, a little questioning hesitation—it was almost as though he expected Paul to take his arm—they set off up the broad slope of the marketplace, Paul instead earnestly gripping his briefcase, while Mr. Keeping, with his raincoat over his arm, had the air of a mildly curious visitor to the town.

Paul wished Geoff hadn't told him about Mr. Keeping's mental problems—and felt anxiously uncertain whether Mr. Keeping himself would expect him to know about them. Smiling vaguely, he took in nothing of the shops and people he was staring at with such apparent alertness. His sense of the walk as an opportunity to get in the Manager's good books was undermined by his fear that he'd been singled out for some kind of correction or discomfiting pep-talk. He saw Hannah Gearing across the square climbing into the Shrivenham bus as if leaving him to his fate. "And how is your mother?" said Mr. Keeping.

"All right, thank you, sir," said Paul. "She manages pretty well."

"I hope she can manage without you for the week."

"Well, my aunt lives quite near us. It's not really a problem." He was relieved but a little disconcerted by these kind questions. "We're fairly used to it."

"Terrible thing," said Mr. Keeping, raising his hat to an approaching lady with a murmur and his unsettling smile, as if to say he remembered exactly the size of her overdraft.

They went up into the quieter reaches of Church Walk, with its fanlights and front railings and lace curtains. A week ago Paul had known almost no one in the town, and now he had been put into an odd grim privileged relation with hundreds of them, over the counter, through the little mahogany doorway of his "position." He was their servant and also an adjudicator, a strange young man granted intimate knowledge of at least one aspect of their lives, which was how much money they had, or didn't have, and how much they wanted. He spoke to them courteously, amid tacit understandings, muted embarrassments: the loan, the "arrangement." Now he glanced at Church Walk, grey veils of the cur-

tains, glints of polished tables, porcelain, clocks, with a sense of arrangements reaching rooms-deep, years-deep into the shadows. Mr. Keeping
said nothing else, and seemed satisfied by silence.

Opposite the church they turned into an unmade road, Glebe Lane,
with larger houses on one side and a view over a hedge into fields on the
other. Long brambly strands of dog-roses swayed in the breeze along the
top of the hedge. The lane had its own atmosphere, exclusive and a little
neglected. It was odd to find yourself here two minutes from the centre
of town. Grass and daisies grew patchily along the ridge of the road. Paul
glanced through gateways at squareish villas set back behind gravel
sweeps in broad gardens; between one or two of them humbler modern
houses had been awkwardly inserted—"The Orchard," "The Cottage."
"This is a private road, you see, Paul," said Mr. Keeping, reverting to his
ironical tone: "hence the countless potholes and unchecked vegetation. I
advise you never to bring a motor-car along here." Paul felt he could
pretty safely promise that. "Here we are . . . ," and they turned into the
driveway of the penultimate house: the lane was sloping down already
and narrowing, as if to lose itself in the approaching fields.

The house was another wide grey villa, with bay-windowed rooms
either side of the front door, and its Victorian name, "Carraveen," in
stucco above it. The front door was wide open, as though the house had
surrendered itself to the sunny day. A pale blue Morris Oxford stood in
the drive with its windows down, and in its shadow a fat little Jack Russell lay on the gravel alternately panting and thinking. Paul squatted
down to talk to the dog, which let him scratch it behind the ears but
never really got interested. Mr. Keeping had gone into the house, and it
seemed so unlikely that he had simply forgotten him that Paul stood and
waited with a consciously unassuming expression. He saw the drive had
an In and an Out, not marked as such, but the fact sank down in him to
some buried childhood idea of grandeur.

There was a thick flower-border, colourful but weedy and overgrown,
around the edge of the drive, and over the top of it he looked into the
garden beside the house, which stretched away through mysterious shadows of two or three large trees to a bright mown lawn that must run
across the back. The whole place, at this indefinable time of day—late
afternoon, late June, work over but hours of sunlight still ahead—made
a peculiar impression on him. The time, like the light, seemed somehow
viscous. He studied the name "Carraveen," a bit like caravan, a bit like
carrageen, the stuff his mother used to set a blancmange, but clearly

romantic too, Scottish perhaps, some now completely forgotten home or holiday place that someone had loved long ago. He felt seduced, and delicately stifled, by something he couldn't yet explain. Through the left-hand bay-window he could see a grand piano in what appeared to be a dining-room, though the table in the centre was covered with books. The church clock struck the quarter-hour, and the silence afterwards seemed discreetly enhanced. Really, all you could hear was the birds.

He heard a voice and looked again through the shadows to the bright back lawn, where he saw a woman in a wide straw hat with a red flower on the brim talking to someone out of view as she moved slowly towards the house. She was a largeish figure, in a shapeless blue dress, and carrying a large tapestry bag. Could this be the disdainful Mrs. Keeping, mother of Julian and John? Surely too old. Mr. Keeping's own mother perhaps, a friend or relative who was visiting. She stopped for a moment, as if stumped by what she'd just been told, and gazed at the ground, and then unseeingly along the side of the house, where she did in fact see Paul. She said something to the person—now Paul heard another woman's voice—and when she looked back he raised his head with a slight smile and then waved weakly, unsure if he wanted to announce himself or efface himself. There was another exchange; she nodded distantly, not exactly at Paul, and then strolled on out of view behind the house.

Paul went to the front door to call goodbye. He felt he'd been placed now as a low-level intruder, a peerer through other people's windows. A middle-aged woman with a wide pale face and black hair that was swept up and set in a stiff, broad helmet was coming towards him. "Oh, hello," he said, "I'm Paul Bryant—from the bank . . ."

She gave him a practical look. "Did you want to see my husband?"

"Well, actually I've just walked here with him," said Paul.

"Oh . . . ," she said, with an air of momentary concession. She had strongly drawn black eyebrows which made her look hard to please. "Was there something else?"

"Well, I don't know," said Paul; and feeling he shouldn't be put in the wrong, "He just left me here."

"Ah . . . !" said Mrs. Keeping, and half-turning she called out, "Leslie!" Mr. Keeping appeared at the end of the hall. "This young man doesn't know if he's been dismissed or not"—and she stared rather drolly at Paul, as if to say the joke was on everyone but her.

"Ah, yes," said Mr. Keeping. "This is Paul Bryant. He's just joined us from Wantage."

"From Wantage . . . !" said Mrs. Keeping, as if this were droller still.

"We all have to come from somewhere, you know," said Mr. Keeping.

Paul had grown up in the mild but untested belief that Wantage was a fine little town. "Well, sir, it was good enough for King Alfred," he said.

Mrs. Keeping half-allowed the protest, and the joke. "Mm, you're going back a bit," she said. Though something else had occurred to her. She set her head on one side and frowned at his shoulders, his posture. "How strong are you?" she said.

"Well, reasonably," said Paul, confused by the scrutiny. "Yes, I suppose . . ."

"Then I think I can use you. Come through," a tiny glow of cajolement now in her tone.

"Paul may have other plans, darling," said Mr. Keeping, but in easy surrender to his wife.

"I shan't need him for long."

"I've certainly got a couple of minutes," said Paul.

They went down the hall and into the room at the end. "I don't want my husband risking his back," said Mrs. Keeping. The sitting-room was densely furnished, large easy-chairs and sofas arm to arm on a thick gold carpet, nests of tables, standard-lamps, and a pair of surprising Victorian portraits, very large in the room, a woman in red and a man in black, looking out over the stereogram and the teak TV cabinet that flanked the fireplace. On top of the TV were several framed photos, in which Paul made out two boys, surely Julian and John, in yachting gear. They stepped out through the open french windows on to a wide patio. "This is Mr. Bryant," said Mrs. Keeping. "You can leave your briefcase there."

"Oh . . . right . . . ," said Paul, nodding at the two females who were sitting in deckchairs. They were identified as "My mother, Mrs. Jacobs"—this was the old lady in the straw hat, whom he'd already seen—and "Jenny Ralph . . . my niece, yes, my *half*-brother's daughter!" as if she'd just worked it out for the first time. Paul himself only pretended to do so, nodded again and murmured hello as he sidled past. Jenny Ralph was a frowning dark-haired girl a bit younger than he was, with a book and a notepad on her knee—he felt himself sidestepping some sulky challenge she seemed to throw out.

The problem was a stone trough on the far side of the lawn, which had somehow slipped or been pushed off one of the two squat blocks it sat on, earth strewn on the grass and a clump of disoriented wallflowers, orangey-black, leaning out and up. "I jolly well hope you can shift it," said Mrs. Keeping, with a return of her unjolly tone, almost as though Paul had pushed it over himself. "I don't want it falling on Roger," she said.

Paul stooped down and gave the trough a preliminary heave. The only effect of this was to rock it very slightly on the skewed axis of the other block. "You don't want to bring the whole thing down," said Mrs. Keeping. She stood several yards away, perhaps to be clear of any such accident.

"No . . . ," said Paul; and then, "It's quite heavy actually, isn't it."

"You'd stand a better chance with your jacket off."

Paul obeyed, and seeing that Mrs. Keeping showed no intention of taking the jacket from him hung it on a lichenous garden seat nearby. Without the jacket he felt even less able, his skinny frame more exposed. "Right!" he said, and laughed rather fatuously. His hostess, as he tried to think of her, gave him a provisional sort of smile. He worked his hands in under the near corner of the trough, where it lay on the grass, but after a couple of hefts in the shuddering manner of a caber-tosser he could only raise it an inch and let it down again heavily just where it had been. He shook his head, and glanced across at the figures on the patio thirty yards off. Mr. Keeping had joined his mother-in-law and niece, and they were gazing generally in his direction as they talked but, perhaps from politeness, not showing any detailed interest. He felt simultaneously important and completely insignificant.

"You're going to have to empty it, you know," said Mrs. Keeping, as though Paul had been actively refusing to do this.

He saw a certain stoical humour was going to be necessary—a smiling surrender of his time and plans. "Have you got a spade, please?" he said.

"You'll need something to put the soil on, of course. And do be careful with my wallflowers, won't you," she said, with a hint of graciousness now they'd come to such niceties. "Do you know, I'm going to get that girl involved."

"Oh, I think I can manage . . . ," said Paul.

"It will do her absolutely no harm," said Mrs. Keeping. "She's going up to Oxford next term and she does nothing but sit and read. Her parents are in Malaya, which is why she's stuck with us"—with a fairly clear suggestion she felt they were stuck with her. She moved off across the lawn, chin raised already, calling out.

Jenny Ralph took Paul off to the far side of the garden, and through a rustic arch into the sunless corner that sheltered the compost-heap and a cobweb-windowed shed. At first she treated him with the nervous snootiness of a child to an unknown servant. "You should find whatever you need in there," she said, watching him edge in among the clutter of the shed. The mower blocked the way, its bin caked at the rim with dung-like clots of dried grass. He reached over for a spade and kicked a loosely propped stack of canes that spilled and clattered ungraspably in every direction. There was a stifling smell of creosote and two-stroke fuel. "It's rather hell in there," said Jenny from outside. She had a notably posh voice, but casual where her aunt was crisp. The accent was more striking, more revealing, in a young person. She sounded mildly fed up with it, but with no real intention of abandoning it.

"No, it's fine," Paul called back. He covered the awkwardness he felt with a girl in a brisk bit of business, passing out the spade, some old plastic sacks—he must be five or six years older than her, but the advantage felt frail. Her poor skin and the oily shine of her dark curly hair were signs of the troubles he'd hardly emerged from himself. The fact that she wasn't especially pretty, though in some ways a relief, seemed also to put some subtly chivalrous pressure on him. He emerged, a trowel in his raised hand, just a little satirical.

"I don't suppose you want to be doing this for a minute," Jenny said, with a slyly commiserating smile. "I'm afraid they're always getting people involved."

"Oh, I don't mind," said Paul.

"You know it's a test. Aunt Corinna's always testing people, she can't help it. I've seen it masses of times. I don't just mean on the piano, either."

"Oh, have you?" said Paul, amused by her frankness, which seemed original and upper-class too. He looked out nervously as they came on to the lawn. Aunt Corinna was in the far corner, inspecting a sagging trellis and, quite possibly, lining up further tasks or tests for him. Beside her a large weeping beech-tree spread awkwardly but romantically, a table sheltered under its skirts.

"You know, she should have been a concert pianist. That's what everyone says, at least; I don't know if it's actually true. I mean anyone can say they should have been something. Anyway now she teaches the piano. She gets fantastic results, of course, though you can see the children are simply terrified of her. Julian says she's a sadist," she said, a touch self-consciously.

"Oh . . . !" said Paul, with a frown and disparaging laugh and then, from the mention of anything taboo, a sure-fire, searching blush. Sometimes they ebbed unnoticed, sometimes kept coming, self-compounding. He stooped and half-hid himself spreading the plastic sacks on the grass. "So Julian's her younger son," he said, still with his back to her.

"Oh, John wouldn't say that, he's far too square."

"So Julian isn't square . . . ?"

"What's Julian? Julian's sort of . . . elliptical." They both laughed. "Have I embarrassed you?" said Jenny.

"Not at all," said Paul, recovering. "The whole of your family's new to me, you see. I'm from Wantage."

"Oh, I see," said Jenny—as if this was in fact a bit of a drawback. "Well, they're rather a nightmare to sort out . . . the old lady you met over there is my grandmother."

"You mean Mrs. Jacobs?"

"Yes, she married again when my father was quite small. She's been married three times."

"Goodness."

"I know . . . She's about to be seventy, and we're going to have a huge enormous party."

Paul started gingerly unearthing the plants from the trough—they trembled under this further assault on their dignity. He stood them, in their trailing tangle of earth and roots, on the old Fisons sack. Soft clots of some kind of manure, loosely forked into the soil, were still slightly slimy. "I hope I'm doing this right," he said.

"Oh, I should think so," said Jenny, who like the others was watching but not exactly paying attention.

"So your aunt said you're going up to Oxford." He tried to disguise his envy, if that's what it was, in a genial avuncular tone.

"Did she. Yes, I am."

"What are you going to study?"

"I'm reading French at St. Anne's." She made it sound beautifully exclusive, the rich simplicity of the proper nouns. He had taken his mother all round Oxford, gaping at the colleges, as a kind of masochistic treat for both of them before he went off to Loughborough to train for the bank; but they hadn't bothered with the women's colleges. "Julian's applying to Univ this year."

"Mm, so you might be there together."

"Which would be rather fab," said Jenny.

When he'd dug out all the earth he rocked the trough with both hands and it moved more readily. Still, he laughed at the second looming failure. "Here goes," he said, and squatted down again. Over the lawn he saw Mrs. Keeping bearing down, with her keen sense of timing. With a violent force that in the moment itself seemed almost comical he heaved up the great stone object and with a stifled shout he lodged it on its other block, on the edge of it at least, but the job was done. "Aha!" said Mrs. Keeping, "we're getting there at last," and as he held it steady and smiled almost devotedly up at her he felt it turn under his hand; if he hadn't jumped back in the second it slipped and fell it would have crushed his foot—the block underneath had lurched over, and now the trough itself, massive and unmoving, lay sideways on the grass. "Oh god, are you all right?" said Jenny, gripping his arm with a welcome note of hysteria. Mrs. Keeping herself made a kind of panting noise. "Now we're jig-gered," she said. "Oh look," said Jenny, "your hand's bleeding." How it had happened he didn't know, and it was only now she said it that it began to hurt, a dull deep pang in the ball of the thumb and needle-like stinging of the grazed flesh. He supposed the pain had been held in check by the knowledge, so far his alone, that the trough had cracked in two.

Ten minutes later he found himself—clown, hero, victim, he couldn't tell which—in a low garden chair with a large gin-and-tonic in his right hand. His left hand was impressively bandaged, the fingers hard to move in their tight sheath. Mrs. Keeping, with a smirk of remorse, had bandaged it herself, the remorse turning steadily more aggressive as the long strip of stuff was bound tighter and tighter. Now the family glanced at his hand with concern and regret and a touch of self-satisfaction. Paul, tongue-tied, reached out to scratch Roger the Jack Russell, who had come round to the back of the house and was sitting, panting, in one of the broad purple cushions of aubrietia which spread over the flagstones. Mr. Keeping was in the drawing-room, fixing drinks for the others; he called out through the french windows, "Your usual, darling?"

"Absolutely!" said Mrs. Keeping, with a tight little laugh and shake of the head, as if to say she'd earned it. She perched on the wooden bench, and tore at the cellophane on a packet of Kensitas.

"And what about Daphne?"

"Gin and It!" shouted Mrs. Jacobs, as if taking part in a game.

"Large one?"

"Vast!"

Paul and Jenny laughed at this, but Mrs. Keeping gave a barely amused grunt. Mrs. Jacobs was sitting facing Paul, and between them was a low metal-framed table with a mosaic top. Over the rim of the table he had, if he wanted it, a direct view into the beige-coloured mysteries of her underwear. In her shapeless sundress and wide floppy hat she had an air of collapse, but her expression was friendly and alert, if ready, with age and perhaps a degree of deafness, to let one or two things slip past her. She wore large glasses with clear lower rims and tops like tawny eyebrows. When her drink was set in front of her on the mosaic table, she gave it a keen but illusionless smile, as if to say she knew what would become of it. Her smile showed surprisingly brown teeth—a smoker's smile that went with the smoky catch in her voice. "Well, cheers!"

"Cheerio . . ." Mr. Keeping sat down, still in his bank manager's suit, which made his own large g-and-t look slightly surreal.

"Cheers," said Jenny.

"What are you drinking, child?" said Mrs. Jacobs.

"Oh, cider, Granny . . ."

"I didn't know you liked cider."

"Well, I don't particularly, but I'm not allowed spirits yet, and one has to get drunk on something, doesn't one."

"I suppose one *does* . . . ," said Mrs. Jacobs, as if weighing up a completely new theory.

"Paul's just started at the bank this week, Daphne," said Mr. Keeping. "He's joined us from Wantage."

"Oh, I love Wantage," said Mrs. Jacobs; and after a moment, "In fact I once ran away to Wantage."

"Oh, Mother, really," said Mrs. Keeping.

"Just for a night or two, when your father was being especially beastly." Paul had never heard anyone speak like this, and couldn't say at first if it was real or theatrical, truly sophisticated or simply embarrassing. He glanced at Mrs. Keeping, who was smiling tightly and batting her eyelids with contained impatience. "I took you and Wilfie under my wing and drove like hell to Wantage. We stayed with Mark for a day or two. Mark Gibbons, you know," she said to Paul, "the marvellous painter. We stayed with him till the heat died down."

"Anyway," muttered Mrs. Keeping, drawing on her cigarette.

"We did, darling. You're probably too young to remember." She sounded slightly wounded, but used to being so.

"You didn't know how to drive, Mother," Mrs. Keeping went on brightly, but unable to stop herself.

"Of course I could drive . . ."

Mrs. Keeping blew out smoke with a hard humorous expression. "We needn't bore Mr. Bryant with our family nonsense," she said.

Paul, in the first nice giddiness of a very strong gin-and-tonic, smiled, ducked his head, showed he didn't mind the mild bewilderment at unexplained names and facts. As often with older people he was both bored and unaccountably involved at the same time. "No, no," he said, and grinned at Mr. Keeping, who surveyed the whole scene with quizzical composure. The evening had swollen to a shape entirely unimagined an hour before.

"You see, I think our family *is* jolly interesting," said Mrs. Jacobs. "I think you underestimate its interest. You should take more pride in it." She reached down beside her chair and brought up her bag, the large tapestry bag with wooden jaws that Paul had seen earlier. She started going through it.

Mrs. Keeping sighed and was more conciliatory. "Well, I am proud of one or two of them, Mother, you know that very well. Cecil's not exactly my cup of tea, but my father, for all his . . . oddities, has moments of genius."

"Well, he's certainly very clever," said Mrs. Jacobs, brows lightly furrowed over her bag. Paul had the impression of a small-scale chaos of papers, powder compacts, glasses cases, pills. She stopped for a moment and looked up at him, her hand in the bag marking her place. "Jenny's grandfather was a marvellous painter, too. You may have heard of him, Revel Ralph? No . . . he was, well, he was very different from Mark Gibbons. I suppose you'd say more decorative."

"I think Mark's a bit over the hill, Granny," said Jenny.

"Well, possibly, my dear, since he's almost as old as me." Paul knew how old this was, of course, but didn't know if it was a secret. "You probably think Revel's hopelessly old hat too."

Jenny made a moue and raised her eyebrows as if to say she could reach her own negative judgements. "No, I like Grandpa's things. I find them rather *piquant*, actually. Particularly the late ones." Again Paul was amused and impressed by the confidence of her views. She spoke with a small frown as if she was at Oxford already. He said,

"Is he . . . not still alive?"

"He was killed in the War," said Mrs. Keeping, with a quick shake of the head, stubbing out her cigarette.

"Well, he was extraordinarily brave," said Mrs. Jacobs. "He had two tanks blown up under him, and he was running to reach a third one when a shell got him." Her cigarette was in one hand, her lighter in the other, but she went on, before anyone else could, "He was a hero, actually. He got a posthumous gong, you know . . ."

"What became of that, Granny?" said Jenny in a more docile tone.

"Oh, I have it," said Mrs. Jacobs, quickly puffing, "of course I have it." Paul wasn't clear whom her indignation was aimed at. She gave him a look as if they were united against the others. "You know, people think he was flighty and gay and what-have-you, but in fact he could be quite fearless."

"Yes," said Paul, "I'm sure . . . ," slightly mesmerized by her and already an admirer of this man he had never heard of a minute ago.

AT THE GATE Paul turned and waved his bandaged hand but Jenny, who'd been told to see him out, had already vanished from the front step. Still, the small muscular contractions of pleasure and politeness remained almost unconsciously on his face as he swung and scuffed along the lane. He smiled at the view over the hedge, at the other front gardens, at the approaching Rover and then its driver, squinting in a rictus of his own against the evening sun, and making Paul feel again like an intruder, or now perhaps an absconder. The sun was still hot on his back. Among the trees the church clock chimed the quarter-hour once more—he checked his watch: 7:15 of course; the hour just gone had taken about twenty minutes, and some compensating sense made him wonder if it shouldn't in fact be 8:15. Here he was in Church Walk. Here was the marketplace. He had never really touched spirits before, and the second gin-and-tonic, as wildly drinkable as the first, had brought him to a state of grinning elation just touched by notes of worry and confusion. He'd been talking and telling himself not to talk, things he normally avoided saying, about his father's plane being shot down, and his mother's illness, and even his exploits at school, things that must have made him sound childish and simple. But no one had seemed to mind. Now he wondered if Mr. Keeping, who said very little, hadn't thought him a fool—it was actually rather creepy of him to get Paul drunk and just sit there watching, with his unnerving smile. He imagined some sarcasm about it, in the office tomorrow. On the other hand, he felt he'd been quite a success with old Daphne Jacobs, who seemed grateful for a new listener, and he'd laughed and winced sympathetically at her stories without necessarily following them. He often found, when he concentrated really hard on what someone was saying, that nothing much went in. The intoxication was partly that of being in the home of people who knew writers, in this case quite famous ones. He was barely aware of Dudley Valance, but he quoted whole verses of Cecil Valance's to the old lady, who smiled indulgently and then began to look slightly impatient. She had a soft uncanny light about her, somehow, from having been his lover—it turned out "Two Acres" had been written specifically for her. She told Paul about it quite frankly, over the second Gin and It (whatever It was), and Jenny had said, "I think Uncle Cecil's poems are awfully imperialist, Granny," which she pretended not to hear. In Vale Street he looked through the windows of the International Stores, closed and shadowy. Something shockingly sad caught at him—he was free, buoyant and squiffy, twenty-three years old, and he was entirely alone, with hours still before sunset and no one to share them with.

The way to his digs took him out of the town, past the closed and overgrown yards of the old goods station, past the new secondary modern school, hard and transparent in the evening sun. Then he crossed into Marlborough Gardens, which was a loop, or noose, with one exit on to the main road. From the pavement he saw people eating in kitchens, or finished already and out in the garden, mowing and watering. The houses were a strange economy that there wasn't a word for, built in threes, two semis with the central house in common, like segments of a terrace. Mrs. Marsh at least had an end house, with a view behind on to a field of barley. Her husband was a coach-driver, with odd hours, taking a party up to London, or sometimes away overnight on a run to Bournemouth or the Isle of Wight. Now she was in the front room with the curtains pulled against the sun and the box blaring—it was the start of *Z-Cars*. She had a pleasant way of not bothering her lodger—she turned her head and nodded; in the kitchen there was a ham salad for him under a cloth, and a redirected letter with a note saying "This came for you, Mrs. Marsh." Paul went upstairs two at a time, used the bathroom, which was where he felt most a stranger, among the couple's shaving-soap and flannels, Mrs. Marsh's other things in the cabinet. The bathroom had a frosted glass panel in the door, which showed if it was occupied at night, and made going to the lavatory especially seem audible and almost visible and even vaguely culpable. Paul's designated bath nights were Tuesday and Thursday: so tonight! Saturdays the bank worked through till one, then he would be off on the bus to Wantage, and his first week of work here would be over.

After his supper he went back upstairs and got down his diary from the top of the wardrobe. He had hardly made his mark on the room—his slippers and dressing-gown, a few books he'd stuffed into his bag. He had the new Angus Wilson out of the library, and was getting through it in his own way, with a restless eye running ahead for the appearances of Marcus, the queer son, whose antics he pondered as if for portents or advice. He didn't want to read this at home and risk his mother asking questions. Also the latest Penguin Modern Poets, *The Mersey Sound*, which he didn't really think was poetry at all; and *Poems of To-day*, in fact published over fifty years ago, and full of things that he loved and knew by heart, such as Drinkwater's "Moonlit Apples" and Valance's "Soldiers Dreaming." The room had a hard square armchair in prickly moquette and up against the window a ladies' dressing-table with three mirrors and a stool, which was where Paul sat each night to do his writing. Whenever he looked up he saw himself, the Bryant nose in triumphant triplicate, his two profiles playing hide and seek with each other. He'd been keeping his diary since he left school, a top-secret record, and the volumes themselves, black quarto notebooks, were growing harder to hide as they amassed. At home he had a box under the bed in which old school projects and browning newsprint concealed a lower layer of private things, frail mementoes of boys at school, three issues of *Manifique!*, with muscle-men in posing pouches, sometimes clearly drawn on afterwards, and then the diaries themselves, in which Paul let himself go in a way that these publications weren't allowed to.

Now he leant forward, like a schoolboy shielding his work, and wrote: "June 29th 1967: hot and sunny all day." As he wrote he pressed very hard with his biro into the page, so that the paper itself seemed to spread and rise in a curl at the margins. When closed, the book showed exactly how much of it had been used up. The written pages, their edges crinkly and darkened, were a pleasing proof of industry, the rest of the book, clean, trim and dense, a pleasing challenge. This week had been rich in material, and he had summed up the girls at work and given Geoff Viner a franker appraisal than was possible in the bank itself. Now he had his chat with Geoff in the toilets to write up, and the whole unexpected adventure at "Carraveen." "It turns out Mrs. J was married to Dudley Valance, C's brother. But she also had big affair with Cecil V before WWI, said he was her first love, he was madly attractive but bad with women. I said what did she mean. She said, 'He didn't really understand women, you know, but he was completely irresistible to them. Of course he was only 25 when he was killed.'" At the foot of the page, where the edge of his writing hand had rested, the greasy paper resisted the ink, and he had to go over some of the words twice: "completely irresistible," he wrote again, "only 25"—the effect bold and clumsy, like the writing of someone who was still drunk or slightly mad.

2

PETER ROWE CAME OUT of his room on the top floor, crossed the landing, and looked over the banister into the great square stairwell. Below him he could hear and then for a moment see a small boy hurrying downwards, saw a raised arm struggling into a jacket. "Don't run!" Peter shouted, with such abrupt and godlike effect that the boy looked up in horror, lost his footing, and slid down bump bump bump on the hard oak treads into the hall. "Now you know why," Peter said, more quietly, and went back into his room.

He had the first period free, then it was the Fifth Form for singing. He filled his kettle at the basin, vaguely rinsed a mug for his Nescafé: the granules started melting and fizzing on the wet bottom. Then he lit himself a cigarette, first of the day, and squinting in the smoke tugged his bed up fairly straight and covered its irregularities with his rug. Along the corridor, he knew, Matron would be going from dorm to dorm, head down, breathing through her mouth. Wherever she found a bed improperly made, its corners loose, its top sheet less than taut, she stooped and tossed it, like a bull, made a total mess of it, and wrote the offending boy's name on a card. The card was then pinned on the board by the staff-room, and in break the delinquents would have to pant upstairs and set about making the whole thing again from scratch, square and smooth and tight as a strait-jacket. Peter felt a twinge of guilty relief at his exemption from this regime.

He started on his weekly letter to his parents, a practice he did keep up as strictly as the boys. "Dearest Mum and Dad," he wrote, "What a beautiful week it has been. I'm glad, because it's the semi-final of the garden competition on Sunday. The HM is to be the judge, and as he knows nothing at all about gardens it's hard to know what he'll be looking for, colour or 'concept.' The boy Dupont whom I've told you about has built a rockery with a waterfall, but the HM, who has very plain tastes, may find this too 'fiddly.' Besides that, things are building up nicely to Open Day. Colonel Sprague is very involved with organizing it all. He is true to type and rather a monster. I call him the Infolonel Colonel." Peter smoked for a bit, and drank his coffee. He thought he probably couldn't divert his parents with the Headmaster's latest obsession, the spread of supposedly sexy books among the higher forms. It was on the agenda for next week's staff-meeting. Already this term the HM had confiscated *Peyton Place* and *The Carpetbaggers,* both on hearsay rather than any knowledge of their contents, which was doubtless why the boys themselves slogged through them. *Dr. No,* found in Walters's tuck-box, had been passed to Peter, as being possibly "more broad-minded," for a judgement. He'd read it last night at a sitting and found three sentences in it unexpectedly arousing; of course he'd seen the film, which was much more exciting: on the page the plot looked slight and awkward, the whole thing explained by the villain himself in an enormous monologue. He noted a sort of tight-lipped sadism in the accounts of James Bond's body and the injuries inflicted on it, but as in a movie the wounds all healed by the scene after next. The boys, of course, in the first derangement of puberty, could be "turned on" by just about anything. Peter knew he had been so himself, and so saw the present purge as inherently futile. He stubbed out his cigarette, and told his parents instead about the First XI match against Beasleys.

At 9:35, with the recurrent momentary dread and resolve that come with living by a timetable, Peter opened his door again and went out on to the landing. In the glance he gave back into his room he saw it as a stranger might, as an appalling mess. He went down one circuit of the main staircase, and set off along the broad first-floor corridor. The classrooms at Corley Court occupied six rooms on the ground floor, but the room with the piano was isolated, with the sick-bay, in the rambling far end of the floor above. Boys with temperatures or infectious diseases were harassed through the wall by ragged bursts of folksong or the torturous practice of scales. He passed the Headmaster's sitting-room, which must once have been a principal bedroom of the house: its high Gothic oriel looked out down the axis of the formal gardens, which now survived only in photographs but had once been a dazzling floral maze. A melancholy fishpond at the centre of the lawn was all that was left.

Peter had got the Corley job in the middle of the year, after the clouded departure of a man called Holdsworth, and took to the house from the start, in part out of natural sympathy for something so widely abused. "A Victorian monstrosity" was the smug routine phrase. He had heard a boy in the First Form opine that Corley Court was "a Victorian monstrosity, and one of the very worst," with just the same humourless laugh the boy's father must have used when describing the place. In fact, the house was perfect for a boarding-school—secluded, labyrinthine, faintly menacing, with its own tree-lined park now mown and marked out in pitches. No one, it was felt, could want to live in such a place, but as an institution of learning it was pretty much ideal. Peter had started to research its history. Last year he had signed a petition to save St. Pancras Station, and at Corley too he loved the polychrome brick and the fierce Gothic detail which were such an amusing challenge to more gracious notions of the English country house—though the rooms inside, which had been altered between the wars, were disappointingly bright and inoffensive. Only the chapel, the library and the great oak staircase, with its shield-bearing wyverns on the newels, had completely escaped the hygienic clean-up of the 1920s. The library was useful as it was, and the chapel, a real High Victorian gem, was also the site of the school's strangest feature, the white marble tomb of the poet Cecil Valance.

Peter went into the sun-baked music-room and flung open the window; there was a pleasant sally of cool morning air over the sill. With a few kicks and long-armed tweaks he straightened the two rows of wooden chairs on the brown linoleum. The room's single adornment, above the blocked-off fireplace, was an oleograph of Brahms, "Presented by his Family in Memory of N. E. Harding 1938–53"; Peter sometimes tried to imagine the family deciding on this particular gift.

He set the Acorn Songbook on the stand of the upright piano and went quickly through today's songs. Most of the boys couldn't read music, so it was a matter of drumming and coaxing the tune into them by remorseless repetition. They paid no more attention to the words than they did with hymns. The words were a given: high-flown, old-fashioned, accepted with a childish mixture of respect and complete indifference. Now the bell rang, the whole school held its breath, and then let go in a babble and clatter that rose dimly upstairs from the floor below. Again the momentary and instantly mastered sense of dread. He started playing "Für Elise," waiting for the noise beyond to particularize in the slap of sandals and knock at the door. He always let them catch him in mid-performance, and when he'd shouted "Come in!" he carried on playing, imposing a nice uncertainty on the class as to whether or not they could talk.

The piano was at right angles to the rows of boys, so he glanced at them along his left shoulder as he played. One day he meant to stun them with the Liszt Sonata, but for now he kept prudently to this simple piece, which some of the boys themselves played with Mrs. Keeping; he was nearer their level than he intended to admit. "Good morning," he murmured, concentrating rather hard on the second section; one or two replied. The different forms had quite distinct atmospheres. He liked the Fifth Form, for their humour and ingenuity, and because it was clear that they liked him; sometimes the humour had to be kept in check. He stood up and looked at them, his frown as he went along the rows stirring odd gleams and doubts in their attentive faces. He was firm in suppressing any hint of favouritism, though he saw the flame of it rise expectantly in Dupont and Milsom 1.

"Well, my little song-birds," said Peter, "I hope you're all in the mood to make a din."

"Yes, sir," came a dutiful chorus.

"I asked you a question," said Peter.

"Yes, sir!" came a lustier sound, breaking into giggles. Peter gazed round the room in deep abstraction, at last noticing the boys and raising his eyebrows in mild anxiety:

"I'm sorry . . . did you say something?"

"YES! SIR!" they shouted, the laughter at this awful old gag contained by an undeniable excitement. The sense of being free to give a wildly corny performance was one of the pleasures of teaching in a prepschool. A great innocence was there to be tapped, even in the surlier and spottier boys, the nocturnal students of *Peyton Place*. Peter glanced past them, through the open window, at the wide hazy vista of fields and woods. It would be horribly shaming if Chris or Charlie or any of his London friends saw him carrying on like this, but the fact was the boys loved it.

"Let's have that in scales," he said, going over and striking the A below middle C, and in his large unembarrassed baritone, crescendo: "Yes! Yes! Yes! Yes! Yes! Yes! Yes! *Sir!*" So the boys sang it, climbing inexorably through the keys, in rapid repeated climaxes of assent that soon became mere yapping syllables.

Peter started them off with "The Saucy *Arethusa*," "page thirty-seven as you must surely know by now . . . ," and as they were still finding the place he launched out with enormous relish on the first verse: "Come all ye jolly sailors bold, Whose hearts are cast in honour's mould, While

English glory I unfold"—head shaking with the jolliness and boldness, chin tucked in for the gravelly descent on "English glory," the risk of comedy brazened out: "Hurrah for the *Arethusa*!" He felt he could sing to them all day. A hand was up: the feeble Peebles, as Colonel Sprague called him, had no book. "Well, share with Ackerley, use your nous," and then they were off. There was something Peter was expecting to happen, and he thought he would listen out for it and wait. For the moment he corrected nothing, the thing was to get them moving: "Not a sheet or a tack or a brace did she slack . . ." They had sung the song every week this term and could belt it out with their strange uncaring glee; it was he himself, frowning over the piano, who sometimes forgot where they were and joined in furiously with the wrong words. "And now we've driven the foe ashore, / Never to fight with Britons more"—a reckless boast, overtaken in a moment by an immense bass crack in the air above the roof of the house, far away and right on top of them, so that the room shook and the piano itself gave out a faint jangling thrum. They broke off raggedly, then rushed to the window, but the plane was so far beyond them and moving so fast that they saw nothing. The great scientific fact seemed all the more eloquent and exemplary for that. On the back-drive below, the Headmaster too was standing and gazing at the sky over the tree-tops, his upper lip raised rodent-like as he squinted into the blue. "Come on, back to your places," said Peter carryingly, before the HM himself could do so; but in fact in the presence, or rather the immediate absence, of this sublime phenomenon, a minute's mutual wonder seemed to be allowed.

"Did you see it, sir?" Brookings called down. But the Headmaster shook his head, with a shifty smile, almost as if he'd missed it with his gun. Peter leant out above the three boys who were jammed in the open casement. Though he thought the HM was a fool, he didn't want to be shown up by him, and the HM found fault in the most unaccountable things. He picked up fag-ends, he brooded ingeniously on things he had misheard. Peter was a young master, far closer in age to the boys than the HM was to him. There was sometimes an imputation in the older man's tone that Peter himself must be kept in check. Now he said,

"They'd let me know this might happen," something slightly absurd in half-shouting this at a first-floor window.

"Had they, sir?"

"Oh, yes: I'm in touch with the Commander at the Base. He keeps me in the picture."

"What was it, sir?" said Brookings.

The Headmaster peered again at the sky, with a genially proprietary air. "Well, back to your lessons, come on!" and nodding uncertainly at Peter he trudged on down the drive towards the garages.

"Anyone know what it was?" said Peter, as they took their places again; with their Airfix and their Biggles and their War Picture Libraries they lived a constant battle in the air.

"Was it a Hustler, sir?" said Sloane.

"Why would a Hustler make that noise?" said Peter, pretty sure he knew, but taking a donnish tone.

"Sonic boom, sir!" said several of the boys.

"So when we speak of a Hustler, what do we mean?" said Peter.

"It's a B-58 bomber, sir," said Sloane, and someone else made a stupid booming noise. "They can do Mach 2, and of course they carry a nuclear weapon, sir."

"I hope they don't bomb us, sir," said Peebles, with that utter feebleness that only provoked the others.

"I don't think we'd know much about it, if they did," said Peter.

"The Americans don't just go round bombing people, you idiot," said Milsom 1, to Peebles, not to Peter, though there was a slight sense of things getting out of hand.

"Right, where were we?" said Peter, and with a sudden intense boredom, which seemed the natural counterpart of his desire to be thorough and exciting: "OK, I've had enough of the ruddy *Arethusa,* let's do something else. 'Cherry Ripe,' perhaps?"

"Oh, no, sir . . . !" There were sickened protests.

"Fine, fine . . . *Fine,* what about 'Hearts of Oak.' "

"Mm, all right, sir," said Sloane, who was still exhilarated by the magic eruption of the sonic boom, and seemed to have promoted himself to class leader, or bargainer.

" 'Hearts of Oak' is a fine old song," said Peter. "Come, cheer up, my lads, 'tis to glory we steer!" And a minute later he had them all at it.

> *Hearts of oak are our ships, jolly tars are our men,*
> *We always are ready—Steady, boys, steady!*

and he joined them to stiffen up the sinew: "We'll fight and we'll conquer again and again!" There was undoubtedly something wrong, but he got them into the next verse and shouting "Keep going!" he left the piano and walked along just in front of the front row and then behind the back row, pausing and leaning in as if to share a confidence with each child. There was a standard place for giggles in this song, as reliable as some old music-hall gag, and Peter hardened his face against it:

> But should their flat bottoms in darkness get o'er
> Still Britons they'll find to receive them on shore.

"Yes, thank you very much, Prowse 2," said Peter. "Sing on, sing on!" As a master, one could make the boys laugh, but one couldn't be made to laugh by them—in class it meant a notable loss of authority, and out of class it was oddly too intimate. Even so, the sheer idiocy of their jokes could be hard to resist.

"Aha!" he said, "yes, I thought as much." He sounded much more bad-tempered than he really meant. Poor Dupont coloured up and dried up too, but Peter had got the proof he needed. The singing trailed off at the promise of an incident, less exciting than a sonic boom but with a human interest that had them all peering round in happy relief that someone else was in trouble. It had happened before—in the first week of term red-headed Macpherson had been sent out smirking and shrugging into his new freedom. "Just give me the first verse," said Peter. Dupont stared at him with a mixture of anxiety and indignation he hadn't seen before; cleared his throat; and then started singing, very quietly, "Come, cheer up, my lads . . ." in a voice that wouldn't obey him. There were sniggers from along the row, and Peter supported him, nodding firmly, holding his eye—" 'Tis to *glory* we *steer!* / To *add* something *more* to this *wonderful year* . . ."—Dupont burning red and looking away as the tune cracked and lurched out of control—"Ah well— I'm sorry," said Peter, and pursed his lips in friendly regret. In the front row Morgan-Williams uttered a croaky warble. Peter ignored the laughter that followed. "It will happen to you too," he said. "We'll all enjoy laughing at you then." He went back to the piano. But he sensed something more was in the air. When he sat down, and turned to look at them, Dupont was still hovering at the end of the row. Peter smiled at him, to say goodbye, a little flash of favouritism after all—in a way it was cause for congratulation, like being confirmed. He would soon settle down, in the Sixth Form next term, long trousers, a teenage voice, he could hear him already. Milsom 1 was looking with furrowed interest at his friend. Sloane said, "You're meant to go, Dupe." Dupont's mortification made Peter himself feel uncomfortable. This clever and unusual child felt for the first time like a figure of fun, perhaps, or of superstition, sent out awkwardly into the future on the other boys' behalf. "You can go and read in the library, if you like," said Peter, which properly was a Sixth Form privilege. Still, there was a crackle of mockery as Dupont went smiling through his blushes to the door.

3

PAUL LEANT FORWARD, raised the brass bolt, and opened the little doors of his position. In less than a minute the bank itself would open; through the frosted glass in the lower half of the windows the grey shapes of three or four waiting customers could be seen outside, blurred and overlapping. But for now the Public Space was deserted, its dark linoleum unscuffed, the ashtrays sparkling, the ink-wells full, *The Times* and the *Financial Times* untouched on the table. There was something beautiful in the sheer old-fashioned dullness of the place. On the notice-board above the table were advertisements for 5% Defence Bonds and Premium Savings Bonds, and under a bold sans-serif heading a state-ment on **BANK RAIDS** which lent the Public Space its one note of possible excitement.

Already he and Geoff had emptied the Night Deposit Safe, and spent a friendly ten minutes checking the contents of the locked leather wal-lets. As the bank closed at three, most shopkeepers dropped off their tak-ings later, in the swivelling chute of the safe. Counting and entering the paid-in cash and cheques was the first task of the day. Geoff counted money with eye-puzzling speed, the rubber thimble on his right fore-finger pulsing over the notes. Paul was lightly distracted by the sense of competition, as well as by Geoff's sleepy but determined morning pres-ence, hair still damp, aftershave new and sharp. He sighed and started on a batch again. Mrs. Marsh had reduced his military bandage to a neat pad at the base of his thumb, but he still felt clumsy and went cautiously. Ten-shilling notes were the dirtiest and most torn, and had sometimes to be set aside. Ten-pound notes he always took more slowly, out of respect. Susie had asked him about his bandage, and the story of last night had come out and given him a first enjoyable taste of being a character, with comical adventures. He heard her say, "Did you hear what happened to young Paul?"

There were three positions on the counter—Jack nearest the door from the street, Geoff in the centre, and Paul waiting to be discovered at the far end, closest to the Manager's office. Geoff was informally keeping an eye on Paul, and Paul even more informally, in fact quite furtively, was keeping an eye on Geoff. It was absurd to have a thing about Geoff, but there he was all day long, on view, in his tight-fitting suit and zip-up ankle-boots with built-up heels hooked over the bar of his stool. Mr. Keeping made sardonic allusions to Geoff's boots, but didn't actually ban them. Among the girls, too, at their desks and typewriters behind them, Geoff's looks were a bit of a joke, one of those jokes that of course allowed them to be talked about. Paul felt no such freedom. When they ribbed Geoff about Sandra, the girl he was seeing from the National Provincial, it was Paul who blushed and felt his pulse quicken at the curiosity in the air. He imagined being kissed by Geoff, suddenly but inevitably, in the staff-room Gents, and then Geoff—"Opening!" said Hannah, as the front door was unlocked, and with a flutter of nerves Paul sat back on his stool and squared his hands on the counter in front of him.

His first customer was a farmer paying in cheques and drawing a large cash sum for his men's wages—Fridays were heavily to do with paying wages and banking the week's takings, alarming queues building up while he tallied fifty or sixty cheques. Hundreds of pounds could pass through his window at a time. He felt the farmer, George Hethersedge, was treating him as a bit of a fool for never having seen him before. He seemed to suggest he would look back on this moment of ignorance with rueful embarrassment. Paul had a rough sense, as he counted the notes and totted up the cheques on his adding-machine, that the name Hethersedge had implications, a weight and a place in the light and shade of local opinion. Like many of these quick-set local names, it also had a terrifying overdraft attached to it. He saw how strange it was, in normal social terms, for him to know this. This slight social awkwardness seemed to lie at the heart of their professional relations.

Quite hidden by Mr. Hethersedge was a little old lady, Miss M. A. Lane, whose hand trembled and who seemed distraught by the business of cashing a cheque for £2. She peeped at Paul through the scrap of coarse veil on the front of her hat. He liked old people, and enjoyed her anxious respect and even slight fear of him as a quick-witted official.

Then there was Tommy Hobday, the chemist from next door, who was in and out all the time and knew his name; and then the little shock of contact and novelty began to dull, and his own fear, of error or exposure, subsided slowly into the routine of a very busy day. Inside the front door was a shallow lobby with a further glass door that had a tightly sprung closer—the snap and swallow of the closer announced the incessant unrhythmical coming and going of the customers.

Just before lunch Paul heard a voice in the Public Space, and sensed a small commotion with it—now Miss Cobb had appeared and was speaking in a strange delighted tone like someone at a party: then the voice again, sharply gracious, Mrs. Keeping, of course, "No, no, no, *absolutely*," pretending not to demand attention, people glancing round. Paul's customer went, leaving him with a clear view of her, in a pale blue frock with a white handbag and looking quite like someone at a party herself. She had picked up the *Financial Times* and was scanning the headlines, her hard black eyebrows raised. Paul watched her nervously, from his ambiguous position, both invisible and on show. She looked up over the page, ran her eye abstractedly across the room, but gave no sign at all of seeing him. He let the smile fade from his face as if preoccupied by something else, his heart quickening for a minute in a muddle of protest and shame. When the lobby door opened she turned slightly and nodded. In a moment Paul saw Mrs. Jacobs, with her heavy tread and humorous questing look, come into view, peer across at him and then approach—"Now then . . ."—dumping her tapestry bag on the counter between them.

"Good morning, madam," Paul said almost humorously, unsure if he should use her name.

"Good morning," said Mrs. Jacobs, genial, rummaging, perhaps herself unaware who he was. Out on to the counter came glasses case, headscarf, twenty Peter Stuyvesants, a paper bag from Hobday's with the rattle of tablets, an orange paperback upside-down, a novel . . . Paul couldn't quite see . . . at last a cheque-book. Then the changing of the glasses, the puzzled reach for the pen. She wrote her cheque in a raffish, off-hand way, keeping up a vague air of absurdity, as if money were an amusing mystery to her. Paul smiled patiently back, scanned and stamped the cheque, which was for £25, and asked her how she would like it. It was only then, with a brief stare, that she took in who he was. "Oh, you're you!" she said, in a jolly tone but none the less placing him, as the funny little man of the night before, whose name she had probably forgotten. Paul smiled as he leant over the cash drawer by his left knee, freed a bundle of clean green oners from its paper wrapper. Rather lovely, it seemed to him, the fine mechanical sameness of the Queen's face under his counting fingers. He counted them out again for her, at a pace she could follow—"There you are, Mrs. Jacobs."

"And your hand, yes," she said, confirming it was him. Paul raised it to show the dressing, and wiggled his fingers to show it was working.

"Good for you," said Mrs. Jacobs, finding her purse, and cramming the notes into it—again as if she found money somewhat unmanageable. "It's our young man," she murmured to her daughter as she rejoined her; but she herself was now murmuring to Mr. Keeping, who had emerged from his office, with his trilby in his hand and his raincoat over his arm, despite the cloudless splendour of the sky as seen through the clear upper halves of the bank windows. Paul supposed they were going to walk him home.

TODAY HE HAD A LATE LUNCH-BREAK, which he preferred—he had the staff-room to himself and read his Angus Wilson over his sandwich without anyone asking questions; and when he got back, it was only an hour to closing time. In the afternoons he felt more confined, on his high stool, swivelling fractionally between the deep cash drawer by his left knee and the wooden bowls of pins, paper-clips and rubber-bands on the counter to the right. Where he'd felt purposeful and efficient in the morning he now felt stiff and disenchanted. The cash drawer boxed him in. His knees were raised, the balls of his feet taut against the metal foot-rest, his thighs spread as he leant forwards; he jiggled his knees for relief from the numbness in his upper thighs and buttocks. The low curved back to the stool nodded forward if it wasn't leant on; though it turned upwards nicely when he pressed and arched against it. He got a faint tingling, an odd compound of numbness and arousal, in the hidden zone between the legs. Queues formed in front of him, with their shuffle of private faces—vacant, amiable, accusing, resigned—glimpsed only by him, and half the time he had a half-erection, seen by no one, caused by no one, under the counter.

Just before closing he came back to his seat from the chief clerk's desk, and found that he had no customers—he glanced out, saw Heather cross the Public Space to stand by the door, and sensed already the little shift of perspective that would come about when she locked it shut, and the team were left alone again. Perhaps it was just a new boy's self-consciousness, but he felt a mood of solidarity settled on the staff when the public had gone. They barely showed it, of course—"No, you're *just* in time!" said Heather, with a grudging laugh, and Paul saw a large young man scoot in past her, smiling keenly, though in fact it was 3:28, he was within his rights, and the smile expressed confidence more than apology. He was feeling in his breast pocket, his smile now slightly mischievous as he homed in on Geoff's position, where a customer was already waiting. Paul had an impression of quirky liveliness and scruffiness, such as you didn't see much in a town like this, something artistic and a little preoccupied, more like a person from London or it could be Oxford, only fifteen miles away. He could well be an Oxford type, with his pale linen jacket curling at the lapels and his blue knitted tie. A pen had made a red ink stain, not far from his heart. His dark curly hair half-covered his ears, there was something witty and attractive in his expression, though he wasn't exactly handsome. Paul leant forward and for a few expanded, trance-like seconds watched him gazing at Geoff, over the shoulder of the man in front of him. His head was on one side, with the vacantly calculating frown of impatience, the tip of his tongue on his lower lip; and then, just for a moment, his face stiffened, his eyes widened as if to fill themselves with Geoff, and then narrowed into a slow blink of amused indulgence; and of course Paul knew, and his heart thumped with feelings he couldn't disentangle, of curiosity, envy and alarm. "Can I help you?" he said, and his own voice sounded loud and almost mocking.

The man looked at him without moving his head, and then with a widening smile, as if he knew he'd been caught out. He came over. "Hello," he said, "you're new!"

"Yes, I'm the new boy," said Paul, pleasantly, and feeling a bit silly.

The man looked at him appreciatively as he felt in his breast pocket. "Well, me too," he said, his voice quick and deep, with a curl of humour in it.

"Oh, yes?" said Paul, wary of being too familiar, but laughing a little.

"Well, new master, but it's much the same. Now I've got to pay this in for the Colonel." He had a paying-in book, the slip all made out, and a cheque for £94: *Corley Court School, General Account.* Paul saw, in the moment he stamped it, an image of the school, teeming and condensed, wealthy and famous, he was sure, though he had never heard of it.

"Where is it, actually?" he said.

"What, Corley?"—the man said the word as one might London, perhaps, or Dijon, with cultured certainty and polite surprise. "It's out on the Oxford road, about three miles away. It's a prep-a-ra-turry school," he said, in a Noël Coward voice.

"The bank is about to close, ladies and gentlemen!" announced Heather.

"Look, you'd better give me some money," said the man. "Don't they have drinking-up time in here?"

"Afraid not," said Paul, with a nod and a smile, in the way one always conceded a customer might have a point; but with some further concession of this one's charm. The man looked at him acutely for a moment before getting out his pen; he had one of those thick biros with four different colours, red, green, black and blue. He wrote a cheque for £5, in neat but imaginative writing, having chosen the green ink. His name was P. D. Rowe. Peter Rowe in the signature.

"End of the month," he said, "we're paid today."

"How would you like it?"

"Oh, god . . . four pound notes and a pound in silver. Yes," said Peter Rowe, as he watched, nodding his head, "time to go *really wild* this weekend."

Paul tittered without looking at him, and then said, "Where can you go wild round here, I wonder?" very quietly, as he really didn't want Susie to hear him.

"Hmm, yes, I take your point," said Peter Rowe. Paul felt oddly conscious of at last having a personal conversation, as the other cashiers did with the customers they knew, and though he didn't know Peter Rowe at all, he was very interested in the answer. "I always think there must be something going on, don't you?" He received the money and slid the coins into a D-shaped leather purse he had. "Though in a little place like this, it may take some finding." He smiled, with a flicker of eyebrows.

Paul heard himself saying, "Well, let me know!" Whatever this going wild entailed had only the vaguest form in his head, and his excitement was mixed with a feeling he was out of his depth.

"Okay, I will," said Peter Rowe. As he crossed the Public Space he glanced in at Geoff again with another little flicker of comic surmise, which Paul felt in a horrified rush of understanding was meant as a sign to him too, and then looked back with a flash of a grin as he went out through the door.

On the way home Paul thought about Peter Rowe and wondered if he'd see him again straight away in the town. But most of the shops were shut and the pubs not yet open and a mood of premature vacancy had settled on the sun-raked length of Vale Street. He felt weary but restless, shut out from the normal play of a Friday night. All down the street, house-doors were protected by striped awnings, or stood open behind bead curtains to let in the air. He caught radio talk, music, a man raising his voice as he went into another room. The drapers and outfitters had covered their shop-windows with cellophane to keep the goods from bleaching in the sun. It was the sugary gold of the cellophane on a bottle of Lucozade, and changed all the clothes inside into unappealing greens and greys. On the tiny stage of Mews' window a woman stepped forward, through the amber light, in a cotton frock, her blank face and pointed fingers raised in genteel animation; while a man stood dependably, in flannels and a cravat, with an endlessly patient smile. They had been like that all week, flies buzzing and dying at their feet, and would surely remain there till the season changed, when one day the peg-board screen behind would shift, and a living arm come groping through. Paul went on, glancing unhappily at his strolling reflection. In the chemists' window there were those enormous tear-shaped bottles of murky liquid, blue, green or yellow, which must have some ancient symbolic function. Dim sediment gathered in them. He wondered what happened at a wild weekend—he saw Peter dancing to "Twist and Shout" with a roomful of friends from Oxford. Perhaps he was going to Oxford for the party; a preparatory school was hardly the place for a rave-up. He didn't fancy Peter, he felt slightly threatened by him, and saw their friendship stirring suspicions in the bank. Already he seemed to be a week or two ahead.

After supper he went up to write his diary, but felt oddly reluctant to describe his own mood. He lay on the bed, staring. He wrote, "Mrs. Keeping came into the bank before lunch, but she totally ignored me, it was quite emb. Mr. K v cool too, and only said he hoped my hand was all right. Also Mrs. Jacobs took ages to realize who I was, though then she was reasonably friendly. She drew out £25. I don't think she could remember my name, she referred to me as 'our young man.' " Something about the clashing curtains and the carpet, both nice enough in themselves, made Paul feel acutely lonely, the three mirrors of the dressing-table blocking the evening sun. The bulb in the ceiling light glowed in weak competition with it. There was the matching suite, dressing-table, wardrobe, bed with quilted headboard, and then nothing that went with anything else. They had the air of things not wanted elsewhere in the house, the scratchy armchair, the wrought-iron lamp, the souvenir ash-trays, the brown wool rug made by Mr. Marsh himself, at what must have been a low moment. Paul started on a sentence about Peter Rowe coming into the bank, but a superstitious impulse made him cross it out after three or four words. He blocked out the words with his biro till the place shone.

He put the diary away and felt on the top of the wardrobe for the copy of *Films and Filming* that he'd hidden there. There was a still on the cover from the new film *Privilege,* starring Jean Shrimpton and Paul Jones. They seemed to be in bed together. Jean Shrimpton's pale profile hovered over Paul Jones, whose eyes were closed, and his lips, and teeth, slightly parted. At first Paul had thought she must be watching him sleep, too entranced by his pretty face to want to wake him. Then he'd guessed, with a strange prickly rush, that they must be making love, and that the pop-star's open mouth wasn't snoring but gasping in surrender. Though actually you couldn't be sure. There was a suggestion of his naked shoulder and chest, and thus of other things you might get to see if you went to the film. It wouldn't come here, of course, he'd have to go into Swindon or Oxford on the bus. In the angle between the two faces there was a disconcerting limb, perhaps Jean's right arm crooked back insect-like as she crouched over him, or maybe Paul Jones's own left elbow, oddly twisted. He saw for the first time it could be his left wrist, much closer, the hand hidden in Jean's hair. In the grey and white close-up Paul Jones's puppyish neck looked fleshy and pitted. Also he had no ear-lobes, a weird thing you couldn't entirely overlook once you'd noticed it. Paul Bryant wasn't sure about Paul Jones. His mother had fan-cied him quite openly once, on *Top of the Pops,* and you couldn't very eas-ily share a fantasy with your mother. His own desire, in its way very modest, was simply to kiss Paul Jones.

He sat propped up on the bed to look through the small ads for the third or fourth time. It was like a mild hallucination, or one of those drawings in the paper containing ten hidden objects: it made him shiver to see the concealed invitations. He went systematically through Serv-ices, domestic work sought by "refined young men" in "private flats and houses," or by "masculine" odd-job men, "anything considered." He wasn't seeking Services himself, but he was keenly preoccupied by their being offered. There were various masseurs. Someone called Mr. Young, a "manipulative therapist," could visit between 10:45 and 3 in north-west

London only. Paul felt he would be rather intimidated by Mr. Young, even if he managed to be in the area at the specified time. His eye worked through the tiny type of "For Sale and Wanted," the ads all looking alike, so that you could lose one and find it again with a slightly magical sense of significance. Mainly it was magazines and films. There were hysterical pleas: "Stills, Photos, Articles, Magazines, ANYTHING dealing with Cliff Richard." An unnamed "studio" offered "physique and glamour movies" for "artists, students and connoisseurs"; someone else sold "50-foot action films," however long that was. Paul imagined the reel going round on a projector . . . he didn't think you could get much action into fifty feet, it would surely be over in no time. Anyway, he didn't have a projector; and couldn't see himself getting one on his present salary. Not that there would really be room in here . . . and then he'd need a screen as well . . . Quite a few people were fans of something called "tapesponding," where it seemed you recorded a message and sent it through the post, which might be romantic, but then he didn't have a tape-recorder either, and even if he did Mrs. Marsh would think he'd gone mad, talking away for hours on end in his room. He wasn't a very confident talker, and couldn't imagine how he'd fill up a tape.

The Personals were the climax of his solitary ritual, the words themselves bulging and bending with outrageous meaning: "Undisciplined bachelor (32) would like to meet strong-minded person with modern outlook." "Motorcyclist, ex-Navy, seeks another for riding weekends." It was 6d a word, but some people went on as garrulously as any tapesponder: "Motorcyclist, 30, but still a novice, seeks further instruction and would also particularly like to contact a qualified watersports trainer. North London/Hertfordshire area preferred." Paul read all this with a beating pulse, smiling narrowly, in a sustained state of fascinated shock. Only one man seemed to have completely missed the point, and asked to meet a girl with an interest in gardening. Otherwise it was a world of "bachelors," many of them with "flats," and most of those flats in London. "Central London flat, large and comfortable. Young bachelor needed to share with another. No restrictions." Paul looked up at the floral curtains and the evening sky above the mirror. "Energetic bachelor (26), own flat, seeks others, similar interests"—he hadn't said what his interests were, it must be taken as read. "Interests cinema, theatre, etc." said some, or just "interests varied." *"Interests universal,"* said "bachelor, late forties," leaving nothing, or was it everything, to chance.

Paul closed his eyes in a heavy-hearted dream of bachelor flats, his gaze slowly making out, among the pools of lamplight, the shared sofa, the muddled slippers, the advanced pictures, opening the door on to the bathroom, where he himself was shaving as Peter Rowe, now looking oddly like Geoff Viner, lolled in the bath, reading, smoking and washing his hair all at the same time, then opening, through a sort of purple vapour, the door of the bedroom, on to a shadowy scene more thrilling and scandalous than anything described in *Films and Filming*—in fact a scene that, as far as he knew, had never been described at all.

4

PETER SAT in the Museum, writing up the labels with his four-coloured biro. "Whose is the sword, again?"

"Oh, the sword, sir? Brookson's, sir," said Milsom 1, coming over and watching intently for a moment.

"He claims it was his grandfather's, sir," said Dupont.

"Admiral's Dress Sword," Peter wrote, in black, and then, flicking to red, "Lent by Giles Brookson, Form 4." He felt the boys themselves ought really to do the labels, but they had a thing about his handwriting. Already he saw his Greek *e,* his looped *d,* his big scrolly *B,* seeping through the school, infecting the print-like hand they had hitherto based on the Headmaster's. It was funny, and flattering in a way, but of course habitual; ten years before, he had copied those *B*s from a favourite master of his own. "Voilà!"

"Merci, monsieur!" said Milsom, and took the card over to the display cabinet, where the more precious and dangerous exhibits were to be housed. There was a lovely set of Indian clay figures in the dress of different ranks and trades—military piper, water-seller, chokidar—very trustingly lent by Newman's aunt. The shelf above was home to a hand-grenade, it was assumed unarmed, a flintlock pistol, Brookson's grandfather's sword, and a Gurkha kukri knife, which Dupont had taken down and was working on now with a wad of Duraglit. He and Milsom were talking about their favourite words.

"I think I'd have to say," said Milsom, "that my favourite word is *glorious.*"

"Not *gorgeous?*" said Dupont.

"No, no, I far prefer *glorious.*"

"Ah well . . . ," said Dupont.

"All right, what's yours? And don't don't *don't* say, you know . . . sort of *pig,* or *and* . . . or, you know . . ."

Dupont merely raised an eyebrow at this. "At the moment," he said, "my favourite word would have to be *Churrigueresque.*" Milsom gasped and shook his head and Dupont glanced at Peter for a second to judge the effect of his announcement. "But on the other hand," he went on airily, "perhaps it's just something very simple like *lithe.*"

"Lithe?"

"Lithe," said Dupont, waving the kukri sinuously in the air. "Just one little syllable, but you'll find it takes as long to say it as glorious, which has three. Lithe . . . *lithe* . . ."

"For god's sake be careful with that weapon, won't you. It's designed for chopping chaps' heads off."

"I am being careful, sir," said Dupont, wounded into a blush. Since his removal from the music-room he'd been slightly wary of Peter, and seemed not to trust his own voice, with its weird octave leaps in the middle of a word. In a minute Peter came and looked over his shoulder at the wide blade: it was the angle in the middle that made the back of his thighs prickle.

"It's a vicious-looking thing, Nigel . . ."

"Indeed it is, sir!" said Dupont, with a grateful glance. Strictly speaking, only prefects were addressed by their first names. He turned the kukri over, one side gleaming steel, the other a still dimly shiny blue-black. His fingers themselves were black from the wadding. "It's perfectly balanced, you see, sir." He held it tremblingly upright, one stained finger in the notch at the foot of the blade. It swung there, like a parrot on a perch.

There were a number of pictures to be hung, and Peter asked the boys where they should go. It was their Museum—surely Dupont's idea, but loyally co-authored with Milsom 1; Peebles and one or two others were involved but had melted away once the hard work of cleaning out the stable and whitewashing the walls had begun. It was clear they just wanted to play with the exhibits. "Let's hang the Headmaster's mother," said Peter, and saw the boys giggle and look at each other. He held up a gloomy canvas in a shiny gilt frame. "Very generous of the Headmaster to lend this, I feel, don't you?" They all gazed at it in the state of comic uncertainty that Peter liked to create. A round-faced woman in a grey dress peered out as if in suppressed anxiety at having produced the

Headmaster. "Where shall we put the late Mrs. Watson?" Horses had clearly been thought to need little light—just the half-door at the front, and one small window high up at the back. The overhead bulb in a tin shade left the upper walls in shadow. "Right up at the top, perhaps . . . ?"

"Does that mean she's dead, sir?" said Milsom.

"Alas, yes," said Peter, with a certain firmness. There were some things they shouldn't be encouraged to joke about—though her death was surely the reason she'd been unhooked at last from the Headmaster's sitting-room wall.

"We do need more lights, sir," said Dupont. He had ideas of using the Victorian oil-lamp lent by Hethersedge, but this was a hazard even Peter had drawn the line at.

"I know we do—I'll have a word with Mr. Sands about it."

"I feel we should put her in a prominent position, sir," said Milsom.

Peter smiled down at him, with a moment's conjecture about what lay ahead in life for such a respectful boy. "I feel you're right," he said, and climbed up to fix the old girl on the wall above the weapons cabinet. It was a central spot, though it turned out the edge of the lampshade threw everything above her chin into deep shadow. "Ah, well," said Peter, rather imposing on the boys his own belief that it didn't matter. They went to get on with their work, glancing up at her doubtfully from time to time.

Peter opened a cardboard box and picked out the framed photograph of Cecil Valance, huffed and then spat discreetly on the glass, and gave it a vigorous wipe with his handkerchief. Inside, between the glass and the mount, were many tiny black specks of harvesters, which had got in there and died perhaps decades ago. "Where shall we hang our handsome poet?" he said. "Our very own bard . . ."

"Oh, sir . . . ," said Milsom; and Dupont dropped the kukri and came over.

"Shall we put him here, sir, right above the desk?" he said.

"We could, couldn't we?" The desk itself was an exhibit—part of a jumble of Victorian furniture and household objects, clothes-baskets, clothes-horses, coal-scuttles, that had been roughly stacked and locked away in the adjacent stable at some unknown date. It was immensely heavy, with two rows of Gothic pigeon-holes, and oak battlements, now rather gap-toothed, running along the top.

"Do you think Cecil Valance might actually have written his poetry at this desk, sir?" said Milsom.

"I bet he did, sir," said Dupont.

"Well, I suppose it's possible . . . ," said Peter. "The early ones, perhaps—as you know, he wrote the later ones in France."

"In the trenches, sir, of course."

"That's right. Though the handy thing about poems is you can write them wherever you happen to be." Peter had been doing some of Valance's work with the Fifth Form—not just the famous anthology pieces but other things from the *Collected Poems* that he'd found in the library, with the Stokes memoir. The boys had been tickled to read poems about their own school, and young enough not to see without prompting how bad most of them were.

Dupont was looking closely at the photograph. "Can we say when it was taken, sir?"

"Tricky, isn't it?" There was just the gilt stamp of Elliott and Fry, Baker Street, on the blue-grey mount. Little evidence in the clothes— dark striped suit, wing-collar, soft silk tie with a gemmed tie-pin. He was in half-profile, looking down to the left. Dark wavy hair oiled back but springing up at the brow in a temperamental crest. Eyes of uncertain colour, large and slightly bulbous. Peter had called him handsome, not quite knowing what he meant. If you thought of Rupert Brooke, say, then Valance looked beady and hawkish; if you thought of Sean Connery or Elvis, he looked inbred, antique, a glinting specimen of a breed you rarely saw today. "He died very young, so he's probably"—Peter didn't say "about my age"—"in his early twenties." Strange to think, if he'd lived, he'd have been the same age as Peter's grandfather, who still played a round of golf a week, and loved jazz, if not quite "Jailhouse Rock."

"Was he ever married, sir?" asked Milsom earnestly.

"I don't believe he was," said Peter, "no . . ." And climbing on to the desk he asked the boys to pass him the hammer, and drove a nail into the whitewashed wall.

AT THE STAFF-MEETING in the Headmaster's sitting-room, the talk this week was all about Open Day. "So we'll have the First XI against Templers, starting at 1:30. What's the lookout there?"

"A walkover, Headmaster," said Neil McAll.

The Headmaster smiled at him keenly for a moment, almost enviously. "Well done."

"Well, Templers are a pretty feeble side," said McAll drily, but not refusing the praise. "And I'd like to take a couple of extra nets this week, after prep . . . ? Just to knock them into shape." The Headmaster seemed ready to grant him anything. Peter glanced at McAll across the table, with uncertain feelings. Black-haired, blue-eyed, dressed in sports kit at improbable times of day, he was adored by many of the boys, and instinctively avoided by others. He breathed competition. In his two years at Corley Court, he was credited with dragging the school up from its long-term resting-place at the bottom of the Kennet League.

"Clean whites, of course, Matron?"

"I'll do my best," said Matron; "though by tenth week . . ."

"Well, see what you can do, will you."

"I'm bringing the seniors' bath night forward to Thursday," said Matron, with an air of great strategy.

"Mm? Oh, I see, quite right," said the HM, frowning over a slight blush. He consulted his list. "Any other activities . . . ? Now, I see I have the Museum."

"Ah, yes," said Peter, surprised at how nervous the HM made him, the whole half-watchful, half-indifferent gathering of the staff. He looked across at John Dawes, the most avuncular of the masters, flicking his lighter for the third or fourth time over the bowl of his pipe; and Mike Rawlins beside him, deep in the systematic doodle with which each week he obliterated the roneoed order of business. They'd been sitting at these meetings for twenty years. "Yes, I think we'll have something to show by Open Day. They've got some interesting things together, as well as some rather silly things. It won't be, you know, the Ashmolean . . ."—Peter grinned and looked down.

"No, well," said the Headmaster, who resented his Oxford allusions.

"I'm assuming the place is locked securely at night?" said Colonel Sprague. "As I understand it, it contains various items lent by parents?"

"Yes, of course," said Peter. "Dupont is officially the curator, and he gets the key off me."

"We don't want any trouble of that kind," said the Colonel.

"I must try to get down and see it," said Dorothy Dawes, as if it would require a certain amount of planning. She taught the "Babies" in the First Form, and seemed set apart from the rest of the school in a nest of knitting-wool and gummed paper. She was always equipped with two treats, Polos and Rolos, which she handed out liberally to reward and console. It wasn't clear to Peter if the Daweses had had children of their own.

"I've lent them a couple of things myself," said the Headmaster. "A portrait and a set of antlers. Just to get them started."

"No, much appreciated," said Peter solemnly. "And we've also got a few interesting items from the Valances' days."

"Ah, yes . . . ," said the Headmaster, a wary look coming over him. "Now this leads me to a somewhat delicate matter, which I must ask you to keep very much to yourselves." Peter assumed they'd got to the sex part, and was suddenly doubting the witty remarks he'd been planning to make about *Dr. No* and Ursula Andress's bust. "Well, you know already, John, and . . . It's to do with Mrs. Keeping."

There was obviously something thrilling about this, since Mrs. Keeping was such a hard nut and not at all popular with the other staff; a ripely responsible look settled over them.

"I've had a few, shall we say, comments before, but now Mrs. Garfitt has written to complain. She claims Mrs. Keeping has been hitting young Garfitt with a book, I'm not quite clear where, and also"—the Headmaster peered at his notes—" 'flicking his ears as a punishment for playing wrong notes.' "

"God, is that all," murmured John Dawes, and Matron gave a short illusionless laugh. "Not that it will do any good."

"I've told Mrs. Garfitt that judicious corporal punishment is one of the things that keep a school like Corley Court ticking over. But I'm not quite happy about it, all the same."

"The trouble is she doesn't consider herself to be a school-teacher," said Mike Rawlins, without losing the track of his doodle.

"No, well, she has no qualifications," said Dorothy, with a slightly shifty look.

"Ah, well . . . ," said Mike, now with a very heavy face. As far as Peter could make out only he and the Headmaster could boast university degrees, the others having various antique diplomas and in one case a medal. Neil McAll was the most exotic, with his Dip. Phys. Ed. (Kuala Lumpur), on the strength of which he taught History and French.

"Well, she is the daughter of Captain Sir Dudley Valance, Bart," said Colonel Sprague, humorously but with feeling. Sprague himself, though only the bursar, showed a keen consciousness of long-erased ranks and sometimes assumed quite imaginary superiority over Captain Dawes and of course over Mike and the HM, who had both been in the RAF.

"Well, that can't have made for an easy upbringing," said Mike.

"Corley Court was her childhood home."

"I don't know . . . ," said the Headmaster, with a deplorably tactical air of vagueness, his eye wandering round the table, "but I was wondering if you might not best be able to have a word with her about all this . . . um, *Peter*."

Peter coloured and blinked, and said at once, "With respect, Headmaster, I don't think I can start disciplining other members of staff, especially if they're twice my age."

"Poor Peter!" said Dorothy, rustling protectively. "He's only just got here."

"No, no, not disciplining . . . obviously!" said the HM, flushing too. "I was thinking more of a . . . a subtle chat, a roundabout sort of conversation, that might be more effective than a dressing-down from me. I believe you play duets with her, or . . . ?"

"Well . . . ," said Peter, almost guiltily startled that the Headmaster should know this. "Not really. We're practising a couple of four-hand pieces we're going to play for her mother's seventieth birthday next week. I really don't know her at all well."

"So it's Lady Valance's seventieth?" said Colonel Sprague. "Perhaps the school should offer some form of congratulations."

"No, no, she's not Lady Valance any more," said Peter quite sharply.

"The present Lady Valance is about twenty-five, from the look of her," said Mike.

"She was a model, wasn't she," said Matron.

The fact was that Corinna Keeping frightened Peter, but he did feel he'd got somewhere with her. Some snobbish thing in her had picked him out, and believed it could impress him if not seduce him. He'd been to Oxford, loved music, had read her father's books. Of course she played ten times as well as he did, but she never showed any desire to flick his ears. In fact she gave him cigarettes, and gossiped with him caustically about the running of the school. He probably was in a position to talk to her, but didn't want to forgo her favour by doing so. He thought there would be interesting people at the party, and she had mentioned her clever son Julian, who had "gone off the rails" in the Sixth Form at Oundle, and whom she too thought Peter might usefully have a chat with. "You probably are on the best footing with her," said John Dawes, with his air of drowsy impartiality. And Peter found himself saying,

"Well, I'll have a subtle chat, if you like."

"It would be best," said the Headmaster, stern now he'd won his point.

"Though it may be far too subtle to do the trick," Peter said.

After this the talk moved to particular boys who were cause for com-
ment of some kind, which passed Peter by as he dwelt regretfully on
what he'd just agreed to. He started on a doodle of his own, in green ink,
putting a pediment and pillars around the word Museum. It could be an
Ashmolean after all. He wondered if Julian Keeping was attractive, and if
there was anything queer about his going off the rails. In a public school
the queer ones didn't generally need to rebel, they fitted in beautifully;
especially, of course, if they were beautiful themselves. He was surround-
ing the words *Open Day* in red stars when he heard the Headmaster say,
"Now, Other Business, um, yes, now, Peter, all this pornography and
what have you." In his slight confusion, Peter carried on doodling as he
smiled and said,

"I haven't much to report, Headmaster." When he looked up he saw
the strange preoccupied look around the table, a long slip of John
Dawes's pipe-smoke hanging and slowly dissolving between them.

"Dorothy, I don't know if you'd rather leave us?"

"Good heavens, Headmaster"—Dorothy shook her head, and then
as if she'd forgotten something rummaged in her bag for a Polo.

"I read *Dr. No,* as requested," said Peter, pulling the confiscated book
from under his papers. On the cover Ursula Andress's right arm was half-
obstructed by her bosom as she reached for the knife at her left hip. The
belt seemed a bit kinky, worn with a bikini. On the back there was a
quote from Ian Fleming: "I write for warm-blooded heterosexuals in
railway trains, aeroplanes, and beds." Neil McAll reached over and
turned the book to face him.

" 'The world's most beautiful woman!' " he said. "I wonder." He
angled the book for John Dawes to see. "Odd, low-slung chest she's got."

Old John, acutely embarrassed, appeared to study it. "Mm, has she?"
Peter tried to picture Gina McAll's bosom; he supposed one judged a
film-star and one's wife by rather different standards.

"The cover is much the . . . naughtiest thing about it," said Peter,
"and since many of the boys will have seen the film I can't think there's
any reason to worry about it. It's actually not badly written." He looked
around, frank-faced. "There's a very good description of a diesel engine
on page ninety-one."

"Hmm . . ." The Headmaster gave a wintry smile at this flippancy.
"Very well. Thank you." Again Peter had the suspicion that to the HM
he was a figure of advanced worldliness. "Since then, a search of the

Fourth Form cupboard has produced . . . this"—he felt in his jacket pocket, as if for some treasured handbook, and brought out a dog-eared paperback, which was passed round with very natural curiosity. It was Diana Dors' autobiography, *Swingin' Dors:* beneath her equally salient bosom on the cover ran the tag-line *I've been a naughty girl.* Mike had a good look at the photo inside of the Swindon-born actress in a mink bikini. "Absolute filth, of course," the Headmaster reminded them, "though I fear it now pales into insignificance. Matron, I'm sorry to say, has discovered the most revolting publications hidden behind the radiators in the Sixth Form."

"Well, yes," said Matron, her face rigid. Peter knew that these radiators were boxed in behind thick grilles, but presumably Matron tore those off as readily as she tossed the badly made beds in the air.

The Headmaster had the magazines in a folder behind him, which he pulled on to his lap and went through them under the table, mentioning the titles in a brusque murmur. They were all standard top-shelf fare, though *Health and Efficiency* was a bit different, having naked men and boys in it too. "Of course no one's owned up to putting them there," he said, with a further flinch of disgust. Peter had a pretty good idea who it was, but had no intention of saying. It was all to be expected. "I think you were saying you'd heard some pretty putrid things being said, too, Matron?"

"I have indeed," said Matron, but clearly she wasn't going to elaborate. Whatever it might have been took on a phantom presence in the curious but baffled faces round the table.

Neil McAll said, "I know I've mentioned this before, but isn't it time we gave them some sex education, at least in the Fifth and Sixth Form?"

"Now as you know I've talked to the Governors about this, and they don't think it's desirable," said the Headmaster rather shiftily.

"The parents don't want it," said Matron, more implacably, "and nor do the boys." They frowned together like some intensely odd couple, and Peter couldn't help wondering if either of them was entirely clear about the facts of life themselves. The older boys sometimes pictured them obscenely entwined, but he felt fairly sure that they were both virgins. Their stubbornness on the matter was certainly peculiar, in view of the long tradition of the confidential chat. And so the boys carried on into puberty, in a colourful muddle of hearsay and experiment, fed by the arousing pictures of tribal women in *National Geographic* and by dimly lubricious novels and artfully touched-up magazines.

After this as it happened Peter had a free period, when he was due to meet Corinna Keeping, an arrangement that now took on a certain charge. He doubted very much he would say anything. There was undeniable intimacy in the four-hand sessions with Corinna. Sharing her piano stool, he had a sense of the complete firmness of her person, her corseted side and hard bust, their hips rolling together as they reached and occasionally crossed on the keyboard. As the secondo player he did all the pedalling, but her legs sometimes jerked against his as if fighting the impulse to pedal herself. The contact was technical, of course, like that in sport, and not to be confused with other kinds of touching. None the less he felt she enjoyed it, she liked the businesslike rigour of its not being sexual as well as the unmentionable fraction by which it was. After a practice, Peter would find her mixed trace of smoke and lily-of-the-valley on his shirt. The meetings had no amorous interest for him at all, but he was naturally flirtatious and without really thinking he found they gave him a pleasant hold on someone generally considered a dragon.

She was waiting in the music-room, having just had Donaldson, who was doing Grade 7, for an hour. "Ah, well done, you've escaped," she said, with a mischievous jet of smoke, stubbing out her cigarette on the side of the tin waste-paper basket. "You got away from all those dear old bores."

Peter merely grinned, took his jacket off and opened a window as if absent-mindedly. Far too soon to mention bullying, and though it had been on the tip of his tongue he saw clearly, now he was in her presence, that she would not be amused by an account of the pornography debate. He said, "Well, a lot of fuss about Open Day, as you can imagine."

"I suppose I can," she said, with a flick of her hard black eyebrows. "Of course I'm not asked to these highly important gatherings . . . I'm rather sorry you have to waste your time with them." It was her sly way of reaching to him over the heads of the other staff. Underneath it, he assumed, must lie wounded pride at coming back to teach music in the house she had lived in as a girl. Once he had asked her what the music-room had been in her day: the housekeeper's bedroom, apparently, and the sick-bay next door the cook's. "Have you looked at the Gerald Berners?"

"I've looked at it long and hard," said Peter.

"Rather dotty, isn't it," said Corinna. "Mother will be thrilled, she adored Gerald."

"Well, I'm glad you've let me off the other two morceaux." It was just the simpler middle one they were doing, the so-called "Valse sentimentale."

Corinna steadied the music on the stand. "Can you think of any other composers who were peers of the realm?"

"What about . . . Lord Kitchener?" Peter said.

"Lord Kitchener? Now you're being silly," said Corinna, and coloured slightly, but smiled too.

First of all they played straight through the piece. "I should just say," said Peter at the end, "that I assume it's meant to sound as though I can't play to save my life."

"Absolutely. You've really got it." With Corinna there was somehow a risk that one might revert to the age of eleven oneself, and get whacked round the head with a book. They went through it again, much more confidently, then she stood up for another cigarette.

"Isn't this main tune oddly familiar?" Peter said.

"Is it? I shouldn't have thought any of Gerald's stuff was familiar."

"No . . . I mean, I think he's pinched it. It's Ravel, isn't it, it's definitely French."

"Aha . . . ?"

Peter played the tune again, very plainly. "God, you're right," said Corinna, "it's the *Tombeau de Couperin*"—and sitting back down she shunted him off the stool and played the Ravel, or a bit of it, with her cigarette between her teeth, like a pianist in a speakeasy.

"There you are!"

"Naughty old Gerald," said Peter, which was a liberty she allowed; though she then said,

"It might just be naughty old Maurice, of course. You'll have to check the dates. Anyway, we'd better look at the Mozart for ten minutes, then I must get back, I have to take my husband to the cricket club."

"Oh, in Stanford Lane?" It was a pleasant ten-minute stroll from the bank. "I must say you spoil your husband."

Though not cross, Corinna didn't look pleased by this. She pushed the *Trois Morceaux* into her music-case, and then flattened the Mozart sonata on the stand. "I suppose you haven't heard about him?" she said.

"Oh, no, I'm sorry . . . Has something happened?" Peter saw him being knocked down in the Market Square.

"Ah, you don't know." She shook her head as if exonerating Peter, but still somewhat nettled. "People say it's agoraphobia, but it's not actually."

"Oh . . . ?"

She sat down again. "My husband had a very bad war," she said, with her little quiver of irritable tension. "It's something that's very hard for people to understand."

"I'm afraid I only met him for three minutes when I opened my account," said Peter. "He couldn't have been nicer—even to someone who had more than forty-five pounds."

"He's a brilliant man," said Corinna, ignoring this pleasantry, "he should be running a far more important branch, but he finds many things difficult that other people don't."

"I'm sorry."

"I think people need to know that, though of course he loathes having any special exceptions made for him. Probably he'd hate me telling you this. Essentially he cannot tolerate being alone."

"Yes, I see." Peter glanced at her face, unsure if this explanation marked a new intimacy. She jetted up the last bit of smoke, and stubbed the cigarette out in the bin.

"He was escaping from a German POW camp when the tunnel collapsed." She beamed at the top line of the opening Allegro. "No light, no air—can you imagine? He thought he'd die there, but they rescued him just in time."

"Goodness," said Peter.

"So that, my dear," said Corinna, with a sharp frown, "is why I need to take him to the cricket club," and she fired off the first bars with a snap of the jaw before he was nearly ready.

5

"I can't believe you're doing this," said Jenny Ralph.

"Oh, I don't mind, honestly."

She approached him awkwardly over the gravel in her high heels, her glass held away from her. "They're using you again!"

"It's only while people are arriving—I like having something to do." Paul stood in the gateway and watched a large black Rover 3-litre coming very slowly along the lane, like a car at a funeral. He said as happily as he could, "I'm a bit of an outsider here, anyway."

"Well, you needn't be shy," Jenny said. She was wearing a wide-skirted dress like a ballroom-dancer's and a lot of eye-shadow, and the fact was she did make him feel a bit shy, despite his greater age. He was wearing his work suit, and wished he had something else. "And you've obviously hit it off with Granny."

"Oh . . . well, she's interesting, I like her."

"Mm, well, she adores you," said Jenny, rather tartly.

"Oh, does she?"

" 'The bank clerk who quotes darling Cecil!' "

"Oh, I see . . . ," said Paul, laughing as he stepped out from the gate, but wondering again if he was just a figure of fun to them all. He smiled and waved at the car. The visors were down against the lowering sun, and the deafish old couple inside seemed a little bemused. The plan was that they were to go on past the house and leave their cars in the field opposite, walking back across the lane and in through the further entrance to the drive. If they were extremely frail, they could park in the drive proper. It was delicate work deciding if the numerous quite elderly arrivals were frail enough to qualify. In the field itself there was a further just possible hazard from cow-shit, which Paul thought it better not to mention explicitly. "Do mind your footing," he called out, as the car crept off.

"No," he said, "we had to learn 'Soldiers Dreaming' by heart."

"I beg your pardon . . . ?"

"The poem by Valance."

"Okay . . . ," said Jenny.

" 'Some stroll through farms and vales unmarked by war, / Not knowing in their dreams / They are at war for just such tranquil fields, / Such fleet-foot streams.' "

"I see . . . ," said Jenny. "By the way, you know there's a dance at the Corn Hall tonight."

"Yes, I know—well, I know someone who's going."

"Oh really . . . do you want to go later?"

"Would you be allowed?" Geoff had been talking about it, he was taking Sandra, and Paul felt suddenly heavy with the idea—then saw in a second that he couldn't possibly take Jenny.

"It's the Locomotives, a group from Swindon . . . Too thrilling. Actually don't say anything about it," said Jenny, turning round to smile at young John Keeping, who was crossing the drive, also with a tumbler in his hand. He had changed into a dark double-breasted suit, with a red silk handkerchief in his breast pocket, and looked immediately like a successful businessman. "My grandmother thought you might care for a drop of the fruit-cup," he said. He brought a heavy irony to being, for a moment, a waiter.

"How kind of her," said Paul, taking the glass, not sure what fruit-cup was.

Jenny made a sharp little face. "I just caught Granny tipping in another half-bottle of gin, so I should be a bit careful, if I were you."

"Oh lord, well, watch out," said John, with a lazy guffaw.

Paul blushed as he took a sip. "Mm, not bad actually," he said, trying not to cough as the gin cut through the momentary illusion of something like orange squash. He took another sip.

John looked at him narrowly, then swivelled on his heel to take in the view down the lane, the half-circle of the drive. He said, "When my grandfather gets here, do you know? Sir Dudley Valance?"

"Oh, yes . . . ," said Paul.

"Can we save a spot for him by the front door. He won't appreciate being made to walk."

"Right . . ."

"He has a war-wound, you know," said John, with some satisfaction. "Well, here you are," he said, nodding at an approaching Austin Princess, and set off back over the gravel to find a drink of his own.

"He can walk perfectly well," said Jenny. "It's just that everyone's frightened of him."

"Why's that?" said Paul.

"Oh . . ."—Jenny puffed, and shook her head, as if it was all too tedious to explain to him. "Oh, god, it's Uncle George," she said. "Here, let me take your drink." She put it down on a flat stone by the gate-post and shouted, "Hello, Uncle George!" and with a kind of weary cheerfulness, "Aunt Madeleine . . ."

Paul leaned a hand on the sun-baked edge of the roof and smiled in through the open window. Uncle George, in the passenger seat, was a man in his seventies, perhaps, with a sun-burnt pate and neat white beard. Craning past him was a strong-jawed woman with crimped grey hair and oddly gaudy make-up and ear-rings. Uncle George himself wore a deep red shirt with a floral green bow-tie. He squinted up at Paul as if determined to solve a puzzle without help. "Now which one are you?" he said.

"Um . . . ," said Paul.

"He isn't any of them," said Aunt Madeleine sharply, "are you?"

"You're not one of Corinna's boys?"

"No, sir, I'm . . . I'm just a colleague, a friend—"

"You remember Corinna's boys, surely," said Madeleine.

"Forgive me, I thought you might be Julian."

"No," said Paul, with a gasp, and a muddled sense of protest at being taken for a schoolboy, however pretty and charming.

"So who's he?" said Paul, once he'd sent them on towards the field.

"Uncle George? He's Granny's brother; well, there were two brothers, in fact, but one was killed in the War—in the *First* World War, I mean: he was called Uncle Hubert. You should ask her about it, if you're interested in the First World War. Uncle George and Aunt Madeleine used to be history professors. They wrote quite a well-known book together called *An Everyday History of England*," said Jenny, almost yawning with casual pride.

"Oh—not G. F. Sawle?"

"That's right, yes . . ."

"What, G. F. Sawle and Madeleine Sawle!—we had it at school."

"There you are then."

Paul pictured the title-page on which he had boxed the names G. F. SAWLE and MADELEINE SAWLE in a complex Elizabethan doodle. "Is everyone in your family a famous writer?"

Jenny giggled. "And you know Granny's writing her memoirs . . ."

"Yes, I know, she told me."

"She's been writing them for yonks, actually. We all rather wonder if they'll ever see the light of day."

Paul took another swig of fruit-cup, already feeling weirdly giddy in the evening sunshine. He said, "I hope you won't mind me saying but I find your family a bit complicated to work out."

"Mm, I did warn you."

"I don't know, for instance, is there a Mr. Jacobs?"

"Dead, I'm afraid. Granny's always had bad luck, in a way," said Jenny, as if she'd been there at the time. "First she married Dudley, who was probably very exciting but a bit unhinged by the War and he was beastly to her; so she ran away with . . . my grandfather"—she took a swig of whatever she was drinking—

"Whatsisname . . . Ralph . . ."

"Revel Ralph, the artist, who everyone thought was queer, you know, but anyway they somehow managed to have . . . my father . . . and in due course . . ."

"*Really?*" said Paul, as if amused and delighted, moving away, his face burning at this sudden eruption of *queer*, the word and the fact, and going a few yards down the lane . . . such a casual eruption, too, as if no one much cared. *Everyone thought he was queer*. Thank god, here was a car, at least, which he prayed was coming to Carraveen. He looked at it fondly, full of hospitable feelings, ignoring his blush in the fervent hope it would go away. A pea-green Hillman Imp, sounding rough in a low gear, windscreen white with dust, perhaps a farmer's car, the visor flipped down against the glare full in the driver's face. Paul watched almost impatiently as it approached, looked with odd camaraderie at the large hands on the wheel, the wrinkled nose, the involuntary grin of the man perhaps barely able to see him waiting, in silhouette, then saw, with a reeling adjustment of memory to the re-encountered fact, that it was Peter Rowe. Something providential in the drink brought him smiling to the open window.

"Oh, hello," said Peter Rowe, "it's you!"

"Hello!" said Paul, looking at his actual face, which seemed unaccountably both plainer and more lovable than he'd remembered, while his sense of the evening ahead seemed to shift around and beneath him, like stage scenery. The inside of the car smelt headily of oil and hot plastic. On the passenger seat lay a clutch of sheet music—"W. A. Mozart," he read, "Duetti." He felt whimsical. "You're not frail or elderly, are you?" he said.

"Absolutely not," said Peter Rowe, with a warm affronted tone and a sly smile.

"Then I'm afraid you'll need to park in the field over there," said Paul; and stayed smiling into the car without thinking of what to say next.

Peter Rowe gave the gear-knob a struggling thrust into first. "Well, I'll see you in a minute," he said, "what fun . . . !" Paul felt the hot car slip away under his fingers, which left a long scuffled trace in the dirt on the roof. "Watch your footing!" he called out, over the popping roar of the engine, which for some reason in a Hillman Imp was at the back, where the boot should be; and the word *footing*, odd from the start, sounded now quite surreal and hilarious to him. He watched the car nose up through the gate and into the field, while the reek of its exhaust sank sweetly into the mild scent of grass.

"Do you know Peter Rowe?" said Jenny.

"Well, I've met him," said Paul, feeling strangely fortified, so that he could say, "I didn't know he'd be here tonight, though—that's great."

"No, well, he's going to play duets with Aunt Corinna—it's a surprise for Granny."

"Oh, I see," said Paul. He thought this was a pretty tame kind of surprise; but then he wasn't really musical. Music always struck him as a bit of a performance. Still, he started to see the scene, himself watching, admiring, possessive, even slightly resentful of Peter's confidence and ability. As a contribution to the party it certainly beat telling people where to park.

"*How* do you know him?" said Jenny, with a mischievous look.

"Oh, he banks with us. I've cashed his cheques." Paul was blandness itself, just tinged with pink.

Jenny glanced over her shoulder, where Peter was now crossing the lane to go in by the other gate, with his music in his hand—he brandished it at them in a wave that was cheerful though suddenly not quite enough. Though perhaps he had to get ready, he had to practise. Paul watched him for these few seconds with a half-smile, an air, he hoped, of untroubled interest—a brisk, heavy walk, he found he knew it already. "He teaches at Corley Court as well," said Jenny; and dropping her voice, "We call him Peter Rowe-my-dear."

"Oh, yes . . . ?" said Paul, now a little critical of Jenny.

Again she gave him a droll look. "He's rather full of himself," she said, in a plonking voice, so he saw that she was quoting someone—Aunt Corinna, very probably.

AS THE SHADOWS SHIFTED and lengthened and the church clock struck eight and then a quarter past, Paul's happy excitement began to dim. In between cars he finished his drink, and the tipsy rush was followed by a less pleasant state of dry-mouthed impatience, as he found himself saying the same thing over and over. Jenny had gone in to find Julian and hadn't come back—anyway they were only kids, even if Jenny treated Paul as somehow younger than herself. Roger wandered out for a sniff around the verge and pissed concisely at four different spots, but made no further sign of solidarity. The arrivals grew fewer. The dreaded Sir Dudley perhaps wasn't coming—thus far Paul had let only one small car, which was virtually an invalid carriage, on to the drive itself. He thought of Peter's smile, and the little throb in his voice as he said "Absolutely not!"—there was a giddy sense of an understanding, like the kick and lift of the booze itself, undamaged, stronger in fact since their first meeting, that made Paul's heart race again. It was almost as though Peter knew what he'd done in Paul's daydreams, knew all about the bath and the bachelor flat. And now this vaguely headachy thirst, and a little doubt, like the cooling and quickening of the air, pushing among the hedge-tops in front of him and then leaving off. He could hear the cheery, faintly contentious noise of fifty or sixty people talking, on the big lawn at the back of the house, where tables and chairs had been set out. Peter was in there somewhere, among the family and friends, happily getting drunk, Peter Rowe-my-dear, rather full of himself. Certain things Paul didn't quite like about him came dully to the light. Did he truly fancy him, now he'd seen him again? Could he really imagine getting undressed with that heavy-footed prep-school master? He thought of Geoff's tight zip, and then of beautiful Dennis Flowers, at King Alfred's in Wantage, Captain of Cricket, not a master but a boy. Paul stared in a kind of abstruse distress at the stretch of the lane by the gate, its chalky potholes, the parched grass and tough, half-pretty groundsel, knotty and yellow-flowered, that grew along its crown. Then the church clock struck 8:30, the two bright notes with their unusual interval that seemed to tell him, in their complete indifference, to get in to the house at once.

HE STEPPED OUT with a racing heart on to the patio, where the drinks table was. They'd all met him, of course, but none of them knew who he was. He sensed nodding curiosity mixed with something cooler as he edged among these mainly grand and grey-haired people. Some women from the Bell had been brought in as waitresses, in black dresses with white aprons and caps—they ladled him out a fresh beaker of the fruit-cup, and there was something slightly comic about it, with the bits of orange and so on plopping in. "Do you want more bits, dear?" said the woman. "No, just drink, please," said Paul, and they all laughed.

He saw Peter on the far side of the lawn, talking to a woman in a tight green dress—he was getting her to hold his glass while he fished out cigarettes from his pocket, there was a clumsy bit of business, and then she was raising her face to him, charmed as well as grateful for the light. Paul approached, heard the chuckling run of Peter's voice, his impatient murmur as he lit his own cigarette, saw their shared smile and toss of the head as they blew out smoke—"What? in the second act, you mean," Peter said; now he was almost in front of them, with a tense tiny smile, but still eerily unseen, and abruptly not sure of a welcome—in a moment he had sidled off, his smile now wounded and preoccupied, round the edge of the chattering groups, looking round as if searching for someone else, till he found himself stuck, by himself, in a corner beside a high stand of pampas grass. He sipped repeatedly at his drink, which seemed much less toxic than his first helping. He was staggered by his own timidity, but he argued in a minute that his little scamper away had been so quick it could surely be reversed. The conversations close by were a blur of wilful absurdity. "I don't think you ever will, with Geraldine," the woman nearest him was saying to a crumpled-looking man whose elbow virtually knocked Paul's drink. He couldn't stay here. Through a momentary opening among the shifting and swaying backs of the guests he saw Mrs. Jacobs herself, in the middle of the lawn, in a blue dress and a dark-red necklace, her glasses gleaming as she turned, her face somehow spot-lit by the fact of this being her own party. "Now, we can't have this . . . !"—Corinna Keeping, in red and black, and all the more alarming in grinning high spirits, had found him out.

She took him, like some bashful hero, though also (she couldn't help it) like a culprit who'd stupidly thought he could escape her, through the thick of the party to the far side of the lawn. "There's someone who wants to meet you!" she said, unable fully to conceal her surprise at this, and in a moment she had delivered him to Peter Rowe—"And Sue Jacobs—well, you can introduce yourselves," though she stood there, with her defiant smile, to make sure they did. They shook hands, and Peter said quietly, "At last," as he blew out smoke.

"I didn't catch your name," said Sue Jacobs.

"Oh, *Paul Bryant*," said Paul, with the queer little effort of clarity and breathless laugh that always came with saying who he was. And Peter nodded, "Paul . . . yes"—of course, he'd only just found out his name.

"We'll have supper in a minute," said Corinna, "and then bring everyone in for the concert." She rested a black-gloved hand on Sue Jacobs's forearm. "Is that all right, love?"

"Absolutely!" said Sue, and grinned back, as if trying to match Corinna's abnormal good humour.

"Are you playing too?" said Paul, not able to look at Peter yet.

"I'm singing," said Sue, her smile vanishing as Corinna moved off. "I'd hoped for a run-through, but we had a hellish drive down." He saw that she was older than he'd thought, perhaps forty, but lean and energetic and somehow competitive.

"Where do you live?"

"Mm?—in Blackheath. Right on the other side. We could perfectly well have had the party there, rather than dragging everyone down into darkest Berkshire."

"But you couldn't?" said Peter.

"Corinna wanted it here, and what Corinna wants . . . Sorry, I'm Daphne's step-daughter," she said to Paul. "She married my father." She made this sound rather a regrettable turn of events.

"Ah, yes!" said Paul, laughing nervously, and not sure where Blackheath was—he pictured something like the New Forest. He saw that just behind them in the edge of the flower-bed, the broken trough was sitting, its end apparently cemented back on and hidden by some quickly arranged nasturtiums; on his hand too the graze had scabbed and been picked back to pink. He said to Peter, "Jenny says you're playing tonight." It was magical as well as completely straightforward having him just a foot away. He had a commonplace smell of smoke mixed with some unusual aftershave that made Paul confusedly imagine being held by him and kissed on the top of his head.

"I could have done with a run-through too, god knows," Peter said. "We bashed through it at school, but she's ten times as good as me."

"I shouldn't smoke if I'm singing," said Sue, opening her little evening bag.

Peter squashed his own cigarette under foot before getting out his lighter for her. "I don't know the Bliss songs," he said.

"I'm only doing the Valance," said Sue. "Mm, thanks . . . It's Five Songs opus something, but we're just doing the one, thank god."

"Aha . . . ! Which poem, I wonder?"

"I expect you'll know—it's about a hammock. He's supposed to have written it for Daphne . . . apparently!"

"I must ask her about Cecil Valance," said Peter. "I've just been doing him with my Fifth Form."

"Well, you should. She seems to think he wrote pretty well everything for her."

"Do you think she'd come and talk to the boys?"

"She might, I suppose. I don't know if she's ever been back to Corley, has she? It will all be in the famous memoirs, of course."

"Oh, is she writing them?" said Peter, putting his hand on Paul's arm for a long moment, as if not to lose him, with talk about strangers, and surely conveying something rather more. In fact, Paul said,

"She's been writing them for yonks."

"Oh, you know about it," said Sue.

"Well, a bit . . ."—and then: "Isn't it the poem that starts, 'A larch tree at your head, and at your feet / A weeping willow'?"

"You do know," said Sue again, sounding slightly put out.

"I'd better get *you* to talk to the Fifth Form!" said Peter, the hint of mockery in his tone dissolving in his long, brown-eyed gaze, as if he too felt excitements teeming softly around and ahead of them. It was a look of a kind Paul had never had before, and in his happiness and alarm he found he had completely finished his drink.

"Well, supper, perhaps," said Sue, in a way that made Paul think she'd become aware of something.

"MAY WE JOIN YOU, sir?" said Peter.

George Sawle's sunburnt face settled into a vague smile as he gestured at the chairs. In the shade, or by now the midge-haunted shadow, of the weeping beech, it was the most secluded of the supper-tables. The old boy seemed almost to be hiding. "I'm Daphne's brother," he said.

"Oh, I know who you are," said Peter, with his suggestive chuckle, putting down his plate next to him. "I'm Peter Rowe. I teach at Corley Court."

"Oh, goodness . . . !" said old Sawle, in a tone that suggested there was a lot to be said on the subject, if one were ever to get round to it. Paul grinned but didn't know if it would be right to say what an honour it was to meet him. He'd sometimes seen John Betjeman in Wantage but had never actually met an author before. The *Everyday History,* with its old-fashioned pictures of strip-farming and horse-drawn transport, had come out some time before the War. It was slightly magical that G. F. Sawle and Madeleine Sawle should even be alive, much less battering round the country in an Austin Princess. Paul sat down next to Peter—it seemed this was what they were doing, it was so absurdly new and easy, and he was trying to keep his head as they sallied around together. This large glass of white wine was clearly going to help. "We met earlier—I'm Paul Bryant." The chair lurched and sank slightly under him in the rough grass.

"Yes, indeed . . . ," said Sawle, nodding and then pulling a little shyly at the longer white tufts of beard under his chin. He quizzed the salmon and new potatoes on their plates through his thick-lensed spectacles.

"Are you not eating, Professor?" said Peter.

"Ah, my wife, I believe . . . ," said Sawle, and after a moment looked round. "Here she comes . . . !" There seemed to be some fleeting invitation to find them comical as a couple, in their devotion or their eccentricity.

Paul looked out and saw Madeleine Sawle stepping warily across the patio with a plate in each hand, and then working towards them among the white-clothed tables where other guests were bagging seats and saying, "My dear, of course you may . . . !" to the people they had just been trying to avoid. The whole social tone was new to him, the top notes of the upper class above a more general mix, with one or two loud local voices, and he was glad to be hidden away here, under the raised flounce of the old beech-tree. He felt the evening's quickening swell of good luck, and with it the usual suspicion that it was all a mistake—surely any minute Mrs. Keeping would send him back to stand by the gate.

"We're tucked under this obliging tree, dear, just as you suggested," said George Sawle, very clearly, as Madeleine set down the plates with a flicker of a frown, and opened her bag to take out the cutlery she'd transported in it. Paul was struck again by the bold oddity of the red ear-rings flanking her square mannish face. "You've met, um . . ."

Paul and Peter introduced themselves—Peter smiled and said "Peter Rowe," warmly and almost forgivingly, as if it were a delightful fact Mrs. Sawle might perhaps have been expected to know. "I'm Paul Bryant," said Paul, and felt he made a slenderer claim. She tilted her head—of course she was rather deaf.

"*Peter* . . . and *Paul*," she said, with amiable sternness. Paul was pleased at the coupling, though he felt like a school-child under her gaze. He wondered if the Sawles themselves had children. She seemed very much the helpmeet of the *Everyday History*, something industrious and educational about her. Paul saw them toiling together in an oak-beamed interior, with perhaps a hand-loom of their own in the background. Otherwise he knew nothing about who she was or what she had done. He thought it was a bit odd that the Sawles were hiding away here, and not joining the rest of the family for dinner. "Are you old friends?"

"Oh, we are," said Peter, "we met about fifteen minutes ago."

"Well, a couple of weeks . . . ," Paul said, laughing, slightly put out.

"Of Daphne's, I mean?"

"Oh, I'm sorry—not yet," said Peter, "though of course I'm hoping to be." He smiled his way broadly through these bits of silliness, and Paul found his admiration for him wrapped up with just a tinge of embarrassment. "I like her enormously"—and at the same moment, as he sat forward to start eating, Paul felt Peter's knee push roughly against his own and stay there, almost as though he thought it was a strut of the table. His heart was beating as he edged his knee away, just an inch. Peter's moved with it, he shifted forwards a bit in his chair to keep the contact more easily. His smile showed he was enjoying that as well as everything else. The warmth transfused from leg to leg and quickly travelled on up to lovely but confusing effect—Paul hunched forward himself and spread his napkin in his lap. He felt a hollow ache, a kind of stored and treasured hunger, in his chest and down his thighs. He found his hand was shaking, and he had another big gulp from his glass, smiling thinly as if in a trance of respectful pleasure at the company and the occasion.

"Oh, Daphne . . . well, of course," Madeleine Sawle was saying, and gave Peter a sparring look as she settled next to her husband, leaving an empty chair between herself and Paul. "You're not in the theatre?" she said.

"It sometimes feels like it," said Peter, "but no, I'm a school-master."

"He teaches at Corley, dear," said George.

"Oh, goodness," said Mrs. Sawle, and tutted as she spread her napkin and checked her husband's readiness to start eating. "I've not been to Corley in forty years. I expect it makes a rather better school than it did a private house."

"Ghastly pile," said the Professor.

"Ooh . . . !" said Peter, flushing slightly in humorous protest, which Sawle didn't notice.

"We used to go there, of course," said Mrs. Sawle, "when Daphne was married to Dudley, as I expect you know."

"Not a very happy time," said the Professor, in a blandly confidential tone.

"It wasn't a very happy time," said Mrs. Sawle, "or I fear a very happy marriage," and gave a firm smile at her plate.

Peter said, "I've just been reading the Stokes memoir of Cecil Valance—it strikes me you must have known him, sir."

"Oh, I knew Cecil," said Sawle.

"You knew him very well, George," said Mrs. Sawle. "That was the last time we were there, to meet Sebastian Stokes, when he was getting his materials together."

"Mm, I remember all too clearly," said old Sawle. "Dudley got us pie-eyed and we danced all night in the hall."

Mrs. Sawle said, "It was on the very eve of the General Strike! I remember we talked of little else."

"Do you know this book?" Peter said, jiggling his knee now and moving his calf too against Paul's.

"I'm afraid I don't," said Paul, finding it very hard to concentrate on talking or eating; he felt sure the Sawles must be able to see what was going on; and anyway, he might know "Soldiers Dreaming" by heart, but they came at things from another angle here, out of a world of family gossip and connections. He held his leg firm against Peter's, which seemed to matter more. He reached out again and drank solemnly from his glass to cover his confusion, thinking at the same time he shouldn't drink so fast, but feeling too there was something fated and irresistible about it. Across the party, half-hidden by the trailing fronds of the tree above, candles had started to flicker, at each little table, against the half-light. In a minute, young Julian appeared, as if raising a curtain, with a lit white candle in a jar held in front of him. "Here you are, Great-Uncle George!" he said, reaching over Madeleine's shoulder to put the jar on the table, his own sleek face, brown eyes, glossy fringe, lit up by the quickly settling flame. Paul felt a new pressure of attention in Peter's knee, as they all gazed up fondly at him. "Are you all right out here—you should be in with Gran," he said. His voice, at seventeen, still had a boy's rawness. He stood smiling at them with that cheerful little consciousness of behaving well, to his worthy old relations, and light-heartedly clinging to his decorum after quite a few drinks.

"Oh, we don't expect special treatment, you know," said George Sawle in a gently ironic voice.

"I don't know if it's just me," said Peter smoothly, watching Julian go, "but I thought that Stokes thing was almost unreadable."

Sawle gave a cluck of a laugh. "Deplorable publication altogether."

"Oh, I'm glad I'm not wrong."

"What . . . !"—old Sawle looked at Peter with some enviable shared understanding. It was a whole way of talking that had Oxford and Cambridge in it, to Paul's ears.

"There hasn't been a proper Life, has there?" Peter said.

"I don't suppose there's enough for a full biography," Sawle said. "To be perfectly honest, I have old Cecil somewhat on my conscience."

"Well, you've no need to, George," said his wife.

Sawle cleared his throat. "I'm supposed to have turned in an edition of his letters quite some time ago."

"Oh, really?" said Peter.

"Well, Louisa asked me originally, oh goodness, some time after the War—his mother."

"She must have lived to a great age, then?" Peter said.

"Well, she was in her eighties, I suppose," said Sawle, with the faint touchiness of someone getting on himself. "She was a very difficult woman. She made a sort of cult of Cecil. There was a very awkward occasion when I was asked down, it was rather like when the poems were being done, to talk about it all. She wasn't living at Corley Court any more by then, she'd moved to a house in Stanford-in-the-Vale. I went for the weekend. 'Let's lay them all out, and decide what ought to go in,' she said. Of course no editor could work under such conditions. I knew I'd have to wait till she was dead."

"Wait as long as you like, dear," said Mrs. Sawle. "You expect too much of yourself. And I can't believe anyone's crying out for these letters."

"Oh, some of them are marvellous—the War letters, love. But Louisa had no idea of course of the sort of thing Cecil wrote in letters to his men friends."

"Is there some quite racy stuff?"

Sawle gave a fond apologetic look to his wife, but didn't exactly answer. "I think all sorts of stuff's going to come out, don't you. I was talking just now to someone about Strachey."

"You must have known him too, I suppose?" Peter said.

"Oh, a bit, you know."

"Didn't really care for Strachey, did you, George?" said Madeleine Sawle, again looking quizzically over her husband's food.

"There's this young chap . . . Hopkirk." Sawle looked at her.

"Holroyd," she said.

"Who's about to tell all about old Lytton."

"Oh, I can't wait," said Peter.

"Mark Holroyd," said Madeleine firmly.

"He came to see me. Very young, charming, clever, and extremely tenacious"—Sawle laughed as though to admit he'd been got the better of. "I don't suppose I helped him much, but it seems he's got some people to agree to the most amazing revelations."

"Quite a tale, by all accounts!" said Madeleine, with a grim pretence of enthusiasm.

"I think if people ever do get to learn the real details of what went on among the Bloomsbury Group," Sawle said, "they'll be pretty astonished."

"We barely knew that world," said Madeleine.

"Well, we were in Birmingham, dear," said Sawle.

"We still are!" she said.

"Mm, I was just thinking," said Peter, "that if this Bill goes through next week it could open the way for a lot more frankness."

Paul, who hadn't been able to discuss the Bill with anybody, felt the grip of the crisis again, but less upsettingly than in the drive with Jenny. "Yes . . . indeed," he said quite calmly, and looking up in the candlelight he felt (though of course you could never really measure it) he was blushing much less than on that occasion.

"Oh, Leo Abse's Bill, you mean," said Sawle, in an abstracted tone, and perhaps to avoid the charged phrase "Sexual Offences." He seemed fixed on some distant and subtle calculation. "It could certainly change the atmosphere, couldn't it"—with a tiny suggestion that prominent and public though it was it had better not be mentioned in front of his wife. He picked up with a little apologetic gasp from where he had been a minute before—"No, to go back to Cecil, I came to feel all his rather wilful behaviour was really an attempt to do one of two things—either to appease his mother or to get as far away from her as possible. Going to war was the perfect combination."

"Ah, yes . . ." Paul glanced at George Sawle almost superstitiously. It wasn't just that he'd known Lytton Strachey and Cecil Valance, but that he spoke so illusionlessly about them. Cecil loomed in the background for him, less as a poet than as some awkward piece of lumber in the family attic.

"Dudley was a very different character," Sawle went on, "but equally under her spell. She appalled them and she fascinated them. He writes very well about her in his autobiography. I don't know if you've read that?"

Paul gazed, hardly bothering to shake his head, and Peter of course said, "I certainly have."

"Awfully good, isn't it?"

Paul said, "I wondered if he'd be coming tonight, actually," with a certain confidence, but Sawle said almost brusquely,

"I'd be astonished if he did."

And having said one thing, Paul thought he'd better immediately say the other thing he'd been nursing and rehearsing, "I wondered what you thought of Valance's poetry, actually?" looking from husband to wife, oracular sources. He felt he must be prepared for a tough answer; but in fact they seemed barely interested.

Madeleine said, "I'm honestly not a poetry person."

The Professor seemed to muse a little longer, and said with regret, "It's hard to say, when you remember them being written. They're probably not much cop, are they?"

Peter glanced rather sweetly at Paul, and at his tender question, but seemed unwilling to disagree with the Sawles; so Paul kept silent about how much they had always meant to him.

"I don't mean to say, incidentally," said Sawle, in his way of not letting others drive him off-course, "that Louisa wasn't heart-broken by Cecil's death—I'm sure she was. But she made the most of it . . . you know. They did, those women. The memorial volumes, the stained-glass windows. Cecil indeed got a marble tomb by some Italian sculptor."

"Well, I know . . . ," said Peter.

"Of course you know all about it."

"What's that?" said Paul.

"Oh, at school," said Peter: "Cecil Valance is buried in the chapel."

"Really?" said Paul, and gasped, the whole subject like a dream taking substance in the candle-lit bell of the beech-tree.

"You must come and see him," said Peter, "if you like the poems; he's rather splendid."

"Thank you," said Paul, "I'd like to very much," his pop-eyed look of earnest gratitude covering his surprise as Peter's hand, stroking the napkin in his lap, wandered as if unawares on to Paul's thigh, and lay there lightly for several seconds.

ON THE WAY in after supper Paul stuck with the Sawles for a moment, but they latched on to others with sudden warmth and relief, and so he slipped off. They'd been polite, even kind to him, but he knew it was really Peter they were interested in. In the deepening shadows between pools of candlelight, the guests, gathering up bags and glasses, conversations stretching and breaking, in an amiable jostle as they bunched in through the french windows, seemed to Paul like a flickering frieze, unknowable faces all bending willingly to something perhaps none of them individually would have chosen to do. He was drunk, and he bunched in too, the drink making him less conspicuous. Everyone was friendlier and noisier. The drawing-room appeared blocked with rows of chairs. The connecting doors into the dining-room had been flung open, and the piano turned round. Mr. Keeping stood to one side with his mocking smile, asking people to go to the front, to fill up the rows. Paul buttoned his jacket and smiled politely at him as he squeezed past. The effects of the drink, free and easy outside, felt a bit more critical in the glare of the crowded room. Could people tell how drunk he was? Before anything happened he would need the lavatory; where there was a queue, of course; some of the old ladies took two minutes, nearly three minutes. He smiled at the woman in front of him and she smiled back tightly and looked away, as though they were both after the same bargain. Then he was alone in the hall with the colourful chaos of presents and cards, most of them unopened, piled on the table and under it. Books obviously, and loosely swathed plants, and soft things it was difficult to wrap neatly. His jiggling desperation grew painful with the knowledge he hadn't bought Mrs. Jacobs a present or even a card himself. When the woman at last emerged and hurried into the drawing-room Paul heard a loud rapping, a hush, a scatter of applause, and then Mrs. Keeping starting to talk. Well he couldn't not go. Better to miss the concert altogether. All he really wanted was to see Peter play, to watch him, with the beautiful and alarming new certainty that he was about to . . . he looked in the mirror, hardly knowing, now it came to it, what it was they might be going to do.

He finished as fast as he could, and listened—awful to pull the great clanking flush during Mrs. Keeping's opening bars. But no, they were still laughing. They must all be as drunk as he was by now. He hung about in the shadow of the door from the hall, there were two empty seats, but in the middle of rows, there was a burst of laughter which he thought for a mad second was aimed at him, and he slipped in pink-faced at the side of the room and stood against the wall, behind a row of dining chairs. Here he could see everything—but so too could everyone see him. There were two or three others standing, and at the back of the room the french windows were still open, with further guests gathered outside in what already looked like darkness. Mrs. Keeping was erect in front of the piano, hands clasped, in the posture of a child reciting. He didn't take in what she was saying. Peter was at the end of the front row, smiling at his hands, or at the floor; Mrs. Jacobs in the middle of the row, the place of honour, sipping at her drink and blinking up at her daughter with delighted reproach as the surprise got under way. Paul smiled anxiously himself, and when everyone laughed he laughed too. "Now Mother is awfully fond of music," Mrs. Keeping said, "so we thought we'd better humour her by playing some." Laughter again—he looked at Mrs. Jacobs, enjoying the collective sense of treasuring and teasing her; a woman just behind her exclaimed, "Dear Daphne," and people laughed at that too. Mrs. Keeping pulled her black wrap around her upper arms and pushed back her shoulders—"So, to start with, her favourite composer."

"Aha . . . !" said Mrs. Jacobs, with an accepting smile, though perhaps a tiny uncertainty as to who that would turn out to be.

"Chopin?" said one old boy to the woman beside him.

"You'll see soon enough!" said Mrs. Keeping. She sat down on the piano stool, and then looked round. "We can't run to the original, I fear, so this is a paraphrase by Liszt." There was a murmur of humorous apprehension. "It's *very hard*!" She fixed the music on the stand with a furious glare, and then she was off.

She could really play, couldn't she?—that was Paul's first feeling. He looked around hastily at the others, with a bashful grin on his face. Was it Chopin? He saw them all deciding, staring at each other, frowning or nodding, some leaning to whisper. There was a noiseless sigh, a wave of collective recognition and relief that almost made the music itself unimportant: they'd got it. He didn't want to show that he hadn't. He had never seen anyone play the piano seriously and at close range, and it locked him into a state of mesmerized embarrassment, made worse by the desire to conceal it. There was the noise itself, which he thought of vaguely as the noise of classical music, sameish and rhetorical, full of feelings people surely never had, and there was the sight of Mrs. Keeping in action, the plunges and stabs of her bare arms up and down the keyboard. She wasn't a large woman—it was only her presence that was crushing. Her little hands looked brave and comical as they stretched and rumbled and tinkled. She rocked and jumped from one buttock to the other, in her stiff red dress, her black wrap slipping—it twitched and drooped behind her as she moved, with a worrying life of its own. The riveting, but almost unwatchable, thing was her profile, powdered and severe, shaken by twitches and nods, like tics only just kept under control. He stared, smiling tightly, and covering his mouth and chin pensively with his hand.

Mrs. Jacobs looked self-conscious too, but in a happy way, her head on one side. Her own responses were almost a part of the performance. The over-active first section of the music had ended, and now a slow tune came in, with a definite air, even on a first hearing, of being what they were waiting for. Mrs. Jacobs raised and then dropped her right hand in greeting to it, and shook her head slowly as it went on. Paul thought she was probably very drunk—he felt the glow of his friendly understanding with her, from that first evening; though he somehow saw that to her being drunk had its whole long sentimental history, whereas to him it was a freakish novelty. Somewhere at the back there was a frail bit of humming and a little giggle when someone shushed. Then here came the song again, and as his eyes slid over the heads of the audience to find Peter he found Peter turned sideways and looking back at him, and the rapid pressure on his own heart and the glow of his face were fitted by the music, like a theme tune: they both smiled just in the moment of turning away.

After that Paul looked around casually, to see if anyone had seen; he watched Julian, also standing, on the other side, pink with drink and the comical effort to look sober. Jenny sat just beside him, with a similar frown of critical concentration, pinned in beside a large old man with a farmer's face and a mass of white hair, and politely ignoring the loud dejected noise of his breathing. Paul turned with a remote smile, as if transported by the music, and found Mr. Keeping, standing at the back, pressed against the red velvet curtains, and staring intently at his wife, also with a hint of a smile, his unreadable mask. She was on display, physical and passionate, and Paul realized he would never see Mr. Keeping himself in quite the same way again. Then his gaze dropped to the woman seated in front of him—the clasp of her necklace, the label at the neck of her dress turned out . . . *Anne-Marie Paris London*—he read it upside-down. When she twitched her head at a sudden loud chord the tips of her hair tickled his fingers. She glanced round, apology just ruffled by accusal. A little later she murmured something to her husband, who absorbed it with a quick tutting nod. Paul had a strange and intense apprehension, for three or four seconds that might have been a long tranced minute, of this unknown woman's life, which would never cross with his again, and the hypnotic detail of her label showing, which she herself was unaware of.

The door beside him into the hall was propped open, and now and then he heard a clatter of plates or a forgetful raised voice from the kitchen, where the women from the Bell were washing up. The front door was open too, and by moments cool air with a distant smell of firs to it ran in and then ebbed away. There was the quiet section, the theme tune again—he didn't dare look at Peter—and he heard the jingle of something on Roger's collar, unconcernedly out of tune and time, as he nosed round on the edge of the drive. Then there were footsteps on the gravel, stopping uncertainly, but an unselfconscious few words of greeting to the dog, which barked uncertainly itself a couple of times. Paul thought of a policeman, for some reason, and then of Sir Dudley

Valance, with his war wound, whom he now seemed to be slightly obsessed by. There was a throat-clearing, a light knock, several people looked round, with the lively interest of an audience in any disturbance . . . Paul made a cringing face and slipped out into the hall.

"Ah, hullo—good evening . . . !"—a man peering in, too absorbed in the moment to lower his voice, and giving at once a sense of awkwardness, in his tight brown suit. "I'm fearfully late—but I didn't want to miss it." A posh, silvery voice, with, not a stammer but pauses between phrases. Paul came out on to the doorstep, and shook his hand firmly and without exactly encouraging him, he thought. Surely this wasn't Sir Dudley. They nodded at each other, as though they were both in a bit of a fix.

"We're just having . . . some music," said Paul tactfully, with a hesitation of his own.

"Ah!" No, this man was about fifty, but with something boyish in his wide bony face as he turned his head and listened. Paul looked at the tufts of badly cut hair, thick and greying around a sun-blistered bald patch. "Well, yes indeed," he said, "and *Senta's . . . Ballad*, always her favourite." They heard the music grow very emphatic and loud, Paul pictured Mrs. Keeping shaking herself to pieces, and then at once there was applause. He thought someone else might come out and help.

"Will you . . . ?"—he gestured into the hall.

"Yes—thank you." Now they could talk normally. "Hello, Barbara!" said the man. One of the women had come out from the kitchen.

"Hello, Wilfrid," she said. "You've missed your dinner."

"That—doesn't matter," said the man, again with his air of monkish simplicity and tiny hesitation.

"We weren't sure we'd be seeing you," said Barbara, with the same odd lack of respect. "Mrs. K's got a concert on so you'll have to be quiet."

"I know—I know," said Wilfrid, frowning a little at Barbara's tone.

"Would you like to go in?" said Paul. He watched the man watching the people inside, one or two faces turned, while Mrs. Keeping was announcing the next item. His brown suit must once have been someone else's, all three buttons done up, the sleeves short, and the trousers too, and a sense of large square objects trapped in tight pockets. Paul wondered if the other guests knew him and a scene was about to occur that he would be blamed for.

"Is she going on long?" said Wilfrid, pleasantly but as if out of earshot. There were one or two more curious glances.

"I don't really know . . . ," said Paul, detaching himself.

"Have you had something to eat?" said Barbara, softening a little. "Or do you want to come into the kitchen?"

"I think perhaps . . ."—Wilfrid gazed at her and flinched. "Is it an awful bore?"

"Ah, that's all right."

"I got a lift into Stanford, and then the bus, then I walked up."

"Well, you must be hungry," said Paul, adopting the condescending tone. He could hear Peter saying something, in his Oxford voice, making them laugh, and he realized that something had happened, and the voice was now a trigger to jolts of excitement and anxiety that ran through him and made him half-unaware of anything else that was going on. The music began. Wilfrid followed Barbara, but turned in the doorway, came back to the hall table, took a small parcel in shiny red paper out of his pocket and added it to the base of the pile. When he had gone, Paul looked at the label: "Happy Birthday Mummy, Love Wilfrid."

The little puzzle of this didn't hold him long. He leant in the doorway to listen, or at least to watch Peter play. This must be the Mozart, surely. He thought there was something daft but also impressive and mysterious about big clever Peter stooped over this dainty but tedious piece of music and giving it his fullest attention. The large hands that had recently stroked his knee under the table were now hopping and pecking around on the deep end of the keyboard, in a remarkable show of fake solemnity. Mrs. Keeping was having more fun up at the other end, making Peter look like an anxious but courtly attendant; her nods and grimaces now seemed like slightly impatient instructions to him, or tight-lipped confirmation that he had or hadn't got something right. And turning the page was a bit of a worry, with both players busy at once. After a minute Paul noticed that Peter did any pedalling that was called for, and got interested in his legs as much as his hands. Mrs. Keeping's legs jumped as she played, and Peter's occasional toeing of a pedal was like a courteous version of the footsie he'd just been playing with him under the table. Paul was warmed by this secret, and admiring of Peter, and jealous that he couldn't play with him himself. At the end he applauded loudly, and made a point of making the very last clap, as they used to at school.

After this there was a very odd piece, which Paul thought from the awful grin on Peter's face must be someone's idea of a joke. The time after the concert, and all the momentous things that were waiting to happen then, weighed so heavily on Paul that he couldn't concentrate.

He sensed Peter's own little knack for being embarrassing and hoped he wasn't making a fool of himself now. And in a moment it was all over, and they were standing up and bowing, the applause now full of laughter, warm-hearted but with something provisional in it too, so perhaps the joke still needed to be explained to them as well. Peter's gaze swept across the room and he seemed almost to lick Paul with his conceited smile, nodding, chuckling, tongue on lip.

This still wasn't the end, of course, and Paul hardly knew if he was happy or relieved when Corinna sat down again at the piano, Peter withdrew to the front row and Sue Jacobs came forward, with a rather furious expression, to sing "The Hammock" by Bliss. It was strange knowing the words so well, and he tried to follow them against what seemed to him the quite pointless interference of the music. The peculiar things a singer did with words, the vowels that turned into other vowels under the strain of a high note, made it all harder and weirder. Picturing the poem, somehow written across the air, was also an escape from watching Sue herself, her bared teeth and humorous roving glare at one person after another in the audience. "And every sleeping garden flower, / Immortal in this mortal hour." All Paul knew about Bliss was that he was the Master of the Queen's Music, but he found it hard to imagine Her Majesty enjoying this particular offering. At the end Mrs. Jacobs got up and kissed them both, and clapped in the air to reignite the general applause. She appeared to be moved, but Paul thought he saw that under the general requirement to be so she was finding it rather a strain.

As people started talking and stood up, Paul caught Peter's eye and comic grimace, and grinned back as if to say how marvellous he'd been. What he was actually going to say he had no idea—he dodged out to the kitchen to get a glass. When he came back and joined the group round Mrs. Jacobs he hardly dared look at him, distracted with nerves and longing and a sense of unshirkable duty about what he imagined was going to happen next.

A few minutes later they were crossing the garden, bumping lightly as they made way for each other between the tables where candles were still burning in jars; some had guttered, there was a veil of mystery, of concealed identity, over the guests who had come back out and were drinking and chatting under the stars. A cake had been cut up and was being taken round, with paper napkins. "I thought you were going to talk to the old girl all night," said Peter.

"Sorry!"—Paul reaching for but not touching his arm.

"Now let's see. The garden's quite big, isn't it."

"Oh, it is," said Paul. "There's a part at the back I think we really must explore." He felt he'd never been so witty or so terrified.

"We loved what you played!" said a woman passing them on her way back to the house.

"Oh, thank you . . . !"—the skein of celebrity made their little sortie more conspicuous and perhaps odd. Away from the lights now, Peter appeared both intimate and alien, a figure sensed by touch more than sight. Someone had put a Glenn Miller record on the stereogram, and the music filtered out among the trees with a tenuous air of romance. They passed the weeping beech—"Hmm, not here, I think," said Peter, with his air, reassuring and fateful, of having a fairly clear plan.

"I think this part of the garden is most attractive." Paul kept up the game, turning warily in the dark under the rose arch into the unkempt corner where the shed and compost were. He was speaking too as if he knew what he was doing, or was going to do. Surely it was time just to seize Peter but something about the dark kept them apart as naturally as it promised to bring them together.

He half-saw Peter fling open the shed door, with rakish impatience, and heard the clatter of canes—"Oh, shit! Oh shit . . ."—a sense of the shed like a booby-trap. "Mm, it's rather hell in there," Paul said, giggling at his own drollery more than he could quite explain. He was drunk, it was one of the hilarious uncorrectable disasters of being drunk. Now Peter was stooping and furiously thrusting and jamming the tumbled canes back in and failing to get the door shut. He shut it; at once it creaked open again. "I should leave it," said Paul.

He'd brushed against Peter uncertainly as he giggled; now Peter's hand was round his neck, their faces close together in the spidery light through bushes, their eyes unreadable, a huddle of smiles and sighs, and then they kissed, smoke and metal, a weird mutual tasting, to which Paul gave himself with a shudder of disbelief. Peter pressed against him, with a slight squirming stoop to fit himself to him, the instant and unambiguous fact of his erection more shocking than the taste of his mouth. In the fierce close-up and the near-dark Paul saw only the curve of Peter's head, his hair in silhouette and the ragged crown of bushes beyond, black against the night sky. He took his cue from his movements, tried to mimic him, but the sudden stifling violence of another man's wants, all at once, instinctive and mechanical, was too much for him. He twisted his head in Peter's two-handed grasp, tried to turn it to a humorous wistful nuzzle against his chin, his chest. "What an amazing party," he heard himself say. "I'm so glad Mrs. Keeping asked me to help with the parking."

"Mm?"

"I meant to say I like your tie, by the way . . ."

Peter was holding him at arm's length with a serene, almost humorous, almost smug look, Paul felt, as if he were measuring him on some scale of previous kisses and conquests. "Oh, my dear," he murmured, with a sort of swallowed laugh, that suggested some shyness after all. They held each other, cheek to cheek, Peter's evening stubble a further part of the dreadful strangeness of being with a man. Paul wasn't sure if he had fluffed it hopelessly, like his frightened scuttle behind the pampas grass when he'd first arrived; or if this could be taken as a natural amorous pause in which his own confusion would be smoothly concealed and forgiven. He knew he had already been found wanting. And quite quickly he thought, well, it was a sort of triumph just to have kissed another man. "I suppose we should go back," he said.

Peter merely sighed at this, and slid his hands tighter round Paul's waist. "You see, I rather thought we might stay out here a bit longer. We've both earned it, don't you think?" Paul found himself laughing, curving to him, suddenly gripping him hard so as to keep him with him and somehow immobilize him at the same time.

DRINK AND KISSING seemed to move to their own clock. When the two of them got back to the house the crowds were already thinning, though a few of the oldsters had settled in, in new arrangements of the crowded chairs in the drawing-room. Paul felt that he and Peter must be bringing a gleam of the unspeakable with them out of the night beyond the french windows, though everyone amiably pretended not to notice. Drink seemed to have captivated them all, reducing some to silent smiles, others to excitable gabble. John Keeping, very drunk, was raptly explaining the virtues of the port he was drinking to a man three times his age. Even Mr. Keeping, with the globe of a brandy glass in his hand, looked unselfconsciously happy; then when he saw Paul he glanced awkwardly away. There had been another change of music, it was some old dance number that sounded to Paul like a scene from a wartime movie, and on the clear square of floor beside the piano, barely moving but with a captivated look of their own, Mrs. Jacobs was dancing with the farmer man, who turned out to be Mark Gibbons, the marvellous painter she'd mentioned, who'd lived in Wantage. Another couple Paul didn't know revolved at twice the speed beyond them. Paul smiled at them mildly and benevolently, from beyond the enormous dark distance he had just travelled, which made everything else appear charming but weirdly beside the point. "I think I've got to go," Peter said to Julian, resting his hand on his shoulder, and Paul painfully half-believed the story even though he knew they were meeting up again by the car.

Outside the loo he was waylaid by Jenny. "Do you want to come to the Corn Hall with us?" she said.

Julian looked surprised, then deliciously shifty. "Yeah, do you think we can . . . yeah, come with us, that would be good, actually . . . Do you want to ask Dad?" he said to Paul.

"Um . . . I think probably *not*," said Paul, pleased that his tone of voice got a laugh. He ought to thank Mr. Keeping for the evening before he left—the gratitude suddenly keen and guilty, and haunted by a new suspicion that perhaps he hadn't been meant to stay for the whole party, and had made a large and unmentionable mistake.

"I mean it goes on till midnight, what is it now?"

Paul couldn't tell them that he had promised to go with Peter and sit—where?—he pictured a shadowy lay-by where he'd seen courting couples in cars. It was a further shock when Peter said, "Oh, why not?— just for half an hour—I feel like dancing"—just as if their own plans didn't matter at all.

"OK . . . ," said Julian—a slight sense inexpressible in the air that though he needed them as a cover he wasn't completely thrilled at the idea of dancing at the Corn Hall with them.

"Is your brother coming?"

"God, don't tell him," said Jenny.

"I love dancing," said Peter.

"Mm, me too," said Jenny, and to Paul's confusion the two of them started rolling their hips and twitching their shoulders at each other. "Don't you think," she said.

In the hall Mrs. Keeping was standing in rapid, muttered conversation with another woman. "He really can't," she was saying, as Paul hung guiltily back. Out on the drive, at the edge of the spread of light from the front door, Uncle Wilfrid was standing, arms folded tightly but face turned up to admire the heavens as if the rest of him were not knotted up with tension and rejection. "I've got Jenny in the box-room, Mother in the spare room, both the boys home . . . he should have said he was coming."

"I'm sure we could find a corner for him," the other woman said.

"Why can't he get a taxi back?"

"It's a bit late, darling," said the woman.

"Is it?"

"I don't suppose he's got his jim-jams . . . ?"

A sort of desperate solidarity seemed to take over Julian's face, even if it meant not going to the Corn Hall after all. He slipped out into the drive—"Hullo, Uncle Wilfrid . . . ," taking him aside, a bit further off.

"You can see the Crab, Julian," said Wilfrid.

And a minute later they were all in the Imp, in the sharp little comedy of sudden proximity, everyone being witty, everyone laughing, shifting the books and litter from under their bottoms as the car bounced at getaway speed along Glebe Lane. They could hear the grass in the crown of the road swiftly scouring the underside of the car. Wilfrid was in the front, Paul, Jenny and Julian in a painfully funny squash in the back. Julian's hot thigh pressed against Paul's thigh, and Paul found the boy was gripping his hand, he thought just out of general abandon and selfless high spirits. He didn't dare squeeze it back. They rattled out into Church Lane, down the Market Place into the surprising surviving outside world, which included a police car and two officers standing by it just outside the Bell. Peter was supremely unimpressed, shot past them, pulled up and turned off the lights, the engine, just in front of the Midland Bank. A sense of reckless disorder overcame Paul for a moment. But tomorrow was Sunday . . .

They clambered out of the car, a small adjustment taking place. Wilfrid said, "I haven't gone dancing since just after the War."

"You'll love it," Jenny told him, with a confident nod. She was in effect, in this lopsided group, his partner.

"Everybody danced with everybody then."

Peter locked the car, and gave Paul a helpless but happy look, a shrug and a smirking shake of the head.

People were leaving the Corn Hall, the women scantily dressed in the summer night, but clinging to the men. Paul disguised his reawoken tension about seeing Geoff, and chatted pointedly to Jenny as they went into the lobby. As he squinted through the glass doors, the high-raftered hall, under the slow sweep of coloured lights, was thick with the promise of his presence. A boomingly lively song was going on, and Jenny was dancing a bit already—"Can we just go in?"

"Only another twenty minutes, my love," said the woman at the door.

"You're not charging us, are you?" Jenny said, defying her to ask her her age.

The woman gazed at her, but the tickets and the cash were all put away, people pushed past, waiting and staggering out past the cloakroom, the lavatories with their stained-glass doors. So in they went.

Paul thanked god for the drink—he strode straight across the hall, round by the stage, smiling into the shadows, as if he lived in places like this—but no, Geoff wasn't here . . . he came back to the others with a pang of sadness and relief; then remembered his tie, and pulled it off impatiently. He felt almost as shy about dancing as kissing, but this time it was Jenny who took him in hand—their little group started bopping together, Paul smiling at all of them with mixed-up eagerness and anxiety, Wilfrid studying Jenny but not quite getting her rhythm as she rocked in her jutting-out frock and waved her hands in front of her, perhaps waiting for someone to take them, while Julian lit and voraciously smoked a cigarette. Beyond him, peeping mischievously at Paul through the patterned light, Peter did his own dance, a kind of loose-limbed twist. Around them other couples made way, looked at them with slight puzzlement, made remarks, surely . . . Surely people in the town knew Jenny; Julian certainly got frowns and smiles of surprise. Paul followed two couples jiving rapturously together, with sober precision despite the abandon of their faces, back and forth in front of the stage.

A big red-faced woman in a spangled frock picked up Wilfrid . . . did she know him?—no, it seemed not, but he was ready for her, a gentleman, truly sober, and with a certain serious determination to do well. Paul watched them move off, with a smile covering his faint sense of shock, and Jenny leant in towards Paul and nodded, "A friend of yours."

Paul's hand on her shoulder for a second, prickly fabric, warm skin, strangeness of a girl—"Mm?"

"Young Paul?"

He hunched into himself as he turned and there was Geoff, reaching out to him but rearing back in broad astonishment; then his face very close, Geoff's hot boozy breath as if he was about to kiss him too, careless and friendly—"What are you doing here!"—and showing Sandra, who shook hands and was inaudibly introduced, looking only half-amused, but Paul was a colleague, perhaps he'd mentioned him. She crossed her arms under her bosom and then looked aside, at others making for the door. "Christ, is old Keeping here too?"—Geoff big with his own joke. "Just *young* Keeping," said Paul, nodding at Julian, but he didn't seem to get it, stood nodding as the lights came teasingly hiding and colouring the contours of his tight pale slacks and the deep V of his open-necked shirt, a first heart-stopping glimpse of naked Geoff. He leant in again, his rough sideburn brushed Paul's cheek for a half-second, "Well, we're off"—Sandra tugging, smiling but moody, as if to say Paul mustn't encourage him. "See you Monday!"—and then his arm was round Sandra's waist as he escorted her in a gallant grown-up way towards the lit square of the exit.

"Well, he's rather fab!" said Jenny.

"Oh, do you think?" said Paul and raised an eyebrow, as if to say girls were a push-over, turning to look for him as he went out into the light, and then into the dark, as though he were a real missed opportunity, then grinning gamely at Peter as he swayed and sloped towards them, biting his lower lip, and gripped them both in a loose very drunken embrace and whispered in Paul's ear, "Tell me when you want to go."

"A mad one and a slow one," announced the lead guitarist of the Locomotives, the words heavy and resonant in the high roof of the hall. "Then it's goodnight."

"Let's stay a bit longer," said Paul, "now we're here."

The final dance, the watch showing five past twelve, and the two policemen standing genially by the open door in the bright light there, talking to the woman that took the coats. They looked in, across the floor, now sparsely occupied by the dancers who felt the lonely space expanding about them, the night air flowing in, Jenny and Julian locked together in a stiff experimental way, his chin heavy on her shoulder, Paul and Peter now leaning by the wall, swaying in time but a few feet apart, their faces in fixed smiles of uncertain pleasure, and out in the middle, Wilfrid and his new friend, who'd adjusted herself imaginatively to her partner's rhythms and was making up a kind of military twostep with him to the tune of "The Green, Green Grass of Home."

6

PETER ROARED along Oxford Street, so very different from its famous namesake, the few shops here with their blinds down in the early torpor of the summer evening, and just before he came into the square he wondered with disconcerting coolness if he did fancy Paul, and what he would feel when he saw him again. He wasn't exactly sure what he

looked like. In the days since he'd kissed him at the Keepings' party his
face had become a blur of glimpses, pallor and blushes, eyes . . . grey,
surely, hair with red in it under the light, a strange little person to be so
excited by, young for his age, slight but hard and smooth under his
shirt, in fact rather fierce, though extremely drunk of course on that
occasion—well, there he was, standing by the market-hall, oh yes, that's
right . . . Peter thought it would be all right. He saw him in strange close
focus against the insubstantial background, the person waiting who is
also the person you are waiting for. Peter was a little late—in the four or
five seconds as the car slowed and neared he saw Paul glance at the watch
on his inside wrist, and then up at the Midland Bank opposite, as if he
was keen to get away from it, then saw him take in the car and with a little shiver pretend he hadn't, and then, as Peter came alongside, his jump
of surprise. He'd changed after work into clean snug jeans, a red pullover
slung round his shoulders; the attempt to look nice was more touching
than sexy. Peter stopped and jumped out, grinning—he wanted to kiss
him at once, but of course all that would have to keep. "Your Imp
awaits!" he said, and tugged open the passenger door, which made a terrible squawking sound. He saw perhaps he could have tidied the car up a
bit more; he shifted a pile of papers off the floor, half-obstructed Paul
with his tidying hands as he got in. Paul was one of those lean young
men with a bum as fetchingly round and hard as a cyclist's. Peter got in
himself, and when he put the car in gear he let his hand rest on Paul's
knee for two seconds, and felt it shiver with tension and the instant
desire to disguise it. "Ready for Cecil?" he said, since this was the pretext
for the visit. It seemed Cecil had already become their codeword.

"Mm, I've never been to a boarding-school before," said Paul, as if
this were his main worry.

"Oh, really?" said Peter. "Well, I hope you'll like it," and they swept
off round the square, the car making its unavoidable coarse noise. It was
something a bit comic about a rear-engined car, the departing fart, not
the advancing roar.

"So how was your day?" said Peter, as they went back up Oxford
Street. It was three miles to Corley, and he felt Paul's self-consciousness
threatening him too as he smiled ahead over the wheel. It was something
he would have to override from the start.

"Oh, fine," said Paul. "We've got the inspectors in, so everyone's a bit
jumpy."

"Oh my dear. Do they ever catch you out?"

"I don't think they have yet," said Paul, rather circumspectly; and then, "Actually I was a bit distracted today because of tonight, you know."

"Oh, I know," said Peter, pleased by this and glancing at Paul, who was half-turned away from him, as if abashed by his own remark.

"I'll be interested to see the tomb."

"Oh, well, of course, that too," said Peter.

Outside the town a dusty breeze blew off the wheat-fields through the open windows, and mixed with the smell that he knew was slightly sickening of hot plastic and motor oil. In the noisy bluster of air perhaps they didn't need to say very much; he explained about the imminent Open Day, the cricket match and the new Museum, but without feeling Paul took it in; and then: "Well, here we are"—the line of woods was approaching, and he hoped Paul saw, far back from the main road, the flèche on the chapel sticking up among the trees. Here was the lodge-house, a diminutive foretaste of the mansion itself, a cluster of red gables, with a corner turret and a spirelet of its own. The huge wrought-iron gates stood perpetually open. And what Peter always thought a lovely thing happened. As he slowed and changed down and turned off into the chestnut-shadowed drive they seemed to slip the noose of the world, they entered a peculiar secret—in the rear-view mirror, quickly dwindling, the cars and lorries still rushed past the gateway; in a moment they could no longer be heard. There was a magical mood, made out of privilege and play-acting, laid over some truer childhood memory, the involuntary dread of returning to school—Peter tested and even heightened his own feelings by peeping for them in the face of this new friend he barely knew, and yet suspected he knew better than anyone had before. On their right, through the wide strip of woodland, the playing-fields could be glimpsed, the thatched black shed of the cricket pavilion. "These woods are out of bounds, by the way," he said. "If you spot a boy in there you can give him the hairbrush."

"The hairbrush . . ."

"On the BTM."

"Oh," said Paul after a moment. "Oh, I see. Well, let's have a look for one later," and blushed again at the surprise of what he'd said. Peter laughed and glanced at him, and thought he had never met a grown man so easily and transparently embarrassed by anything remotely risqué. He was a hot little bundle of repressed emotions and ideas—perhaps this was what made the thought of sex with him (which he planned to have in the next hour or two) almost experimentally exciting. Though what colour he would turn then . . . "Now, here we are." There had been some talk about Corley at Corinna's party, but Peter hadn't told him what to expect. He slowed again at the second set of gate-piers, and there suddenly it was. "Voilà!"

Some form of stifling good manners, or perhaps mere self-absorption, seemed to keep Paul from seeing the house at all. Peter let his own smile fade as they trundled across the gravel sweep and came to a halt outside the Fourth Form windows, the sashes up and down to let in air, and the curious heads of boys doing prep turning to look out. The indescribable atmosphere of school routine and all the furtive energies beneath it seemed to hang in the air, in the jar and scrape of a chair on the floor, the inaudible question, the raised voice telling them all to get on with their work.

In the front hall Peter said quietly, "I'm sure you're dying for a drink." In his room he had plenty of gin and an unopened bottle of Noilly Prat.

"Oh . . . thank you," said Paul, but wandered off round the hall table to gaze with unexpected interest at the Honours Boards. On the two black panels scholarships and exhibitions to obscure public schools were recorded in gold capitals. There were annoying variations in the size and angle of the lettering.

"You notice D. L. Kitson?"

"Oh, yes . . . ?"

"Donald Kitson . . . No? Anyway, he's an actor. The school's main claim to fame." There were squeaky footsteps behind them, on the polished oak of the stairs, the Headmaster's crepe soles. He came towards them with his usual air of having leapt to a conclusion—this time, perhaps, a favourable one.

"Ah, Peter, good. Praising our famous men." He must have seen the car return, the stranger come in.

"Headmaster, this is my friend Paul Bryant—Paul . . ."—and he rather mumbled the HM's name, as if it were either confidential or unnecessary. He had the keenest sense yet of breaking the rules.

"Well, welcome to Corley Court," said the Headmaster, standing with them to look at the Honours Boards. "I rather fear after this term we're going to be in need of a new board." It was in fact notable that the frequency had picked up, after a hopeless five years, 1959 to '64, in which there were no honours at all. "Peter's working wonders with the Sixth Form," the Headmaster said, almost as if speaking to a parent. It was possible of course that he'd seen him in the bank, and was trying to place him.

"Is it all right if I show Paul round a bit, Headmaster?"

The HM seemed to welcome the idea. "Keep out of prep, if you can. You'll want to see the chapel. And the library. Actually," he said, with a glance at the window, practical and proprietary, as if regretting he couldn't join them, "it's not a bad evening for a hike round the Park."

"There's a thought," said Peter, with a deadpan stare at Paul.

"Get out on the Upper Tads! Get into the woods! What . . . !"

"Well, we could . . ." The old fool seemed to be chasing them into each other's arms.

"Now, I'm just going to check on the repairs," he said, moving away towards the door of the Fifth Form.

"Well, I rather want Paul to see that too, if that's all right," said Peter.

"Most unfortunate, just before our Open Day," the HM continued in a confidential tone to Paul. He opened the left half of the double door and peered in in his brusquely suspicious way. "Well, they've made some progress"—allowing Paul and Peter to follow him into the room, where instead of the bowed heads of boys doing prep they found the tables pushed back against the walls, sacks of rubble, and at the far end, above an improvised scaffold of ladders and planks, a large ragged hole in the ceiling. There was a smell of damp, and a layer of gritty dust over every surface. During Musical Appreciation on Tuesday evening, Matron's bath had overflowed, the water finding its way down through the old ceiling beneath, where it must have built up for a while above the suspended 1920s ceiling before dripping, and pouring, and then crashing down excitingly in a mass of plaster on to a desk that the boys had only just vacated. The programme was still on the blackboard, in Peter's famous handwriting, Webern's *Six Pieces for Orchestra* and the *William Tell* overture, which had barely hit its stride when the first warm splat of water hit Phillipson's neck.

"Have you had a chance to admire the original ceiling, Headmaster?" said Peter, unsure if he meant to amuse him or annoy him.

"My whole concern," said the Headmaster, with that snuffling frankness that was his nearest shot at humour, "has been to get the thing patched up by Saturday!"

Peter scrunched his way among the herded chairs, Paul following, perhaps unsure of the seriousness of the event, peering around with a half-smile in the little primitive shock of being back in a classroom.

"Matron must be mortified," Peter said, attributing finer feelings to her than she had given vent to at the time. He climbed up one of the A-shaped ladders supporting the platform Mr. Sands and his son had been working from. "I've taken some photographs for the archives, by the way, Headmaster," he said, looking down with a precarious sense of advantage. The archives were a purely imaginary resource that the HM none the less wouldn't want to deny. He and Paul gazed up at him with the usual mingled concern and impatience of the earthbound. "It'll be wonderful if we can open up the whole thing."

"I advise you to make the most of it now," said the Headmaster. "It's the last chance you'll ever get." And again he glanced with a rough suspicion of humour at Paul.

"Perhaps we could open it all up during the long vac?"

The Headmaster grunted, drawn against his will into a slightly undignified game. "When Sir Dudley Valance covered it up he knew exactly what he was doing."

But Peter got Paul to climb up too, the planks jumping and yielding under their joint weight, and gripped his arm with insouciant firmness as they raised their heads and peered into the shadowy space between one ceiling and another. Their shoulders blocked most of the light through the hole, and towards the far end of the room this unexpected attic stretched away into complete darkness. It was perhaps two foot six high, the old dry timber smell confused with the rich smell of recent damp. "It's hard to see," said Peter. "Hold on . . . ," and moving slowly he felt for his lighter in his jacket pocket, brought it up to head height and thumbed the flint. "Ruddy thing . . ." Then he got it going and as he swept his arm in a slow arc they saw festive gleams and quickly swallowing shadows flow in and out of the little gilded domelets overhead. Between these there was shallow coffering, painted crimson and gold, and where the water had come through, bare laths and hanging fragments of horse-hair plaster. It seemed far from the architecture of everyday life, it was like finding a ruined pleasure palace, or burial chamber long since pillaged. Where the ceiling joined the nearest wall you could make out an ornate cornice, two gilded capitals and the murky apex of a large mirror.

"Don't set the place on fire, will you," said the Headmaster.

"I promise not to," Peter said.

"Fire and flood in one week . . . ," the Headmaster complained.

Peter winked at Paul by lighter-light, gazed slyly at his prim little mouth, slightly open as he peered upwards. "I've worked out this used to be the dining-room, you see," he said, the sound echoing secretively in the space. Then stooping down, "I was talking to the former Lady Valance about it the other night, Headmaster, she said it was her favourite room at Corley, with these absolutely marvellous jelly-mould domes."

"I'm not happy about you being up there," said the Headmaster.

"I'm sure she'd love to come and see it again."

"Now, now, come on down."

"We're coming," said Peter, squeezing Paul's shoulder, and snapped the lighter shut. He wasn't sure Paul was any more interested than the Headmaster himself. But the vision of the lost decoration, a glimpse of an uncharted further dimension of the house he was living in, was so stirring to him that it hardly mattered. It was a dream, a craze, put aside now almost ruefully in favour of his other craze, his bank-clerk friend.

"Well, good to have met you," said the Headmaster as they went back into the hall. "And do bear in mind, if you want us to have your boy, put him down early: a number of OCs have been putting their boys down at birth—which is really the best advertisement a school can have."

"Oh . . . well, um . . . putting them down?" said Paul—but the HM turned, and with a glance at his watch crossed to the huge hall table, an indestructible relic of the Valance days, snatched up the handbell which stood on it and rang it with implacable violence for ten seconds, as if repudiating by his stern management all the nonsense Peter had just been talking. And at once another old noise, high-pitched, echoing, with just a tinge of sadness for the lost silence, rose to life in the rooms beyond. Paul shivered, perhaps surprised by memory, and Peter pressed his hand in the small of his back as they moved towards the main stairs. Almost instantaneously, doors opened, and boys appeared in the hall. "Steady!" the Headmaster shouted wearily. "Don't run," and the boys curbed themselves and looked curiously at Paul as they went past. There was a strange atmosphere whenever someone from the outside world appeared in school, and Peter knew it would be talked about. He didn't normally mind the lack of privacy, but for a moment it felt like being back at school himself. "Let's get upstairs and have a drink," he murmured, with a pleasant but unencouraging nod to Milsom 1 as he filed past, clutching his Bible.

"But what about Cecil?" said Paul, hanging back on the third or fourth stair, with a regretful look.

"Do you want to see him first? Okay, just a quick peek"—Peter smiling narrowly at him and wondering if perhaps Cecil wasn't a codeword after all. He led him back down, and off through the arch into the glazed cloister that ran along the side of the house. Work had already been put up here for the art exhibition. He bumped into Paul, as he halted politely to look at the watercolour sunsets pinned to boards. Here and there there was a sign of talent, something hopeful among the childish splodge. Art, which required technique as well as vision, was the subject Peter found most frustrating to teach; he wasn't much good at it himself. He taught them perspective, in a strict way, which was something they might be grateful for. He wanted the warmth of Paul's body, he leant on him and laid a hand along his shoulder, peering at a blotchy jam-jar of poppies by Priestman, which was thought to show promise. On what Neil McAll called "the sex front" Peter's time at Corley had been a desert, apart from a drunken night in London at half-term; it was shamingly clear that the thirteen- and fourteen-year-old boys had more fun than he did. Well, that was the age he'd started himself—he'd been at it ever since. He squeezed the back of Paul's neck, a claim and a promise. Again it seemed strange that he fancied him as much as he did; and the mystery of it, which he had no desire to solve, only made the whole episode more compelling. In the chapel he was certainly going to kiss him, and get inside his clothes in one way or another; barring of course some possible rectitude of Paul's about places of worship. "Come on," he said, taking his arm. But then as he turned the iron ring and eased open the chapel door, he heard the flagging wail of the harmonium. "Oh, Christ . . ."

Dusk came early to the chapel, and in the gloom a little tin lamp lit up the anxious features of a boy, in such an odd way Peter couldn't see at first who it was. "Ah, Donaldson . . ."—the sound faltered and broke off with a squeak.

"Sorry, sir."

"That's all right . . . Carry on." The boy, not bad at the piano, had been given permission to explore this more troublesome instrument. "Don't mind us!" But he had lost confidence for a moment, he was all arms and legs with the treadles and the knee-flaps and pinning down the music. He picked a respectfully nasal stop, and began again on "All is safely gathered in."

Paul had already gone towards the tomb, which seemed to float forward among the dark pews. Peter reached behind the door to click the stiff old switches, but no light came on. Donaldson glanced at him, and said, "I think the fuse must have gone, sir." Well, so much the better, it would be a twilit visit. The vivid glass by Clayton & Bell had closed down, in the sad way of church windows when the light is going, into sombre neutrality; the colours had become a dignified secret. This seemed somehow religious, a renewable mystery. Peter crossed himself as he approached, and frowned because he wasn't sure what he meant by it, or even if he wanted Paul to see. It was certainly an unusual setting for a first date, and very different from others he had had, which had tended to be in pubs.

To fit in the whole school they had a line of chairs in the space on either side of Cecil. It was evident that the tomb, which the school was more or less proud of, was also a bit of a nuisance. The boys fixed pretend cigarettes between the poet's marble lips, and one particularly stupid child long ago had carved his initials on the side of the chest. Peter moved chairs out of the way, with a foul scraping noise. Paul went up close, followed the inscription round, "CECIL TEUCER VALANCE MC . . ." Peter saw it freshly himself, second-rate art but a wonderful thing to have in the house; he felt happy and forgiving, having someone to show it to, someone who actually liked Valance, and perhaps hadn't noticed he was second-rate too. The tomb made some grander case for Cecil, in the face of any such levelling quibble. "What do you think?"

It was still hard to tell if Paul's solemn, self-conscious look expressed emotion or mere beetling politeness. He came back close to Peter to speak, as if the chapel imposed a certain discretion. "Funny, it doesn't say he was a poet."

"No . . . no, that's true," said Peter, moved himself and aroused by their repeated touching; "though the Horace, I suppose . . ."

"Mm?"

He touched the plaited Gothic letters. "Tomorrow we shall set forth upon the boundless sea"—trying not to sound too like a teacher as he translated.

"Oh, yes . . ."

Getting into his stride, Donaldson pulled out something bigger, the Bourdon stop perhaps, for the next verse of the hymn, its loud plonking drone giving them a kind of cover. "Have you seen the Shelley Memorial in Oxford?"

"Yes, I have."

"Surely the only portrait of a poet to show his cock," said Peter, and glanced over at Donaldson's mirror to see if he'd been heard.

"Mm, I expect it is," murmured Paul, but seemed too startled to catch his eye. He went up to look at the poet's head, with Peter close behind him, blandly pretending to share his curiosity. Again he put his arm lightly across Paul's shoulders, where his red sweater was slung round—"Handsome fellow," he said, "don't you think?"—and then with tense luxuriance let his hand drift slowly downwards, just the thin shirt here between his fingers and the warm hard curve of his spine—"I mean, not that he really looked like that"—to that magical spot called the sacral chakra, which an Indian boy at Magdalen had told him one night was the pressure-point of all desires. So he pressed on it, tenderly, with a little questioning and promising movement of his middle finger, and felt Paul gasp and curl his back against him as if in some trap where the effort to escape only caught you the more tightly.

"Fell at Maricourt," said Paul, now leaning forward as though he was going to kiss Cecil.

"Well, quite," said Peter. He was entranced by his secret mischief, the ache of expectation like vertigo in his thighs and his chest. Paul half-turned towards him, flushed and shifty, worried perhaps by his own arousal. There was a comically disconcerting suggestion that Cecil himself had something to do with it. Now they had to be careful. As if archly colluding, Donaldson engaged the octave coupler for a further verse. Peter half expected to see his smirk in the mirror, but the boy was responding too hard to the querulous demands of his own instrument. Under the piping blare ("free from sorrow, free from sin") Peter said humorously and straightforwardly, "I really think we'd better go up to my room, don't you."

"Oh . . . oh all right." Paul seemed to think ahead, as if at an unexpected change of plan.

Peter took him up the nearest back-stairs, and the first-floor corridor brought them past the laundry-room—at some point he wanted to take Paul up through the skylight there and on to the roof, which was for good reason the most out-of-bounds thing in the whole school. But he saw at once that the door was open—Matron was fossicking round in there, just her large white rump showing now to the passer-by. "Well, if you come again," he murmured; and saw Paul himself uncertain of such a prospect, eagerness struggling with some entrenched habit of disappointment. They went on, climbed the grand stairs to the second floor, there was the creak of the floorboard that Paul was hearing for the first time, and then they were in Peter's room, with the door snapped shut between them and the world. He pulled Paul towards him and kissed him, and the door he was leaning on rattled in its lock at the sudden impact of their two bodies.

What he'd forgotten was that Paul would immediately start talking—his mouth two inches from Peter's cheek, about how nice this first kiss had been, and how he liked Peter's tie, and he'd been thinking all week . . . his colour at the happy end of the spectrum of embarrassment, his head hot and glowing, and the string of words, half-candid, half-senseless, a jerking safety-line . . . so Peter kissed him again, a long almost motionless kiss to calm him and shut him up and then, perhaps, to break him down. Focused as he was, he took in the familiar creak and rustle, way off behind him, through a mere thickness of oak, and then the short groan, like a polite but determined cough, of the floorboard just outside the door. There was a sharp knock, which they both felt. They froze for one second, Peter letting Paul slide out of his arms, then quickly buttoning his jacket, while still leaning heavily against the door. The handle turned, and the door budged slightly. None of the rooms at Corley had a key. He saw Paul had picked up a book, with a horrified pretence of calm, like a schoolboy about to be caught. Peter called, "Sorry, Matron!" in a hollow voice, and with a funny impromptu kick at the door spun round and snatched it wide open.

Matron was holding a stack of folded sheets, with the grey starchy gleam of all the laundry at Corley. She peered into the room. "Oh, you've got a visitor," she said, apology and disapproval struggling uncertainly. There was her slight wheeze, having toiled up from the laundry-room, and the almost subliminal whistle of the clean sheets against her white-coated bosom. Peter smiled and stared. "I'm giving out clean sheets tonight, because of Open Day," Matron said. There was quite a charge of antagonism, a combative resistance to Peter's charm, and, to be fair, his mockery.

"I hope my room's not going to be open too, Matron," he said. She grappled off the top sheet. "Here, let me . . ." Really he should introduce Paul, but he preferred to excite her suspicion.

"We all need to get ahead," she said, with a tight smile.

"Oh, absolutely." It wasn't clear if she expected him to change the bed right now. She looked narrowly towards it.

"Well, then . . . ! I'll leave you to it," she said. "Top to bottom."

"Of course."

And with that she withdrew. Peter closed the door firmly, gave Paul a queasy grin and poured out two glasses of gin and vermouth. "Sorry about that. Have a drink . . . chin chin." They clinked their glasses, and Peter watched over his own raised rim as Paul sipped, with a little grimace, a swallowed urge to cough, and then put the glass down on the desk. He said, "God, you look so sexy," exciting himself more by his own choked sound. Paul gasped, and picked up his drink, and said something inaudible, which Peter felt sure must be along the same lines.

He thought the Park would offer more shelter than a room with a chair jammed under the door-handle, but as soon as they got outside he was aware of the unusual hum and crepitation of activity, a mower running, voices not far off. Still, the school seemed more delightfully surreal after a large gin drunk in two minutes. The evening had a lift and a stride to it. He remembered summer evenings at his own prep-school, and the haunting mystery, lit only by glimpses, of what the masters did after the boys were tucked up in bed. He wondered now if any of them had done what he was about to do. Paul seemed changed by the gin too, loosened up and at once a little wary of what he might say and do as a result. Peter asked him on a hunch if he was an only child, and Paul said, "Yes—I am," with a narrow smile, that seemed both to question the question and show exactly the only child's sly self-reliance. "What about you?"

"I've got a sister."

"I can't imagine having a sister."

"And what about the rest of your family?"—it was first-date talk, and Peter felt already he might not remember the answer. He wanted to get Paul into the Out-of-Bounds Woods. He took him quickly past the bleak little fishpond, and on towards the stone gate.

"Well, there's my mum."

"And what does she do?"

"I'm afraid she doesn't do anything, really."

"No, nor does mine, but I thought I should ask."

Paul paused, and then said quietly, "She got polio when I was eight."

"Oh, god, I'm sorry."

"Yeah . . . it's been quite difficult, actually." Something flavourless in his words, from embarrassment perhaps and repetition.

"Where does she have it?"

"Her . . . *left* leg is quite bad. She wears a caliper . . . you know. Though she often uses a wheelchair when she goes out."

"And what about your father?"

"He was killed in the War, in fact," said Paul, with a strange, almost apologetic look. "He was a fighter pilot—but he went missing."

"My god," said Peter, with genuine sympathy, and seeing in a blundering way that all these things might help to explain Paul's oddity and inhibition. "It must have been right at the end of the War."

"Well, that's right."

"I mean, when were you born?"

"March '44."

"So you don't remember him at all . . ." Paul pursed his lips and shook his head. "God, I'm really sorry. So you have to support your mother?"

"Well, more or less," said Paul, again with his air of hesitant acceptance, and familiarity with the fumbling sympathy of others when told the news.

"But she gets an Air Force pension, presumably?" Peter's Aunt Gwen did, so he knew about these things.

Paul seemed slightly irritated by this. "Yes, she does," he said; but then, more warmly, "No, that's really important, obviously."

"Oh, my dear," said Peter quietly. He was naturally troubled, and half wished he hadn't asked. He saw the flickering energy of the evening going out in sexless supportiveness; and some more shadowy sense of Paul having too many problems not to be a problem in himself.

"It's sort of why I didn't apply to university," Paul said, with a shrug at this awkward conclusion.

"Mm, you see I didn't realize . . . ," said Peter, and left it at that. He thought, in a momentary montage, of what he had done at university, and tried to blink away the further faint sense of pity and disappointment that seemed to hover between him and this possible new boyfriend. He glanced at him walking along beside him, in his neat brown shoes, quite a springy step, hands awkwardly in his jeans pockets then out of them again, and his agonized look at saying anything at all personal about himself. Well, best to see these problems clearly from the start; a more experienced lover would conceal them till the honeymoon was over. They went past the Ionic temple, where the boys' pets hopped and fluttered in their cages, and Brookings and Pearson in their dungarees were mawkishly grooming their rabbits. They went past the fenced square of the boys' gardens, a place, as everyone said, like a graveyard, with its two dozen flowered plots. Again there were a few of the senior boys, let out in this magic hour after prep, on their knees with trowels, or watering their pansies and nasturtiums. Peter thought he saw from Paul's smile that he was slightly frightened of the boys. In the far corner, looking vulnerable in the open air, was the fairy construction of Dupont's garden, a miniature alp of balanced rocks with a gap at the top through which water could be poured from a can down a twisting cascade and into the wilderness of heathers and mosses below. Equally vulnerable was its aching claim on First Prize in the competition, to be judged by Craven's mother, who was very much a salvia and marigold kind of woman. "They're like graves, aren't they!" said Paul, and Peter touched him again forgivingly in the small of the back and they went on.

In the middle of the High Ground Mike Rawlins was mowing the sacred chain of the cricket pitch, in readiness for Saturday's trouncing of Templers. Peter waved to him, and before they were near him he took Paul's arm firmly and turned him round. "Now there you are . . ." There was the house, massive and intense, and the farmlands beyond, flat and painterly in the heavy light, with the con-trails of planes from Brize Norton slowly lifting and dissolving in the clearer air above. Peter said, "You must admit." He wanted to get something out of Paul, as he might out of some promising but stubborn child. Though it occurred to him that the shyness he was trying to overcome might merely be a dullness he would always have to overlook.

"Amazing," said Paul.

"It's all coming back, you know," Peter said, with a tight smile and shake of the head.

"How do you mean?"

"Victoriana. People are starting to understand it." Last year at St. Pancras Station he had joined a small rally headed by John Betjeman; he dreamed of getting Betjeman to come and talk to the boys about Corley Court—he pictured his pleasure in the jelly-mould ceiling. "That's my room, of course," he said, without pointing, and saw Paul had no idea which one he meant. In one or two other windows strip lights showed against the evening sun, and in the end room on the first floor the curtains were closed, the Babies already in bed, in the barely muted light.

"Do you think Cecil Valance actually had an affair with Mrs. Jacobs?" said Paul.

"Oh! Well, I suppose only one person alive knows for sure, and that's what she says. Of course you never know exactly what people mean by 'an affair.' "

"No . . . ," said Paul, and sure enough he blushed again.

"I think Cecil was probably queer, don't you?" said Peter, which was a mixture of a hunch and a certain amount of cheerfully wishful thinking, but Paul just gasped and looked away. There was a strange disturbance, almost subliminal at first. Over the rattling roar of the mower a few yards off a larger and darker noise began to drone and wallow, and then, not quite where they were looking, a military aircraft trawling low over the woods, steady, heavy-bellied, throbbing and majestic, and somehow aware, as if its pilot had waved, that its passage overhead was a marvel to the craning and turning figures below. Its four propellers gave it a patient, old-fashioned look, unlike the sleek unanswerable jets they saw long before they heard them. As it passed overhead and then over the house it appeared to rise a little before homing in through the lower haze towards the aerodrome five miles away. Mike sheltered his eyes with a raised right arm that seemed also to make a friendly claim or greeting. They went over, Peter introduced Paul, and Mike explained, amid the sweet and sharp smells of two-stroke exhaust and cut grass and his own sweat, that it was one of the big Belfast freighters they'd just brought in. "Sluggish old bus," he said, "but it'll carry anything." In upper windows of the school, boys who'd been watching stood down and melted away. And then the evening re-established itself, but perceptibly at a later phase, as if the past two minutes had been a tranced half-hour.

Ahead of them the little creosoted cottage of the cricket pavilion waited under the lengthening shadow of the woods, a possible place for a snog, at least, but still too much in Mike's view. Peter put his arm round Paul's shoulders, and they strolled on stiffly for a few seconds, Paul again unsure what to do with his hands. "No," said Peter smoothly, "I'd like to write something about old Cecil one day—I don't think any-one has, since that Stokes memoir, you know."

"Right . . ."

"Which is something of a period piece. Unreadable, really. That's why I was asking George Sawle the other night."

"Do you write then?"

"Well, I'm always writing something or other. And of course I keep a sensational diary."

"Oh, so do I," said Paul, and Peter saw him tremble and focus, "well, sensationally dull." There it was, the tiny treasured bit of wit in him. Peter fell on it with a laugh.

Just beyond the whited boundary lay the slipcatch, mown all around, but little used, tall grass growing up through its silvery slats. Peter liked the shape of it, like some archaic boat, and sometimes on evening walks by himself he lay down in it and blew cigarette-smoke at the midges overhead. He imagined lying in it now, with Paul close beside him. It was another of those sites where half-glimpsed fantasies, always in the air, touched down questioningly for a minute, and then flitted on.

Paul had found a cricket ball in the long grass, and stepping back a few yards he threw it swerving through the dip of the slipcatch and up into the air, where no one of course was waiting to receive it—it bounced once and ran off quickly towards the old parked roller, leaving Paul looking both smug and abashed. "I can see you're rather good," said Peter drily; and nervous that he might be asked to put the slipcatch to its proper use, and lob a ball to and fro through it with Paul for half an hour, pretending not to care that he could neither catch nor throw, he walked smilingly on. There was something expert and even vicious in the flick of Paul's arm and the hard momentary trundle of the ball along the curving rails.

It felt sweetly momentous to walk in under the edge of the wood. Here again the evening seemed suddenly advanced. Even the near distances were mysteriously barred and crowded with green, shadows blurred the massive tree-boles while the roof of the wood formed a far-off, slowly stirring dazzle. The horse-chestnuts and limes that made a great undulating wall around the playing-fields were mixed further in with large oaks and sinister clusters of yews. The children climbed and hid in the unchecked brushwood round the base of the limes, and scratched out their tunnels in the rooty soil beneath. Here and there the undergrowth thickened artificially with barricades of dead branches, the camouflaged camps they made, with hidden entrances too small for any master to crawl through. You couldn't be sure if a rustling noise was a child at his spy-hole or a blackbird among the dead leaves.

Paul's behaviour was more anxious now, he hung back again, craned round at the trees, found inexplicable interest among the leaves underfoot; his thin stiff smile of admiration was almost comical to see. "Come here," said Peter, and when Paul came to him, as if good-naturedly leaving something more involving, which still half-held his attention, he locked an arm tight under his elbow, making a quick necessary joke of that too, and marched him briskly along. "You're coming with me!" he said, and found himself shivering and swallowing with excitement and a kind of latent violence. He really wasn't waiting for more than a minute longer—it was only the dim consciousness that outside this hot-faced rush of beautiful necessity there might still be boys about, among the trees, in the dugout of a camp, that kept him from seizing him roughly there and then. He saw of course that Paul needed this treatment, needed someone to override him. Still, he had to give in, after a few ducking and face-shielding yards of scrambling through the saplings and thick undergrowth, to Paul's "Um, actually . . . !," his tug and grimace less scared than indignant.

"Sorry, my dear, am I hurting you?" Peter's grasp became a reasonable stroke, a clumsy holding hands, two fingers plaited for a moment, his endearment gleaming with his humorous annoyance at being checked. He looked around as if thinking of something else; it seemed all right, and then, with a moment's courteous questioning pause in the air, he kissed him fully but gently on the lips. He made the promise of withdrawing a part of the advance, a tantalizing tremor. And again, as if overcome, Paul yielded; and again, when Peter pulled back and smiled, he started talking. "Oh god . . . ," he said, in a sort of tragical quiet voice Peter hadn't heard before. "Oh my god."

"Come on then," said Peter quietly, and they walked on with a new sense of purpose, surely, towards the massive old wreck of a tree which Peter thought of as a kind of Herne's Oak. Beyond here was the line, invisible but potent as any prep-school law or prohibition, dividing the In-Bounds from the Out-of-Bounds Woods.

PETER DROPPED PAUL in Marlborough Gardens, watched from behind the wheel as he let himself in, with a quick turn of the head in the lighted doorway but no wave. At a bedroom window a light already showed through unlined pink curtains; in a minute the bathroom light went on. He had a sense of the private but simple life of the household marked out in lights, and Paul reabsorbed into its routines, which both were and weren't his own; relieved to be back, in a way, but glowing and inattentive surely with new knowledge. Peter wrestled the car into gear and made off with his usual air of helpless indiscretion round the loop of the Gardens.

He wondered if Paul might be too strange for him after all. It might be hard work having such a silent boyfriend, his reserve seemed like a judgement on you. Still, certainly worth holding on to him in the present dearth of opportunity. Someone else might not see the point of him at all—someone who hadn't touched his hot sleek skin, felt his hesitations and his burning little stabs at letting go. He had a charming, slightly tapering cock, hard as a hat-peg, which he had clearly been astonished, and almost appalled, to see in the hands of someone other than himself, and then in the mouth. He had panted and giggled at the shock. And then quickly, afterwards, he started to fret—he let Peter hold him, and hold his hand, but he had a troubled look, as if he felt he had let himself down. They almost rushed, then, to get him back home; they parted with only a "See you soon" and the darting, deniable kiss on the cheek in the insecure shadow of the car. Yet all these little awkwardnesses raised the game for Peter, and excited him more. It wasn't at all like other affairs he had had, but he felt the same disorienting rush of insight, the roll and lift of some larger conveyance than a rattling Hillman Imp. On the main road back to Corley, with the windows down, a new smell blew in, the moist sweet night smell off the fields and trees, all the more mysterious when the nights were so short. The sun would be up a little after four: and find them both waking to their separate sense of how things had changed. Peter saw his thoughts drifting during lessons, and Paul with the paying-in books, preoccupied by his sensations, perched on his swivel stool in a distracting new awareness of being thought about and wanted.

He slowed and indicated to the empty road, and turned in through the gates to the heavier occluded darkness of the Park. *The lights of home . . . the mile of scented darkness . . .* The woods had grown up a lot, clearly, since Cecil's day: now the lights of the school were hidden. That mile, too, was a purely poetical distance—or a social one, perhaps, designed to impress. It was one of Cecil's many invitations to admire him, though not, presumably, to turn up at Corley Court in person. He appeared to the reader on fast-moving horse-back, this latterday world of cheap cars and jet-planes superbly unimagined.

> *Between the White Horse downs and Radcot Bridge*
> *Nothing but corn and copse and shadowed grazing,*
> *Grey village spires and sleeping thatch, and stems*
> *Of moon-faced mayweed under poplars gazing*
> *Upon their moon-cast shadows in the Thames.*

It was one of his better pre-war poems, though with that tendency to sonorous padding that spoiled almost everything he wrote if judged by the sternest standard.

Peter parked on the front gravel and made a poor attempt to shut the car door quietly. The moon was up, among streaky clouds, and before going in he walked round in front of the house, across the lawn by the fishpond, and back up the rise towards the gate into the High Ground. He seemed to stride through the complex calm of sexual gratification, borne along by running and looping images of what had happened—he saw himself enhancing it, warming it by little touches, then felt the countervailing cool of something like unease, the cool of loneliness. If Paul were with him still, they would make it better, do it over again. No doubt it was painful for anyone who was courting, but for two men . . . He stopped in front of the Ionic temple and peered into the deep shadow, oddly wary of the warm life caged invisibly there. Perhaps disturbed by him, a rabbit or hamster rustled and scratched, a budgie hopped and fluttered and tinkled its bell. He went on and stood by the gate, looking back, the moonlight and its shadows making the house insubstantial, for all its pinnacled bulk, as if half in ruin. The dorms were all dark but the light of the Headmaster's television flickered inside the oriel window. The moon gleamed sharply on the pointed vane of the chapel roof, and on the dial of the stopped clock in the central gable, under the pale stone banner of the Valance motto, "Seize the Day."

It was funny how Paul had been turned on by Cecil's tomb, and by the fact of Corley having been his home. Cecil's brother, of course, had stayed on here for thirty years more, till the military took over. It was surely good luck in the end that all the Victorian work was boxed in—there was nothing for the army to ruin. Dudley Valance's hatred for the house was what had preserved it. It would be worth trying to talk to him about the early days, about Cecil as a boy. In *Black Flowers* he dealt very coolly with his brother—there was quite a sarcastic tone to some of it. Still, what a subject, two writers growing up in this astonishing place, the whole age that had built it riding for a fall. Perhaps he should seize the day himself, and start gathering materials, talking to people like old Daphne Jacobs who still remembered Cecil, and had loved him, and apparently been loved back.

Were people interested in Cecil? How did he rank? Undeniably a very minor poet, who just happened to have written lines here and there that had stuck . . . But his life was dramatic as well as short, and now everyone was mad about the First World War—the Sixth Form all learned "Anthem for Doomed Youth" by heart, and they liked the Valance war poems he had shown them. There was something a little bit queer about several of these poems; something he suspected in Dudley, too. Dudley seemed if anything the queerer one, with his intense devotion to the man he called Billy Prideaux, who'd been shot beside him on a night recce, and seemed to have triggered a nervous breakdown, powerfully but obscurely described in his book.

Peter came back to the stone bench by the fishpond and lit a cigarette. Cecil's letters would be the thing to get a look at—Peter hoped his charm had worked last week on George Sawle, who must have all sorts of useful memories. Interesting what he'd said about Lytton Strachey too, and this book that was about to come out. Was the era of hearsay about to give way to an age of documentation? He looked at the house, as if it enshrined the mystery and in its Victorian way imposed the task. Was he up to writing a biography? It would take a much more orderly existence than any he'd managed so far . . . It was odd, it often struck him, being here in the country with these eighty children and a group of adults he would never have chosen as friends. But it would be at least a symbolic advantage, if he were to write the book. The stars thickened in the outer sky and the sinking moon threw the steep black profile of the roof into Gothic relief. It was windless and warm, the near-stasis of an ideal English summer. It all looked very good for the Open Day. He got up and strolled back towards the house in the nice tired mood of prospective exertion.

What was that? A hand stroked the back of his neck as the shadow of a tall brick chimney high above the Headmaster's window wobbled and shifted. A kite-like form detached itself, and moved with dreamy-looking wariness across the sloping upper leads; five seconds later another, hesitant but committed, and making it seem that the inky shadow might harbour many more of them. They were strangely antique, these two figures, of uncertain size and height, and seemed to flow like oily shadows themselves, in dressing-gowns left open like cloaks. They crept from chimney-stack to chimney-stack, towards the higher slope of the chapel roof, with its crowning spirelet still far above their heads. Once or twice Peter could hear very faintly the patter or slither of their slippered feet.

FOUR

Something of a Poet

Mrs. Failing found in his remains a sentence that puzzled her. "I see the respectable mansion. I see the smug fortress of culture. The doors are shut. The windows are shut. But on the roof the children go dancing for ever."

—E. M. Forster, *The Longest Journey*, chapter 12

I

THE RAIN WASN'T MUCH, but the wind was wild, and he hurried round the square with his brolly held low in front of him and half-blocking his view. The plane trees roared in the dark overhead, and wide wet leaves shot past him or pressed blindly against his coat. In his left hand he had his briefcase, black leather, streaked by the rain. He'd been reading poetry in the library, in the dwindling evening crew. When the dark-haired man, called R. Simpson, who seemed to be working on Browning's plays, started packing up, he had packed up too; but at the street-door, in the downpour, Simpson had hurried right, while he had gone left, in the usual muddle of gloom and relief, towards the Underground. He found the tussle with the weather oddly satisfying.

After dusk in Bedford Square you could see into the high first-floor windows of publishers' offices, the walls of bookshelves and often a huddle of figures at a glaringly lit party. Such a party was going on now, at the front door below a few guests were leaving, and the bright rectangle widened and narrowed as they slipped out into the night, laughing and exclaiming about the weather. A couple emerged, heads lowered, and behind them he saw a small figure, an old woman surely, framed in the doorway as she buttoned her coat, secured her hat, hung her bag on her arm, and then, as she stepped out on to the pavement, pushed up a flimsy umbrella, which the wind snatched instantly and jerked upwards inside-out behind her head. Her words whipped back to him distinctly, "Oh, bugger it!" He saw her grappling with the thing as he drew nearer, his own umbrella swerving and struggling in the face of the wind. She staggered a little, more or less righted it, and moved quickly away, almost stumbling, though a spoke stuck up at a hopeless angle, the pink fabric flared loose, there was a lull and then a sudden slam of wind which wrenched the brolly out of her hands and off into the road, where it skidded and then leapt away in long hops between the parked cars. Of course he should help her, run after it, but she seemed, with a certain reckless good sense, to have given the thing up. She turned for a moment, glint of street-lamp on glasses, then ducked back into the wind, the rain now only a kind of roaring dampness, and as she hurried on Paul felt such a twisting stab of anxious excitement that he hid behind his umbrella for ten seconds, not knowing what to do. He slowed down, almost as though to let her get away; then pulled himself together. Trudging forward against the wind she seemed alarmingly vulnerable, to the weather, to the London night, and also to him. Why had no one come with her, or seen her to a cab? It was with a sort of ache he came up behind her, the painful comedy of having her for a further ten seconds, fifteen seconds, within arm's reach, her red felt hat pulled down tight and her white hair beneath it tugging in clumps in the storm. There was a pink silk scarf around her neck, and her mac was shabby, the collar darkened. He picked up very faintly its musty, perennial smell, before he swept his umbrella up and then down between her and the gale. "There you are . . . ," he said.

"I know," she said, "isn't it awful," walking on, with a quick doubtful glance at him but perhaps a touch of reassurance too.

"You shouldn't be out in this, Mrs. Jacobs," he said, very capably.

"The rain's pretty well stopped, I think."

Paul grinned, perhaps rather stared at her. "Where are you going?" He felt buoyant with his nerves and his own, perhaps unshared, sense of hilarity in the meeting. He slowed his step to hers.

"Were you at the party?" she said, with a slightly sentimental look, as if still savouring it.

Before he could think better of it, he said, "Yes, I was, but I didn't get a chance to speak to you."

"Caroline has so many young friends . . ." She made sense of it for herself. He could see she'd had quite a bit to drink—the grip of the drink at these parties and the nonsense you talked: then you came hurtling out, parched and light-headed and you hoped not alone. Night had fallen while you drank. He was straightforward, though still teasing her for some reason:

"Do you remember me, Mrs. Jacobs?"

She said, as if she'd been waiting a long time patiently for this question, and without looking at him, "I'm not sure."

"Why should you!" he said. "We haven't seen each other for a good ten years . . ."

"Ah, well," she said, relieved but still non-committal.

"No, it's *Paul*—Paul Bryant. I used to be in the bank at Foxleigh. I came to your . . . your big birthday party, all those years ago." That perhaps wasn't tactful.

"Oh, did you," and then Mrs. Jacobs gave a strange gasp, or grunt—Paul saw it too late, like a hazard in the black gleam of the pavement just ahead. Could they chat on casually around that double tragedy? It was also perhaps an opportunity, for sympathy, for showing that he knew her story and she could trust him. "Yes, indeed," she said.

"I was so very sorry to hear about . . . Corinna, and . . ."

She almost stopped, put a hand on his sleeve, perhaps in silent thanks, though there was something corrective in it too. She looked up at him. "You couldn't find me a taxi, I suppose, could you?"

"Yes, of course," said Paul, chastened as if by several reminders at once, but relieved he could be of service. Above them towered the grey bulk of the new YMCA, and beyond it there was the glitter and hiss of traffic in the Tottenham Court Road. "Where do you want to go?"

"I have to get to Paddington."

"Oh, you're not living in London any more?"

"I think there's a train at about ten to nine."

Now the rain started pattering on the umbrella. They were by the bright doorway of the Y, young men coming out, with a glow of self-worth about them, putting up hoods, making a dash for it. "Would you like to wait here—I'll find you a cab." Under the light he saw more plainly how shabby she was. She wore a lot of powder, over a face that now appeared both gaunt and pouchy. The rain had splashed her brownish stockings and her scuffed court shoes. The workings of time were sordid, slightly frightening to him, and he steadied himself with the thought of what she had been long ago. These glowing and darting boys coming out of the gym and the sauna had no idea of her interest. He spoke to her loudly and charmingly to show them she was worth it. She was a Victorian, she had seen two wars, and she was the sister-in-law, in a strange posthumous way, of the poet he was writing about. To Paul her natural habitat was an English garden, not a gusty defile off the Tottenham Court Road. Poems had been written for her, and set to music. She remembered intimacies that by now were nearly legendary. Whether she remembered Paul, however, he couldn't tell.

It took five minutes to get a cab on the main road, and signal it round to where she was standing. Running back to her, seeing her expression, anxious but somehow inattentive, he knew he would go with her to Paddington, and on the way he would make an arrangement to see her again. He spoke to the driver, and then strode across with the brolly to bring her to the car. "The silly thing is," she said, "I'm not sure I've the fare for the cab."

"Ah!" Paul said, almost sternly, "don't worry," wondering if he could in fact afford this. "Anyway, I'm coming with you." And adopting a bland, unhearing expression he more or less pushed her into the taxi, and went round the other side to get in himself. He supposed they had fifteen minutes.

They settled, rather tensely; the cabby kept up talk through the partition about the diabolical weather, till Paul sat forward and shut the screen. He glanced at Mrs. Jacobs for approval, though she seemed for a moment, in the underwater gloom of the cab, to be ignoring him. Her soft face was oddly haggard in the running shadows and gleams.

Paul said, "I can't get over just bumping into you like that."

"I know . . ." It was a struggle for her between being grateful, embarrassed and, he sensed, somewhat offended.

The cab had a food-like smell of earlier occupants, and the seat was still slippery from their wet clothes. He unbuttoned his coat, sat at an angle, with one leg drawn up, eager but casual. She had the transparent aura of old age, was notable and ignorable at the same time. She had her bag on her knee, both gloved hands on top of it. It wasn't the same bag of twelve years earlier, but another, closely related, with the family trait of being shapelessly bulky—too bulky, really, to count as a handbag. It admitted as much in its helpless slump. He said, "So how have you been?"—giving the question a solicitous, tentative note. He thought it was three years since Corinna's death, and Leslie Keeping's suicide.

"Mm, very well, really. Considering, you know . . . !"—a dry chuckle, quite like the old days, though her face retained its look of anxiety and preoccupation. She wiped the window beside her ineffectively and peered out, as if to check where they were going.

"But you're not living in London? I think the last time I saw you, you were in . . . Blackheath?"

"Ah, yes. No, I've moved, I've moved back to the country."

"You don't miss London?" he said amiably. He wanted to find out where she lived, and sensed already a certain resistance to telling him. She merely sighed, peered at the blotted world outside, sat forward to push down the window a crack, though in a moment the throb of the engine shivered it shut. "I've been in London myself for three years now."

She tucked in her chin. "Well, you're young, aren't you. London's fine when you're young. I liked London fifty years ago."

"Well, I know," said Paul. In some absurd way her account in her book of living in Chelsea with Revel Ralph had coloured his own sense of what London life might offer: freedom, adventure, success. "I got out of the bank, you see. I think I always really wanted to be a writer."

"Ah, yes . . ."

"It seems to be going quite well, I'm pleased to say."

"I'm so glad." She smiled anxiously. "We're sure he is going to Paddington, aren't we?"

Paul entered into it as a little joke, leaning forward. Through a wiped arc he saw for a moment a blurred corner pub, a hospital entrance, all unrecognizable. "We're fine," he said. "No, I've been doing a bit of reviewing. You may have seen a piece of mine in the *Telegraph* a couple of months ago . . ."

"I don't see the *Telegraph,* as a rule," she said, with droll relief more than regret.

"I know what you mean," Paul said, "but actually I think the books pages are as good as any." What he really wanted to know, but somehow couldn't ask, was if she'd seen his review of *The Short Gallery* in the *New Statesman,* a paper he felt she was unlikely to take. He'd done it as a gesture of friendship, finding all that was best in the book, the tiny criticisms themselves clearly affectionate, the corrections of fact surely useful for any future edition. Whenever he reviewed a book he read all its other reviews as keenly as if he were the author of the book himself. Daphne's memoir had been covered either by fellow survivors, some loyal, some sneering, or by youngsters with their own points to make; but a more or less open suggestion that she had made a good deal of it up hung over all of them. Paul blushed when he read about errors he had failed to spot, but drew a stubborn assurance of his own niceness from the fact of having been so gentle with her. His was much the best notice she had received. As he wrote it, he imagined her gratitude, phrased it for her in different ways and savoured it, and for weeks after the review appeared—rather cut, unfortunately, but its main drift still plain to see—he waited for her letter, thanking him, recalling their old friendship, and suggesting they meet up again, perhaps for lunch, which he pictured variously at a quiet hotel or in her own house in Blackheath, among the distracting memorabilia of her eighty-two years. In fact the only response had been a letter to the Editor from Sir Dudley Valance, pointing out a trifling error Paul had made in alluding to his novel *The Long Gallery,* on which Daphne's title was a pawky in-joke. If even Sir Dudley, who lived abroad, saw the *New Statesman,* perhaps Daphne did too; or the publisher might have sent it on. Paul thought a certain well-bred reserve might have kept her from writing anything to a reviewer. She was pulling off her gloves. "You won't mind if I have a cigarette?"

"Not at all," said Paul; and when she'd found one in her bag he took the lighter from her and gently held her arm for a second as she leant to the flame. The smoke soured the fetid air almost pleasantly. And at once, with the little shake of her head as she exhaled, her face, even the uptilted gleam of her glasses, seemed restored to how they had been twelve years before. Encouraged, he said, "I'm very pleased to see you, because in fact I'm writing something about *Cecil* . . . Cecil Valance"—with a gasp of a laugh, quickly deferential. He didn't come out with the full scale of his plans. "Actually, I was about to write to you, and ask if I could come and see you."

"Well, I don't know," she said, but quite nicely. She blew out smoke as if at something very distant. "I wrote a book myself, I don't know if you saw that. I sort of put it all in there."

"Well, yes, of course!"—he laughed again. "I reviewed it, in fact."

"Were you horrid?" she said, with another touch of the droll tone he remembered.

"No, I loved it. It was a rave."

"Some of them were stinkers."

He paused sympathetically. "I just felt it would be very valuable to be able to speak to you—of course I don't want to be a nuisance. If you like, I'll just come for an hour when it suits you."

She frowned and thought. "You know, I never pretended to be a wonderful writer, but I have known some very interesting people." Her quiet laugh now was slightly grim.

Paul made a vague noise of indignant dismissal of all her critics. "Of course I saw your interview in the *Tatler,* but I thought there might be a bit more to say!"

"Ah, yes." Again she seemed both flattered and wary.

"I don't know if you'd prefer the morning or the afternoon."

"Mm?" She didn't commit herself to a time, or to anything really. "Who was that very nice young man at the party—I expect you know him? I can't remember anyone's name. *He* was asking me about Cecil." She seemed to take some slightly mischievous pleasure in this.

"I hope he's not writing about him!"

"Well, I'm not at all sure he isn't."

"Oh dear . . . !"—Paul felt rattled, but managed to say smoothly, "I'm sure since your book came out there's been a lot more interest in him."

She took in a deep draught of smoke and then let it out in a sleepy wave up her face. "It's the War, too, of course. People can't get enough of the War."

"Oh, I know," said Paul, as if he too thought it rather overdone. In fact he was counting on it heavily.

She peered at him, in the streaking glare and shadow, almost haughtily. "I think I do remember you," she said. "Don't you play the piano?"

"Aha!" said Paul. "Yes, I know what you're thinking of."

"You played duets with my daughter."

He enjoyed this passive imposture, though it was uncomfortable too to be taken for Peter. "It was great fun, that evening," he said modestly.

"I know," she said. "Wasn't it."

"They were happy times in Foxleigh, in many ways." He spread a warm glaze over the place and time, as if they were much more distant than was the case. "Well, they introduced me to your family!" He thought she saw this as pure flattery. He wanted to ask about Julian, and Jenny, but any questions were darkened by the awful larger question of Corinna and Leslie Keeping. Was it proper to talk about them, or presumptuous and intrusive? The effort of keeping the talk going stalled him for a minute.

"Ah! Here we are . . . !" she said as the cab swung down the long ramp into the station. He saw that for her the moment of escape was also one of obligation. At the setting-down place he jumped out, and stood with his brolly hooked over his forearm and his wallet open in his hand. He only took a taxi about twice a year, but he tipped the driver with the jovial inattention of young men he had seen in the City. Mrs. Jacobs had clambered out on the other side, and waited in a ladylike fashion for the business to be done. Paul rejoined her with a happy but submissive smile.

"Why don't you give me your address, anyway, and I can write to you."

"Yes, that would be fine," she said quietly, as though she'd been thinking it over.

"And then we can take it from there . . . !" He had a pad in his brief-case, and he lent it to her, looking away as she wrote her details down. "Thank you very much," he said, still businesslike.

"Well, thank you—for rescuing me."

He stared at her stout, slightly stooped and shabby person, the cheer-ful glasses under the sad red hat, the clutched bag, and shook his head, as if at a chance meeting of devoted old friends. "I just can't believe it!" he said.

"Well, there you are," she said, doing her best.

"See you very soon, I hope"—and they shook hands. She was getting, what was it?, a Worcester train, from the nearest platform—he hadn't looked yet at her address. She turned away, went a few determined steps, then looked back with a hesitant and slightly conspiratorial air that he found immediately charming.

She said, "Just tell me your name again."

"Oh! *Paul Bryant* . . ."

She nodded and clenched her hand in the air, as if catching at a moth. "Au revoir," she said.

2

"DEAR GEORGIE," Paul read, "At luncheon today the General was moved to remark that your visit to Corley Court had been *reasonably quiet,* and pressed a little further said you had 'hardly put a foot wrong.' That *hardly* may give you pause: but she would say no more. Overall, I take her to mean that further visits will not be frowned on. [. . .] I will of course convey her good wishes to you in person, tomorrow afternoon, at 5:27 precisely. Praise the Lord for Bentley Park and Horner's Van (Homer's—can't read? Not *the* Homer, dare I hope, the writer?). Then Middlesex will be all before us. Your CTV." Outside the train window, Middlesex itself was opening and then hiding again in the curves of the line. Paul kept his finger in the *Letters of Cecil Valance* as he stared into the bright afternoon—low sun over suburban houses, bare trees between playing-fields, now a tunnel. He looked down at Cecil's face, the promi-nent dark eyes, wavy dark hair oiled almost flat, the sepia knot of his tie, with a pin behind it, the brass-buttoned epaulettes and wide serge lapels with a regimental badge on each, and the buckled leather strap that cut across his chest like a sash. "Edited by G. F. Sawle" beneath the picture. Then the flickering townscape jumped in again and they were slowing to a station.

Paul had formed a general idea, from studying the *London A–Z,* of where "Two Acres" was. But a small-scale map in black-and-white, with the street names squeezing like juggernauts through the streets and the odd vague rhombuses and triangles of blank space in the outer suburbs, might have been showing him almost anything. The half-dozen letters of Cecil's to George that survived were addressed, in the confident bygone style, to "Two Acres, Stanmore, Mddx." There was no suggestion the house stood on a particular street, or that any functionary could fail to know it and its occupants. Horner's van would have offered a lift from the station. But now it was impossible to arrive as Cecil had done: the station itself, "built to look like a church," according to George Sawle's meticulous footnotes, "with battlemented tower and steeple," had been closed to passengers in 1956. Paul had a sense, as of some neglected worry, that a search in the British Library, or indeed in the Stanmore Library, might have turned up a detailed historical map. But for now the poem was his guide. There was a road called Stanmore Hill, and Cecil referred to the "beechy crown of Stanmore Hill," so that was a useful start. The garden was described as running down a slope, pretty clearly (its "goatfoot paths and mimic tor," its "steps dissolving in the dusk / Through scented belts of rose and green / Into the little twilit dene"), and the house itself Paul imagined, on even slighter evidence, perched at the top, for the view. Bentley Priory, a large empty pentagon marked "Royal Air Force" in the *A–Z,* but with dotted footpaths through it, and the blank lozenge of a lake, seemed to climb the hillside too. George's notes explained that the Priory, "once the home of the widowed Queen Adelaide, had later been a hotel; the branch-line from Harrow and Wealdstone to Stanmore had been opened to bring in the guests; trains ran hourly; subsequently the Priory became a girls' school; during the Battle of Britain, it was the headquarters of Fighter Command." Sawle pointed out the reference to *Paradise Lost,* but was something else meant by Cecil's references to Middlesex? Throughout the book he looked back on the landscape of his own youth strictly as a historian; the initials GFS replaced the first person singular; he was patiently impartial. And yet there were omissions, like the one in this short letter, marked by the scrupulous square brackets. What could possibly have offended, sixty years on?

Outside the Tube station, Paul felt the little breathless shock of disorientation, swiftly denied. His thing in London was never to show that he didn't know where he was going; he was less worried about being lost than about asking the way. And then the fact of doing research on the ground, the strange heart-race of crossing the physical terrain of his subject's past, such as he'd felt when Peter first took him to Corley Court and showed him Cecil's tomb, was like a secret guidance. He went along steadily, among the lunch-time shoppers, the office-workers going for a pint, with a completely private sense of purpose: no one knew who he was or what he was doing, or sensed the larger rhythm of his day that lay beyond their routines. It was freedom too, with its prickle of trepidation, since Paul had once been as routine-bound as them.

Stanmore Hill began like a village street, but soon opened out into a long straight climb out of town, already cheerless in the November afternoon. He passed a large pub, the Abercorn Arms, which was mentioned in one of the handful of letters from Cecil to George that survived: the boys had had a pint there themselves. Paul saw the appeal of it, as part of his research, but he felt self-conscious entering pubs alone and pressed on up the road. Boys are what they had been, of course, George only half Paul's present age when he met Cecil, and yet they seemed to occupy their lives with a peculiar unselfconscious authority Paul had never felt in his own. Towards the top of the hill there was a small weather-vaned clock-tower on a stable block, half-covered by trees, and though he felt sure it couldn't be "Two Acres," it seemed in some incoherent way like a promise of it.

After that the road flattened out and on the far side was a long black pond, surrounded by scruffy trees, and the beginning of Stanmore Common. He saw a woman walking a dog, a white poodle that looked alarmingly too big, and since they were the only walkers about, Paul felt conspicuous. He turned down a side-road, thinking that he could have asked her, and for ten or fifteen minutes he wandered round a modest little network of lanes that none the less had something mysterious about them, the sun lowish already among the nearly bare trees, further murky ponds, woodlands sloping away on the far side, and here and there, half-hidden by hedges and fences and large gardens, a number of houses. He wished he were more expert at looking at houses, and knowing how old they were. George Sawle said "Two Acres" was red-brick, and had been built in the 1880s; his father had bought it from its first owner in 1890; his mother had sold it in 1920. Paul checked each name as he passed: "The Kennels" . . . "Old Charlocks" . . . "Jubilee Cottage."

Could he have missed it? He thought of the tests he had just read about in an earlier letter of Cecil's, from his first weeks at Marlborough, where he had had to prove to a senior boy that he knew where things were and the meaning of ridiculous names. "I got them all," Cecil told his mother, "except for Cotton's kish, and for this it is Daubeny who must have forty lashes, for failing to instil this vital fact in my teeming brain. I fear you will think this unjust."

He was almost back at the main road and here was the woman with the poodle coming towards him. She gave him a quick hard smile, a man roaming round with a briefcase in the afternoon. "You look lost," she said.

"I'm okay now," said Paul, nodding at the road ahead. "Thanks so much!" And then, "Well, actually," when she had passed him, "sorry . . . I'm looking for a house called 'Two Acres.' "

She half-stopped and turned, the dog pulling her on. "*Two* Acres? No . . . I don't know it. Are you sure it's round here?"

"Pretty sure," said Paul. "A famous poem was written about it."

"Mm, not a poetry reader, I'm afraid."

"I thought you might have heard of it."

"Stop it, Jingo! No . . . ," she frowned back to him, "I mean, two acres is quite big, you realize."

"Well . . . yes," Paul agreed.

"We have a third of an acre, and believe me that takes a good deal of work."

"I suppose in the old days . . . ," said Paul.

"Oh, well in the old days . . . Jingo—*Jingo!*—mad dog! I'm so sorry . . . Who lives in this house you're looking for?"

"That I don't know," said Paul, the intimate and whimsical nature of his quest exposed, as he'd known it would be if he stooped to asking anyone. It seemed beyond the woman, too: she winced at his briefcase, which must hold the reason for his search, which she wasn't going to ask—some rep or agent no doubt.

"Well, good luck," she said, as if seeing she had wasted her time. And as she went on, "Try the other side of the hill!"

Which Paul did, going down a narrow road that was perhaps a private driveway—there seemed to be a new development of houses whose roofs he could see further down the slope. The lane turned a corner, running for thirty yards under a tall dark larch-lap fence that gave off, even on this chilly day, a dim scent of creosote. Just behind it, a house stood, only the long ridge of its roof and two tall chimneys visible. At the far end, gates, of the same height and material as the fence, chained and padlocked; but allowing, through the narrow gap between hinge and frame, a one-eyed view of a weedy bit of gravel and a downstairs window of the house, disconcertingly close. After this, a dense screen of leylandii, much taller than the fence, ran back from the road, cutting close to the corner of the house itself, and shielding it from the tarmacked drive beyond, at the head of which was a big display board, with an artist's impression of another red-roofed house, and the words "Old Acres—Six Executive Homes, Two Remaining."

The small dislocation in the name was dreamlike for him, though almost meaningless in the light of day. He supposed to have kept "Two Acres" would only have brought home to the executives just how tiny their properties were; perhaps "Old Acres" lent atmosphere to the still raw-looking properties packed in at artful angles to each other among trees which must be survivors from the Sawles' garden. To those who knew, it preserved a word, at least, of the old order. But he saw already that the "airy-chambered garden" had gone; and even the house itself, which Paul had no doubt was the house, seemed resistant to being looked at. He got out his camera from his bag and crossing the lane took a picture of the fence.

This wasn't quite enough. Going back, he stared concernedly at the entranceway of the house before "Two Acres," "Cosgroves," a drive curving out of sight behind rhododendrons, the house itself too far off to keep a watch on its gate. As he strolled in he was smiling mildly, the smooth compulsion of the trespasser just hedged by a far-fetched pretence that he was lost. His movements felt almost involuntary, though everything about him was alert. On his right a wide lawn opened out, dead leaves drifted by the wind into ridges and spirals. An empty teak seat, a stone table. A blue sack wrapping a plant he took for a moment for a stooping person. The boundary with "Two Acres" on this side was a dense run of shrubbery, and then a wall of old firs, bulging and decrepit, pressing down on an ancient wooden garage and a little tar-roofed potting-shed with cobwebbed windows. He caught the sound though not the words of a woman's voice, somewhere outside but in monologue, as if on the telephone. The space between garage and shed gave him cover; he slid between them, and then going at a squat and for a yard or two on hands and knees, shielding his face with his briefcase, he pushed through the dense harsh fronds between the trunks of the firs, and emerged, scratched and dishevelled, in the back garden of "Two Acres" itself.

He stood where he was for a minute, and looked round. He felt almost comically cheated but his excitement worked over and around his disappointment, with cunning persistence. There was little enough to see. The defensive wall of conifers turned a corner and cut across behind the house as well, robbing it of a last glimpse of the trees beyond and below, which must be the parkland of Bentley Priory. The enclosed space was dead and already sunless. The short slope of tangled grass, dead thistles and nettles had a track through it of the kind a fox might make— Paul saw it would live undisturbed here, the house condemned by its own urge for privacy. Taken by a sudden urge, territorial as much as physical, he turned his back on the house, put down his briefcase, and had a short fierce piss into the long grass.

Somehow he couldn't take the house in; but he would take photographs, so as to see it all later. He wandered up to a small window in the side wall, a shadowy kitchen, a steel sink just in front of him, a door open beyond into a brighter space. The little translucent mill set in the pane span round fitfully when he breathed on it. The feeling he'd had, that the house might still somehow be lived in, left him completely. It was empty, and therefore in a way his; he felt a lurching certainty that he could and should get into it. Then as he stepped back he saw high up under the eaves the badge-shaped red-and-white box of a burglar alarm, Albion Security, which was a challenge he didn't mean to take up. It looked new and alert and immune to the plea made by the books in his briefcase that he was only here to research the life of a poet. He went round the corner on to the front drive, just a narrow strip in front of the house; the horrible fence, with its creosote smell, concealed him completely from the road. A short brick path ran up to the front door. On the door-frame at chest height was a small oblong box with three circular holes in it, a wire trailing from one of them. So at some stage, before this latest degradation, "Two Acres" had been divided up, three flats, probably—like almost every house in London. Well, there were sixty years unaccounted for, since the day the Sawle family had relinquished the place. Paul wondered dimly how it had been done—new bathrooms, firedoors; his eyes ran over the black gleam of the little upstairs windows; who had got Daphne's room, had the room where Cecil slept become a living-room, another kitchen?

Paul spent ten minutes at the house, magnetized but baffled, drawn to each window in turn. He looked out all the time for something detachable, and small enough to join the books in his bag. Not a flower-pot, or twig, but something that had been there unquestionably since before the First World War. A rusty horseshoe over the front door had swung sideways on its nail, the luck spilling out—he could reach it easily, but he didn't like to; he pushed it up straight, but in a second it dropped back again. There were overgrown flower-beds in front of the windows, such as burglars leave footprints in, and he leant in across them. Beneath the visor of his hand he stared into the shadowy spaces, where electric sockets and dark lines and squares on the wallpaper were now the sole decoration. A big room on the garden side with french windows must have been the sitting-room. He could just about imagine Cecil flirting with Daphne in front of the brick fireplace. A square of worn and stained beige carpet covered part of the parquet floor. At the end of the room he could make out a shadowy alcove, under a huge oak beam, and he thought he saw what might have been romantic and even beautiful about it; but when he stepped away, and roamed off through the long grass to take some more photographs, he thought the house looked rather a hulk. He saw now that something had been knocked down—there was a broad black arrow on the brickwork where a roof must have abutted. A new bathroom window had been punched through the wall, out of line with everything else. You could strip all the romance from a place if you were determined enough, even the romance of decay. He'd had the idea that he would find things more or less as they had been in 1913—more deeply settled in, of course, discreetly modernized, tastefully adapted, but the rockery still there, the "glinting spinney" a beautiful wood, and the trees where the hammock had been slung still bearing the ridges of the ropes in their bark. He thought other resourceful people would have come, over the years, to look at it, and that the house would wear its own mild frown of self-regard, a certain half-friendly awareness of being admired. It would live up to its fame. But really there was nothing to see. The upstairs windows seemed to ponder blankly on the reflections of clouds.

3

CECIL VALANCE'S EARLIEST KNOWN WRITING was a short composition produced for his mother when he was six years old. It was faithfully reproduced in the Memoir by Sebastian Stokes that prefaced the 1926 *Collected Poems:*

VII April MCCML~~XXX~~XCVII

ALL ABOUT ME

My Name is CECIL TEUCER VALANCE. Teucer was a Famous Soldier he was a Grate Archer and Cecil was a Famous Lord by the way. My Father is called Sir Edwin Valance (2nd Bt) and my grashious Mother is known to all as Lady Valance. She has a beautifull red dress which made Lady Adleen extreemly jelous to see it. My home is called Corley Court in Berkshire, if you don't know it It is one of the Grate Houses of that county. Oh if you meet a small boy calling himself Dudley Valance it is probably my small brother. He can be trying I shoud probally tell you here and now. On Monday on the Farm I saw IX new carves— they are the Sweetest Things on theyre wobbly legs. To-day we were all stuned by the news Lord PORTSCATHO has been killed in a explosin he was only ~~XXXX~~ XLIIV. My poor Father was very nearly in Tears at the sad news. I have had quit a bad caugh but am considerably recovered. Today I have red "How Rain is Made" in the Home "Cyclopaidea" and quit a fair number of Poems for my age as Nanny likes to say, among them "The Brook" by LORD TENNOSYN, I am Determined to learn all IX of its verses, it is one of the best know of all poems of course. I emitted to say I am something of A Poet, this year I have written no fure than VII Poems "humbly deadicated" to my Mother (Lady Valance).

What that same Lady Valance took to be Cecil's last communications were described by Dudley Valance in his autobiography *Black Flowers* (1944):

My mother, who never wasted time (except, of course, other people's), was nonetheless much involved in attempts to converse with the spirit-world. Her belief that Cecil might be reached and spoken to preoccupied her with the mingled gloom and determination of some hopeless love affair. Though notably reserved, as a rule, in her personal feelings, she allowed her tender yearnings for contact with the "other side" to be seen by her family and by one or two friends with surprising candour. She was not perhaps likely to be embarrassed by emotions founded in her duty and suffering as the mother of a fallen hero. It was in the library at Corley that she undertook many lengthy and bewildering "book-tests," upon a system taught to her by a clergyman in Croydon, and through the agency of Mrs. Leland Aubrey, a notorious medium of the time, who mined the pitiful hopes of well-connected mourners for twenty years after the War. Mrs. Leland Aubrey was herself under the "control" of a spirit called Lara, a Hindoo lady some three hundred years old, so it will be seen that the chain of communication was by no means direct. This remoteness, however, with its clear resemblance to a game of Chinese Whispers, was the very thing claimed in its favour by my mother, who had absorbed it as a point of doctrine from her medium and from the clergyman, a very high authority with her. It was precisely because Mrs. Aubrey had never been to Corley, had had no contact with its occupants, possessed no knowledge of the library there or of the disposition of any of the rooms, that she was seen as least susceptible to any kind of improper suggestion, and least capable of any kind of fraud. Her very remoteness argued for her probity. It was a bold advancement of the confidence-trickster's art, bold but also subtle: since when this point of doctrine was absorbed it gave licence to the wildest and most arcane forms of self-delusion. Any message of such impeccable provenance must of necessity be meaningful, and the random scraps thrown up by the tests were raked over by my mother for esoteric messages as keenly as the entrails of a fowl by some ancient divinator. That act of interpretation was a responsibility that fell solely to her, or to her occasional companions in these sessions, its further beauty, to a woman as private as my mother, being that the message itself was apparently quite unknown to the medium, who merely indicated to her where it was to be found. It was as if she had opened a letter from her dead son which Mrs. Aubrey had chanced to deliver.

What seems first to have happened was this: my mother received a letter (a real one, with a penny-halfpenny stamp on it) from the clergyman in Croydon, who had himself lost a son in the War, claiming that during a sitting with Mrs. Leland Aubrey, at which he had received book-tests from his dead boy, Lara had also transmitted a message which was evidently from Cecil, and intended for his mother, Lady Valance. Might he have her permission to forward the test to her? A request can rarely have fallen on readier ears; and doubtless the impression of a longed-for miracle was just what the medium and the parson had calculated. My mother had already shown some interest in spiritualism, and in the year after Cecil's death had even attended a number of séances at the house of Lady Adeline Strange-Paget, mother of my great friend Arthur, whose younger brother had been drowned at Gallipoli; these had left her with clear misgivings, but also perhaps with a sense of avenues still unexplored. The medium on that occasion was an associate of Mrs. Aubrey's and was later indicted on several charges of blackmail. But it turned out too that the parson's son had been in the Royal Berkshire Regiment, and had been drafted into Cecil's company in the weeks before the Somme offensive; he had outlived Cecil by a mere three days. In letters home the boy had written of his love and admiration for my brother. In many cases soldiers who had served with Cecil had written to my parents after his death, or the soldiers' own parents had sent letters of condolence containing tributes from the letters of their sons, themselves now dead, to the officer they had admired. The parson from Croydon, however, stored up his tribute, until a time when he could use it to greater profit.

This first test my parents performed alone, but I can speak from direct experience of their later repetitions. The general form of a book-test was that Mrs. Aubrey would go into a trance, in which Lara would communicate with Cecil, the result being taken down on the spot by the clergyman, since a trance very naturally impeded the medium's capacity to write for herself. The message would then be sent to my mother, who would at once act upon its instructions. She kept all these messages, in the same place as she kept Cecil's letters, regarding them as merely a further phase of their correspondence. This is a sample, and one at which my wife and I happened also to be present.

Lara speaking. "This is a message for Cecil's mother. It is in the

library. When you go in it is on a short shelf on the left, before the cor-
ner, the third shelf up from the floor, the seventh book. Cecil says it is
a green book, it has green on it or in it. Page 32 or 34, a page with very
little printed on it, but what there is makes a particular message for
her. He wants to tell her that he loves her and is always with her."

This final sentence, which appeared with minor variations at
the end of most of the messages, was clearly added by the medium
as a kind of insurance. The rest of the message, just as typically,
created the impression of something exact while containing various ambiguities. There were, for instance, three doors into the
library, the principal one from the hall, and two smaller ones,
leading into the drawing-room on one side and the morning-
room on the other. The instructions therefore might have led to
three quite different locations. The morning-room was my
mother's own sanctum, and she had little doubt that Cecil envisaged her entering the library from that side. My father, who often
in the evenings came into the library from the drawing-room,
would naturally have taken the diametrically opposite view; but
in this, as in so many things, he tended to give precedence to my
mother. On the present occasion, I recall there was some uncertainty, none the less. The directions to the short shelf on the left
and before the corner were very generous, since the first corner
was at the far end of the room. On each slip my mother wrote the
name of the book and its author, and the quotation itself. Here
she has put: "Short shelf. The 7th book, Wingfield's 'Charity'—
has no green. On trying on far side (enter from Dr-Room) 'History of Lancashire' by Bunning, no green on it. On entering from
Hall, 7th book, counting from the right, 'The Silver Charger' by
E. Manning GREENE, page 34 has only, 'it could be said that the
knight was returned, and all well about him, save that his heart
went out in the night to his dear ones left behind.' A true message
from Cecil." In this careful record her natural honesty is shown as
clearly as her credulity; the phrase "counting from the right"
shows her awareness that books are normally counted from the
left, but her conviction at the outcome is undimmed. Even her
square, rather unformed, hand seems eloquent to me now of her
stubbornness and innocence. Beneath this she has written, as
always, "Present": and each witness has put his signature, as if sub-
scribing to the larger truth of the proceedings. "Louisa Valance.

Edwin Valance. Dudley Valance. Daphne Valance. 23rd March
1918." (On the matter of my father's participation, it was notable
that Lara's messages never referred to him—until, once this fact
had been commented on in a telephone conversation, the following week brought one expressly for him.)

I have spoken facetiously, but out of distaste, for there was an
atmosphere, indescribable but unforgettable, in the library on
these occasions; and one that came increasingly to linger, so that
even at other times it seemed to darken the air in that already
gloomy chamber. It was not at all, to my sense, that of a supernat-
ural presence, but rather of hopes, and therefore fears, painfully
laid bare. In a way it was the library I would most have liked to do
away with, when I remodelled the house; the air of bogus method,
of wilful tampering with broken hearts, seemed to haunt its dark
alcoves and peer forth from the little carved faces on the bookshelves. You may think it strange, and weak-willed in me not to
have broached the matter directly with my mother; to which I can
only say that in all probability you never knew her.

There were other friends, no doubt, who acquiesced and even
looked hopefully on the outcome of this psychical quackery—
Lady Adeline, old Brigadier Aston at Uffington, who had lost all
three of his boys. But my wife and I quickly came to deplore the
hold Mrs. Aubrey had over my mother. Interspersed with evidently random book-tests came others so pointedly specific as to
arouse suspicion in us (though in my mother, of course, only
heightened conviction). One week the test led us to a *Westminster
Review* with a poem of Cecil's own in it, and the lines, "When you
were there, and I away / But scenting in the Alpine air the roses of
an English May"—a poem written in fact to a Newnham girl he
was keen on, but to my mother's eye a perfectly adequate parable
of the afterlife. Another gave her a line from Swinburne (a poet
she hadn't previously approved of), "I will go back to the great
sweet mother"; she didn't seem to mind that the great sweet
mother in question was the English Channel. She was accustomed to receiving answers to her questions and satisfaction of
her demands; had it not been so pathetic I might have been more
moved to laughter at the spectacle of her determination, brought
face to face with the meaningless results of these latterday *sortes
Virgilianae*. My wife was once so bold as to ask her mother-in-law

why, if Cecil had wanted to tell her "Love is love alway," he had
not simply said as much to Lara, rather than putting her through
the paper-chase in the library? It was one of a number of remarks
taken by the older lady to typify the younger one's unsuitability as
the future mistress of Corley.

My wife and I, who lived at Naughton's Cottage until my
father's death, were naturally unable to measure, even less control,
these activities. But our suspicions grew, and for a while threatened to corrupt the whole character of domestic life at Corley,
already under great strain from the War. Mrs. Aubrey was clever
enough to fire a number of blanks (one test led unequivocally to a
page of quadratic equations, which even my mother's best efforts
could not bring out right). But the incidence of gratifying bro-
mide grew so high that we began to wonder whether there were
not some accomplice within the house, a maid or footman confirming the location of certain volumes. On occasion the book in
question was out of its normal run—a fact interpreted no doubt
as proof of Cecil's absolute up-to-dateness and all-seeing eye. I
enlisted Wilkes, who had risen to be butler during the War, and
who I knew was above reproach, but his discreet enquiries among
the staff led nowhere. I don't know if I am more embarrassed or
proud of a trick I played myself. I had learned to use my limp in
various ways, so as to get what I wanted or simply to get in the
way. On this occasion, seizing the letter from my mother, I
lurched off as fast as I could down the room, rather as an eager
shop assistant might run for a packet of tea, and concealing the
shelves from her view I called out "The *fourth* book, Mamma, on
the *second* shelf" whilst taking at random a volume from the shelf
above. I have forgotten the volume, but will always remember the
sentence: "Its want of volitary powers led inevitably to its extirpa-
tion," the subject being, I believe, the Giant Moa: "What does he
mean?" worried my mother, faced with this bleakly Darwinian
pronouncement from my brother. Ah, had Cecil been able to fly,
how different things might have been!

One had wondered from the start, of course, what Mrs.
Aubrey was getting out of it. It slowly became clear that she was in
receipt of cheques for sums unmatched by even the most charita-
ble of the causes my mother espoused. She had a rich old lady
where she wanted her, a victim passionate to be duped. But then,

by slight, almost deniable, degrees, my mother seemed to let the thing go; she mentioned it rarely, she grew somewhat furtive— not about the tests but about stopping the tests, with the implication that doubt had won out over painful desire. I suspect that by the time my father had his stroke they had completely stopped. The strange timorous delicacy imposed on others by a very forceful personality ensured that we did not ask. She herself recovered much of the humourless cheerfulness that had been so typical of her before the War. Her good works redoubled in mass and effort. With my father indisposed, the present-day concerns of a large estate consumed the energies lately devoted to the past. She was still careful to spend some minutes of each morning in the chapel, alone with her first-born; but grief itself perhaps had run its course.

Paul re-read this passage with a rather silly feeling of excitement, thinking how useful it might be to get some messages from Cecil for himself. An appendix in G. F. Sawle's edition of Cecil's Letters seemed to suggest the book-test slips still existed, in the Valance archive, which Paul imagined bundled haphazardly in a large locked bureau like the one in *The Aspern Papers;* George gave them short shrift, but noted their significance as evidence of the spiritualist craze during and after the First World War. Paul's copy of *Black Flowers* was the old red Penguin edition, 1957, and he peered again at the tiny author photo on the back: a shadowy sneer in a one-inch square. Beneath it there was a ramblingly circumstantial biographical note:

Sir Dudley Valance was born in 1895 at Corley Court in Berkshire, the younger son of Sir Edwin Valance, Bt., and educated at Wellington and at Balliol College, Oxford, where he read English Language and Literature, taking a First in Honour Moderations in 1913. On the outbreak of War he enlisted with the Wiltshire Regiment (Duke of Edinburgh's), quickly rising to the rank of Captain, but after being wounded at the Battle of Loos in September 1915 was unable to return to active service. His experiences during the War are memorably recorded in the present volume, largely written in the 1920s, though not published until twenty years later. His first book, *The Long Gallery,* came out to great acclaim in 1922. A satirical country-house novel, in the tradition

of Peacock, it cast a merrily merciless eye over three generations of
the ancient Mersham family, and added such figures as the jingo-
istic General Sir Gareth "Jo-boy" Mersham and his "artistic" paci-
fist grandson Lionel to the great roll-call of British comic
characters. On the death of his father in 1925, Dudley Valance
succeeded to the baronetcy, his elder brother having been killed in
the War. When war broke out again, Corley Court was requisi-
tioned as a military hospital, and in 1946 Sir Dudley deemed it
best to sell the family home. England he felt was a changed land,
and thenceforth he and his wife have chosen to spend much of
each year at their fortified sixteenth-century house near Antequera in Andalusia. A further volume of his memoirs, *The Woods
Decay*, appeared in 1954. Sir Dudley Valance is a Fellow of the
Royal Society of Literature and President of British Friends of
Sherry.

Paul imagined the meetings of these two groups had fairly similar trajec-
tories. Of course he had nearly met Dudley; he remembered preparing to
do so, at Daphne's seventieth, out in the twilit lane, and his relief (apparently shared by everyone) when he failed to turn up. Now he was the
person that he most wanted, or anyway needed, to talk to—he was considerably more frightened of him now he'd read his books, with their
extended exasperated portrait of his mother and their puzzled coolness
about Cecil himself, whom Dudley clearly thought very overrated. They
were masculine books, in a way that seemed, from the viewpoint of the
late 1970s, when so much was coming into the open, to be interestingly
"gay," in a suppressed English fashion—"deniable," as Dudley would say.
It was hard not to feel that his relations with the soldier whose death gave
the book its title had been much more of a romance than his marriage to
Daphne Sawle. The funny thing about the Penguin note was the mixture
of cranky candour and evasion—of the two figures who really interested
Paul, Cecil was only obliquely referred to, and the first Lady Valance
might never have existed. It followed of course that their two children
could not exist either. Even in the book itself they featured hardly at all.
There was a sentence towards the end which began, almost comically,
"By now the father of two children, I began to take a different view of
the Corley entail"—the first mention of Corinna and Wilfrid's existence.

Dudley, naturally, was the first person Paul had written to, care of his
agent, but the letter, like the one he had written soon after to Daphne,

remained unanswered, creating a very uncertain mood. George Sawle needed to be approached, but Paul put off writing to him, out of muddled emotions of rivalry and inadequacy. At this stage of the project he had a sense of dotted items, an archipelago of documents, images, odd facts that fed his private belief that he was meant to write Cecil Valance's Life. Sawle's long-delayed edition of the Letters had done a lot of his work for him, in its drily scholarly way. Beside it on his bookshelf in Tooting Graveney stood his small collection of related items, some with a very thin but magical thread of connection; the books that only mentioned Cecil in a footnote gave him the strongest sense of uncovering a mystery. In front of him now he saw the torn and Sellotaped wrapper of Winton Parfitt's *Sebastian Stokes: A Double Life;* the black quarto notebooks in which he'd transcribed in pencil the letters between Cecil and Elkin Mathews, the publisher of *Night Wake,* in the British Library; the strange stiff binding of a privately printed register of Kingsmen killed in the Great War, with its peculiar heady smell of gum. On a barrow in the Farringdon Road he had found a copy of Sir Edwin Valance's *Cattle Feeds and Cattle Care* (1910), 25p, which he felt in its very intractability conveyed something almost mystical about his subject's family. He also had "the Galleries": Dudley's novel of 1922, which certainly drew on the Valances for its deranged Mersham family, and of course Daphne's recent memoir.

He had written to Winton Parfitt and asked him straightforwardly if he knew of material on Stokes's dealings with Cecil that had come to light since his book had been published twenty years earlier. The subtitle *A Double Life* referred disappointingly to Stokes's dual careers as man of letters and discreet Tory fixer; Parfitt nowhere revealed that his subject had been queer, or drew what seemed to Paul to be the obvious inference, that he had been in love with Cecil. His waffling memoir of the "joyous" and "splendid" young poet, doubtless highly acceptable to old Lady Valance, was also a surreptitious love-letter of his own. In fact Parfitt was as much of a diplomatic clam as old "Sebby" himself, and the royal-blue jacket of his huge biography, covered with praise from the leading reviewers, was now among those features that make all second-hand bookshops look inescapably the same. There was something "splendid" about the book—an "event," a "milestone," a "labour of love"—and something inescapably dodgy and second rate. It seemed a kind of warning to Paul. Still, he had grown familiar with half-a-dozen pages of it. There was a short paragraph mentioning Stokes's visit to the

Valances to gather materials for the memoir, but it was overshadowed by the frantic negotiations preceding the General Strike. That weekend at Corley was something he planned to ask Daphne herself about, when he managed to speak to her: it seemed a pregnant moment, an unrepeatable Cecil-focused gathering at which he longed to have been present himself. Parfitt had written back promptly, from his Dorset manor-house, in a fine italic hand, to say he knew of nothing significant, but offering warm encouragement before slipping in, with ingenuous briskness, the awful final sentence: "You will no doubt be in touch with Dr. Nigel Dupont, of Sussex, who has also written to me in connection with his work on the ever-intriguing Cecil."

Paul was very unhappy about Dr. Nigel Dupont, but he didn't know what to do about him. He couldn't help thinking he must be the unknown person Daphne had met at the party in Bedford Square, the sinister "nice young man" who'd been asking her all about Cecil. "Sussex" presumably meant Sussex University, not merely that Dr. Dupont lived somewhere in that county. He would be an ambitious young academic, an Englishman presumably, but with an incalculable element of Gallic arrogance and appetite for theory. Could he be writing a life of Cecil too? There were a number of obvious ways of finding out, but Paul was unable to take any of them. He saw himself at another party, being introduced to his rival, at which point the scenario halted and dithered in the mists of his ignorance and worry. He had a sense of the "ever-intriguing Cecil" actively encouraging both biographers, as if through "Lara" herself, in a spirit of mischief and self-importance.

At Tooting Graveney they lived on first-name terms with the dead. Karen, Paul's landlady and would-be accomplice in what she called "the Cecil job," worked at Peel's Bookshop in Putney, and read a lot of things in drab-looking but exclusive bound proofs long before they were published. In his nine months as her lodger he'd grown used to daily gossip about Leonard and Virginia, Lytton and Morgan and the rest, whom she spoke of almost as personal friends; Duncan and Vanessa strayed into the conversation as easily as customers into the shop. It seemed a teenage meeting with Frances Partridge had set her off on a craze for Bloomsbury, and as books on the subject now came out about once a month she lived in an addictive state of constantly renewed expectation. Cecil hadn't been strictly Bloomsbury, of course, but he'd known most of the Cambridge branch, and Karen clearly thought it a great stroke of luck to have his biographer as a lodger. She mothered him, and took a solemn interest in the "job" (whose appeal to Paul was precisely that it wasn't one); and Paul himself, who liked to preserve a certain mystery around his work, none the less shared almost everything with her. Karen's kitchen became the nerve-centre for the project, and many plans and speculations were explored over the wandering vines of the William Morris tablecloth and the second bottle of Rioja. He enjoyed her admiring interest, looked forward to telling her things that otherwise only went in his diary, and worried intermittently that she was coming to see the job as a joint effort.

In the strange week after Christmas, Paul got home early from the library and saw that a letter with a Spanish stamp had come for him. Karen had propped it on the hall table, in a way that suggested great restraint in not opening it herself. There it was, with a typed address, his name misspelt. He took it to the kitchen to open it neatly. He saw now that it would say one of two things, and his knife seemed to dawdle even as it snicked it open.

> El Almazán
> Sabasona
> Antequera

> Dear Mr. Bryan
> My husband is unwell, and has asked me to reply to your letter of November 26. He is very sorry, but he will not be able to see you. As you may know, we live in Spain for much of the year, and my husband is rarely in London.
> Yours sincerely,
> Linette Valance

For a moment he felt oddly embarrassed, and was glad Karen wasn't here to see it. It was unquestionably a blow: so much depended on Dudley, and his locked bureau of family papers. He put the letter back in the envelope, and a few minutes later got it out again, with an excited feeling that he couldn't quite remember it; but it seemed to say more or less what he'd thought it had before. Unless, perhaps, something else was conveyed by its very perfunctoriness? Even a rejection was a communication, after all—the letter, sparse and snooty though it was, yielded a small charge of contact. In a way, it was an adjunct to the family archive itself. He left it lying on the kitchen table as he boiled the kettle and prepared the teapot. At each inspection it looked just a little less disheartening. It was a brush-off, which needed to be brief to be effective, but was-n't it also a bit feeble? A strong response would have been to say, "Sir Dudley Valance refuses to see you, and furthermore is implacably opposed to your writing the life of his brother, Captain Cecil Valance MC." No such veto was even hinted at. He started to feel that Linette herself didn't think it was over yet. There was almost something defeatist in it, a mere delaying gesture in the face of the inevitable. The objections given, that they were "rarely in London" and in Spain "for much of the year," were vague and obviously not insuperable—was there not very nearly a suggestion that they didn't want to be a nuisance to Paul him-self? And he started to wonder if he couldn't somehow arrange to get out to Antequera and talk to them there, rather than troubling them on their rare and brief visits to London. His commitment in doing so would cer-tainly impress them, even move them, and he began to see a warm and subtle friendship developing, of the kind that would be life-blood to his book.

Later on, upstairs in his room and writing up the arrival of the letter in his diary, Paul sat back and stared out of the window with a sudden pang of sympathy for the poor old Valances, a moment of insight that he felt at once was of the essence of being a biographer. What he'd taken as snootiness was surely a sign of their acute vulnerability, something the upper classes were often at pains to conceal from the lower ones. Dudley was under the weather, and at eighty-four finding the prospect of meet-ing strangers a strain—for all he knew Paul might be just another hack, it was quite understandable; and Linette herself, half-comprehendingly taking instruction from a sick man, had written in haste before returning to his bedside to nurse him. A conversation with Paul, when it actually happened, might be a huge and happy relief to both of them. He decided that over the coming days he would write another letter, more personal and accommodating, and building on the warm contact that was now established between them.

4

THE FIRST INTERVIEW Paul conducted for the book had been with someone whose very survival seemed a little uncanny, one of the servants at "Two Acres" at the time when Cecil had first visited the Sawles. On the phone, the old boy said he was jiggered if he knew how Paul had tracked him down, and Paul read him the passage in Cecil's letter to Freda Sawle where he said he wanted to "kidnap young Jonah at the station and demand an impossible ransom." "What's that?" said old Jonah indignantly, as if he thought Paul himself was making some improper suggestion; he was very deaf. Paul said, "You've got an unusual name!" George had footnoted the reference punctiliously: "Jonah Trickett (b. 1898), the 'boy' at 'Two Acres,' who had been detailed to act as CV's valet; employed by FS from 1912 to 1915, when enlisted with Middlesex Regiment. From 1919 gardener and chauffeur to H. R. Hewitt (see also below, p137, 139n)." Paul wasn't sure he'd understood, on the phone, what the proposed visit was about. He agreed to let him come, though still sounded vaguely offended that anyone could think it necessary. "You're one of the few people left alive who remember Cecil Valance!" Paul said. That of course was the uncanny thing: there were thousands of eighty-one-year-olds, but surely no one else left in the world who had handled the intimate effects of this poet who had died in 1916, helped him to dress and undress and done whatever it was for him that a valet did. "Oh, yes? Ah well," said the sharp old voice, "whatever you say . . . ," as if catching a first glimpse of his own potential importance in the story.

It was another great trek across Middlesex, twenty-seven stops to Edgware, the very end of the Northern line, a reassuring eternity steadily shrinking, Paul rehearsing the questions and imagining the answers, and the questions they prompted in turn. He had the suspicion Jonah wouldn't volunteer much; he would have to bring him out, and then help him to discover what he really had to say. The prospect made him extremely nervous, as though he were going for an intervew himself. In his briefcase he had a letter from Peter Rowe that he hadn't looked at this morning when it arrived, and he opened it now, with slight misgivings, in the wintry sunlight of the empty train. The envelope contained a postcard, which in Peter's case was always an old painting of a preferably naked man, this time a St. Sebastian by one of the millions of Italians Paul had never heard of; the message, in small brown italic, read:

> Dearie! I distinctly felt an arrow go in, just under the heart, when I heard that you are writing the life of CTV. However, the agony is somewhat abated. That's a book I always thought I would write myself, one day, though I'm not sure I could have done it as well as I know you will. Of course I feel I have a hand in it, from having led you one evening long ago to the Poet's tomb. Wd love to talk about it with you—I have a few hunches about old C that might be worth exploring!
>
> Sempre, P.
> ps my book out in March

Paul wished he hadn't read it, since Peter's handwriting alone, with its quick cultured command of any space it alighted on, crossed his feelings with anxiety. And the Sebastian too, a huge foreshortened hunk shackled to a tree, and not at all like Peter to look at, was still an eerie reminder of his life when Peter was in it, and that critical summer of 1967. Now he had a book of his own coming out, on Victorian churches, he was planning a TV programme as well as giving interval talks, apparently, on Radio 3. Paul thought of him with an uneasy mixture of envy, admiration and regret.

Arnold Close was a terrace of pebble-dashed cottages with playing-fields beyond. Paul approached the second house and unlatched the front gate with a new flinch of dread and determination. The little garden was all brown and tidied for winter, a few pink buds surviving the frost. He pretended not to look into the front room, where a lamp was on, framed photographs with their backs to him on the window-sill. The house seemed both watchful and defenceless. He hoped he would get something valuable out of it—and that in the process he would give it something back, an interest and distinction it didn't know it had.

He lifted the knocker and dropped it with a mightier noise than he meant to. He was dully aware that the door, with its four thick bull's-eye panes above the letter-box, was the same as his mother's had been; and there was something vaguer, shouts and football whistles on the air, the meagre romance of suburbs petering out into country, that took him back to his Uncle Terry's council house in Shrivenham. He knew little

houses like this, almost knew the voice in the hall, and the shape looming and slipping in the curls of the glass. He felt the clutch of nerves, and
set his face sternly when the door opened—a large middle-aged woman
who kept her hand on the latch. "Oh, good afternoon . . . I've come to
see Mr. Trickett . . ."

"And you are . . . ?"

"Paul Bryant!"

She nodded and stepped back. "Dad's expecting you," she said, without exactly welcoming him herself. She was wearing a thick overcoat in a
gloomy brown tartan pattern, and tight brown leather gloves. Paul sidled
past her into the narrow hall, catching his look of polite apprehension in
the mirror. The glamorous opening that he represented, putting her
father in a book, seemed indifferent to her, or perhaps even undesirable.
"Dad!" she called out, as if knowing she wouldn't be heard, "he's here,"
and closing the door, she edged back past Paul and went into the front
room. "Mr. Bryant's here," she said. "Now, will you be all right?" Paul
gulped a large breath and seemed to be sighing with gratification as he
followed her into the room. The eagerness and charm, the smile confidently friendly but not hilarious, the note of respect with a hint of
conspiracy—all this he hoped to sustain in his swoop towards the total
stranger struggling up from his armchair with silvery head slightly
cocked and the questioning look of a deaf person. "You'll have to speak
up," said the woman.

Paul shook his hand and said, "Hello, Mr. Trickett!"—he'd somehow
forgotten about the deafness, and now he heard his own forced note.

"Are you Paul?" asked Mr. Trickett, with a nervy laugh and again a
bird-like way of looking for the answer.

"That's right," said Paul, finding of course that he was like a child to
the old man, or like one of a number of confusing grandchildren. This
too was annoying, but he would make the best of it. Jonah Trickett was
small but broad-shouldered, with a wide friendly face very finely lined,
and large blue eyes that seemed keener from listening as well as watching. He had a full head of hair and the perfect but impersonal dentures
that give their own helpless eagerness to an old man's face. Paul could see
that as a boy he might have been appealing; he had something boy-like
in him still. Now he lurched slightly as he moved.

"I've got a new hip," he said, a half-embarrassed boast. "Take the
young man's coat, Gillian." His voice was a bit breathy, and like the road
he lived in, London with a hint of country to it.

As he put down his briefcase and unbuttoned his coat Paul glanced round the room—some plates on the wall but no pictures, the photos in the window black-and-white weddings, and one more recent gathering in colour. The gas fire made the room disorientingly hot. On top of the TV was a photo of Jonah with a woman, who must surely be, or have been, his wife. Paul felt he should seem appreciative but not nosey, oddly the opposite of the case. "Well, I'll be off then," said Gillian, taking his coat with her into the hall. When the front door slammed, he felt a horrible self-consciousness crawling over both of them, and he watched through the window with a paralysed smile as Gillian went up the path and closed the gate behind her. It was as if something intensely embarrassing had just been said. He supposed he need only stay twenty minutes if it didn't work out. They sat down on either side of the gas fire, with a bowl of water on the hearth. The little bone pipes glowed and fluttered. He had a sense that the occasion had been prepared for: on the table beside Jonah there was a cardboard folder and his own letter under a coloured glass paperweight. He got out the tape-recorder, which had a mike on a stand, and took a minute or two to fit up; Jonah seemed to think this was a bit of a liberty as well as a novelty, but Paul said, "Every word you say is important to me," which he accepted with a wary smile. Paul pressed the Record button. "So how are you today?" he said.

"What's that?" said Jonah.

KAREN, WHO HAD SECRETARIAL TRAINING, offered to transcribe the tape for Paul on her golfball typewriter, and after two tense evenings of sporadic clatter and the sound of men's voices coming in five-second bursts from her room, incessantly stopped and replayed (his own voice not exactly his, and with its own unsuspected country burr), she came downstairs and handed over a thick sheaf of foolscap paper. "There were some bits I couldn't be sure of," she said. "I've put guesses in brackets."

"Oh, okay," said Paul, smiling to suggest he wasn't worried and quickly taking the document off on the search for his glasses. At a glance it seemed both professional and a serious problem. She had set it out in a narrow column, like a play-script, though the play itself would have been some absurdist ordeal of pauses and cross-purposes. "We still have the tapes, don't we?" Paul said. "We'll keep everything like that for the archive."

"I'm not sure that tape-recorder's much good."

"It was quite expensive."

"Jonah's all right, it's you that's sometimes very faint."

"Well, the mike was by him. It's what he said that's important."

The point was, of course, that Karen often couldn't make out the questions. He read a bit at random:

PB: Did George Sawle (*inaudible*)?

JT: Oh, no, he didn't.

PB: Really? how interesting!

JT: Oh, lord, no! (*Cackles*)

PB: So was Cecil himself at all (*inaudible: fortunate?*)

JT: Well he could be, yes. Though I don't suppose anybody knows that!

PB: I'm sure they don't! That's not what you expect! (*giggles*)

Karen was very free with the exclamation marks, and Shavian stage-directions (*sniggers, pauses regretfully, with sudden feeling* etc.) attached to quite ordinary-looking statements. Well, she was trying to help, keen to help, and then, as so easily happens, getting in the way. Sometimes Jonah's deafness itself came to the rescue, and he asked Paul to repeat a question louder. Elsewhere Paul was worried to find he already had no memory of the inaudible thing that had been said; at moments, too, he had let the machine do the listening, when Jonah was talking about the War, for instance, stuff he didn't need for the book. Perhaps his anxiety at the time had made it hard to listen. His whole interest was in finding out what Jonah knew about Cecil's dealings with Daphne and with George, and an awkward sense of strategy, of distractedly biding his time, interfered with his concentration. So he found himself next day, when Karen had gone to work, replaying the tapes as he read the transcript, to see if he could make out what she had missed or misinterpreted, and with a muddled angry sense of having got off to a bad start.

He saw that in too much of the interview he had let Jonah wander off the subject of Cecil to talk about life in "the old days" in general, and about his life after the War, with Harry Hewitt, a rich businessman of whom he was clearly much fonder than he had been of the Sawles. The Sawles seemed the subject of some vague unplaceable disapproval, which perhaps outlasted the now forgotten things that caused it.

PB: So you're saying that Freda Sawle drank too much?

JT: Well, I don't know it was too much.

PB: I mean, how did you know about it?

JT: Well, you know what you know. What they said in the
   (*unclear: kitchen?*) She had a weakness.

PB: A weakness? I see.

JT: There was Mrs. Masters (*?check*), her maid, she got the stuff
   for her.

PB: You mean, she bought drink for her?

JT: Well, Bombay gin, it was, I can see it now.

He had asked Jonah if he'd been back to the house lately, and Jonah
had said, "Oh, I haven't been over that way for years," as if it were really
quite a journey. Paul thought it couldn't be more than two miles away.
Jonah's lack of sentiment for the house and the family extended to Cecil
himself.

PB: You knew he was a famous poet, I suppose.

JT: Well, we knew that.

PB: Of course he wrote one of his most famous poems there, as
   you probably know.

JT: Oh, yes?

PB: It's called "Two Acres."

JT: (*doubtful*) Ah, yes, I think I heard about that.

PB: Do you remember him coming to the house?

JT: (*Hesitates*) Oh, he was a (*unclear: gentleman?*), he was! [Paul
   played the tape again to confirm his recollection that the word,
   covered by his own cough and rustle of papers, was "devil."]

PB: Really? In what way? What was he like?

Here Paul had arrived, quite effectively after all, at the great simple question; but it seemed that of Cecil's visits to "Two Acres" Jonah could
remember next to nothing; it all looked very promising for a minute or
two, but it thinned and dissolved under Paul's questioning. What
remained, offered with a kind of compensatory certainty, was first that
Cecil had been "a horror!," which appeared to mean no more than
"extremely untidy." Second, that he had silk underwear, very expensive
("Hmm, was that unusual?" "Well, I never saw it before. Like a woman's,
it was. I'll never forget it.") And third, that he was very generous—he
tipped Jonah a guinea, and "when he came the second time, two
guineas," which since Jonah was only paid £12 a year, plus meals, by
Freda Sawle, was surely a staggering amount.

PB: You must have done some (*inaudible*) for him?

JT: I hadn't done nothing!

PB: I'm not really sure what would happen if you valeted someone.

JT: It wasn't proper valeting, not at the Sawles'. They didn't know about it. "Just make it look right," young George said, I remember that. "Do whatever he says."

PB: And what did he ask you to do?

JT: I don't rightly remember.

PB: (*laughs*) Well, you must have really hit it off with him!

JT: (*inaudible*) . . . anything like that.

PB: But was it different the second time he came?

JT: I don't recall.

PB: No particular—

JT: (*impatient*) It was seventy years ago, damn nearly!

PB: I know, sorry! I mean, did you do something extra the second time to get the double tip? Sorry, that sounds rude.

JT: (*pause*) I daresay I was glad of the extra.

Paul had stopped to turn the cassette over, with a feeling, just in the little interval, while Jonah shifted on his new hip and twitched his cushion, that he'd rattled the old man; and with a novice's indecision about whether he should back off or press him harder.

PB: I wondered if you remembered anything Cecil said?

JT: (*pauses; awkward laugh*) Well, all I know is, he said he was a heathen. He wouldn't go to church with the others on Sunday.

PB: A pagan . . . ?

JT: That was it. He said, "I recommend it, Jonah. It means you can do what you like without having to worry about it afterwards." I was a bit thrown by that! I said it wouldn't go down so well if you were in service!

PB: (*laughs*) Anything else?

JT: I just remember that. I know he liked to talk. He liked the sound of his own voice. But I don't remember.

PB: What was his voice like?

JT: Oh, very (*inaudible*). Like a proper gentleman.

Soon, because he was nervous and dry-mouthed, Paul had asked for a glass of water. He thought it a bit unfriendly that he hadn't been offered anything, a cup of tea; but he'd come at 2:30, an odd between-times. They didn't know what to do for an interview any more than he did. Jonah let him go into the kitchen. Gillian had left it all wiped down, the dish-cloth shrouding the two taps. Through the window Paul saw the back garden with a small greenhouse, and beyond a privet hedge the white frame of a soccer goal some way off. Again, it was a room he felt he knew. He stood, slowly gulping the cold water, in a brief unexpected trance, as if he could see decade after decade pass through this house, this square of garden, school terms and years, new generations of boys shouting, and Jonah's long life, with all its own routines and duties, wife and daughter, all these unheeded but reassuring bits and bobs in the kitchen and the sitting-room, and thoughts of Cecil Valance as rare as holidays. On the tape, which continued to run in Paul's absence, Jonah could be heard moving things around near the microphone, speaking indistinctly under his breath, and emitting a quietly musical fart.

PB: And what was Cecil like with George Sawle?
JT: What was he like?
PB: (*inaudible*) George, you know?
JT: I'm not sure what you mean. (*nervous laugh*)
PB: They were great friends, weren't they?
JT: I think he met him at college. I don't know much about that.
PB: You didn't mix much with the Sawle children yourself?
JT: Good grief, no! (*laughs wheezily*) No, no, it wasn't like that at all.
PB: Did you know Daphne was (*inaudible*) with Cecil?
JT: Well, I don't recall. We didn't know about that.
PB: (*pauses*) What hours did you work, do you remember?
JT: Well, I do, I worked six till six, I remember that very well.
PB: But you didn't sleep at the house?
JT: I went back home. Then up every morning at five! We didn't mind it, you know! [And here Jonah had gone on, with what seemed to Paul like relief, to a detailed description of a servant's day—a day in which the principal figures in Paul's story were oddly seen as mere ineffectual walk-ons.]

When Jonah got out his photo album the taped record became too cryptic altogether for Karen. Paul listened, fast-forwarded for ten seconds, cut in again—murmurs, grunts and rueful laughs like the sounds of some intimacy from which he was now bizarrely excluded. He had stooped over Jonah in his armchair, staying his hand sometimes as he turned the pages. It was a shared task, each of them somehow guiding the other, Jonah still puzzled and touchy about the undue interest Paul was taking in it all. "Well, there's not much to it," he said, which was true in a way, though as always the "not much" stared out like a provocation. Those old snapshots, two inches by three—the few Paul had seen of himself as a child were almost as small. Jonah hovered over them and partly concealed them with the oblong magnifying glass he used for reading the paper, the miniature faces swelling and darting as he muttered comments on one or two of them. There was a group photo of the staff at "Two Acres," it must be just before the War, Jonah grinning in a work-coat buttoned at the neck, standing between two taller maids in caps and aprons, with a huge-bosomed woman behind them, who sure enough was the cook; Paul really didn't recognize the door and window behind, but Jonah was unmistakable, and so glowingly pretty that the older Jonah seemed to grow self-conscious on his behalf; at sixteen he had a look of being happy in his place as well as slyly curious about what lay outside it. Then there were several of the family. "So that was their mother? May I?" Paul said—steadying the glass: a sturdy-looking woman with a wide appealing face and the guesswork smile that went with short-sightedness. He saw a lot of Daphne in her, not the teenager of the photos but Daphne as he knew her, older than her mother had been then. "Freda looks very nice." "Yes, well," said Jonah, "she was all right," though now her weakness, as he had called it, seemed to swim to the surface under the lens—Hubert Sawle, balding and responsible, standing next to her, surely knew about it too. They had the indefinable air of figures in an ongoing crisis, which their smiles didn't quite expect to conceal. "What about George?—ah, yes, that must be him." George played up to the camera, pointing at Daphne, or posing just behind her with a silly face. Daphne herself had the vulnerable look of a girl hoping to get away for longer than five minutes with the pretence of being grown-up. She sat smiling graciously under a large hat with a silk flower on the side. Then George crept up, like a villain in a silent film, and made her jump. "Now is that . . . ? I've got an idea," said Jonah, and let Paul take the glass again and square it over the cornermost snap—two young men almost level with the ground in deckchairs, George in a boater, the other's face cast in primitive photographic shadow by the brim of his hat, save for a gleam of a nose and a smile. "That's your

young man, I think, isn't it?" said Jonah—really it could have been anybody, but Paul said, "Yes, of course it is . . . !" and when he had done so
he tingled at the certainty that it was.

He hadn't expected Jonah to have such a hoard; it seemed the mysterious but omnipresent Harry Hewitt had given Hubert a camera, and
Hubert had kept on dutifully taking snapshots and presenting them to
all and sundry. Jonah showed him a photograph of the two men
together; under the glass his square brown fingers half-hid what he was
pointing out. "I see . . . yes . . ."—Hubert was quite different here, peeping at the camera, a cigarette held uncertainly just by his trouser-pocket,
while beside him, with an arm round his shoulder, as if escorting him
towards some challenge he had been shyly avoiding, stood a darker,
rather older man, very smartly dressed, with a long gaunt face, large ears,
and a wide moustache drawn out into uncertain points. "So that was the
man you worked for after the War . . ." There was something so evidently
gay about the photograph that the question sounded insinuating to himself, and perhaps to Jonah too. Later on he found the place in the transcript where he'd come back to questions about Hewitt.

JT: Mr. Hewitt was a friend of the Sawles. He was a great friend of
   Mr. Hubert. So I knew him already, in a way. He'd always been
   kind to me. He lived in Harrow Weald (*unclear: Paddocks?*)
PB: I'm sorry?
JT: That's what his house was called.
PB: Oh!
JT: Well, it's an old folks' home now. The old dears are in there!
   (*chuckles wheezily*)
PB: Right. A big house, then.
JT: He was an art collector, wasn't he, Harry Hewitt. I believe he
   left it all to a museum, would it be the Victoria and Albert
   Museum?
PB: He didn't have children?
JT: Ooh no, no. He was a bachelor gentleman. He was always very
   generous to me.

Then, over the page, Jonah had changed his servant's coat for lumpy
serge and a too-large peaked cap, and in a line of recruits all taller than
himself looked even younger than he had two years before, the smile of
curiosity now a crooked look of childish worry. Paul straightened up,

gazed down abstractedly for a minute at the neat old man with the album on his knee; then bent down again into his sharp clean odour of shaving-soap and hair-tonic.

In a minute, Jonah had to go to the loo, which was upstairs, and with his new hip was likely to take him a while. When he was safely halfway up, Paul stopped the tape, mooched across the room, glanced amiably through the window at the front garden and the lane, then lifted the paperweight from the folder on the table by Jonah's chair, looked over his own letter again with interest, as it were from the recipient's point of view, and with one finger raised the cardboard cover. Some brittle and sun-browned newspaper cuttings, words lost at the corners and folds, brown envelopes rubbed and softened with use. These must be Jonah's demob papers. Then a prize certificate for carnations that he'd won in 1965. Then there was a folded review of a school play. A photograph from the local paper of what must be Gillian's wedding. It struck him poor Jonah didn't have enough treasures for separate folders—everything precious must be in here together. Paul leafed through the papers in loose groups. It was all just family stuff, of the most routine kind, very distant and pathetic, but put here ready perhaps, in the belief the inter-view was to be about Jonah's own life. Then laying it all back again, and having a last look as he did so, Paul saw a large brown envelope addressed to Hubert Sawle Esq., "Two Acres," the address struck through in ink: he lifted it out with a sudden heaviness of heart. Peering into it quickly but intently, half-pulling out the top two or three sheets, he saw letters, one signed H. O. Sawle, so perhaps these were just Jonah's scraps and mem-orabilia from that time. "Wishing you good luck!"—May 1915 . . . in large backward-leaning writing. And then under it he found himself staring, in a sudden accusing rush of colour to his face, at a quite differ-ent hand, the hand he was only starting to know apart from all others, like the hand of a new lover. A tiny envelope, addressed to Pte J. Trickett, at the Middlesex Regiment barracks in Mill Hill. The large black post-mark was smudged, but the year stood out, "1916." Setting down the other papers, he was about to open it when he saw with astonishment that he had turned over something else in Cecil's writing, several sheets of paper, torn in half, and covered in densely written and corrected verse. His fingers were trembling as he lifted the first one, which seemed to oscillate under his eyes like something out of focus. He knew it and he didn't know it. He knew it so well that he couldn't think what it was, and then when he understood he found it wasn't what he knew. "Hearty, lusty, true and bold . . ." The lavatory upstairs flushed, a sequence of muted sighs and whines spread through the plumbing system of the house; then he heard Jonah's careful but not unduly slow tread coming down. It was a teetering five seconds of bewildered indecision. He squared up the papers, closed the folder, and set the paperweight back on top, calling up his mental photograph of how it had been before he touched it; he was completely confident it looked just as it had—even the paperweight was the right way round; but when Jonah came back in his eye seemed to go straight to it, and Paul wondered if the final impression wasn't so meticulously accurate as to be in some way unconvincing.

Later on, listening to the tapes, so muffled and unprofessional, and leafing back and forth through the embarrassing half-clarification of the transcript, Paul had a growing gnawing sense that he'd already lost something of great value, though he wasn't quite sure how he'd done so, or even what it was. Did Jonah know more than he said about Cecil's friendship with George? It was natural enough that he wouldn't say, perhaps wouldn't know how to say; and though he didn't seem to have much patience for George, or Daphne either, he was hardly going to go on record with the sort of claim Paul was hoping for about people who were still alive, whom he hadn't seen for sixty-five years . . . Obscurely related there was the matter of Cecil's massive tip, more than a month's wages, and doubled on his second visit. Why had he done that? Because he knew he had been a "horror," perhaps—though what did that word really mean? And why did Jonah remember that, and almost nothing else? Paul wondered if Cecil had bought his silence about something—perhaps so effectively that he had indeed entirely forgotten it. Or was that the matter he had written to him about, at the Mill Hill barracks? Paul felt sick that he hadn't simply taken that letter. Why on earth would an aristocratic young officer be writing to a private in another regiment? It was striking enough that Cecil had even mentioned Jonah to Freda— Paul knew from other such letters he'd read that upper-class people never mentioned servants, unless it was some figure of great age and eccentric dignity, like a butler or old nanny. And then what seemed to be a manuscript of "Two Acres" itself, glimpsed like something in a dream and, at a glimpse, full of dreamlike variants.

The mortifying thing, as Paul had packed up his tape-recorder, put on his coat and been followed to the front door, was the lingering presence in the air, and in his own tight smile, of Jonah's rebuff—his wheezy, regretful head-shake of insistence that no, he had no letter, nothing written by Cecil Valance at all; so that Paul had been trapped, in the moment he was leaving, in a kind of impasse. He must have looked shifty, even coyly wounded—some new narrowing of suspicion and rejection had seemed to enter Jonah's blue eyes. Paul didn't tell Karen any of this, but it had made the long journey back to Tooting Graveney more uncomfortable than the journey out.

5

"SHOVE?"

"Mm?"

"Fredegond Shove."

"Oh, yes! . . . um . . ."

"It's the *Collected Poems*."

"Aha . . ."

"Or . . . wait a minute, what about this . . ."—he handed Paul a precious-looking volume, in a black slipcase: *A Funny Kind of Friendship: Letters of Sir Henry Newbolt to Sebastian Stokes*. "Interest you at all?"

"Well, *actually* . . ." It just might be interesting, for his own research; and anything he took away could be sold, sooner or later.

"Private press, we don't have to do it."

Paul balanced the stack of books he'd already chosen on the edge of a table scattered with sugar and ground coffee. Here the reek of Gitanes smoke was laced with that of sour milk. In cracked old mugs with comic logos, bluish crusts of mould were forming. The books table itself, ten volumes deep, had a broken leg propped up on other books that presumably would never be reviewed. The squalor was remarkable, but no one who worked here—young men in olive-green corduroy, goodlooking women chatting on the phone about Yeats or Poussin—appeared to notice it. They sat in their low cubicles, walled in by rubbish, books and boxes, half-eaten meals, old clothes, and great slews of scrawled-over galley-proofs.

"So—gay things," said Jake, rubbing his hands.

"That's right!" said Paul, and was furious to find himself blushing.

"We get quite a lot of those these days . . ." Jake wore a wedding-ring, but he seemed very glad for Paul to be gay. He was the same age, younger perhaps, clearly proud of working at the *TLS,* and cheerfully corporate—"we do this," "we had that." Paul imagined sharing his cubicle, high up above the traffic, deciding the fate of books together. "Bloomsbury, I suppose . . . ?"

"Bloomsbury . . . First World War." Paul saw a promising mauve cover deep down, gay books keeping generally to that end of the spectrum, but when he dug it out it was a survey of historic thimbles, which wasn't quite gay enough. "I *think* there's a new volume of Virginia Woolf's Letters coming up . . ."

"Ah," said Jake, "yes, that's gone, I'm afraid—Norman's doing it."

"Ah, well . . ." Paul flinched and nodded, as if at the evident justice of this commission, and wondered who the hell Norman could be; he felt Norman wasn't his surname. So far Paul had had only two things in the paper, both very cut, and very far back, almost in the Classified section: a piece about Drinkwater's plays, and a regretful demolition of a novel by the retired diplomat Cedric Burrell. This caused a bit of a stir, as Burrell had immediately cancelled his subscription to the *TLS,* which he'd had since going up to Oxford in 1923. But no one seemed to mind, they were even rather pleased, and Jake had asked him to drop in and "look at the books," if he was ever around. Paul let a day and a half pass before turning up.

"Remind me what you're working on?"

"I'm writing a biography of Cecil Valance," said Paul firmly, and the claim sounded foolishly bold in this new setting. But one day, no doubt, his book would appear on the table in front of him. Someone would ask to do it. Maybe Norman would get a crack at it.

"That's right, 'Two blessèd acres of English ground.' "

"Among other things . . ."

"Didn't we have something on him recently?"

"Oh, well the *Letters,* perhaps? That was a couple of years ago now . . ."

"That must be it. So he was gay too, was he?"

"Again . . . among other things."

Again Jake was delighted. "They all were, weren't they?" he said.

Paul felt he should be a bit more cautious: "I mean, he did have affairs with women, but I have the feeling he really preferred boys. That's one of the things I want to find out."

An older man, in his fifties perhaps, with oiled black hair and a paisley bow-tie, had emerged from his cubicle to get coffee, and stayed looking at the new books and looking at Paul too, over his half-moon glasses, with a certain air of strategy. Jake said, "Robin, this is Paul Bryant, who's been doing some things for us. Robin Gray."

"Ah, yes," said Robin Gray, in a friendly patrician tone, tucking his chin in. He had the blue eyes of a schoolboy in the face of a don or a judge.

"Paul's writing about Cecil Valance, you know, the poet."

"Yes, indeed." Robin glanced to left and right, as if at the enjoyable delicacy of the matter. "Indeed, I had heard . . ."

"Oh, really?" said Paul, smiling back, and feeling suddenly uneasy. "Goodness!"

Robin said, "I believe you bumped into Daphne Jacobs." And now he scratched his head, with an air almost of embarrassment.

"Oh, yes . . . ," said Paul.

"And who might Daphne Jacobs be?" said Jake. "One of your golden oldies, Robin?"

Robin gave a curt laugh while still holding Paul's eye. Paul felt he shouldn't answer the question for him. He half-wondered himself what the answer would be. "Well," said Robin, "she is now the widowed Mrs. Basil Jacobs, but once upon a time she was Lady Valance."

"Don't tell me she was married to Cecil," said Jake.

"Cecil!" said Robin, as if Jake had a lot to learn. "No, no. She was the first wife of Cecil's younger brother Dudley."

"I should explain, Robin knows everyone," said Jake, but just then he was called to the phone at the far end of the office, leaving the two of them in their unexpected new relation. They went into the semi-privacy of Robin's cubicle, where he set down his coffee on the desk; unlike the others he kept a china cup and saucer, and there was a degree of order in the books, a parade of Loeb classics, archaeology, ancient history. On the radiator a brown towel and swimming-trunks were spread out to dry. There was a strong sense of a bachelor life, of rigorous routine. Robin shifted papers from a second chair. "I'm the ancient history editor," he said, "which everyone thinks is very apt." Paul smiled cautiously as he sat down; beside him was a shelf of *Debrett's* and *Who's Who,* and those eerily useful volumes of *Who Was Who,* giving the hobbies and phone-numbers of the long dead. Late one night he and Karen had rung Sebastian Stokes himself: a moment's silence and then the busily negative drone of non-existence. Of course you had to convert the old exchanges to the new numbers—they might have got it wrong. "Don't lean back in that chair, by the way, or you'll land on the floor."

"I was a bit worried about . . . *Daphne,*" Paul said, sitting forward, making his own thoughtful claim on knowing her. "No one seemed to be looking after her."

"I'm sure you were kind to her," said Robin, a touch cautiously.

"Well, I didn't do much . . . you know . . . Have you known her a long time?"

Robin stared and grunted as if at the effort it would take to explain properly, and at last said, very slowly, "Daphne's second husband's half-sister married my father's elder brother."

"Right . . . *right!* . . . so . . ."—Paul gazed at the world beyond the dirty window, the top floor of a pub across the Gray's Inn Road.

"So Daphne is my step-aunt by marriage."

"Exactly," said Paul. "Well, I'm very glad to meet you. You see, I'm hoping to interview her, but she hasn't replied to a letter I sent her in November, which is three months ago now . . ."

"Well, you know she's been ill," said Robin, tucking his chin in again.

Paul winced. "I was afraid that might be the reason."

"She has this macular problem."

"Oh, yes?"

"It means she can't really see—her sight's very bad. And as you may know she also has emphysema."

"Doesn't that come from smoking?"

"I fear they both do," said Robin, with a sigh at his own ashtray.

"Is she getting better?"

"Well, I'm not sure one ever really gets better."

Paul had a sickening feeling she might smoke herself to death before he'd had a chance to speak to her. "I was surprised to see she still smoked, after Corinna . . . you know."

"Mmm." Robin looked at him keenly. "So you knew Corinna, did you?"

"Oh, very much so," said Paul, noting as if from the corner of his eye how indulgently he thought of her now that she wasn't there to expose him and put him down; she'd become a useful element in his own plans. "That was how I met Daphne, you see. I worked under Leslie Keeping for several years."

"Oh, you were in the bank," said Robin, "I see," and squared his lighter and cigarette-packet on the table, as if making some subtle calculation. "I wonder if you were there when Leslie died?"

"No, I'd already left."

"Right, right."

"But I heard all about it, of course." It was the most grimly sensational piece of news that Paul had had anything to do with, and he felt, for all its horror, a keen attachment to it.

"All that hit Daphne very hard, of course."

"Well, of course . . ." Paul waited respectfully. "I first met them all in 1967," he said, "though I'm not sure Daphne remembered that when I saw her again."

"Her memory is certainly somewhat . . . um . . . tactical," said Robin.

Paul giggled, "Yes, I see . . . but I wondered, she's not living by herself, is she?"

"No, no—her son Wilfrid, from her first marriage—do you know?—is living with her."

"I do know Wilfrid," said Paul, and instantly pictured his strange determined amorous dance in the Corn Hall at Foxleigh, the first and last time he'd met him. He couldn't see him being a very practical nurse or housekeeper. "And what about her son by her second marriage?" Robin shook his head rapidly, a sort of shudder. "Okay . . . !" Paul laughed. "And the Keeping boys, they don't see her?"

"Oh, John's far too busy," said Robin, firmly but perhaps ironically. "And you know Julian has become a *drop-out* . . ."—with an air of marvelling hearsay, like a magistrate. "Of course before long, Wilfrid will inherit the title."

"Yes, of course . . ."

"He'll be the fourth baronet." They looked ponderingly at each other, then laughed in minor embarrassment as if at some misunderstanding. Paul felt there was a certain sexual undertone to the chat, even to the way they'd quickly got off on this topic amid the business of the office.

"To be absolutely frank—," said Robin, and here he did reach for his cigarettes, and kept Paul waiting uneasily while he lit one and inhaled and fixed him again with a blue gaze over the top of his spectacles, "I think Daphne was rather put out by your review of her book in the *New Statesman*." He sounded a bit stern about it himself. "She felt you'd rather gone for her."

"Oh, no!" said Paul, with a guilty face, though a prickle of pride at his own sharpness very slightly offset the lurching feeling he'd been tactless and clumsy. "The piece was heavily cut, I did tell her that."

"I'm sure."

"They took out a lot of the nice things I said." He pictured her in the taxi to Paddington, and heard her saying how some reviewers had been horrid. To pretend she hadn't seen his review seemed now to be dignified good manners of a crushingly high order. She had managed to reproach him and excuse him all at the same time. "It was supposed to be a bit of a fan letter."

"I'm not sure it read like that," said Robin. "Though you were by no means the worst."

"I certainly wasn't." ("Unhappy fantasies of a rejected wife" had been Derek Messenger's verdict in the *Sunday Times*.)

Robin sipped at his coffee and drew on his cigarette, as if measuring regrets and pondering possibilities. He was indefinably in his element, and Paul sensed it was a stroke of luck to have met him, and if he could get him on his side he might get Daphne too. "I must say, I enjoyed the book," Robin said, with a further head-shake of frankness.

"No, I enjoyed it too. There were things I wanted to know more about, of course . . ." Paul gave him an almost sly smile, but asked something harmless first: "I'm not clear really who Basil Jacobs was."

"Oh, Basil"—Robin sounded impatient himself with this tame question. "Well, Basil was certainly the nicest of her husbands, though in a way as . . . as hopeless as the others."

"Oh, dear! Was Revel Ralph hopeless too?"

Robin pulled on his cigarette as if to steady himself. He said, "Revel was completely impossible."

Paul grinned—"Really? You can't have known him, surely."

"Well . . ." Robin toyed with this flattery; "I was born in 1919, so you can work it out."

"Mm, I see!" said Paul, which he didn't altogether—was Robin claiming to have tangled with Revel himself? Revel was only forty-one when he was killed, so doubtless still pretty active, as it were, and Robin he could just about see as a naughty young soldier—it was too much to ask about.

"Oh, god yes," said Robin, suddenly disgusted by his cigarette, stubbing it out and folding it under his thumb in the ashtray. "Basil wasn't hopeless like that, he was much more conventional. I imagine Daphne felt she'd had enough of temperamental artists."

"What did he do?"

"He was a businessman—he had a small factory that made something, I can't remember what, a sort of . . . washer or something."

"Right."

"Anyway, he went bust. He had a daughter from an earlier marriage, and they went to live with her. I think it was all rather a nightmare."

"Oh, yes, Sue."

"Sue, exactly . . . ," said Robin, with a cautious smile. "You seem to know most of the family."

"Well . . . ," said Paul. "They're not actually all that useful when it comes to Cecil. But it's good to know they're on my side." He found he had stood up, smiling, as if to go, and only then said, with a pitying shake of the head, "I mean, what do you think really went on between Daphne and Cecil?"

Robin laughed drily, as if to say there were limits. Paul knew already that information was a form of property—people who had it liked to protect it, and enhance its value by hints and withholdings. Then, perhaps, they could move on to enjoying the glow of self-esteem and surrender in telling what they knew. "Well," he said, and went slightly pink, under the pressure of his own discretion.

"I mean, would you like to have a drink some time? I don't want to bother you now." Paul thought a discreet encounter, something with almost the colour of a date, might appeal to Robin. He saw, because it was a habit he had himself, elsewhere, how his eyes paused a fraction of a second in each upward or sideways sweep at the convergence of his black-jeaned legs. But Robin hesitated, as if to grope round some other obstacle.

"You see, I don't drink during Lent," he said. "But after that . . ."—with a suggestion he drank like a fish through the rest of the liturgical year. "Ah, Jake . . . ," and there was Jake again, standing behind them, with the twinkle of someone detecting a secret.

"I hope I'm not breaking something up."

"Not a bit," said Robin suavely.

"I'll give you a ring if I may," said Paul, "—after Easter!"

Jake led Paul back to have his books entered in the system, an unfollowable procedure of typed slips and cards. "I've just had a word with the Editor," he said. "We wondered if you'd be interested in covering this for us?" He passed him a sheet of paper—"Ignore that stuff at the top": two other names with question-marks and phone-numbers, heavily inked over during phone-calls surely, which as surely had not borne fruit. "You'd have to stay overnight—it would just be seven hundred words for the Commentary pages." It was hard to take in, Balliol College, Oxford, a conference, dinner, the Warton Professor of English . . . a shiver of panic went through him, which he turned into a breathy laugh.

"Well, if you think I'd be right for it."

"You're not a Balliol man, are you?"

"Ooh, no!" said Paul with a little shudder. "Not I. Well, thank you—ah, I see, Dudley Valance is speaking."

"That's partly what made me wonder—I didn't know he was still alive."

"Not in good health, I'm afraid," said Paul.

"You must know him . . ."

"A bit, you know . . . He and Linette live in Spain for most of the year." He felt the prickle of the uncanny again, the secret sign, the reasserted intention that he should write his book. There were times in one's life that one only knew as one passed through them, the decisive moments, when one saw that the decisions had been taken for one.

Jake walked him to the door of the office and they stood talking there a little longer, but had to move aside for a big fat boy in jeans and a T-shirt pushing a trolley stacked high with tightly bound bales of newsprint; he threw one down with a pleasant thump on to the floor. "Read all about it!" he said, and watched with a curious cynical smile as they reacted. "Ah, yes . . . now . . . ," said Jake, showing off, but charmingly, to entertain his guest. One or two others got up and circled, looking for scissors, a sharp knife, and ignoring the delivery boy, who wheeled back into the corridor, still smiling thinly. In a moment the plastic tape was snipped, and the top copy plucked up and turned and presented to Paul with a casual flourish: "For you!"—the new *TLS*—Friday's *TLS*, ready two days early, "hot off the press" someone said, enjoying his reactions, though in fact the paper was cool to the touch, even slightly damp. There was a cursory checking, in which Paul politely shared—that pictures had come out, that a last-minute correction had been made—while an enviable sense of professional satisfaction seemed to fill the air and then (since this momentous occurrence was a weekly routine) to fade almost at once as people went back to their desks and focused again on issues weeks and months ahead. Paul said goodbye to Jake, and went away with the clear idea of more such meetings already in his mind.

On the way along the dreary corridor he turned off into the Gents and had only just unzipped when he heard the yawn of the door behind him and a second later a half-pleased, half-embarrassed "Aha . . . !" He glanced round. Slightly disconcertingly, Robin Gray didn't follow the normal etiquette but came to the urinal right next to Paul's, leaving three further stalls untenanted. There was a droll murmur and frowning fidget as he got himself going, a certain sturdiness of stance, as if on a rolling ship, and a quick candid gaze, friendly but businesslike, at Paul's own progress on the other side of the porcelain partition. Then looking ahead, he said, "You were quite right, by the way, in what you said earlier."

"Oh . . . really?" said Paul, glancing at him, a little confused. "What was that?"

"About Cecil Valance and boys."

Now it was Paul's turn to say, "Aha! . . . Well, I thought it must be."

Robin tucked in his chin, with his air of heavily flagged discretion. "Not for now, I think." He gave a cough of a laugh. "But I believe you'll find it amusing. Well, I'll tell you all about it when we meet." And with that plump promise he zipped himself up and went back to the office.

Paul sauntered down the broad stairs and into the lobby of the *Times* building with a smile on his face. He had *A Funny Kind of Friendship* in his briefcase and a feeling of something much funnier—the first sense of a welcome from the literary family, of curtains held back, doors opening into half-seen rooms full of oddities and treasures that seemed virtually normal to the people who lived in them. In the long lobby, belatedly gleaming with afternoon light, low tables between leather armchairs were spread with copies of today's *Times,* and *Sun,* and the three *Times* supplements, thrilling evidence of what went on upstairs. He nodded goodbye as he passed the uniformed receptionist. The revolving door from the street brought in a courier in helmet and whistling leggings, red URGENT stickers on the packet in his hand; Paul stepped into the still-revolving quadrant and emerged on to the pavement with a graciously busy half-smile at the passers-by who would never have access to these mysteries. He kept his copy of the day-after-tomorrow's *TLS* under his arm, which he wanted very much to be seen with. He didn't think the people in the street here were getting the point of it—but back in the North Reading-Room of the British Library he felt it might stir a good deal of envy and conjecture.

6

PAUL TROTTED DOWN the long stone staircase and out into the quad with a preoccupied frown and a curious feeling of imposture. Though old enough to be a don, he was visited in waves by the nervous ignorance of a freshman. He skirted the lawn respectfully, beneath ranged Gothic windows, clutching his briefcase and picturing the evening to come, with its sequence of challenges, drinks in the Senior Common Room, dinner in Hall, social contacts and collisions all the more daunting for the tacit codes that college life was steeped in. But at some point, he was almost sure, tonight or perhaps tomorrow, he would get his chance. Of course it was still possible the old boy wouldn't turn up; at the age of eighty-four he had excuses readily to hand. With excited foreboding Paul pictured his dark autocratic face, as he knew it from photographs, and when he went up the three steps into the gatehouse there he was—under the arch, by the porter's lodge, in a dark overcoat, leaning on a stick.

Paul nearly greeted him, gasped and suppressed a smile as he went past; his heart was racing at the sudden opportunity—he turned and then stood near him, at an angle, as though waiting for someone else. Awful of course if it wasn't him; but no, the wide, hawkish face was unmistakable, stretched rather than furrowed by age, the full mouth a little thinner and down-turned, impressive dark eyes staring ahead, grey hair sleeked back into curls around the collar. Paul stepped aside to look at the glassed-in notice-boards, over which his own slightly smirking face floated in reflection. The old man remained immobile, only poking now and then at the flagstones with the rubber tip of his stick. He was evidently someone for whom arrangements had always been made. Paul cleared his throat and paced around, choosing his words. Through the inner window of the lodge, before the dark wall of pigeon-holes, he could see a woman talking to the porter. Surely, Linette—with thick stiff hair, an improbable auburn, mingling with the upturned collar of her fox-fur jacket. A hard, good-looking face, thoroughly made up, and a manner he knew at once, from its tight smiles and frowns, of getting people to do things. The porter made a brief phone-call, and then came out, opening the door for her, and bringing her suitcase. "Good evening, Sir Dudley! The Master's coming down himself to meet you"—a flourish in which Paul heard a doubling-up of respect, of everyday loyalty to the Master and deference to the visitor. Linette had now made an approach impossible, and Paul went to look for his imaginary friend by the gate on to Broad Street. He could hear the tone but not quite the words of the muttered conversation between the Valances. In front of him, students cycling past, university life rattling on although it was the vacation. In a minute there were calls and wheezy laughs behind him, and as Paul turned round he saw a tiny grey-haired man in a gown come whirling up the steps from the quad and greet his guests—not exactly as old friends but on the footing of some clear shared understanding, which seemed to smile out of his keen, rather spiritual face. Sir Dudley said, "You needn't have come down yourself," in a voice of chuffing, almost supercilious grandeur, and his wife said, "Good evening, Master!" which for all its submissiveness showed she had got what she wanted.

Off they went, the Master offering Sir Dudley an arm on the steps. "What year did you go down?" he said, and Paul heard, "Nineteen fourteen, you see . . . I never took my degree . . . I got married . . ." Lady Valance laughed for the Master, as though to show how little this lack of a degree had mattered, and perhaps to indulge the mention of this earlier marriage. Well, they must have been together for fifty years themselves, after the mere nine or ten with Daphne, whom Paul thought of now more fondly. What a contrast—he pictured her in her shabby mac and hat, in the place of this highly preserved woman, who still moved with the dawdling strut of a model. Paul watched them from the steps. Now two muscular boys in white rowing shorts burst out from a doorway, and slowed and ran on the spot to let the Master and his guests go by; then they were off, coming up past Paul in a rush and out through the gate into the street. For once it was the old man who held his interest, and seemed in fact almost miraculous, from the lordly jabs of his stick to the yap of his vowels. As they went off through an arch on the far side of the quad, Dudley still visibly a casualty of the Battle of Loos, other less palpable things seemed to hover about him, which were famous phrases of his brother, in *Georgian Poetry*, or the *Oxford Dictionary of Quotations*. Paul felt, in some idiotic but undeniable way, that he had very nearly seen Cecil himself.

He went on, as planned, along Broad Street, to look at the bookshops. The rowing boys had already vanished into the thickening light of the late afternoon—the sun in the west struck right along the street, and dazzled the people who were coming towards him, leaving him, a mere looming silhouette, free to examine them closely. As he loitered around the biography table in Blackwell's, picking up the expensive new books and looking at their indexes and acknowledgements, he had Dudley's hunched but handsome figure on his mind, and was starting to hear answers to his questions in that extraordinary voice. Paul thought he would like his own acknowledgements page to begin with thanks to his subject's brother, ideally perhaps by that stage "the late Sir Dudley Valance," who "gave so generously of his time" and "made his archives available without questions or conditions." The author of this new life of

Percy Slater had even been "welcomed warmly into the family home"—
something Paul now sensed was less likely to happen in his case.

He had always opened such books at the grey-black seams that
marked the inserts of pictures. His daydreams for his own book often
dwelt on this last, almost decorative addition to the work—the quickly
passed-over photos of unappealing forebears, the birthplace or childhood residence, the subject sharpening into focus in his teens, the
momentarily confusing captions—*lower right, opposite, over*—one or
two of the pictures thought worthy of a full page, the defining portraits.
Would Dudley ever make such things available to him? Paul felt some
kind of subterfuge might be necessary. Percy Slater had lived into his seventies so there was all the proliferation of wives and children, snapshots
from Kenya and Japan, a late picture in doctoral robes of this very university, chatting to Harold Macmillan, the Chancellor. None of that for
Cecil, of course, just a photograph of his tomb, perhaps.

And there, at the end of the table, in a sober brown jacket with the
title in red and yellow, was *The Letters of Evelyn Waugh,* a book with an
aura, it seemed to Paul, and fat with confidence of its own interest—he
looked at something else first, just to savour and focus his anticipation,
and then after a minute casually picked up the heavy volume and
hopped backwards through the index in his now systematic way—
Valance, then Sawle, then Ralph. Two mentions of Dudley, one of Cecil,
which turned out to be in the footnote identifying Dudley as "younger
brother of the First World War poet." He coveted it, but the price, £15, a
week's rent—hardly possible. A familiar but still extraordinary calm
came over him. He made his way into the History department, chose a
huge book on medieval England, itself part of a massively scholarly
series, pale blue wrappers, Clarendon Press, price £40, and a minute later
took it off upstairs. In his bag he had a compliments slip from Jake at the
TLS, with his name on and the scribbled message, "800 words by end of
March," and he tucked it into the front of the book as he went. Stopping
at a mezzanine where Classics were displayed, he got out his notebook to
write down a title, and squatting down to a low shelf behind a table he
pencilled three or four page numbers and a question-mark on the fly-
leaf of his volume of Plantagenet history. From here it was a further
turn of the stairs up to the second-hand department, where he asked the
bearded young man if they bought review copies in good condition.
The Plantagenets were given a quick glance, the review-slip almost
subliminally noted, the book checked for any devaluing marginalia.
"We can only offer half-price," said the man. "Oh, really?" said Paul,

chewing his cheek—"well, okay, fine, I guess, if that's your standard practice. Sorry . . . let me just take that review-slip . . ." The item was written
in a ledger, the book itself translated to a trolley of new acquisitions,
and two clean £10 notes handed over. A few minutes later he strolled
back into college with *The Letters of Evelyn Waugh* in his briefcase and
a happy surplus of £5 in his back pocket.

The room he'd been given, at the top of a long stone staircase, had the
name Greg Hudson on the door, and though the sheets and towel were
fresh he felt like an unwanted guest among all the books, records and
clothes that Greg had left behind over the vac. There were muddy plim-
solls under the bed, a Blondie poster above the desk. In a sweet-smelling
cupboard full of jam and coffee he found a bottle of malt whisky, half-
full, and poured a finger of it into a tumbler. He stood sipping at it, with
one foot on the hearthstone. There was a poem by Stephen Spender that
began, very oddly, "Marston, dropping it in the grate, broke his pipe." It
had come into his mind the moment he'd unlocked the door, amid the
uneasy displeasure, and covert excitement, of finding the room was full
of someone else's things. The line about Marston was part of his illusion
of Oxford, a glimpse of pipe-smoking students known by their sur-
names; and though he'd forgotten what happened in the rest of the
poem, he saw Marston dropping his pipe on the stone hearth just here,
as easily as he could let slip this glass of treasured Glenfiddich.

He read the postcards from Paris and Sydney propped on the mantelpiece, both signed Jacqui with a lot of crosses, and took down the
mounted photo of the college's Second XV, which had the names written
underneath in a crazily ornate script. So that was Greg, the grinning
giant standing off-centre, his mid-parts hidden by the shaggy round
head of the man seated in front of him. How his great sweaty body must
labour in this schoolboy-size bed—and when Jacqui came round, what a
terrible squash it must be for them. He pulled open the top drawer of the
desk, but it was so jammed with papers that he couldn't face going
through it just yet. Otherwise, there was nothing much to read except
chemistry books. For some reason, he left his new purchase, if that's
what it was, untouched.

He decided that before going down to dinner in half an hour he
would look again at Dudley's *Black Flowers,* to have something to quote,
or to ask, if he got a chance over drinks. "I was wondering, Sir Dudley,
when you said . . ." Since he knew Corley Court, it seemed a sound
starting-point. He peered at the author photo with fresh interest, and a
suspicion that Dudley looked almost younger now—the style of the

1950s man of letters seemed deliberately ageing. He sat self-consciously under the bright ceiling-lamp, with his glass of whisky. A red tartan rug thrown over the armchair disguised the probing state of the springs, deranged presumably by the recurrent impact of Greg. About the changes at Corley, Dudley had written:

My father had been laid low and effectively silenced by a stroke a year after the War ended; he lived on until 1925, the patient prisoner of a bath chair, his essential geniality apparently undimmed. When he spoke it was in a cheerful language of his own, and with no awareness that the sounds issuing from his mouth were nonsense to his listeners. One saw from his expression that what he was saying was generally fond and amusing. And he appeared to follow our conversation with perfect clarity. It took a great deal of patience in us, and then a certain amount of kindly pretence, to keep up any sustained talk with him. His own demeanour, however, suggested that he drew great satisfaction from these agonizing encounters.

Of course all work on *The Incidence of Red Calves Among Black Angus,* meant as his major contribution to agricultural science, was suspended for ever. My mother very capably extended her control of domestic life at Corley to that of a large estate; my own efforts to assist her were, if not rebuffed, then treated as impractical and rather tiresome. It was suggested (fancifully, it seemed to me) that my brother Cecil had known all about farming, both "horn and corn" as my mother liked to put it, but that I had never shown any aptitude for the matter. The fact that in due course I must surely take over the running of Corley weighed oddly little with her. I was myself, it is true, a *mutilé de guerre,* subject to various cautions and exemptions; but idleness did not sit easily with me. Perhaps the silencing of the other writers in our family, the poet and the agronomist, opened a door to the younger son. A psychologist of family life might find some such pattern of subconscious motivations and opportunities. At any rate I looked again at sketches I had published long before in the *Cherwell* and the *Isis,* and found myself pleased by their youthful sarcasm. The habit, so familiar to many of us after the War, of thinking of our earlier selves as foreign beings, Arcadian innocents, proved refreshingly a merely partial truth.

I wrote *The Long Gallery* at great speed, in a little under three months, in a mood of irritable tension and ferocious high spirits. I have already said something of its reception, and of the changes, some amusing and many tedious, that the success of that little book brought to our lives. But thereafter the more serious work I knew it in me to do refused to come. I felt as if there was much that I needed to clear away; and on this too no doubt our psychologist would have something to report. Some such need, I think, lay behind my strong desire, once my father had died, to clear out Corley itself. A deepening distaste for all Victoriana became a kind of mission for me, who had inherited by default a large Victorian house of exorbitant ugliness and inconvenience. Sometimes, it is true, I wondered if in later years its ugliness might recommend itself as a quaint kind of charm to generations yet unborn. In few places did I sanction the complete demolition of the heavy and garish decorative schemes of my grandfather—the ornate ceilings, the sombre panelling, the childish and clumsy outcrops of stone-carving and mosaic—but with the help of an interior designer of a thoroughly modern kind I saw to it that they were all "boxed in." Waterhouse, whose dismal Gothic buildings had despoiled my own College, was sometimes credited with the design, which in its ability to inflict pain on the eye was certainly up to his best standard. It is quite possible my grandfather consulted him. But the drawings surviving at Corley were all from the hand of a Mr. Money, a local practitioner known otherwise only for the draughty Town Hall at Newbury (a building whose discomforts my brother and I knew well from our annual visits as children to observe our father presenting trophies to local livestock breeders). At Corley, of course, certain things were sacrosanct—the chapel in the best Middle Pointed that money (or Money) could provide, and where my brother was laid to rest under a great quantity of Carrara marble. That could never be touched. And the library I left, at my mother's stern request, in its original state of caliginous gloom. But in all the other principal rooms, a modern brightness and simplicity effectively overlaid the ingenious horrors of an earlier age.

Paul had finished his drink, and felt a small top-up would be undetectable, and if detected untraceable. He went back to the cupboard with righteous impatience. Was this building, this spartan attic room, part of Waterhouse's work, he wondered? He peered at the stone-framed window, the notched and stained oak sill, the boarded-up fireplace, which perhaps had a general kinship with those at Corley Court. Peter's room there had had a fireplace just the same, grey stone, with a wide flat pointed arch . . . He remembered the time he had made him examine a hole in the ceiling, in a state of high excitement. Really, such things meant nothing to him—but Peter would certainly have known. He had been at Exeter College—but had he had friends across the road here in Balliol? Paul saw him entirely at home in the university, as if they had been destined for each other. He went out to the lavatory, in a queer little angled turret, and when he looked down from the window into the gloomy quad he saw a dark-haired figure moving swiftly through the shadows and into the lit doorway of a staircase who might almost have been Peter, before he knew him, fifteen years ago, calling on a friend, some earlier lover—that was what his unselfconscious evenings had been like.

By the time he set off for drinks, Paul already felt cautiously cheerful. In the large lamp-lit Common Room, a surprisingly sleek modern building, he rather got stuck with a secretary from the English faculty office, a nice young woman who'd been responsible for much of the conference arrangements. A mutual shyness tethered them in their corner, beside the table on which all the papers were laid out, including the *TLS*. "Well, there you are!" said Ruth, his friend, blushing with satisfaction, so that Paul formed the wary idea she had taken a shine to him. The room itself, full of confident noise, brisk introductions, loud reunions, was a breathtaking plunge for him. He realized the man standing near him was Professor Stallworthy, whose life of Wilfred Owen had fought rather shy of Owen's feelings for other men. Paul suddenly felt shy of them too. Beyond him was a white-haired man in military uniform of some splendour—General Colthorpe, Ruth said, who was going to speak about Wavell. She confirmed that the broad-faced, genially pugnacious-looking man talking to the Master was Paul Fussell, whose book on the Great War had moved and enlightened Paul more than anything he'd read on the subject—though sadly, like Evelyn Waugh's *Letters*, it had only mentioned Cecil in a footnote ("a less neurotic—and less talented—epigone of Brooke"). Paul looked around admiringly and restlessly, his tiny empty sherry glass cupped behind his hand, waiting for the Valances to come in. "Were you at Oxford?" said Ruth.

"No, I wasn't," Paul said, with an almost bashful smile, as though to say he understood and forgave her error.

He was introduced to a young English don, and chatted to him in a keen but rather circular way about Cecil, the long sleeves of the don's gown brushing over Paul's hands as he moved and turned. Paul couldn't always follow what he meant; he found himself in the role of lowly sapper while Martin (was he called?) talked in larger strategic terms, with a pervasive air of irony—"Well, quite!" Paul found himself saying, two or three times. He felt he was boring him, and he himself was soon achingly tense and distracted by the presence of the Valances in the room, and merely nodded genially when Martin moved off. Dudley's voice, both clipped and drawling, the historic vowels perhaps further pickled and preserved by thirty years' exile in sherry country, could be heard now and then through the general yammer. He was easy to lose, among the taller, younger figures milling round him, the swoop of gowns, the odd barbaric intensity of people connecting. Linette's sparkly green evening jacket was a help in tracking their gradual movement through the crowd. Then for a minute they were alongside, Linette with her back to Paul, Dudley in stooped profile, and again with a look of short-winded good-humour as he tried to follow what a young Indian man was saying to him, in fashionably theoretical terms, about life in the trenches.

"Yes, I don't know," said Dudley, maintaining a precarious balance between mild modesty and his fairly clear belief that the Indian was talking rot. He smiled at him widely in a way that showed Paul the conversation was over, but which the Indian scholar took as a cue for a further convoluted question:

"But would you agree, sir, that, in a very real sense, the experience of most writers about war is predicated on the idea that—"

"Darling, you mustn't tire yourself!" said Linette sharply, so that the Indian, mortified, apologized and backed away from her flicker of a smile. Well, it was a little lesson for Paul in how not to proceed with them. In the moment of uncomfortable silence that followed he perhaps had his chance: he raised his chin to speak, but a weird paralysis left him murmuring and blinking, looking almost as apologetic as the retreating questioner. He could have asked Ruth to introduce him, but he didn't want Linette in particular to learn his name at this early stage—whether Dudley himself had ever seen his letters he doubted. Stiff-necked, Dudley seemed rarely to turn his head, and a call from his other side made him swivel his whole body away, with a well-practised lurch of his weight on to his stick. Paul was left with a sense of astonished near-contact, of greatness, it almost seemed, within arm's reach.

At dinner it turned out he'd been placed next to Ruth again, and when he said, "Oh that's nice!" he half-meant it, and half felt a kind of emasculation. The seating was on long benches, and they all remained standing, one or two bestriding the bench as they talked, until everyone was in. Dudley stumped past in a swaying line that was heading for the High Table, and proper chairs. Now the Master made a more official welcome to the conference, and said a long scurrying Latin grace, as if apologetically reminding them of something they knew far better than he did.

Paul was drunk enough to introduce himself to the very unattractive little man on his other side (there were far more men than women), but he soon found his shoulder turned against him, and for an awkward ten minutes he strained the patience of the two men opposite who were involved in complex discussion of faculty affairs into which there was no real point in trying to induct Paul, whose *TLS* credentials started to wear thin. He leant towards them with a smile of forced interest to which they were rudely immune. "I'm writing up the conference for the *TLS*"— Paul felt he'd said this too often—"though also, as it happens, I'm working on a biography of Cecil Valance."

"Did he ever finish his work on the Cathars?" said the man on the right.

"Not as far as we know," said Paul, absorbing the horror of the question with some aplomb, he felt. Was the man thinking of someone else? Cecil's work at Cambridge had been on the Indian Mutiny, for some reason. Was that anything to do with the Cathars? Who were the Cathars, in the first place?

"Or have I got that wrong?"

"Well . . ." Paul paused. "His research—which he never finished, by the way—was on General Havelock."

"Oh, well, not the Cathars at all," said the man, though with a critical look at Paul, as though the mistake had somehow been his.

The other man, who was a little bit nicer, said, "I was just speaking to Dudley Valance, whom you must know, obviously, before dinner—he was up with Aldous Huxley and Macmillan, of course. Never took his degree."

"Well, nor did Macmillan, come to that," said the first man.

"Didn't stop him becoming Chancellor," said Paul.

"That's right," said the nicer man, and laughed cautiously.

"That was all bloody Trevor-Roper's doing," said the first man, with a bitter look, so that Paul saw he had ambled well-meaningly into some other academic minefield.

The meal unrolled in a further fuddle of wines, time was speeding past unnoticed and unmourned, he knew he was drinking too much, the fear of his own clumsiness mixing with a peculiar new sense of competence. He made it pretty clear to Ruth that he wasn't interested in girls, but this only seemed to put them on to a more confusingly intimate footing. The Master clapped his hands and said a few words, and then everyone stood while the High Table filed out, the rest of them being invited to use a room whose name Paul didn't catch for coffee and further refreshments. So perhaps tonight he wouldn't get a shot at Dudley after all. But then outside in the quad, as cigarettes were lit and new groups formed and drifted off, Ruth kept him back, and then said, "Why don't you slip into Common Room with me?"

"Well, if you think that would be all right . . ."

"I don't want you to miss anything," she said.

So back they went, Paul now rather shy at getting what he wanted. At a first quick survey, over his coffee cup, he saw that Linette had been separated from her husband, and was standing talking to a group of men, one almost her own age, a couple of them younger than Paul. He attached himself to another small group round Jon Stallworthy, from which he could watch while nodding appreciatively at the conversation. Dudley was sitting on a long sofa at the other side of the room, with various Fellows and a good-looking younger woman who seemed to be flirting with him. His magnetism was physical, even in old age, and to certain minds no doubt class would come into it. Without him Linette seemed disoriented, an Englishwoman in her seventies, who lived much of the year abroad. She exacted some gallantry from the men, which went on in nervous swoops and laughs, small faltering sequences of jokes, perhaps to cover their own slight boredom and disorientation with her. And then, in a strange nerveless trance, Paul found himself accepting a glass of brandy, crossing the floor and joining the group around her—he didn't know what he would say, it felt pointless and even perverse and yet, as a self-imposed dare, inescapable. She had a large jet brooch on her green jacket, a black flower in effect, which he examined as she talked. Her face, close-to, had a mesmerizing quality, fixed and photogenic, somehow consciously the face Dudley Valance had been pleased and proud to gaze on every day for half a century, as handsome as his own, in its way, and as disdainful of the impertinent modern world. She was having to say something about his work, but Paul had the feeling their lives and the people they saw were far from literary. He pictured them sitting in their fortified house, knocking back their fortified wine, their friends presumably the fellow expats of Antequera. And there was something else, about that stiff auburn mane, and those long black lashes—Paul knew in his bones that she hadn't been born into Dudley's world, even though she now wore its lacquered carapace. Anyway, it seemed his arrival had been more or less what the others were waiting for, and after a minute, with various courteous murmurs and nods they all moved off in different directions, leaving the two of them together. "I really must check on my husband," she said, looking past him, the gracious smile not yet entirely faded from her face. Paul had a feeling that all that was going to change when he said who he was. He said,

"I'm so looking forward to your husband's talk tomorrow, Lady Valance."

"Yes, I know," she said, and he almost laughed, and then saw it was merely a general term of assent. She meant, what she then said, "It's a great coup for you all to have got him here."

"I think everyone thinks the same," said Paul, then went on quickly, "I'm hoping he'll be saying something about his brother."

Linette's head went back a little. It was as if she'd only vaguely heard that he had a brother. "Oh, good lord, no," she said, with a little shake. "No, no—he'll be discussing his own work." And a new suspicion floated in her eyes, in the quick pinch of her lips and angling of the head. "I don't think I caught your name."

"Oh—Paul Bryant." It semed absurd to be skulking around the truth, but he was glad to be able to say, "I'm covering the conference for the *TLS*."

"For the . . . ?"—she turned an ear.

"*The Times* . . ."

"Oh, really?" And with a slightly awkward hesitation, "Did you write to my husband?"

Paul looked puzzled. "Oh, about Cecil, you mean? Yes, I did, as it happens . . ."

She glanced approvingly at Dudley. "I'm afraid all requests such as yours fall on very stony ground."

"Well, I don't want to be any trouble to him . . ." Paul seemed to glimpse the barren hillsides of Andalusia. "So you've had others . . ."

"Oh, every few years, you know, someone wants to poke about in Cecil's papers, and one just knows from the start that it would be a disaster, so it's best simply to say no." She was rather jolly about it. "I mean, his letters were published—I don't know if you saw those?"

"Well, of course!" said Paul, unable to tell if anything here was in his favour. She seemed to be inviting him to agree he was a disaster in the making.

"And you've read my husband's books?"

"I certainly have." It was time to be sternly flattering. "*Black Flowers,* obviously, is a classic—"

"Then I'm sorry to tell you you've really read everything he has to say about old . . . um . . . Cecil."

Paul smiled as if at the great bonus of what Dudley had already given them; but did go on, "There are still one or two things . . ."

Linette was distracted. But she turned back to him after five seconds, again with her look of haughty humour, which made him unsure if she was mocking him or inviting him to share in her mockery of something else. "There's been some extraordinary nonsense written."

"Has there . . . ?" Paul rather wanted to know what it was.

She made an oh-crikey face: "Extraordinary nonsense!"

"Lady Valance? I don't know if this would be a good moment?" The elderly don had come back. "Forgive my breaking in . . ."

"Oh, for the . . . um . . . ?"

"Indeed, if you'd like to see . . ." The smiling old man left just enough sense of a chore in his voice to make it clear he was doing her a favour which she couldn't decline.

"I don't know if my husband . . ." But her husband seemed perfectly happy. And by a miracle the old chap took her off, out of the room, the slight flirty wobble of her high heels glimpsed beneath the raised wing of his gown, leaving Paul free at last to approach his prize.

In fact it was Martin who brought him in—"Sir Dudley, I'm not sure if you've met—"

"Well, no, we haven't yet," said Paul, bending to shake hands, which seemed to irritate Dudley, and went on cheerfully, before anyone could say his name, "I'm writing up the conference for the *TLS.*" Martin of course knew about the Cecil job, but probably not about Dudley's resistance to it.

"Ah, yes, the *TLS,*" said Dudley, as Paul further found himself being offered the low armchair at right-angles to him at the end of the sofa. He was in the presence, with a need no doubt to say his piece. "I've got a bone to pick with the *TLS*," Dudley went on, with a narrow smile that wasn't exactly humorous.

"Oh, dear!" said Paul, his clutched brandy glass seeming to impose a new way of performing on him, a sort of simmering joviality. But Dudley's smile remained fixed on his next remark:

"They once gave me a very poor review."

"Oh, I'm surprised . . . what was that for?"

"Eh? A book of mine called *The Long Gallery*."

The mock-modesty of the formulation made this less amusing, though a man on the other side laughed and said, "That would be what, sixty years ago?"

"Mm, a bit before my time," Paul said, and put his head back rather steeply to get at the brandy in the bottom of his glass. He found Dudley disconcerting, in his sharpness and odd passive disregard for things around him, as if conserving his energy, perhaps just a question of age. He seemed to show he had fairly low expectations of the present company and the larger event they were part of, whilst no doubt thinking his own part in it quite important. Paul wanted to bring the talk round to Cecil before Linette got back, but without disclosing his plans. Then he heard an American graduate he'd met briefly earlier say, "I don't know how you would rate your brother's work, sir?"

"Oh . . ." Dudley slumped slightly; but he was courteous enough, perhaps liked to be asked for a bad opinion. "Well, you know . . . it looks very much of its time now, doesn't it? Some pretty phrases—but it didn't ever amount to anything very much. When I looked at 'Two Acres' again a few years ago I thought it had really needed the War to make its point—it seems hopelessly sentimental now."

"Oh, I grew up on it," said another man, half-laughing, not exactly disagreeing.

"Mm, so did I . . . ," said Paul quietly over his balloon.

"It always rather amused me," said Dudley, "that my brother, who was heir to three thousand acres, should be best known for his ode to a mere two." This was exactly the joke that he had made in *Black Flowers*, and it didn't go down very well in the Balliol SCR—there was a little sycophantic laughter, most prominently from Paul himself. "Ah . . . !" General Colthorpe had come back in, and even in a civilian context there was an uneasy movement among a number of them to stand up.

"Whom are you discussing?" he said.

"My brother Sizzle, General," Dudley seemed to say.

"Ah, indeed," said the General, declining an offered space on the sofa but fetching a hard chair as he came round and making a square circle of the group, which took on a suddenly strategic air. "Yes, a tragic case. And a very promising writer."

"Yes . . ."—Dudley was more cautious now.

"Wavell had several of them by heart, you know. It's 'Soldiers Dreaming,' isn't it, he puts in *Other Men's Flowers,* but he had a great deal of time for 'The Old Company.' "

"Oh, well, yes," said Dudley.

"I'll be saying something about it tomorrow. He used to quote it"—the General batted his eyelids—" 'It's the old company, all right, / But without the old companions'—one of the truest things said about the experience of many young officers." He looked around—"They came back and they came back, do you see, if they came through at all, and the company was completely changed, they'd all been killed. There was always a company tradition, keenly maintained, but the only people who remembered the old soldiers were soon dead themselves—no one remembered the rememberers. No, a great poem in its way." He shook his head in candid submission. Paul sensed there were demurrers in the group, but the General's claim for the poem's truth made them hesitate.

"It's a subject, of course, I wrote about myself," said Dudley, in a strange airy tone.

"Well—indeed," said the General, perhaps less on top of the younger brother's work, or uneasy with its tone about army life in general. As a cultured person from the world of action and power, General Colthorpe, with his long intellectual face and keen inescapable eye, was so imposing that Dudley himself began to look rather pansy and decadent in comparison, with his beautiful cuff-links and his silver-headed stick, and the grey curls over his collar at the back. The General frowned apologetically. "I was wondering—there's not been a Life, I think, has there?"

Paul's heart began to race, and he blushed at the naming of this still half-secret desire. "Well . . . !" said Martin, and smiled across at him.

"Of Sizzle, no," said Dudley. "There's really not enough there. George Sawle did a very thorough job on the Letters a few years back—almost too thorough, dug out a lot of stuff about the girlfriends and so on: my brother had a great appetite for romantic young women. Anyway, I gave Sawle a free hand—he's a sound fellow, I've known him for years." Dudley looked around with a hint of caution in this academic setting. "And of course there's the old memoir, you know, that Sebby Stokes did—perfectly good, shows its age a bit, but it tells you all the facts."

This left Paul in a very absurd position. He sat forward, and had just started to say, "As a matter of fact, Sir Dudley, I was wondering—" when Linette reappeared, alone, at the far end of the room.

"Ah, there you are . . . ," Dudley called out, with an odd mixture of mockery and relief.

Linette came towards them, in her still fascinating way, pleased to be looked at, smiling as if nursing something just a little too wicked to say. The General stood up, and then one or two others, half-ashamed not to have thought of it. Linette knew she had to speak, but hesitated appealingly. "Darling, the . . . *Senior* Dean's just been showing me the most marvellous . . . what would one call it . . . ?"—she smiled uncertainly.

"I don't know, my love."

She gave a pant of a laugh. "It was a sort of . . . very large . . . *very* lovely . . ."—she raised a hand, which described it even more vaguely.

"Animal, vegetable or mineral," said Dudley.

"Now you're being horrid," she said, with a playful pout, so that Paul felt admitted for a second to a semi-public performance, such as friends might see on the patio or whatever it was in Antequera: it was a little embarrassing, but carried off by their quite unselfconscious confidence of being a fascinating couple. "I was going to say, I hope they're not tiring you, but now I rather hope they are!"

"Lady Valance," said General Colthorpe, offering his chair.

"Thank you so much, General, but I'm really rather tired myself." She looked across at Dudley with teasing reproach. "Don't you think?" she said.

"You go, my love, I'm going to sit and jaw a bit longer with these good people"—again the courtesy unsettled by the flash of a smile, like a sarcasm; though perhaps he really did want to make the most of this rare occasion to talk with young readers and scholars; or perhaps, Paul thought, as Martin jumped up to conduct her back to the Master's lodgings, what Dudley really wanted was another large whisky.

THE NEXT MORNING Paul woke to the sound of a tolling bell, with a hangover that felt much worse for the comfortless strangeness of Greg Hudson's room. He lay with a knuckle pressed hard against the pain in his forehead, as if in intensive thought. All he thought about was last night, in startling jumps and queasy circlings of recollection. He felt contempt for his juvenile weakness as a drinker, pitted against the octogenarian's glassy-eyed appetite and capacity. He remembered with a squeezing of the gut the moment when he found himself talking about Corinna, and Dudley's stare, at a spot just beyond Paul's right shoulder, which he'd mistaken at first for tender gratitude, even a sort of bashful encouragement, but which turned out after twenty-five seconds to be the opposite, an icy refusal of any such intimacy. Thank god Martin the young English don had come back at that point. And yet at the end, perhaps because of the drink, there had been something forthright and friendly, hadn't there, in the way they'd parted? On the doorstep of the Master's lodgings, under the lamp, Dudley's wincing gloom broken up in a grin, a seizing of the moment, an effusive goodnight: Paul could hear it now—no one had spoken to him since, and the sound of the words remained available, unerased. "Yes, see you in the morning!" If he could get round Linette, there might be a chance of another conversation, with the tape running. Most of the other things Dudley had said last night he'd completely forgotten.

When he got out of bed, Paul was lurchingly surprised to find Greg's unwashed jock-strap and one or two other intimate items scattered across the floor, but the awful blurred recollections of his late-night antics were overwhelmed by the need to get to the lavatory; which he did just in time. After he'd been sick, in one great comprehensive paragraph, he felt an almost delicious weakness and near-simultaneous improvement; his headache didn't vanish, but it lightened and receded, and when he shaved a few minutes later he watched his face reappearing in stripes with a kind of proud fascination.

Dudley didn't come to breakfast in hall, of course, so at 9:20 Paul went down to the phone at the foot of the staircase and dialled the extension of the lodgings. He felt still the oddly enjoyable tingle of weakness and disorientation. The phone was answered by a helpful secretary, and almost at once Dudley was saying, in a nice gentlemanly way, and with perhaps a hint of tactical frailty to pre-empt any unwelcome request, "Dudley Valance . . . ?"

"Oh, good morning, Sir Dudley—it's Paul . . . !" It was simply the sort of contact he had dreamed of.

There was a moment's thoughtful and potentially worrying silence, and then a completely charming "Paul, oh, thank god . . ."

"Ah . . . !"—Paul laughed with relief, and after a second Dudley did the same. "I hope this isn't too early to call you."

"Not at all. Good of you to ring. I'm sorry, for a ghastly moment just then I thought it was Paul *Bryant*."

Paul didn't know why he was sniggering too, as the colour rushed to his face and he looked round quickly to check that no one could see or hear him. "Oh . . . um . . ." It was as bad as something overheard, a shocking glimpse of himself—and of Dudley too: he saw in a moment the intractable delicacy of the problem, the shouldering of the insult was the exposure of the gaffe . . . and yet already he was blurting out, "Actually it is Paul Bryant, um . . ."

"Oh, it *is*," said Dudley, "I'm so sorry!" with a momentary bleak laugh. "How very unfortunate!"

Still too confused to feel the shock fully, Paul said incoherently, "I won't trouble you now, Sir Dudley. I'll see you at your lecture." And he hung up the phone again and stood staring at it incredulously.

It was during General Colthorpe's talk on Wavell that Paul suddenly understood, and blushed again, with the indignant but helpless blush of foolish recognition. Very discreetly, under the desk, he got out Daphne Jacobs's book from his briefcase. It was somewhere in the passage on Dudley's exploits as a practical joker, those efforts she retailed as classics of wit and cleverly left it to the reader to wonder at their cruelty or pointlessness. As before, he felt General Colthorpe was watching him particularly, and even accusingly, from behind his lectern, but with infinite dissimulation he found the place, her account of her first visit to Corley, and looking up devotedly at the General between sentences he read the now obvious description of Dudley taking a telephone call from his brother:

> The well-known voice came through, on a very poor line, from the telegraph office in Wantage: "Dud, old man, it's Cecil here, can you hear me?" Dudley paused, with the grin of feline villainy that was so amusing to anyone not the subject of his pranks, and then said, with a quick laugh of pretended relief, "Oh, thank god!" Cecil could be heard faintly, but with genuine surprise and concern, "Everything all right?" To which Dudley, his eye on himself in the mirror and on me in the hallway behind him, replied, "For a frightful moment I thought you were my brother Cecil." I was confused at first, and then astonished. I knew all about teasing from my own brothers, but this was the most audacious bit of teasing even I had ever heard. It was a joke I later heard him play on several other friends, or enemies, as they then unexpectedly found themselves to be. Cecil, of course, merely said "You silly

ass!" and carried on with the call; but the trick came back to my mind often, in later years, when a telephone call from Cecil was no longer remotely on the cards.

7

PAUL WROTE in his diary:

April 13, 1980 (Cecil's 89th birthday!) /10:30pm.

I'm writing this up from skeleton notes while I can still remember it fairly well. On the coach back from Birmingham I started to play back the tape of the interview and found it goes completely dead after a couple of minutes: the battery in the mike must have given out. Amazing after twenty interviews that it should happen with this one—now I have no documentary proof for the most important material so far. Astounding revelations (if true!)

My appt was for 2:30. The Sawles have lived in the same house (17 Chilcot Ave, Solihull) since the 1930s: a large semi, red brick, with a black-and-white gable at the front. It was new when they bought it. George Sawle walked me round the garden before I left, and pointed out the "Tudor half-timbering": he said everyone at the university thought it was screamingly funny that 2 historians lived in a mock-Tudor house. A pond in the back garden, full of tadpoles, which interested him greatly, and a rockery. He held my arm as we went round. He said there had been a "very ambitious rockery" at "Two Acres," where he and Hubert and Daphne had played games as children—he has always liked rockeries. Hubert was killed in the First World War. Their father died of diphtheria in 1903 "or thereabouts" and Freda Sawle in "about 1938" ("I'm afraid I'm rather bad with dates"). GFS told me with some pride that he was 84, but earlier he'd said 76. (He is 85.)

Madeleine opened the door when I arrived—she complained at some length about her arthritis, which she seemed to blame largely on me. Walks with an elbow-crutch (shades of Mum). Said, "I don't know if you'll get much sense out of him." She was

candid, but not friendly; not sure if she remembered me from
Daphne's 70th. Her deafness much worse than thirteen years ago,
but she looks just the same. Her sense of humour is really no more
than an irritable suspicion that someone else might find something funny. She said, "I'm only giving you an hour—even that
may be too much"—which was a completely new condition, and
put me in a bit of a flap.

GFS was in his study—looked confused when I came in, but
then brightened up when I said why I was there. "Ah, yes, poor
old Cecil, dear old Cecil!" A kind of slyness, as if to imply he
really knew all along, but much more friendly than I remember at
D's 70th—in fact by the end rather too friendly (see below!) Now
completely bald on top, the white beard long and straggly, looks a
bit mad. Bright mixed-up clothes, red check shirt under green
pullover, old pin-stripe suit-trousers hitched up so tight you don't
quite know where to look. I reminded him we'd met before, and
he accepted the idea cheerfully, but later he said, "It's a great
shame we didn't meet before." At first I was emb by his forgetfulness—why is it emb when people repeat themselves? Then I felt
that as he didn't know, and there was no one else there, it didn't
matter; it was a completely private drama. He sat in the chair
beside his desk and I sat in a low armchair—I felt it must be like a
tutorial. Books on 3 walls, the room lived-in but dreary.

I asked him straight away how he had met Cecil (which oddly
he doesn't say in the intro to the Letters). "At Cambridge. He got
me elected to the Apostles. I'm not supposed to talk about that, of
course" (looking rather coy). What they called "suitable" under-
graduates were singled out and assessed, but the Society was so
secret they didn't know they were being vetted for it. "C was my
'father,' as they called it. He took a shine to me, for some reason."
I said he must have been suitable. "I must, mustn't I?" he said and
gave me a funny look. Said, "I was extremely shy, and C was the
opposite. You felt thrilled to be noticed by him." What was he like
in those days? He was "a great figure in the college," but he did
too many things. Missed a First in the History tripos, because he
was always off doing something else; he was easily bored, with
activities and people. He sat for a fellowship twice but didn't get
it. He was always playing rugger or rowing or mountaineering.
"Not in Cambs, presumably?" GFS laughed. "He climbed in

Scotland, and sometimes in the Dolomites. He was very strong, and had very large hands. The figure on his tomb is quite wrong, it shows him with almost a girl's hands."

C also loved acting—he was in a French play they did every year for several years. "But he was a very bad actor. He made all the characters he played just like himself. In Dom Juan by Molière (check) he played the servant, which was quite beyond him." Did C not understand other people? GFS said it was his upbringing, he (C) believed his family and home were very important, and in a "rather innocent" way thought everyone else would be interested in them too. Was he a snob? "It wasn't snobbery exactly, more an unthinking social confidence." What about his writing? GFS said he was self-confident about that too, wrote all those poems about Corley Court. I said he wrote love poems as well. "Yes, people thought he was a sort of upper-class Rupert Brooke. Upper class but second rate." I said I couldn't work out from the Letters how well C knew Brooke—there are 2 or 3 sarcastic mentions, and nothing in Keynes's edition of RB's letters. "Oh, he knew him—he was in the Society too, of course. RB was 3 or 4 years older. They didn't get on." He said C was jealous of RB in many ways, C was naturally competitive and he was overshadowed by him, as a poet and "a beauty." Wasn't C v good-looking? GFS said "he was very striking, with wicked dark eyes that he used to seduce people with. Rupert was a flawless beauty, but Cecil was much stronger and more masculine. He had an enormous cock." I checked that the tape was still going round nicely and wrote this down before I looked at GFS again—he was matter-of-fact but did look vaguely surprised at what he'd just heard himself say. I said I supposed he'd gone swimming with C. "Well, on occasion," he said, as if not seeing the point of the question. "C was always taking his clothes off, he was famous for it." Hard to know what to say next. I said were there real people behind all the love-poems? This was really my central question. He said, "Oh, yes." I said Margaret Ingham and D of course. "Miss Ingham was a blue stocking and a red herring" (laughed). I felt I should come out with it. Did C seduce men as well as women? He looked at me as if there'd been a slight misunderstanding. "C would fuck anyone," he said.

At this point MS's crutch whacked against the door and she

came in with a couple of coffees on a tray. GFS has prostate trouble, but says coffee is good for his memory. "I'm starting to get a bit forgetful," he said. "A bit!" said MS. GFS (quietly): "Well, you don't always hear what I say, you know, dear." She said coffee excited him and made him confused about things; he continually got things wrong. She talked about him in the third person. GFS said, "Peter's asking me about Cecil at Cambridge." She didn't correct him, and nor did I (later I became Simon, and by the time I left I was Ian). "I remember C very well, though, dear." MS rather squashed me, perching on the arm of my chair; she said she'd never met C, but she took a dim view of the other Valances. Old Sir Edwin seemed nice enough, though he only talked nonsense by the time she knew him, and before that apparently he had only talked about cows; he'd always been a great bore. C's mother was a tyrant and a bully. Dudley was unstable—he'd had a bad war and afterwards he used it as an excuse to attack friend and foe alike. I said, could he not be charming too? His first novel was very funny, and D's book describes him as "magnetic." "Perhaps to a certain type of woman. Daphne was always easily charmed. I was relieved when they split up, and we never had to go there again. Corley Court was a ghastly place." Having soured the atmosphere thoroughly, she went out again. GFS however seems not to take much notice of her—he makes the requisite signals and potters along in serene vagueness about the recent past, though events of 60 or more years ago are clear to him ("clearer than ever," he said, as if to say I was in luck). Still, he jumps around and is hard to follow. (He now spoke incoherently about WWI, when he was in military intelligence—nothing to do with C.)

I wanted to bring him back to what he'd been saying before we were interrupted. It took me a while to realize he'd lost what little sense he'd had of who I was—I reminded him tactfully. I said I'd recently met Dudley for the first time. "Oh, Dudley Valance, you mean?" GFS then launched into a thing about Dud, how he'd been "stunningly attractive, but in a very dangerous way, very sexy." Much more than C—he had marvellous legs and teeth. Dud was always naughty, satirical. C was his parents' favourite, and Dud resented this, he was always making trouble. Later he became a frightful shit. I said in one of C's letters he called Dud a womanizer. GFS said this was just a word they all used then for a heterosexual man, it didn't mean anything. "Lytton and people always said it—they were all terrified of women." But C wasn't, I said. "He was and he wasn't, he didn't understand women any more than he did servants." I said he (GFS) hadn't made it clear about "womanizer" in the Letters. Didn't it create a misleading impression? He said Dud had read the book and didn't object. He probably quite liked people to think he had been a Lothario. The thing about Dud in fact was that he wasn't very keen on "all that": he liked to play with women. After Wilf was born it more or less stopped—it was very hard for D. It was all part of his mental trouble after the War.

I asked had he been surprised when D suddenly married Dud? GFS: "It happened all the time. Women often married the brother of someone they were engaged to who was killed in the War. It was a form of remembrance in a way, it was a form of loyalty, and there was some kind of auto-suggestion to it. The young woman didn't have to go searching for another man when there was a similar one already to hand." Were C and Dud particularly similar? "They lived in the same house, and D had a thing about Corley from the day she met C. C was D's first love, but she was in awe of him. She was closer in age to Dud, and got on well with him from the start." I said how C had written to both D and Ingham from France saying "will you be my widow?" but was he actually engaged to D? He said, "I don't think so, though of course there was the child." What child was that? Here GFS looked genuinely confused for a minute, then he said, "Well, the girl, wasn't it . . ." He sipped at his coffee, still looking doubtful. "You see I'm not sure she knows about it." I said did he mean Corinna? He said yes. I said, well you know she died three years ago. It was an awful moment, his old face looked really helpless with worry, and then anger coming through, as if I was lying to him. I said she'd had lung cancer, and this did make some sort of sense to him. "Poor old Leslie," he said, but I didn't feel I could say anything about Leslie's suicide. He muttered about how awful it was, but I saw him coming to accept it, with a rather sulky look. He said, "Well, it doesn't matter then." I still didn't know what he meant. I said, "What about Corinna?" Now I must get this right: he said that on C's last leave, two weeks before he was killed, he had spent the night with D in London, and got her pregnant. (In her book D says they had supper in a restaurant and then she went home.) So did Dud think he was Corinna's father? GFS didn't know.

Of course I was incredibly excited by this, but at the same time I was worrying about the dates. Corinna was born in 1917, but when? I was furious that she was dead: the discovery of a living child would have been the making of the book! It gave me goose-bumps to think that that woman I'd seen several times a week until I left the bank might have been C's daughter. Even her diffi-cult and snobbish aspects, and her clear sense of having come down in the world, took on a more romantic and forgivable char-acter. All that time, and I hadn't known. And now she's gone. Bad pangs of missed-chance syndrome, so that I'm telling myself, and even half-hoping, that it isn't true. I said to GFS that Corinna and Wilf both look(ed) exactly like Dud. It seemed rude, and proba-bly fairly pointless, to challenge him. I said, had D herself told him this? He said, "Well, you know . . ."

I decided I needed to go to the loo. MS was sitting in the hall by the telephone, as if ready to call for my taxi. Wondered if I could ask her what she knew, but some desire to protect GFS himself prevented me. Wondered about their marriage. I suppose she is anxious about him misbehaving in some way, she is grim but her worries come out; she said he is on heart drugs that react badly with his dementia, they can be very disinhibiting; alcohol is completely banned. I didn't like to say that he seemed fairly disin-hibited without alcohol. (What I don't know, of course, is if he shares all these secrets—or speculations?—with her.)

When I got back I had to help him back again into what we were doing. I thought I'd ask him about Revel Ralph. (Not strictly relevant for the book, but I wanted to know.) "Oh, I loved RR, he was a charmer, very attractive, very sexy, though not in a conven-tional way. You know he married my sister. She ran away with him—it was a great scandal at the time, because Dud was always in the papers. He despised publicity, but he couldn't do without it. Actually he didn't seem to mind very much—he married a model, you know, a leggy blonde. She was a frightful bitch." I asked if D and RR were happy together. He said RR was much nicer than Dud, and younger of course—they didn't have much money, but they became quite a famous couple too—they lived in Chelsea. "I used to say they lived on the mere luxuries of life. [This is the phrase D uses in her own book.] You know, Picassos on the wall, and the children with holes in their clothes. Wilf adored Revel, but Corinna disapproved of him. RR was a well-known stage designer. He was queer, and rather a weak character. D always fell for difficult men who couldn't love her properly—they couldn't give her what she wanted. RR became a drug addict, and they both drank like fishes." I asked if D had taken drugs. "I expect so. I wouldn't be a bit surprised if she had tried it." Had he seen much of her in the 1930s? "We were never at all close. Well, she's still alive, you know." Me: "But you don't see her?" I think he was genuinely unsure about this: "I don't think we see much of each other now."

Was RR unfaithful to D? (The questions were very basic, but I felt the "disinhibition" combined with the forgetfulness made it perfectly all right.) "I'm sure he was. RR was very highly sexed, he would fuck anyone." (I laughed at this, but he seemed not to know why. Sensed he felt everyone else had had a lot more sex than he had.) Me: "What about the son she had with RR, Jenny Ralph's father, had he known him?" "Well, there was a son, but of course RR wasn't the father." Again, I thought I mustn't startle him by showing my surprise. Again he gave me the confidential look: "Well, I don't think it's any secret that the child's father was a painter called Mark Gibbons. They had an affair." I imagined Mark Gibbons would fuck anyone too, but didn't like to ask. Remembered seeing him at D's 70th, dancing with her, so perhaps something in it. (Note: is MG still alive? Could he have known C? Also does Jenny Ralph know who her grandfather is?) "I'm pretty sure that's right," he said, "but you'd better keep it under your hat." I didn't promise this.

I asked if he had any photos of C. "I'm sure I have!" He went over to a low shelf on the far side of the room, where dozens of what looked like old albums and scrapbooks were stacked up, and started hoicking them out on to a table there. Looking at him stooping, arse in the air, his tongue between his teeth as he grunted and squinted, I thought of the pictures in Jonah's book of GFS at 19, that prim but secretive look that I'd thought was a bit like me. I said there were some good photos in the Letters. "Oh, were there?" he said. But what I wanted was photos of GFS and C together. "That's just what I'm looking for," he said. He pulled up a large album in floppy covers, and as he lifted it on to the table a number of small photos slid out and fell to the floor here and there. Obviously the old mounts had perished. I picked up one or two of them, and noted where others had fallen (inc the fantastic one of C reading aloud to Blanchard and Ragley, which was in the Letters).

"Now, let me see . . ."—there was a definite sense that neither of us knew what we were going to find. He supported himself lightly on my arm, stooping across in front of me to peer at particular pictures, so that his bald head and beard blocked my view, though he nattered on as if I could see what he was looking at. The albums go right back to late-Victorian sepia portraits of his parents' families (Freda Sawle was half-Welsh, apparently, her uncle a well-known singer). GFS was easily distracted, squinting to read the inscriptions in white ink, puzzling things out and correcting himself, breathing in hot gasps over the page. I said I believed Hubert had had a camera. "Quite so. I remember Harry Hewitt gave it to him." Here was old HH again—I wondered what GFS's line on him would be. "HH was a v rich man, who lived in Harrow Weald. He was in import/export, glass and china and so on, with Germany. Some people thought he was a spy." Me: "But he wasn't?" GFS squeezed my arm and giggled: "I don't think so. He was queer, you know, he was in love with my brother Hubert, who was killed in the War." But Hubert didn't reciprocate? "Hubert wasn't at all that way himself. He was very shy. HH kept giving him expensive presents, which became emb for him." I said hadn't C known HH? "They met when C was staying at 2A one time, and became friends of a sort." Was HH in love with C too? "Probably not, he was very loyal—he wanted someone to protect and help. C had too much money for HH to fancy him." Would C have flirted with him? "More than likely" (laughed).

"Now, here we are, Simon!" A number of pictures of "poor old C"—the best of them already in the Letters, the one of C in shorts with a rugger ball, looking furious: "You can see what marvellous legs he had!" Me: "I'd like to reproduce that one." GFS: "Where would you do it?" Me: "In the book I'm writing about C." GFS: "Oh, yes, I think you should. What a good idea. You know there's never been a book about him. I'm glad you're going to do that, it will be quite an eye-opener." There was a little group at 2A, on the lawn with the house behind, so that I could recognize it, C and D and GFS and a large old woman in black. "That was a German woman who lived near us—my mother took pity on her. She was at the Wagner festival in Germany when the War broke out, and she couldn't get back to England. Her house was smashed up by the local people. When she came back after the war my mother sort of took her under her wing. We all rather dreaded her, though probably she was perfectly all right. Now, here's C and me—that's an interesting picture, though my wife doesn't think it's very good of me." I leant forward to look at it, GFS resting his hand on my shoulder. "That's at Corley Court—you could get out on to the roof." After a moment I recognized the place exactly, from the two or three times Peter took me up there. I said, "You could climb up through the laundry-room." GFS: "Yes, that was it, you see." It showed C and GFS, leaning against a chimney, C with no shirt on, GFS with his shirt half undone, looking bashful but excited. A tiny photo, of course, but clear—C's strong wiry body, bit of black hair on his chest, and running down his stomach, one arm raised against the chimney with biceps standing up sharp. He is smiling in a sneering sort of way, and looks much older than GFS, who always seems v self-conscious in the presence of a camera. He was quite handsome at 20—odd glimpse of his white hairless chest: he looks like a schoolboy beside C. Me: "Who took it, I wonder?" GFS: "I wonder too. Possibly my sister"—which might help explain GFS's look of confusion, if she'd just caught them at it. It gave me my first real idea of C's body, and because the camera was like an intruder I suddenly felt what it must have been like to come into his presence—my subject! Very odd, and even a bit of a turn-on—as GFS seemed to feel, too: "I look positively debauched there, don't I?" he said. I said, "And were you?" and felt his hand, rubbing my back encouragingly, move down not quite absent-mindedly to just above my waist. He said, "I'm afraid I probably was, you know."

The atmosphere was now rather tense, and I glanced at him to see how conscious he was of it himself. "In what way, would you say?" (shifting away a bit, but not wanting to startle him). He kept looking at the picture, breathing slowly but heavily, as if undecided: "Well, you know, in the normal ways," which I suppose was quite a good answer. I said something like, "Well, I don't blame you!" "Awful, isn't it? I was quite a dish back then! And look at me now"—turning his face to mine with a jut of his bearded chin while his hand moved down again in a determined little rubbing motion on to my bum.

So there we were, me and the famous (co-)author of *An Everyday History of England,* looking me in the eye with who knows what memories and conjectures, his hand appreciatively cupping my backside. I laughed awkwardly, but held his gaze for a moment, with a sort of curiosity and a sure sense now that C had touched him like this, nearly 70 years ago, and that probably I'd brought this on myself by freeing these memories in him. Also, that it didn't matter in the least, this book-lined room was a place I was shortly going to leave, and leave him in, even the house itself would revert to the house I'd imagined for them before, a real Tudor house full of historical artefacts. I pictured the painstaking doodle I did round his name and Madeleine's name on the title-page of their book when I was twelve or so; and now for a moment I thought he was going to kiss me, and wondered how I would take it—I almost wanted him to, in a way—but he looked down, and as he did so I thought suddenly, well, this is a history I'm going to write. I went on politely, "And what about all C's letters to you? You said they were lost?" He said, "Yes, you see, I couldn't say exactly what happened. My mother destroyed them, she burned almost all of them. By the way"—his hand still clutching my left buttock, but now more as if he needed it for support than for any fun he was getting out of it—"better not mention this to my wife." It wasn't at all clear what the "this" referred to. "All right," I said, and he let go. GFS: "Oh, they were a great loss, a loss to literature. Though fairly hair-raising, some of them!"

As soon as we'd sat down again MS came in and said she was going to ring for a minicab. We went out into the hall. MS insisted on ringing herself: reading glasses, the number looked up in an old address book, an impatient tone when she got through. She frowned into the mirror as she spoke, admiring her own no-nonsense handling of the person she kept mishearing. "Twenty minutes!" she said; so there was a strange gap to fill. She said, "I hope you'll use your judgement about what my husband said to you?" I thought what a scary teacher she must have been; said I hoped so too. "Really I shouldn't have let him see you, he's very confused." I said he probably knew more about C than anyone alive. MS: "And I'm afraid I have to ask you, did he give you anything to take away—any documents or anything?" I said I'd taken nothing apart from notes, but he had promised to lend me photos for the book. She looked at me very squarely, which of course I can deal with; then she considered my briefcase, but at this point the study door opened and GFS came wandering out. "Oh, hello!" he said—looked very interested to see me. "Paul's just going, dear," said MS (a first slip into first-name terms). "Yes, yes . . ."—he has quite a cunning smile for covering up about things which are obviously just at the edge of (very recent) memory, a tone of forbearance towards her, almost. MS: "Did you enjoy your chat, George?" GFS: "Oh, very much, dear, yes," with a look at me that could have been a stealthy attempt to work out who I was or a much more mischievous mental replay of feeling me up. MS: "And what did you talk about? I don't suppose you remember." GFS: "Oh, you'd be surprised." Then he proposed the potter round the garden, which MS allowed, though I was a bit more anxious, after the incident indoors. But clearly my polite pretence that nothing had happened was soon rendered meaningless by his forgetting that anything had. "Have a look at the tadpoles, George," she said. Which we duly did, MS watching from the window the whole time. "Wriggly little buggers," GFS called them.

8

DIDCOT AND THEN SWINDON came by, with remote tugs of allegiance that distracted him, as the half-familiar outskirts slipped away, from the bigger tug of his mission to Worcester Shrub Hill. He treasured the length of the journey, and had a childish feeling, in the bright placeless run among farms and the gentle tilts of the earth one way or the other, that the important interview with Daphne Jacobs was all the time being magically deferred; though with each long deceleration and stop (Stroud, was it?, a little later Stonehouse) the end came inescapably closer. Of course he wanted to be there, in Olga, as Daphne's house was surprisingly called, and he also wanted to be cradled all day in this pleasant underpopulated train. He couldn't even bring himself to prepare; he had written out a series, or flight, of questions, up which he hoped to lead her towards a steady light at the top, but his briefcase, heavy with bookmarked evidence, stayed untouched on the seat beside him.

Some time after Stonehouse, the train made a long threading descent of the western edge of the Cotswolds into what seemed a vast plain beyond, half-hidden in murky sunlight. Paul had never been so far in this direction. The sensation of entering a whole new region of his own island was dreamlike but unsettling. A few minutes later they were sliding quite fast into Gloucester station, the knots of people on the platform, hikers, soldiers, closing in and moving along with their eyes fixed anxiously or threateningly on the rapidly braking train. Well, there was still Cheltenham to come before Worcester.

In a minute, however, he had to move his things for a woman and two children to sit down, she nagging at them distractedly, her own face taut with worry, and when the train began to move again he found the romance of the journey from London, which they knew nothing about, had been left behind for ever, and a period of compromise and cohabitation had begun. Paul kept his briefcase on the table, leaving little room for the boy to spread his colouring book. His dislike of children, with their protean ability to embarrass him, seemed to focus in his scowl over *The Short Gallery*, which he rather brandished in their faces. The fact that he was about to conduct an interview of enormous importance to his own book, and therefore to his future life, was squeezing and trapping him like the onset of some illness undetectable to anyone else. If what George had said was right, then Paul's conversations with Daphne, today and again tomorrow, were bound to be a peculiar game, in which he would have to pretend not to know the thing he was most hoping to get her to own up to.

He looked through the first chapter again, which was her "portrait" of Cecil:

On this fine June night, which was to be the last time I saw him, Cecil took me to Jenner's for a Spartan supper of the kind which seems to a love-struck girl to be a perfect love-feast. Pea soup, I remember, and a leg of chicken, and a strawberry blancmange. Neither of us, I think, cared a hoot what we ate. It was the chance to be together, under the magic cloak of our own strong feelings, out of the noise of war, that counted above all. When we had done we walked the streets for an hour, down to the Embankment, watching the light pass on the broad stretches of the river. The next day, Cecil was to re-embark for France, and the mighty thrust that we knew was coming. He didn't ask me then—it was to be in his last letter, a few days later—if I would marry him, but the evening air seemed charged with the largest questions. Our talk, meanwhile, was of simple and happy things. He saw me into a cab which would take me to my train at Marylebone, and my last sight of him was against the great black columns of St. Martin-in-the-Fields, waving his cap, and then turning abruptly away into the future we both imagined with such excitement, and such dread.

Perhaps it was just a reflection of his own habits, but Paul didn't believe anyone remembered all the courses of a meal they'd eaten four years ago, much less sixty-four; whereas (again perhaps reflecting his own fairly limited experience) they always remembered having sex. The worrying air of cliché and unreality about the whole of this scene was only heightened by the leg of chicken and the strawberry blancmange, which in some way Paul didn't like to think about seemed to stand in for the blandly concealed truth of a night spent at the Valances' Marylebone flat—even the naming of the station was a cover. And what, come to that, of Cecil preparing for a "mighty thrust"?

Chewing his lip, Paul examined Daphne's photo on the back flap of the jacket. She appeared three-quarter length, in a plain dark suit and blouse and a single string of pearls, looking out with a half-smile and a certain generalized charm, caused perhaps by her not having her glasses on. Immediately behind her was an archway, through which a grand hall and staircase could dimly be made out. When you looked very closely at her face you saw it was a subtly worked blur, silvery smooth from touching up around the eyes and under the chin; the photographer had taken fifteen or twenty years off her. The whole thing gave the impression of a good-looking, even marriageable woman of means in a setting whose splendour needed only to be hinted at. It was hard to relate her to the bedraggled old figure he'd rescued in the street. None the less, the suggestion that the other persona existed was subtly unnerving.

At Worcester he was suddenly cheerful to be on the move; he queued for a taxi, the first one he had taken since their joint journey the previous November: Cathedral Cars. He mustered a breezy tone with the driver as they left the city and the meter started flickering in cheerful green increments. He thought he would enjoy the small country roads more on the way back—as yet he was looking straight through the barns and hedges to the imagined scene he had set up at Olga. They came into Staunton St. Giles, past the lodge-gates of a big house and then along a wide unattractive street of semi-detached council houses; a war memorial, with a church beyond, a village shop and Post Office, a pub, the Black Bear, where he almost felt like stopping first, but it was a minute or two from closing time. "Do you know where Olga is?" Paul asked the driver.

"Ooh, yes," he said, as if Olga were a well-known local character. A handsome stone house, the Old Vicarage, came by, a run of old cottages looking much more pleased with themselves than the rest of the village, a nice place for Daphne to spend her final years. The taxi slowed and turned down a side lane, and pulled up unexpectedly by the gate of a decrepit-looking bungalow. "Twelve pounds exactly," said the driver.

Paul waited till the taxi had turned the corner, then he walked a short way along the lane and took four or five photos of the bungalow, over the low garden wall, a documentary task that held off for a minute his heavy-hearted embarrassment at the state of the place. He came back, hiding the camera in his briefcase until later, when he'd worked out whether Daphne would mind being photographed herself. Sometimes, after the subjective indulgence of an interview, people found the crude fact of a photograph too jarring and intrusive.

The name OLGA was fashioned out of wrought iron, on the wrought-iron gate. Paul stepped in over the weedy gravel, and gazed round at the neglected garden, the grass tall and green in the roof-gutters, the dead climbing rose left swaying over the porch, an old Renault 12 with a rusty dent in the offside wing and green moss growing along the rubber sills of the windows. Two or three stripes of the lawn had been mown, perhaps a week ago, and the mower abandoned where it stood. The flower-beds were full of last year's dead leaves. It all made him more flinchingly apprehensive about what he was going to find once he got indoors. He pressed the bell, a sleepy ding-dong that then repeated, all by itself, as if showing some impatience the caller might have hoped to conceal, and saw his face scarily distorted in the rippled glass of the front door; he seemed to run forward into their lives in waves. It was Wilfrid Valance who answered. He was just as Paul had remembered, and also, after thirteen more years of bumbling along as he was, alarmingly different, a wide-faced child with furrowed cheeks, and one defiant central tuft of grey hair fronting the bald plateau above. "How *are* you?" said Paul.

"Mm, you found us all right," said Wilfrid, with a twitch of a smile but not meeting his eye. Paul thought he saw that his visit was quite an occasion.

"Well, just about . . . ," he said meaninglessly, and handed over his coat and scarf. The hall was tiny, with other glass-panelled doors opening off it—a look of sixties brightness that had already become obscurely depressing. "And how is your mother?" For a moment he felt a kind of awe, repressed till now, at being about to see her, the survivor, the friend of the long dead. And a twinge of something like envy at the thought of the friendship they might have had themselves if he hadn't been a biographer.

"Oh, she's . . ."—Wilfrid shook his head and grinned; Paul remembered his hesitations, like a suppressed stammer, in the middle of sentences, but this time the rest of the statement wasn't forthcoming.

The sitting-room was stifling from a two-bar electric fire—a great thing like a fire-basket, with glowing fake coals showing dimly in the sunlight. There was a strong smell of burnt dust. Paul came in with a cheerful "Hello, Mrs. Jacobs," determined not to show his shock at the state of the room. She was sitting almost with her back to him, in a wing-chair covered in shabby pink chintz. All around her was an astounding chaos of junk, so extreme that he knew he must simply ignore it. There was a worrying sense of the temporary grown permanent, piled-up objects adapting into furniture, covered by tablecloths and tipsily topped with lamps and vases and figurines.

"It's all right," she said, half-turning her head, but not looking at him, "Wilfrid's put me right about you."

"Oh, yes . . . ?"—he laughed cautiously: so she was tackling the question of his review straight off.

"You're not the pianist."

"No, I'm not—you're quite right," said Paul.

"I have an excellent memory, Mummy, as you know," said Wilfrid, as if still contradicting her. "The pianist was a big . . . handsome fellow."

"Oh, what was he called? that charming young man . . . so talented . . ."

Paul groped round this for a moment, almost as if struggling to remember himself. "Peter Rowe, do you mean?"

"Peter—you see, I rather liked him."

"Oh, yes, well . . . ," murmured Paul, coming round in front of her; she didn't seem interested in shaking hands. She was wearing a thick grey skirt and a blouse under a shabby sleeveless cardigan. She gave him a calculating look, perhaps only the result of her not seeing him properly. After the first awkward moments, he absorbed this as a likely hazard of the hours ahead.

"What became of him, I wonder?"

"Peter? Oh, he's doing all right, I think," said Paul blandly. He was standing in the small area between the fire and a low coffee-table heaped with books and newspapers, it was almost like a childish dare as the back of his calves got hotter and hotter.

"Of course he taught at Corley Court—he was extremely interested in that house, you know."

"Oh, he was," said Wilfrid, with a shake of the head.

"Extremely interested. He wanted to put back all the jelly-mould ceilings and what-have-you that Dudley did away with."

"During your time, of course," said Paul encouragingly, as if the interview had already started. He moved round towards the armchair facing hers, and got out the tape-recorder from his briefcase in a slightly furtive way.

"You see, he's the one I might have expected to be writing about Cecil," she said. "He was extremely interested in him, as well."

"What wasn't he interested in!" said Paul.

Daphne said, "I'm having a certain amount of trouble with my eyes," reaching on the little table beside her with its lamp and books. Could she still read? Paul wondered. He half-expected to see his own letters there.

"Yes, so I gathered from *Robin*," he said, with a fond tone towards this mutual friend.

"You didn't block the drive, did you?" said Daphne.

"Oh . . . no—I got a taxi at Worcester station."

"Oh, you got a Cathedral. Aren't they expensive?" said Daphne, with a hint of satisfaction. "Can you find somewhere to sit? One day quite soon Wilfrid's going to sort this room out, but until that day I fear we live in chaos and disorder. It's funny to think I once lived in a house with thirty-five servants."

"Goodness . . . !" said Paul, lifting a leather *Radio Times* folder and a heap of thick woollen socks, perhaps waiting to be darned, from the armchair. In her book he was sure she'd said twenty-five servants. He rigged up the microphone on top of the books on the coffee-table between them. "Why is this house called Olga, I wonder?" he said, just to test the levels.

"Ah! You see, Lady Caroline had it built for her old housekeeper," said Wilfrid in a pious tone, "whose name was Olga. She retired here . . . out of sight but not quite . . . out of reach."

"And now Lady Caroline lets it to you," said Paul, watching the bobbing red finger which dropped, as if by gravity, when no one spoke.

"Well, we hardly pay a thing . . ."

Daphne chuckled narrowly. "What have you got there?" she said.

"I hope you don't mind if I tape our conversation . . ." Paul clicked the button and rewound.

"Perhaps as well to get it right," said Daphne uncertainly. It was the tape-recorder's odd insinuations of flattery and mistrust. Some people glanced at it as an awkward third person in the room, others were calmed by the just-detectable turning of the spool, some, like old Joan Valance, a second cousin of Cecil's whom he'd tracked down in Sidmouth, were moved to gabbling relief at having so impartial and receptive an audience. Daphne fidgeted with her cushions. "I'll have to be careful what I say."

"Oh, I hope not," with his ear to the idiotic tone of the playback.

"Very careful."

"If you want to tell me anything off the record, you can: just say, and I'll stop the tape."

"No, I don't think I'll be doing that," said Daphne, with a quick smile. "Aren't we having any refreshments, Wilfrid?"

"Well, if you care to ask for them . . ."

They both said coffee. "Bring us a couple of coffees, Wilfrid, and then find something useful to do. You could make a start on clearing up those things in the garage."

"Oh, that's a very big job, Mummy," said Wilfrid, as if not so easily fooled.

When he had gone out of the room, she said, "It's only a very big job because he will keep putting it off. Oh, he's so . . . disorganized," and she shifted her cushion again, flinched and half-turned, the powder-and-smoke-smudged discs of her glasses blank for a second in the light. This irritable nervousness might be hard to deal with. Paul wanted to remind her of their old connections, but he was wary of mentioning Corinna. He said, just while they waited,

"I was wondering, do you see much of John, and Julian, and Jenny?" They sounded like characters in a children's book.

"We're a bit cut off here, to be perfectly frank," she said. He saw she wouldn't want to admit to feeling neglected.

"What are they doing now?"—with a glance at the red needle.

"Well . . ." She was slow to warm to the question. "Well, they're all extremely busy, and successful, as you might expect. Jennifer's a doctor—I mean, not an actual doctor, obviously. She's teaching at Edinburgh, I think it's Edinburgh. Wilfrid will put me right if it's not."

"Teaching French literature?"

"Yes . . . and John of course has his very successful wine business."

"He takes after his grandfather," said Paul, almost fondly.

"His grandfather doesn't have a wine business."

"No, I meant—I believe Sir Dudley is involved in the sherry world, isn't he."

"Oh, I see . . . And Julian—well Julian's the artistic one. He's very creative."

Paul could tell from her tone, which was also fond, but final, that he shouldn't ask what form this creativity took. He felt his own secret interest in Julian as a sixth-former might somehow burn through. Daphne said, "Why, have you met Dudley?"

"Yes, I have," said Paul simply, with no idea as yet what line to take about him. He told her a bit about the Oxford conference, in what felt to him a very fair-minded way, and finding he had already somehow both censored and excused Dudley's crushing put-down over the phone; as an anecdote it had a value that went some way to compensate for the further talk they had never had. "He was quite controversial. He said that war poems, being written at the time, were usually not much good, 'inept and amateurish' I think were his words; whereas the great war writing was all in prose, and appeared ten years later—or more in his case, of course."

"That sounds like Dudley."

"He wouldn't say anything much about Cecil."

She pondered for a minute, and he thought she might say something about him herself. "Of course they've made him an honorary fellow, haven't they," she said.

"I didn't know that."

"Yes, they have. We're talking about your father," Daphne said, as Wilfrid came back in.

"Oh . . . !" said Wilfrid, with a surprising cold grimace.

"Not Wilfie's favourite person," said Daphne.

When Wilfrid had gone out again, there was swiftly a new atmosphere, of involuntary intimacy, as if Paul were a doctor and about to ask her to undo her blouse. He checked the tape again. Daphne had a look of conditional resignation. He cleared his throat and looked at his notes, his plan, designed to make the whole thing more like a conversation, and for both of them more convincing. Still, it sounded more stilted than he'd meant: "I was wondering about the way you wrote your memoirs, er, *The Short Gallery*, as a set of portraits of other people, rather than one of yourself." He was afraid she couldn't see his respectful smile.

"Oh, yes." Her head went back an inch. No doubt the shadowy question of his review of that book lurked somewhere beyond the actual question—beyond all of them. "Well . . ."

"I mean"—Paul laughed—"why did you do it like that? Of course, I remember when I first met you, you said you were writing your memoirs then, so I know it occupied you for a long time. That was thirteen years ago!"

"No, it did," said Daphne. "Much longer than that, even."

"And may I just say that I admired the book a great deal."

"Oh—that's kind of you," she said, pretty drily. "Well, I suppose the main reason was that I was lucky enough to know a lot of people more talented and interesting than myself."

"Of course, in a way I wish you'd written more about yourself."

"Well, there's a certain amount that gets in, I hope." She squinted at the tape-recorder, aware it was capturing this flannel, and her reaction to it. "I was very much brought up in the understanding that the men all around me were the ones who were doing the important things. A lot of them wrote their own memoirs, or, you know, their lives are being written about now—there's this new life of Mark Gibbons that's going to come out."

"Oh, yes, I've heard about it," Paul said; Karen had got the proofs—unindexed, but a quick read-through had produced only passing references to Daphne; Daphne, it seemed, had them too.

"The publisher sent it. Wilfrid's been reading it to me, because I can't read any more. But of course she's got all sorts of things wrong."

"Were you consulted for that book?"

"Oh yes, the woman wrote to me. But really, I put it all in my own book—everything I thought worth saying about Mark, who was a dear friend, of course."

"Well, I know," said Paul, and looked at her rather cannily; but it was instantly clear from her hard half-smile that no confessions about bearing his child were remotely on the cards. "I remember meeting him at your seventieth."

"Ah, do you . . ."—she accepted this. "Yes, he must have been there. Isn't it awful, I've forgotten," she said, and smiled more sweetly, as if she'd just seen a good way out of his future questions.

"Well, of course I'm hoping not to get it wrong," said Paul, "with your help!" He sipped a little of the weak coffee. It struck him that if Daphne had helped her a bit more, the biographer of Mark Gibbons might not have made the mistakes that she was now deploring. It was a recurrent little knot of self-defeating resistance that perhaps all biographers of recent subjects had to confront and undo. People wouldn't tell you things, and then they blamed you for not knowing them—unless they were George Sawle, of course, where the flow of secrets had been so disinhibited as to be almost unusable. Still, Daphne was an old lady, of whom he was reasonably fond, and he said gently, "I suppose you wanted to put the record straight a bit, though."

"Well, a bit—about 'Two Acres' and things, you see. In the poem I'm merely referred to as 'you.' And of course in Sebby Stokes's thing I'm 'Miss S.'!"

Paul laughed sympathetically, half-embarrassed by his own new suspicion that the "you" of the poem was really George. "There's more about you in . . . Sir Dudley's book."

"Yes . . . but then he's always so down on everybody."

"I was surprised by how little he says about Cecil."

"I know . . ."—she sounded amiable but bored at once by talk of *Black Flowers.*

"I suppose Cecil must have been the first real writer you'd met."

"Oh, yes, well as I said in the book, he was the most famous person I had met before I was married, though he wasn't actually terribly famous at the time. I mean, he'd had poems here and there, but he hadn't yet published a book or anything."

"*Night Wake* wasn't till 1916, was it, only a few months before he was killed?"

"That's probably right," said Daphne. "And then after that of course he emerged as quite an important figure."

"But you'd read some of his poems before you met him?"

"I think one or two."

"So to you he would have been a glamorous figure before you'd even set eyes on him."

"We were all quite curious to meet him."

"What do you remember about his first visit to 'Two Acres'? Why don't you just tell me about that."

She tucked in her chin. "*Well,* he *arrived,*" she said, as if resolved to tackle the question squarely.

"He arrived at 5:27," said Paul.

"*Did* he . . . ? Yes."

"I think . . . your brother . . . must have met him."

"Well, of course he had."

"No . . . ! I mean, he was at the station."

"Oh, quite possibly."

"Do you remember when you first saw Cecil yourself?"

"Well, it would have been then."

"And did you feel an immediate attraction to him?"

"Well, he was very striking, you know. I was only sixteen . . . very innocent . . . well, we all were in those days—I'd certainly never had a boyfriend, or anything like that—I was a great reader, I read romantic novels, but I had no knowledge of romance myself—and a lot of poetry, of course, Keats, and Tennyson we all loved . . ."—Paul saw her easing into a routine, something sweet and artificial in her voice. He let her run on, his own face abstracted and impatient as he saw the shape of his next question, a rather tougher one. When she seemed to have finished, and turned to pick up her coffee, he said,

"Can I ask you, what did you think about your brother's friendship with Cecil?"

"Oh . . . ," she huffed over her mug. "Well, it was very unusual."

"In what way?" said Paul, with a small shake of the head.

"Mm? He'd never had a friend before, poor George. I think we were all rather tickled when he suddenly produced one."

Paul grinned at this with the reluctant sense of kinship that sometimes ghosted his interviews. "And could you see why they were such friends? Did they seem very close?"

Again Daphne sighed out, as if to say she might as well be candid. "I think it was just a clear case of old-fashioned"—she paused and sipped—"well, hero-worship, really, wasn't it? George was very young for his age, emotionally. I suppose Cambridge brought him out a bit." She winced. "To be honest, George has always been a bit of a cold fish."

Paul played for a pondering moment or two with even more candid phrases, but looking at her he was doubtful, and frightened of disgusting her. He said, "I just wondered if you felt he was jealous of your affair with Cecil?"

"George? No, no"; and as if not satisfied with her earlier put-down, or feeling that by now it didn't matter anyway, "George never exactly had normal human emotions, you see. I don't know why. And I dare say it hasn't done him any harm—life's probably much simpler without them, though a bit dull, wouldn't you think!" Paul pictured George with the half-naked Cecil on the roof at Corley, and smiled distantly, at a loss as to how much of this she believed or expected him to believe; and to how much she might quite willingly have forgotten. "If you'd come a few years ago, I'd have suggested you go and talk to him, but I'm afraid he's rather lost it now—up top, you know. I think poor Madeleine has quite a struggle with him."

"I'm sorry to hear that," said Paul.

"No, he'd have been a useful person for you to talk to. I don't mean to suggest he was ever a bore, by the way. He was an intellectual, he was always the brains of the family."

Paul let a moment pass, while he looked at his papers, his little mime of being an interviewer, which seemed more for his own benefit than for hers. "Do you mind if I ask you—you say in the book that it was, well, a love-affair—you and Cecil, I mean . . . !"

"Well, indeed."

"You wrote to each other, but did you see each other?"

"Didn't I say . . . ? No, we saw each other fairly often, I think."

"The War, I suppose, intervened."

"Well, the War, quite. We didn't see each other so often then."

"I've been trying to work out from the Letters when he was in England—he signed up almost at once, September 1914."

"Yes, well he loved the War."

"So he was out in France by December, and then only home quite rarely on leave, until he—until he was killed, eighteen months later."

"That must be right, yes," said Daphne, with a small cough of impatience.

Paul said, in a tactical tone, but with a quick apologetic smile, "Can I jump forward to the last time you saw him?"

"Oh, yes . . . ," she gasped, as if momentarily dizzy.

"What happened then?"

"Well, again . . ." She shook her head, as if to say that she'd have liked to help. "I think it was all very much as I said in my little book."

So Paul read out, rather skimmingly, the passage he'd read on the train earlier, which she listened to with an air of curiosity as well as mild defiance. Again he wasn't sure how to do it: how did you ask an eighty-three-year-old woman if someone had—he hardly liked to say it even to himself. And if Cecil had got her pregnant—well, of course she could get the whole thing off her chest at last, in a tearful rush of relief, but something told Paul it wasn't going to happen in the present atmosphere. Still, when he looked up, it seemed she was moved by her own words. "Well, there you are!" she said, and shook her head again. It was one of those disorienting moments, all too common in Paul's life, when he saw he'd missed something, and thinking back he still couldn't see what had triggered the very quick change of emotion in the other person. He wondered if she was about to cry. Socially awkward, but wonderful for the book if the trick had worked and he'd stirred some brand new memory; he glanced at the patient revolution of the tape. Then he saw he'd got it wrong again—or else she was brusquely shutting him out from her unexpected turn of feeling. She said, "To tell the truth I sometimes feel I'm shackled to old Cecil. It's partly his fault, for getting killed—if he'd lived we would just have been figures in each other's pasts, and I don't suppose anyone would have cared two hoots."

"Oh, I think they might have done . . . !"—was he teasing her or reassuring her? "I understand you were planning to get married?"

"Well . . . Even if we had I don't imagine it would have been a great success."

"There's the letter where he says, 'will you be my widow?' " Paul thought it wasn't tactful, even now, to mention the fact, exposed by the Letters, that Cecil had also asked Margaret Ingham to be his widow on the very same day. "But I suppose he was rather . . . fickle, perhaps?"

"Well, of course he was. But the thing you have to understand is that Cecil made you feel you were at the absolute centre of his universe." And at this Paul felt both pity and a hint of envy.

Quite soon it was time for the customary, necessary, and often useful visit to the loo—a welcome escape into privacy, a gape in the mirror, and a chance to pry unobserved into the subject's habits and attitude to hygiene and sense of humour. At Olga perhaps a touch of mad humour showed in the junk that had been piled and propped in the gloomy and mouldy-smelling little room. Behind the door there was a stack of pictures with cracked glass and a folding card-table, and under the basin the long box of a croquet set with JACOBS stencilled on the lid. Opposite the basin his shoulder brushed a large murky painting in a fancy gilt frame with various bits chipped off: it showed a pale young man with a black hat and a snooty expression, and was streaked across as though someone had tried to clean it with a muddy sponge. The lavatory, which could never have been a bright room, was made all the gloomier by Virginia creeper which covered the lower part of the frosted-glass window and had forced its way in through the opening top light, a long strand feeling its way across the wall, above a stack of large objects covered in a tablecloth. Paul hardly liked to use the loo itself, dark as peat below the water-line, and with what Peter Rowe used to call a lesbian seat, that had to be held up. Under the tablecloth it turned out there were wine boxes, sealed with brittle yellow Sellotape, which might be worth exploring on a later visit. Along the wall beside the loo, books and magazines were stacked several feet high. On top was the issue of the *Tatler* with Daphne's interview in it, and a six-year-old *Country Life* with a feature on Staunton Hall, "the home of Lady Caroline Messent"—he supposed they must be kept there for some small ritual of reassurance. The books were like a jumble sale in which you might find something—it was clearly either Daphne's or Wilfrid's habit to mark their place each time with a torn-off sheet of toilet-paper. The cohabitation of mother and son oppressed Paul here more than he could explain. He sat down for a minute, and looked sideways at the titles. And there, just above floor level, and tricky to prise out, was *Black Flowers,* in its dust-jacket, torn and stained, but the first edition, 1944, on cheap wartime paper, signed: "For Wilfrid, Dudley Valance." It was too stark and sad and valuable to leave here, and Paul placed it where he would be able to get it later. He washed his hands and looked at himself in the mirror to assess his progress and give himself a quick pep-talk, slightly thrown by the murky sneer of the young man in the frame behind him.

Wilfrid, sensing his brief absence, had come back in and was edging round the end of the sitting-room, apparently looking for something. "And I really must ask you," Paul said in a rush, "if you still have the book with the manuscript of 'Two Acres' in it. I'd love to see it."

"Well, you're out of luck, I'm afraid," said Daphne.

"You don't have it?"

She frowned almost crossly. "Where is it, Wilfrid?"

"I believe it's in London, Mother," said Wilfrid, peering into a large wicker basket on top of a pile of old curtains, "it's gone to be photographed."

"It's being photographed," she confirmed. "It's extraordinarily delicate, well, it's seventy years old, isn't it?—nearly seventy."

"No, that's a very good idea," Paul said. "Who's doing it for you?"

"I can't remember his name—he's doing the new edition of Cecil's poems."

"Oh, well you're in good hands," Paul said.

"What is his name?"

"I think he's called Dr. Nigel Dupont."

"Exactly. He told me he feels a very personal connection with Cecil because he was at school at Corley."

"Oh, really?"

"He got interested in him from seeing his tomb all the time in the chapel."

"How interesting," said Paul, as the heavy likelihood that Dupont had been a pupil of Peter's closed sickeningly about him. "Did Nigel . . . um . . . come to see you?"

"No, it was all very easy, we did it by mail."

"Recorded delivery," said Wilfrid.

"He doesn't give two pins about, you know, the biographical side," said Daphne, "he's very much a textual editor, would you call it."

"Well, indeed."

"All the different editions and what have you."

"Fascinating . . ." Paul edged back towards his chair. Outside, the afternoon was beginning to lower, late sunlight making the dirty windows opaque.

"Well, it is rather fascinating. He says they're full of mistakes. It was Sebby Stokes, you know, he messed around with them quite a bit, apparently, I suppose he thought he was improving them."

"Perhaps he was!"

Daphne turned and said, "Why don't you and Mr. Bryant get out round the village."

"We don't know that he wants to," Wilfrid said.

"Walk down to the farm, you like that."

It was a bold distraction on Daphne's part, cutting short the interview, but Paul had been hoping for a chance to talk to Wilfrid in private at some point. So out they went, Paul borrowing a large loose pair of old black wellingtons, which Wilfrid told him, once they'd got into the road, had "formerly belonged to Basil."

"Oh, really?" said Paul, disliking the thought of wearing a dead man's shoes; they dragged and clunked on the tarmac. "For some reason I hadn't imagined he was so big . . ." Later he thought it odd that Daphne had hung on to them, moved house with them. Wilfrid had put on a pair of mud-caked workman's boots, and a kind of car-coat over his fleece. His big monkish head, with its tufts of grey hair, was bare.

"This isn't one of the attractive, picturesque villages," Wilfrid said. They strode back down the lane, past the shop with its steamed-up window, past the council houses, and then into another lane that ran up the side of some fenced-off parkland, ploughed fields on the other side. Away from the bungalow Wilfrid became both franker and more anxious; he said twice, "She can look after herself for half an hour."

"She's lucky to have you," Paul said, sounding feebly polite.

"Oh, she drives me potty!" said Wilfrid, with a grin of guilty excitement. Now they mounted the verge to let a tractor and trailer go past, great clots of silage dropping off behind it into the lane. Wilfrid stared at the driver but didn't greet him. Paul wasn't sure what to say—he felt both mother and son were cheered up and somehow kept going by driving each other potty.

"Well, she's made a very good recovery," said Paul.

"Thanks to Nurse Valance," said Wilfrid, in an odd pert tone.

Paul couldn't think what Wilfrid would have been doing if he hadn't had his mother to look after. "But you have some help?"

"Nothing worth mentioning. And of course the whole thing makes it . . . very hard for me to have a girlfriend."

Paul managed to raise his eyebrows in sympathy. "No, I can imagine . . ."

"But there you are!" said Wilfrid. "I'm with her till the end now. Now that's Staunton Hall over there, she'd want me to . . . point that out. That's where Lady Caroline lives."

"Olga's former employer."

"Olga is what she calls her . . . Petit Trianon." Paul made out the bulk of a large square house among the trees a couple of fields away. The sun was now very low over the hedges behind them, and the small attic windows of the mansion glowed as if all the lights were on. "Do you want to see the farm?"

"I don't mind," said Paul.

"I wouldn't have minded being a farmer," said Wilfrid.

They walked on for a while and Paul said, "Well, of course!—your grandfather . . ."

"I always liked animals. There were two farms at Corley. One very much . . . grew up amongst all that"—with a return of his precise, clerical tone, perhaps to cover the strange disjunction between then and now. As Robin had reminded him, Wilfrid would soon be the fourth baronet.

"Do you remember your grandfather at all?"

"Oh, hardly. He died when I was . . . four or five. You know, I called him . . . Grandpa Olly-olly—because that was all he could say."

"He had a stroke, didn't he."

"He could only make that sort of olly-olly noise."

"Were you frightened of him?"

"I expect a bit," said Wilfrid. "I was a rather nervous child"—as if looking back on some quite alien state.

"Your father was fond of him."

"I don't think my father had much time for him."

"Ah . . . he writes about him very nicely."

"Yes, he does," said Wilfrid.

A steady increase in the mud in the lane, and round a right-angled bend was the entrance to the farmyard, a concrete platform for the milk-churns at the gate, and beyond it a glistening oily-brown quagmire of cow-shit stretching away to the open doors of a corrugated-iron barn. "Well, this must be it!" said Paul. He didn't see the point of fouling up the late Basil Jacobs's wellies, and Wilfrid's boots were hardly up to it. Wilfrid seemed to feel some irritable embarrassment, having brought him here, but then said,

"We'd probably better be getting back anyway."

"Do you ever see your father?" said Paul, as they turned round.

"Not often," said Wilfrid firmly, and looked out across the fields.

"He must have been very upset about . . . your sister."

"You'd think . . . wouldn't you?"

Paul sensed he'd pressed him enough, and changed the subject to his hotel, which he was worried about getting back to.

"The bad thing was," Wilfrid cut in, "that he didn't come to the funeral. He *said* he was going to come over, but that week of course Leslie . . . blew his brains out, and my sister's funeral was put back, as a result, and he didn't come after all. He just had a horrible wreath . . . delivered."

"That's awful," said Paul. He wanted to say hadn't Dudley had various mental problems, but he rather gathered that Wilfrid had had them too, so he merely looked at him respectfully for a moment.

"But then he never much cared for my sister," Wilfrid said, "so though bad, it wasn't perhaps . . . surprising."

"No, I see . . ."

"Though sometimes there's something . . . almost surprising in a person being so completely true to type."

"You mean on this one occasion you really thought he'd do the right thing."

"Stupidly, we did," said Wilfrid, and there seemed little more to say after that; though a good deal for Paul to think about.

Now the sun had sunk among the black cloud-bars to the west, and the back of the village huddled clear but bleak in the neutral light of the early evening. Chicken-runs, garden sheds, heaps of garden refuse thrown over the hedge all year long; a car on bricks, a greenhouse painted white, the jostle of tall TV aerials against the cold sky. Paul pictured his street in Tooting and the lit red buses with a shiver of longing. It was what Peter used to call his *nostalgie du pavé,* the panicky longing for London. "Oh, my dear," he would say, in Wantage or Foxleigh, "I'm not dying here."

When they got back to the bungalow, Paul said, "Thanks so much, I should probably push off now," but to his surprise Daphne said, "Have a drink first." She made her way, holding on to table and chair, to the corner of the room where on a crowded surface there was a cluster of bottles with an ice-bucket, phials of Tabasco and bitters, all the paraphernalia of the cocktail hour. Wilfrid was sent out to the garage to get ice from the freezer. "He knows we need it, and then he makes such a face!" said Daphne. "G-and-t?" Paul said yes, and smiled at the thought of the time he'd first met her, over the same drink, when he'd sat in the garden trying not to look up her skirt. Daphne opened a tonic bottle with a practised snap, the tonic fizzing out round the top and dripping down her wrist. "Have you got it?" she said, as Wilfrid returned with the silver plastic bucket. "Oh, look, it's all an enormous lump, you'll have to break it up, I can't possibly use this. Really, Wilfrid!"—making a half-hearted comedy out of her annoyance for the sake of their guest.

When they were settled, Daphne came back with a genial but purposeful look to the new book on Mark Gibbons that she'd been reading, which she said again wasn't good at all, and anyway half the point of

Mark was lost if the pictures were in black-and-white. (Paul guessed she meant Wilfrid had been reading it to her, but as usual his agency was somehow elided.) She said it was funny how some people emerged from the great backward and abyss while others were wholly forgotten. Mark had had a sort of handy-man, called Dick Mint, who was a bit of a character, fixed the car, looked after the garden, and was often to be found sitting in Mark's kitchen at Wantage jawing endlessly with his employer. A pretty fair bore, actually, but he had his remarks: he thought the Post-Impressionists were something to do with the GPO. Perhaps, what? twenty people in the whole world knew him, hardly a household name. Lived in a caravan. And now, thanks to this book, thousands of people, probably, were going to know about him—he'd become a character on a world stage. People in America would know about him. Whereas the woman who came in, whose name Daphne thought was Jean, who did all the washing and cleaning, wasn't mentioned at all—in fact nobody now thought of her from one year to the next.

"I must read the Mark Gibbons book," Paul said, wishing he'd had the tape-recorder on through this spiel.

"Really I shouldn't bother," said Daphne.

Paul laughed. "This must happen to you quite a lot."

"Mm?"

"You must know a lot of people whose lives have been written."

"Yes, or they turn up in someone else's, you know."

"Like you, yourself, indeed, Mummy!" said Wilfrid.

"The thing is, they all get it wrong." She'd now got back into that irritable mood that she clearly enjoyed.

"The best ones don't, perhaps," said Paul.

"They take against people," said Daphne, "or someone they talk to bears a grudge, and tells them things that aren't right. And they put it all in as if it was gospel!" This was obviously meant as a warning, but was said as if it had completely slipped her mind that he was writing a biography himself. She glowed, chin tucked in, eyes turned on him but, as he had to remind himself, barely seeing him; though a tremor of contact seemed to pass between them through the quivering heat of the electric fire.

"Well . . . !" Paul paused respectfully. The first rush of the gin seemed to present him with a view of all the things it was in his grasp to ask her, the numerous doubts and rumours and aspersions he had heard, about her and her family. Did she have any idea what had gone on between

George and Cecil, for instance? Did Wilfrid himself know the theory that his sister was Cecil's child? He had to tread carefully, but he saw more clearly than ever that the writer of a life didn't only write about the past, and that the secrets he dealt in might have all kinds of consequences in other lives, in years to come. With Wilfrid present, knocking back an orange squash, he could hardly say or ask anything intimate; though Daphne too was more open and cheerful after a drink—it might have been worth trying.

Still, something warned Paul not to accept a second gin, and at seven o'clock he asked if he could call a taxi. Daphne smiled firmly at this, and Wilfrid said he'd be happy to drive him into Worcester in the Renault.

"I really don't want to make you turn out at night," Paul said, his courteous demurral covering a natural nervousness about the car as well as the driver.

"Oh, I like to take her out for a spin," said Wilfrid, so that for a moment Paul thought Daphne was coming too. "It's not good for her just to . . . stand in the drive from one week to the next."

Daphne stood up, and hanging on to the large oak chest got across the room with a new air of warmth and enthusiasm. "Where do you live?" she said, almost as if thinking of a return visit.

"I live in Tooting Graveney."

"Oh, yes . . . Is that near Oxford?"

"Not really, no . . . It's near Streatham."

"Streatham, oh!"—even this seemed rather a lark.

They now shook hands. "Well, thank you so much." It was perhaps a moment to call her Daphne, but he held off till their second session. "I'll see you tomorrow, same time."

Paul wondered afterwards if it was a true misunderstanding or a bit of Dudleyesque fooling. She halted by the door into the hall, head cocked in confusion. "Oh, are you coming back?" she said.

"Oh . . . well"—Paul gasped. "I think that was . . . what we agreed!" He'd got nothing out of her today, but was resignedly treating it as a warm-up for the real explorations the following afternoon.

"What are we doing tomorrow, Wilfrid?"

"I should be surprised if we were doing anything very much," said Wilfrid, in a way that made Paul wonder whether all his patient simplicities weren't perhaps a very cool kind of sarcasm.

In the Renault it was rather as if a child drove an adult, both of them pretending that it wasn't worrying or surprising. It emerged that the dip-switch was broken, so that they had either to crawl along on side-lights, the hedges looming dimly above them, or to be flashed at by on-coming motorists blinded by the headlights on full beam. Wilfrid coped with both things with his usual whimsical patience. Paul didn't want to distract him, but when they got on to the main road he said, "I hope I'm not tiring your mother."

"I think she's enjoying it," Wilfrid said; and with a glance in the mirror, as if to check she wasn't there, "She likes telling a story."

Paul very much wished she would tell him a story. He said, "I'm afraid it was all so long ago."

"There are things she won't talk about . . . I hope we can trust you on that," said Wilfrid, with an unexpected note of solidarity after his earlier grumbling about her.

"Well . . ."—Paul was torn between the discretion just requested of him and the wish to ask Wilfrid what he was talking about. "I obviously don't want to say anything that would upset her—or any of the family." Might Wilfrid himself tell him things? Paul had no idea what he was capable of, mentally. He clearly loved his mother and more or less hated his father, but he might not be the ally Paul needed for his further prying into the dealings of the Sawles and Valances. If Corinna was really Cecil's daughter, then Dudley's shocking coolness towards her might have some deeper cause.

"I don't think you're married, are you?" Wilfrid asked, peering forward over the wheel into the muddled glare on the edge of Worcester.

"No, I'm not . . ."

"No, Mother thought not."

"Ah, yes . . . well, hmm."

"Poor old Worcester," said Wilfrid a minute later, as the car swerved through a sort of urban motorway right next to the Cathedral; up above, too close to see properly, reared floodlit masonry, the great Gothic tower. "How could they have butchered the old place like this?" Paul heard this as a catch-phrase, saw mother and son on their trips into town coming out with it each time. "Right next to the Cathedral," said Wilfrid, craning out to encourage Paul to do the same, while the car wandered over into the fast lane—there was a massive blast on a horn, a lit truck as tall as the tower screeching behind them, then thundering past.

Turning left, and then passing staunchly through a No Entry sign, they travelled the length of a one-way street in the wrong direction, Wilfrid mildly offended by the rudeness of on-coming drivers, turned another corner, and there they were outside the front door of the Feathers. "Amazing," said Paul.

"I know this old town backwards," said Wilfrid.

"Well, I'll see you tomorrow," said Paul, opening the door.

"Shall I pick you up?" said Wilfrid, with just a hint of breathlessness, Paul thought, a glimpse of excitement at having this visitor in their lives. But Paul insisted he was perfectly happy to get a Cathedral. He stood and watched as Wilfrid drove off into the night.

9

DAPHNE FOLLOWED HER REGIME as usual that evening—there was the hot milk, and then the tiny glass of cherry brandy, to take the sickening sleepy taste away. Her sleeping pill itself was swallowed with the last cooled inch of the milk, and after that a pleasant certainty that the day was wound up suffused her, well before the physical surrender to temazepam. Tonight the cherry brandy seemed to celebrate the fact. She said, "What time is he coming back?" just to have it confirmed that it wasn't till after lunch. Wilfrid started on the film that followed the News, but her macular thing made the telly both boring and upsetting. So she left him to it, going out of the room with a passing pat at his arm or shoulder, and made her way to the other end (in so far as Olga had another end) of the house.

Book at Bedtime this week was the autobiography of a woman—she couldn't remember her name, or what exactly she'd been up to in Kenya last night when sleep had come with just enough warning for her to switch off the radio and the bedside light. On the dressing-table, an awful cheap white and gilt thing, stood the photographs she never really looked at, but she peered at them now, in her sidelong way, as she smeared on her face cream. Their interest seemed enhanced after the visit from the young man, and she was glad he hadn't seen them. The one of her with Corinna and Wilfrid by the fishpond at Corley was her favourite—so small but clear: she turned it to the light with a creamy thumb. Who had taken it, she wondered? . . . The photo, known by heart, was the proof of an occasion she couldn't remember at all. The Beaton photo of Revel in uniform was, pleasingly, almost famous: other portraits from the same session had appeared in books, one of them in her own book, but this exact photograph, with its momentary drop of the pose, the mischievous tongue-tip on the upper lip, was hers alone. A pictorial virtue, of the kind that Revel himself had taught her to understand, had been made of the hideous great-coat. His lean head and fresh-cropped poll were framed by the upturned collar—he looked like some immensely wicked schoolboy, though she knew if you looked closely you could see the fine lines round the eyes and the mouth that Beaton had touched out in the published images.

She woke in the dark out of dreams of her own mother, very nearly a nightmare; it was wartime and she was searching for her, going in and out of shops and cafés asking if anyone had seen her. Daphne never remembered her dreams, but even so she felt sure she had never dreamt about her mother before—she was a novelty, an intruder! It was bracing, disconcerting, amusing even, once she had felt for the switch at the neck of the lamp, and squinted at the time, and had a small drink of water. Freda had died in 1940, so the Blitz setting made almost too much sense. And no doubt talking to the young man, trying to cope with all his silly and rather unpleasant questions, had brought her back. In talking, she had only touched on her mother, whose actual presence in 1913 she could no longer see at all, but that must have been enough to set the old girl going, as if greedy for more attention. Daphne kept the light on for a while longer, with a barely conscious sense that in childhood she would have done the same, longing for her mother but too proud to call for her.

In the dark again she found she was at the tipping-point, relief at the closing-down of yesterday was ebbing irrecoverably, and already the dread of tomorrow (which of course was already today) was thickening like regret around her heart. Why on earth had she said he could come back? Why had she let him come at all, after that idiotic condescending piece about her book in the *Listener,* or perhaps the *New Statesman*? He was only pretending to be a friend—something no interviewer, probably, had ever been. Paul Bryant . . . he was like some little wire-haired ratter, with his long nose and his tweed jacket and his bloody-minded way of going at things. Daphne turned over in a spasm of confused annoyance, at him and at herself. She didn't know what was worse, the genial vague questions or the stern particular ones. He called him Cecil all the time, not as if he'd known him, exactly, but as if he could help him. "What was Cecil like?"—what a stupid question . . . "When you say in your book he made love to you, what happened exactly?" She'd said "Pass!" to that one, rather good, as if she were on *Mastermind.* She thought tomorrow she would just say "Pass!" to everything.

And Robin, too—there was a good deal of Robin this and that. She couldn't think what he meant by sending him, recommending him; though then a shadowy understanding, grim, frivolous, almost word-less—the old thing that she didn't even picture—turned over and after a minute lay down again at the side of her mind. As well as which, there was something else, which maybe was actually a blessing in its way, that for quite long stretches of the conversation young Paul Bryant had clearly not been listening to a word she said. He thought she couldn't see him at all, reading something while she talked; then he hurried her along, or he came in suddenly with some completely irrelevant other thing. Maybe he thought he knew all the answers already, but in that case why ask questions? Of course he had it all on his blasted tape-recorder, but that didn't exempt him from the normal courtesies. She thought in the morning she would ring up Robin at the office and give him a very hard time about it.

She turned over once more and settled with a spasm of self-righteousness; and was on the very edge of sleep again when the obvious idea that she could put Paul Bryant off altogether made her suddenly and beautifully alert. Wilfrid had taken him back to the Feathers, that fearful dump—she was glad he was staying there. He seemed to think it was quite the thing! Only two stars, he'd said, but very comfortable . . . She'd get her son to ring up for her first thing in the morning. She lay there, half-plotting, half-drowsing, imagining it, the afternoon without him, freedom tinged, but not irreparably spoilt, by guilt. She was pretty sure she had said he could come twice, and besides he had come from London specially. But why should she be put upon, at the age of eighty-three? She wasn't at all well, she was having a lot of trouble with her eyes . . . She really mustn't worry about it. He'd been through all Cecil's letters to her, which he claimed were manipulative and self-pitying—perfectly true, perhaps, but then what more did he want from her? He was asking for memories, too young himself to know that memories were only memories of memories. It was diamond-rare to remember something fresh. And she felt that if she did, Paul Bryant was hardly the person she would want to share it with.

Daphne was supposed to have a good memory, and this reputation sustained her uneasily in face of the thousands of things she couldn't remember. People had been amazed by what she'd dredged up for her book, but much of it, as she'd nearly admitted to Paul Bryant, was, not fiction, which one really mustn't do about actual people, but a sort of poetical reconstruction. The fact was that all the interesting and decisive things in her adult life had happened when she was more or less tight: she had little recall of anything that occurred after about 6:45, and the blur of the evenings, for the past sixty years and more, had leaked into the days as well. Her first problem, in doing her book, had been to recall what anyone said; in fact she had made up all the conversations, based (if one was strictly truthful) on odd words the person almost certainly had said, and within about five, or at the outside ten, years of the incident recorded. Was this just her failing? Now and then people gave her the most astonishing reports of what *she* had said, drolleries they would never forget, and rather gratifying to her—though perhaps these should be treated with comparable suspicion? Sometimes she knew for sure that they were mixing her up with someone else. She had probably taken too long with her memoirs. Basil had encouraged her, told her quite freely to write all about Revel, and Dudley before him, "significant figures!" he'd said, self-mockingly. But it had taken thirty years to bring it off, over which time she'd naturally forgotten a great deal that she'd known very well when she started out. If she'd kept a diary it would have been different, but she never had, and her experience as a memoirist, if typical, couldn't help but throw the most worrying light over half the memoirs that were written. Certain of her incidents were tied indubitably to Berkshire or Chelsea, but a host of others took place against a general-purpose scenery, as in some repertory theatre, of drinks-tray and mirrors and chintz-covered sofas, blending all social life into one staggeringly extended run.

She felt something similar, but worse in a way, about hundreds and hundreds of books she'd read, novels, biographies, occasional books about music and art—she could remember nothing about them at all, so that it seemed rather pointless even to say that she had read them; such claims were a thing people set great store by but she hardly supposed they recalled any more than she did. Sometimes a book persisted as a coloured shadow at the edge of sight, as vague and unrecapturable as something seen in the rain from a passing vehicle: looked at directly it vanished altogether. Sometimes there were atmospheres, even the rudiments of a scene: a man in an office looking over Regent's Park, rain in the streets outside—a little blurred etching of a situation she would never, could never, trace back to its source in a novel she had read some time, she thought, in the past thirty years.

She woke to find grey light spreading above the curtains, and made a wary assessment of the time. These early wakings were anxious countings of loss and gain—was it late enough not to mind being woken? Might it still be early enough to lay a presentable claim on more sleep? With the coming on of spring one was more defenceless. Five-fifty: not too bad. And as soon as she wondered about whether she had to go to the loo she found she did. Out of bed, into slippers, dressing-gown on over pyjamas—she was glad she couldn't see herself in the mirror as more than a blurred bundle. Light on, out past Wilfrid's door, the click of the loose parquet, but it wouldn't wake him. He had the large capacity for sleep of a child. She had a picture, not much changed in fifty years, of his head on the pillow, and nothing ever happening to him, at least that she knew of. And now there was this Birgit, with her shadowy plans. Poor Wilfrid was so naïve that he couldn't see the woman for the fortune-hunter she was—and what a fortune! . . . Daphne tutted as she groped her way through the shadowy cupboard in which the wash-basin and lavatory were like surreal intrusions in a mountain of rubbish.

IN THE MORNING, bright and early, Lady Caroline Messent rang to invite her to tea. The phone at Olga was fixed to the kitchen wall, Caroline perhaps having pictured Olga herself as habitually in that room, and standing more or less to attention when she spoke to her. "I can't, my dear," said Daphne, "I've got this young man coming back."

"Oh, do put him off," said Caroline in her droll scurry of a voice. "Who is he?"

"He's called—he's interrogating me, I'm like a prisoner in my own home."

"Darling . . . ," said Caroline, allowing that for the present at least it was Daphne's home. "I wouldn't stand for it. Is he from the gas board?"

"Oh, much worse." Daphne steadied herself against the worktop which she could dimly see was a dangerous muddle of dirty dishes, half-empty bottles and pill-packets. "He turned up yesterday—he's like the Kleeneze man."

"You mean hawking?"

"He says I met him at Corinna and Leslie's, but I have absolutely no recollection of it."

"Oh, I see . . . ," said Caroline, as if now siding slightly with the intruder. "But what does he want?"

Daphne sighed heavily. "Smut, essentially."

"Smut?"

"He's trying to write a book about Cecil."

"Cecil? Oh, Valance, you mean? Yes, I see."

"You know, I've already written all about it."

Caroline paused. "I suppose it was only a matter of time," she said.

"Hmm? I don't know what he's got into his head. He's insinuating, if you know what I mean. He's more or less saying that I didn't come clean in some way in my book."

"No, that must be awfully annoying."

"Well, less awfully, more bloody, actually, as Alfred, Lord Tennyson said to my father."

"So funny, that," said Caroline.

"Really Cecil means nothing to me—I was potty about him for five minutes sixty years ago. The significant thing about Cecil, as far as I'm concerned," said Daphne, half-hearing herself go on, "is that he led to Dud, and the children, and all the grown-up part of my life, which naturally he had no part in himself!"

"Well, tell that to your Kleeneze man, darling," said Caroline, evidently thinking Daphne protested too much.

"I suppose I should." And she saw there was a little shameful reluctance to do so, and thus reduce even further her interest for the young man. It struck her suddenly that Caroline must already know him. "I'm fairly sure he was at your launch party," she said. "Paul Bryant."

"You don't mean the young man from . . . was it Canterbury . . . one of the red-bricks."

"He might be, I suppose. He used to work in the bank with Leslie."

"Ah, no. But there certainly was a clever young man, you're quite right, doing something on Cecil's poetry."

"No, I know who you mean, I can't remember his name. I've dealt with him already. This is *another* young man."

"Mm, my dear, it's obviously Cecil's moment," said Caroline.

10

NEXT MORNING Paul sat in his hotel room, going over his notes, with a coffee tray beside him: the pitted metal pot with the untouchable handle, the lipsticked cup, the bowl of white sugar in soft paper tubes which he emptied serially into the three strong cupfuls he took, getting quickly excited and overheated. On a plate with a doily were five biscuits, and though he'd only just had breakfast he ate them all, the types so familiar—the Bourbon, the sugared Nice, the rebarbative ginger-nut, popped in whole—that he was touched for a moment by a sense of the inseparable poverty and consistency of English life, as crystallized in the Peek Frean assortment box. He sat back in his chair as he munched and levelled a look at his own industrious jaw movements in the mirror; and a less comfortable sensation came over him. The fact was he had never watched himself eating, and was astonished at his forceful, rodent-like look, the odd sag of his neck on one side as he chewed, the working flicker of his temples. This must be what his company was like to others, what Karen faced each night over dinner, and the realization made him run down pensively, stop chewing mid-biscuit and then start up again as if to catch himself unawares. He wasn't at all sure he would want to confide his own secrets to such a man.

He was writing up further aspects of yesterday's meeting in his diary—a book in which the sparse record of his own life was now largely replaced by the ramifying details of others'. Now and then he played back the tape, more for the feel of it than because he believed he would get much out of it. There was a fair amount he had forgotten, but he knew too that there were spells in any interview when he didn't listen to the other person: it was partly the perennial self-consciousness, his sense of playing a role—laughing, sighing, sadly nodding—eclipsing any likelihood of taking in whatever was being said; and it was partly some colder sense that the interviewee was evasive or repetitive, deliberately boring him and wasting his time. It was appalling what they couldn't remember, and with his primary witnesses, all in their eighties, he had a view of them stuck in a rut, or a wheel, doggedly chasing the same few time-smoothed memories along with their nose and their paws. When he'd gone through "The Hammock" with Daphne, hoping to goad her memory, she had carried on using the same words and phrases as she had in her book, and probably had for fifty years before that. In her book she'd made such a thing of this youthful romance, and he could see that the thing that she'd made had replaced the now remote original experience, and couldn't usefully be interrogated for any further unrevealed details. She didn't actually seem at all interested in Cecil, much less in the chance Paul was giving her, at the end of her life, to put things straight. He laughed warily when he thought of her little snub, as he was leaving ("Are you coming back?"); but in a way it simply made him more determined.

George's theory about Corinna, if true, threw a very strange light on to Dudley. Perhaps today he should try to get her on to the subject of her first marriage, and trick her, almost, into some revelation. George had said such marriages happened a great deal at that time. Obviously Paul would have to track down Corinna's birth certificate. How complicit was Dudley in the whole thing? It was a most peculiar love triangle. In *Black Flowers* Dudley coped with his brother's affairs in his customary ramblingly cutting style.

My wife had met Cecil before the War, when he had been something of a mentor to her brother George Sawle, and it was after a visit to the Sawles' cottage in Harrow that he had written "Two Acres," a poem that attained some celebrity in the war years, and after. I suspect she was a good deal dazzled by his energy and his profile, and as an ardent consumer of romantic verse she was surely impressed to meet a real live poet, dark-eyed and raven-haired. There are certainly signs that he was fond of her, though these should not be exaggerated; my brother was accustomed to admiration, and as a rule was gracious to those who provided it. He wrote his famous poem at her request for some memento in her visitors' book, but he had only known her at the time for two days. It amused me somewhat that Cecil, heir to three thousand acres, should have been best-known for his ode to a mere two. Very thoughtfully, he invited her to Corley once when her brother also was staying with us.

There followed various sarcasms about George's visits to the Valances.

He showed a keen interest in both house and estate. If he had the unintended air at times of an agent or bailiff, his preoccupations were no doubt largely intellectual. He and Cecil were sometimes absent for hours, returning with tales of what they had found in the labyrinthine cellars or secluded attics of the house, or with reports, which pleased my father, of the quality of the grazing or the woodsmanship shown on the Corley farms.

Paul thought again about George and Cecil on the roof, the whole rich difficult range of unspoken testimony, in images and implications. Surely Dudley was hinting here at something he couldn't possibly have said outright?

Daphne, two or three years younger, was more open and at ease, and spoke her mind in a manner that sometimes startled my mother but habitually delighted me. She had grown up with two elder brothers of her own, and was used to their spoiling. I was thrown together with her by the somewhat exclusive nature of George and Cecil's pursuits, and our own relations were at first fraternal; it was clear that she idolized Cecil, but to me she was an amusingly artless companion, unaffected by the family view of me as, if not a black, then certainly a greyish sheep. She loved to talk, and her face lit up with amusement at the simplest pleasantries. To her Corley Court was less a matter for the social historian than a vision out of some old romance. Its inhuman aspects were part of its charm. The stained glass windows that kept out the light, the high ceilings that baffled all attempts at heating, the barely penetrable thickets of overladen tables, chairs and potted palms that filled the rooms, were invested with a kind of magic. "I should like very much to live in a house like this," she said, on the occasion of that first visit. Four years later she was married in the chapel at Corley, and in due course, if for a limited span, was herself the mistress of the house.

Paul decided hotels were hardly the best place to work. All around there was noise—a late riser above had pulled the bath-plug and the waste fell with an unembarrassed frothing and gargling sound through a pipe apparently inches from his desk; the maid had come in twice, even though check-out wasn't till eleven; baffled but unbeaten, she toiled in the hallway with the hoover or went up and down opening and slamming the doors; in a room immediately to his left, and previously unsuspected, some sort of business meeting had got under way, with periodic laughter and the rambling voice of a man addressing them, a completely meaningless phrase now and then discernible through the thin wall. Paul sat back with a yelp of frustration; yet he saw the scene had already a kind of anecdotal quality, and he wrote it up too in his diary, as a reminder of the biographer's difficult existence.

When he got back to Olga, just before two o'clock, he found the front door open and heard Wilfrid's voice coming from the kitchen, speaking more regularly and emphatically than usual. Even so, he couldn't make out at first what he was saying. He felt he'd chanced on something awkwardly private. There was a sense of possible crisis. Rather than ring the bell, Paul stepped into the hall and gripping his briefcase stood leaning forward with an apologetic expression. It dawned on him that Wilfrid was reading to his mother. " 'Ah hammer . . . dryers ever seen,' " he seemed to say. For a dislocated second Paul couldn't place it; then of course he knew. *Are Hamadryads ever seen / Between the dancing veils of green . . . ?* He was reading "Two Acres" for her, and she was making a grumbling noise or coming in on the words herself as if to say the reading was hardly necessary; it was a sort of briefing perhaps for her second day's interview, and Paul found something reassuring in that—and something oddly touching in the reversal of roles, son reading to mother. " 'Or pause, then take the hidden turn, / The path amid—' " " 'The path amid the hip-high fern,' " Daphne came in. "You don't read it at all well."

"Perhaps you would rather I didn't?" said Wilfrid in his usual tone of dry forbearance.

"Poetry, I mean, you have no idea how to read poetry. It's not the football results . . ."

"Well, I'm sorry . . ."

"The curfew tolls the knell of passing day: *one;* The ploughman homeward plods his weary way: *nil,*" said Daphne, getting a bit carried away. "When I'm gone, you should get a job on the telly."

"Don't . . . talk like that," said Wilfrid, and Paul, not seeing their faces, took a moment to realize it was not her mockery but the mention of her going that he was objecting to. And what indeed would he do then? Puzzled for a moment by his own muddled feelings of affection and irritation towards Daphne, Paul tiptoed back out again and rang the bell.

Exactly as yesterday, but with determined new warmth, Paul said to Wilfrid in the hall, "And how is your mother?"

"I fear she didn't sleep at all well," said Wilfrid, not meeting his eye; "you might keep it . . . pretty short today." Paul went into the sitting-room and set up the mike and looked over his notes with a clear sense they were blaming him for her bad night. But in fact when Daphne came through she seemed if anything rather more spry than yesterday. She made her way among the helpful obstacles of the room with the inward smile of an elderly person who knows they're not done yet. He felt something had happened in the interim; of course she would have been thinking, reassessing her position as she lay awake, and he would have to find out as he went along if the spryness was a sign of compliance or resistance.

"Rather a lovely day," she said as she sat down; and then cocking her head to check Wilfrid was still in the kitchen making coffee, "Has he been telling you about his popsy?"

"Oh—well, I gathered . . ." Paul smiled distractedly as he checked the tape-recorder.

"I mean, he's sixty! He can't look after a lively young woman—he can hardly look after me!"

"Perhaps she would look after him."

But she gave a rather earthy chuckle at this. "He's not a bad person, he wouldn't hurt a fly, or even a flea probably, but he's totally impractical. I mean look at this house! It's a miracle I haven't tripped over something and broken my leg; or my wrist; or my neck!"

"Does she live locally?"

"Thank god, no—she lives in Norway."

"Oh, I see . . ."

"Birgit. She's a pen-pal, didn't he tell you that?"

"Well, Norway's a long way away."

"That's not what Birgit thinks. Well, she's got designs on him."

"Do you think?"

Daphne was quietly candid. "She wants to be the next Lady Valance. Ah, tea, Wilfie, how splendid!"

"Coffee, you said, Mummy." She took it cautiously from the tray. "Shall I go over to Smiths' for those things, then?"

"No, no," she said, "stay and talk with us—it will be more fun for Mr. Bryant, and you can help me out—I forget so much!"

"Do call me Paul," said Paul, with a glare of a smile at Wilfrid—if he stayed it was certain Daphne would say nothing remotely interesting; he needed to be sent off on some sort of errand, but it was hard for Paul to know what.

"Well, of course I'm very interested in . . . Paul's great project."

"Well, I know you are." She sipped. "Mm, delicious."

Paul wondered how to cope with this. As always he had plans, which as often proved impossible to follow, and he had never been good at improvising: he clung to the discarded plan still when he could. He reminded her about Corley Court, and the times he'd visited the house, and how he was hoping to go again, he'd written to the Headmaster; but she couldn't be got to show any interest in the topic at all. "Do you have much from those days, I wonder?" Paul said. Perhaps under the table-cloths and blankets in this room there were Valance heirlooms, little dusty things that Cecil might have owned and handled. The sense of the whole unexamined terrain of Cecil's life lying so close and yet so stubbornly out of view came over him at times in waves of dreamlike opportunity and bafflement.

"I didn't get much. I got the Raphael."

"Oh, well . . . ?"—Paul narrowed his eyes at her tone.

"You probably saw it in the loo."

"Oh . . . oh, the picture of the man, do you mean . . . Goodness . . . Well, that must be worth quite a lot!" Paul hated his own snigger—he really had no idea.

"Well, so one had hoped. Unfortunately it's a copy, done when was it, Wilfie?"

"About 1840, I believe," said Wilfrid, sportingly, but with a certain pride too.

"But you didn't know that at the time?"

"Well, I think . . . you know. And what else?"—she gazed around as if against a bright glare.

"The ashtray," said Wilfrid.

"Oh, yes—I got the ashtray." On the little table, beside her coffee cup, was a small silver bowl, with a scalloped edge. "Have a look." She lifted it and Paul got up to take it from her. It was just the sort of thing people used to keep in old suitcases in the strong-room at the bank, but tarnished and scratched by the protracted attentions of a heavy smoker.

"Look on the bottom," said Wilfrid.

"Oh, I see . . ."

"I suppose Dudley had a sort of complex or something about property. He had that done to all sorts of valuable things, no doubt greatly reducing their value in the process." In flowing letters, like some more conventional inscription stamped in the silver, were the words *Stolen from Corley Court*. He handed it back, with a blush at the naming of this particular vice.

"I was wondering about the picture behind you," he said, to distract her. Somehow the nightmare of the room was yielding small treasures, consolation prizes for the talk that Daphne was trying to prevent from happening.

"Oh, well, that's Revel, of course," said Daphne, as though now referring to an undisputed master.

"And it's obviously . . . you!" said Paul.

"I'm very attached to that drawing, aren't I, Wilfie."

"Yes . . . you are," Wilfrid agreed.

"So when was it done?" Paul got up, and edged around between the back of Daphne's chair and the standard-lamp to have a closer look. It struck him that the Victorian "thicket" of furniture and stuff at Corley had been re-created here by Daphne willy-nilly. Perhaps clutter always won in the end.

"It's a very fine picture," said Daphne. It showed a round-faced young woman with dark hair in bunches on either side of her head. A light scarf was tied loosely in the open neck of her blouse. She leant forward, lips parted, as if waiting for the punchline of a joke. It was done in what Paul thought was red chalk, and signed *For Daphne—RR April 1926.* "We both had the most appalling hangovers at the time, but I don't believe you can tell with either of us."

Paul giggled, but didn't hazard a view. When he thought about the date, it began to seem significant. "I'd like to see more of his pictures," he said, sad to hear himself surrender to a further diversion from the subject of Cecil, but with a feeling she could still be brought back to it.

"Would you, really?" Daphne sounded surprised, but was ready to oblige. "What have we got? Well, have a look at Revel's albums, I suppose. You know where they are, Wilfie."

"Yes . . . now then . . . ," said Wilfrid, nodding his head from side to side as he fetched them out from a chest of drawers behind his chair. Paul began to suspect Wilfrid's years-long failure to tidy the house was really a cover for a highly personal but efficient system of his own. "Well, there's this one anyway." And Paul was shown, more hastily than he would have liked, a large black-covered sketchbook of Revel Ralph's; it was laid open across Daphne's knee, and Paul and Wilfrid flanked her, craning down politely while she peered from odd ingenious angles and quickly turned the pages, as if regretting showing them after all. There were pages of Georgian-looking houses, whether real or invented Paul had no idea, pretty but rather boring, which Wilfrid then said were designs for *The School for Scandal;* some sketches of another woman in a dark hat, which Daphne said were studies for a portrait of Lady somebody, "a very trying woman"; and then a rapid and much more inspired-looking series of drawings, over ten or twelve pages, of a naked young man, lying, sitting, standing, in a range of ideal but natural-looking positions, everything about him wonderfully brought out, except his cock and balls which were consigned to the imagination by a swoop of the pencil, ostentatiously discreet, pretending it wasn't the point. Daphne seemed to sense Paul's interest—"What's that?" pushing the book away so she could see it—"Oh, you remember him, Wilfie, the Scotch boy at Corley. Revel was awfully taken with him—he did a lot of drawings of him—I remember they became great friends."

"I was too young to remember him," said Wilfrid, and looking at Paul over Daphne's head, "I was only seven when we . . . er, moved to London."

Even so, Paul wondered whether Wilfrid wasn't abashed by looking at these sketches, all the bolder for being private things, the little studies of the Scotch boy's thighs, buttocks and nipples, in the presence of his mother; and what on earth Daphne herself thought, having married a man who produced such work. "I remember he came to several of our parties at the studio," she said, as if in fact recommending her husband's roving eye. Paul thought for a moment she might be teasing him.

"These ought to be in a museum," he said awkwardly.

"And soon I dare say they will be. But I like having them around, so for now I'm hanging on to them, thanks very much"—and she shut the book halfway through as if to say she'd indulged him quite enough.

"Actually I wanted to ask if you have any pictures of 'Two Acres'?"— something told him it was cleverer to ask for pictures of the house than pictures of people: it sounded more disinterested, and no doubt both kinds of photo would be mounted in the same album. Once more Wilfrid obliged. "This was Granny Sawle's album," he said.

"It was a dear house," said Daphne, again holding the album down by her left knee and raising her eyebrows suspiciously. "That's the view from the lane, isn't it, yes, that was the dining-room window, and there were the four cherry-trees in front of it, of course."

"A cloud of snow at Eastertide!" said Paul (it wasn't Cecil's most original line).

"Aha!" said Wilfrid from the far side of the room.

"There you are . . . ," said Daphne. "And the rockery, look. Goodness, how it all comes back."

"Well, I'm glad," said Paul, with a frank laugh.

"Now who's that? Wilfie, is it Granny?"

"Oh . . . ," said Paul. It was the stout old German woman again, that George had told him about, but of course he didn't know her name. Already Paul felt annoyed by her, a figure of no interest who kept demanding attention. He remembered George had said she was a great bore. She sat in light-absorbing black in a deckchair from which it was hard to see how she would ever get up.

"What?" said Wilfrid, coming over. "I don't know who everyone is, I wasn't even born yet, remember? Oh, good grief—no, no, that's not Granny. No, no." He laughed breathily. "Granny was really a rather— lovely woman, with lovely auburn hair."

"Well, I wouldn't say it was auburn," said Daphne. "She was a dark blonde. She was very proud of her hair." It probably wasn't something Daphne would say of herself. Paul looked to Wilfrid, and said,

"She was the German woman, wasn't she?"

"That's right . . . ," said Wilfrid, already abstracted, leaning forward quickly to turn the page. "I haven't seen these for a long time," he said.

"I wonder what's become of the house," said Daphne.

"It probably doesn't even exist any more, Mother," said Wilfrid. It was one of those little moments when Paul found it in his power to inform and perhaps upset the person he had himself come to for information.

"Oh, it does, actually," he said.

"You've seen it, I suppose, have you," Daphne said, in an irritable tone.

Paul pursed his lips regretfully. "Well, I'm not sure you'd recognize the old place."

"Oh, really?" she said, lightly but grimly.

"Well, no—you would," said Paul, "of course you would"—and he thought, *but you never will go there, you'll never see the place again.* He had a feeling she was blaming him already for the changes, the years of flats, the sold-off garden, blaming him for knowing what he knew and what she had hoped never to know.

"Actually don't tell me," she said.

"Anyway, we've got the poem, haven't we," said Wilfrid.

"Well, of course," said Daphne, "there's always the poem."

There were no photos of Cecil in the album, which since he'd only spent six nights of his life at "Two Acres" was hardly surprising, but of course disappointing. Paul looked closely at George whenever he appeared, from sailor-suited six-year-old to boatered Cambridge man, and with less and less doubt that whatever warmth this cold fish had felt had been directed at other young men. He asked Daphne if she would let him reproduce two photos of the house and garden, and she said she didn't see why not, but she fidgeted until she was sure that Wilfrid had returned the album to its hiding-place. When they were all sitting down again, Paul cleared his throat and looked at her more narrowly than before, and with a greater cumulative sense that it didn't matter how he looked at her, she wasn't going to see him. He said airily, "There's one thing—," just as Daphne, with a little chuckle, almost grinning, as if at some great mutual satisfaction, said, "Well! I'm sorry to say that I've promised to be at my friend Caroline's by four o'clock, so alas we'll have to bring the meeting to a conclusion, with a vote of thanks to Wilfrid Valance for the refreshments!"

Paul's face reddened and stiffened, but he wasn't going to be outdone. He made a thing of nodding regretfully at his watch. "Well, if I'm to catch the 5:10," he said.

"Oh, well, there you are, perfect," said Daphne smoothly.

It wasn't clear if Wilfrid would want to drive him again; Paul was ready to phone for a Cathedral. He stood up, and started putting the tape-recorder and his papers into his briefcase with as little discomfiture as possible, in fact with a few delaying and normalizing remarks. "I'm so grateful to you," he said.

"Well, I don't suppose I've been much help to you," she said.

"You've been very kind!" said Paul, in a full embrace of untruth. He took out his copy of *The Short Gallery:* "I wonder—would you sign this for me?"—it was the copy he had had for review. He hoped she was no longer up to reading the pencilled marginalia, even if she thought to look.

"What's that . . . ?"

"Oh, Paul wants you to sign your book for him, Mummy," said Wilfrid, clearly pleased by the request.

"Oh, well, if you like"—and after a scrabble for a biro and with an awkward squint at the title page, Daphne wrote something, in her large loping hand—Paul didn't look but it took him back in a complex moment to the night she had written down her address for him at Paddington, and then much further to the morning at Foxleigh long before when he'd seen her make out a cheque with a comic precautionary air of not knowing what she was doing. There was something about her writing, with its big squareish loops and above-normal scale, that seemed to show her to him as a girl, something unguarded and almost unaltered by time, the same swelling *D*s and crook-like *p*s she would have signed in letters to Cecil Valance before the First World War, and that now she was signing for him. She closed the book and handed it back; then stood up too, with the uncertain look of having come through something without too much harm. He clipped his briefcase shut.

"Well! I'll be in touch," he said. He wasn't at all sure he would ever see

her again. "And as I say, I'll let you know about the book-launch, whenever it happens. You have to be there!" She was completely impassive at
this, and Paul moved forward with a quick amiable gasp and touched her
upper arm—she hadn't seen it coming: it was only after he'd planted the
first kiss and was already committed to the second that her resistance
showed, a little bewildered grunt and recoil, as if from the sheer scale of
his misunderstanding.

FIVE

The Old Companions

No one remembers you at all.

—Mick Imlah,
"In Memoriam Alfred Lord Tennyson"

I

THE WOMAN SITTING next to him said, "I don't know if Julian's coming, do you?"

"I don't, I'm afraid . . . ," said Rob.

"I believe they were great friends. I'm not sure I'd recognize him now." She craned round. Her black hat had an inch of veil at the front, and a mauve silk flower over her right ear. No wedding-ring, but several other fine old rings, heirlooms perhaps, on other fingers. Her clothes were soft crumpled velvet and silk, black and deep red, stylish but not exactly fashionable. She smiled at him again, and he wasn't sure if she thought she knew him, or thought quite naturally that she didn't need to know him to speak to him. Her firm, clipped voice had a hint of mischief. "I fear a number of these people are going to have to stand." She looked round with satisfaction at the embarrassed struggles of the latest arrivals, as they clambered along the rows, or sat down abruptly and as if they didn't mind on some impossible ledge or radiator; one old man had perched like a tennis umpire at the top of the library steps. It was still only ten to two, but events like this brought out a strange zeal in people. Rob had been lucky to find this seat, at the end of a row, but near the front. "Did you go to the funeral?"

"I didn't, I'm afraid," he said.

"Nor did I. Not a fan."

"Oh . . ."

"Of funerals, I mean. I've reached the age where one finds, with sore dismay, that one goes to more funerals than parties."

"I suppose you could say this was somewhere between the two . . ." He opened the folded order of events, on which nine readers and speakers were listed. Inevitably, out of emotion, inexperience or sheer self-importance, almost all of them would go on too long, and the glinting wineglasses and shrouded buffet just visible at the far end of the library would not be reached till about four o'clock. The library itself was fune-really splendid—Rob gazed at the tiers of leather-bound books with the sceptical, secretive eye of a professional. A broad arc of chairs filled the space and a low podium had been set up, with a lectern and a micro-phone. The servants, in their black jackets, were growing flustered, more chairs were brought in. An event like this must be a challenge to the rou-tine of a club; the automatic deference due to a deceased member stretched a little thinner over this very mixed crowd. A couple of young-sters had been made to put on ties, but one group of men in leather were too far outside the dress-code for any such remedial action and had been let in unchallenged. The only other man without a tie was a lilac-vested bishop.

From his seat Rob had a view along the front row in profile, unmis-takably members of the family, as well as people who were due to speak: he recognized Sarah Barfoot, Nigel Dupont and Desmond, Peter's hus-band. Rob had had a fling with Desmond himself, ten or twelve years ago, and looked at him now with that eerie awareness of the unforeseen that lurks beneath the reassurances of any reunion. The other readers could be identified perhaps from the list. Dr. James Brooke he didn't know at all. At the far end was a man of about sixty, with a long nose and glasses on a string, looking over the typed sheets he was going to read from. He seemed somehow outside the nervous but supportive mood of the rest of the team, his own nerves perhaps concealed behind his frown and the sudden impatient glare he turned on the audience behind him; then he saw someone he knew, and gave a curt but humorous nod. Rob thought this must be Paul Bryant, the biographer.

Rob's neighbour said, "How old was he?" getting out her reading glasses.

He looked at the front of the card with its small black-and-white photo and the words PETER ROWE—9 OCTOBER 1945–8 JUNE 2008—A CELEBRATION. "Um—sixty-two." The photo was more typical than flat-tering, Peter at a party, making a point, with a glass of wine in his hand. At these memorials great fondness was often shown for the foibles of the deceased. Rob found it brought back immediately the sound of Peter's voice, plummy, funny, carrying—a sound which Peter himself had been very fond of.

"You probably knew him well."

"Not really, I'm afraid. I mean, I grew up on his TV series, but I only got to know him much later."

"I loved those, didn't you."

"We did a lot of business with him . . . Sorry, I should say, I'm a book-dealer," and here Rob reached in his suit pocket for the little translucent case and presented her with his business card: *Rob Salter, Garsaint.com, Books and Manuscripts.*

"Aha! very good . . ." She peered at it.

"He had a great art library."

"I imagine so. Is that your field?"

"We're mainly post-1880—literature, art and design."

She tucked the card in her handbag. "You don't do French books, I suppose?"

"We can search for specific things, if you need them." He shrugged pleasantly. "We can find you anything you want."

"Mm, I may well have to call on you."

"Now that all information is retrievable . . ."

"Quite a thought, isn't it," she said, and here she fished out her own card, rubbed at the corners, and with a private phone-number inked in: *Professor Jennifer Ralph, St. Hilda's College, Oxford.* "There you are."

"Oh . . . ," said Rob, "yes, indeed . . . Villiers de L'Isle-Adam, I think?"

"How clever of you."

"I've sold several copies of your book."

"Ah," she said, delighted but dry—"which one?"

But here a horrible lancing whine was heard from the speakers as the tall figure of Nigel Dupont approached and ducked grinningly away from the microphone. Then he approached again, and had said no more than "Ladies and Gentlemen" when again the savage noise leapt into the room and echoed off the walls and ceiling. Though it wasn't his fault, it made him look a bit of a fool, which he plainly wasn't used to. He swept his strikingly blond forelock back with a distracted hand. When the problem had been more or less sorted out, all he said, squinting at a text on his iPhone, was, "I'm sure you'll understand, there will be a slight delay, Peter's sister's held up by traffic."

"The famous Dupont, I presume," said Jennifer, quite loudly, as talk resumed. "We are honoured."

"I know . . . ," said Rob. Dupont had a long, unseasonally suntanned face with almost invisible rimless glasses, and a suit that in itself con-veyed the sheer superiority of a well-endowed chair at a Southern Cali-fornian university.

"And do you know by any chance the name of the man at the far end—with the, um, green tie?" said Jennifer, picking his least personal identifying feature.

"Well, I think," said Rob, "it must be Paul Bryant, mustn't it, who writes all those biographies—there was that one that caused all the fuss about the Bishop of Durham."

Jennifer nodded slowly. "Good . . . *god* . . . yes, it is! I can't have seen him for forty years."

Rob was amused by her half-abstracted, half-mocking gaze across the room. "How did you come to know him?"

"Hmm? Well," said Jennifer, sliding down a little in her chair, as though to hide from Bryant but also to enter a more confidential phase with Rob, "years ago he wrote one of his books, his first one, actually— which also caused a good deal of fuss—about my . . . sort of great-uncle." She shook away the unnecessary explanation.

"Yes . . . that was Cecil Valance?"

"Exactly."

"Your great-uncle was Cecil Valance . . . ," said Rob, marvelling, almost teasing.

"Well"—she snatched a breath, and he saw her in her College room, in a trying tutorial on Mallarmé or some other subject beyond the student's reach: "I mean, do you really want to know?"

"Very much," said Rob, quite truthfully, and with a sense now it would be rather annoying when the event started. He'd been a student when the Valance biography came out, and he remembered reading extracts from it in a Sunday paper, and enjoying the atmosphere of revelations without being specially interested in the people involved.

"My grandmother," said Jennifer, "was married to Cecil's brother Dudley Valance, who was also a writer, rather forgotten now."

"Well, *Black Flowers*," said Rob.

"Exactly—I mustn't forget you're a bookseller! But anyway she left him, and married my grandfather, the artist Revel Ralph."

"Yes—absolutely," said Rob, seeing her quick raised eyebrow.

"Now my father worked mainly in Malaya, he was very big in rubber, but I was sent to school in England, of course, and in the holidays I often stayed with my aunt Corinna, who was Dudley's daughter. That was when I met Peter, by the way. He played duets with her. She was a very fine pianist—could have been a concert pianist."

"I see," said Rob, distracted by the image of her father in rubber, though the lewd subtext flickered only as an encouraging smile. "How interesting."

"Well it *is* interesting," said Jennifer drily, tucking in her chin, "but according to Paul Bryant everything I've just told you is untrue. Let me see . . . My aunt wasn't really Dudley's daughter, but Cecil's, Dudley was gay, though he managed to father a son with my grandmother, and my father's father wasn't Revel Ralph, who really was gay, but a painter called Mark Gibbons. I may be simplifying a bit."

Rob grinned and nodded, not taking all of this in. "And this wasn't the case?" he said.

"Oh, who knows?" said Jennifer. "Paul was something of a fantasist, we all knew that. But it caused a fair old stink at the time. Dudley's wife even tried to take out an injunction against it."

"Yes, of course"—it was that sense he'd had of the old guard trying and failing to close ranks.

"Do you remember? And of course it cast my poor grandmother in rather an unenviable light."

"Yes, I see that."

"She'd been married three times as it was, and now he was claiming that two of her three children hadn't been sired by her husbands, and also, did I mention that Cecil had had an affair with her brother? Yup, that too."

"Oh dear!" said Rob, who couldn't quite see where Jennifer stood on the subject. She seemed to deplore Paul Bryant, but wasn't exactly disputing what he'd said. Her droll academic tone had something county in it too, a little snobbish reserve she hadn't wholly wanted to disown. "I presume she wasn't still alive?"

"Mm, well she was, I'm afraid, though extremely old, and virtually blind, so there was no chance of her actually reading it. Everyone tried to keep it from her." Jennifer flinched with her evident sense of the humour as well as the horror of the situation. "Though as I'm sure you know there will always be one very dear friend who feels they have to put you in the picture. I think it sort of finished her off. As it happened she'd written a rather feeble book of her own about her affair with Uncle Cecil, so it was a bit of a shock to be told he'd also had an affair with her brother."

"Well, outing gay writers was all the rage then, of course."

"Well, fine," she said, with a candid shake of the head. "If that's all it had been . . ."

Rob looked at her as he found the title. *"England Trembles,"* he said. Long out of print, though an American paperback had surfaced later— he could see the photo of Valance on the front— *"Sensational!"*—*Times of London*—something like that.

"England Trembles," said Jennifer, "exactly . . . ," turning down the corners of her mouth in a rather French expression of indifference. "The thing was—"

A loud purring sound, a preparatory burble of self-pleasure, rose above the talk, and then "Ladies and gentlemen, thank you so much, my name's Nigel Dupont . . ."

"Ah—" Rob winced.

"There's quite a story about Master Bryant as well," said Jennifer, with a rapid nod and grimace of a promise to carry on with it later. "All was not as it seemed . . ." Rob sat back, smiling appreciatively, but amused too to be reserving judgement on the matter.

It seemed Dupont had been asked by the family to be a sort of MC for the occasion—he assumed the role with evident willingness and nat- ural authority and just a hint of allowable muddle, as if to remind them he was good-naturedly helping out. "So, we're all here," he said, peering down with a smile of exaggerated patience at the confused figure of Peter's sister, red-faced from a horrible rush across London, still settling her bags and papers in the front row. Then, the smile running across the rows, "I'm aware many people in this very splendid room knew . . . er, Peter far better than I did, and we'll be hearing from some of them in a moment. Peter was a hugely popular guy, with a huge variety of friends. I can see many different types of people here"—surveying the room humorously, with his expat's eye, and producing confusion and even laughter in persons suddenly considering what type they might belong to—"and perhaps this gathering of his friends can best be thought of as the last of Peter's famous parties, at which one might meet anyone from a duke to a . . . to a DJ, a bishop to a barrow-boy"—Dupont perhaps suggesting a certain loss of touch with contemporary English life; the bishop in the second row smiled tolerantly. "Many friendships of course were initiated at those parties. I know some of my own best work might never have been done if it hadn't been for meetings brought about by, um . . . Peter." He reflected for a moment—it seemed he was going to speak without notes, which created its own small tension of latent embarrassment and renewed relief when he went on. Peter's name itself seemed constantly about to elude him. "However, for now, Terence—

Peter's father—has suggested I say a few words about the period when I first knew him, when he was in his early twenties, and I was a tender twelve years old." Dupont smiled distantly and high-mindedly at this memory as the vaguely disturbing sound of what he had said sank in— Rob glanced across the room, and caught a tall fair-haired man smiling too, and smiling at Rob specifically through his more general air of amusement. Rob thought he might have seen him around, but his cataloguing mind couldn't yet place him. He looked down, and saw that Jennifer, beneath her own air of polite attention, was discreetly drawing on the back of the service card with a propelling pencil: an expert little sketch of Professor Dupont.

"For a brief period, just over three years, Peter taught at a prep-school in Berkshire called Corley Court. It was his first proper job—I believe he had worked in the men's department at Harrods for a few months before, which was what gave him his first taste for London—life in the inside leg as he used to call it! He had come down from Oxford with a decent second, but true academic endeavour was never going to be Peter's *Fach*." Dupont gazed complacently at the tiers of leather-bound books, while a frown of uncertainty about what he'd just said passed through the audience. "He had a passion for knowledge, of course, but he wasn't a specialist—which was just as well at Corley, where he had to teach everything, except I think math, and sport. Corley Court was a High Victorian country house of a kind then much reviled, though Peter was fascinated by it from the start. It had been built by a man called Eustace Valance, who had made his fortune from grass seed, and been created a baronet on the strength of it. His son was also an agriculturalist, but his two grandsons, Cecil and Dudley, were both in their ways to become quite well-known writers." Here Rob looked at Jennifer, who gave a little nod as she strengthened the boyish curl of Dupont's forelock.

"You probably all know lines of Cecil's by heart," he went on, smiling along the densely packed rows and eliciting again a mixture of resistance and eagerness; it was as though he might ask any one of them to quote the lines they knew. "He was a first-rate example of the second-rate poet who enters into common consciousness more deeply than many greater masters. 'All England trembles in the spray / Of dog-rose in the front of May' . . . 'Two blessèd acres of English ground' "—he looked almost teasingly at them, as though he were a prep-school master himself. "Some of you perhaps know that I went on to edit Cecil Valance's poems, a project that might never have come about had it not been for

Peter's early encouragement." And he nodded slowly, as if at the providential nature of this. Rob had forgotten this fact, which linked Jennifer and Dupont in the sort of unexpected way he liked.

"So . . ." Dupont paused, as if to recover his bearings, some clever little vanity again in the invitation to watch him improvise. Half the audience seemed seduced by it; others, older colleagues of Peter's, friends of the family who had never heard of Dupont, and were yet to see the point of him, had the air of mildly offended blankness which is the default expression of any congregation. One or two, of course, would have read Dupont's milestone works in Queer Theory, and perhaps be pleasantly surprised to find he could talk in straightforward English when necessary. Rob felt again he didn't have to take a view; he looked humorously and enquiringly at Jennifer's knee, and she offered her service card with her little down-turned smile: she had got Dupont exactly, in a sketch that was somewhere between a portrait and a cartoon. Rob gave an almost noiseless snort and as he looked across the rows again he found the tall blond man smiling at him and then blinking slowly before he turned away. Rob's feeling it wasn't proper to cruise at a memorial service was mixed with a feeling that Peter himself wouldn't have minded. He looked aside and his gaze fell, with a kind of respectful curiosity, on Desmond, sitting very straight, but with his eyes fixed on Dupont's black brogues. "So," Dupont was saying: "what . . . er, Peter used to call a 'violently Victorian house,' and a poet of the First World War, with an interesting private life. We can see now that Corley Court was as seminal to Peter's work, as it was to be to my own. His two ground-breaking series, *Writers at War,* for Granada, and *The Victorian Dream,* for BBC2, were in a way incubated in that extraordinary place, cut off from the outside world and yet"—here he smiled persuasively at the beauty of his own thought—"bearing witness to it . . . in so many ways."

Rob's eye ran on along the curve of the front row, where the later speakers were smiling at Dupont with polite impatience and anxiety. At the far end Paul Bryant was scribbling on his printed text, like someone at a debate. Peter's father had a grief-stricken but curious look, as though he were still finding out important things about his son. The timing of the event, four months after Peter's death, was surely not easy for him. But something else, both awkward and comic, was now becoming unignorable. Very slowly, Dupont's loud purr, a kind of maximized intimacy filling the high-ceilinged room impartially from the two large speakers on stands, had been dwindling to a sound of more modest reach, clearer at first, as the short masking echo was removed, then quieter altogether, as though a humble functionary were revealed working some splendid machine. He himself seemed to notice that his words weren't coming back at him at quite the optimal volume. "When Peter drove some of us into Oxford in his car," he was saying, "the first thing he took us to see was Keble College chapel . . ."—"Can't! hear!" came a lordly shout from the back, enjoying its own petulance, and others more politely and help-fully joined in. Dupont looked down and found the microphone on its stand had drooped like a flower, and was now pointing at his crotch.

Rob smiled at this, glanced over to the blond man, only to find him sharing a grin with one of the men in leather on the far side of the room. Faintly annoyed, Rob turned in his seat while the mike was sorted out, and gazed up at the shelves closest to him. He thought it must be a sec-tion where books by members were placed. A few famous names stood out, to the pride of the Club; other writers Rob had never heard of must dutifully and determinedly have given copies of everything they pub-lished—now fading, foxing, sunning, untouched surely, for decade after decade. He liked the effect of recession, of work proudly presented and immediately forgotten—hidden in full view, overlooked surely even by those members whose eyes swept over the shelves each day; it was the sort of shadowy terrain the well-armed book-dealer hunted in.

"I could talk about Peter for hours," Dupont was saying, "but now let's have some music." He stepped down from the podium and they listened to Janet Baker singing Mahler's "Ich bin der Welt abhanden gekommen," so loudly that the system flared and crackled, and the young man in charge of the sound abruptly turned her down, and then, seeing the little searching smiles of some of the audience, turned her up again, grinning and tucking his hair behind his ears. Rob got out his fountain-pen and made a few notes of his own on the back of his service card.

Next Nick Powell, who had been at Oxford with Peter, described the journey to Turkey they had made together one summer—reading from a text, though with a more hesitant and personal effect than Dupont had managed while improvising; he didn't say exactly that he'd had an affair with Peter, but the likelihood seemed to fill the vague well-intentioned space between his spoken memories and the listeners' imagining of them. And then again, at first as if cloaked by emotion, the voice grew dry and withdrawn, and the long rising whine of a motorcycle speeding the length of Pall Mall lent a sudden sad sense of the world outside.

There was the chink of workmen's hammers, a faint squeal of brakes. A more sympathetic woman rose in her seat to point out the problem with the mike. And again came the voice from the back, "Can't hear!" as if the speaker's failure to get through to him confirmed the very low opinion of him that he already held.

The feebleness of the mike now became a trying and subtly undermining part of the programme itself. Everyone's patience was stretched by it: the sound-boy, with his inane air of knowing less about sound than anyone present, kept getting up and tightening the wing-nut that held the mike in place, while irritation with him grew and advice was called out. In some barely conscious way it made the audience fed up with the readers and speakers too. Eventually the mike was detached from the stand, and they had to hold it, like a singer or comedian, which led to further problems with ringing feedback or again the slow fade as they lowered it unawares away from their faces. It was difficult to manage, and Sarah Barfoot's hand shook visibly as she held it.

As the others spoke, Rob noted down a few things—that Peter had learned to play the tuba "to an almost bearable standard," that he had built a temple in his parents' garden, but abandoned it halfway through, and called it a sham ruin. This was said to be typical of him. "Peter was an ideal media don," said someone from the BBC, "without actually being a don—or indeed having much technical grasp of the media. The producers he worked with were crucial to the success of the series." At least three people said he'd been "a great communicator," a phrase which in Rob's experience usually meant someone was an egomaniacal bore. Though he hadn't known Peter at all well, Rob was struck by the odd tone of several remarks, the not quite suppressed implication that though Peter was "marvellous," "inspiring" and "howlingly funny," and everyone who knew him adored him, he was really no more than a dabbler, prevented by the very haste and fervour of his enthusiasms from looking at anything in proper scholarly detail. Of course it was a "celebration," so a veil was drawn over these shortcomings, but not so completely that one didn't catch a glimpse of the hand drawing it, the prim display of tact. Then they played ninety seconds of Peter himself on *Private Passions,* talking about Liszt, and his voice, with its rich boozy throb and its restless dry wit, seemed to possess the room and put them all, half-forgivingly, in their place, as if he were alive and watching them from the walls of books, as well as being irrecoverably far away. There was even laughter along the rows, grateful and attentive to the shock of his presence, though Peter was hardly being funny. Rob had never heard the piece before—"Aux cyprès de la Villa d'Este," played at almost painful volume, so that it was hard to judge what Peter had said about it as a "vision of death": that Liszt had rejected the title "Elegy" as too "tender and consoling," and had called it a "Threnody" instead, which he said was a song of mourning for life itself. Rob wrote the two words, with their distinct etymological claims, on the back of his card. Glancing along the front row, he saw Paul Bryant, who was up next, and evidently unsure how long the Liszt was going on, discreetly applying ChapStick, then sitting forward and staring at the floor with a tight but forbearing smile. Then he was up at the lectern, and seized the mike with the look of someone who'd long wanted to have such a thing in his hand.

Rob glanced at Jennifer, her eyes narrowed, revolving her pencil abstractedly between her fingers. Bryant was a good subject, short but ponderous, with a long decisive nose in a flushed, rather sensitive face, frizzly grey hair trained carefully from side to side across his pale crown. He stood just beside the lectern, stroking down his tie with his free hand. He said that, as a literary biographer, he'd been asked to talk about Peter's literary interests, which of course was absurd in a mere seven minutes: Peter deserved a literary biography of his own, and maybe he would write it—anyone with stories to tell should see him afterwards, in strictest confidence, of course. This got a surprisingly warm laugh, though Rob was unsure, after what Jennifer had said, whether he was sending himself up as a teller of other people's secrets.

Bryant made it clear, in the way Nick Powell had sweetly avoided, that Peter had been his lover—Rob glanced at Desmond, who remained impassive; the thirty-year difference in their ages certainly said something about Peter's tenacity and appeal. He said he hadn't had the advantage of a university education, "but in many ways Peter Rowe was my education. Peter was that magic person we all meet, if we're lucky, who shows us how to live our lives, and be ourselves." This stirred vague wonderings about the completely unknown subject of Bryant's private life. "Like . . . Professor Dupont, I too was brought closer to Cecil Valance by Peter. I well remember him showing me the poet's tomb at Corley on our very first date—an unusual sort of first date, but that was Peter for you! He even talked at that time of writing something about Valance, but I think we're all agreed that he would never have had the patience, or the stamina, to write a proper biography—as soon as I started on my own life of Valance he sent me a letter, that was very typical of him, saying that he knew I was the right man for the job." Rob was looking at Jennifer's card as she swiftly and elegantly wrote "NOT!" on it. "When I'd made my way somewhat in the literary world, it was a pleasure to be able to recommend Peter as a reviewer, and he did some marvellous pieces in the *TLS* and elsewhere—though deadlines, I believe, remained a bit of an 'issue' for him . . ."

It was true of course that the lyric of grief was often attended, or followed soon after, by a more prosaic little compulsion, the unseemly grasp of the chance to tell the truth—and since the person involved could no longer mind . . . There was a special tone of indulgent candour, amusing putting-straight of the record, that wandered all too easily and invisibly into settling of scores and something a bit shy of objective fact. "He once more or less admitted to me," Bryant said with a rueful laugh, "that he could hardly play the piano at all, but in front of an audience of prep-school boys he could generally get away with it." (Here Jennifer shook her head and sighed, as if disappointed but unsurprised.) By the time he sat down again, he had said almost nothing about Peter Rowe's life in books, beyond his failure to produce anything but "TV spin-offs." Was it envy? It was fairly clear that they hadn't seen much of each other for the past forty years, so the talk was a wasted opportunity—Rob thought of what he could have said himself about Peter's book collection.

The final speaker was Desmond, who gripped the mike in both hands with a much less humorous look. There were perhaps a dozen people of colour in the room, but Desmond was the only black speaker, and Rob felt the small complex adjustment of sympathy and self-consciousness that passed through the audience; and then an unexpected squeeze of emotion of his own, at the thought of Desmond ten years ago. He was heavier and squarer-faced now, the lovely boyish thing in him was lost, except in his tremor of determination. Rob frowned gently as he remembered the scar on Desmond's back, his almost hairless body and knobbly navel; but he saw that the magic of sexual feeling for him lingered only as a kind of loyal and sentimental sadness. He knew that in the six years he'd been with Peter, Desmond had divided opinion, especially among Peter's old friends: was he a godsend or a frightful bore? Now he had the awkward dignity of the less amusing survivor from a couple, testing the loyalty of those very friends. Perhaps grief itself had subtly unsexed him, just at the moment he would have, in one way or another, to start again.

He spoke clearly, and rather stiffly, with a hint of reproof in his face for all the trivialities that had gone before. The nice square Nigerian diction, with its softened consonants and strong hard vowels, had been slowly effaced by London in the years since Rob had met him at a party and taken him home shivering in a taxi. He said how being Peter's friend had been the greatest privilege of his life, and that being married to him for two years had been not only wonderfully happy but a celebration of everything Peter had believed in and worked for. He had always said how important the changes in the law in 1967 had been to him and to so many others like him, when he was a young man teaching at Corley Court, but that it was very imperfect, only a beginning, there were many more battles to be won, and the coming of civil partnerships for same-sex couples was a great development not just for them but for civil life in general. This was met by a few seconds of firm applause, and flustered but generally supportive looks among those who didn't clap. Rob clapped, and Jennifer, surprised but willing, a moment later clapped too. It was good to see the gay subject, which after all had bubbled through Peter's life more keenly and challengingly than it did in his own, brought home here under the gilded Corinthian capitals of a famous London club. There was a sort of yearning in some of the older faces not to be startled by it. Then Desmond said he was going to read a poem, and drew out a folded sheet of paper from the breast pocket of his pin-stripe suit. "Oh, do not smile on me if at the last / Your lips must yield their beauty to another . . ." Rob didn't think he knew it, and felt the awkwardness of poetry in the mouths of people untrained to read it; then abruptly felt the reverse, the stiff poignancy of words which an actor would have made into a dubious show of technique. "Let yours be the blue eye, the laughing lips / That at the last and always smile on me." Rob gave Jennifer a quizzical glance, she leant towards him and whispered behind her hand, "Uncle Cecil."

Rob escorted Jennifer through the clearing and stacking of the chairs towards the crowd around the buffet table, Jennifer making confidential but fairly loud remarks about some of the speakers while Rob discreetly switched on his phone. "A shame about the sound," she said. "That young man was absolutely hopeless!"

"I know . . ."

"You'd have thought they'd have something as basic as that sorted out." Rob saw he had a text from Gareth. "I thought that Scotsman was awfully boring, didn't you?"

see u 7 @ Style bar—cant wait! XxG

"He was rather . . . ," said Rob—distracted for a moment in the mental blush of disorientation, then pocketing his phone and glancing round. The blond man had attached himself to the group of leather queens. But the idea of picking him up, so simply initiated by a sly shared smile, didn't wholly dissolve under the reminder of his imminent date with someone else.

There were rows and rows of white cups and saucers, for tea and coffee, but Jennifer said, "I'm having a drink," and Rob, who never drank during the day, said, "I'm going to join you." She picked up a glass of red with a quick shiver—and then, seeing platters of sandwiches already reduced to cress-strewn doilies, she pushed in between two other people waiting and built herself a little plateful of sausage rolls and chocolate fingers. She had the look of someone making the most of a day out— Rob thought the arrangements at St. Hilda's College might be fairly spartan; and then a visit to London . . . She held her plate and glass expertly in one hand, and ate swiftly, almost greedily. He wondered what her emotional history had been—not women, he felt. She had a quiver of sexual energy about her, unexpectantly tucked under her crushed velvet hat. They moved away together, each looking round as if prepared to free the other. He felt she liked him, without being interested in him— it was a consciously temporary thing, and none the less happy for that. He said, "Well, you were saying . . . !" and she said, "What?—oh, well, *yes* . . . so, Paul Bryant started out, before he became a great literary figure, as a humble bank-clerk . . ." Rob glanced round—"Oh, actually," he said, and touched her arm. The readers and speakers of course were moving among the crowd, with uncertain status, as mourners and performers. Now Bryant was just beside them, making for the buffet, talking to a large woman and a handsome young Chinese man with glasses and a tie-clip. "Oh, I know!" Bryant was saying, "it's an absolute outrage—the whole thing!" There was something camp and declamatory about him— Rob saw he was still riding the wave of his performance; to himself he was still the focus of attention. "I need a drink!" he said, sounding just like Peter, cutting in behind Jennifer, with a busy but gracious nod, an unguarded blank glance at her, two heavy seconds of possible recognition, a breathless turn, surely, and denial—"Andrea, what are you having?" But Jennifer, curious and fearless, touched his shoulder: "Paul?" she said, and as he twitched and turned, her face was a wonderful hesitant mask of mockery, greeting and reproach. Rob thought she must be the most terrifying teacher.

Bryant stepped back, gripped her forearm, stared as if he were being tricked, while some rushed but extremely complex calculation unfurled behind his eyes. Then, "Jenny, my dear, I don't believe it!"

"Well, here I am."

"Oh, Peter would have been thrilled," shaking his head in wonderment. Was it a fight or a reunion? He craned forward—"I can't believe it!" again; and kissed her.

She laughed, "Oh!," coloured slightly and went on at once, "Well, Peter meant a lot to me, long ago."

"Oh, the dear old tart that he was . . . ," Bryant said, glancing narrowly at Rob, not knowing of course what role he might have played in Peter's life. "No, a great man. Peter Rowe-my-dear, you used to call him, do you remember?"—he was sticking to the fondly proprietary view of the deceased, barbs in an indulgent tone of voice. "Andrea, this is Jenny Ralph—or was—I don't know . . . ?"

"Still is," said Jenny firmly.

"A very old friend. Andrea . . . who was Peter's next-door neighbour, am I right?"

"Rob," said Rob, nodding, not giving them much to go on, though Jennifer endorsed him, in a supportive murmur, "Yes, Rob . . ."

"Rob . . . hello, and this is—where are you?—*come here!*—Bobby"— to the patient Chinese man he'd turned his back on—"my partner."

Rob shook hands with Bobby, and smiled at him through the knowing shimmer of gay introductions, the surprise and speculation. "Civil?" he said.

Bryant said, "Hmm, well, some of the time," and Bobby, with a sweet but tired grin at him, said politely,

"Yes, we're civil partners."

In a minute glasses of wine were raised, Bryant peeping over his a bit cautiously at Jennifer, who said, in her candid way, "Well, I read your book."

"Oh, my dear," he said, with a little shake of the head; then, "Which one?"

"You know—Uncle Cecil . . ."

"Oh, *England Trembles*, yes . . ."

"You caused quite a stir with that one," said Jennifer.

"Tell me about it!" said Bryant. "Oh, the trouble I had with that book." He explained to Andrea, "It's the book I mentioned in my speech just now, if you remember—the life of Cecil Valance. My first book, actually." He turned to Jennifer. "There were times I felt I'd bitten off more than I could chew."

"Yes, I'm sure," said Jennifer.

"Didn't he write 'Two Acres'?" said Andrea. "I had to learn that at school."

"Then you probably still know it," Jennifer assured her.

"Something about the something path of love . . ."

"It was written for my grandmother," said Jennifer.

"Or, as I contend, for your great-uncle!" said Bryant gamely.

"That's amazing." Andrea looked round. "I must introduce you to my husband, he's really the poetry lover."

Bryant chuckled uneasily. "It was your dear grandmother who gave me so much trouble."

"Well, you certainly reciprocated," said Jennifer, so that Rob thought perhaps it was a fight after all.

"Was I awful? I just couldn't get anything out of her."

"That could have been because she wanted to keep it to herself, I suppose."

"Mm, Jenny, I can tell you disapprove."

"Who was this?" said Andrea.

"My grandmother, Daphne Sawle," said Jennifer, as if this needed no further explanation.

"I knew she'd never see it, of course, so . . ."

But Jennifer didn't give ground on this, and Rob, who imagined they were both wrong in different ways, was not in the mood for a row. He said to Bobby, "So did you ever meet Peter?" and drew him aside as he got a second glass of wine. He glanced round, thinking with a touch of relief of the two hundred other people here he could talk to if he wanted. He saw the blond man look over the shoulder of the man he was joking with and give him a frank saucy look, as though he thought Rob had picked Bobby up. Bobby had a wide smile, short shiny black hair, and a strong uncritical belief in his husband's work. He dismissed his own work in IT—"Too boring!" He told Rob they lived out in Streatham, and though Paul often worked in the British Library, Bobby rarely came into Town. They had been together for nine years. "And you?" said Bobby. "Oh, I'm very much single," said Rob, and grinned, and felt Bobby was slightly sorry for him. He looked round and saw that Nigel Dupont was coming through towards the buffet. "That woman is being quite aggressive to Paul!" said Bobby. "Yes, I know . . . ," said Rob. In fact Bryant himself had half-turned away from Jennifer.

"About my present project? I can't tell you," he was confessing to a woman in a black suit. "Oh, yes, another Life. Still rather hush-hush—I'm sure you'll understand!—ah, Nigel . . ."—with a clever little air of deflation.

"Hello, Paul!" said Dupont, warily genial, and rather oddly too, since they'd just been sharing a podium.

"Oh, I loved what you said," said the woman. "Very moving."

"Thanks . . . ," said Dupont. "Thanks so much."

"Do you know Jenny Ralph?" said Bryant.

"Ah! nice to see you," said Dupont warmly, allowing the possibility they had met before.

"Bobby you've met, and . . ."

"Rob Salter."

"Rob . . . hi!"—shaking his hand gratefully, and holding his eye.

Rob smiled back. "Interesting to hear about your school—and the Valance connection."

"That's right . . . Old times . . ."

"So here we have his editor—"

". . . in the red corner . . . !" said Bryant—

"hah—and his biographer!"

"That's right . . . ," said Dupont again.

"No, we're old friends," said Bryant, curving against him, as if he'd just been kidding. "It worked out quite well, didn't it. We were both digging away like mad, from quite different angles." He tilted his head from side to side. "I'd get one thing, old Nigel would get another."

"It worked out fine," said Dupont, in a tone that showed he had a forgiving nature and it had all been a long time ago. From here the Valance work seemed a distant prolegomenon to far more sensational achievements.

"Of course I put you on to the Trickett MS," said Bryant, wagging his finger.

"That's right . . . If only you'd been able to track down the lost poems as well . . . ," said Dupont, with a playful shake of the head.

"Oh, they're gone, don't you think? I'm sure Louisa burnt them—if they ever existed!"

"What was the Trickett thing?" said Rob, piqued by the talk of manuscripts and lost poems.

Dupont, whom Rob now found, with the sudden surrender of a prejudice, completely charming, even sexy, paused on the brink of a shift into academic talk—"Oh, it was an unpublished part of one of the poems, which turned out to be a sort of queer manifesto, except in tetrameter couplets . . ."

"Really?"

"Written in 1913, quite interesting . . ."

"You know, I had to take issue with one thing you said," said Bryant.

"Oh, lord," said Dupont, with a comical cringe.

"Just now, I mean, when you said dear old Pete's famous Imp was pea-green."

"Yes"—Dupont looked nonplussed.

"I could swear it was sort of beige." Bryant grinned and narrowed his eyes.

"I don't think so," said Dupont. "I went in that car a lot. In fact I even washed it once, before a group of us went to Windsor Castle in it, just in case we saw the Queen."

"Well, I won't tell you what I did in it!" said Bryant with a gasp—"no, but I'm sure you're wrong."

"Maybe you're colour-blind," said the woman in black.

"Not at all," said Bryant. "Anyway, it doesn't matter!"

"It sometimes looked beige with dirt, I suppose," Dupont said in a cleverly bemused tone.

Jennifer said, "I'm very much of Professor Dupont's view."

Rob thought it rather comical that these two who'd tussled over Cecil Valance were doing it again over Peter Rowe. He saw that Bryant, a moderately successful writer, after all, and in his mid-sixties, had a look of exasperation, as though never given the credit due to him, and almost provokingly determined to get it. Rob thought he might get hold of *England Trembles,* and judge for himself.

Half an hour later, after three drinks, and a trip downstairs to the marble and mahogany loo, where Peter's father emerged from a cubicle and engaged him in earnest talk by the basins while a dozen tipsy guests darted or staggered in and out, he accompanied the old man up the grand stairs and thought about saying his goodbyes and going. The huge brass chandeliers had been switched on, and the room was thinning. It seemed the blond man had already left, and at this Rob felt almost relieved. And really this wasn't the moment . . . and with the eager young Gareth to see in an hour, at the Style Bar . . . He looked round for Desmond, whom he had, not quite purposely, been avoiding.

He saw him talking to an elderly couple, with a resolute air of courtesy which Rob found lightly chastening as he slid towards him. He gave him the warm little smile of a prior claim, over their two grey heads. Desmond caught his eye but carried on talking, "Well, we'll speak to Anne about it—that should work out well," still standing stiffly, so that Rob, in momentary confusion, merely gave him a hug, sideways on; and was then introduced to Mr. and Mrs. Sorley.

"Did you know Peter well?" asked Mrs. Sorley, small and sweet-faced, a bit thrown perhaps by a glass of wine in the afternoon, and the crowded occasion. They were Yorkshire, it seemed lived there still.

"Not well," said Rob, "I sold him a lot of expensive books."

"Oh . . . oh, I see! No, we're old friends of Terry and Rose—well, Bill was in the army with Terry, and of course I knew Rose in the Wrens—all those years ago!"—a guileless promptness of exposure. Rob said,

"So you knew Peter all his life," and smiled back.

"Oh yes," she said, with a conscientious little shake of the head. "I was just saying to Desmond, how Petie used to put on plays when he was quite small—him and his sister played all the parts. Proper grown-up plays, you know—*Julius Caesar.*"

"I can just imagine!" Rob thought they could hardly have expected then to have been up in London half a century later, at Peter's own memorial, talking to his male partner. He wanted to commiserate with them and also in a way to congratulate them.

"Well, I must have a word with Sir Edward," said Desmond, with a dutiful smile.

"Well, well done today," said Rob, mournful, head on one side.

"Yeah, thanks, Rob. We'll be in touch—we've got your e-mail, I think"—so was there a new man on the scene already? Or was the "we" a mere habit, the way he thought of his and Peter's home? With a kiss for Mrs. Sorley, though not for Rob, he went off across the room, amid sympathetic smiles and blank but lingering glances.

Rob spoke a bit longer to the Sorleys, feeling stung by Desmond's coldness, and of course completely unable to protest or explain. It was true he hadn't been to the funeral, hadn't been in touch with Desmond at all since 1995. He meant nothing to Desmond. And it occurred to him, as he gazed a little distractedly over Bill Sorley's shoulder, that perhaps Desmond thought Rob had only come today out of some idea he had of making an offer for Peter's library—which was, in truth, at the back of his mind. Though there was more to it than that, much more.

He could see the Sorleys rather sticking to him, now they'd got him, among all these strangers and alarming if sometimes unnameable celebrities. Paul Bryant and Bobby were leaving, Bobby turning and giving Rob a finger wave. They went out through the double doors, arm in arm for a moment, so that he felt abashed by their evident contentment and self-sufficiency. "That's very funny," he said to Bill Sorley, "yes . . .": they seemed happy to do most of the talking. He spotted Jennifer, by the white marble fireplace, talking to a man he'd seen arrive about half an hour ago, as if unavoidably detained or really as if appointments of any kind were beyond him. He had a soft, intelligent but very nervous face, and thick shoulder-length grey hair, unwashed and unmanageable, which he ran his hands through incessantly as he spoke. His suit was old and shiny and scuffed at the heels, and Rob imagined he might have had some difficulty getting past the porter downstairs. He couldn't tell from Jennifer's expression, which seemed to hover between grief and hilarity, if she needed rescuing. He smiled and slumped regretfully—"Well, I think I really have to go . . ."

As he approached her, she looked up and nodded at him, as if they were partners themselves, or at least had some useful and chivalrous agreement for the occasion. The man half turned—"Well, it was marvellous to see you, darling," a cultured voice, terrible teeth, a flinching smile, the look of being fed up with being a nuisance to people.

"And you!" said Jennifer, warm in the moment of escape; but perhaps here there was more to it too. "Shall we?" she said to Rob. And then, "This is Julian Keeping."

"Hello." Rob smiled keenly at him, leant in and shook his hand, which had a bony grip.

Keeping flapped his other hand, as if to say he wouldn't bother them further. "An old friend of Peter's, from way back," he said, shaking his head. "Too long ago!" He had a sad smell to him—Rob didn't think it was drink, that sweet and sour choke to the nose; but smoke certainly, his finger ends and nails were tanned; and beyond that perhaps just long and compounded neglect. Rob nodded to him again, and then followed Jennifer to the door.

"Are you getting a taxi?" she said, at the top of the stairs, and Rob saw, which he hadn't a minute before, that she was pretty drunk. She went down with high-stepping wariness, smiling faintly, preoccupied perhaps by thoughts of this unfortunate man. Rob was bright and speedy with drink himself, laughing half-guiltily at the echo of his own voice off the marble stairwell. "Believe it or not," she said, "that was my first sweetheart."

"Really," said Rob. "Well . . ." He glanced at her, still unsure of her feelings, or what she would let him see of them.

"He couldn't be said to have worn well."

"Um, no . . ."

"Corinna's son, in fact," she said.

"Oh, really?" Rob looked narrowly at her. "So, your cousin, and, let me get this right, Cecil Valance's grandson!"

"Well, if you believe all that," she said; she shook her head and laughed, "Oh god!"

They went to their separate cloakrooms, and then he waited for her under the columns of the hall—the lights on now and a glimpse through the glass doors of evening already in possession of the street outside. She came back out with a humorous smile of accepted courtesy, a little flushed, but clearly, even determinedly, refocused on the present. Her coat was long, dark, made of some softly crinkling and glowing material, shyly extravagant, and again with an air of being a fashion all of her own. "So funny seeing Paul Bryant," she said, as they went through into the lobby, her tone again very dry.

"Oh, yes," said Rob, glad she hadn't forgotten her promise.

"I probably shouldn't say this . . ."

"Oh, surely?"—catching her mischievous look under the flowered hat, and giddily aware of the contrasting sobriety of the porter, in his striped trousers. Jennifer glanced over her shoulder. "He was always somewhat of a fantasist, you see. He told the most pitiful stories about his father, being a fighter pilot, shot down at the end of the war— somewhere or other."

"You don't remember?"

"No, *he* was the one who didn't remember. The story kept changing. My aunt and I picked up on it, she thought it was odd, she had a terrifying eye for any kind of nonsense."

"This is Corinna, you mean?"

"Yes . . . Anyway, of course, the point was he never had a father, he was a bastard," she said in her candid old-fashioned way. "His mother had been in a factory in the war, and got pregnant by someone there. There was some story about her being ill, as well, I can't quite recall. That may have been true, of course, but one started to treat anything he said with a degree of suspicion."

Rob glanced again at the porter, whose stare seemed simultaneously offended and indifferent. He himself didn't see this as quite such a point against Bryant as Jennifer seemed to—in fact it made him if anything more intriguing and sympathetic. "So you said he used to be a bank-clerk?" (He had the examples of T. S. Eliot and P. G. Wodehouse at the ready.)

"Used, yes, in my uncle's bank. No, the rather awful thing was, my uncle had to fire him: I believe he was jolly lucky it didn't go to court." They went out and down the steps into the waiting chill of Pall Mall, car headlights, briefly stalled, advancing on them with the bright impersonal rush of the London night. "Some sort of fiddle. He was quite clever—he is clever, Paul Bryant, in his odd way—and I think it was difficult to prove, but Uncle Leslie had no doubt about it, and Paul himself some-how wasn't surprised, from what I gathered, to be thrown out of the bank. I was doing my doctorate then, and he sent me a card, right out of the blue, to say he was leaving the world of banking to pursue a career as a writer."

Rob said, vaguely humorously, looking around, "To spend more time with his family."

"Well, to spend more time with *my* family, as it turned out," said Jennifer.

"And the rest is biography," said Rob with a wise grin, as the cab he had waved at came to a halt and he opened the door for her.

2

WHAT ROB THOUGHT of as Raymond's was properly Chadwick's, Antiques and Second-Hand, though it had started out, a century ago, as the best dress-shop in Harrow. In the floor of the set-back doorway the words "MADAME CLAIRE" could still be read in the dulled mosaic, circling the barely legible "MODES." Now the two broad display win-dows, where headless Edwardian mannequins had once been stationed (hats shown on separate stands, like cakes), were barricaded with old fur-niture, the rough deal backs of wardrobes, tables stacked on tables, among which an individual item, a plaster bust of Beethoven or a real glass cake-stand, was sometimes artlessly exhibited to the public. Rob had never set eyes on Hector Chadwick himself—it was always Ray-mond he saw, if he was in the area, or if Raymond let him know he had something for him. The old Harrow houses yielded treasures, now and then, among the van-loads of almost unsaleable books that found their way into the shop and then on, into junk shops and musty charity stores all over North London.

Rob shoved open the door, and a leisurely bell rang, and then rang again, in a part of the shop that was out of view. The showroom, as Raymond called it, was partitioned by ramparts of furniture into gloomy alleys, and it was hard to tell if there was anyone else in it. Not much natural light got through, and lamps that were notionally for sale glowed here and there on desks and sideboards. The feeling of secrecy and safety was shadowed by a childish sense of unease. At the back was a wall of books Rob had sometimes looked over, torn wrappers, dun-coloured cloth, obscure possibilities, the wary flicker of excitement snuffed out, as often as not, in the odour of dust and disuse. The smell of the books was like a drug, a promise of pleasure shot through with a kind of foreknown regret. In dreams he clambered or floated up bookshelves like these, where indefinably significant copies of editions that never existed hid among themselves in shy dull colours, old greens and ochres and faded yellows. Undeveloped prototypes for books, the novel by Woolf of which only one copy was printed, the unknown Compton-Burnett with its ever-mutating title, *Helpers and Hinderers, A House and Its Horse, Friend and Fraud.* He worked his way round—"Raymond?"

"Hey, Rob?" There was the clatter of his keyboard. "With you in a sec." Raymond and his computer lived together in intense co-dependency, as if they shared a brain, his arcane undiscriminating memory backed up on the machine and perpetually enlarged by it. Raymond himself was vast, in a cheerfully challenging way. What his life was like beyond the confines of the shop Rob had no idea. "Just uploaded a new thing for you."

"Oh yeah . . . ?"

"You're going to like this one."

"Mm, I wonder."

At the side of the shop, a chaotic cubicle made a kind of office. Rob grinned in over the heaped papers and coiling dusty cables at Raymond's round face gleaming in the light from the screen; he bounced slightly on his office chair as he nodded. His reddish beard, grown long and wild like a martyr's, spread out over his T-shirt, half-covering the slogan for his website, "Poets Alive! Houndvoice.com," above an implausibly cheerful picture of W. B. Yeats. He looked up and nodded. "I've just done Tennyson—want to see?"

On Houndvoice Raymond posted eerie little videos of long-dead poets reading, authentic sound recordings emerging from the mouths of digitally animated photographs. It was clear from the Comments that some viewers thought they were really seeing Alfred Noyes read "The Highwayman," while even those who weren't taken in were apparently impressed by the fish-like gaping of the poet's lips and the rhythmical flicker of his eyebrows.

"Yeah, I guess . . . ," said Rob, coming round as Raymond pushed back his chair. "They're a bit spooky, aren't they."

"Yeah?" said Raymond, clearly pleased. "Yeah, I suppose people might be a bit spooked by them."

Rob didn't think the films were remotely convincing, but in a way this made them more disturbing. The dummy-like dropping of the jaw, the cheesy melting and setting of the features, were like the evidence of other impostures—the doctored photos of early séances, more creepy and depressing to Rob than the thought of real communication with the dead. Rob met up with his dead friends in witty and poignant dreams, where they didn't look at all like these bundles of mouthing matter. "Here we go," said Raymond, maximizing the player and whacking up the volume. Lord Tennyson's notable head and shoulders filled the screen—hollow-cheeked, high-domed, hair tangled and greasy, the straggly dark beard with a lot of grey in it. The beard, at least, was a blessing, as it completely covered the poet's mouth, preventing any ghoulish working of the lips. Raymond clicked the Play button and against a rainstorm of hissing and the galloping thump of the cylinder the determined quavering voice of the great poet began its familiar rush through "Come Into the Garden, Maud." Rob had always thought the recording uncanny in itself—the effect whenever he'd heard it before was comic and touching and awe-inspiring by turns. He saw Raymond was watching him watch the video, and he smiled thinly, as if only just reserving judgement. The bard's beard quivered like a beast in a hedge, as the famous face made repetitive mincing and chewing movements. Rob felt the peculiar look in the older Tennyson's eyes, the air of almost belligerent anxiety, appealing to him critically and directly through the shame that was being inflicted on his lower features. Then it came to its abrupt end, and Raymond's copyright line—not in the recording or the image, but in the puppet-show he'd made with them—appeared across Tennyson's frozen face.

"Almost incredible," Rob said, "listening to a man read a poem he wrote a hundred and fifty years ago."

"Ah—yes," said Raymond, seeing this rather skirted the issue.

Rob stood back. "I suppose that's the earliest you can go, isn't it," with a quick grasp for reassurance. "That must be the earliest recording of a poet."

"Well, strictly speaking," said Raymond, "though of course you can fake the voices, if you want to," peeping at Rob with that strange look, in a middle-aged man, of a teenager trying his luck.

"Oh, for god's sake," said Rob.

"No, a bit naff, perhaps." Raymond shielded his feelings with a genial-sounding change of subject. "So what can I do for you, Rob?"

Rob narrowed his eyes. "You said you might have something for me . . ."

"Oh, yes . . . Yes, indeed." Raymond swivelled his chair and peered bemusedly around the office—a moment's teasing to cover his excitement. He raked his beard as his eyes ran over the shelves. "I thought, this is quite up Rob's street . . . if I can only find it. Oh, I know, I put it in my naughty drawer"—and leaning forward over himself, Raymond tugged open the bottom drawer of a filing-cabinet. The naughty drawer was where he kept things he didn't want the Harrow schoolboys to find, in their occasional lingering searches in the more hidden parts of the shop. Sometimes a house clearance turned up a stash of girlie mags or even muscle mags, which by now were antique collectibles in themselves. Raymond was the mere dealer—to Rob's eye he seemed to survey an old *Penthouse* and an issue of *Physique Pictorial* with the same gruff detachment. Now he brought out a red leather-bound book, a thickish quarto, at a glance a journal or manuscript book, with a rounded spine to enable it to open flat. He swivelled back, weighing the book in both hands, as if he shouldn't let it go without certain warnings and preconditions. "What do you know about someone called Harry Hewitt?"

"Nothing whatever." Rob saw that the book had a clasp, a lockable diary, perhaps; on the front, under Raymond's thumb, an embossed gold *H*.

"No . . ." Raymond nodded. "Quite an interesting character. Died in the sixties. Businessman, art collector—left some stuff to the V and A?" Rob shook his head obligingly. "Lived up the road—Harrow Weald. Big house called Mattocks, sort of Arts and Crafts. Never married," said Raymond reasonably.

"I get the picture."

"Lived with his sister, who died in the mid-seventies. After which

Mattocks became an old people's home. Closed down a few years ago—place boarded up, kids got in, a bit of vandalism, not too bad. Now about to be demolished."

"I assume Hector's been over it . . . ?"

"There wasn't much left."

"No, well, those old folks . . ."

Raymond grunted. "Thieves got the best stained-glass windows. Hector salvaged a fireplace or two. But there was a strong-room no one had got into, which didn't hold Hector back for long. Nothing valuable in it, apparently, just papers and stuff from Hewitt's days."

"Including what you have in your hand."

Raymond passed it over—and as he did so the hinged brass bar of the lock dropped open. "We had to cut it, I'm afraid."

"Oh . . ." It seemed to Rob a bit rum that a man who could unlock a strong-room had to take a hacksaw to a book. A handsome book, too, the inner border of the binding tooled in gold, thick gold on the page-edges, the endpapers with gold-seamed crimson marbling, bound by Webster's, "By Appointment to Queen Alexandra." Rob winced at the violation, quite apart from the damage to the price. Inside perhaps a hundred pages densely written over in greyish blue-black ink, a sheet of mauve blotting-paper half-way through marking where the writing stopped.

"Have a look at it," said Raymond. "Cup of tea?"

And so he settled Rob down, after jarring shunting of a large wardrobe, in a tiny improvised sitting-room, made out of a chaise-longue, a bedside cupboard and a standard-lamp. The tea was served in a bone-china cup and saucer. Beyond the wardrobe, he could hear Raymond back at his computer, moments of music and talk.

At first, Rob wasn't sure what he was reading. "December 27, 1911—My dear Harry—I can never thank you enough for the Gramophone, or 'Sheraton Upright Grand' to give it its official title! It is the most splendid gift anyone ever had, Harry old boy. You should have seen my sister's face when the lid was first opened—it was a Study, Harry. My mother says it is quite unearthly to have Mr. McCormack singing his heart out in her own humble Drawing room! You must come and hear him yourself soon Harry. Mere Thanks are inadequate Harry old boy—Best love from Yours ever Hubert." The handwriting was small, vigorous and compacted. Under a ruled line another letter began immediately: "January 11, 1912—My dear old Harry—A Thousand thanks for the Books.

The binding alone is most handsome and Sheridan one of the best writers I am sure. My mother says we must read the plays out Harry she is keen for you to take a Part! Daphne is all set to dress up too! You know I am not much of an actor Harry old boy. We will see you tomorrow at 7:30. Really you are too kind to us all. Tons of love from yours Hubert."

So, a letter-book, copies kept by the grateful "Hubert"? It seemed a bit unlikely he would show such pride in them. In which case, letters transcribed by their recipient, also "H" of course, to immortalize them, if that was the word? So many of them were thank-you letters that it seemed little more than a vanity project. He had an image of this wealthy old queen in effect writing thank-you letters to himself (" 'My dear Harry,' wrote Harry"). Rob skimmed on, with lowish expectations, eye out for proper nouns . . . Harrow, Mattocks, Stanmore, the whole thing parochial in the extreme, and then Hamburg, "when you get back from Germany, Harry"—well, we knew Harry was a businessman. Rob sipped frowningly at his tea. It was slightly chilly in the shop. "You will not find me much use at bridge, Harry, Old maid is about my level!"

Jumping ahead, Rob started to see there was something else going on, a kind of shadow side to the glow of gratitude. June 4, 1913—"My dear old Harry, I am very sorry but you know by now I am not the demonstrative type, it is not in my nature Harry." September 14, 1913—"Harry, you must not think me ungrateful, no one ever had a better friend, however I'm afraid I do rather shun, and Dislike, displays of physical affection between men. It is not in my way Harry." In fact—of course—the two strands often came together, *thanks* and *no thanks*. Perhaps the book of vanity was also a covert record of mortification—or success: Rob didn't know how it was going to end. He tried to picture the displays of physical affection—what were they? More than hugs, kisses, perhaps, begun with tense negligence, then growing more insistent and difficult. And meanwhile the presents escalated. May 1913, "The gun arrived this morning—it's an absolute ripper, Harry old boy"; October 1913, "Harry, I can't thank you enough for the truly splendid wardrobe. My poor old suits look quite shabby in their new home!"—and a quaint reflection, "Creature comforts in life do matter Harry, whatever the Divines may say!" Then January 1914, "My dear old Harry, the little car is a joy—I went out with Daphne for a spin in her—we did 48mph several times! She says a Straker is the best car in the world, and I am bound to agree. Only a large Wolseley overhauled us." Was there a certain hardening, the half-hidden note of covetousness, poor puzzled Hubert very slightly corrupted by all this generosity? Perhaps Harry would give him a Wolseley next. To an ardent gay man the recurrent *old*s that tolled through the letters—"My dear old Harry," "Harry old boy"—however cheerfully meant, might have palled after a bit: "I cannot believe you are 37 tomorrow, Harry old boy!" in November 1912. Well, it was a curiosity—clever of Raymond to see that, and worth paying a bit for. One of Garsaint's customers would probably go for it, the collectors of Gay Lives, which Rob had made a speciality of. And then of course the date.

He leafed forward, something resistant in the dense exclamatory crawl of the writing, the words themselves. There was very little after the end of 1914—a few short letters from France, it seemed: BEF Rouen, more whole-hearted letters now they were apart, perhaps, and the whole perspective had changed. Then a letter of April 5, 1917: "My dear old Harry—A quick letter as we are moving shortly but don't know where. They don't give us much notice as a rule. A glorious day, which makes life feel much more worth living. We had our Easter service today, as we shall probably be moved by then, and I stayed to Communion afterwards. You will keep an eye on Hazel won't you Harry old boy—she is a dear sweet girl—and on Mother and Daphne too. Goodnight Harry and best love from Hubert." After which Harry had written, "My last letter from my darling boy: FINIS." But underneath, in a ruled ink box, there was a little memorial:

> HUBERT OWEN SAWLE
> 1st Lieut "The Blues"
> Born Stanmore, Mddx, January 15, 1891
> Killed at Ivry April 8, 1917
> Aged Twenty-six

At the counter Raymond raked his beard. "Ah, Rob—any interest?"

"This Hubert Sawle—any relation of G. F. Sawle and Madeleine Sawle?"

"Very good, Rob . . . yes . . . Hubert was G. F.'s brother."

"Totally unheard-of."

"Till now . . ."—Raymond nodded at the book.

"And Daphne Sawle was the sister. You see, I met this woman last week who was Daphne Sawle's grand-daughter."

"Right . . ."

"I got a bit lost in her story, about the biography of Cecil Valance, you know. She said her grandmother had written her memoirs. I meant to chase it up."

"I don't know," said Raymond; and as this was something he didn't like saying, he got to work.

"Of course the house in 'Two Acres' was round here, wasn't it?"

"Stanmore, yep."

"Anything there?"

Raymond peered, scrolled down and up, tongue on lip. "Demolished five or six years ago—well, it was a ruin already. No, Rob, there's no one called Sawle except G. F. and Madeleine, who I happen to know was his wife."

"Are you on Abe?"

"G. F. edited Valance's letters, of course."

"That's right," said Rob, again with the private glow of perceived connections, the protective feeling for his quarry that came up in any extended search. "I've an idea Daphne wrote under the name Jacobs."

"Oh yes . . ." Raymond's large hands made their darting wobble above the keyboard.

"She's totally forgotten now, but she published this book of memoirs about thirty years ago—she was married to Dudley Valance, then to an artist called Revel Ralph."

"Right . . . here we are . . . Daphne Jacobs: *Assyrian Woodwind Instruments*—that the one?"

"Um . . ."

"*Bronze Ornaments of Ancient Mesopotamia.*"

"I don't think she goes back quite that far."

"*Corpus Mesopotamianum . . .*"—that slowed him up for a second. "There's loads of this stuff."

"I think her book's called *The Short Gallery.*"

"*O*-kay—here we go—*The Short Gallery: Portraits from Life.* Aha, seven copies . . . Plymbridge Press, 1979, 212 pp . . . First Edition, £1. There you are!"

Rob came round and looked over Raymond's shoulder. "Scroll down a bit." There were the usual anomalies—fine copy in fine dj, £2.50; ex-library, with no dj, damp-staining to rear boards, some light underlining, £18, with an excitable sales pitch, "Contains candid portraits of leading writers and artists A Huxley, Mary Gibbons, Lord Berners, Revd Ralph &c sensational account of teenage affair with WW1 Poet Dudley Valance."

"Wrong!" said Raymond. "Right?"

"Love 'Revd Ralph,' " said Rob. "Now that's amusing. 'Inscribed by the author "To Paul Bryant, April 18, 1980." ' " With it was the sixteen-page catalogue, which Garsaint sometimes had, for the Revel Ralph "Scenes and Portraits" exhibition at the Michael Parkin Gallery in 1984, with a posthumous foreword by Daphne Jacobs—reassuringly un-signed: £25.

The final copy, from Delirium Books in LA, floated aloft in a book-man's empyrean of its own: "Sir Dudley Valance's copy, with his book-plate designed by St. John Hall, inscribed and signed by the author 'To Dudley from Duffel,' with numerous comments and corrections in pen-cil and ink by Dudley Valance. Book condition: fair. Dust-jacket, losses to head of spine, 1cm repaired tear to rear panel. In protective red morocco slipcase. An exceptional association copy. $1,500."

"Take your pick," said Raymond.

"Mm, I will," said Rob. Jennifer Ralph's description of the book as "rather feeble" tugged against his more indulgent curiosity. Of course she would have known some of the figures whose portraits appeared in it, which made a difference. "And how much do you want for Hewitt?"

"Hundred?"

Rob raised an eyebrow. "Raymond?"

"You saw the Valance letters?"

"I'm sorry . . . ?" Rob raised an eyebrow too, coloured slightly.

"Oh, yes." And taking the book back from him, Raymond showed him that a few blank pages further on from the mid-volume FINIS there was another small section of transcribed letters, very different in tone. "That's really the interest, Robson, my friend."

"Dear Hewitt," the first one began, in September 1913; modulating to "Dear Harry" in the third letter, sent from France. Five letters in total, the last dated June 27, 1916, signed, "Yours ever, Cecil."

"Have these been published, I wonder?"

"You'd have to check."

"I bet they haven't." Rob looked over them as quickly as the writing allowed. The idea that Valance might have had a thing with Hewitt too . . . No sign of it, which was itself somehow suggestive. "And why did the old fool transcribe them—I mean, what did he do with the originals?"

"Ah, you see, he failed to think of the needs of a twenty-first-century bookseller—quite a common failing of the past."

"Thanks for that." Rob looked at the last letter more narrowly.

It was bad luck you couldn't get to up to Stokes's—you would like him, I think. It occurred to me to send you the new poems before we get stuck in to the next big show—I will send them tomorrow, all being well, when I have gone over them once more. They are for your eyes only—you will see they are not publishable in my life-time—or England's! Stokes has seen some (not all). One of them draws, you will see, on our last meeting. Let me know you have them safe. My love (is that too fresh?) to Elspeth the strict scholar.

Yours ever, Cecil.

"So the house has been completely cleared, has it?"

"They're getting out the last stuff this week."

"Mm, what sort of stuff?" Rob thought he saw the colour creep up behind Raymond's beard as he turned away and rummaged on the desk—a distraction, though at first Rob thought it was a search for some further evidence.

"I haven't been down there myself. I think Debbie's there now."

"Well, why didn't you say so before?"—to Rob the slow afternoon, the mild trance of autumn in North London, the musty otherworld of Chadwick's shop, were revealed as a decoy, a disastrous waste of time, like the stifling obstacles and digressions of a certain kind of dream. "How far is it to the house?"

"Well, how are you going?"

There was a taxi-rank down the road towards the school, as if ready to whisk the boys off to their homes, or the shops, or the airport . . . Rob ran down to the first car, but there was no driver: he was over the road, at the café, picking up a tea and a sandwich, and it was more than the driver of the second cab's life was worth to take his fare . . . the cabbies' tedious etiquette. Rob sensed there was something offputting in his own urgency, a hint of unwelcome trouble—he went grinning impatiently to the café, and after a minute the driver followed him out to the taxi. "It's a house called Mattocks—was an old people's home. Do you know it?"

"Well, I did know it," said the cabbie, slow in the pleasure of his own irony. "There's not much going on down there now."

"No, I know."

"They'll have the wreckers' balls down there, any day now." And he looked at Rob in the mirror as he slid into his seat, doubtless toying with some dismal joke.

"Let's see if we can get there first," said Rob. He leant coaxingly forward and saw his own eyes and nose in the mirror, in surreal isolation.

They turned and headed out north again, up through the most densely congested junctions of Harrow-on-the-Hill, the driver's courtesy extending to any number of undecided road-crossers, reversing delivery-vans and anxious would-be joiners from side-roads; he was a great letter-in. Then in the leafy residential streets and avenues of the Weald his vaguely smiling dawdle on the brink of third gear suggested almost that he didn't know where he was going. He started joking about something Rob seemed to have missed, Rob said "Sorry?" and then saw he was talking on his phone, deploring something with a friend, laughing, the loud unguarded half of a conversation in which Rob's needs seemed to shrink even further, the mere transient ticking of the fare. Above the pavements the tall horse-chestnuts were dropping their leaves, the oaks just beginning to rust and wither. So many of the big old houses had come down, their long gardens built over. There was a low wall with a sloped coping, the railings gone, a broken and leaning board fence behind. "Just a minute, Andy," said the driver, and set Rob down with a pleasant nod as he gave the change, a faint retroactive suggestion they'd had a nice time together.

Rob picked his way past the black puddles in the ruts of the drive. The house was set fifty yards back from the road, though its privacy had long been surrendered—on either side new developments looked in over the boundary walls. It was one of those big red-brick villas, of the 1880s perhaps, with gables and a turret, a lot of timber and tile-hanging, and very high ground-floor rooms that would take a fortune to furnish and heat, and so easily (Rob had seen them all over London) turned bleak and barely habitable in their latter-day lives. Now there were holes in the steep slate roof, small bushes seeded in the gutters, stripes of moss and slime down the walls. A JCB was backed up under the trees, and beside it a blue Focus presumably belonging to Debbie.

The front door was boarded up, and Rob made his way round to the side. There was a smell of smoke, cutting and toxic, not the good autumn-leaf smell. The ground sloped down, so that the broken veranda along the side of the house rose up to shoulder height. Then there was the round turret, and then a high brick wall with a door on to a tiny yard, the service entrance, the door here wide open—Rob slipped into the house through a dark scullery with huge tin sinks, a dim kitchen with a gas range, broken chairs, nothing worth salvaging. The floor was gritty underfoot, and there was a penetrating smell of raw damp—then he pushed open a fire-door into what must have been the dining-room and there was the smell of smoke again. He saw the awful wiring and boxing-in—the old house had been too disfigured thirty years before for any real sense of marvelment or discovery. He wrote it off. Into the hall—fire-doors again concealing the stairs, but light through double doors on to a room on the garden side of the house. He heard a child's voice, the carefree note with its little edge of determination.

"Are you Debbie?" Out on the lawn, a shrubby tangle trampled back, a red-faced woman in jeans and a T-shirt was picking up items around the smouldering bonfire and throwing them on top—some old magazines caught, doubtfully, a moment of flame curling outwards as they slithered back down.

"Don't get too close, now"—a boy of six or seven, red-faced too in his small anorak, bringing random things forward: a cardboard box, a handful of grass and twigs that fell back over his feet as he tossed it.

Debbie didn't know who Rob was: he saw the curbing of curiosity, her provisional stance of responsibility for what was going on. "Raymond sent me down, I'm Rob."

"Oh, yes, right," said Debbie. "I was just about to call him, we're nearly done."

Rob looked into the fire, which seemed dense and half-digested, colour still showing in old floor-mats, were they?—that the fire had given up on, pink edges of a blackened curtain. "How long's it been burning?"

"What was it, Jack, day before yesterday?"

But the boy ran off at this to find something else to burn. Rob disguised his anxiety, picked up a stick and flipped some loose bits of wood back into the pyre. He had the almost absurd idea that other items might still be lying unconsumed at the bottom of it all; he saw them raking it out with a sense of excitement and purpose greater than that of the burning—already it seemed a story. "Raymond said you'd cleared the strong-room?"

Debbie had a wary eye out for the child. "Yes, that can go on, my love." Though little Jack had his own caprices and changes of mind.

"I'm saving this one, Mummy."

"Well, all right . . . ," Debbie said, with a glance at Rob, the mime of patience. "Sorry . . . yes"—he saw she was neither for him nor against him. "We got all that out on Monday—it was just old papers, account books." She snubbed her nose as she nodded. "Rubbish, no use to anyone."

Rob looked round at the house rearing behind them, the curved flight of broken stone steps he had come down into the garden; and down which Harry Hewitt must have come a thousand times, and his beloved Hubert, now and then perhaps, before the Great War, having motored over in the Straker with his sister Daphne for protection.

"Mind if I have a look round?"

"Help yourself. Electric's off, though—you won't see much." She told him where the strong-room was, beyond the TV room, was it?—well, all the functions were muddled up. He wondered if he really wanted to go in.

"Mum? Mum?" Jack holding a wicker basket aloft in both hands.

"No, that can go on—god, it's Victorian, some of this stuff!"—with a first look of humorous collusion with Rob. Jack had his own pile of salvage, items he was pointedly saving from the flames, and another pile of things to be gleefully thrown on. Sometimes an item was moved from one pile to the other with the proper arbitrariness of fate.

Back through the french doors into the sitting-room—with a shadowy hole in the wall: a fireplace Hector had rescued, perhaps. Through the door on the left into the TV room, lit up as if underwater by a small bramble-covered window; and beyond this a short passage, almost dark, with a white-painted door on the right standing open to reveal the black steel door of the strong-room immediately behind it, also just ajar. Rob's curiosity was as much about the secret room as its contents, when he gripped the handle. He supposed a collector needed such a place; perhaps Hewitt was a hoarder who took more pleasure in possession than display. Well, it had kept one secret pretty closely, for ninety years. He wondered when he'd copied the letters out—as they arrived, or when he was grieving, or much later, in a painful search for lost feelings? With a wary murmur Rob slid his foot forward over the threshold, breathed the smell, unlike the rest of the place, dry wood. Then he thought of his phone, snapped it open and shone its faint spy's light in front of him. The space was only an arm's reach deep, slatted wooden shelves on three sides, like an airing-cupboard. A stone floor, a bulb hanging above. The phone's light dimmed unwastefully and went out: he lit it again, ran it quickly round. Debbie had left nothing, except something whiteish on the floor, under the shelf on the left, a piece of newspaper. Rob picked it up, a sheet of the *Daily Telegraph,* and uncrumpled it: November 6, 1948.

When the light went again, he stood for a moment, daring himself, in the near dark, testing the emptiness and the quickly stifled echo; then he got out. And puzzling vaguely over it as he came back into the relative brightness of the sitting-room, he realized from the stiffened folds that the page of the *Telegraph* had been used to wrap some square object, it was a wholly random survival, of no interest in itself. He took it out to throw on to the fire.

There was now quite a show, some broken chairs had been tossed on and the whole thing had a wild dangerous heat and snap to it, loud cracks and sparks, a roll of black smoke from a foam-rubber cushion. Little Jack was awed, standing back beside his mother, but with a look of calculation about dares of his own. They seemed to stretch ahead.

"Find anything?" said Debbie. Of course it was a sign of her excellence that he hadn't. It occurred to him, as he went back down the drive and on to the unknown street, that Valance had never sent the promised letter, on the eve of the Somme, after all—if he had done, the careful memorious Hewitt would surely have transcribed it too. And now Rob had to get back into Town—he had a date at seven with . . . for a moment he couldn't think of his name. He looked on his phone for the text, and caught the smell of smoke on his hands.

ALAN HOLLINGHURST is the author of *The Swimming-Pool Library,*
The Folding Star, The Spell, and *The Line of Beauty,* which won the Man
Booker Prize and was a finalist for the National Book Critics Circle
Award. He has received the Somerset Maugham Award, the E. M. For-
ster Award of the American Academy of Arts and Letters, and the James
Tait Black Memorial Prize for Fiction. He lives in London.

A NOTE ON THE TYPE

THIS BOOK was set in Adobe Garamond. Designed for the Adobe Corporation by Robert Slimbach, the fonts are based on types first cut by Claude Garamond (c. 1480–1561). Garamond was a pupil of Geoffroy Tory and is believed to have followed the Venetian models, although he introduced a number of important differences, and it is to him that we owe the letter we now know as "old style." He gave to his letters a certain elegance and feeling of movement that won their creator an immediate reputation and the patronage of Francis I of France.

Typeset by Scribe,
Philadelphia, Pennsylvania
Printed and bound by Berryville Graphics,
Berryville, Virginia
Designed by Virginia Tan